FORTY-SEVEN   W9-AMM-874

GIBBSVILLE, PA

GIBBSVILLE, PA

The Classic Stories

John O'Hara

Edited by Matthew J. Bruccoli

Preface by George V. Higgins

Carroll & Graf Publishers, Inc.
New York

Published by arrangement with Random House, Inc.

First Carroll & Graf Edition 1992

Carroll & Graf Publishers, Inc.
260 Fifth Avenue
New York, NY 10001

Library of Congress Cataloging-in-Publication Data is available.

ISBN: 0-88184-899-9

Manufactured in the United States of America

Contents

Contents

Preface

A Man of Measured Discontents— John O'Hara and His Losses

by George V. Higgins*

It's a long time now since 1934, when Harcourt, Brace & Company published an American classic to moderate applause and scattered, righteous catcalls. *Appointment in Samarra,* John O'Hara's first book, rattled many Americans bold enough to read it. Regardless of their actual participation in Scott Fitzgerald's Rich Kids' whirling spree, their voices full of money and their breaths steeped in gin— very few Americans had done that, after all, or made and then lost fortunes on the New York Stock Exchange—the readers that O'Hara greeted were accustomed to that stuff, F. Scott's carefree pictures that he'd shot through gentle lenses. They had read Fitzgerald's fables with quite justified assurance of escape, much as tonight's evening TV viewers will tune in on bubble gum, and there is nothing wrong with that. But that comfortable habit had not prepared them for this rookie coming out of the grease-stained Depression just as mean and scared as they; he seemed to lack, well, polish.

O'Hara told the story of the self-doomed Julian English, Gibbs-ville, Pa., Cadillac dealer. He did it with understated verve, laconic fatalism, and a sexual insouciance that troubled some onlookers. Then twenty-nine, O'Hara was a fresh veteran of a crippled marriage built upon a hotshot New York reporter's life, itself erected on a desultory and undisciplined prep school career which precluded Yale matriculation and deprived him of the badges. He was on the wagon,

* George V. Higgins is a professor in the Creative Writing Program at Boston University; he has published nineteen novels, a collection of short stories, four books of nonfiction, and hundreds of articles, columns, and reviews. This introduction was adapted from "John O'Hara and His Hounds," *Harper's,* September 1984: 73–75.

for the first of several times—the last would be permanent, a result of a stomach blowout that bled him flat in 1953. He had the eye of a recording angel, and about as much mercy.

He brought all of that equipment to the Julian English story. He described the random despair just beneath the surface of fashionable young married life in a small Pennsylvania coal city. He said the people who lived it were bubbling despair up to the surface with bootleg booze from Ed Charney, grabbing the thighs of others' spouses at the Lantenengo Country Club. He said they were suicidal, mean, and far too brittle. There wasn't much romance in it, Julian closing the garage doors and checking the windows before he fired up the Cadillac and gassed himself, dead drunk in all respects. It was squalid and a downer, and it didn't make one laugh. O'Hara said that those who escaped death were lucky, and on no account to be admired. That view did not beguile all readers; it attracted harder minds.

That attraction lasted, though. *Appointment in Samarra* did no better than tenth place on the *Publishers Weekly* best-seller list for October 1934, but it's still in print today, as reliable as its durable and sturdy author proved to be in his thirty-six remaining years of life. He had thirty-three more books left in him—novels, collections of his surgical stories, plays, and stuff he wrote for the papers. Now, twenty-three years after his death on April 11, 1970, nearly sixty years after his debut, thirteen of his other books survive in print, along with *Appointment*.

This is an extraordinary accomplishment, especially for a writer with this generation that reads as heedlessly as it bolts down fast food. Paradoxically, postmortem, it precludes a febrile rediscovery of him now, accompanied by loud hosannas tardily acknowledging his neglected mastery. Revivals are not held for those whose work is plainly living, as John O'Hara's is. He was a Caterpillar diesel of a storyteller, no wasted motion, no regrets, sometimes rough but mostly smooth, taking his first prosperity as the means that would permit him to do just what he'd intended ever since he started out: become one prodigious writer and discharge his obligations.

The ferocity of his commitment to the telling of his stories did not win him unmixed blessings, as he clearly had expected. His production did maintain himself, two more wives, and one beloved daughter in comfortable quarters and expensive motorcars. His publishers made money which he took in moderation, limiting himself for a good many years to an annual draw of $25,000 from his royalties—uncollected earnings piled up to exceed a million on deposit at no interest at Random House. He passively acquired the reputation of being a snob, and acquiesced to it, but just about the only showy thing he did was write. He had that Jansenist strain of lapsed Irish Catholicism that so strikingly resembles the dour Calvinist work ethic: *laborare est orare*. He thought work in general was good, and he thought his own work was particularly good.

He was therefore vulnerable to the mistaken expectation that his work would win widespread approval for its excellence. He was injured when reviewers recoiled from his realism and lambasted him for being too explicit about sex. Henry Seidel Canby lashed out at him with the mores of the 1930s, hitching "vulgar" to his name in a pompous screed in the *Saturday Review of Literature,* and he was not alone. O'Hara was aware that such reactions sold books and titillated the hesitant who might otherwise have missed him. But he was angry at the implied extension of the tawdriness he described to the writer who described it. He wrote stories edged like razors and they made reviewers bleed; then he griped that they were spattering their blood upon his name. He thought that was unjust.

O'Hara had a lively sense of injustice. The early death of his father, Dr. Patrick O'Hara, had dashed whatever hopes might have lingered after that fractious prep school career for four spacious years at Yale. That death demoted him and his mother from the well-fixed stratum of small-town society in Pottsville, Pa., to a station where the bread was a day old and the shirt cuffs frayed. His immediate predecessors in the limelight of American literature—Fitzgerald, Ernest Hemingway, and William Faulkner—lacked complete college training too, but they seemed to feel it less and very seldom to resent it. O'Hara nursed his defensive resentment of the life he thought he'd missed time and time again through his long years of fame, and never quite surrendered to the fact that he had missed it. That is why the Yale library has the manuscript of *Butterfield 8* and the galley proofs of *Appointment in Samarra;* Rutgers has *A Rage to Live;* Harvard, *From the Terrace;* the University of Pennsylvania, *Ourselves to Know;* Princeton, *Ten North Frederick;* and Penn State all the papers he had not distributed before designating it as his repository in 1964—he was foraging for honors, but he didn't get them from Penn State any more than from any of the others. He was scheduled to receive an honorary degree from American International College in Springfield, Massachusetts, in 1964, but bad weather grounded his plane and the college refused to grant the degree unless he showed up. Former Yale President Kingman Brewster was forthright—and supercilious—in his explanation of O'Hara's disappointments in New Haven; he said Yale didn't give him an LL.D. degree "because he asked for it."

Out of the unhappiness he derived from the literary critics and the sniffy professors who downgraded his hard work, on top of the vengefulness he felt toward Pottsville's secure well-to-do, O'Hara made a small, mean art of harboring a grudge. He gave grudges a green rancor that endures unto this day.

Thirty years after *Appointment*—and thus, Gibbsville, first appeared—O'Hara's editor at Random House, Albert Erskine, thought it would be nice if John O'Hara let the Literary Guild reprint some of what he'd written. That would bring more (unneeded) money to O'Hara, while publicizing his books further and giving Random House a profit without any new exertion. The difficulty was that John O'Hara hated book clubs, and was quite capable of turning down fifty thousand dollars in the interest of fidelity to his stern principles.

Albert Erskine knew his man. Through Bennett Cerf, the head of Random House, he contrived to have the Literary Guild's owners at Doubleday increase the proposal to $50,050. The extra fifty dollars represented Doubleday's repayment of the fee it had exacted from O'Hara back in 1934 for permission to reprint the short passage from W. Somerset Maugham's play *Sheppey* in which Death explains the meaning of an appointment in Samarra. O'Hara's vanity was sopped, and the Literary Guild reprinted *Samarra, Hope of Heaven,* and *Butterfield 8.*

That was a rare success for him in fighting his tormentors. They outnumbered him, of course, all the critics and reviewers, and he stubbornly refused to do what it appeared they wanted: stop writing for a while, or at least stop publishing, and thus derive from time and silence the patina of high art. He categorically declined to play by the established rules, and that was reckless conduct, as he knew.

The conventional and baseless wisdom of the American literary industry requires that a writer, to assert a lofty purpose and have any chance at all of being heard in that assertion, must agonize in the approved, feckless, artistic fashion for a minimum of two years for each one that he spends writing. Three mute years are even better; four or five bring much respect. A writer who can choke back the words for a decade is a genius, and will surely be anointed, if he ever does some work, as the creator of a novel that is—what else?—"long awaited." Writing is the only trade I know of in which sniveling confessions of extreme incompetence are taken as credentials probative of powers to astound the multitude. The received image of the writer is that of an unproductive sensitive who suffers from the vapors, is enslaved by his gonads, falls victim to romantic swoons, and passes out at deadlines. *Writer's block,* an occupational hazard in the same sense that the search for Bridey Murphy—and the resurrected Elvis—are theological inquiries, trails only rhinovirus, priapism, and debilitating drug addictions on the list of disabling and humiliating and loathsome complaints publicly and joyfully confessed by people who should be mortified to claim them. Strong men and healthy women unabashedly admit in front of God and all the people that they have taken advance money to do work beyond their gifts, confessing that they have perpetrated scams the likes of which would bring indictment in a well-run society, and get not only absolution but loud praise for their cheap swindles.

Publishers, at first impression victims of this con game, enthusiastically abet it, solemnly assuring all who may inquire that the book so long delayed by sexual dalliance, addiction, or sloth is sure to be a masterpiece when and if it turns up. One suspects that they connive in this charade of hoax and buncombe partly because they get greasy satisfaction from presenting further evidence that all writers are children—spoiled, mewling, drooling infants unaccountably equipped with more artistic temperament than the entire duty roster of La Scala's opera season. The greater motive, though, is that the lazy scribblers by their indolence permit the editors to languish also at an even, idle speed, taking lunch and cocktails in the company of those who advertise, promote, and review the dribbled works, so that no one breaks a sweat.

Cavalierly, John O'Hara would have none of that. "As to the Annual Model vs the Triennial Model that the publishers seem to prefer," he wrote to Hollywood producer David Brown in 1959, "I really don't think publishers know very much about publishing. As to laziness, I am lazy except where writing is concerned." Therefore, he said, he had determined to put out *Ourselves to Know* fourteen or fifteen months after his "giant," *From the Terrace,* "and take all the risks of wearing out my welcome." He told Brown that Hemingway didn't publish half enough. He told Mark Schorer that "it was time-wasting that destroyed [Sinclair] Lewis, not work." And he informed Bennett Cerf that most novelists were "plodders," "partly because they stall and partly because they don't know their business."

Confident as he was of the rectitude of his position—that what writers do is write, and that they should go ahead and do it—and assured of his great skill, O'Hara went ahead and did it, and incurred the unjust punishment. In the abstract he was right. But he lived in the real world, where envy complicates things, and the shunning was imposed. Thus four years after he permitted *Los Angeles Times* critic Robert Kirsch to publish his letter admitting that he coveted the Nobel Prize, O'Hara declared in the *New York Herald Tribune* that the critics "hate me. And they better for I despise them." This did not include the critics he shamelessly cultivated, of course—Charles Poore of *The New York Times* and John Hutchens of the *Trib*, along with Kirsch and several others—but it did remind any establishment figure who might have forgotten that John O'Hara was still sulking and could easily be further baited and then injured with a casual word or two.

It was thus in a proud, partly self-inflicted loneliness that John O'Hara spent his prodigiously productive lifetime, creating a body of work of magnificent dimensions. Between 1960 and 1968 he published seven collections of short fiction, some 137 terse and extended stories that all by themselves would supply credentials for a towering reputation in the world of perfect justice that he never did quite find. Those works, appearing in the spaces between the six novels published in those years, brought his career production of stories to 402. Starting with *Sermons and Soda-Water*, soldiering on through *Assembly, The Cape Cod Lighter, The Hat on the Bed, The Horse Knows the Way, Waiting for Winter,* and *And Other Stories,* he performed a feat of the storyteller's art that Scheherazade would honor. With his best novels—*Appointment in Samarra, Butterfield 8, Ten North Frederick*— and his play, *Pal Joey,* those stories seize in crystal amber the lives of sad and funny people whose yearnings, sorrows, and small joys are real today and solid to the touch. He knew how those people talked, and what they talked about, and what they meant when they were saying something else. He knew intimately all the details of their daily lives, the ones of the emotions as surely as the ones of their automobiles. He was exact and sympathetic, but clear-eyed and resolute, when he wrote about them. And as wrathful as he was, for all the many hurts he cherished, he wrote fearlessly and bravely, with his pride on the line. Very likely no one was ever quite as good as John O'Hara thought he was, not even John O'Hara, but no writer in this country in this century has tried harder to achieve the excellence he claimed.

It isn't bragging if the guy does what he says he's going to do.

Introduction

John O'Hara called it "my Pennsylvania protectorate." His fiction set in Gibbsville and the surrounding terrain established a truthful, lasting territory in American literature. What might be called the "locale à clef"—that is, the development of a fictionalized but recognizable setting in a series of stories and novels—is notably represented in twentieth-century American fiction by Sherwood Anderson's Winesburg (Clyde, Ohio), William Faulkner's Yoknapatawpha (Lafayette County, Mississippi), Thomas Wolfe's Altamont (Asheville, North Carolina), and O'Hara's Gibbsville (Pottsville, Schuylkill County). Anderson's approach was restrictive; he assembled one volume of loosely connected stories that have been charitably regarded as an episodic novel.* Faulkner, Wolfe, and O'Hara maintained an open-ended or evolving approach to their territories, adding or altering characters and events through many works.

Pottsville is 100 miles northwest of Philadelphia. O'Hara was born there in 1905. This part of the state was locally referred to as "The Region"—short for the anthracite coal region, which encompassed a thirty-mile radius around Pottsville, including all of Schuylkill County (O'Hara's Lantenengo County). Schuylkill County had a 1920 population of 217,745, of whom 21,876 were in Pottsville. The communities in the county were Tamaqua (O'Hara's Taqua), Minersville (Collieryville), Schuylkill Haven (Swedish Haven), Frackville (Mountain City), Cressona (Fair Grounds), Pine Grove (Richtersville), Shenandoah, Ashland, Mahanoy City, Port Carbon, Palo Alto, Mount Carbon, Mechanicsville, St. Clair, and Orwigsburg—all directly or indirectly dependent on coal. Lykens in Dauphin County, the home town of O'Hara's mother, became Lyons. In addition to the towns, The Region was pockmarked with patches, the company shacks at mine sites.

F. Scott Fitzgerald, whose writing O'Hara greatly admired, com-

* O'Hara mentioned *Winesburg, Ohio,* in "A Case History": " 'Full of plain, unpleasant truths. Very gloomy little stories that could have happened right here in Gibbsville. And did, some of them.' "

mented that "A writer can spin on about his adventures after thirty, after forty, after fifty, but the criteria by which these adventures are weighed and valued are irrevocably settled at the age of twenty-five." During the early decades of the twentieth century, when coal was king, Pottsville was a very prosperous city, and The Region presented a complex social structure, from Pottsville's Mahantongo Street to the patches. The ready explanation that O'Hara's Gibbsville fiction expresses the resentments of an Irish-Catholic outsider for the snubs he endured from the Protestant aristocracy is both facile and misleading. The oldest son of Dr. Patrick O'Hara, an affluent surgeon, grew up with great expectations that collapsed when his father died in 1925.

After apprenticeship as a reporter in Pottsville* and New York, O'Hara began writing short stories in 1928. His first novel, *Appointment in Samarra*, published in 1934, established Gibbsville and The Region. As the result of this novel's success and notoriety, O'Hara and his fiction became identified with Gibbsville, and critics conveyed the misleading impression that most of O'Hara's work was set in The Region. Between *Samarra* and *The Farmers Hotel* (1951) there were only six Gibbsville stories—including the key long story "The Doctor's Son" (1935). In 1949 O'Hara stopped writing short stories when he broke with *The New Yorker,* his primary story market, following the magazine's disrespectful review of *A Rage To Live* (a Pennsylvania novel, but not set in The Region). The 1955 novel *Ten North Frederick* initiated a return to Gibbsville, releasing a flow of material that resulted in a resumption of short stories and the development of an extended story form. "A Family Party" appeared in *Collier's* in 1956 and was separately published; a long story set in Lyons, it was O'Hara's first Region story in a decade. In 1960 he returned to *The New Yorker* with the long story "Imagine Kissing Pete" in which O'Hara documents, through the narrator Jimmy Malloy, his reawakened commitment to The Region:

> After I became reconciled to middle age and the quieter life I made another discovery: that the sweetness of my early youth was a persistent and enduring thing, so long as I kept it at the distance of years. Moments would come back to me, of love and excitement and music and laughter that filled my breast as they had thirty years earlier. It was not nostalgia, which only means homesickness, nor was it a wish to be living that excitement again. It was a splendid contentment with the knowledge that once I had felt those things so deeply

---

* Between 1924 and 1926 O'Hara was a reporter on the *Pottsville Journal.* No file of the newspaper for that period has been located.

and well that the throbbing urging of George Gershwin's "Do It Again" could evoke the original sensation and the pictures that went with it: a tea dance at the club and a girl in a long black satin dress and my furious jealousy of a fellow who wore a yellow foulard tie. I wanted none of it ever again, but all I had I wanted to keep. I could remember precisely the tone in which her brother had said to her: "Are you coming or aren't you?" and the sounds of his galoshes after she said: "I'm going home with Mr. Malloy." They were the things I knew before we knew everything, and, I suppose, before we began to learn. There was always a girl, and nearly always there was music; if the Gershwin tune belonged to that girl, a Romberg tune belonged to another and "When Hearts Are Young" became a personal anthem, enduringly sweet and safe from all harm, among the protected memories. In middle age I was proud to have lived according to my emotions at the right time, and content to live that way vicariously and at a distance. I had missed almost nothing, escaped very little, and at fifty I had begun to devote my energy and time to the last, simple but big task of putting it all down as well as I knew how.

This paragraph provides a striking demonstration of the force of memory in O'Hara's fiction: the Gershwin song, the girl's dress, and the yellow foulard tie preserved for thirty years.

O'Hara did not attempt to write a Region cycle or saga; the novels and stories have no structural connections or causal links. The only character who might have been utilized as a unifying device, Jimmy Malloy, is more often absent than he is present. Malloy resembles O'Hara in obvious ways; but Malloy's experiences are fictional or fictionalized, although his responses to them may be assumed to be O'Hara's.

The Region stories were not written from research; O'Hara rarely returned to Pottsville after 1927. When he submitted "Zero" to *New Yorker* editor William Maxwell, O'Hara recalled:

In 1922 I was in love with a girl named Gladys Suender, who was known in our set as The Creole. A real beauty, and to some extent the Natalie in *From the Terrace*. Her younger sister and husband were here last Saturday after the Yale game, and Jane told me that Gladys is in the hospital and may die. Kidney. Gladys has had a cruel life. A lousy marriage, ending in a desertion; family lost their dough, etc. Anyway, the Suenders lived in Frackville, up the Mountain, the second coldest town in the Commonwealth, next to Snowshoe, Pa. In 1922 the new road had not been completed (a new road which has now been abandoned, by the way) and on one side of the road there was a sheer drop of maybe 500 feet and never room for three cars abreast. So one night I was on my way back to Pottsville after a date with Gladys. If you got going right you could *coast* six miles in neutral from Frackville into the town of St. Clair. I had my old man's Buick Phaeton and I got going right, all right, but half way down I discovered that while I was at Gladys's house the foot brake had frozen tight. So had the hand brake, and I was moving along at about 40 m.p.h. Nothing else was on the road, but sometimes the bootleggers in their Reo Speedwagons would come through in convoy at about that hour and they didn't give a damn about anyone. The only thing I could do, I did, which was to ease the right fenders and running board against the bushes and rocks on the edge of the road, which slowed me down, until I was able to run the car up against the embankment without crashing. I got to St. Clair in second gear. The town Frackville is, of course, the town in "Zero."

The story does not use any of these events; but it is about O'Hara's responses to his memories of that time, that place.

O'Hara's technique is memorial. But it is an error to read the Gibbsville/Region stories as straight reportage. They are fictions developed from his recollections of and feelings about time, place, and character. In a 1955 interview about Gibbsville O'Hara stipulated:

> The physical design is Pottsville, as it exists. I left there in '27, when I was twenty-two. . . . But there were a solid eighteen years of impressions, which I've gone back and referred to. But what it amounts to is that I've just taken a real town and made it conform to a novelist's idea. . . . A novelist is lucky to create a place like . . . Gibbsville. He can fill it with people of his own invention, and can go on inventing. I could do a novel a year for twenty-five years on Gibbsville.

O'Hara's Region has staying power because he was unsurpassed at evoking the *way it was* and the *way it felt* by getting the actualities right: the words, the clothes, the cars, the songs. All great fiction writers are great social historians.

When O'Hara returned to stories he found that the form of his earlier *New Yorker* stories was constrictive; 2,000 words were not enough for the background material he now regarded as necessary. He explained his historical rationale in the foreword to *Sermons and Soda-Water* (1960):

> I have another reason for publishing these stories in novella form; I want to get it all down on paper while I can. I am now fifty-five years old and I have lived with as well as in the Twentieth Century

from its earliest days. The United States in this Century is what I know, and it is my business to write about it to the best of my ability, with the sometimes special knowledge I have. The Twenties, the Thirties, and the Forties are already history, but I cannot be content to leave their story in the hands of the historians and the editors of picture books. I want to record the way people talked and thought and felt, and do it with complete honesty and variety. I have done that in these three novellas, within, of course, the limits of my own observations. I have written these novellas from memory, with a minimum of research, which is one reason why the novella is the right form.

The scope of O'Hara's fiction is extraordinary. His muse was not restricted to Pennsylvania. Most of his work is set outside The Region. All of it cuts across levels of social stratification; but careless commentators have assigned his characters to the upper classes ("the country-club set")—which in certain critical schools renders these characters unworthy of serious attention. Indeed, much of O'Hara's work belongs with the novel of manners: fiction in which the customs and conventions of a social class determine the values and conduct of the characters. The novel of manners is traditionally concerned with the upper classes or the rising middle class, and O'Hara was an acute observer of class determiners. Nonetheless, in all of his fiction—and especially in the Gibbsville/ Region stories— he crosses all the social boundaries. Among the strongest stories in this volume are those about shopkeepers, barbers, and bartenders.

John O'Hara is a leading contender for the title as Best American Short-Story Writer. This truth has few adherents because he possessed a strong capacity to outrage the literary opinion-makers— particularly those on the academic dole—who deprecated his work as "limited" (meaning an absence of fashionable themes) and "materialistic" (meaning a concern with the effects of money). The same critics—most of whom had never been farther south than the last downtown stop on the IRT—who proclaimed the universality of Yoknapatawpha belittled the achievement of Gibbsville. Should readers in the nineties care about stories set in a quasi-fictional Pennsylvania city during the twenties? What is there in The Region for readers who have never left Utah? Even if these stories are superb repositories of American social history, what qualifies some of them as masterpieces?

The art of fiction is the art of character creation. Plot is not enough. In 402 stories and novellas O'Hara created hundreds of believable characters whose actions are buttressed by accurately observed details. A writer who can't be trusted for details can't be trusted for anything else. Fit readers will respond to the right details; but even readers who have never seen or heard of a Pierce-Arrow or a Locomobile or a Mercer ought to be able to sense that these cars have been used deliberately and therefore meaningfully. O'Hara's details are never trivial. They support the truth of fiction. He insisted that accurate speech is essential to character creation; and his detracters conceded that he had "a sharp ear." There are readers and writers who are indifferent to accuracy in fiction: people who don't notice much in life don't notice much in print. O'Hara did not write for them.

O'Hara did not express noble claims about the human spirit. His recurring themes are loneliness and cruelty. These themes frequently coalesce in O'Hara's studies of the loss of love and of the effects of social exclusion. The objectivity of his writing—his so-called reportorial point of view—was a method for controlling his response to the pain endured by his characters. His work was not impersonal; his characters' nastiness that has repelled readers conveys O'Hara's sensitivity to pain.

John O'Hara's adherents tend toward bellicosity. So did O'Hara. We believe that an American master has been disparaged for reasons that have little to do with the quality of his genius and much to do with distortions of his work. O'Hara was condemned by critics who felt ignorant or deprived because he wrote about things they didn't know about. Thus he has been denounced for snobbery, although writing about snobbery is not the same as advocating it. We are all snobs of some kind. Reviewing O'Hara's 1945 story collection *Pipe Night,* Prof. Lionel Trilling of Columbia University observed:

> More than anyone now writing, O'Hara understands the complex, contradictory asymmetrical society in which we live. He has the most precise knowledge of the content of our subtlest snobberies, of our points of social honor and idiosyncrasies of personal prestige. He knows, and persuades us to believe, that life's deepest emotions may be expressed by the angle at which a hat is worn, the pattern of a neck-tie, the size of a monogram, the pitch of a voice, the turn of a phrase of slang, a gesture of courtesy and the way it is received. . . . For him customs and manners are morals.

As George V. Higgins testifies, O'Hara was charged with writing too much. But after 1960 he was working against the last deadline, and his compulsion to write was part of a large literary concern. Attempting to encourage his friend Clifford Odets in 1963, O'Hara wrote: "The good ones bring to their work a competence that results in first-rate work, and which is more desirable than single pieces of good work. Our first-rate failures belong in the body of work precisely because they are to be judged not merely as individual pieces but as parts of the whole." This creed provides a rationale for assessing the literature of John O'Hara's Pennsylvania protectorate.

—Matthew J. Bruccoli
16 August 1992

Editorial Note

This volume includes fifty-three stories set in The Region and written over a thirty-year span. Seven stories that treat Region characters have been omitted; their settings are not stipulated or they are not primarily within The Region: "The Three Musketeers" (1946), "In the Silence" (1961), "Ninety Minutes Away" (1963), "Arnold Stone" (1964), "I Can't Thank You Enough" (1964), "Andrea" (1966), "The Strong Man" (1968), and "The Mechanical Man" (1974). *A Few Good Trips and Some Poetry* (1968) was reluctantly omitted because it is a short novel.

It has proved impossible to organize the stories by character or theme. The order is chronological by date of first publication, demonstrating John O'Hara's incremental method of composition: invention catalyzed by memory. Five of the stories included in this volume were published posthumously.

The stories are reprinted from their first appearance in an O'Hara collection; a few typographical problems have been solved by reference to the original magazine publication of the stories.

GIBBSVILLE, PA

Mary

Her father was a foreman in a Pennsylvania coal mine, and her mother was a fat and pretty Polish woman who always wanted the best for her daughters. Mary's father never interfered with her mother's plans. He loved his daughters in a manner of habit: he was their father, he put a roof over their heads, fed them, bought their clothes, gave them a little money for to now spend on whatever girls spend money on, and if one of them got into trouble, he'd see to it that the guy married her. He seldom spoke to them. Didn't know what to say.

Her home was a clean little house in a dirty little town. Her mother had taken "painting" in the Sisters' school, and the parlor was decorated with two or three of her works. When I first knew Mary there were no ashtrays in the house. Her father smoked his pipe in the kitchen, where all meals were served, or on the porch or at the Polish-American Republican Club. He never smoked in the front of the house. Mary used to want to love her father, to fight with him and go to Mass with him. But he wasn't very friendly; he gave her two dollars a week for her allowance, but he went to six o'clock Mass on Sunday because he couldn't sleep after the sun came up, so Mary couldn't take him by the arm and go up the aisle with him at eleven-thirty Mass, the way Betty O'Connor did with her father, the wealthy undertaker.

Mary was tall and beautiful, crafty, quiet, and passionate. She suddenly leapt from *Film Fun* to Michael Arlen's books and stories in *Cosmopolitan*. And she went from me to Philadelphia and an artist of a certain local reputation. I saw her a short time after she first began to pose in the nude. "You know, Doc, if Mom—Mother ever knew that, she'd die, so don't you ever let on. But it isn't anything. I mean he don't look at me as a person. He just sees the lines of my body. *You* know. The contours. That's the way artists are, Doc."

* * *

New Yorker (2 May 1931); *The Doctor's Son*

She used to write to me and tell me that she still loved me, and knew I still loved her, but she thought ". . . if we would ever enter the so-called state of holy matrimony, that it would only lead to unhappiness because on account of two such temperaments like ours being as far apart as the two poles." She often would tell me that she admired my mind, and if we were in Paris things could be different because people are more broad-minded over there, but Philadelphia —well, she was always running into people from home there, and if tales got back to Mom, why, Mom would make her come home. She said she'd go to Paris with me because the artist had told her all about it, about how the people over there are so *free* and all. She said she had told the artist about me and he was very nice and sympathetic. He said that was the best place for anybody that wanted to do any writing. That place was just made for artists and writers.

On one visit to Philadelphia, when I neglected to call her, I saw her in the Club Madrid with one of the city's most notorious roués.

The next time I saw her was three or four months later. It was at a revue opening in New York. She was with one of those faces-above-dinner-coats that go to all the openings, one of those persons who gladly pay twenty-four dollars to attend a première. She had done something to her hair, because it was much lighter than I'd ever seen it, and God knows how—because it was February—but she had contrived to have a grand healthy tan. Anyone who saw her thought exactly what she wanted everyone to think: that she had been in Florida. Maybe she had. I didn't ask.

After that I saw her frequently, at least once a fortnight, and I noticed her taste in men was steadily improving. I danced with her at the Casino one night, and she offered the information that she was modelling—Saks, or Bergdorf, or some place—and got a swell reduction on clothes. I went home just a little bit sad because she had found it necessary to explain.

She gave me her address and phone number. She lived at one of those apartment hotels in the East Fifties that I never can identify unless the awnings are in place over the sidewalk. One night I called her and she had nothing to do, so I went to see her. I was very careful of my behavior, never batting an eye when she said "eyether," and drinking my highball in a chair that was the room's width away from her. The telephone rang. She answered it and made a date with the voice at the other end of the wire. She hung up and smiled at me. "That was Ted Frisbee, the polo-player," she said. "I'm awf'ly fond of him. He has such a nice sense of hoomer."

It Must Have Been Spring

I t must have been one of the very first days of spring. I was wearing my boots and my new corduroy habit, and carrying my spurs in my pocket. I always carried my spurs on the way to the stable, because it was eight squares from home to the stable, and I usually had to pass a group of newsboys on the way, and when I wore the spurs they would yell at me, even my friends among them. The spurs seemed to make a difference. The newsboys were used to seeing me in riding breeches and boots or leather puttees, but when I wore the spurs they always seemed to notice it, and they would yell "Cowboy-crazy!", and once I got in a fight about it and got a tooth knocked out. It was not only because I hated what they called me. I hated their ignorance; I could not stop and explain to them that I was not cowboy-crazy, that I rode an English saddle and posted to the trot. I could not explain to a bunch of newsboys that Julia was a five-gaited mare, a full sister to Golden Firefly, and that she herself could have been shown if she hadn't had a blanket scald.

This day that I remember, which must have been one of the very first days of spring, becomes clearer in my memory. I remember the sounds: the woop-woop of my new breeches each time I took a step, and the clop sound of the draught horses' hooves in the thawed ground of the streets. The draught horses were pulling wagon-loads of coal from the near-by mines up the hill, and when they got half-way up the driver would give them a rest; there would be a ratchety noise as he pulled on the brake, and then the sound of the breast chains and trace chains loosening up while the horses rested. Then presently the loud slap of the brake handle against the iron guard, and the driver yelling "Gee opp!", and then the clop sound again as the horses' hooves sank into the sloppy roadway.

My father's office was on the way to the stable, and we must have been at peace that day. Oh, I know we were, because I remember it was the first time I wore the new breeches and jacket. They had

New Yorker (21 April 1934); *The Doctor's Son*

come from Philadelphia that day. At school, which was across the
street from our house, I had looked out the window and there was
Wanamaker's truck in front of our house, and I knew that The
Things had come. Probably crates and burlap rolls containing furniture and rugs and other things that did not concern me; but also a
box in which I knew would be my breeches and jacket. I went home
for dinner, at noon, but there was no time for me to try on the new
things until after school. Then I did hurry home and changed, because I thought I might find my father in his office if I hurried,
although it would be after office hours, and I wanted him to see me
in the new things.

Now, I guess my mother had telephoned him to wait, but then I
only knew that when I got within two squares of the office, he came
out and stood on the porch. He was standing with his legs spread
apart, with his hands dug deep in his hip pockets and the skirt of his
tweed coat stuck out behind like a sparrow's tail. He was wearing a
gray soft hat with a black ribbon and with white piping around the
edge of the brim. He was talking across the street to Mr. George
McRoberts, the lawyer, and his teeth gleamed under his black mustache. He glanced in my direction and saw me and nodded, and put
one foot up on the porch seat and went on talking until I got there.

I moved toward him, as always, with my eyes cast down, and I felt
my riding crop getting sticky in my hand and I changed my grip on it
and held the bone handle. I never could tell anything by my father's
nod, whether he was pleased with me or otherwise. As I approached
him, I had no way of telling whether he was pleased with me for
something or annoyed because someone might have told him they
had seen me smoking. I had a package of Melachrinos in my pocket,
and I wanted to throw them in the Johnstons' garden, but it was too
late now; I was in plain sight. He would wait until I got there, even
though he might only nod again when I did, as he sometimes did.

I stood at the foot of the porch. "Hello," I said.

He did not answer me for a few seconds. Then he said, "Come up
here till I have a look at you."

I went up on the porch. He looked at my boots. "Well," he said.
"Did you polish them?"

"No. I had Mike do it. I charged it. It was a quarter, but you
said—"

"I know. Well, you look all right. How are the breeches? You don't
want to get them too tight across the knee or they'll hurt you."

I raised my knees to show him that the breeches felt all right.

"Mm-hmm," he said. And then, "Good Lord!" He took off his hat
and laid it on the porch seat, and then began to tie my stock over

again. I never did learn to tie it the way he wanted it, the way it should have been. Now I was terribly afraid, because he could always smell smoke—he didn't smoke himself—and I remembered I had had a cigarette at recess. But he finished tying the stock and then drew away and commenced to smile.

He called across the street to Mr. McRoberts. "Well, George. How does he look?"

"Like a million, Doctor. Regular English country squire, eh?"

"English, hell!"

"Going horseback riding?" said Mr. McRoberts to me.

"Yes," I said.

"Wonderful exercise. How about you, Doctor? You ought to be going, too."

"Me? I'm a working man. I'm going to trephine a man at four-thirty. No, this is the horseman in my family. Best horseman in Eastern Pennsylvania," said my father. He turned to me. "Where to this afternoon? See that the mare's hooves are clean and see if that nigger is bedding her the way I told him. Give her a good five-mile exercise out to Indian Run and then back the Old Road. All right."

I started to go. I went down the porch steps and we both said goodbye, and then, when I was a few steps away, he called to me to wait.

"You look fine," he said. "You really look like something. Here." He gave me a five-dollar bill. "Save it. Give it to your mother to put in the bank for you."

"Thank you," I said, and turned away, because suddenly I was crying. I went up the street to the stable with my head bent down, because I could let the tears roll right out of my eyes and down to the ground without putting my hand up to my face. I knew he was still looking.

Dr. Wyeth's Son

There were many things that made Johnny Wyeth stand apart from the rest of our gang. For one thing, his accent. He had a Southern accent. He had come to our town only the winter before that summer, and his accent was unchanged, although he went to school with us and we all had at least traces of Pennsylvania Dutch inflections and sentence structure in our talk. But being with us did not change his accent, although being with him may have had its effect on ours. But besides his accent there was his way of dressing that made him different from the rest of us. We all wore, in the summer, a sort of uniform for all but dress-up occasions. When we had to dress, we wore white duck knickerbockers and blue Norfolk jackets, but other times in the evening we wore khaki (we pronounced it "ky-ky") knickerbockers and blue shirts and "Scout" shoes, which were ordinary brown high shoes except they had a cap on the toes. But Johnny, in the summer evenings, wore white linen suits and white buckskin Oxfords, which had the advantage of being noiseless when we played games like Run, Sheepie, Run, and a game which we simply called Chase. Then, Johnny was different from the rest of us because he wore glasses. He was cross-eyed, and to boys of that age being cross-eyed is not unattractive. At least in Johnny's case it gave him a wild look which I suppose caused us to credit him with a lot more daring than we all had.

Johnny's father, like mine, was a doctor, and I used to hear my father say that Dr. Wyeth was the best diagnostician who had come to our town in years, but that "it was too bad he drank." This was a curious admission to come from my father, who was a total abstainer and a rabid dry. I knew Dr. Wyeth drank, all right. Nights he used to come home and leave his car with the engine running, in front of the Markwith house, where the Wyeths lived. (They didn't own their home, as we all knew.) He would sit in the car for a few minutes and then get out and stagger in, and Johnny would leave us—we hung

New Yorker (28 July 1934); *The Doctor's Son*

around Victoria Jones's porch—and go up and turn off the motor. I remember the switch, a shiny Bosch switch it was, and Johnny never would let us turn it; he had to do it himself.

There was one other thing that kept Johnny from being like us, and that was his language. He cursed and swore all the time. We were pretty clean of speech; the majority of us were Catholics and we had to tell it in confession when we used bad language, but Johnny was Presbyterian and he didn't care what he said. One of his favorite words was "baster." He did not know what it meant, and neither did we, but he said it was the worst thing you could call anybody, and he said his father had told him that if anyone ever called him that, to go right ahead and kill him, hit him with a rock or anything else. Johnny used it whenever he was extremely angry. The rest of the time he simply cursed and swore and used dirty words. The Holding twins, Gerald and Francis, in whose back yard we had our headquarters, in a dusty, dirt-smelling tool house, were the ones who most frequently told Johnny to cut out his language. But they had no effect on Johnny.

However, one afternoon that summer, late one afternoon, we were playing Million-Dollar Mystery in the Holdings' tool house. "The Million-Dollar Mystery" was the name of a movie serial which we were all following, and we would use the scenario of each episode to provide us with a game from Friday to Friday. It was quite late, almost supper time, and we were playing hard, and Gerald or Francis, I forget which, had an old, rusty Daisy air rifle, which he stuck in Johnny's stomach with too much force behind it, and Johnny let out a yell you could have heard up at the courthouse. "God damn you! What's the idea you doing that?" And so on, with a lot of profanity.

"Oh, come on," we all said. "Don't get so sore about nothing. Quit swearing and put up your hands. He has you covered."

"No, sir, I won't do anything of the kind," said Johnny. "This no-good baster ain't gonna do that to me."

"Don't you call *me* that," said the Holding twin.

"Oh, I won't, eh? Who says I won't, you baster." Johnny raised his voice and the argument went on, everybody getting in it one way or another, but always Johnny's voice and the words he said were more distinguishable than anything else. And then suddenly we looked around as the door of the tool shed opened, and there was Mr. Holding. Mr. Holding in bedroom slippers, spectacles with a little gold chain reaching back to one ear, necktie held against his shirt by a little gold pincher.

"Who's using that language in this yard? John Wyeth, was that you?"

"What if it was? No baster ain't gonna hit me with any God-damn rifle."

"Here, here! Stop that kind of talk this minute. Leave this yard or I'll take you by the ear. Leave this yard this minute, you young guttersnipe, using language like that. I'll show you—" He advanced toward Johnny, and Johnny moved back and grabbed an old garden rake.

"God damn you, don't you put a hand to me! I'll sure hit you with this, you put a finger on me."

"Oh, *ho!* Like father, like son," said Mr. Holding. "Well, we'll see who has the say about what goes on in this yard. Come on, you boys. Hurry up and go home. I'll settle with Johnny. Ought to know what to expect from his kind."

"Go on, *get* out!" Johnny screamed, and called Mr. Holding an old baster and a lot of other things which we did not make out, because we were out of the tool house. Mr. Holding went right to the house, and standing in the areaway beside the house we could hear him on the telephone. "Dr. Wyeth? This is Holding, next door. Will you come over and get that son of yours out of my yard, or will I have to call the police? . . . Decent young boys . . . *my* sons hear talk like that . . . and keep him away from these boys or you'll hear from *all* the fathers in this neighborhood. We're all getting fed up with the goings-on since you moved here." We heard no more, because Mrs. Holding told us to go home.

But that night after supper we met early at Victoria Jones's porch and we all waited for the Holding twins, and at seven or so they came down the street together. Right away we asked them about what had happened after we were sent home.

"Oh, did he get his!" said one Holding.

"Did he get his!" said the other.

"What happened?" we said.

"Papa called up Mr. Wyeth and told him to come over and get Johnny or else he'd get the police to arrest him, and so pretty soon Mr. Wyeth—"

"Doctor Wyeth," I said.

"Aw, well, Doctor. He came over and got Johnny and took him out the back gate, and *then* you should of *heard* it. He had Johnny yelling and cursing. What he beat him with, it must of been at least a cane. He must of beat him with a cane for a half an hour."

"More than once. A couple of times," said the other Holding.

"Oh, a couple of times at least. He was still giving it to him when we sat down for supper. The worst I ever heard anybody get beaten."

We asked them more questions, but they did not know many more details, and after that Victoria Jones came out and sat on the porch and the other girls came one by one, and the argument was about whether Johnny deserved it. Johnny did not show up that night, but along about nine o'clock, when it was just getting dark, we saw Dr. Wyeth drive up in his car and stop in front of his house, and this night he was the worst we'd ever seen him. He could hardly get out of the car. When he did finally get out and go in the house, none of us dared to go over and turn off the motor.

The Doctor's Son

My father came home at four o'clock one morning in the fall of 1918, and plumped down on a couch in the living room. He did not get awake until he heard the noise of us getting breakfast and getting ready to go to school, which had not yet closed down. When he got awake he went out front and shut off the engine of the car, which had been running while he slept, and then he went to bed and stayed, sleeping for nearly two days. Up to that morning he had been going for nearly three days with no more than two hours' sleep at a stretch.

There were two ways to get sleep. At first he would get it by going to his office, locking the rear office door, and stretching out on the floor or the operating table. He would put a revolver on the floor beside him or in the tray that was bracketed to the operating table. He had to have the revolver, because here and there among the people who would come to his office, there would be a wild man or woman, threatening him, shouting that they would not leave until he left with them, and that if their baby died they would come back and kill him. The revolver, lying on the desk, kept the more violent patients from becoming too violent, but it really did no good so far as my father's sleep was concerned; not even a doctor who had kept going for days on coffee and quinine would use a revolver on an Italian who had just come from a bedroom where the last of five children was being strangled by influenza. So my father, with a great deal of profanity, would make it plain to the Italian that he was not being intimidated, but would go, and go without sleep.

There was one other way of getting sleep. We owned the building in which he had his office, so my father made an arrangement with one of the tenants, a painter and paperhanger, so he could sleep in the room where the man stored rolls of wallpaper. This was a good arrangement, but by the time he had thought of it, my father's strength temporarily gave out and he had to come home and go to bed.

Meanwhile there was his practice, which normally was about forty patients a day, including office calls and operations, but which he had lost count of since the epidemic had become really bad. Ordinarily if he had been ill his practice would have been taken over by one of the young physicians; but now every young doctor was as busy as the older men. Italians who knew me would even ask me to prescribe for their children, simply because I was the son of Mister Doctor Malloy. Young general practitioners who would have had to depend upon friends of their families and fraternal orders and accidents and gonorrhea for their start, were seeing—hardly more than seeing—more patients in a day than in normal times they could have hoped to see in a month.

The mines closed down almost with the first whiff of influenza. Men who for years had been drilling rock and had chronic miner's asthma never had a chance against the mysterious new disease; and even younger men were keeling over, so the coal companies had to shut down the mines, leaving only maintenance men, such as pump men, in charge. Then the Commonwealth of Pennsylvania closed down the schools and churches, and forbade all congregating. If you wanted an ice cream soda you had to have it put in a cardboard container; you couldn't have it at the fountain in a glass. We were glad when school closed, because it meant a holiday, and the epidemic had touched very few of us. We lived in Gibbsville; it was in the tiny mining villages—"patches"—that the epidemic was felt immediately.

The State stepped in, and when a doctor got sick or exhausted so he literally couldn't hold his head up any longer, they would send a young man from the graduating class of one of the Philadelphia medical schools to take over the older man's practice. This was how Doctor Myers came to our town. I was looking at the pictures of the war in the *Review of Reviews*, my father's favorite magazine, when the doorbell rang and I answered it. The young man looked like the young men who came to our door during the summer selling magazines. He was wearing a short coat with a sheepskin collar, which I recognized as an S. A. T. C. issue coat.

"Is this Doctor Malloy's residence?" he said.

"Yes."

"Well, I'm Mr. Myers from the University."

"Oh," I said. "My father's expecting you." I told my father, and he said: "Well, why didn't you bring him right up?"

Doctor Myers went to my father's bedroom and they talked, and

then the maid told me my father wanted to speak to me. When I
went to the bedroom I could see my father and Doctor Myers were
getting along nicely. That was natural: my father and Doctor Myers
were University men, which meant the University of Pennsylvania;
and University men shared a contempt for men who had studied at
Hahnemann or Jefferson or Medico-Chi. Myers was not an M.D.,
but my father called him Doctor, and as I had been brought up to tip
my hat to a doctor as I did to a priest, I called him Doctor too,
although Doctor Myers made me feel like a lumberjack; I was so
much bigger and obviously stronger than he. I was fifteen years old.

"Doctor Myers, this is my boy James," my father said, and without
waiting for either of us to acknowledge the introduction, he went on:
"Doctor Myers will be taking over my practice for the time being
and you're to help him. Take him down to Hendricks' drug store and
introduce him to Mr. Hendricks. Go over the names of our patients
and help him arrange some kind of a schedule. Doctor Myers
doesn't drive a car, you'll drive for him. Now your mother and I
think the rest of the children ought to be on the farm, so you take
them there in the big Buick and then bring it back and have it
overhauled. Leave the little Buick where it is, and you use the Ford.
You'll understand, Doctor, when you see our roads. If you want any
money your mother'll give it to you. And no cigarettes, d'you understand?" Then he handed Doctor Myers a batch of prescription
blanks, upon which were lists of patients to be seen, and said goodbye and lay back on his pillow for more sleep.

Doctor Myers was almost tiny, and that was the reason I could
forgive him for not being in the Army. His hair was so light that you
could hardly see his little moustache. In conversation between sentences his nostrils would twitch and like all doctors he had acquired
a posed gesture which was becoming habitual. His was to stroke the
skin in front of his right ear with his forefinger. He did that now
downstairs in the hall. "Well . . . I'll just take a walk back to the
hotel and wait till you get back from the farm. That suit you,
James?" It did, and he left and I performed the various chores my
father had ordered, and then I went to the hotel in the Ford and
picked up Doctor Myers.

He was catlike and dignified when he jumped in the car. "Well,
here's a list of names. Where do you think we ought to go first?
Here's a couple of prescription blanks with only four names apiece.
Let's clean them up first."

"Well, I don't know about that, Doctor. Each one of those names
means at least twenty patients. For instance Kelly's. That's a saloon,

and there'll be a lot of people waiting. They all meet there and wait for my father. Maybe we'd better go to some single calls first."

"O.K., James. Here's a list." He handed it to me. "Oh, your father said something about going to Collieryville to see a family named Evans."

I laughed. "Which Evans? There's seventy-five thousand Evanses in Collieryville. Evan Evans. William W. Evans. Davis W. Evans. Davis W. Evans, Junior. David Evans?"

"David Evans sounds like it. The way your father spoke they were particular friends of his."

"David Evans," I said. "Well—he didn't say who's sick there, did he?"

"No. I don't think anybody. He just suggested we drop in to see if they're all well."

I was relieved, because I was in love with Edith Evans. She was nearly two years older than I, but I liked girls a little older. I looked at his list and said: "I think the best idea is to go there first and then go around and see some of the single cases in Collieryville." He was ready to do anything I suggested. He was affable and trying to make me feel that we were pals, but I could tell he was nervous, and I had sense enough to know that he had better look at some flue before tackling one of those groups at the saloons.

We drove to Collieryville to the David Evans home. Mr. Evans was district superintendent of one of the largest mining corporations, and therefore Collieryville's third citizen. He would not be there all the time, because he was a good man and due for promotion to a bigger district, but so long as he was there he was ranked with the leading doctor and the leading lawyer. After him came the Irish priest, the cashier of the larger bank (of which the doctor or the lawyer or the superintendent of the mines is president), the brewer, and the leading merchant. David Evans had been born in Collieryville, the son of a superintendent, and was popular, a thirty-second degree Mason, a graduate of Lehigh, and a friend of my father's. They would see each other less than ten times a year, but they would go hunting rabbit and quail and pheasant together every autumn and always exchanged Christmas gifts. When my mother had large parties she would invite Mrs. Evans, but the two women were not close friends. Mrs. Evans was a Collieryville girl, half Polish, and my mother had gone to an expensive school and spoke French, and played bridge long before Mrs. Evans had learned to play "500." The Evanses had two children: Edith, my girl, and Rebecca, who was about five.

The Evans Cadillac, which was owned by the coal company, was standing in front of the Evans house, which also was owned by the coal company. I called to the driver, who was sitting behind the steering wheel, hunched up in a sheepskin coat and with a checkered cap pulled down over his eyes. "What's the matter, Pete?" I called. "Can't the company get rid of that old Caddy?"

"Go on wid you," said Pete. "What's the wrong wid the doctorin' business? I notice Mike Malloy ain't got nothin' better than Buicks."

"I'll have you fired, you round-headed son of a bitch," I said. "Where's the big lad?"

"Up Mike's. Where'd you t'ink he is?"

I parked the Ford and Doctor Myers and I went to the door and were let in by the pretty Polish maid. Mr. Evans came out of his den, wearing a raccoon coat and carrying his hat. I introduced Doctor Myers. "How do you do, sir," he said. "Doctor Malloy just asked me to stop in and see if everything was all right with your family."

"Oh, fine," said Mr. Evans. "Tell the dad that was very thoughtful, James, and thank you too, Doctor. We're all O.K. here, thank the Lord, but while you're here I'd like to have you meet Mrs. Evans. Adele!"

Mrs. Evans called from upstairs that she would be right down. While we waited in the den Mr. Evans offered Doctor Myers a cigar, which was declined. Doctor Myers, I could see, preferred to sit, because Mr. Evans was so large that he had to look up to him. While Mr. Evans questioned him about his knowledge of the anthracite region, Doctor Myers spoke with a barely discernible pleasant hostility which was lost on Mr. Evans, the simplest of men. Mrs. Evans appeared in a house dress. She looked at me shyly, as she always did. She always embarrassed me, because when I went in a room where she was sitting she would rise to shake hands, and I would feel like telling her to sit down. She was in her middle thirties and still pretty, with rosy cheeks and pale blue eyes and nothing "foreign" looking about her except her high cheek bones and the lines of her eyebrows, which looked as though they had been drawn with crayon. She shook hands with Doctor Myers and then clasped her hands in front of her and looked at Mr. Evans when he spoke, and then at Doctor Myers and then at me, smiling and hanging on Mr. Evans' words. He was used to that. He gave her a half smile without looking at her and suggested we come back for dinner, which in Collieryville was at noon. Doctor Myers asked me if we would be in Collieryville at that time, and I said we would, so we accepted his invitation. Mr. Evans said: "That's fine. Sorry I won't be here, but I have to go to Wilkes-Barre right away." He looked at his watch. "By George! By now I ought to be half way there." He grabbed his hat and kissed his wife and left.

When he had gone Mrs. Evans glanced at me and smiled and then said: "Edith will be glad to see you, James."

"Oh, I'll bet she will," I said. "Where's she been keeping herself anyway?"

"Oh, around the house. She's my eldest," she said to Doctor Myers. "Seventeen."

"Seventeen?" he repeated. "You have a daughter seventeen? I can hardly believe it, Mrs. Evans. Nobody would ever think you had a daughter seventeen." His voice was a polite protest, but there was nothing protesting in what he saw in Mrs. Evans. I looked at her myself now, thinking of her for the first time as someone besides Edith's mother. . . . No, I couldn't see her. We left to make some calls, promising to be back at twelve-thirty.

Our first call was on a family named Loughran, who lived in a neat two-story house near the Collieryville railroad station. Doctor Myers went in. He came out in less than two minutes, followed by Mr. Loughran. Loughran walked over to me. "You," he said. "Ain't we good enough for your dad no more? What for kind of a thing is this he does be sending us?"

"My father is sick in bed, just like everybody else, Mr. Loughran. This is the doctor that is taking all his calls till he gets better."

"It is, is it? So that's what we get, and doctorin' with Mike Malloy since he come from college, and always paid the day after payday. Well, young man, take this back to Mike Malloy. You tell him for me if my woman pulls through it'll be no thanks to him. And if she don't pull through, and dies, I'll come right down to your old man's office and kill him wid a rock. Now you and this one get the hell outa here before I lose my patience."

We drove away. The other calls we made were less difficult, although I noticed that when he was leaving one or two houses the people, who were accustomed to my father's quick, brusque calls, would stare at Doctor Myers' back. He stayed too long, and probably was too sympathetic. We returned to the Evans home.

Mrs. Evans had changed her dress to one that I thought was a little too dressy for the occasion. She asked us if we wanted "a little wine," which we didn't, and Doctor Myers was walking around with his hands in his trousers pockets, telling Mrs. Evans what a comfortable place this was, when Edith appeared. I loved Edith, but the only times I ever saw her were at dancing school, to which she would come every Saturday afternoon. She was quite small, but long since her legs had begun to take shape and she had breasts. It was her father, I guess, who would not let her put her hair up; she often told me he was very strict and I knew that he was making her stay in Collieryville High School a year longer than was necessary because he thought her too young to go away. Edith called me Jimmy—one of the few who did. When we danced together at dancing school she scarcely spoke at all. I suspected her of regarding me as very young. All the little kids at dancing school called me James, and the oldest girls called me sarcastic. "James Malloy," they would say, "you think you're sarcastic. You think you're clever, but you're not. I consider the source of that remark." The remark might be that I had heard that Wallace Reid was waiting for that girl to grow up—and so was I. But I never said things like that to Edith. I would say: "How's everything out in the metropolis of Collieryville?" and she would say they were all right. It was no use trying to be sarcastic or clever with Edith, and no use trying to be romantic. One time I offered her the carnation that we had to wear at dancing school, and she refused it because the pin might tear her dress. It was useless to try to be dirty with her; there was no novelty in it for a girl who had gone to Collieryville High. I told her one story, and she said her grandmother fell out of the cradle laughing at that one.

When Edith came in she took a quick look at Doctor Myers which made me slightly jealous. He turned and smiled at her, and his nostrils began to twitch. Mrs. Evans rubbed her hands together nervously, and it was plain to see that she was not sure how to introduce Doctor Myers. Before she had a chance to make any mistakes I shook hands with Edith and she said, "Oh, hello, Jimmy," in a very offhand way, and I said: "Edith, this is Doctor Myers."

"How do you do?" said Edith.

"How are you?" said the doctor.

"Oh, very well, thank you," Edith said, and realized that it wasn't quite the thing to say.

"Well," said Mrs. Evans. "I don't know if you gentlemen want to wash up. Jimmy, you know where the bathroom is." It was the first time she had called me Jimmy. I glanced at her curiously and then the doctor and I went to wash our hands. Upstairs he said: "That your girl, James?"

"Oh, no," I said. "We're good friends. She isn't that kind."

"What kind? I didn't mean anything." He was amused.

"Well, I didn't know what you meant."

"Edith certainly looks like her mother," he said.

"Oh, I don't think so," I said, not really giving it a thought, but I was annoyed by the idea of talking about Edith in the bathroom. We came downstairs.

Dinner was a typical meal of that part of the country: sauerkraut and pork and some stuff called nep, which was nothing but dough, and mashed potatoes and lima beans, coffee, tea, and two kinds of pie, and you were expected to take both kinds. It was a meal I liked, and I ate a lot. Mrs. Evans got some courage from somewhere and was now talkative, now quiet, addressing most of her remarks to Doctor Myers and then turning to me. Edith kept looking at her and then turning to the doctor. She paid no attention to me except when I had something to say. Rebecca, whose table manners were being neglected, had nothing to contribute except to stick out her plate and say: "More mash potatoes with butter on."

"Say please," said Edith, but Rebecca only looked at her with the scornful blankness of five.

After dinner we went to the den and Doctor Myers and I smoked. I noticed he did not sit down; he was actually a little taller than Edith, and just about the same height as her mother. He walked around the room, standing in front of enlarged snapshots of long-deceased setter dogs, one of which my father had given Mr. Evans. Edith watched him and her mother and said nothing, but just before we were getting ready to leave Mrs. Evans caught Edith staring at her and they exchanged mysterious glances. Edith looked defiant and Mrs. Evans seemed puzzled and somehow alarmed. I could not figure it out.

II

In the afternoon Doctor Myers decided he would like to go to one of the patches where the practice of medicine was wholesale, so I suggested Kelly's. Kelly's was the only saloon in a patch of about one hundred families, mostly Irish, and all except one family were Catholics. In the spring they have processions in honor of the Blessed Virgin at Kelly's patch, and a priest carries the Blessed Sacrament the length of the patch, in the open air, to the public school grounds, where they hold Benediction. The houses are older and stauncher than in most patches, and they look like pictures of Ireland, except that there are no thatched roofs. Most patches were simply unbroken rows of company houses, made of slatty wood, but Kelly's had more ground between the houses and grass for the goats and cows to feed on, and the houses had plastered walls. Kelly's saloon was frequented by the whole patch because it was the postoffice substation, and it had a good reputation. For many years it had the only telephone in the patch.

Mr. Kelly was standing on the stoop in front of the saloon when I swung the Ford around. He took his pipe out of his mouth when he recognized the Ford, and then frowned slightly when he saw that my father was not with me. He came to my side of the car. "Where's the dad? Does he be down wid it now himself?"

"No," I said. "He's just all tired out and is getting some sleep. This is Doctor Myers that's taking his place till he gets better."

Mr. Kelly spat some tobacco juice on the ground and took a wad of tobacco out of his mouth. He was a white-haired, sickly man of middle age. "I'm glad to make your acquaintance," he said.

"How do you do, sir?" said Doctor Myers.

"I guess James here told you what to be expecting?"

"Well, more or less," said Doctor Myers. "Nice country out here. This is the nicest I've seen."

"Yes, all right I guess, but there does be a lot of sickness now. I guess you better wait a minute here till I have a few words with them inside there. I have to keep them orderly, y'understand."

He went in and we could hear his loud voice: ". . . young Malloy said his dad is seriously ill . . . great expense out of his own pocket secured a famous young specialist from Philadelphia so as to not have the people of the patch without a medical man . . . And any lug of a lunkhead that don't stay in line will have me to answer to . . ." Mr. Kelly then made the people line up and he came to the door and asked Doctor Myers to step in.

There were about thirty women in the saloon as Mr. Kelly guided Doctor Myers to an oilcloth-covered table. One Irishman took a contemptuous look at Doctor Myers and said: "Jesus, Mary and Joseph," and walked out, sneering at me before he closed the door. The others probably doubted that the doctor was a famous specialist, but they had not had a doctor in two or three days. Two others left quietly but the rest remained. "I guess we're ready, Mr. Kelly," said Doctor Myers.

Most of the people were Irish, but there were a few Hunkies in the patch, although not enough to warrant Mr. Kelly's learning any of their languages as the Irish had had to do in certain other patches. It was easy enough to deal with the Irish: a woman would come to the table and describe for Doctor Myers the symptoms of her sick man and kids in language that was painfully polite. My father had trained them to use terms like "bowel movement" instead of those that came more quickly to mind. After a few such encounters and wasting a lot of time, Doctor Myers more or less got the swing of prescribing for absent patients. I stood leaning against the bar, taking down the names of patients I didn't know by sight, and wishing I could have a cigarette, but that was out of the question because Mr. Kelly did not approve of cigarettes and might have told my father. I was standing there when the first of the Hunkie women had her turn. She was a worried-looking woman who even I could see was pregnant and had been many times before, judging by her breasts. She had on a white knitted cap and a black silk shirtwaist—nothing underneath—and a nondescript skirt. She was wearing a man's overcoat and a pair of Pacs, which are short rubber boots that men wear in the mines. When Doctor Myers spoke to her she became voluble in her own tongue. Mr. Kelly interrupted: "Wait a minute, wait a minute," he said. "You sick?"

"No, no. No me sick. Man sick." She lapsed again into her own language.

"She has a kid can speak English," said Mr. Kelly. "Hey, you. Leetle girl Mary, you daughter, her sick?" He made so-high with his hand. The woman caught on.

"Mary. Sick. Yah, Mary sick." She beamed.

Mr. Kelly looked at the line of patients and spoke to a woman. "Mame," he said. "You live near this lady. How many has she got sick?"

Mame said: "Well, there's the man for one. Dyin' from the way they was carryin' on yesterday and the day before. I ain't seen none of the kids. There's four little girls and they ain't been out of the house for a couple of days. And no wonder they're sick, runnin' around wild widout no—"

"Never mind about that, now," said Mr. Kelly. "I guess, Doctor, the only thing for you to do is go to this woman's house and take a look at them."

The woman Mame said: "To be sure, and ain't that nice? Dya hear that, everybody? Payin' a personal visit to the likes of that but the decent people take what they get. A fine how-do-ya-do."

"You'll take what you get in the shape of a puck in the nose," said Mr. Kelly. "A fine way you do be talkin' wid the poor dumb Hunkie not knowing how to talk good enough to say what's the matter wid her gang. So keep your two cents out of this, Mame Brannigan, and get back into line."

Mame made a noise with her mouth, but she got back into line. Doctor Myers got through the rest pretty well, except for another Hunkie who spoke some English but knew no euphemisms. Mr. Kelly finally told her to use monosyllables, which embarrassed Doctor Myers because there were some Irishwomen still in line. But "We can't be wasting no time on politeness," said Mr. Kelly. "This here's a doctor's office now." Finally all the patients except the Hunkie woman were seen to.

Mr. Kelly said: "Well, Doctor, bein's this is your first visit here you gotta take a little something on the house. Would you care for a brandy?"

"Why, yes, that'd be fine," said the doctor.

"James, what about you? A sass?"

"Yes, thank you," I said. A sass was a sarsaparilla.

Mr. Kelly opened a closet at the back of the bar and brought out a bottle. He set it on the bar and told the doctor to help himself. The doctor poured himself a drink and Mr. Kelly poured one and handed it to the Hunkie woman. "There y'are, Mary," he said. "Put hair on your chest." He winked at the doctor.

"Not joining us, Mr. Kelly?" said the doctor.

Mr. Kelly smiled. "Ask James there. No, I never drink a drop. Handle too much of it. Why, if I took a short beer every time I was asked to, I'd be drunk three quarters of the time. And another advantage is when this here Pro'bition goes into effect I won't miss it. Except financially. Well, I'll take a bottle of temperance just to be sociable." He opened a bottle of ginger ale and took half a glassful. The Hunkie woman raised her glass and said something that sounded more like a prayer than a toast, and put her whole mouth around the mouth of the glass and drank. She was happy and grateful. Doctor Myers wanted to buy another round, but Mr. Kelly said his money was no good there that day; if he wanted another drink he was to help himself. The doctor did not want another, but he said he would like to buy one for the Hunkie woman, and Mr. Kelly permitted him to pay for it, then we said goodbye to Mr. Kelly and departed, the Hunkie woman getting in the car timidly, but once in the car her bottom was so large that the doctor had to stand on the running board until we reached her house.

A herd of goats in various stages of parturition gave us the razz when we stopped at the house. The ground around the house had a goaty odor because the wire which was supposed to keep them out was torn in several places. The yard was full of old wash boilers and rubber boots, tin cans and the framework of an abandoned baby carriage. The house was a one and a half story building. We walked around to the back door, as the front door is reserved for the use of the priest when he comes on sick calls. The Hunkie woman seemed happier and encouraged, and prattled away as we followed her into the house, the doctor carefully picking his way through stuff in the yard.

The woman hung up her coat and hat on a couple of pegs on the kitchen wall, from which also hung a lunch can and a tin coffee bottle, the can suspended on a thick black strap, and the bottle on a braided black cord. A miner's cap with a safety lamp and a dozen buttons of the United Mine Workers of America was on another peg, and in a pile on the floor were dirty overalls and jumper and shirt. The woman sat down on a backless kitchen chair and hurriedly removed her boots, which left her barefoot. There was an awful stink of cabbage and dirty feet in the house, and I began to feel nauseated as I watched the woman flopping around, putting a kettle on the stove and starting the fire, which she indicated she wanted to do before going to look at the sick. Her breasts swung to and fro and her large hips jounced up and down, and the doctor smirked at these things, knowing that I was watching, but not knowing that I was trying to think of the skinniest girl I knew, and in the presence of so much woman I was sorry for all past thoughts or desires. Finally the woman led the way to the front of the house. In one of the two front rooms was an old-fashioned bed. The windows were curtained, but when our eyes became accustomed to the darkness we could see four children lying on the bed. The youngest and oldest were lying together. The oldest, a girl about five years old, was only half covered by the torn quilt that covered the others. The baby coughed as we came in. The other two were sound asleep. The half-covered little girl got awake, or opened her eyes and looked at the ceiling. She had a half-sneering look about her nose and mouth, and her eyes were expressionless. Doctor Myers leaned over her and so did her mother, speaking to the girl, but the girl apparently made no sense even in the Hunkie language. She sounded as though she were trying to clear her throat of phlegm. The doctor turned to me and said dramatically: "James, take this woman out and get her to boil some water, and go out to the car and get your father's instrument case." I grabbed the woman's arm and pulled her to the kitchen and made signs for her to boil some water, then I went out to the Ford and wrestled with the lid of the rear compartment, wondering what the hell Myers wanted with the instrument case, wondering whether he himself knew what he wanted with it. At last I yanked the lid open and was walking back with the leather case in my hands when I heard a loud scream. It sounded more deliberate than wild, it started so low and suddenly went so high. I hurried back to the bedroom and saw Doctor Myers trying to pull the heavy woman away from her daughter. He was not strong enough for her, but he kept pulling and there were tears in his eyes: "Come away, God damn it! Come away from her, you God damn fool!" He turned to me for help and said: "Oh, Jesus, James, this is awful. The little girl just died. Keep away from her. She had diphtheria!"

"I couldn't open the back of the car," I said.

"Oh, it wasn't your fault. Even a tracheotomy wouldn't have saved her, the poor little thing. But we've got to do something for these others. The baby has plenty of spots, and I haven't even looked at the other two." The other two had been awakened by their mother's screams and were sitting up and crying, not very loud. The woman had the dead girl in her arms. She did not need the English language to know that the child was dead. She was rocking her back and forth and kissing her and looking up at us with fat streams of tears running from her eyes. She would stop crying for a second, but would start again, crying with her mouth open and the tears, unheeded, sliding in over her upper lip.

Doctor Myers took some coins from his pocket and tried to make friends with the in-between kids, but they did not know what money was, so I left him to go in to see how the man was. I walked across the hall to the other bedroom and pulled up the curtains. The man was lying in his underwear; gaunt, bearded, and dead.

I knew he was dead, but I said: "Hyuh, John, hyuh." The sound of my voice made me feel silly, then sacrilegious, and then I had to vomit. I had seen men brought in from railroad wrecks and mine explosions and other violent-accident cases, but I had been prepared for them if only by the sound of the ambulance bell. This was different. Doctor Myers heard me being sick and came in. I was crying. He took a few seconds to see that the man was dead and then he took me by the arm and said: "That's all right, kid. Come out in the air." He led me outside into the cold afternoon and I felt better and hungry.

He let go of my arm. "Listen," he said. "As soon as you feel well enough, take the car and go to the hospital. The first thing you do there is get them to give you twenty thousand units of antitoxin, and while you're doing that tell them to send an ambulance out here right away. Don't go near anybody if you can help it except a doctor." He paused. "You'd better find out about an undertaker."

"You'll need more than twenty thousand units of antitoxin," I said. I had had that much in my own back when I was eight years old.

"Oh, no. You didn't understand me. The antitoxin's for you. You tell whoever's in charge at the hospital how many are sick out here, and they'll know what to send."

"What about you?"

"Oh, I'll stay here and go back in the ambulance. Don't worry about me. I want to stay here and do what I can for these kids." I suddenly had a lot of respect for him. I got into the Ford and drove away. Doctors' cars carried cardboard signs which said By Order State Department of Health, which gave them the right to break speed laws, and I broke them on my way to the hospital. I pulled in at the porte-cochère and met Doctor Kleiber, a friend of my father's and told him everything. He gave me antitoxin. He smiled when I mentioned getting an undertaker. "Lucky if they get a wooden rough box, even, James. These people aren't patients of Daddy's, are they, James?"

"No."

"Well then, I guess maybe we have to send an Army doctor. I'm full up so I haven't a minute except for Daddy's patients. Now go home and I'll take care of everything. You'll be stiff in the back and you want to rest. Goodbye now." So I drove home and went to bed.

III

I was stiff the next morning from the antitoxin, but it had not been so bad as the other time I had taken it, and I was able to pick up Doctor Myers at the hotel. "I feel pretty damn useless, not being able to drive a car," he said. "But I never had much chance to learn. My mother never had enough money to get one. You know that joke: we can't afford a Ford."

"Oh, well," I said, "in Philadelphia you don't need one. They're a nuisance in the city."

"All the same I'd like to have one. I guess I'll have to when I start practicing. Well, where to first?" We outlined a schedule, and for the next couple of days we were on the go almost continually. We hardly noticed how the character of the region was changed. There was little traffic in the streets, but the few cars tore madly. Most of them were Cadillacs: black, company-owned Cadillacs which were at the disposal of young men like Doctor Myers and the two drunken Gibbsville doctors who did not own cars; and gray Cadillacs from the USAAC base in Allentown, which took officers of the Army Medical Corps around to the emergency hospitals. At night the officers would use the cars for their fun, and there were a few scandals. One of my friends, a Boy Scout who was acting as errand boy—"courier," he called himself—at one of the hospitals, swore he witnessed an entire assignation between an Army major and a local girl who was a clerk in the hospital office. One officer was rumored to be homosexual and had to be sent elsewhere. Opinion among us boys was divided: some said he was taken away and shot, some said he was sent to Leavenworth, others said he was dishonorably discharged. The ambulances were being driven by members of the militia, who wore uniforms resembling those of the marine corps. The militia was made up of young men who were exempt from active service. They had to make one ambulance driver give up his job, because he would drive as fast as the ambulance would go even when he was only going to a drug store for a carton of soap. Another volunteer driver made so much noise with the ambulance bell that the sick persons inside would be worse off than if they had walked. The women of wealth who could drive their own cars drove them, fetching and carrying blankets and cots, towels and cotton, but their husbands made some of the women stop because of the dangers of influenza and Army medical officers. Mrs. Barlow, the leader of society, did not stop, and her husband knew better than to try to insist. She was charming and stylish and looked very English in her Red Cross canteen division uniform. She assumed charge of the emergency hospital in the armory and bossed the Catholic sisters and the graduate nurses around and made them like it. Her husband gave money and continued to ride a sorrel hunter about the countryside. The rector of the Second Presbyterian Church appeared before the Board of Health and demanded that the nuns be taken out of the hospitals on the ground that they were baptizing men and women who were about to die, without ascertaining whether they were Catholics or Protestants. The *Standard* had a story on the front page which accused unnamed undertakers of profiteering on "rough boxes," charging as much for pine board boxes as they had for mahogany caskets before the epidemic.

Doctor Myers at first wore a mask over his nose and mouth when making calls, and so did I, but the gauze stuck to my lips and I stopped wearing it and so did the doctor. It was too much of a nuisance to put them on and take them off every time we would go to a place like Kelly's, and also it was rather insulting to walk in on a group of people with a mask on your face when nobody in the group was wearing one. I was very healthy and was always glad to go in with the doctor because it gave me something to do. Of course I could have cleaned spark plugs or shot some air into the tires while waiting for the doctor, but I hated to monkey around the car almost as much as I liked to drive it.

In a few days Doctor Myers had begun to acquire some standing among the patients, and he became more confident. One time after coming from my father's bedroom he got in the car with some prescriptions in his hand and we started out. To himself he said, looking up from a prescription: "Digitalis . . . now I wonder?" I turned suddenly, because it was the first time in my life I had heard anyone criticize a prescription of my father's. "Oh, I'm sorry, Jimmy," he said.

"You better not ever let him hear you say anything about his prescriptions."

"Yes, I know. He doesn't want anyone to argue with him. He doesn't think I'm seeing as many people as I should."

"What does he expect?" I said.

"Oh, he isn't unreasonable, but he doesn't want his patients to think he's neglecting them. By the way, he wants us to stop in at the Evanses in Collieryville. The David Evanses. Mrs. Evans phoned and said their maid is sick."

"That's O.K. with me," I said.

"I thought it would be," he said.

Collieryville seemed strange with the streets so deserted as on some new kind of holiday. The mines did not work on holydays of obligation, and the miners would get dressed and stand around in front of poolrooms and saloons, but now they were not standing around, and there was none of the activity of a working day, when coal wagons and trucks rumble through the town, and ten-horse teams, guided by the shouted "gee" and "haw" of the driver, would pull loads of timber through the streets on the way to the mines. Collieryville, a town of about four thousand persons, was quiet as though the people were afraid to come out in the cold November gray.

We were driving along the main street when I saw Edith. She was coming out of the P. O. S. of A. Hall, which was a poolroom on the first floor and had lodge rooms on the two upper stories. It was being used as an emergency hospital. I pulled up at the curb and called to Edith. "Come on, I'll give you a ride home," I said.

"Can't. I have to get some things at the drug store," she said.

"Well, we're going to your house anyway. I'll see you there," I said.

We drove to the Evans house and I told the doctor I would wait outside until Edith came. She appeared in about five minutes and I told her to sit in the car and talk to me. She said she would.

"Well, I'm a nurse, Jimmy," she said.

"Yes, you are," I said scornfully. "That's probably how your maid got sick."

"What!"

"Why, you hanging around at the P. O. S. of A. Hall is probably the way your maid got sick. You probably brought home the flu—"

"Oh, my God!" she said. She was nervous and pale. She suddenly jumped out of the car and I followed her. She swung open the front door and ran towards the kitchen, and I was glad she did; for although I followed her to the kitchen, I caught a glimpse of Mrs.

Evans and Doctor Myers in Mr. Evans' den. Through the half-closed doors I could see they were kissing.

I didn't stop, I know, although I felt I had slowed up. I followed Edith into the kitchen and saw she was half crying, shaking her hands up and down. I couldn't tell whether she had seen what I had seen, but something was wrong that she knew about. I blurted out, "Don't go in your father's den," and was immediately sorry I had said it; but then I saw that she had guessed. She looked weak and took hold of my arms; not looking at me, not even speaking to me, she said: "Oh, my God, now it's him. Oh, why didn't I come home with you? Sarah isn't sick at all. That was just an excuse to get that Myers to come here." She bit her lip and squeezed my arms. "Jimmy, you mustn't ever let on. Promise me."

"I give you my word of honor," I said. "God can strike me dead if I ever say anything."

Edith kissed me, then she called out: "Hey, where is everybody?" She whispered to me: "Pretend you're chasing me like as if I pulled your necktie."

"Let go!" I yelled, as loud as I could. Then we left the kitchen, and Edith would pull my necktie at every step.

Mrs. Evans came out of the den. "Here, what's going on here?"

"I'm after your daughter for pulling my tie," I said.

"Now, Edith, be a good girl and don't fight with James. I don't understand what's the matter with you two. You usedn't to ever fight, and now you fight like cats and dogs. You oughtn't to. It's not nice."

"Oh—" Edith said, and then she burst into tears and went upstairs.

I was genuinely surprised, and said: "I'm sorry, Mrs. Evans, we were only fooling."

"Oh, it's not your fault, James. She feels nervous anyhow and I guess the running was too much for her." She looked at the doctor as if to imply that it was something he would understand.

"I guess I'll go out and sit in the car," I said.

"I'll be right out," said the doctor.

I sat in the car and smoked, now and then looking at the second floor window where I knew Edith's room was, but Edith did not come to the window and in about twenty minutes the doctor came out.

"The maid wasn't sick after all," he said. "It was Mrs. Evans. She has a slight cold but she didn't want to worry your father. I guess she thought if she said she was sick, your father'd come out himself."

"Uh-huh," I said. "Where to now?"

"Oh, that Polish saloon out near the big coal banks."

"You mean Wisniewski's," I said.

IV

Doctor Myers must have known I suspected him, and he might even have suspected that I had *seen* him kissing Mrs. Evans. I was not very good at hiding my likes and dislikes, and I began to dislike him, but I tried not to show it. I didn't care, for he might have told my father I was unsatisfactory, and my father would have given me hell. Or if I had told my father what I'd seen, he'd have given Doctor Myers a terrible beating. My father never drank or smoked, and he was a good, savage amateur boxer, with no scruples against punching anyone smaller than himself. Less than a year before all this took place my father had been stopped by a traffic policeman while he was hurrying to an "OBS." The policeman knew my father's car, and could have guessed why he was in a hurry, but he stopped him. My father got out of the car, walked to the front of it, and in the middle of a fairly busy intersection he took a crack at the policeman and broke his jaw. Then he got back and drove around the unconscious policeman and on to the confinement case. It cost my father nearly a thousand dollars, and the policeman's friends and my father's enemies said: "God damn Mike Malloy, he ought to be put in jail." But my father was a staunch Republican and he got away with it.

I thought of this now and I thought of what my father would have done to Doctor Myers if he found out. Not only would he have beaten him up, but I am sure he would have used his influence at the University to keep Myers from getting his degree.

So I hid, as well as I could, my dislike for Doctor Myers, and the next day, when we stopped at my home, I was glad I did. My father had invented a signal system to save time. Whenever there was a white slip stuck in the window at home or at the office, that meant he was to stop and pick up a message. This day the message in the window read: "Mrs. David Evans, Collieryville."

Doctor Myers looked at it and showed it to me. "Well, on to Collieryville," he said.

"O.K., but would you mind waiting a second? I want to see my mother."

He was slightly suspicious. "You don't need any money, do you? I have some."

"No, I just wanted to see if she would get my father to let me have the car tonight." So I went in and telephoned to the Evanses. I got

Edith on the phone and told her that her mother had sent for Doctor Myers.

"I know," she said. "I knew she would. She didn't get up this morning, and she's faking sick."

"Well, when we get there you go upstairs with the doctor, and if he wants you to leave the bedroom, you'll have to leave, but tell your mother you'll be right outside, see?"

"O.K.," said Edith.

I returned to the car. "How'd you make out?" said Doctor Myers.

"She thinks she can get him to let me have it," I said, meaning that my father would let me have the car.

When we arrived at the Evans house I had an inspiration. I didn't want him to suspect that we had any plan in regard to him, so I told him I was going in with him to apologize to Edith for our fight of the day before. There was the chance that Edith would fail to follow my advice and would come downstairs, but there was the equally good chance that she would stay upstairs.

The plan worked. In some respects Edith was dumb, but not in this. Doctor Myers stayed upstairs scarcely five minutes, but it was another five before Edith came down. Doctor Myers had gone out to wait in the Ford.

Edith appeared. "Oh, Jimmy, you're so nice to me, and I'm often mean to you. Why is that?"

"Because I love you." I kissed her and she kissed me.

"Listen, if my dad ever finds this out he'll kill her. It's funny, you and me. I mean if you ever told me a dirty story, like about *you* know —people—"

"I did once."

"Did you? I mustn't have been listening. Anyhow it's funny to think of you and me, and I'm older than you, but we know something that fellows and girls our age, they only guess at."

"Oh, I've known about it a long time, ever since I went to sisters' school."

"And I guess from your father's doctor books. But this isn't the same when it's your own mother, and I bet this isn't the first time. My dad must have suspicions, because why didn't he send me away to boarding school this year? I graduated from high last year. I bet he wanted me to be here to keep an eye on her."

"Who was the other man?"

"Oh, I can't tell you. Nobody you know. Anyhow, I'm not sure, so I wouldn't tell you. Listen, Jimmy, promise to telephone me every time before he comes here. If I'm not here I'll be at the Bordelmans' or at the Haltensteins', or if not there, the Callaways'. I'll stay home as much as I can, though. How long is he going to be around here, that doctor?"

"Lord knows," I said.

"Oh, I hope he goes. Now give me a goodbye kiss, Jimmy, and then you have to go." I kissed her. "I'm worse than she is," she said.

"No, you're not," I said. "You're the most darling girl there is. Goodbye, Ede," I said.

Doctor Myers was rubbing the skin in front of his ear when I came out. "Well, did you kiss and make up?"

"Oh, we don't go in for that mushy stuff," I said.

"Well, you will," he said. "Well . . . on to Wizziski's."

"It's a good thing you're not going to be around here long," I said.

"Why? Why do you say that?"

"Because you couldn't be in business or practice medicine without learning Hunkie names. If you stayed around here you'd have to be able to pronounce them and spell them." I started the car. I was glad to talk. "But I tell you where you'd have trouble. That's in the patches where they're all Irish with twenty or thirty cousins living in the same patch and all with the same name."

"Oh, come on."

"Well, it isn't as bad as it used to be," I said. "But my father told me about one time he went to Mass at Forganville, about fifteen miles from here, where they used to be all Irish. Now it's half Polack. Anyhow my father said the priest read the list of those that gave to the monthly collection, and the list was like this: John J. Coyle, $5; Jack Coyle, $2; Johnny Coyle, $2; J. J. Coyle, $5; Big John Coyle, $5; Mrs. John Coyle the saloonkeeper's widow, $10; the Widow Coyle, $2. And then a lot of other Coyles."

He did not quite believe this, but he thought it was a good story, and we talked about college—my father had told me I could go to Oxford or Trinity College, Dublin, if I promised to study medicine—until we reached Wisniewski's.

This was a saloon in a newer patch than Kelly's. It was entirely surrounded by mine shafts and breakers and railroads and mule yards, a flat area broken only by culm banks until half a mile away there was a steep, partly wooded hill which was not safe to walk on because it was all undermined and cave-ins occurred so frequently that they did not bother to build fences around them. The houses were the same height as in Kelly's Patch, but they were built in blocks of four and six houses each. Technically Wisniewski's saloon was not in the Patch; that is, it was not on company ground, but at a crossroads at one end of the rows of houses. It was an old stone house which had been a tavern in the days of the King's Highway.

Now it was a beery smelling place with a tall bar and no tables or chairs. It was crowded, but still it had a deserted appearance. The reason was that there was no one behind the bar, and no cigars or cartons of chewing tabacco on the back bar. The only decorations were a calendar from which the October leaf had not been torn, depicting a voluptuous woman stretched out on a divan, and an Old Overholt sign, hanging askew on the toilet door.

The men and women recognized Doctor Myers and me, and made a lane for us to pass through. Wisniewski himself was sick in bed, and everybody understood that the doctor would see him first, before prescribing for the mob in the barroom.

Doctor Myers and I went to Wisniewski's room, which was on the first floor. Wisniewski was an affable man, between forty and fifty, with a Teutonic haircut that never needed brushing. His body under the covers made big lumps. He was shaking hands with another Polack whose name was Stiney. He said to us: "Oh, hyuh, Cheem, hyuh, Cheem. Hyuh, Doc."

"Hyuh, Steve," I said. "Yoksheemosh?"

"Oh, fine dandy. How's yaself? How's Poppa? You tell Poppa what he needs is lay off this here booze." He roared at this joke. "Ya, you tell him I said so, lay off this booze." He looked around at the others in the room, and they all laughed, because my father used to pretend that he was going to have Steve's saloon closed by the County. "You wanna drink, Cheem?" he asked, and reached under the bed and pulled out a bottle. I reached for it, and he pulled the bottle away. "Na na na na na. Poppa close up my place wit' the County, I give you a drink. Ya know, miners drink here, but no minors under eighteen, hey?" He passed the bottle around, and all the other men in the room took swigs.

Doctor Myers was horrified. "You oughtn't to do that. You'll give the others the flu."

"Too late now, Doc," he said. "T'ree bottle now already."

"You'll lose all your customers, Steve," I said.

"How ya figure dat out?" said Steve. "Dis flu make me die, dis bottle make dem die. Fwit! Me and my customers all togeder in hell, so I open a place in hell. Fwit!"

"Well, anyhow, how are you feeling?" said the doctor. He placed a thermometer under Steve's arm. The others and Steve were silent until the temperature had been taken. "Hm," said Doctor Myers. He frowned at the thermometer.

"'M gonna die, huh, Doc?" said Steve.

"Well, maybe not, but you—" he stopped talking. The door

opened and there was a blast of sweaty air from the barroom, and Mr. Evans stood in the doorway, his hand on the knob. I felt weak.

"Doctor Myers, I'd like to see you a minute please," said Mr. Evans.

"Hyuh, Meester Ivvins," called Steve. Evans is one name which is constantly pronounced the same by the Irish, Slavs, Germans, and even the Portuguese and Negroes in the anthracite.

"Hello, Steve, I see you're drunk," said Mr. Evans.

"Not yet, Meester Ivvins. Wanna drink?"

"No, thanks. Doctor, will you step outside with me?"

Doctor Myers stalled. "I haven't prescribed for this man, Mr. Evans. If you'll wait?"

"My God, man! I can't wait. It's about my wife. I want to know about her."

"What about her?" asked the doctor.

"For God's sake," cried Mr. Evans. "She's sick, isn't she? Aren't you attending her, or don't you remember your patients?"

I sighed, and Doctor Myers sighed louder. "Oh," he said. "You certainly—frightened me, Mr. Evans. I was afraid something had happened. Why, you have no need to worry, sir. She has hardly any temperature. A very slight cold, and she did just the sensible thing by going to bed. Probably be up in a day or two."

"Well, why didn't you say so?" Mr. Evans sat down. "Go ahead, then, finish with Steve. I'll wait till you get through. I'm sorry if I seemed rude, but I was worried. You see I just heard from my timber boss that he saw Doctor Malloy's car in front of my house, and I called up and found out that Mrs. Evans was sick in bed, and my daughter sounded so excited I thought it must be serious. I'll take a drink now, Steve."

"Better not drink out of that bottle, Mr. Evans," said the doctor, who was sitting on the edge of the bed, writing a prescription.

"Oh, hell, it won't hurt me. So anyhow, where was I? Oh, yes. Well, I went home and found Mrs. Evans in bed and she seemed very pale, so I wanted to be sure it wasn't flu. I found out you were headed this way so I came right out to ask if you wouldn't come back and take another look. That's good liquor, Steve. I'll buy a case of that." He raised the bottle to his lips again.

"I'll give you a case, Meester Ivvins. Glad to give you a case any time," said Steve.

"All right, we'll call it a Christmas present," said Mr. Evans. "Thanks very much." He was sweating, and he opened his raccoon coat. He took another drink, then he handed the bottle to Stiney. "Well, James, I hear you and Edith were at it again."

"Oh, it was just in fun. You know. Pulling my tie," I said.

"Well, don't let her get fresh with you," he said. "You have to keep these women in their place." He punched me playfully. "Doctor, I wonder if you could come to the house now and make sure everything's all right."

"I would gladly, Mr. Evans, but there's all that crowd in the barroom, and frankly, Mrs. Evans isn't what you'd call a sick woman, so my duty as a—physician is right here. I'll be only too glad to come if you'd like to wait."

The Hunkies, hearing the Super talked to in this manner, probably expected Meester Ivvins to get up and belt the doctor across the face, but he only said: "Well, if you're sure an hour couldn't make any difference."

"Couldn't possibly, Mr. Evans," said Doctor Myers. He finished with Steve and told him to stop drinking and take his medicine, then he turned to leave. Steve reached under his pillow and drew out a bundle of money. He peeled off a fifty-dollar bill and handed it to the doctor.

"Oh, no, thanks," said Doctor Myers. "Doctor Malloy will send you a bill."

"Aw, don't worry about him, eh, Cheem? I always pay him firs' the mont', eh, Cheem? Naw, Doc, dis for you. Go have a good time. Get twenty-five woman, maybe get drunk wit' boilo." I could imagine Doctor Myers drinking boilo, which is hot moonshine. I nudged him, and he took the money and we went to the barroom.

I carried the chair and table and set them in place, and the Hunkies lined up docilely. Mr. Evans waited in Steve's room, taking a swig out of the bottle now and then until Doctor Myers had finished with the crowd. It was the same as usual. It was impractical to get detailed descriptions from each patient, so the flu doctor would ask each person three or four questions and then pretend to prescribe for each case individually. Actually they gave the same prescription to almost all of the patients, not only to save time, but because drug supplies in the village and city pharmacies were inadequate, and it was physically impossible for druggists to meet the demand. They would make up large batches of each doctor's standard prescription and dole out boxes and bottles as the patrons presented the prescriptions.

It took about two hours to dispose of the crowd at Steve's. Mr. Evans told Doctor Myers to come in the Cadillac because it was faster than the Ford—which I denied. I followed in the Ford and got to the Evans house about three minutes after the Cadillac. Edith met me at the door. "Oh, what a scare!" she said.

"If you think you were scared, what about me?" I said. I told her how I had felt when her father appeared at Steve's.

"Your father phoned and wants you to take that Myers home," she said, when I had finished.

"Did he say why?" I asked.

"No, he just said you weren't to make any more calls this afternoon."

"I wonder why."

"I hope it hasn't got anything to do with him and my mother," she said.

"How could it? Only four people know about it. He couldn't guess it, and nobody would tell him. Maybe he's got up and wants me to drive for him."

"Maybe . . . I can't think. I'm afraid of them up there. Oh, I hope he goes away." I kissed her, and she pushed me away. "You're a bad actor, James Malloy. You're bad enough now, but wait till you grow up."

"What do you mean grow up? I'm almost six feet."

"But you're only a kid. I'm seventeen, and you're only fifteen."

"I'll be in my seventeenth year soon." We heard footsteps on the stairs, and Doctor Myers' voice: ". . . absolutely nothing to worry about. I'll come in again tomorrow. Goodbye, Mr. Evans. Goodbye, Edith. Ready, Jim?"

I gave him my father's message and we drove home fast. When we got there one of the Buicks was in front of the house, and we went in the living-room.

"Well, Doctor Myers," my father said. "Back in harness again. Fit as a fiddle, and I want to thank you for the splendid attention you've given my practice. I don't know what my patients would have done without you."

"Oh, it's been a privilege, Doctor. I'd like to be able to tell you how much I've appreciated working for you. I wouldn't have missed it for the world. I think I'd like to serve my internship in a place like this."

"Well, I'm glad to hear it. I'm chief of staff at our hospital, and I'm sorry I can't offer you anything here, but you ought to try some place like Scranton General. Get the benefit of these mining cases. God damn interesting fractures, by the way. I trephined a man, forty-eight years old—all right, James, I'll call you when I need you." I left the room and they talked for half an hour, and then my father called me. "Doctor Myers wants to say goodbye."

"I couldn't leave without saying goodbye to my partner," said the doctor. "And by the way, Doctor Malloy, I think I ought to give part of this cheque to James. He did half the work."

"If he did I'll see that he gets his share. James knows that. He wants one of these God damn raccoon coats. When I was a boy the only people that wore them drove hearses. Well—" My father indicated that it was time for the doctor and me to shake hands.

"Quite a grip James has," said the doctor.

"Perfect hands for a surgeon. Wasted though," my father said. "Probably send him to some God damn agricultural school and make a farmer out of him. I want him to go to Dublin, then Vienna. That's where the surgeons are. Dublin and Vienna. Well, if you ever meet Doctor Deaver tell him I won't be able to come down for the Wednesday clinics till this damn thing is over. Good luck, Doctor."

"Thank you, many thanks, Doctor Malloy."

"James will drive you to the hotel."

I took him to the hotel and we shook hands. "If you ever want a place to stay in Philadelphia you're always welcome at my house." He gave me the address of a fraternity house. "Say goodbye to the Evanses for me, will you, Jim?"

"Sure," I said, and left.

My father was standing on the porch, waiting impatiently. "We'll use the Buick," he said. "That Ford probably isn't worth the powder to blow it to hell after you've been using it. Do you really want one of those livery stable coats?"

"Sure I do."

"All right. Now, ah, drive to Kelly's." We drove to Kelly's, where there was an ovation, not too loud, because there were one or two in the crowd on whom my father was liable to turn and say: "You, ya son of a bitch, you haven't paid me a cent since last February. What are you cheering for?" We paid a few personal visits in the Patch. At one of them my father slapped a pretty Irish girl's bottom; at another he gave a little boy a dollar and told him to stop picking his nose; at another he sent me for the priest, and when I came back he had gone on foot to two other houses, and was waiting for me at the second. "What the hell kept you? Go to Terry Loughran's, unless the skunk got another doctor."

"He probably did," I said jovially. "He probably got Lucas."

"*Doctor* Lucas. Doctor Lucashinsky. Ivan the Terrible. Well, if he got Lucas it serves him right. Go to Hartenstein's."

We drove until one o'clock the next morning, taking coffee now and then, and once we stopped for a fried egg sandwich. Twice I very nearly fell asleep while driving. The second time I awoke to hear my father saying: ". . . And my God! To think that a son of mine would rather rot in a dirty stinking newspaper office than to do this. Why, I do more good and make more money in twenty minutes in the operating room than you'll be able to make the first three years you're out of college. If you *go* to college. Don't drive so fast!"

It was like that for the next two days. I slept when he allowed me to. We were out late at night and out again early in the morning. We drove fast, and a couple of times I bounded along corduroy roads with tanks of oxygen (my father was one of the first, if not the first, to use oxygen in pneumonia) ready to blow me to hell. I developed a fine cigarette cough, but my father kept quiet about it, because I was not taking quinine, and he was. We got on each other's nerves and had one terrible scene. He became angered by my driving and punched me on the shoulder. I stopped the car and took a tire iron from the floor of the car.

"Now just try that again," I said.

He did not move from the back seat. "Get back in this car." And I got back. But that night we got home fairly early and the next morning, when we had to go out at four o'clock, he drove the car himself and let me sleep. I was beginning to miss Doctor Myers. It was about eight o'clock when I came down for breakfast, and I saw my father sitting in the living-room, looking very tired, staring straight ahead, his arms lying on the arms of the chair. I said hello, but he did not answer.

My mother brought me my breakfast. "Did you speak to your father?"

"Oh, I said hello, but he's in a stupor or something. I'm getting sick of all this."

"Hold your tongue. Your father has good reason to be unhappy this morning. He just lost one of the dearest friends he had in the world. Mr. Evans."

"Mr. Evans!" I said. "When'd he die?"

"At about four o'clock this morning. They called your father but he died before he got there. Poor Mrs. Evans—"

"What he die of? The flu?"

"Yes." I thought of the bottle that he had shared with Steve and the other Hunkies, and Mrs. Evans' illness, and Doctor Myers. It was all mixed up in my mind. "Now you be careful how you behave with your father today," my mother said.

I called up Edith, but she would not come to the phone. I wrote her a note, and drove to Collieryville with some flowers, but she would not see me.

Even after the epidemic died down and the schools were reopened she would not see me. Then she went away to school and did not come home for the Easter holidays, and in May or June I fell in love with another girl and was surprised, but only surprised, when Edith eloped. Now I never can remember her married name.

Mrs. Whitman

(The following, apparently the rough draft of a letter, was picked up on South Broad Street near Walnut in Philadelphia. It is printed here for its value as an American document.)

Dear (blurred): This is not the story of Ella Miller Whitman. The story of Ella Miller Whitman and her lifelong devotion to the Gibbsville (Pa.) *Standard* could only have been written by one man: Bob Hooker, editor and publisher of the *Standard,* and he not only has written the story, but published it in a beautifully bound presentation volume which was one of the nicest surprises at the dinner given Mrs. Whitman recently upon the occasion of her retirement from the *Standard.* Mrs. Whitman had been with the *Standard* for forty-five years. Indeed, as Bob Hooker said in his speech: "Not only has Mrs. Whitman been with the *Standard* for five and forty years. There have been times when you might even say that Ella has *been* the *Standard!*" At this there was a suspicious moisture in Mrs. Whitman's usually twinkling eyes, but the smile never left her unlined face. It had been hoped that Mrs. Whitman might round out the full fifty years of devotion to the *Standard,* but Herbert Hooker, Bob's nephew and business manager of the *Standard,* wisely realized that although Mrs. Whitman's health seemed as good as can be reasonably expected at her age, there was always the chance that she might not be around five years longer. Herbert was above all things a business man, a realist, and reluctantly or not he also faced the possibility that his Uncle Bob might not be in the land of living on the day that Mrs. Whitman achieved the half-century mark of her career. He therefore wrote his uncle, then vacationing in one of the less ostentatious Florida resorts, and suggested tactfully that Mrs. Whitman be retired and a commemorative dinner be given in her honor. With the full approval of Bob Hooker the nephew went about lining up many

of the important folk of Gibbsville to be present at the event or at
least to send messages to the honored guest. It is true that the
mayor, the fire chief, the honorable county judges, and several other
locally famed figures did not know Mrs. Whitman personally, or at
any rate had been unaware that she had been serving the *Standard*
these many years, but that was an inevitable consequence of Mrs.
Whitman's lifelong avoidance of the limelight. So long as she is
spared Mrs. Whitman may derive daily satisfaction from the beautifully bound volume containing the pretty tributes from her grateful
employers and from virtually all persons of importance in Gibbsville.
These included the briefer messages as well as the speeches by the
mayor, the presiding judge, the secretary of the chamber of commerce, Mrs. Whitman's own pastor, and, of course, Bob Hooker
himself. In addition the leading merchants were afforded the opportunity to participate in the celebration, just as they had been a few
years earlier when "Fighting Bob" was discovered to have passed a
full fifty years as a newspaper man. At that time only full-page con-
gratulatory advertisements were accepted. For Mrs. Whitman this
regulation was relaxed as was the rate, in order to enable a more
representative group, including Mrs. Whitman's neighborhood
shops, to be represented in the volume. So cooperative, however,
were the department stores, specialty shops, nationally famous newsprint manufacturers, the Mergenthaler and Hoe people, insurance
firms and private individuals (several of whom were content to remain, simply, "A Friend") that not only was the expense of the dinner itself defrayed, but a neat purse was turned over to Mrs. Whitman. Although not officially announced at the dinner or in the
Standard's account on the following day, the amount of the purse
was said to be in the neighborhood of four figures. This sum, of
course, was over and above Mrs. Whitman's pension, under the
terms of which she is to receive half pay so long as she is spared.
Moreover, mention at this junction should be made of the beautiful
silver coffee set—coffee pot with ebonized handles, cream pitcher,
sugar bowl, and tray—which was the gift of Mrs. Whitman's fellow
workers. This beautiful, useful, and long-lasting gift was made possible through popular subscription, but 'tis said the lion's share was
borne by the editor and publisher. At any rate the tray bears the
legend: "To Ella M. Whitman, In Appreciation of Forty-five Years of
Service—From Bob Hooker and The Gang at The Gibbsville Standard."

The presentation volume mentioned above was, as may be inferred, the dinner program in a special leather-and-gold binding,
hand tooled. On the front cover is a golden replica of the *Standard*'s

masthead, a superb example of the bookbinder's art. Directly beneath the masthead is the dedication: "To Ella M. Whitman, In Appreciation of Forty-five Years of Service—From Bob Hooker and The Gang at The Gibbsville Standard." On the spine are Mrs. Whitman's initials, the year, and the word *Standard,* also in gold. But beautiful as is the bookbinder's contribution to the presentation volume, it is the contents of the program itself which one may assume will bring forth a tiny tear when in her richly earned years of retirement Mrs. Whitman pauses to peruse the happy memento.

As one opens the book first to greet the eye is a full-page reproduction of the most recent available photograph of Mrs. Whitman. There is a sentimental touch to the inclusion of this photograph which could be recognized only by those in the know. This same picture was made in the *Standard*'s own "shop" by Murray Weiss, staff photographer and assistant sports editor of the *Standard.* Originally it was taken for inclusion along with the other members of the *Standard*'s "Twenty-five Year Club," an informal organization which was founded by Herbert Hooker while he was preparing the celebration of Fighting Bob's fiftieth anniversary in the newspaper business. Mrs. Whitman, of course, more than qualified for "membership" in the "club" for at that time she had been with the *Standard* approximately forty years, but it is believed that Herbert in making Mrs. Whitman a member of the "Twenty-five Year" group was exercising tact in two ways: it was, after all, his uncle's day, and too it may have passed through his mind that a lady's age is her own secret. At any rate the photograph remained in the *Standard*'s files until the program for her own celebration was being prepared. With characteristic fairness Herbert Hooker gave Mrs. Whitman her day: her photograph is the first in the book; Bob Hooker's does not appear until the second following page, and Herbert's two pages after that.

What might be called the title page reads as follows: "Programme —Testimonial Banquet to Ella M. Whitman, In Appreciation of Forty-five Years of Service—Tendered by Bob Hooker and The Gang at The Gibbsville Standard." The date appears at the bottom of the page, along with the name of the hotel, which was, of course, the Gibbs Hotel. A word here may for all time clear up the single minute criticism which was directed against the *Standard*'s sincere and touching tribute to Mrs. Whitman. It is customary in Gibbsville to hold affairs of the kind in the King Coal Room of the Gibbs House, as it formerly was known. The King Coal Room was the name given the main dining-room when the hotel was completely redecorated and refurnished in 1929, and the room is regarded as one of the most attractive rooms of its kind in that section of Pennsylvania, if not in the entire State. The murals are regional in theme, depicting as they do coal-mining scenes which were painted by a professional artist from Philadelphia. To residents of Gibbsville and the surrounding territory the words King Coal Room are so well known that the room need not be otherwise identified. It has been the scene of countless fashionable banquets, wedding receptions, and balls, and throughout the Thirties it was the scene of the regular Saturday night dances, which were attended by leading members of Gibbsville society, although open to the public. In the course of the pleasant but by no means small task of arranging for Mrs. Whitman's celebration Herbert Hooker inevitably and automatically decided upon the King Coal Room, but, as he later confided to friends, when this decision was casually mentioned to Bob Hooker the latter voiced his doubt that the King Coal Room was suitable. He pointed out that a lady of Mrs. Whitman's retiring habits might find herself so ill at ease in such worldly surroundings that she would be completely ill at ease, with the result that what had been intended as an occasion for her own personal enjoyment might turn out to be little short of a trying ordeal. Herbert therefore changed the plan and the banquet was held in the more informal, more friendly Coffee Shoppe, where Mrs. Whitman was wont to lunch each working day. Also, if pressed Herbert will admit that he had Mrs. Whitman's best interests in mind in another direction: the *Standard*, of course, assumed the entire expense of the celebration and a certain sum was budgeted to cover that expense. Since the per-plate cost of dinner in the King Coal Room is nearly double that of the Coffee Shoppe it stood to reason that within the limitations of the budgeted sum the Coffee Shoppe was the more desirable, since it left a tidy amount which could be and was devoted to the purse which was tendered Mrs. Whitman as the climax of the banquet. And later in the evening Mrs. Whitman had her King Coal Room after all, for at the conclusion of the festivities she was hostess to a small party of friends among whom were City Editor Jack O'Brien, Sports Editor Walt Southard, Composing Room Foreman Jake Spitz, and their wives. Also present as one of Mrs. Whitman's guests was J. Russell Meredith, for thirty years political and county editor of the *Standard*. (Mr. Meredith had resigned from the *Standard* shortly after the banquet plans were announced, giving ill health as his reason. He was not present at the banquet. Mr. Meredith's many friends will be delighted to hear that he is well on the way to recovery and has accepted a position in the County Recorder's office under County Recorder Will M. Templeton.)

For obvious mechanical reasons it was possible to include in the printed program only those laudatory messages which had been prepared in advance. Mrs. Whitman herself had, as was to be expected, declined the opportunity to present her own response to these tributes in the program. In fact she had consented to the celebration on condition that she not be called upon for any speech. But in that she reckoned without the persuasiveness of Editor Bob Hooker, who departed from the announced program and led the assemblage in applause which had the desired effect of bringing Mrs. Whitman to her feet to say a few words. It was a never-to-be-forgotten sight as the well-loved jovial editor-in-chief placed his arm about the shoulders of the faithful employee, now on her way to a well-earned rest. "And now," said Editor Bob, "I yield, as, truth to tell, I have more than once yielded in the past, to my favorite co-worker, and permit me to state, permit me to admit right here in open court, as it were, that many times in the five decades past I have had good reason to be happy in deferring to the wise judgment of Ella Whitman on such occasions as I have consulted her. Boys and girls of the *Standard* gang, I give you Ella M. Whitman." At this there was renewed applause which must have drowned out the sound of the orchestra playing in the King Coal Room on the floor above. Mrs. Whitman waited until the applause had died down and then she spoke with all the assurance of a veteran speaker. As reported in the *Standard* the next day, her remarks were simple but eloquent: "Mr. Hooker, ladies and gentlemen: I am very grateful to you all, not only for what has been said here this evening, but even more so for the friendships and the kindnesses I have been shown during my forty-five years with the *Standard.* Forty-five years is a long time, and I suppose I am an old lady and that my usefulness is at an end, and so I shall not be with you after this evening. Some of you know what is in my heart tonight and to you I say thank you, and thirty." This last, the word thirty, is the traditional signing-off signal of the newspaper business, which Mrs. Whitman had learned as typesetter and proofreader on the *Standard,* before taking charge of the classified advertising of the paper, a position which she occupied for twenty-three of her forty-five years' service. When she finished her graceful speech the assemblage rose as one man, and with Herbert Hooker at the piano and Editor Bob Hooker leading, all present sang *Auld Lang Syne* and Ella Whitman had entered upon the *emerita* phase of her career.

No, this is not the story of Ella Miller Whitman. It is a bigger story than that. It is the story of Free Enterprise in a Free Country. It is the story of employer and employee working hand-in-hand, one for the other in a manner all too rare in these times. If it be the story of Ella Miller Whitman, then it is also the story of Bob Hooker. Truly, it is the story of neither, and of both.

With (blurred)

The Lady Takes an Interest

[T]he following is a copy of an intra-office communication. The original is presumed to be in the files and/or records, if any, of Mrs. Robert Hooker, president of the Gibbsville (Pa.) *Standard* and widow of the late "Fighting Bob" Hooker, owner, editor, and publisher. The memorandum was written by Doug Campbell, now managing editor, formerly city editor, sports editor, etc., of the *Standard*.]

To: Mrs. Hooker
From: Doug Campbell
Subject: Ray B. Hoffner Memorial

I hope you will forgive the delay in answering your memos regarding the Ray B. Hoffner Memorial, but I am sure you will understand when I explain that due to our recent retrenchment program and the difficulty your nephew Karl and I have been having in getting newsprint, I have had to put off writing this memo. Also I have been expecting to see you in the office and left word downstairs that when you came in I was to be notified immediately. I of course understand that aside from your duties as president of the paper you have numerous other commitments and, parenthetically, I trust that we have been handling the news items to your satisfaction. We are all very grateful to you for sending in these items, especially when you include lists of names of the prominent women with whom you are associated in the charitable and other enterprises. Mary Dobbs, our new young society editor, has been doing a fine job and I know I speak for her as well as myself when I express my thanks for your sending the items instead of telephoning them. In addition to her job as society editor, Mary has been helping out "on the street," as we say, and it is almost impossible for her to take long lists of names over the phone after lunch. Our county edition goes to press at 2:50

in the afternoon, which means that Mary, for instance, is writing from about 11:30 A.M., when she comes in from her tour of news sources. Her deadline for society-page items is 12 noon, unless we have to hold for items of extreme importance. Another difficulty when some items are telephoned is that because of the nature of many of your charitable and civic enterprises it is desirable to have such news published not only in our paper but by our competition as well. I believe I explained to you that the *Leader* will not print an item which appeared first in our paper. But thanks to your new system of writing out the "stories" and lists of names we now are able to hand over the items to one of the stenographers downstairs, who makes a carbon which we shoot over to the *Leader* office. You thus get double, or complete, coverage for your charitable and civic interests. We all hope that you will drop in on us in the editorial room very soon, preferably after four o'clock, when we are under somewhat less pressure than at other times of the day, although I need not tell you we are always honored by your visits. Since we are a little short-handed at the moment I suggest that if you wish to bring friends who are interested in seeing how a newspaper is brought out, it probably would be pleasanter for them if you notify me a day or two in advance so that I can assign one of the staff to escort you and provide the necessary explanations. I also suggest that you wear old clothes if you wish to go through the whole plant.

And so to the matter of the Ray B. Hoffner Memorial. Unfortunately I have mislaid the originals of your memos to me, but I have had several conversations with your nephew Karl and I think I know substantially what you have in mind. Perhaps it would be advisable to review the suggestions, before passing on my comments, and, in so doing, check my perhaps faulty memory.

As I remember it, when Ray Hoffner died last January you were in Phoenix, Arizona, and did not hear of his death until your return to town. As I understand it, you were on your way East by train when you read in one of the Denver papers that a police officer had been killed in line of duty, and that the local paper had created a fund for his family. This left so strong an impression that you quite rightly decided it would be a good thing if we were to do likewise, and when you learned, upon returning to town, that Sergeant Hoffner had died, you decided that this was an excellent opportunity to emulate our esteemed Denver contemporary. You discussed the matter with Karl, who of course agreed, and you thereupon wrote me the first memorandum, which I carelessly mislaid. I did, however, discuss the matter briefly with Karl, who knew Ray Hoffner very slightly, if at all, owing to his (Karl's) fairly recent residence in town and also to the fact that as business manager his duties do not place him in contact with police officers. In our first discussion I suggested to Karl that perhaps we would be wiser to postpone the creation of a fund until another time. That is my belief now, and I urge you to consider all the facts before issuing an actual order in the Hoffner matter.

It is too soon after Hoffner's death to establish a fund for the future without causing some comment. I suggest that privately we decide upon certain conditions of an award, and then in the regrettable event of a police officer's death, either in line of duty or some such praiseworthy condition, we announce the award simultaneously with the appearance of the story covering his death. I respectfully suggest that to qualify for the award, which should be given to the wife and/or family of the deceased police officer, said officer shall have died as a result of injury or illness sustained in police activity. We can work out details, but that, in my opinion, should be our guiding principle.

Sergeant Hoffner, unfortunately, would not qualify under those terms. I have known Ray Hoffner all my life and while what I am about to say is a confidential report, I have no doubt it would be corroborated by anyone who has had any connection with Police Headquarters or with Ray. The cause of death was correctly given as pneumonia. The preceding circumstances have, however, not been publicized. He had gone off duty shortly after two o'clock A.M., and paid his nightly visit to a house on Railway Avenue which since has been closed. The house is what we call in the paper a house of "ill repute." Shortly after four o'clock Patrolmen Wilkes and Velusky, on duty in the prowl car in the western end of town, received an order to go at once to the house on Railway Avenue to investigate the firing of shots. There they found Sergeant Hoffner, who had been drinking. He had emptied his revolver while taking target practice at a row of beer bottles. He was not in a belligerent mood and when the woman proprietor of the house assured the officers that he could pass the night there to "sleep it off," the officers relieved Hoffner of his revolver and departed. About an hour later, however, Wilkes and Velusky received a message to look for Hoffner, who had left the house in search of the prowl car in order to retrieve his revolver. He now was in a belligerent mood and before leaving had threatened and struck several of the inmates. In spite of the severely cold weather he left without his cap and overcoat. Wilkes and Velusky proceeded to search the neighborhood without success. They went off duty at eight A.M. and were relieved by Patrolmen Shea and Wintergarten, who continued the search. Hoffner was found asleep in the tool shed of the St. Stanislaus Polish Cemetery, more than a mile and one half from the house on Railway Avenue, when two part-time gravediggers appeared for work at ten A.M. Police were notified and Hoffner was taken to headquarters, although not booked, and then removed by ambulance to St. Mary's Hospital, where he died three days later. Surviving were two sons by his first marriage, which ended in divorce. They are believed to be living in Allentown, Pa., with Hoffner's married sister. His second wife, from whom he was separated in 1935, operates a beauty parlor in Milwaukee, Wis. Hoffner was buried in the Odd Fellows Cemetery by the Police Benevolent Fund, after Milwaukee police reported to local headquarters that the second wife "wanted no part of him, alive or dead."

I would be glad to work out details either for some kind of coöperation with the Police Benevolent Fund or to establish a Fund of our own, but I think you will agree that to do so in memory of Ray Hoffner would not be to the best interests of the paper, and I am sure that if Mr. Hooker were alive he would agree. We are, of course, always delighted to receive your most welcome suggestions for the good of the paper, and perhaps as a small stockholder I may be permitted to offer one or two of my own at some future time. Your inspired wartime idea to run a cut of the American flag on the editorial page was typically patriotic and you no doubt recall how much I personally appreciated your suggestion several years ago that women's golf scores properly belong on the society page. Thus by tokens of your interest we are made aware that we are all pulling together—you in the mansion on the hill, and we here.

(Signed) DOUG CAMPBELL,
Managing Editor

A Family Party

Stenographic Report

*T*he following is a stenographic report of an address by Mr. Albert
W. Shoemaker, president of the Shoemaker Printing Company
and former editor and publisher of the Lyons Republican, at a
dinner in honor of Dr. Samuel G. Merritt. The dinner, which
took place on September 17, 1955, in the main dining room of the
Lyons Hotel, Lyons, Pennsylvania, commemorated the forty years of Dr.
Merritt's service to Lyons and surrounding communities and to wish
him well upon his retirement from active practice of his profession.

The affair was sponsored jointly by the Lyons Rotary Club, Kiwanis,
Lions, Junior Chamber of Commerce, Patriotic Order Sons of America,
Knights of Columbus, Benevolent & Protective Order of Elks, Ancient
Order of Hibernians, Knights of Pythias, Ministerial Association, Holy
Name Society, Veterans of Foreign Wars, American Legion, Lyons Gun
Club, Merchants Association, Boy Scouts of America, Order of the
Eastern Star, American Red Cross, Daughters of Isabella, Delphian
Society, United Mine Workers of America, and the Nesquehela County
Medical Society.

More than two hundred persons, including many prominent in business, labor, industry and the professions, were present at the dinner. The
invocation was by the Reverend Father Alexis P. Smirnolinski, pastor of
St. Boniface R. C. Church, after which the toastmaster, Mr. Cyril V.
Longenecker, introduced several leading out-of-town visitors, who were
called upon for brief remarks. They were followed by the address by Mr.
Shoemaker, who was the principal speaker of the evening.

The benediction was asked by the Reverend Eustace Muhlenberg Fry,
rector of the Lyons Methodist Episcopal Church. Music was provided
by the Lyons High School Orchestra under the leadership of Miss Char-
line K. Smith, B.M.

Collier's (2 March 1956); A Family Party

* * *

Mr. Toastmaster, Distinguished Guests, Reverend Members of the Clergy, and Ladies and Gentlemen:

Back in February of this year, when a few of us old-timers accidentally discovered that we had in our midst a man who had held the same job for close on to forty years, that seemed such a remarkable accomplishment in these days that a few of us decided we ought to do something about it. This town of ours used to be an important railroad center, before they put in the buses and before the business of mining coal was all shot to—well, a certain place that I understand they have all the coal they need, if the reverend clergy will pardon me.

I mention the railroads because when they were prosperous, one of the greatest honors a man could have was the watch that the railroad company gave a man when he retired. I used to sometimes wonder why they gave a railroader a watch when he retired instead of when he started out, but of course the railroads used to do a lot of things I could never understand, but that's not saying I don't wish we still had them with us. But as I was saying, it was an honor when the company gave a man a watch, and incidentally you never hear of a bus driver bragging about the watch the bus company gave him. Well, be that as it may, the reason why a man was so proud of his watch was because it meant something. It represented something.

What did it represent? It represented that a man had given thirty or forty years of faithful service to his company and to his community, out in all kinds of weather, often performing his duties at the risk of his very life. It represented to one and all that a man had not only done his job and obeyed orders, but oftentimes did that little extra something that meant his train reached its destination on time and without damage to the cargo or injury to the passengers. Railroading was hard work and not only hard work physically. A man had to keep on his toes. If you wanted to go from brakeman to fireman or fireman to engineman, you had to study the rules and pass difficult examinations that if you ever saw the examination for fireman, I wonder how many college graduates could pass it today.

Well, ladies and gentlemen, the more we thought of it the more we decided that we had in our midst a friend of ours who had held a job for forty years, or nearly forty, and while he wasn't a brakeman on the railroad, or a fireman, or an engineman, or for that matter a trackwalker, still he had been serving his community that long, and he was entitled to some recognition. Of course you all know who I am talking about, so I guess I can take the liberty of saying that this old friend of ours, he held his job for forty years. Sure he held his job for forty years. Why? Nobody could fire him.

But seriously, if you want to look at it that way, I'm wrong, because to put it another way, there wasn't a man or woman in Lyons or nearby communities that couldn't fire him. On the railroad there's only a few that can fire you, but this friend of ours, anybody could fire him. But nobody ever did, at least that I know of, so we had to give him credit for keeping his job for forty years with more bosses than anybody I can think of. Not to take anything away from those of you who worked on the railroads, or had fathers or brothers or uncles that were railroaders, but this friend of ours was every bit as important as any engineman or fireman or conductor, and I'm sure some of you will agree with me that maybe he was a little more important. I could look around this room right now and see the faces of some former railroaders that wouldn't be here tonight if it hadn't of been for the friend we are honoring this evening.

And I guess anybody that's old enough can remember how desperately he worked the night of the Short Mountain wreck. That was the time when an 1800-type locomotive ran away and plowed into the Bug loaded with a hundred and eighty miners on their way home from work. For the benefit of the younger ones present, the Bug was the name they gave to the miners' train that took the miners up to Short Mountain and Outerbridge Colliery. They killed fourteen miners not counting members of the crew, and when I was in the Army in France in 1918 I still never saw anything to compare with that rear car of the Bug. They used to back it up to Outerbridge Colliery, so when the 1800-type ran away she plowed right into that rear car and I don't want to turn your stomachs with a description of the carnage that evening.

I was reporting on my father's newspaper, the good old Lyons *Republican* that I unfortunately couldn't keep its head above water after 1929, and when we heard there was a wreck up on Short Mountain my father sent me up there to cover it, and all I can tell you is that I wish it had been my day off. Only I didn't have a day off. But I wished I had gone for a swim out in the Glen. Anything so I wouldn't have to be there when my father got word about the wreck. We got the word just about as soon as anybody because we used to publish the *Republican* in the building where Hartman's Garage is now, but then it was our office and we had our printing plant there, and of course it was right across the street from the old freight station and down the street from the passenger, and somebody mentioned it to my father and they were making up a train consisting of a baggage car and a locomotive to go up there to the scene of the wreck. They had young boys going around to the doctors' offices and trying to get miners that had first-aid experience, first-aid crewmen, and any National Guard men that could be of assistance.

We only had the three doctors in town then and I remember thinking when I got on the train, they had two of the doctors, but I didn't see Sam Merritt. "Where is Sam Merritt?" I asked myself. Well, I could have saved my breath, because when we reached the scene of the wreck, Sam was there already. But I'll tell you this much. At first I couldn't recognize him. And I'll leave it to your imagination what his face was covered with that I couldn't recognize him.

How did Sam Merritt get there? How did he happen to be the first there? The first doctor? Well, it's a good question, but tonight we can ask ourselves how Sam Merritt was often the first one to be there, on the scene when he was needed. I'm not taking anything from the other two doctors we had then, or any we had since, but I never knew a man like Sam Merritt for being there when he was needed.

Well, I took a look at Sam and he took a look at me, and then he put me to work. I wasn't a reporter. I was an orderly, or a nurse. There was nobody standing around that night, taking notes. He worked us all so hard that we hardly got any chance to show any signs of weakness. I tell you what the only thing I can compare it to that I ever saw was, and that was a field hospital. Or more like a dressing station before you got to the field hospital. We got other help from Johnsville, and also from Singerstown and Mountain View and Holtz's and Singers Crossing, and by the time it was dark, some of the doctors and nurses from Gibbsville and Fort Penn, but the commander in chief was Sam Merritt, and we'll never know how many miners had their lives saved because Sam was on the scene so quickly after it happened.

Later on, weeks later, I happened to think of that and I asked Sam, I said, "How did you happen to get there so soon the evening of the wreck?" And do you know what his answer was? His answer was typical, I mean typical of how a doctor can never call his time his own. He said he had a new 16-gauge, a Fox I remember it was, 16-gauge Fox in the back of his tin lizzie and he'd been meaning for days to take it out and fire a few rounds just to get the feel of it, and this particular day he decided that he'd put it off long enough and he was going to fire that gun no matter whose baby didn't get delivered or who got the croup.

So he took the back road out by Schwarzwald's and was looking for a place to stop and get in a little shooting and suddenly he heard the crash. It was suppertime almost, but he had no trouble locating the crash because the boiler blew up and the rear car caught fire. Right away he guessed what happened. Back went the new gun and Sam drove as near as he could to the scene of the wreck and went the rest on foot. And just to show you that the world isn't full of men like Sam Merritt, somebody stole the new gun from the back of the Ford. While he was tending to the injured and dying, somebody went up to his car and stole the shotgun out of the back seat of the car and he never laid eyes on it again.

Well, maybe some of you good people are wondering a little about this speech of mine, if you can call it a speech, so I guess I better tell you how it all happened. I think everybody, or at least everybody from town, all know that Sam Merritt is my best friend and has been since we were boys together. As boys we weren't too close. We didn't get along very well. I never thought much of him and he never thought much of me, but there weren't so many boys the same age, so there was only the four or five white boys and two colored that played together then, and Sam and I were in that bunch. We all used to go out the Glen swimming, or get chased off coal cars and empty freights, and sometimes get caught stealing apples out of Mrs. Fiddler's orchard. Hallowe'en we used to take gates off people's fences, and hold ticktacks up against their windows, or chalk up their sidewalks—where there were sidewalks—or barns, if they didn't have any sidewalks.

Lyons was a great deal different then than it is now, when we were boys. When we were boys they didn't have any radio or television and Sol Pollock hadn't even started up his movie house. You could count the automobiles on the fingers of one hand, and the hose company didn't have the combination truck they have now. We had a hand pumper that we also pulled by hand, or the firemen did. We just ran along after them. I heard my nephew talking the other day about the bucket brigade, as if a bucket brigade was something typical of the Revolutionary War. Well, they had them in the Revolutionary War, but they had them in my time, too, and I don't go back quite that far.

Oh, there were a great many things we have now that we didn't have then, like paved streets, and sidewalks on every street in town. But I can tell you a few things we had then that we don't have now and one of them is trees. You wouldn't know it now, but almost every house in Lyons had its tree in front of it, and sometimes two, and I know in our back yard we had four apple trees and two oxheart cherry trees and two or maybe three sickle pears and a grape arbor.

We have this modern hotel where we are having this banquet this evening, but where this hotel stands there used to be the old Exchange Hotel run by Martin Angstadt, and I can remember him how he used to get very angry if a man's horse chewed the bark off one of the trees in front of his hotel. It meant there was something wrong with the horse but Martin didn't care about the horse. All he cared about was what they were doing to his trees. All I have to do is shut my eyes and remember how Lyons looked thirty, forty years ago when we still had trees. Now instead of trees we have parking meters on Main Street and Market Street and very few trees anywheres else.

But I started to tell you good people how I happened to be making this speech this evening. I didn't ask to do it, I guarantee you that. But when we began talking among ourselves about giving a banquet in honor of Sam Merritt we had several discussions about asking somebody prominent like the Governor or maybe some famous doctor or somebody like that. But the more we thought of it the more we wanted to make it what you might call a family party. You won't find anybody here tonight that's a stranger to Sam Merritt. We're all either his friends or related to him, and that includes those from out of town that you heard earlier this evening.

We could have got the Governor to come here this evening and you'll notice on the program you'll see printed the names of former Lyons boys that left Lyons and went out to become successful in New York City, Philadelphia, Detroit, Michigan, and other distant places. They all wanted to take some part in the celebration, as Cy told you earlier, so we very graciously permitted them to buy tickets for the dinner even if they couldn't be here to eat it. But we decided that if we got somebody like the Governor it would make it a different kind of a party. Sam Merritt was never one that was much for show and I doubt if he would have permitted us to hold this dinner if it got too elaborate. In fact he said so. If we wanted to hold a banquet for him it had to be kept simple and confined to Lyons people and a few from out of town that he himself would like to have present.

Well, you can't have a party like this without there being a speaker, and the more we went ahead with the preparations the more I noticed that they didn't say anything about who the speaker was going to be. Then finally about two weeks ago I brought it up at a meeting of the committee and the other fellows looked at each other and laughed and I think it was Reese Evans said to me, "Bert, you're it."

"Me?" I said.

"That's right. You. Bert Shoemaker."

"But the dinner's only about two weeks off," I said. I said, "I can't go to work and prepare a speech in two weeks."

"We know that," said Reese. "That's why we didn't tell you before.

We don't want a speech. If you prepare a speech it'll be formal and stiff. All we want you to do is stand up on your two feet and kind of reminisce about Sam. You're his best friend and you know him bet- ter than anybody else and you won't spill all over with sentimental hogwash."

"That you can be sure of," I said. "Because if I did the first person to leave the room would be Samuel G. Merritt, M.D." So that's how I happened to get picked as the speaker. They allowed me to write down a few notes that I could refer to in case I got stuck for some- thing to say, but that's all. I have these notes here, and just let me hold them up for you to see and you'll readily understand that I wasn't allowed to do much preparation.

So far I haven't referred to my notes but I think I ought to start touching on some of the highlights and I notice I have written down here the word *Family*. I had the experience the other day where there were these two young fellows in their early thirties and one of them made a disparaging remark about the other and I said to him it was no way to talk about his cousin. His cousin? he said. Well, be- lieve it or not, this one young fellow didn't know he was a cousin of the other and it was up to me to explain the relationship. They don't seem to care so much about that any more, and that being the case, I wouldn't be surprised if half the people in this room, especially the younger ones, don't know a great deal about Sam's family history.

Not that I intend to give you a whole family tree, but for their benefit, Sam was born right here in Lyons in the year 1887. His father was Isaac Merritt and Isaac was born here too. Here I have to look at my notes and it says Isaac was born 1860. Eighteen sixty. Well, that was ninety-five years ago, almost a hundred years ago. Mr. Merritt went through school here, first public and then high, then I understand he took the two-year commercial course at Fort Penn Commercial Institute.

What Mr. Merritt's father, Sam's grandfather did, I don't know and I should have found that out before getting up here and talking. However, I do know the family originally came here from Connecti- cut by way of York State, and I understand the road they have called the Merritt Parkway was named after some family connection, al- though you'll have to verify that with Sam as that's only my impres- sion and I don't want to make a positive statement to that effect. But that's what the stock was. New England. Then in 1883 Sam's father married Miss Frieda Langendorf, and the Langendorfs are an old Lyons family, which most of you know. The Langendorfs built the first trolley line here and I guess there wasn't much accomplished around here that the Langendorfs didn't have something to do with.

Sam was the second son of that union. He had an older brother, Isaac Junior, known as Boo for some reason I couldn't fathom. Boo Merritt was always known as Boo even in the privacy of the home. Boo received an appointment to the United States Naval Academy at Annapolis, Maryland, and he was in his third year there doing extremely well when he contracted spinal meningitis and passed away at the age of twenty. He was the tallest of the Merritt family and some said he grew too fast. That may be, but I can tell you all the girls fell for him when he came home on vacation in his Annapolis midshipman's uniform. In those days we used to have a dance at Christmas at the Odd Fellows Hall and the rest of us weren't in it when Boo was around.

Boo passing away was very hard on Sam not only because they were very close for two brothers about the same age, but also he had the responsibility of being the oldest of the Merritt children. There was Victoria, now Mrs. J. J. Singer, and Dorothy, Mrs. D. W. Schleicher, of Johnsville, both ladies it is my pleasure to see here tonight observing the affair in honor of their older brother. Then there was Oscar Merritt, Sam's younger brother, born 1891 and passed away at the age of six of typhoid, so I guess you couldn't call him a responsibility when Boo died, although naturally Mr. and Mrs. Merritt must have thought back to their early loss when Boo died, and that was a sort of a responsibility for Sam.

I often think it was Boo that decided Sam to become a doctor. When he passed away, that is. Up to then I don't remember Sam ever saying much about being a doctor. This is only what I think, but when we were young boys together I would have said Sam would grow up to be a carpenter. Carpenter and builder. In those days a master carpenter could build a house and all the help he needed was an apprentice, and by the time Sam was fourteen or fifteen years of age, he was the handiest with tools in our bunch, and one summer when he was fifteen or sixteen, he put in new shelves and bins and one counter in his father's store. He did it all by himself.

Today I guess Sam has the best amateur carpentry shop in town down in the cellar at his house, and a lot of us here tonight have articles of furniture that Sam made in his own shop, just for pleasure. Very fine workmanship, too. Not only articles of furniture, but also the gavel they use at Rotary, that was made by Sam. The pulpit at the M. E. church, that was made by Sam, not to mention countless cigar humidors and things for the ladies to keep their sewing in.

I often heard Sam say he could make more cash money as a carpenter than as a doctor, because people pay their carpenter before they pay their doctor, but I promised I wouldn't say anything about that tonight because I don't think anybody'd have the nerve to show their face here tonight if they owed Sam for an unpaid bill. I wouldn't think of mentioning that, because I don't think anybody'd drive here in a nice new sedan if they still owed Sam for medical attention a year or two ago. So I won't say anything about that.

Nobody has to make excuses for not paying Sam the money they owe him, because Sam makes up their excuses himself. I remember saying to him some years ago, I said I noticed that a certain family were sending their son away to college and they seemed to forget they owed Sam over eight hundred dollars. "Well," said Sam, "eight hundred dollars will only pay for one semester and if the boy's no good and flunks out at the end of the one semester, that'll be a heartache for the parents. And if the boy finishes and makes a good showing, I'll get some satisfaction out of knowing that I helped put him through." That's the kind of story that everybody here can tell about Sam Merritt.

I used to try to persuade him to leave his money at home when he went out on his calls because if he had twenty-five dollars in his pocket when he went out, that was no guarantee that he was going to have twenty-five when he got home. And don't forget, friends, some of his patients used to pay him cash by the visit.

"At least don't give away more than you earn in a day," I used to say to him. But Sam would take a look at some poor family and how they were living, or existing, and before he got home that evening he'd have an order of groceries and meat and clothes for the children on their way to the poor family.

Not that the poor weren't grateful. It wasn't the poor he should have worried about. I guess if there's one man here tonight that knows more about that than I do it's Reverend Smirnolinski, because he had more poor people in his parish than the other denomina-. tions. If you want to know what the Irish think of Sam Merritt you ought to take a look at some of the embroidery tablecloths and napkins the Sisters made for the Merritt family. And don't think that makes Sam any the less a good Methodist, because it doesn't. Sam's a good Mason and I don't have to say any more on that subject because I just got the signal to pipe down, but I think you all got my meaning.

I was saying a minute ago that when he was a young fellow in his teens, I didn't think Sam Merritt would ever be a doctor. I never even gave it a thought. Take high school. In botany he was all right, but when he had biology Sam would turn green when he had to dissect a frog. As far as any of us know, there was never a doctor in the Merritt or the Langendorf family, and the nearest thing to it was I understand the Merritt store did a thriving business in Peruna. That was a medicine that you didn't need a prescription for and it cured all your aches and pains. Some people took Peruna that wouldn't permit you to mention the name of Old Overholt, but the one made you feel just as good as the other.

One summer Sam got a job tending the soda fountain at Brown's but he didn't learn anything about medicine that summer. I had the same job another summer and we used to close at half past nine, but it was always near eleven before I got home by the time I got finished washing the soda glasses and ice-cream dishes and packing down those cans with ice and mixing syrup for the next day. Nobody had time to learn anything on that job. Except how smart old Doc Brown was, hiring a young fellow that thought he was going to gorge himself on ice cream and paying him two dollars a week and working him so hard he didn't even have time to eat up the profits.

But I'm not up here to pay compliments to old Doc Brown and his business ability. You wanted somebody to take a cinder out of your eye, Doc was as efficient at that as any professional man. Or, a little indigestion, Doc would give you a glass of soda water, or somebody'd faint and they'd be revived in Doc Brown's drugstore. In fact, Brown's drugstore in those days was the closest we had to a hospital here in Lyons. The collieries had shacks where injured men would be taken and put in bed till it was time to move them to the hospital in Fort Penn. But if there was a runaway horse and somebody got hurt, or for instance somebody fell on the ice and broke a leg, if it happened anywhere near Doc Brown's drugstore, that's where they'd take him.

And all those things meant expense to old Doc and usually there wasn't anybody to send a bill to, not to mention who had to clean up the drugstore after an accident. In a way Doc Brown should be here tonight, because although he didn't start Sam Merritt to becoming a doctor, I know that when Sam finally did go away to medical college, when he came home for vacation he always used to sit and talk to Doc Brown in those two big easy chairs Doc had in the back of the drugstore.

Doc would sit there in one of those big easy chairs and without getting up he could see who was in the store, and usually he could guess what they wanted. I guess a lot of people used to wonder how Doc Brown would know they were in the store. Well, I'll tell you. He had a peephole. It wasn't a regular peephole, such as they have in the curtain on a theatrical stage. Doc's peephole was this way: there was a row of medicine bottles on a shelf that stood between the store proper and the back room. Well, there was an empty place in that row of bottles and from where he sat Doc could sit in the chair and see through that vacant place and watch the people come in the front door.

I remember one time when I was about fourteen years old, I went in the store and Doc was in the back and I didn't think he heard me. So I reached down in the cigar counter and helped myself to two Philadelphia Hand-Mades and stuck them in my pocket. Then I called out, "Anybody here?" and Doc came out and waited on me. I guess I was getting something for my mother or father, and whatever it was, I said to charge it, and Doc said to me, "Want me to put the cigars on the bill or will you pay for them yourself? Since when did your father start smoking cigars?"

Well, I guess Doc Brown and Sam Merritt had many an interesting chat after Sam started going to medical college. I noticed since then that other Lyons boys that went away to study medicine used to drop in and loaf around at Doc Brown's. One way of keeping in touch with the profession and learning about prescriptions. Even after they got their degree they used to be in Doc Brown's till they got started building up a practice, although in a town like Lyons there was always plenty of work for a doctor if he didn't care when he got paid. I guess that's the same everywhere, not only Lyons.

The older men, the established ones, they got so much a year being company doctor at one of the collieries, and so much for various lodges, and usually the Protestant doctors got all the Protestants and the Catholic doctor got all the Catholics, and one of the older doctors would get the Reading Railway and the other would get the Pennsy. What was left for the young fellow just starting out was pretty slim pickings and some of it we don't have to talk about in mixed company. I know this much, that in 1915, when Sam Merritt hung out his shingle, I was getting eighteen a week working for my father on the old *Republican* and Sam was Dr. Samuel G. Merritt, or Dr. S. G. Merritt, I was a married man with a wife and daughter and Sam didn't feel he could afford to get married yet. Of course I didn't have to have my own tin lizzie and buy surgical instruments and things like that.

Surgical instruments. I want to ask Sam Merritt here and now, yes or no, is it true what I heard thirty-five or more years ago that one day he and four or five other fellows were out gunning for deer out in the Valley and they spent the night at a farmhouse out there and the farmer was putting in new timbers in the barn and somehow or other a big stone block fell on him and crushed his foot and they couldn't get the stone off. Now what I want to know, tonight after all these years, is it true that Sam cut off the foot with an ordinary handsaw? Sam says yes, he's nodding to me. That's all I wanted to know. I've been waiting thirty-five years for the answer to that, but Sam would never tell me. I don't know why. If you can do as good a job—well, some of the ladies don't appear to be very pleased with this kind of talk, so I'll change the subject.

Perhaps it would be more fitting if I went back to what I was saying about Boo Merritt and how when he passed away it decided Sam to be a doctor. Up to then Sam wouldn't even help out if a mare was having a colt, and I told you how he felt about dissecting. I'll tell you this much too, and I don't think it will make anybody sick. Sam Merritt the first time he ever saw a real operation fainted. He told me that himself. That was at the Jefferson Medical College in Philadelphia and he just keeled over. He got used to it, but the first time, he and I think two other students fell flat on their faces. Well, a man that wanted to be a doctor that bad must have had some underlying reason for it, and according to the way I look at it, Sam was so incensed over what happened to Boo that he began to wonder or say to himself, "If I can prevent that, it's my job to prevent it."

Why do I say that? Well, I don't think Sam said it in so many words. But if you look at Sam's whole career as a doctor and as a man, I never saw anybody like Sam for wanting to right a wrong. A doctor is always righting wrongs. That's his business, or profession, if you prefer. He is supposed to cure people, which is the same thing as righting a wrong. But now there was brother Boo, passing away just when he ought to be starting life. I don't say Sam resolved to find a cure for spinal meningitis, nothing like that. But Boo passing away just showed Sam that there was a way he could right wrongs and make it his lifework.

Maybe when Oscar passed away that had something to do with it, but by the time Boo passed away Sam was a little older and more likely to think about such things. Up to then Sam was destined to be a carpenter, if the signs meant anything, but shortly after Boo passed away Sam began taking an interest in doctoring and have long talks with Dr. George Steever, and there is a man that ought to be here tonight to give us the full story of how Sam finally made his decision, because if it hadn't of been for Dr. George Steever, in my opinion Sam never would have gone to medical college.

Looking around, my guess is that Dr. George Steever is responsible for over half the people in this room. Those he didn't personally bring into the world, he brought one or both of their parents. In my case he brought me into the world and Sam Merritt and all Sam's brothers and sisters. But they gave Dr. Steever a celebration years

ago when he retired to St. Petersburg, Florida, and this party is for
Sam Merritt. But it wouldn't be complete if I didn't mention the late
Dr. George Steever. He used to let Sam go along with him on his
calls and that way Sam got a first-hand look at what it would be like
to be a doctor, and of course we have to give Dr. Steever credit for
recognizing Sam's ability. Or maybe not ability, because Sam didn't
have any ability then, but Dr. Steever had the insight to realize that
Sam would make a good doctor and helped him get into medical
college and also convinced Mr. Isaac Merritt that it was worth going
to all that expense. I just remembered now that I made a note of Dr.
Steever and here I mentioned him without consulting my notes.

Well, since I took a look at my notes I might as well take a good
look at them and see what I have down here. *Hobbies.* I guess if you
didn't know it before you know it now, that Sam always liked to go
gunning. That was one hobby I wouldn't be surprised if Sam brought
down as many as fifteen deer in the space of thirty years. That's
nothing unusual in Lyons, but I'll bet some of you will be surprised
to hear that Sam was I think the last man to get a bear in this town. I
mean by that, within ten miles of town. I haven't even heard of a
bear being seen the last twenty years, but there were still some in the
woods on Klinger's Mountain as late as 1916, the year Sam got his.
That's still pretty wild country through there but I never heard of
anybody from town getting a bear since Sam shot his. What would
that be? Thirty-five years ago. I mean thirty-nine. Thank you.

Sam hardly ever took a real vacation but there was one day he
kept sacred and that was the opening day of the hunting season,
even if all he went out for was pheasant. If he ever came back with
an empty pouch I never heard of it, because Sam was a very good
shot with gun or rifle. A little better with the shotgun because he got
more practice, but he was what I call a hunting shooter. Some of our
fellows out at the Gun Club could beat Sam shooting blue rocks or
target, but when you got out in the woods or out where there was
quail, Sam didn't miss very many. He had a lot of patience. I don't
mean that the way you took it. I meant the other kind of patience,
not p-a-t-i-e-n-t-s. He had both kinds, but the kind of patience I have
reference to is the kind whereby you can wait and wait for hours, if
necessary. If Sam was convinced there was deer in a certain locality,
he'd stand there like a statue till he got a shot at the animal. Sam
could stand there with a chew of tobacco in his mouth and never
move a muscle. Maybe I shouldn't have said that about chewing
tobacco. But Sam chewed all his life and half the time I wouldn't
know if he had a chew in or not. Most people didn't know he even
chewed. Well, I guess that about covers gunning.

Carpentry I already spoke of. This do-it-yourself craze you hear so much about nowadays, Sam was ahead of the public by forty years. Other hobbies I won't mention because a Methodist isn't supposed to play cards. Well, anybody that ever played bridge or poker with a certain friend of ours, he didn't violate any religious scruples with the kind of bridge and poker he played. All I can say is that if Methodists aren't supposed to play bridge or poker, this friend of ours played like a Methodist.

Maybe the true test of how fond we are of this man is that I notice there are several people in this room, myself among them, and anybody that speaks to him, let alone attends a banquet for him, must be very fond of him after being his partner at a game of bridge. Suffice it to say that he went right on playing auction after everybody else in the country was playing contract. They tell the famous story of the fellow that was playing bridge one time and after he got set five tricks doubled and redoubled and vulnerable, his partner said to him, "Herman, when did you learn to play bridge? Don't just say today, say what time today." That fits our friend to the letter. Yes, our friend had to have a lot of lovable qualities to overcome his lack of ability when it came to playing cards.

Earlier in this talk, or remarks, or whatever you wish to call them, I spoke of Sam Merritt's service to the community. In my opinion it would have been enough just to have Sam Merritt attending to our aches and pains, great or small, and carrying us through our illnesses, major or minor. The majority of us here tonight have felt the touch of his hand on our pulse or had him tell us to say "Ah" and do all the things a family doctor does in the course of his daily routine. Old or young, rich or poor, we all felt better for having Sam in charge because we had the confidence that with Sam there beside us and looking after us, we had more than a doctor there. We had if not a friend—those that did not know him on that basis—we had the instinctive feeling that here was a man that the thing he wanted most in the world was for us to get well, and if there was anything in his power, he'd see to it that we did.

I look around and see a lot of you nodding in agreement. Yes, so many of us have shared that experience in our acquaintance with Sam. Speaking from personal experience, he saved my life on two separate occasions. Once when I had pneumonia and the other time was when we were both about twenty and out swimming at the Glen I got cramps and it was Sam that not only pulled me out but brought me to. Many of the young people he brought into the world went out and served their country in Africa, Europe, the Pacific and Korea, and there are children in this town tonight that Sam not only delivered them but also both of their parents. Some of us are walking around with both legs or have the use of both hands that if it hadn't of been for Sam's care we would have been minus a limb. In all our memories as long as we live we'll all have some reason to be grateful to Sam Merritt. And it ought to be a great satisfaction to Sam, although the kind of man Sam is, I don't even think he gives that a thought. He would only consider that he had done his duty according to the oath of I am sorry to say I can't recall the name of the famous Greek person that made up the oath that all doctors are supposed to take.

But as though that were not sufficient to make an indelible impression on the history of our community, let us not, my friends, overlook his service to the community as a whole and not merely what we know and recall as individuals. For Samuel G. Merritt made a contribution to this community that is not generally known and to the best of my knowledge and belief, never was given credit for. Perhaps many of you, even those who hold him in high esteem and consider that you are his friends, perhaps many of you will be hearing this for the first time.

Now I see our friend frowning at me because he is beginning to suspect the nature of what I am about to tell you and he would vastly prefer that I maintain silence on the subject. But this is a family party in which I see nobody here that does not belong here. This is a family party and I was delegated to make the principal address because I happen to be the guest of honor's best friend. Therefore in spite of the silent protest of our guest of honor, I consider it my duty at least once and for all to relate to you the true story of a service which he rendered the community that many of us are apt to overlook and many others do not even know about.

Sam, you're just going to have to sit there and let me talk, so stop making faces at me.

Back in the middle of the nineteen twenties, and all the years preceding, if somebody from Lyons had to have a major operation or hospital care, they had their choice of two hospitals. The person could go to Gibbsville, thirty-five miles away, or they could go to Fort Penn, a distance of forty-four miles. Most people preferred to go to Fort Penn because although Gibbsville was nearer by nine miles, it meant mountain travel all the way, whereas Fort Penn meant there was only one mountain between Lyons and there.

In the old days when I was a boy the only ambulance we had was owned by the colliery and it was drawn by mules. If a miner got badly hurt in the mines they would bring him first to the first-aid shack and then put him in the ambulance and put him in the baggage car of the

Pennsy train, the morning one or the evening one, and I don't have to tell you that half the time by the time the train was ready to leave, the injured man was beyond all assistance on this earth.

Later on the collieries had an automobile ambulance, but even that wasn't much of an improvement in bad weather. The roads from here to Gibbsville were usually drifted, or the tires would go bad, or that old Winton would get engine trouble and there they'd be stuck halfway between here and Gibbsville till somebody came along and pulled them out. From here to Fort Penn was better, but not all that better.

Well, then came the great influenza epidemic of 1918 and the people around here were dying like flies. Odd Fellows Hall was turned into an emergency hospital and so was the Moose Hall. Sam and our other doctors used to work till they dropped and then they'd have a cup of coffee and start working some more. But all those conditions convinced Sam that we needed a hospital here in Lyons. Thirty-five miles away, forty-four miles away was too far to take somebody that was dying of illness or accident. So that was when Sam began his one-man campaign to raise funds for a hospital here in Lyons.

You know what the first thing he did was, after he got an estimate on how much the hospital would cost? He put up all his savings, a little over $14,000, mortgaged his house for another ten, got his mother to donate a thousand, and he was in business. In other words, he was able to go around to people and say he had raised $25,000 toward a new hospital for Lyons.

The lowest estimate he could get for a completely equipped small hospital, completely equipped but with nothing fancy, was $300,000. So he went to his sisters and got between them another five thousand, and that way he was able to tell people that ten per cent of the cost was already raised. He didn't bother to tell anybody that all the money had been raised inside his own family, mostly by Sam himself. Some of you easily remember what a campaign he put on. First he started with his friends, and he bled us dry, but we were only too glad. All you had to do was listen to Sam giving his sales talk and he made it seem like a pleasure to dig down in your pocket or your bank account and give till it hurt and then give some more, as they used to say. The other two doctors in town put up five thousand apiece and more credit to them, because it was a lot of money in those days.

Of course everywhere Sam went to collect money or pledges, everybody said what about the coal companies? Why don't you get the money from them? But Sam said he was more anxious to have it a community enterprise first and save the coal companies for big contributions later, when more than half the money was raised and the coal companies couldn't say no. The same with the Union. Sam felt that if Lyons raised most of the money, the Union and the operators would be practically forced into putting up the balance.

Well, Sam was doing fine, pleading and persuading and badgering. All the town churches had euchres and bake sales and sold chances on this or that, and Rotary and Kiwanis and the fraternal organizations all chipped in, and Sam added up one day and realized that he had in money and pledges just a little over $200,000. Now was the time to go to the coal companies and the Union!

Then the ax fell.

The day before he was going to call on the coal companies the miners went out on strike. That turned out to be a strike lasting from the first of September, '25, to the twelfth of February, '26. What a winter that was. Men standing around with nothing to do and no colliery whistles sounding in the hills, everybody short on rations or going to soup kitchens, and merchants wondering if they'd be able to stay open much longer. And who was the most unpopular man in Lyons? Not the superintendent, not the district leader of the Union. No, the most unpopular man was Sam Merritt, because he held onto the cash he had collected and wouldn't give it back. He knew if he gave it back it would be twice as hard to collect again and he held onto it in two special accounts at the two town banks.

I am proud to confess that I gave one fellow a punch in the jaw right out in the middle of Main Street when he hinted that the strike didn't worry Sam Merritt with all that money in the bank. And there was a lot of that kind of talk that I didn't hear first-hand or I would have had to give a few more socks in the jaw. I happened to know that the only meat Sam had in the house during the whole month of December was some venison he shot, and likewise he only had enough heat in the house to warm the first floor where the office was. I think a lot of people went to that office that didn't have much wrong with them but only wanted to keep warm.

Well, the strike was settled on Lincoln's Birthday and Sam and I had a little drink of schnapps to celebrate the occasion and he said he was going to go back to work. "Back to work?" I said.

"Back collecting for the hospital," he said. And so he did. Inside of a week he was around getting a few pledges, then he tackled the coal companies. He got twenty thousand apiece from the two independents, but then when he went and called on the Nesquehela he got nothing but a cold stare.

"Why not?" he said.

"We have other plans," they said.

"Well, let me in on the plans. I've raised most of the money. It's all in the town banks. Every penny accounted for. It didn't cost a cent to collect the money, but we can't start to build without your contribution. We need seventy-five thousand." Sam pleaded with them.

"We have other plans," was all they'd say.

Then about two days later Sam had a visitor. Call him Dr. Blank. He's a blank as far as I'm concerned. He came into Sam's office and said, "Doctor, naturally we've been hearing a lot about your little hospital, or at least your plans for a little hospital."

Sam said yes, and to go ahead.

"Well," the other doctor said, "we've been having the same idea up in Johnsville."

"Oh, you have, have you?" said Sam. "When did you first get your idea?"

"Well, when we got the idea doesn't make any difference. The point is we've raised some money too because we want the hospital to be in Johnsville."

"Why not Lyons? We've been working on this for a year," said Sam.

"Yes, but you've gone as far as you can without the contribution from Nesquehela."

"That's true," said Sam. "Why don't you come in with us and we'll have a Lyons-Johnsville hospital. We can go ahead without Nesquehela."

"Ah, but we have Nesquehela, and we want the hospital for Johnsville."

Sam picked up the phone and called the super and asked if it was true that Nesquehela was backing Johnsville. Yes, he was told, it was true. "And I suppose Dr. Blank is to be superintendent of the new Johnsville Hospital?" said Sam. Yes, that was true.

"All right, Doctor, you'll hear from me," said Sam.

I don't know what must have gone on in Sam's mind the next few hours, but I know that he sat down and wrote a letter that we printed and sent to every single person and organization that had contributed to the Lyons Hospital campaign. I could quote you the whole letter but what's the use. It explained what had happened, that Johnsville was also planning a hospital and had been promised the Nesquehela contribution, without which Lyons could not start to build. He then urged all who had contributed to the Lyons hospital to authorize him to turn the contribution over to Johnsville, because it would mean a much bigger and better-equipped institution, and after all Johnsville was only eight miles away.

Sam worded that letter so carefully that most people were convinced that it was their duty to turn the money over to Johnsville, and over 85 per cent of them did. And this is something that nobody ever knew before tonight—namely, that included in the money that Johnsville got was the $30,000 that Sam raised inside his own family.

That's the kind of man we honor here tonight.

Now I hope Sam forgives me for telling that story. I know he won't hold it against me, because if Sam was the kind of a man that held things against people, that story never would have happened and I wouldn't be telling it tonight. I know this much: I would not have forgiven myself if I hadn't come out with the true facts on why Johnsville has a hospital and Lyons doesn't. And I could tell by the way you good people applauded that many of you were hearing it for the first time, and that does my heart good. I don't know of a better story that illustrates the bigness of Sam Merritt, a bigger man than his own personal, professional disappointment, bigger than envy, bigger than mere personal pride. No one would have blamed Sam for getting out of the hospital deal and withdrawing his support, no one would have been disappointed in Sam. But I'll tell you, my friends, I think we would have been surprised. It was no surprise when he gave the Johnsville Hospital his support, not to mention his money. What would have been a surprise was if he had acted in any other way, because the finest principles is what we take for granted when we think of Sam Merritt. . . .

And now I come to the part of Sam's life that we all make the mistake of pretending it did not exist and therefore, in my opinion, make it worse than it really is. This is a family party and every person in this room is a member of a family and every family has its family secrets. Or so we think, that they are secrets. Yet I say with no hesitation that there is not a man or woman here this evening who has not at some time during the course of the evening said to himself or herself, "How sad that Alice cannot be with us tonight."

You look at me, some of you, as if to say, "Haven't you got sense enough to avoid certain topics? Do you have to speak of Alice tonight of all nights?" I say to you in reply, to pretend to ignore the subject of Alice would be hypocritical to the nth degree. And worse than that, if I got up here and talked about Sam without talking about Alice would be as wrong as if I did not mention Dr. George Steever and the part he played in Sam's medical career, or the sadness that came to Sam when his brother Boo died. And the worst thing of all, I would be cruelly unfair to Alice herself. Yes, unfair to Alice.

I know what is going on in some minds, but I do not agree. We have now been here since half past seven, a good three hours, and yet I have not heard anyone mention Alice by name. Why? Alice is not dead. We all know that. But if I don't risk the displeasure and disapproval of a few, this evening would pass without mentioning her and it would be as though Alice had never existed. And how dishonest and false that would be.

Do some of you think that by not mentioning Alice I would be sparing Sam? If you do, then you don't know the man as I know him. For there is never a minute of the day when Alice is not in his thoughts. And believe me, my friends, if we ignored Alice tonight, I don't think we would earn Sam's gratitude. I know Sam Merritt and I know that when he finally went home tonight, after he turned out the light and was alone with his thoughts and mulling over the events of the evening, I know that he would wish that someone, someone had found the words to express some appreciation for the one person, the one person who more than anybody else in the world was responsible for the position Sam Merritt occupies in our community and in our hearts.

They have a saying that they use nowadays and like so many sayings, they think it's a new one. But it isn't. We used to say it when we were young fellows and girls. It is the expression "going steady." Young people were going steady forty, fifty years ago. It is that long ago that Sam Merritt began going steady with Alice Connor. In fact, Sam started going steady with Alice when he was in high and she was still in grammar because they had the three years' difference in their ages.

Some parents, like today, did not approve of their daughters going steady so early and Mr. and Mrs. Connor were among them. But with Alice it was Sam or nobody and it was the same with Sam. Mr. and Mrs. Connor had nothing against Sam, but they naturally didn't want her to get serious when they were only in high school. Therefore they had a talk with Sam about it and in a friendly way they told him that they thought Alice should be given the chance to get better acquainted with other boys.

But they soon found out that their daughter had no interest in other boys. Luckily they were sensible people and accepted the verdict but they would not allow the young couple to become engaged until Sam finished medical college. Then it was delayed because Sam was interning at a hospital in Philadelphia and then delayed some more while he was getting started. They finally felt they were in a position to get married and I was given the honor of being best man. Now I don't believe there's anybody in this room that would be such a damn fool as to think that I would say anything that would injure

Sam Merritt. I was his best man, he was my best man, and next to my own wife Lou there was never a girl that I revered more than Alice Connor.

They got married and the early years of struggle were happy ones because they were practically the one person. Alice didn't take the training course to be a nurse, but she learned it all. She learned bookkeeping in high, so she was able to keep Sam's books for him. In addition she did all the housework herself and when Sam began doing a little better financially and tried to persuade her to get a hired girl, she said she would rather use the money for some other purpose, such as a new car, or office furniture, or for the new additions to the family. Unfortunately, both times they were expecting, they lost both babies. One died at birth and the other was premature.

Alice was terribly disappointed when the babies did not live but it did not deter her from going right on working to assist Sam in his professional career. But without realizing it, her strength must have been more seriously affected than anyone realized, and soon after that she began to show signs that after the second baby she had not made a complete recovery. She was subject to depression and after a time Sam took her to the best doctors in Fort Penn and they examined her and recommended a complete rest in a private hospital near Fort Penn.

When she came home she was all right for a while, but the old trouble returned and once again Sam accompanied her to Fort Penn. Only a few of their closest friends knew about her condition at the time. We used the excuse that Alice was having a series of operations. The second time she came home from the private hospital Sam brought a trained nurse back and we all made believe that the nurse was there to help Sam in the office, but then I guess the truth got to be known publicly when what we all know happened. One of her moods of depression and she jumped out of the second-story window. Broke both her legs, one arm.

We all know about it. It happened in broad daylight, people walking in the street. I never saw the use of any secrecy after that. As long as there was a chance of recovery, yes. But by the next day it was no more a secret in Lyons than if the borough hall caught fire and burned down. We didn't run anything in the *Republican* about it, but I often thought since then that it would have been better for all concerned if we had. Maybe we would have put a stop to all the idle rumors that circulated.

Well, that was a long time ago, a long time ago. Some twenty-five years, and a little more. We're all getting on. What Alice looks like today, I don't know. But what I do know is how I prefer to think of her, slender, light brown hair, devoted to the only man she ever cared for, working with him, encouraging him until she was no longer able to. Now they have operations that they can cure the kind of illness Alice had, but they didn't have them then and they don't advise it now.

Well, I've brought it out in the open and it isn't a happy story, of course, but would anybody be any the happier if I didn't mention the only woman that Sam ever loved, the woman that loved him? That helped him when he needed help the most? Friends, I don't think anybody, Alice or Sam or anybody, was hurt by any of this, and maybe somebody was even helped.

In fact, I can be sure of that. I don't have to say maybe. Because I have the honor to announce—to you, Sam, because everybody else in this room knows it—that those here tonight have raised the sum of $20,000 for the maternity ward of the Johnsville Hospital, to be known as the Alice C. Merritt Ward. And I take great pleasure in handing you this check, on this engraved silver platter. I will read the engraving:

Presented to
Samuel G. Merritt, M.D.,
at a Family Party in Honor of
His First Forty Years of Service
To His Community.

I thank you.

Imagine Kissing Pete

To those who knew the bride and groom, the marriage of Bobbie Hammersmith and Pete McCrea was the surprise of the year. As late as April of '29 Bobbie was still engaged to a fellow who lived in Greenwich, Connecticut, and she had told friends that the wedding would take place in September. But the engagement was broken and in a matter of weeks the invitations went out for her June wedding to Pete. One of the most frequently uttered comments was that Bobbie was not giving herself much opportunity to change her mind again. The comment was doubly cruel, since it carried the implication that if she gave herself time to think, Pete McCrea would not be her ideal choice. It was not only that she was marrying Pete on the rebound; she seemed to be going out of her way to find someone who was so unlike her other beaus that the contrast was unavoidable. And it was.

I was working in New York and Pete wrote to ask me to be an usher. Pete and I had grown up together, played together as children, and gone to dancing school and to the same parties. But we had never been close friends and when Pete and I went away to our separate prep schools and, later, Pete to Princeton and I to work, we drifted into that relationship of young men who had known each other all their lives without creating anything that was enduring or warm. As a matter of fact, I had never in my life received a written communication from Pete McCrea, and his handwriting on the envelope was new to me, as mine in my reply was to him. He mentioned who the best man and the other ushers would be—all Gibbsville boys —and this somewhat pathetic commentary on his four years in prep school and four years in college made an appeal to home town and boyhood loyalty that I could not reject. I had some extra days coming to me at the office, and so I told Pete I would be honored to be one of his ushers. My next step was to talk to a Gibbsville girl who lived in New York, a friend of Bobbie Hammersmith's. I took her to din-

ner at an Italian speakeasy where my credit was good, and she gave
me what information she had. She was to be a bridesmaid.

"Bobbie isn't saying a word," said Kitty Clark. "That is, nothing
about the inner turmoil. Nothing *intime*. Whatever happened happened the last time she was in New York, four or five weeks ago. All
she'd tell me was that Johnny White was impossible. Impossible.
Well, he'd been very possible all last summer and fall."

"What kind of a guy was he?" I asked.

"Oh—*attractive*," she said. "Sort of wild, I guess, but not a roué.
Maybe he is a roué, but I'd say more just wild. I honestly don't know
a thing about it, but it wouldn't surprise me if Bobbie was ready to
settle down, and he wasn't. She was probably more in love with him
than he was with her."

"I doubt that. She wouldn't turn around and marry Pete if she
were still in love with this White guy."

"Oh, *wouldn't* she? Oh, are you ever wrong there. If she wanted to
thumb her nose at Johnny, I can't think of a better way. Poor Pete.
You know *Pete*. Ichabod McCrea. Remember when Mrs. McCrea
made us stop calling him Ichabod? Lord and Taylor! She went to see
my mother and I guess all the other mothers and said it just had to
stop. Bad enough calling her little Angus by such a common nickname as Pete. But calling a boy Ichabod. I don't suppose Pete ever
knew his mother went around like that."

"Yes he did. It embarrassed him. It always embarrassed him when
Mrs. McCrea did those things."

"Yes, she was uncanny. I can remember when I was going to have
a party, practically before I'd made out the list Mrs. McCrea would
call Mother to be sure Pete wasn't left out. Not that I ever would
have left him out. We all always had the same kids to our parties. But
Mrs. McCrea wasn't leaving anything to chance. I'm dying to hear
what she has to say about this marriage. I'll bet she doesn't like it,
but I'll bet she's in fear and trembling in case Bobbie changes her
mind again. Ichabod McCrea and Bobbie Hammersmith. Beauty and
the beast. And actually he's not even a beast. It would be better if he
were. She's the third of our old bunch to get married, but much as I
hate to say it, I'll bet she'll be the first to get a divorce. Imagine
kissing Pete, let alone any of the rest of it."

The wedding was on a Saturday afternoon; four o'clock in Trinity
Church, and the reception at the country club. It had been two years
since I last saw Bobbie Hammersmith and she was now twenty-two,
but she could have passed for much more than that. She was the only
girl in her crowd who had not bobbed her hair, which was jet-black
and which she always wore with plaited buns over the ears. Except in

the summer her skin was like Chinese white and it was always easy to pick her out first in group photographs; her eyes large dark dots, quite far apart, and her lips small but prominent in the whiteness of her face beneath the two small dots of her nose. In summer, with a tan, she reminded many non-operagoers of Carmen. She was a striking beauty, although it took two years' absence from her for me to realize it. In the theatre they have an expression, "walked through the part," which means that an actress played a role without giving it much of herself. Bobbie walked through the part of bride-to-be. A great deal of social activity was concentrated in the three days— Thursday, Friday, and Saturday—up to and including the wedding reception; but Bobbie walked through the part. Today, thirty years later, it would be assumed that she had been taking tranquilizers, but this was 1929.

Barbara Hammersmith had never been anything but a pretty child; if she had ever been homely it must have been when she was a small baby, when I was not bothering to look at her. We—Pete McCrea and the other boys—were two, three, four years older than Bobbie, but when she was fifteen or sixteen she began to pass among us, from boy to boy, trying one and then another, causing several fist fights, and half promising but never delivering anything more than the "soul kisses" that were all we really expected. By the time she was eighteen she had been in and out of love with all of us with the solitary exception of Pete McCrea. When she broke off with a boy, she would also make up with the girl he had temporarily deserted for Bobbie, and all the girls came to understand that every boy in the crowd had to go through a love affair with her. Consequently Bobbie was popular; the boys remembered her kisses, the girls forgave her because the boys had been returned virtually intact. We used the word hectic a lot in those days; Kitty Clark explained the short duration of Bobbie's love affairs by observing that being in love with Bobbie was too hectic for most boys. It was also true that it was not hectic enough. The boys agreed that Bobbie was a hot little number, but none of us could claim that she was not a virgin. At eighteen Bobbie entered a personal middle age, and for the big social occasions her beaus came from out-of-town. She was also busy at the college proms and football games, as far west as Ann Arbor, as far north as Brunswick, Maine. I was working on the Gibbsville paper during some of those years, the only boy in our crowd who was not away at college, and I remember Ann Arbor because Bobbie went there wearing a Delta Tau Delta pin and came back wearing the somewhat larger Psi U. "Now don't you say anything in front of Mother," she said. "She thinks they're both the same."

We played auction bridge, the social occupation in towns like ours, and Bobbie and I were assimilated into an older crowd: the younger married set and the youngest of the couples who were in their thirties. We played for prizes—flasks, cigarette lighters, vanity cases, cartons of cigarettes—and there was a party at someone's house every week. The hostess of the evening usually asked me to stop for Bobbie, and I saw her often. Her father and mother would be reading the evening paper and sewing when I arrived to pick up Bobbie. Philip Hammersmith was not a native of Gibbsville, but he had lived there long enough to have gone to the Mexican Border in 1916 with the Gibbsville company of mounted engineers, and he had gone to France with them, returning as a first lieutenant and with the Croix de Guerre with palm. He was one of the best golfers in the club, and everyone said he was making money hand-over-fist as an independent coal operator. He wore steel-rim glasses and he had almost completely gray hair, cut short. He inspired trust and confidence. He was slow-moving, taller than six feet, and always thought before speaking. His wife, a Gibbsville girl, was related, as she said, to half the town; a lively little woman who took her husband's arm even if they were walking only two doors away. I always used to feel that whatever he may have wanted out of life, yet unattained or unattainable, she had just what she wanted: a good husband, a nice home, and a pretty daughter who would not long remain unmarried. At home in the evening, and whenever I saw him on the street, Mr. Hammersmith was wearing a dark-gray worsted suit, cut loose and with a soft roll to the lapel; black knit four-in-hand necktie; white shirt; heavy gray woolen socks, and thick-soled brogues. This costume, completely unadorned—he wore a wrist watch—was what he always wore except for formal occasions, and the year-to-year sameness of his attire constituted his only known eccentricity. He was on the board of the second most conservative bank, the trustees of Gibbsville Hospital, the armory board, the Y.M.C.A., and the Gibbsville and Lantenengo country clubs. Nevertheless I sensed that that was not all there was to Philip Hammersmith, that the care he put into the creation of the general picture of himself—hard work, quiet clothes, thoughtful manner, conventional associations—was done with a purpose that was not necessarily sinister but was extraordinarily private. It delighted me to discover, one night while waiting for Bobbie, that he knew more about what was going on than most of us suspected he would know. "Jimmy, you know Ed Charney, of course," he said.

I knew Ed Charney, the principal bootlegger in the area. "Yes, I know him pretty well," I said.

"Then do you happen to know if there's any truth to what I heard? I heard that his wife is threatening to divorce him."

"I doubt it. They're Catholics."

"Do you know her?"

"Yes. I went to Sisters' school with her."

"Oh, then maybe you can tell me something else. I've heard that she's the real brains of those two."

"She quit school after eighth grade, so I don't know about that. I don't remember her being particularly bright. She's about my age but she was two grades behind me."

"I see. And you think their religion will keep them from getting a divorce?"

"Yes, I do. I don't often see Ed at Mass, but I know he carries rosary beads. And she's at the eleven o'clock Mass every Sunday, all dolled up."

This conversation was explained when Repeal came and with it public knowledge that Ed Charney had been quietly buying bank stock, one of several moves he had made in the direction of respectability. But the chief interest to me at the time Mr. Hammersmith and I talked was in the fact that he knew anything at all about the Charneys. It was so unlike him even to mention Ed Charney's name.

To get back to the weekend of Bobbie Hammersmith's wedding: it was throughout that weekend that I first saw Bobbie have what we called that faraway look, that another generation called Cloud 90. If you happened to catch her at the right moment, you would see her smiling up at Pete in a way that must have been reassuring to Mrs. McCrea and to Mrs. Hammersmith, but I also caught her at several wrong moments and I saw something I had never seen before: a resemblance to her father that was a subtler thing than the mere duplication of such features as mouth, nose, and set of the eyes. It was almost the same thing I have mentioned in describing Philip Hammersmith; the wish yet unattained or unattainable. However, the pre-nuptial parties and the wedding and reception went off without a hitch, or so I believed until the day after the wedding.

Kitty Clark and I were on the same train going back to New York and I made some comment about the exceptional sobriety of the ushers and how everything had gone according to plan. "Amazing, considering," said Kitty.

"Considering what?"

"That there was almost no wedding at all," she said. "You must promise word of honor, Jimmy, or I won't tell you."

"I promise. Word of honor."

"Well, after Mrs. McCrea's very-dull-I-must-say luncheon, when we all left to go to Bobbie's? A little after two o'clock?"

"Yes."

"Bobbie asked me if I'd go across the street to our house and put in a long-distance call to Johnny White. I said I couldn't do that, and what on earth was she thinking of. And Bobbie said, 'You're my oldest and best friend. The least you can do is make this one last effort, to keep me from ruining my life.' So I gave in and I dashed over to our house and called Johnny. He was out and they didn't know where he could be reached or what time he was coming home. So I left my name. *My* name, not Bobbie's. Six o'clock, at the reception, I was dancing with—I was dancing with *you.*"

"When the waiter said you were wanted on the phone."

"It was Johnny. He'd been sailing and just got in. I made up some story about why I'd called him, but he didn't swallow it. '*You* didn't call me,' he said. '*Bobbie* did.' Well of course I wouldn't admit that. By that time she was married, and if her life was already ruined it would be a darned sight more ruined if I let him talk to her. Which he wanted to do. Then he tried to pump me. Where were they going on their wedding trip? I said nobody knew, which was a barefaced lie. I knew they were going to Bermuda. Known it since Thursday. But I wouldn't tell Johnny . . . I don't like him a bit after yesterday. I'd thought he was attractive, and he *is,* but he's got a mean streak that I never knew before. Feature this, if you will. When he realized I wasn't going to get Bobbie to come to the phone, or give him any information, he said, 'Well, no use wasting a long-distance call. What are you doing next weekend? How about coming out here?' 'I'm not that hard up,' I said, and banged down the receiver. I hope I shattered his eardrum."

I saw Pete and Bobbie McCrea when I went home the following Christmas. They were living in a small house on Twin Oaks Road, a recent real-estate development that had been instantly successful with the sons and daughters of the big two- and three-servant mansions. They were not going to any of the holiday dances; Bobbie was expecting a baby in April or early May.

"You're not losing any time," I said.

"I don't want to lose any time," said Bobbie. "I want to have a lot of children. Pete's an only child and so am I, and we don't think it's fair, if you can afford to have more."

"If we can afford it. The way that stock market is going, we'll be lucky to pay for this one," said Pete.

"Oh, don't start on that, Pete. That's all Father talks about," said

Bobbie. "My father *was* hit pretty hard, but I wish he didn't have to keep talking about it all the time. Everybody's in the same boat."

"No they're not. *We're* on a *raft.*"

"I asked you, please, Pete. Jimmy didn't come here to listen to our financial woes. Do you see much of Kitty? I've owed her a letter for ages."

"No, I haven't seen her since last summer, we went out a few times," I said.

"Kitty went to New York to try to rope in a millionaire. She isn't going to waste her time on Jim."

"That's not what she went to New York for at all. And as far as wasting her time on Jim, Jim may not want to waste his time on her." She smiled. "Have you got a girl, Jim?"

"Not really."

"Wise. Very wise," said Pete McCrea.

"I don't know how wise. It's just that I have a hell of a hard time supporting myself, without trying to support a wife, too," I said.

"Why I understood you were selling articles to magazines, and going around with all the big shots."

"I've had four jobs in two years, and the jobs didn't last very long. If things get any tougher I may have to come back here. At least I'll have a place to sleep and something to eat."

"But I see your name in magazines," said Pete. "I don't always read your articles, but they must pay you well."

"They don't. At least I can't live on the magazine pieces without a steady job. Excuse me, Bobbie. Now you're getting *my* financial woes."

"She'll listen to yours. It's mine she doesn't want to hear about."

"That's because I know about ours. I'm never allowed to forget them," said Bobbie. "Are you going to all the parties?"

"Yes, stag. I have to bum rides. I haven't got a car."

"We resigned from the club," said Pete.

"Well we didn't *have* to do that," said Bobbie. "Father was going to give it to us for a Christmas present. And you have your job."

"We'll see how much longer I have it. Is that the last of the gin?"

"Yes."

Pete rose. "I'll be back."

"Don't buy any more for me," I said.

"You flatter yourself," he said. "I wasn't only getting it for you." He put on his hat and coat. "No funny business while I'm gone. I remember you two."

He kept a silly grin on his face while saying the ugly things, but the grin was not genuine and the ugly things were.

"I don't know what's the matter with him," said Bobbie. "Oh, I do, but why talk about it?"

"He's only kidding."

"You know better than that. He says worse things, much worse, and I'm only hoping they don't get back to Father. Father has enough on his mind. I thought if I had this baby right away it would —you know—give Pete confidence. But it's had just the opposite effect. He says it isn't his child. *Isn't his child!* Oh, I married him out of spite. I'm sure Kitty must have told you that. But it *is* his child, I swear it, Jim. It couldn't be anybody else's."

"I guess it's the old inferiority complex," I said.

"The first month we were married—Pete was a virgin—and I admit it, I wasn't. I stayed with two boys before I was married. But I was certainly not pregnant when I married Pete, and the first few weeks he was loving and sweet, and grateful. But then something happened to him, and he made a pass at I-won't-say-who. It was more than a pass. It was quite a serious thing. I might as well tell you. It was Phyllis. We were all at a picnic at the Dam and several people got pretty tight, Pete among them. And there's no other word for it, he tried to rape Phyllis. Tore her bathing suit and slapped her and did other things. She got away from him and ran back to the cottage without anyone seeing her. Luckily Joe didn't see her or I'm sure he'd have killed Pete. You know, Joe's strong as an ox and terribly jealous. I found out about it from Phyllis herself. She came here the next day and told me. She said she wasn't going to say anything to Joe, but that we mustn't invite her to our house and she wasn't going to invite us to hers."

"I'm certainly glad Joe didn't hear about it. He would do something drastic," I said. "But didn't he notice that you two weren't going to his house, and they to yours? It's a pretty small group."

She looked at me steadily. "We haven't been going anywhere. My excuse is that I'm pregnant, but the truth is, we're not being asked. It didn't end with Phyllis, Jim. One night at a dinner party Mary Lander just slapped his face, in front of everybody. Everybody laughed and thought Pete must have said something, but it wasn't something he'd said. He'd taken her hand and put it—you know. This is *Pete! Ichabod!* Did you ever know any of this about him?"

"You mean have I heard any of this? No."

"No, I didn't mean that. I meant, did he go around making passes and I never happened to hear about it?"

"No. When we'd talk dirty he'd say, 'Why don't you fellows get your minds above your belts?' "

"I wish your father were still alive. I'd go see him and try to get some advice. I wouldn't think of going to Dr. English."

"Well, you're not the one that needs a doctor. Could you get Pete to go to one? He's a patient of Dr. English's, isn't he?"

"Yes, but so is Mrs. McCrea, and Pete would never confide in Dr. English."

"Or anyone else at this stage, I guess," I said. "I'm not much help, am I?"

"Oh, I didn't expect you to have a solution. You know, Jim, I wish you would come back to Gibbsville. Other girls in our crowd have often said it was nice to have you to talk to. Of course you were a very bad boy, too, but a lot of us miss you."

"That's nice to hear, Bobbie. Thank you. I may be back, if I don't soon make a go of it in New York. I won't have any choice."

During that Christmas visit I heard other stories about Pete Mc-Crea. In general they were told as plain gossip, but two or three times there was a hint of a lack of sympathy for Bobbie. "She knew what she was doing . . . she made her bed . . ." And while there was no lack of righteous indignation over Pete's behavior, he had changed in six months from a semi-comic figure to an unpleasant man, but a man nevertheless. In half a year he had lost most of his old friends; they all said, "You've never seen such a change come over anybody in all your life," but when they remembered to call him Ichabod it was only to emphasize the change.

Bobbie's baby was born in April, but lived only a few weeks. "She was determined to have that baby," Kitty Clark told me. "She had to prove to Pete that it was anyway *conceived* after she married him. But it must have taken all her strength to hold on to it that long. All her strength *and* the baby's. Now would be a good time for her to divorce him. She can't go on like that."

But there was no divorce, and Bobbie was pregnant again when I saw her at Christmas, 1930. They no longer lived in the Twin Oaks Road house, and her father and mother had given up their house on Lantenengo Street. The Hammersmiths were living in an apartment on Market Street, and Bobbie and Pete were living with Mrs. Mc-Crea. "Temporarily, till Pete decides whether to take this job in Tulsa, Oklahoma," said Bobbie.

"Who do you think you're kidding?" said Pete. "It isn't a question of me deciding. It's a cousin of mine deciding. It's a cousin of mine deciding if he'll take me on. And why the hell should he?"

"Well, you've had several years' banking experience," she said.

"Yes. And if I was so good, why did the bank let me go? Jim knows all this. What else have you heard about us, Jim? Did you hear Bobbie was divorcing me?"

"It doesn't look that way from here," I said.

"You mean because she's pregnant? That's elementary biology, and God knows you're acquainted with the facts of life. But if you want to be polite, all right. Pretend you didn't hear she was getting a divorce. You might as well pretend Mr. and Mrs. Hammersmith are still living on Lantenengo Street. If they were, Bobbie'd have got her divorce."

"Everybody tells me what I *was* going to do or *am* going to do," said Bobbie. "Nobody ever consults me."

"I suppose that's a crack at my mother."

"Oh, for Christ's sake, Pete, lay off, at least while I'm here," I said.

"Why? You like to think of yourself as an old friend of the family, so you might as well get a true picture. When you get married, if you ever do, I'll come and see you, and maybe your wife will cry on my shoulder." He got up and left the house.

"Well, it's just like a year ago," said Bobbie. "When you came to call on us last Christmas?"

"Where will he go now?"

"Oh, there are several places where he can charge drinks. They all think Mrs. McCrea has plenty of money, but they're due for a rude awakening. She's living on capital, but she's not going to sell any bonds to pay his liquor bills."

"Then maybe *he's* due for a rude awakening."

"Any awakening would be better than the last three months, since the bank fired him. He sits here all day long, then after Mrs. McCrea goes to bed he goes to one of his speakeasies." She sat up straighter. "He has a lady friend. Or have you heard?"

"No."

"Yes. He graduated from making passes at all my friends. He had to. We were never invited anywhere. Yes, he has a girl friend. Do you remember Muriel Nierhaus?"

"The chiropractor's wife. Sure. Big fat Murial Minzer till she married Nierhaus, then we used to say he gave her some adjustments. Where is Nierhaus?"

"Oh, he's opened several offices. Very prosperous. He divorced her but she gets alimony. She's Pete's girl friend. Murial Minzer is *Angus McCrea's* girl friend."

"You don't seem too displeased," I said.

"Would you be, if you were in my position?"

"I guess I know what you mean. But—well, nothing."

"But why don't I get a divorce?" She shook her head. "A spite marriage is a terrible thing to do to anybody. If I hadn't deliberately selected Pete out of all the boys I knew, he'd have gone on till Mrs. McCrea picked out somebody for him, and it would almost have had to be the female counterpart of Pete. A girl like—oh—Florence. Florence Temple."

"Florence Temple, with her cello. Exactly right."

"But I did that awful thing to Pete, and the first few weeks of marriage were just too much for him. He went haywire. I'd slept with two boys before I was married, so it wasn't as much of a shock to me. But Pete almost wore me out. And such adoration, I can't tell you. Then when we came back from Bermuda he began to see all the other girls he'd known all his life, and he'd ask me about them. It was as though he'd never seen them before, in a way. In other ways, it was as though he'd just been waiting all his life to start ripping their clothes off. He was dangerous, Jim. He really was. I could almost tell who would be next by the questions he'd ask. Before we'd go to a party, he'd say 'Who's going to be there tonight?' And I'd say I thought the usual crowd. Then he'd rattle off the list of names of our friends, and leave out one name. That was supposed to fool me, but it didn't for long. The name he left out, that girl was almost sure to be in for a bad time."

"And now it's all concentrated on Muriel Minzer?"

"As far as I know."

"Well, that's a break for you, *and* the other girls. Did you ever talk to him about the passes he made at the others?"

"Oh, how could we avoid it? Whoever it was, she was always 'that little whore.' "

"Did he ever get anywhere with any of them?"

She nodded. "One, but I won't tell you who. There was one girl that didn't stop him, and when that happened he wanted me to sleep with her husband."

"Swap, eh?"

"Yes. But I said I wasn't interested. Pete wanted to know why not? Why wouldn't I? And I almost told him. The boy was one of the two boys I'd stayed with before I was married—oh, when I was seventeen. And he never told anybody and neither have I, or ever will."

"You mean one of our old crowd actually did get somewhere with you, Bobbie?"

"One did. But don't try to guess. It won't do you any good to guess, because I'd never, never tell."

"Well, whichever one it was, he's the best liar I ever knew. And I guess the nicest guy in our whole crowd. You know, Bobbie, the

whole damn bunch are going to get credit now for being as honorable as one guy."

"You were all nice, even if you all did talk too much. If it had been
you, you would have lied, too."

"No, I don't think I would have."

"You lied about Kitty. Ha ha ha. You didn't know I knew about
you and Kitty. I knew it the next day. The very next day. If you don't
believe me, I'll tell you where it happened and how it happened, and
all about it. That was the great bond we had in common. You and
Kitty, and I and this other boy."

"Then Kitty's a gentleman, because she never told me a word
about you."

"I kissed every boy in our crowd except Pete, and I necked, heavy-
necked two, as you well know, and stayed with one."

"The question is, did you stay with the other one that you heavy-
necked with?"

"You'll never know, Jim, and please don't try to find out."

"I won't, but I won't be able to stop theorizing," I said.

We knew everything, everything there was to know. We were so far
removed from the technical innocence of eighteen, sixteen, nineteen.
I was a man of the world, and Bobbie was indeed a woman, who had
borne a child and lived with a husband who had come the most
recently to the knowledge we had acquired, but was already the most
intricately involved in the complications of sex. We—Bobbie and I—
could discuss him and still remain outside the problems of Pete Mc-
Crea. We could almost remain outside our own problems. We knew
so much, and since what we knew seemed to be all there was to
know, we were shockproof. We had come to our maturity and our
knowledgeability during the long decade of cynicism that was usually
dismissed as "a cynical disregard of the law of the land," but that was
something else, something deeper. The law had been passed with a
"noble" but nevertheless cynical disregard of men's right to drink. It
was a law that had been imposed on some who took pleasure in
drinking by some who did not. And when the law was an instant
failure, it was not admitted to be a failure by those who had imposed
it. They fought to retain the law in spite of its immediate failure and
its proliferating corruption, and they fought as hard as they would
have for a law that had been an immediate success. They gained no
recruits to their own way; they had only deserters, who were not
brave deserters but furtive ones; there was no honest mutiny but
only grumbling and small disobediences. And we grew up listening to
the grumbling, watching the small disobediences; laughing along
when the grumbling was intentionally funny, imitating the small dis-

obediences in other ways besides the customs of drinking. It was not only a cynical disregard for a law of the land; the law was eventually changed. Prohibition, the zealots' attempt to force total abstinence on a temperate nation, made liars of a hundred million men and cheats of their children; the West Point cadets who cheated in examinations, the basketball players who connived with gamblers, the thousands of uncaught cheats in the high schools and colleges. We had grown up and away from our earlier esteem of God and country and valor, and had matured at a moment when riches were vanishing for reasons that we could not understand. We were the losing, not the lost, generation. We could not blame Pete McCrea's troubles—and Bobbie's—on the Southern Baptists and the Northern Methodists. Since we knew everything, we knew that Pete's sudden release from twenty years of frustrations had turned him loose in a world filled with women. But Bobbie and I sat there in her mother-in-law's house, breaking several laws of possession, purchase, transportation and consumption of liquor, and with great calmness discussing the destruction of two lives—one of them hers—and the loss of her father's fortune, the depletion of her mother-in-law's, the allure of a chiropractor's divorcée, and our own promiscuity. We knew everything, but we were incapable of recognizing the meaning of our complacency.

I was wearing my dinner jacket, and someone was going to pick me up and take me to a dinner dance at the club. "Who's stopping for you?" said Bobbie.

"It depends. Either Joe or Frank. Depends on whether they go in Joe's car or Frank's. I'm to be ready when they blow their horn."

"Do me a favor, Jim. Make them come in. Pretend you don't hear the horn."

"If it's Joe, he's liable to drive off without me. You know Joe if he's had a few too many."

In a few minutes there was a blast of a two-tone horn, repeated. "That's Joe's car," said Bobbie. "You'd better go." She went to the hall with me and I kissed her cheek. The front door swung open and it was Joe Whipple.

"Hello, Bobbie," he said.

"Hello, Joe. Won't you all come in? Haven't you got time for one drink?" She was trying not to sound suppliant, but Joe was not deceived.

"Just you and Jim here?" he said.

"Yes. Pete went out a little while ago."

"I'll see what the others say," said Joe. He left to speak to the three in the sedan, and obviously he was not immediately persuasive, but they came in with him. They would not let Bobbie take their coats, but they were nice to her and with the first sips of our drinks we were all six almost back in the days when Bobbie Hammersmith's house was where so many of our parties started from. Then we heard the front door thumping shut and Pete McCrea looked in.

There were sounds of hello, but he stared at us over his horn-rims and said to Bobbie: "You didn't have to invite me, but you could have told me." He turned and again the front door thumped.

"Get dressed and come with us," said Joe Whipple.

"I can't do that," said Bobbie.

"She can't, Joe," said Phyllis Whipple. "That would only make more trouble."

"What trouble? She's going to have to sit here alone till he comes home. She might as well be with us," said Joe.

"Anyway, I haven't got a dress that fits," said Bobbie. "But thanks for asking me."

"I won't have you sitting here—"

"Now don't make matters worse, Joe, for heaven's sake," said his wife.

"I could lend you a dress, Bobbie, but I think Phyllis is right," said Mary Lander. "Whatever *you* want to do."

"*Want* to do! That's not the question," said Bobbie. "Go on before I change my mind. Thanks, everybody. Frank, you haven't said a word."

"Nothing much for me to say," said Frank Lander. But as far as I was concerned he, and Bobbie herself, had said more than anyone else. I caught her looking at me quickly.

"Well, all right, then," said Joe. "I'm outnumbered. Or outpersuaded or something."

I was the last to say goodbye, and I whispered to Bobbie: "Frank, eh?"

"You're only guessing," she said. "Goodnight, Jim." Whatever they would be after we left, her eyes were brighter than they had been in years. She had very nearly gone to a party, and for a minute or two she had been part of it.

I sat in the back seat with Phyllis Whipple and Frank Lander. "If you'd had any sense you'd know there'd be a letdown," said Phyllis.

"Oh, drop it," said Joe.

"It might have been worth it, though, Phyllis," said Mary Lander. "How long is it since she's seen anybody but that old battle-ax, Mrs. McCrea? God, I hate to think what it must be like, living in that house with Mrs. McCrea."

"I'm sure it would have been a *lot* easier if Bobbie'd come with us," said Phyllis. "That would have fixed things just right with Mrs. McCrea. She's just the type that wants Bobbie to go out and have a good time. Especially without Pete. You forget how the old lady used to call up all the mothers as soon as she heard there was a party planned. What Joe did was cruel because it was so downright stupid. Thoughtless. Like getting her all excited and then leaving her hung up."

"You've had too much to drink," said Joe.

"*I* have?"

"Yes, you don't say things like that in front of a bachelor," said Joe.

"Who's—oh, Jim? It is to laugh. Did I shock you, Jim?"

"Not a bit. I didn't know what you meant. Did you say something risqué?"

"My husband thinks I did."

"Went right over my head," I said. "I'm innocent about such things."

"So's your old man," said Joe.

"Do you think she should have come with us, Frank?" I said.

"Why ask me? No. I'm with Phyllis. What's the percentage for Bobbie? You saw that son of a bitch in the doorway, and you know damn well when he gets home from Muriel Nierhaus's, he's going to raise hell with Bobbie."

"Then Bobbie had nothing to lose," said Joe. "If Pete's going to raise hell with her, anyway, she might as well have come with us."

"How does he raise hell with her?" I said.

No one said anything.

"Do you know, Phyllis?" I said.

"What?" said Phyllis.

"Oh, come on. You heard me," I said. "Mary?"

"I'm sure I don't know."

"Oh, nuts," I said.

"Go ahead, tell him," said Frank Lander.

"Nobody ever knew for sure," said Phyllis, quietly.

"That's not true. Caroline English, for one. She knew for sure."

Phyllis spoke: "A few weeks before Bobbie had her baby she rang Caroline's doorbell in the middle of the night and asked Caroline if she could stay there. Naturally Caroline said yes, and she saw that Bobbie had nothing but a coat over her nightgown and had bruises all over her arms and shoulders. Julian was away, a lucky break because he'd have gone over and had a fight with Pete. As it was, Caroline made Bobbie have Dr. English come out and have a look at her, and nothing more was said. I mean, it was kept secret from everybody, especially Mr. Hammersmith. But the story got out some-how. Not widespread, but we all heard about it."

"We don't want it to get back to Mr. Hammersmith," said Mary Lander.

"He knows," said Frank Lander.

"You keep saying that, but I don't believe he does," said Mary.

"I don't either," said Joe Whipple. "Pete wouldn't be alive today if Phil Hammersmith knew."

"That's where I think you're wrong," said Phyllis. "Mr. Hammersmith might want to kill Pete, but killing him is another matter. And what earthly good would it do? The Hammersmiths have lost every penny, so I'm told, and at least with Pete still alive, Mrs. McCrea supports Bobbie. Barely. But they have food and a roof over their heads."

"Phil Hammersmith knows the whole damn story, you can bet anything on that. And it's why he's an old man all of a sudden. Have you seen him this trip, Jim?" said Frank Lander.

"I haven't seen him since the wedding."

"Oh, well—" said Mary.

"You won't—" said Joe.

"You won't recognize him," said Frank Lander. "He's bent over—"

"They say he's had a stroke," said Phyllis Whipple.

"And on top of everything else he got a lot of people sore at him by selling his bank stock to Ed Charney," said Joe. "Well, not a lot of people, but some that could have helped him. My old man, to name one. And I don't think that was so hot. Phil Hammersmith was a carpetbagger himself, and damn lucky to be in the bank. Then to sell his stock to a lousy stinking bootlegger . . . You should hear Harry Reilly on the subject."

"I don't want to hear Harry Reilly on any subject," said Frank Lander. "Cheap Irish Mick."

"I don't like him any better than you do, Frank, but call him something else," I said.

"I'm sorry, Jim. I didn't mean that," said Frank Lander.

"No. It just slipped out," I said.

"I apologize," said Frank Lander.

"Oh, all right."

"Don't be sensitive, Jim," said Mary.

"Stay out of it, Mary," said Frank Lander.

"*Everybody* calm down," said Joe. "Everybody knows that Harry Reilly is a cheap Irish Mick, and nobody knows it better than Jim, an Irish Mick but not a cheap one. So shut the hell up, everybody."

"Another country heard from," said Phyllis.

"Now *you*, for Christ's sake," said Joe. "Who has the quart?"

"I have my quart," said Frank Lander.

"I have mine," I said.

"I asked who has mine. Phyllis?"

"When we get to the club, time enough," said Phyllis.

"Hand it over," said Joe.

"Three quarts of whiskey between five people. I'd like to know how we're going to get home tonight," said Mary Lander.

"Drunk as a monkey, if you really want to know," said Joe. "Tight as a nun's."

"Well, at least we're off the subject of Bobbie and Pete," said Phyllis.

"I'm not. I was coming back to it. Phyllis. The quart," said Joe.

"No," said Phyllis.

"Here," I said. "And remember where it came from." I handed him my bottle.

Joe took a swig in the corner of his mouth, swerving the car only slightly. "Thanks," he said, and returned the bottle. "Now, Mary, if you'll light me a cigarette like a dear little second cousin."

"Once removed," said Mary Lander.

"Once removed, and therefore related to Bobbie through her mother."

"No, *you* are but I'm not," said Mary Lander.

"Well, you're in it some way, through me. Now for the benefit of those who are not related to Bobbie or Mrs. Hammersmith, or Mary or me. Permit me to give you a little family history that will enlighten you on several points."

"Is this going to be about Mr. Hammersmith?" said Phyllis. "I don't think you'd better tell that."

"You're related only by marriage, so kindly keep your trap shut. If I want to tell it, I can."

"Everybody remember that I asked him not to," said Phyllis.

"Don't tell it, Joe, whatever it is," said Mary Lander.

"Yeah, what's the percentage?" said Frank Lander. "They have enough trouble without digging up past history."

"Oh, you're so noble, Lander," said Joe. "You fool nobody."

"If you're going to tell the story, go ahead, but stop insulting Frank," said Mary Lander.

"We'll be at the club before he gets started," said Phyllis.

"Then we'll sit there till I finish. Anyway, it doesn't take that long. So, to begin at the beginning. Phil Hammersmith. Phil Hammersmith came here before the war, just out of Lehigh."

"You're not even telling it right," said Phyllis.

"Phyllis is right. I'm screwing up my own story. Well, I'll begin again. Phil Hammersmith graduated from Lehigh, then a few years *later* he came to Gibbsville."

"That's better," said Phyllis.

"The local Lehigh contingent all knew him. He'd played lacrosse and he was a Sigma Nu around the time Mr. Chew was there. So he already had friends in Gibbsville."

"Now you're on the right track," said Phyllis.

"Thank you, love," said Joe.

"Where was he from originally?" I asked.

"Don't ask questions, Jim. It only throws me. He was from some place in New Jersey. So anyway he arrived in Gibbsville and got a job with the Coal & Iron Company. He was a civil engineer, and he had the job when he arrived. That is, he didn't come here looking for a job. He was hired before he got here."

"You've made that plain," said Phyllis.

"Well, it's important," said Joe.

"Yes, but you don't have to say the same thing over and over again," said Phyllis.

"Yes I do. Anyway, apparently the Coal & Iron people hired him on the strength of his record at Lehigh, plus asking a few questions of the local Lehigh contingent, that knew him, *plus* a very good recommendation he'd had from some firm in Bethlehem. Where he'd worked after getting out of college. But after he'd been here a while, and was getting along all right at the Coal & Iron, one day a construction engineer from New York arrived to talk business at the C. & I. Building. They took him down-cellar to the drafting-room and who should he see but Phil Hammersmith. But apparently Phil didn't see him. Well, the New York guy was a real wet smack, because he tattled on Phil.

"Old Mr. Duncan was general superintendent then and he sent for Phil. Was it true that Phil had once worked in South America, and if so, why hadn't he mentioned it when he applied for a job? Phil gave him the obvious answer. 'Because if I had, you wouldn't have hired me.' 'Not necessarily,' said Mr. Duncan. 'We might have accepted your explanation.' 'You say that now, but I tried telling the truth and I couldn't get a job.' 'Well, tell me the truth now,' said Mr. Duncan. 'All right,' said Phil. So he told Mr. Duncan what had happened.

"He was working in South America. Peru, I think. Or maybe Bolivia. In the jungle. And the one thing they didn't want the natives, the Indians, to get hold of was firearms. But one night he caught a native carrying an armful of rifles from the shanty, and when Phil yelled at him, the native ran, and Phil shot him. Killed him. The next day one of the other engineers was found with his throat cut. And the day after that the native chief came and called on the head man of the construction outfit. Either the Indians thought they'd killed the man that had killed their boy, or they didn't much care. But the chief told the white boss that the next time an Indian was killed, two white men would be killed. And not just killed. Tortured. Well, there were four or maybe five engineers, including Phil and the boss. The only white men in an area as big as Pennsylvania, and I guess they weighed their chances and being mathematicians, the odds didn't look so hot. So they quit. No hero stuff. They just quit. Except Phil. He was fired. The boss blamed Phil for everything and in his report to the New York office he put in a lot of stuff that just about fixed Phil for good. The boss, of course, was the same man that spotted Phil at the C. & I. drafting-room."

"You told it very well," said Phyllis.

"So any time you think of Phil Hammersmith killing Pete McCrea, it wouldn't be the first time," said Joe.

"And the war," I said. "He probably killed a few Germans."

"On the other hand, he never got over blaming himself for the other engineer's getting his throat cut," said Joe. "This is all the straight dope. Mr. Duncan to my old man."

We were used to engineers, their travels and adventures in far-off places, but engineers came and went and only a few became fixtures in our life. Phil Hammersmith's story was all new to Mary and Frank and me, and in the cold moonlight, as we sat in a heated automobile in a snow-covered parking area of a Pennsylvania country club, Joe Whipple had taken us to a dark South American jungle, given us a touch of fear, and in a few minutes covered Phil Hammersmith in mystery and then removed the mystery.

"Tell us more about Mr. Hammersmith," said Mary Lander.

Mary Lander. I had not had time to realize the inference that must accompany my guess that Frank Lander was the one boy in our crowd who had stayed with Bobbie. Mary Lander was the only girl who had not fought off Pete McCrea. She was the last girl I would have suspected of staying with Pete, and yet the one that surprised me the least. She had always been the girl our mothers liked us to take out, a kind of mothers' ideal for their sons, and possibly even for themselves. Mary Morgan Lander was the third generation of a family that had always been in the grocery business, the only store in the county that sold caviar and English biscuits and Sportsmen's Bracer chocolate, as well as the most expensive domestic items of fruit, vegetables, and tinned goods. Her brother Llewellyn Morgan still scooped out dried prunes and operated the rotary ham slicer, but no one seriously believed that all the Morgan money came from the store. Lew Morgan taught Sunday School in the Methodist Episcopal Church and played basketball at the Y.M.C.A., but he had been to Blair Academy and Princeton, and his father had owned one of the first Pierce-Arrows in Gibbsville. Mary had been unfairly judged a teaser, in previous years. She was not a teaser, but a girl who would kiss a boy and allow him to wander all over her body so long as he did not touch bare skin. Nothing surprised me about Mary. It was in character for her to have slapped Pete McCrea at a dinner party, and then to have let him stay with her and to have discussed with him a swap of husbands and wives. No casual dirty remark ever passed unnoticed by Mary; when someone made a slip we would all turn to see how Mary was taking it, and without fail she had heard it, understood it, and taken a pious attitude. But in our crowd she was the one person most conscious of sex and scatology. She was the only one of whom I would say she had a dirty mind, but I kept that observation to myself along with my theory that she hated Frank Lander. My theory, based on no information whatever, was that marriage and Frank Lander had not been enough for her and that Pete McCrea had become attractive to her because he was so awful.

"There's no more to tell," said Joe Whipple. We got out of the car and Mary took Joe's arm, and her evening was predictable: fathers and uncles and older brothers would cut in on her, and older women would comment as they always did that Mary Lander was *such* a sensible girl, *so* considerate of her elders, a *wonderful* wife to Frank. And we of her own age would dance with her because under cover of the dancing crowd Mary would wrap both legs around our right legs with a promise that had fooled us for years. Quiet little Mary Lander, climbing up a boy's leg but never forgetting to smile her Dr. Lyons smile at old Mrs. Ginyan and old Mr. Heff. And yet through some mental process that I did not take time to scrutinize, I was less annoyed with Mary than I had been since we were children. I was determined not to dance with her, and I did not, but my special knowledge about her and Pete McCrea reduced her power to allure. Bobbie had married Pete McCrea and she was still attractive in spite of it; but Mary's seductiveness vanished with the revelation that she had picked Pete as her lover, if only for once, twice, or how many times. I had never laughed at Mary before, but now she was the fool, not we, not I.

I got quite plastered at the dance, and so did a lot of other people. On the way home we sang a little—"Body and Soul" was the song, but Phyllis was the only one who could sing the middle part truly—and Frank Lander tried to tell about an incident in the smoking-room, where Julian English apparently had thrown a drink in Harry Reilly's face. It did not seem worth making a fuss about, and Frank never finished his story. Mary Lander attacked me: "You never danced with me, not once," she said.

"I didn't?"

"No, you didn't, and you know you didn't," she said. "And you always do."

"Well, this time I guess I didn't."

"Well, *why* didn't you?"

"Because he didn't want to," said Frank Lander. "You're making a fool of yourself. I should think you'd have more pride."

"Yeah, why don't you have more pride, Mary?" said Joe Whipple. "You'd think it was an honor to dance with this Malloy guy."

"It is," I said.

"That's it. You're getting so conceited," said Mary. "Well, I'm sure I didn't have to sit any out."

"Then why all the fuss?" said Frank Lander.

"Such popularity must be deserved," I said, quoting an advertising slogan.

"Whose? Mary's or yours?" said Phyllis.

"Well, I was thinking of Mary's, but now that you mention it . . ." I said.

"How many times did he dance with *you*, Phyllis?" said Joe.

"Three or four," said Phyllis.

"In that case, Frank, Jim has insulted your wife. I don't see any other way out of it. You have to at least slap his face. Shall I stop the car?"

"My little trouble-maker," said Phyllis.

"Come on, let's have a fight," said Joe. "Go ahead, Frank. Give him a punch in the nose."

"Yeah, like you did at the Dam, Frank," I said.

"Oh, God. I remember that awful night," said Phyllis. "What did you fight over?"

"Bobbie," I said.

"Bobbie was the cause of *more* fights," said Mary Lander.

"Well, we don't need her to fight over now. We have you," said Joe. "Your honor's been attacked and your husband wants to defend it. The same as I would if Malloy hadn't danced with *my* wife. It's a good thing you danced with Phyllis, Malloy, or you and I'd get out of this car and start slugging."

"Why did you fight over Bobbie? I don't remember that," said Mary.

"Because she came to the picnic with Jim and then went off necking with Frank," said Phyllis. "I remember the whole thing."

"Stop *talking* about fighting and let's *fight,*" said Joe.

"All right, stop the car," I said.

"Now you're talking," said Joe.

"Don't be ridiculous," said Phyllis.

"Oh, shut up," said Joe. He pulled up on the side of the road. "I'll referee." He got out of the car, and so did Frank and I and Phyllis. "All right, put up your dukes." We did so, moved around a bit in the snow and slush. "Go on, mix it," said Joe, whereupon Frank rushed me and hit me on the left cheek. All blows were directed at the head, since all three of us were armored in coonskin coats. "That was a good one, Frank. Now go get him, Jim." I swung my right hand and caught Frank's left eye, and at that moment we were all splashed by slush, taken completely by surprise as Phyllis, whom we had forgotten, drove the car away.

"That bitch!" said Joe. He ran to the car and got hold of a door handle but she increased her speed and he fell in the snow. "God damn that bitch, I should have known she was up to something. Now what? Let's try to bum a ride." The fight, such as it was, was over, and we tried to flag down cars on their way home from the dance. We recognized many of them, but not one would stop.

"Well, thanks to you, we've got a nice three-mile walk to Swedish Haven," said Frank Lander.

"Oh, she'll be back," said Joe.

"I'll bet you five bucks she's not," I said.

"Well, I won't bet, but I'll be damned if I'm going to walk three miles. I'm just going to wait till we can bum a ride."

"If you don't keep moving you'll freeze," said Frank.

"We're nearer the club than we are Swedish Haven. Let's go back there," I said.

"And have my old man see me?" said Joe.

"Your old man went home hours ago," I said.

"Well, somebody'll see me," said Joe.

"Listen, half the club's seen you already, and they wouldn't even stop," I said.

"Who has a cigarette?" said Joe.

"Don't give him one," said Frank.

"I have no intention of giving him one," I said. "Let's go back to the club. My feet are soaking wet."

"So are mine," said Frank. We were wearing pumps, and our feet had been wet since we got out of the car.

"That damn Phyllis, she knows I just got over a cold," said Joe.

"Maybe that's why she did it," I said. "It'd serve you right if you got pneumonia."

We began to walk in the middle of the road, in the direction of the clubhouse, which we could see, warm and comfortable on top of a distant plateau. "That old place never looked so good," said Joe. "Let's spend the night there."

"The rooms are all taken. The orchestra's staying there," I said.

We walked about a mile, our feet getting sorer at every step, and the combination of exhaustion and the amount we had had to drink made even grumbling an effort. Then a Dodge touring car, becurtained, stopped about fifty yards from us and a spotlight was turned on each of our faces. A man in a short overcoat and fur-lined cap came toward us. He was a State Highway patrolman. "What happened to you fellows?" he said. "You have a wreck?"

"I married one," said Joe.

"Oh, a weisscrackah," said the patrolman, a Pennsylvania Dutchman. "Where's your car?"

"We got out to take a leak and my wife drove off with it," said Joe.

"You from the dance at the gulf club?"

"Yes," said Joe. "How about giving us a lift?"

"Let me see you' driwah's license," said the cop.

Joe took out his billfold and handed over the license. "So? From Lantenengo Street yet? All right, get in. Whereabouts you want to go to?"

"The country club," said Joe.

"The hell with that," said Frank. "Let's go on to Gibbsville."

"This aint no taxi service," said the cop. "And I aint taking you to no Gippsfille. I'm on my way to my substation. Swedish Haven. You can phone there for a taxi. Privileged characters, you think you are. A bunch of drunks, you ask me."

I had to go back to New York on the morning train and the events of the next few days, so far as they concerned Joe and Phyllis Whipple and Frank and Mary Lander, were obscured by the suicide, a day or two later, of Julian English, the man who had thrown a drink at Harry Reilly. The domestic crisis of the Whipples and the Landers and even the McCreas seemed very unimportant. And yet when I heard about English, who had not been getting along with his wife, I wondered about my own friends, people my own age but not so very much younger than Julian and Caroline English. English had danced with Phyllis and Mary that night, and now he was dead. I knew very little about the causes of the difficulties between him and Caroline, but they could have been no worse than the problems that existed in Bobbie's marriage and that threatened the marriage of Frank and Mary Lander. I was shocked and saddened by the English suicide; he was an attractive man whose shortcomings seemed out of proportion to the magnitude of killing himself. He had not been a friend of mine, only an acquaintance with whom I had had many drinks and played some golf; but friends of mine, my closest friends in the world, boys-now-men like myself, were at the beginning of the same kind of life and doing the same kind of thing that for Julian English ended in a sealed-up garage with a motor running. I hated what I thought those next few days and weeks. There is nothing young about killing oneself, no matter when it happens, and I hated this being deprived of the sweetness of youth. And that was what it was, that was what was happening to us. I, and I think the others, had looked upon our squabbles as unpleasant incidents but belonging to our youth. Now they were plainly recognizable as symptoms of life without youth, without youth's excuses or youth's recoverability. I wanted to love someone, and during the next year or two I confused the desperate need for love with love itself. I had put a hopeless love out of my life; but that is not part of this story, except to state it and thus to show that I knew what I was looking for.

II

When you have grown up with someone it is much easier to fill in gaps of five years, ten years, in which you do not see him, than to supply those early years in the life of a friend you meet in maturity. I do not know why this is so, unless it is a mere matter of insufficient time. With the friends of later life you may exchange boyhood stories that seem worth telling, but boyhood is not all stories. It is mostly not stories, but day-to-day, unepisodic living. And most of us are too polite to burden our later-life friends with unexciting anecdotes about people they will never meet. (Likewise we hope they will not burden us.) But it is easy to bring old friends up to date in your mental dossiers by the addition of a few vital facts. Have they stayed married? Have they had many more children? Have they made money or lost it? Usually the basic facts will do, and then you tell yourself that Joe Whipple is still Joe Whipple, plus two sons, a new house, a hundred thousand dollars, forty pounds, bifocals, fat in the neck, and a new concern for the state of the nation.

Such additions I made to my friends' dossiers as I heard about them from time to time; by letters from them, conversations with my mother, an occasional newspaper clipping. I received these facts with joy for the happy news, sorrow for the sad, and immediately went about my business, which was far removed from any business of theirs. I seldom went back to Gibbsville during the Thirties—mine and the century's—and when I did I stayed only long enough to stand at a grave, to toast a bride, to spend a few minutes beside a sickbed. In my brief encounters with my old friends I got no information about Bobbie and Pete McCrea, and only after I had returned to New York or California would I remember that I had intended to inquire about them.

There is, of course, some significance in the fact that no one volunteered information about Bobbie and Pete. It was that they had disappeared. They continued to live in Gibbsville, but in parts of the town that were out of the way for their old friends. There is no town so small that that cannot happen, and Gibbsville, a third-class city, was large enough to have all the grades of poverty and wealth and the many half grades in between, in which $10 a month in the husband's income could make a difference in the kind and location of the house in which he lived. No one had volunteered any information about Bobbie and Pete, and I had not remembered to inquire. In five years I had had no new facts about them, none whatever, and their disappearance from my ken might have continued but for a broken shoelace.

I was in Gibbsville for a funeral, and the year was 1938. I had broken a shoelace, it was evening and the stores were closed, and I was about to drive back to New York. The only place open that might have shoelaces was a poolroom that in my youth had had a two-chair bootblack stand. The poolroom was in a shabby section near the railroad stations and a couple of cheap hotels, four or five saloons, an automobile tire agency, a barber shop, and a quick-lunch counter. I opened the poolroom door, saw that the bootblack's chairs were still there, and said to the man behind the cigar counter: "Have you got any shoelaces?"

"Sorry I can't help you, Jim," said the man. He was wearing an eyeshade, but as soon as he spoke I recognized Pete McCrea.

"Pete, for God's sake," I said. We shook hands.

"I thought you might be in town for the funeral," he said. "I should have gone, too, I guess, but I decided I wouldn't. It was nice of you to make the trip."

"Well, you know. He was a friend of my father's. Do you own this place?"

"I run it. I have a silent partner, Bill Charney. You remember Ed

Charney? His younger brother. I don't know where to send you to get a shoelace."

"The hell with the shoelace. How's Bobbie?"

"Oh, Bobbie's fine. *You* know. A lot of changes, but this is better than nothing. Why don't you call her up? She'd love to hear from you. We're living out on Mill Street, but we have a phone. Call her up and say hello. The number is 3385-J. If you have time maybe you could go see her. I have to stay here till I close up at one o'clock, but she's home."

"What number on Mill Street? You call her up and tell her I'm coming? Is that all right?"

"Hell, yes."

Someone thumped the butt of a cue on the floor and called out: "Rack 'em up, Pete?"

"I have to be here. You go on out and I'll call her up," he said. "Keep your shirt on," he said to the pool player, then, to me: "It's 402 Mill Street, across from the open hearth, second house from the corner. I guess I won't see you again, but I'm glad we had a minute. You're looking very well." I could not force a comment on his appearance. His nose was red and larger, his eyes watery, the dewlaps sagging, and he was wearing a blue denim work shirt with a dirty leather bow tie.

"Think I could get in the Ivy Club if I went back to Princeton?" he said. "I didn't make it the first time around, but now I'm a big shot. So long, Jim. Nice to've seen you."

The open hearth had long since gone the way of all the mill equipment; the mill itself had been inactive for years, and as a residential area the mill section was only about a grade and a half above the poorest Negro slums. But in front of most of the houses in the Mc-Creas' row there were cared-for plots; there always had been, even when the mill was running and the air was full of smoke and acid. It was an Irish and Polish neighborhood, but knowledge of that fact did not keep me from locking all the doors of my car. The residents of the neighborhood would not have touched my father's car, but this was not his car and I was not he.

The door of Number 402 opened as soon as I closed my car door. Bobbie waited for me to lock up and when I got to the porch, she said: "*Jim.* Jim, Jim, Jim. How nice. I'm so glad to see you." She quickly closed the door behind me and then kissed me. "Give me a real kiss and a real hug. I didn't dare while the door was open." I kissed her and held her for a moment and then she said: "Hey, I guess we'd better cut this out."

"Yes," I said. "It's nice, though."

"Haven't done that since we were—God!" She stood away and looked at me. "You could lose some weight, but you're not so bad. How about a bottle of beer? Or would you rather have some cheap whiskey?"

"What are you drinking?"

"Cheap whiskey, but I'm used to it," she said.

"Let's both have some cheap whiskey," I said.

"Straight? With water? Or how?"

"Oh, a small slug of whiskey and a large slug of water in it. I'm driving back to New York tonight."

She went to the kitchen and prepared the drinks. I recognized some of the furniture from the Hammersmith and McCrea houses. "Brought together by a shoestring," she said. "Here's to it. How do I look?"

"If you want my frank and candid opinion, good enough to go right upstairs and make up for the time we lost. Pete won't be home till one o'clock."

"If then," she said. "Don't think I wouldn't, but it's too soon after my baby. Didn't Pete tell you I finally produced a healthy son?"

"No."

"You'll hear him in a little while. We have a daughter, two years old, and now a son. Angus McCrea, Junior. Seven pounds two ounces at birth."

"Good for you," I said.

"Not so damn good for me, but it's over, and he's healthy."

"And what about your mother and father?" I said.

"Oh, poor Jim. You didn't know? Obviously you didn't, and you're going to be so sorry you asked. Daddy committed suicide two years ago. He shot himself. And Mother's in Swedish Haven." Swedish Haven was local lore for the insane asylum. "I'm sorry I had to tell you."

"God, why won't they lay off you?" I said.

"Who is they? Oh, you mean just—life?"

"Yes."

"I don't know, Jim," she said. "I've had about as much as I can stand, or so I keep telling myself. But I must be awfully tough, because there's always something else, and I go right on. Will you let me complain for just a minute, and then I'll stop? The only one of the old crowd I ever see is Phyllis. She comes out and never forgets to bring a bottle, so we get tight together. But some things we don't discuss, Phyllis and I. Pete is a closed subject."

"What's he up to?"

"Oh, he has his women. I don't even know who they are any more, and couldn't care less. Just as long as he doesn't catch a disease. I told him that, so he's been careful about it." She sat up straight. "I haven't been the soul of purity, either, but it's Pete's son. Both children are Pete's. But I haven't been withering on the vine."

"Why should you?"

"That's what *I* said. Why should I have nothing? Nothing? The children are mine, and I love them, but I need more than that, Jim. Children don't love you back. All they do is depend on you to feed them and wash them and all the rest of it. But after they're in bed for the night—I never know whether Pete will be home at two o'clock or not at all. So I've had two tawdry romances, I guess you'd call them. Not you, but Mrs. McCrea would."

"Where is dear Mrs. McCrea?"

"She's living in Jenkintown, with an old maid sister. Thank heaven they can't afford carfare, so I'm spared that."

"Who are your gentlemen friends?"

"Well, the first was when we were living on the East Side. A gentleman by the name of Bill Charney. Yes, Ed's brother and Pete's partner. I was crazy about him. Not for one single minute in love with him, but I never even thought about love with him. He wanted to marry me, too, but I was a nasty little snob. I *couldn't* marry Bill Charney, Jim. I just couldn't. So he married a nice little Irish girl and they're living on Lantenengo Street in the house that used to belong to old Mr. Duncan. And I'm holding court on Mill Street, thirty dollars a month rent."

"Do you want some money?"

"Will you give me two hundred dollars?"

"More than that, if you want it."

"No, I'd just like to have two hundred dollars to hide, to keep in case of emergency."

"In case of emergency, you can always send me a telegram in care of my publisher." I gave her $200.

"Thank you. Now I have some money. For the last five or six years I haven't had any money of my own. You don't care how I spend this, do you?"

"As long as you spend it on yourself."

"I've gotten so stingy I probably won't spend any of it. But this is wonderful. Now I can read the ads and say to myself I could have some expensive lingerie. I think I will get a permanent, next month."

"Is that when you'll be back in circulation again?"

"Good guess. Yes, about a month," she said. "But not the same man. I didn't tell you about the second one. You don't know him. He came here after you left Gibbsville. His name is McCormick and he went to Princeton with Pete. They sat next to each other in a lot of classes, McC, McC, and he was sent here to do some kind of an advertising survey and ran into Pete. They'd never been exactly what you'd call pals, but they *knew* each other and Mac took one look and sized up the situation and—well, I thought, why not? He wasn't as exciting as Mr. Charney, but at one time I would have married him. *If* he'd asked me. He doesn't live here any more."

"But you've got the next one picked out?"

"No, but I know there will be a next one. Why lie to myself? And why lie to you? I don't think I ever have."

"Do you ever see Frank?"

"Frank? Frank Lander? What made you think of him?"

"Bobbie," I said.

"Oh, of course. That was a guess of yours, a long time ago," she said. "No, I never see Frank." She was smoking a cigarette, and sitting erect with her elbow on the arm of her chair, holding the cigarette high and with style. If her next words had been "Jeeves, have the black Rolls brought round at four o'clock" she would not have been more naturally grand. But her next words were: "I haven't even thought about Frank. There was another boy, Johnny White, the one I was engaged to. *Engaged to.* That close to spending the rest of my life with him—or at least part of it. But because he wanted me to go away with him before we were married, I broke the engagement and married Pete."

"Is that all it was? That he wanted you to go away with him?"

"That's really all it was. I got huffy and said he couldn't really love me if he wanted to take that risk. Not that we hadn't been taking risks, but a pre-marital trip, that was something else again. My five men, Jim. Frank. Johnny. Bill and Mac. And Pete."

"Why didn't you and Frank ever get engaged?"

"I wonder. I·*have* thought about *that,* so I was wrong when I said I never think of Frank. But Frank in the old days, not Frank now. What may have happened was that Frank was the only boy I'd gone all the way with, and then I got scared because I didn't want to give up the fun, popularity, good times. Jim, I have a confession to make. About you."

"Oh?"

"I told Frank I'd stayed with you. He wouldn't believe he was my first and he kept harping on it, so I really got rid of Frank by telling him you were the first."

"Why me?"

"Because the first time I ever stayed with Frank, or anybody, it was at a picnic at the Dam, and I'd gone to the picnic with you. So you were the logical one."

"Did you tell him that night?"

"No. Later. Days later. But you had a fight with him that night, and the fight made it all the more convincing."

"Well, thanks, little pal," I said.

"Oh, you don't care, do you?"

"No, not really."

"You had Kitty, after all," she said. "Do you ever see Kitty?"

"No. Kitty lives in Cedarhurst and they keep to themselves, Cedarhurst people."

"What was your wife like?"

"She was nice. Pretty. Wanted to be an actress. I still see her once in a while. I like her, and always will, but if ever there were two people that shouldn't have got married . . ."

"I can name two others," said Bobbie.

"You and Pete. But you've stuck to him."

"Don't be polite. I'm stuck with him. Can you imagine what Pete would be like if I left him?"

"Well, to be brutally frank, what's he like anyway? You don't have to go on paying for a dirty trick the rest of your life."

"It wasn't just a dirty trick. It would have been a dirty trick if I'd walked out on him the day we were getting married. But I went through with it, and that made it more than a dirty trick. I *should have* walked out on him, the day we got married. I even tried. And he'd have recovered—then. Don't forget, Pete McCrea was used to dirty tricks being played on him, and he might have got over it if I'd left him at the church. But once I'd married him, he became a different person, took himself much more seriously, and so did everyone else. They began to dislike him, but that was better than being laughed at." She sipped her drink.

"Well, who did it? I did. Your little pal," she said. "How about some more cheap whiskey?"

"No thanks, but you go ahead," I said.

"The first time I ever knew there *was* a Mill Street was the day we rented this house," she said, as she poured herself a drink. "I'd never been out this way before."

"You couldn't have lived here when the mill was operating. The noise and the smoke."

"I can live anywhere," she said. "So can anyone else. And don't be too surprised if you find us back on Lantenengo. Do you know the big thing nowadays? Slot machines and the numbers racket. Pete wants to get into The Numbers, but he hasn't decided how to go about it. Bill Charney is the kingpin in the county, although not the real head. It's run by a syndicate in Jersey City."

"Don't let him do it, Bobbie," I said. "Really don't."

"Why not? He's practically in it already. He has slot machines in the poolroom, and that's where people call up to find out what number won today. He might as well be in it."

"No."

"It's the only way Pete will ever have any money, and if he ever gets his hands on some money, maybe he'll divorce me. Then I could take the children and go away somewhere. California."

"That's a different story. If you're planning it that way. But stay out of The Numbers if you ever have any idea of remaining respectable. You can't just go in for a few years and then quit."

"Respectable? Do you think my son's going to be able to get into Princeton? His father is the proprietor of a poolroom, and they're going to know that when Angus gets older. Pete will never be anything else. He's found his niche. But if I took the children to California they might have a chance. And *I* might have a chance, before it's too late. It's our only hope, Jim. Phyllis agrees with me."

I realized that I would be arguing against a hope and a dream, and if she had that much left, and only that much, I had no right to argue. She very nearly followed my thinking. "It's what I live on, Jim," she said. "That—and this." She held up her glass. "And a little admiration. A little—admiration. Phyllis wants to give me a trip to New York. Would you take us to '21' and those places?"

"Sure."

"Could you get someone for Phyllis?"

"I think so. Sure. Joe wouldn't go on this trip?"

"And give up a chance to be with Mary Lander?"

"So now it's Joe and Mary?"

"Oh, that's old hat in Gibbsville. They don't even pretend otherwise."

"And Frank? What about him?"

"Frank is the forgotten man. If there were any justice he ought to pair off with Phyllis, but they don't like each other. Phyllis calls Frank a wishy-washy namby-pamby, and Frank calls Phyllis a drunken trouble-maker. We've all grown up, Jim. Oh, haven't we just? Joe doesn't like Phyllis to visit me because Mary says all we do is gossip. Although how she'd know *what* we do . . ."

"They were all at the funeral, and I thought what a dull, stuffy little group they've become," I said.

"But that's what they are," said Bobbie. "Very stuffy and very dull. What else is there for them to do? If I were still back there with them I'd be just as bad. Maybe worse. In a way, you know, Pete McCrea has turned out to be the most interesting man in our old crowd, present company excepted. Joe was a very handsome young man and so was Frank, and their families had lots of money and all the rest of it. But you saw Joe and Frank today. I haven't seen them lately, but Joe looks like a professional wrestler and I remember how hairy he was, all over his chest and back and his arms and legs. And Frank just the opposite, skin like a girl's and slender, but now we could almost call *him* Ichabod. He looks like a cranky schoolteacher, and his glasses make him look like an owl. Mary, of course, beautifully dressed I'm sure, and not looking a day older."

"Several days older, but damn good-looking," I said.

A baby cried and Bobbie made no move. "That's my daughter. Teething. Now she'll wake up my son and you're in for a lot of howling." The son began to cry, and Bobbie excused herself. She came back in a few minutes with the infant in her arms. "It's against my rules to pick them up, but I wanted to show him to you. Isn't he an ugly little creature? The answer is yes." She took him away and returned with the daughter. "She's begun to have a face."

"Yes, I can see that. Your face, for which she can be thankful."

"Yes, I wouldn't want a girl to look like Pete. It doesn't matter so much with a boy." She took the girl away and when she rejoined me she refilled her glass.

"Are you sorry you didn't have children?" she said.

"Not the way it turned out, I'm not," I said.

"These two haven't had much of a start in life, the poor little things. They haven't even been christened. Do you know why? There was nobody we could ask to be their godfathers." Her eyes filled with tears. "That was when I really saw what we'd come to."

"Bobbie, I've got a four-hour drive ahead of me, so I think I'd better get started."

"Four hours to New York? In that car?"

"I'm going to stop and have a sandwich halfway."

"I could give you a sandwich and make some coffee."

"I don't want it now, thanks."

We looked at each other. "I'd like to show how much I appreciate your coming out to see me," she said. "But it's probably just as well I can't. But I'll be all right in New York, Jim. That is, if I ever get there. I won't believe that, either, till I'm on the train."

If she came to New York I did not know about it, and during the war years Bobbie and her problems receded from my interest. I heard that Pete was working in a defense plant, from which I inferred that he had not made the grade in the numbers racket. Frank

Lander was in the Navy, Joe Whipple in the War Production Board, and by the time the war was over I discovered that so many other people and things had taken the place of Gibbsville in my thoughts that I had almost no active curiosity about the friends of my youth. I had even had a turnover in my New York friendships. I had married again, I was working hard, and most of my social life originated with my wife's friends. I was making, for me, quite a lot of money, and I was a middle-aged man whose physician had made some honest, unequivocal remarks about my life expectancy. It took a little time and one illness to make me realize that if I wanted to see my child grow to maturity, I had to retire from night life. It was not nearly so difficult as I had always anticipated it would be.

After I became reconciled to middle age and the quieter life I made another discovery: that the sweetness of my early youth was a persistent and enduring thing, so long as I kept it at the distance of years. Moments would come back to me, of love and excitement and music and laughter that filled my breast as they had thirty years earlier. It was not nostalgia, which only means homesickness, nor was it a wish to be living that excitement again. It was a splendid contentment with the knowledge that once I had felt those things so deeply and well that the throbbing urging of George Gershwin's "Do It Again" could evoke the original sensation and the pictures that went with it: a tea dance at the club and a girl in a long black satin dress and my furious jealousy of a fellow who wore a yellow foulard tie. I wanted none of it ever again, but all I had I wanted to keep. I could remember precisely the tone in which her brother had said to her: "Are you coming or aren't you?" and the sounds of his galoshes after she said: "I'm going home with Mr. Malloy." They were the things I knew before we knew everything, and, I suppose, before we began to learn. There was always a girl, and nearly always there was music; if the Gershwin tune belonged to that girl, a Romberg tune belonged to another and "When Hearts Are Young" became a personal anthem, enduringly sweet and safe from all harm, among the protected memories. In middle age I was proud to have lived according to my emotions at the right time, and content to live that way vicariously and at a distance. I had missed almost nothing, escaped very little, and at fifty I had begun to devote my energy and time to the last, simple but big task of putting it all down as well as I knew how.

In the midst of putting it all down, as novels and short stories and plays, I would sometimes think of Bobbie McCrea and the dinginess of her history. But as the reader will presently learn, the "they"—life —that had once made me cry out in anger, were not through with

her yet. (Of course "they" are never through with anyone while he
still lives, and we are not concerned here with the laws of compensa-
tion that seem to test us, giving us just enough strength to carry us in
another trial.) I like to think that Bobbie got enough pleasure out of
a pair of nylons, a permanent wave, a bottle of Phyllis Whipple's
whiskey, to recharge the brightness in her. As we again take up her
story I promise the reader a happy ending, if only because I want it
that way. It happens also to be the true ending. . . .

Pete McCrea did not lose his job at the end of the war. His Princeton degree helped there. He had gone into the plant, which specialized in aluminum extrusion, as a manual laborer, but his IBM card
revealed that he had taken psychology courses in college, and he was
transferred to Personnel. It seemed an odd choice, but it is not hard
to imagine that Pete was better fitted by his experience as a poolroom proprietor than as a two-year student of psychology. At least
he spoke both languages, he liked the work, and in 1945 he was not
bumped by a returning veteran.

Fair Grounds, the town in which the plant was situated, was only
three miles from Gibbsville. For nearly a hundred years it had been
the trading center for the Pennsylvania Dutch farmers in the area,
and its attractions had been Becker's general store, the Fair Grounds
Bank, the freight office of the Reading Railway, the Fair Grounds
Hotel, and five Protestant churches. Clerks at Becker's and at the
bank and the Reading, and bartenders at the hotel and the pastors of
the churches, all had to speak Pennsylvania Dutch. English was desirable but not a requirement. The town was kept scrubbed, dusted
and painted, and until the erection of the aluminum plant, jobs and
trades were kept in the same families. An engineman's son worked
as waterboy until he was old enough to take the examinations for
brakeman; a master mechanic would give his boy calipers for Christmas. There were men and women in Fair Grounds who visited
Gibbsville only to serve on juries or to undergo surgery at the Gibbsville Hospital. There were some men and women who had never
been to Gibbsville at all and regarded Gibbsville as some Gibbsville
citizens regarded Paris, France. That was the pre-aluminum Fair
Grounds.

To this town in 1941 went Pete and Bobbie McCrea. They rented a
house no larger than the house on Mill Street but cleaner and in
better repair. Their landlord and his wife went to live with his
mother-in-law, and collected the $50 legally frozen monthly rent and
$50 side payment for the use of the radio and the gas stove. But in
spite of under-the-table and black-market prices Peter and Bobbie
McCrea were financially better off than they had been since their

marriage, and nylons at black-market prices were preferable to the no nylons she had had on Mill Street. The job, and the fact that he continued to hold it, restored some respectability to Pete, and they discussed rejoining the club. "Don't try it, I warn you," said Phyllis Whipple. "The club isn't run by your friends any more. Now it's been taken over by people that couldn't have got in ten years ago."

"Well, we'd have needed all our old friends to go to bat for us, and I guess some would think twice about it," said Pete. "So we'll do our drinking at the Tavern."

The Dan Patch Tavern, which was a new name for the renovated Fair Grounds Hotel bar, was busy all day and all night, and it was one of the places where Pete could take pleasure in his revived respectability. It was also one of the places where Bobbie could count on getting that little admiration that she needed to live on. On the day of Pearl Harbor she was only thirty-four years old and at the time of the Japanese surrender she was only thirty-eight. She was accorded admiration in abundance. Some afternoons just before the shift changed she would walk the three blocks to the Tavern and wait for Pete. The bartender on duty would say "Hi, Bobbie," and bring her currently favorite drink to her booth. Sometimes there would be four men sitting with her when Pete arrived from the plant; she was never alone for long. If one man tried to persuade her to leave, and became annoyingly insistent, the bartenders came to her rescue. The bartenders and the proprietor knew that in her way Bobbie was as profitable as the juke box. She was an attraction. She was a good-looking broad who was not a whore or a falling-down lush, and all her drinks were paid for. She was the Tavern's favorite customer, male or female, and if she had given the matter any thought she could have been declared in. All she wanted in return was a steady supply of Camels and protection from being mauled. The owner of the Tavern, Rudy Schau, was the only one who was aware that Bobbie and Pete had once lived on Lantenengo Street in Gibbsville, but far from being impressed by their background, he had a German opinion of aristocrats who had lost standing. He was actively suspicious of Bobbie in the beginning, but in time he came to accept her as a wife whose independence he could not condone and a good-looking woman whose morals he had not been able to condemn. And she was good for business. Beer business was good, but at Bobbie's table nobody drank beer, and the real profit was in the hard stuff.

In the Fair Grounds of the pre-aluminum days Bobbie would have had few women friends. No decent woman would have gone to a saloon every day—or any day. She most likely would have received warnings from the Ku Klux Klan, which was concerned with personal conduct in a town that had only a dozen Catholic families, no Negroes and no Jews. But when the aluminum plant (which was called simply The Aluminum or The Loomy) went into war production the population of Fair Grounds immediately doubled and the solid Protestant character of the town was changed in a month. Eight hundred new people came to town and they lived in apartments in a town where there were no apartments: in rooms in private houses, in garages and old stables, in rented rooms and haylofts out in the farming area. The newcomers wasted no time with complaints of double-rent, inadequate heating, holes in the roof, insufficient sanitation. The town was no longer scrubbed, dusted or painted, and thousands of man-hours were lost while a new shift waited for the old to vacate parking space in the streets of the town. Bobbie and Pete were among the lucky early ones: they had a house. That fact of itself gave Bobbie some distinction. The house had two rooms and kitchen on the first floor, three rooms and bath on the second, and it had a cellar and an attic. In the identical houses on both sides there were a total of four families and six roomers. As a member of Personnel it was one of Pete's duties to find housing for workers, but Bobbie would have no roomers. "The money wouldn't do us much good, so let's live like human beings," she said.

"You mean there's nothing to buy with the money," said Pete. "But we could save it."

"If we had it, we'd spend it. You've never saved a cent in your life and neither have I. If you're thinking of the children's education, buy some more war bonds and have it taken out of your pay. But I'm not going to share my bathroom with a lot of dirty men. I'd have to do all the extra work, not you."

"You could make a lot of money doing their laundry. Fifty cents a shirt."

"Are you serious?"

"No."

"It's a good thing you're not, because I could tell you how else I could make a lot more money."

"Yes, a lot more," said Pete.

"Well, then, keep your ideas to yourself. I won't have boarders and I won't do laundry for fifty cents a shirt. That's final."

And so Bobbie had her house, she got the admiration she needed, and she achieved a moderate popularity among the women of her neighborhood by little friendly acts that came spontaneously out of her friendly nature. There was a dinginess to the new phase: the house was not much, the men who admired her and the women who welcomed her help were the ill-advantaged, the cheap, the vulgar, and sometimes the evil. But the next step down from Mill Street would have been hopeless degradation, and the next step up, Fair Grounds, was at least up. She was envied for her dingy house, and when Pete called her the Queen of the Klondike she was not altogether displeased. There was envy in the epithet, and in the envy was the first sign of respect he had shown her in ten years. He had never suspected her of an affair with Mac McCormick, and if he had suspected her during her infatuation with Bill Charney he had been afraid to make an accusation; afraid to anticipate his own feelings in the event that Charney would give him a job in The Numbers. When Charney brought in a Pole from Detroit for the job Pete had wanted, Pete accepted $1,000 for his share of the poolroom and felt only grateful relief. Charney did not always buy out his partners, and Pete refused to wonder if the money and the easy dissolution of the partnership had been paid for by Bobbie. It was not a question he wanted to raise, and when the war in Europe created jobs at Fair Grounds he believed that his luck had begun to change.

Whatever the state of Pete's luck, the pace of his marriage had begun to change. The pace of his marriage—and not his alone—was set by the time he spent at home and what he did during that time. For ten years he had spent little more time at home than was necessary for sleeping and eating. He could not sit still in the same room with Bobbie, and even after the children were born he did not like to have her present during the times he would play with them. He would arrive in a hurry to have his supper, and in a short time he would get out of the house, to be with a girl, to go back to work at the poolroom. He was most conscious of time when he was near Bobbie; everywhere else he moved slowly, spoke deliberately, answered hesitantly. But after the move to Fair Grounds he spent more time in the house, with the children, with Bobbie. He would sit in the front room, doing paper work from the plant, while Bobbie sewed. At the Tavern he would say to Bobbie: "It's time we were getting home." He no longer darted in and out of the house and ate his meals rapidly and in silence.

He had a new girl. Martha—"Martie"—Klinger was a typist at the plant, a Fair Grounds woman whose husband was in the Coast Guard at Lewes, Delaware. She was Bobbie's age and likewise had two children. She retained a young prettiness in the now round face and her figure had not quite reached the stage of plumpness. Sometimes when she moved an arm the flesh of her breast seemed to go all the way up to her neckline, and she had been one of the inspirations for a plant memo to women employees, suggesting that tight sweaters and tight slacks were out of place in wartime industry. Pete brought her to the Tavern one day after work, and she never took her eyes off Bobbie. She looked up and down, up and down, with her mouth half open as though she were listening to Bobbie through her lips. She showed no animosity of a defensive nature and was not openly possessive of Pete, but Bobbie knew on sight that she was Pete's new girl. After several sessions at the Tavern Bobbie could tell which of the men had already slept with Martie and which of them were likely to again. It was impossible to be jealous of Martie, but it was just as impossible not to feel superior to her. Pete, the somewhat changed Pete, kept up the absurd pretense that Martie was just a girl from the plant whom he happened to bring along for a drink, and there was no unpleasantness until one evening Martie said: "Jesus, I gotta go or I won't get any supper."

"Come on back to our house and have supper with us," said Pete. "That's okay by you, isn't it, Bobbie?"

"No, it isn't," said Bobbie.

"Rudy'll give us a steak and we can cook it at home," said Pete.

"I said no," said Bobbie, and offered no explanation.

"I'll see you all tomorrow," said Martie. "Goodnight, people."

"Why wouldn't you let her come home with us? I could have got a steak from Rudy. And Martie's a hell of a good cook."

"When we can afford a cook I may hire her," said Bobbie.

"Oh, that's what it is. The old snob department."

"That's exactly what it is."

"We're not in any position—"

"*You're* not."

"*We're* not. If I can't have my friends to my house," he said, but did not know how to finish.

"It's funny that she's the first one you ever asked. Don't forget what I told you about having boarders, and fifty cents a shirt. You keep your damn Marties out of my house. If you don't, I'll get a job and you'll be just another boarder yourself."

"Oh, why are you making such a stink about Martie?"

"Come *off* it, Pete, for heaven's *sake.*"

The next statement, he knew, would have to be a stupidly transparent lie or an admission, so he made no statement. If there had to be a showdown he preferred to avert it until the woman in question was someone more entertaining than Martie Klinger. And he liked the status quo.

They both liked the status quo. They had hated each other, their house, the dinginess of their existence on Mill Street. When the fire whistle blew it was within the hearing of Mill Street and of

Lantenengo Street; rain from the same shower fell on Mill Street and on Lantenengo Street; Mill Street and Lantenengo Street read the same Gibbsville newspaper at the same time every evening. And the items of their proximity only made the nearness worse, the remoteness of Mill Street from Lantenengo more vexatious. But Fair Grounds was a new town, where they had gone knowing literally nobody. They had spending money, a desirable house, the respectability of a white-collar job, and the restored confidence in a superiority to their neighbors that they had not allowed themselves to feel on Mill Street. In the Dan Patch Tavern they would let things slip out that would have been meaningless on Mill Street, where their neighbors' daily concern was a loaf of bread and a bottle of milk. "Pete, did you know Jimmy Stewart, the movie actor?" "No, he was several classes behind me, but he was in my club." "Bobbie, what's it like on one of them yachts?" "I've only been on one, but it was fun while it lasted." They could talk now about past pleasures and luxuries without being contradicted by their surroundings, and their new friends at the Tavern had no knowledge of the decade of dinginess that lay between that past and this present. If their new friends also guessed that Pete McCrea was carrying on with Martie Klinger, that very fact made Bobbie more credibly and genuinely the woman who had once cruised in a yacht. They would have approved Bobbie's reason for not wanting Martie Klinger as a guest at supper, as they would have fiercely resented Pete's reference to Bobbie as the Queen of the Klondike. Unintentionally they were creating a symbol of order that they wanted in their lives as much as Bobbie needed admiration, and if the symbol and the admiration were slightly ersatz, what, in war years, was not?

There was no one among the Tavern friends whom Bobbie desired to make love with. "I'd give a week's pay to get in bed with you, Bobbie," said one of them.

"Fifty-two weeks' pay, did you say?" said Bobbie.

"No dame is worth fifty-two weeks' pay," said the man, a foreman named Dick Hartenstein.

"Oh, I don't know. In fifty-two weeks you make what?"

"A little over nine thousand. Nine gees, about."

"A lot of women can get that, Dick. I've heard of women getting a diamond necklace for just one night, and they cost a lot more than nine thousand dollars."

"Well, I tell you, Bobby, if I ever hit the crap game for nine gees I'd seriously consider it, but not a year's pay that I worked for."

"You're not romantic enough for me. Sorry."

"Supposing I did hit the crap game and put nine gees on the table in front of you? Would you and me go to bed?"

"No."

"No, I guess not. If I asked you a question would you give me a truthful answer? No. You wouldn't."

"Why should I?"

"Yeah, why should you? I was gonna ask you, what does it take to get you in bed with a guy?"

"I'm a married woman."

"I skipped all that part, Bobbie. You'd go, if it was the right guy."

"You could get to be an awful nuisance, Dick. You're not far from it right this minute."

"I apologize."

"In fact, why don't you take your drink and stand at the bar?"

"What are you sore at? You get propositioned all the time."

"Yes, but you're too persistent, and you're a bore. The others don't keep asking questions when I tell them no. Go on, now, or I'll tell Rudy to keep you out of here."

"You know what you are?"

"Rudy! Will you come here, please?" she called. "All right, Dick. What am I? Say it in front of Rudy."

Rudy Schau made his way around from the bar. "What can I do for you, Bobbie?"

"I think Dick is getting ready to call me a nasty name."

"He won't," said Rudy Schau. He had the build of a man who had handled beer kegs all his life and he was now ready to squeeze the wind out of Hartenstein. "Apolochise to Bobbie and get the hell outa my place. And don't forget you got a forty-dollar tab here. You won't get a drink nowheres else in tahn."

"I'll pay my God damn tab," said Hartenstein.

"That you owe me. Bobbie you owe an apolochy."

"I apologize," said Hartenstein. He was immediately clipped behind the ear, and sunk to the floor.

"I never like that son of a bitch," said Rudy Schau. He looked down at the unconscious Hartenstein and very deliberately kicked him in the ribs.

"Oh, *don't*, Rudy," said Bobbie. *"Please* don't."

Others in the bar, which was now half filled, stood waiting for Rudy's next kick, and some of them looked at each other and then at Rudy, and they were ready to rush him. Bobbie stood up quickly. "Don't, Rudy," she said.

"All right. I learned him. Joe, throw the son of a bitch out," said Rudy. Then suddenly he wheeled and grabbed a man by the belt and lifted him off the floor, holding him tight against his body with one hand and making a hammer of his other hand. "You, you son of a bitch, you was gonna go after me, you was, yeah? Well, go ahead. Let's see you, you son of a bitch. You son of a bitch, I break you in pieces." He let go and the man retreated out of range of Rudy's fist. "Pay your bill and don't come back. Don't ever show your face in my place again. And any other son of a bitch was gonna gang me. You gonna gang Rudy, hey? I kill any two of you." Two of the men picked Hartenstein off the floor before the bartender got to him. "Them two, they paid up, Joe?"

"In the clear, Rudy," said the bartender.

"You two. Don't come back," said Rudy.

"Don't worry. We won't," they said.

Rudy stood at Bobbie's table. "Okay if I sit down with you, Bobbie?"

"Of course," said Bobbie.

"Joe, a beer, please, hey? Bobbie, you ready?"

"Not yet, thanks," she said.

Rudy mopped his forehead with a handkerchief. "You don't have to take it from these bums," said Rudy. "Any time any them get fresh, you tell me. You're what keeps this place decent, Bobbie. I know. As soon as you go home it's a pigpen. I get sick of hearing them, some of the women as bad as the men. Draft-dotchers. Essengial industry! Draft-dotchers. A bunch of 4-F draft-dotchers. I like to hear what your Daddy would say about them."

"Did you know him, my father?"

"Know him? I was in his platoon. Second platoon, C Company. I went over with him and come back with him. Phil Hammersmith."

"I never knew that."

Rudy chuckled. "Sure. Some of these 4-F draft-dotchers from outa town, they think I'm a Nazi because I never learn to speak good English, but my Daddy didn't speak no English at all and he was born out in the Walley. My old woman says put my dischartch papers up over the back-bar. I say what for? So's to make the good impression on a bunch of draft-dotchers? Corporal Rudolph W. Schau. Your Daddy was a good man and a good soldier."

"Why didn't you ever tell me you knew him?"

"Oh, I don't know, Bobbie. I wasn't gonna tell you now, but I did. It don't pay to be a talker in my business. A listener, not a talker."

"You didn't approve of me, did you?"

"I'm a saloonkeeper. A person comes to my—"

"You didn't approve of me. Don't dodge the issue."

"Well, your Daddy wouldn't of liked you coming to a saloon that often. But times change, and you're better off here than the other joints."

"I hope you don't *mind* my coming here."

"Listen, you come here as much as you want."

"Try and stop me," she said, smiling.

Pete joined them. "What happened to Dick Hartenstein?" he said.

"The same as will happen to anybody gets fresh with your wife," said Rudy, and got up and left them.

"There could be a hell of a stink about this. Rudy could lose his license if the Company wanted to press the point."

"Well, you just see that he doesn't," said Bobbie.

"Maybe it isn't such a good idea, your coming here so often."

"Maybe. On the other hand, maybe it's a wonderful idea. I happen to think it's a wonderful idea, so I'm going to keep on coming. If *you* want to go to one of the other places, that's all right. But I like Rudy's. I like it better than ever, now."

No action was taken against Rudy Schau, and Bobbie visited the Tavern as frequently as ever. Hartenstein was an unpopular foreman and the women said he got what had been coming to him for a long time. Bobbie's friends were pleased that their new symbol had such a forthright defender. It was even said that Bobbie had saved Hartenstein from a worse beating, a rumor that added to the respect she was given by the men and the women.

The McCrea children were not being brought up according to Lantenengo Street standards. On the three or four afternoons a week that Bobbie went to the Tavern she would take her son and daughter to a neighbor's yard. On the other afternoons the neighbors' children would play in her yard. During bad weather and the worst of the winter the McCreas' house was in more frequent service as a nursery, since some of the neighbors were living in one- or two-room apartments. But none of the children, the McCreas' or the neighbors', had individual supervision. Children who had learned to walk were separated from those who were still crawling, on the proven theory that the crawling children were still defenseless against the whimsical cruelties of the older ones. Otherwise there was no distinction, and all the children were toughened early in life, as most of their parents had been. "I guess it's all right," Pete once said to Bobbie. "But I hate to think what they'll be like when they get older. Little gangsters."

"Well, that was never your trouble, God knows," said Bobbie. "And I'm no shining example of having a nannie take care of me. Do you remember my nannie?"

"Vaguely."

" 'Let's go and see the horsies,' she'd say. And we'd go to Mr. Duncan's stable and I'd come home covered with scratches from the stable cat. And I guess Patrick was covered with scratches from my nannie. Affectionate scratches, of course. Do you remember Mr. Duncan's Patrick?"

"Sure."

"He must have been quite a man. Phyllis used to go there with her nannie, too. But the cat liked Phyllis."

"I'm not suggesting that we have a nannie."

"No. You're suggesting that I stay away from the Tavern."

"In the afternoon."

"The afternoon is the only time the mothers will watch each other's children, except in rare cases. Our kids are all right. I'm with them all day most of the time, and we're home every evening, seven nights a week."

"What else is there to do?"

"Well, for instance once a month we could go to a movie."

"Where? Gibbsville?"

"Yes. Two gallons of gas at the most."

"Are you getting the itch to move back to Gibbsville?"

"Not at all. Are you?"

"Hell, no."

"We could get some high school kid to watch the children. I'd just like to have a change once in a while."

"All right. The next time there's something good at the Globe."

Their first trip to the Globe was their last. They saw no one they knew in the theatre or in the bar of the John Gibb Hotel, and when they came home the high school kid was naked in bed with a man Pete recognized from the plant. "Get out of here," said Pete.

"Is she your kid, McCrea?"

"No, she's not my kid. But did you ever hear of statutory rape?"

"Rape? This kid? I had to wait downstairs, for God's sake. She took on three other guys tonight. Ten bucks a crack."

The girl put on her clothes in sullen silence. She never spoke except to say to the man: "Do you have a room some place?"

"Well," said Pete, when they had gone. "Where did you get her from? The Junior League?"

"If you'd stared at her any more you'd have had to pay ten dollars too."

"For sixteen she had quite a shape."

"She won't have it much longer."

"You got an eyeful, too, don't pretend you didn't."

"Well, at least she won't get pregnant that way. And she *will* get *rich*," said Bobbie.

Pete laughed. "It was really quite funny. Where *did* you get her?"

"If you want her name and telephone number, I have it downstairs. I got her through one of the neighbors. She certainly got the word around quickly enough, where she'd be. There's the doorbell. Another customer?"

Pete went downstairs and informed the stranger at the door that he had the wrong address.

"Another customer, and I think he had two guys with him in the car. Seventy dollars she was going to make tonight. I guess I'm supposed to report this at the plant. We have a sort of a V-D file of known prostitutes. We sic the law on them before they infect the whole outfit, and I'll bet this little character—"

"Good heavens, yes. I must burn everything. Bed linen. Towels. Why that little bitch. Now I'm getting sore." She collected the linen and took it downstairs and to the trash burner in the yard. When she returned Pete was in bed, staring at the ceiling. "I'm going to sleep in the other room," she said.

"What's the matter?"

"I didn't like that tonight. I don't want to sleep with you."

"Oh, all right then, go to hell," said Pete.

She made up one of the beds in the adjoining room. He came and sat on the edge of her bed in the dark. "Go away, Pete," she said.

"Why?"

"Oh, all right, I'll *tell* you why. Tonight made me think of the time you wanted to exchange with Mary and Frank. That's all I've been able to think of."

"That's all passed, Bobbie. I'm not like that any more."

"You would have got in bed with that girl. I saw you."

"Then I'll tell you something. You would have got in bed with that man. I saw you, too. You were excited."

"How could I help being excited, to suddenly come upon something like that. But I was disgusted, too. And still am. Please go away and let me try to get some sleep."

She did not sleep until first light, and when the alarm clock sounded she prepared his and the children's breakfasts. She was tired and nervous throughout the day. She could not go to the Tavern because it was her turn to watch neighbors' children, and Pete telephoned and said bluntly that he would not be home for supper, offering no excuse. He got home after eleven that night, slightly drunk and with lipstick on his neck.

"Who was it? Martie?" said Bobbie.

"What difference does it make who it was? I've been trying to give up other women, but you're no help."

"I have no patience with that kind of an excuse. It's easy enough to blame me. Remember, Pete, I can pick up a man just as easily as you can make a date with Martie."

"I know you can, and you probably will."

It was the last year of the war, and she had remained faithful to Pete throughout the life of their son Angus. A week later she resumed her affair with Bill Charney. "You never forgot me," he said. "I never forgot you, either, Bobbie. I heard about you and Pete living in Fair Grounds. You know a couple times I took my car and dro' past your house to see which one it was. I didn't know, maybe you'd be sitting out on the front porch and if you saw me, you know. Maybe we just say hello and pass the time of day. But I didn't think no such thing, to tell you the God's honest truth. I got nothing against my wife, only she makes me weary. The house and the kids, she got me going to Mass every Sunday, all like that. But I ain't built that way, Bobbie. I'm the next thing to a hood, and you got that side of you, too. I'll make you any price you say, the other jerks you slept with, they never saw that side of you. You know, you hear a lot about love, Bobbie, but I guess I came closer to it with you than any other woman I ever knew. I never forgot you any more than you ever forgot me. It's what they call a mutual attraction. Like you know one person has it for another person."

"I know."

"I don't see how we stood it as long as we did. Be honest, now, didn't you often wish it was me instead of some other guy?"

"Yes."

"All right, I'll be honest with you. Many's the time in bed with my wife I used to say to myself, 'Peggy, you oughta take lessons from Bobbie McCrea.' But who can give lessons, huh? If you don't have the mutual attraction, you're nothin'. How do you think I look?" He slapped his belly. "You know I weigh the same as I used to weigh? You look good. You put on a little. What? Maybe six pounds?"

"Seven or eight."

"But you got it distributed. In another year Peggy's gonna weigh a hundred and fifty pounds, and I told her, I said either she took some of that off or I'd get another girl. Her heighth, you know. She can't get away with that much weight. I eat everything, but I do a lot of walking and standing. I guess I use up a lot of excess energy. Feel them muscles. Punch me in the belly. I got no fat on me anywhere, Bobbie. For my age I'm a perfect physical specimen. I could get any amount of insurance if I got out of The Numbers. But nobody's

gonna knock me off so why do I want insurance? I may even give up
The Numbers one of these days. I got a couple of things lined up,
strictly, strictly legitimate, and when my kids are ready to go away to
school, I may just give up The Numbers. For a price, naturally."

"That brings up a point."

"You need money? How much do you want? It's yours. I *mean*
like ten, fifteen gees."

"No, no money. But everybody knows you now. Where can we
meet?"

"What's the matter with here? I told you, I own this hotel."

"But I can't just come and go. People know me, too. I have an
idea, though."

"What?"

"Buy a motel."

"Buy a motel. You know, that thought crossed me a year ago, but
you know what I found out? They don't make money. You'd think
they would, but those that come out ahead, you be surprised how
little they make."

"There's one near Swedish Haven. It's only about a mile from my
house."

"We want a big bed, not them twin beds. I tell you what I could do.
I could rent one of the units by the month and move my own furniture in. How would that suit you?"

"I'd like it better if you owned the place."

"Blackmail? Is that what you're thinking about? Who'd blackmail
me, Bobbie? Or my girl? I'm still a hood in the eyes of some people."

There was no set arrangement for their meetings. Bill Charney
postponed the purchase of the motel until she understood he had no
intention of buying it or of making any other arrangement that implied permanence. At first she resented his procrastination, but she
discovered that she preferred his way; he would telephone her, she
would telephone him whenever desire became urgent, and sometimes they would be together within an hour of the telephone call.
They spaced out their meetings so that each one produced novelty
and excitement, and a year passed and another and Bobbie passed
the afternoon of her fortieth birthday with him.

It was characteristic of their relationship that she did not tell him
it was her birthday. He always spoke of his wife and children and his
business enterprises, but he did not notice that she never spoke of
her home life. He was a completely egocentric man, equally admiring of his star sapphire ring on his strong shortfingered hand and of
her slender waist, which in his egocentricity became his possession.

Inevitably, because of the nature of his businesses, he had a reputation for being close-mouthed, but alone with Bobbie he talked freely. "You know, Bobbie, I laid a friend of yours?"

"Was it fun?"

"Aren't you gonna ask me who?"

"You'll tell me."

"At least I guess she's a friend of yours. Mary Lander."

"She used to be a friend of mine. I haven't seen her in years."

"Yeah. While her husband was in the service. Frank."

"You're so busy, with all your women."

"There's seven days in the week, honey, and it don't take up too much of your time. This didn't last very long, anyway. Five, maybe six times I slept with her. I took her to New York twice, that is I met her there. The other times in her house. You know, she's a neighbor of mine."

"And very neighborly."

"Yeah, that's how it started. She come to my house to collect for something, some war drive, and Peggy said I took care of all them things so when I got home I made out a cheque and took it over to the Landers' and inside of fifteen minutes—less than that—we were necking all over the parlor. Hell, I knew the minute she opened the door—"

"One of those mutual attractions?"

"Yeah, sure. I gave her the cheque and she said, 'I don't know how to thank you,' and I said if she had a couple minutes I'd show her how. 'Oh, Mr. Charney,' but she didn't tell me to get out, so I knew I was in."

"What ever broke up this romance?"

"Her. She had some guy in Washington, D.C., she was thinking of marrying, and when I finally got it out of her who the guy was, I powdered out. Joe Whipple. I gotta do business with Joe. We got a home-loan proposition that we're ready to go with any day, and this was three years ago when Joe and I were just talking about it, what they call the talking stage."

"So you're the one that broke it off, not Mary."

"If a guy's looking at you across a desk and thinking you're laying his girl, you stand to get a screwing from that guy. Not that I don't trust Joe, because I do."

"Do you trust Mary?"

"I wondered about that, if she'd blab to Joe. A dame like Mary Lander, is she gonna tell the guy she's thinking of marrying that she's been laying a hood like me? No. By the way, she's queer. She told me she'd go for a girl."

"I'm surprised she hasn't already."

"Maybe she has. I couldn't find out. I always try to find out."

"You never asked me."

"I knew you wouldn't. But a dame like Mary, as soon as she opened the door I knew I was in, but then the next thing is you find out what else she'll go for. In her case, the works, as long as it isn't gonna get around. I guess I always figured her right. I have to figure all angles, men *and* women. That's where my brother Ed was stupid. I used to say to him, find out what kind of a broad a guy goes for before you declare him in. Ed used to say all he had to do was play a game of cards with a guy. But according to my theory, everybody goes into a card game prepared. Both eyes open. But not a guy going after a broad. You find out more from broads, like take for instance Mary. Now I know Frank is married to a dame that is screwing his best friend, laid a hood like me, and will go for a girl. You think I'd ever depend on Frank Lander? No. And Joe Whipple. Married to a lush, and sleeping with his best friend's wife, Mary."

"Then you wouldn't depend on Joe, either?"

"Yes, I would. Women don't bother him. He don't care if his wife is a lush, he'll get his nooky from his best friend's wife, he *isn't* going to marry her because that was three-four years ago, and he's tough about everybody. His wife, his dame, his best friend, *and* the United States government. Because I tell you something, if we ever get going on the home-loan proposition, don't think Joe didn't use his job in Washington every chance he got. The partnership is gonna be me and Joe Whipple, because he's just as tough as I am. And one fine day he'll fall over dead from not taking care of himself, and I'll be the main guy. You know the only thing I don't like about you, Bobbie, is the booze. If you'd lay off the sauce for a year I'd get rid of Peggy, and you and I could get married. But booze is women's weakness like women are men's weakness."

"Men are women's weakness."

"No, you're wrong. Men don't make women talk, men don't make women lose their looks, and women can give up men for a hell of a long time, but a female lush is the worst kind of a lush."

"Am I a lush?"

"You have a couple drinks every day, don't you?"

"Yes."

"Then you're on the way. Maybe you only take three-four drinks a day now, but five years from now three or four drinks will get you stewed, so you'll be stewed every day. That's a lush. Peggy eats like a God damn pig, but if she ever started drinking, I'd kick her out. Fortunately her old man died with the D.T.'s, so she's afraid of it."

"Would you mind getting me a nice double Scotch with a little water?"

"Why should I mind?" He grinned from back molar to back molar. "When you got a little load on, you forget home and mother." He got her the drink, she took it in her right hand and slowly poured it down his furry chest. He jumped when the icy drink touched him.

"Thank you so much," she said. "Been a very pleasant afternoon, but the party's over."

"You sore at me?"

"Yes, I am. I don't like being called a lush, and I certainly don't like you to think I'd make a good substitute for Peggy."

"You *are* sore."

"Yes."

The children did not know it was her birthday, but when Pete came home he handed her two parcels. "For me?" she said.

"Not very much imagination, but I didn't have a chance to go to Gibbsville," he said.

One package contained half a dozen nylons, the other a bottle of Chanel Number 5. "Thank you. Just what I wanted. I really did."

He suddenly began to cry, and rushed out of the room.

"Why is Daddy crying?" said their daughter.

"Because it's my birthday and he did a very sweet thing."

"Why should he cry?" said their son. He was nine years old, the daughter eleven.

"Because he's sentimental," said the daughter.

"And it's a very nice thing to be," said Bobbie.

"Aren't you going to go to him?"

"Not quite yet. In a minute. Angus, will you go down to the drug store and get a quart of ice cream? Here's a dollar, and you and your sister may keep the change, divided."

"What flavor?" said the boy.

"Vanilla and strawberry, or whatever else they have."

Pete returned. "Kids gone to bed?"

"I sent them for some ice cream."

"Did they see me bawling?"

"Yes, and I think it did them good. Marjorie understood it. Angus was a little mystified. But it was good for both of them."

"Marjorie understood it? Did you?"

"She said it was because you were sentimental."

He shook his head. "I don't know if you'd call it sentimental. I just couldn't help thinking you were forty years old. Forty. You forty. Bobbie Hammersmith. And all we've been through, and what I've done to you. I know why you married me, Bobbie, but why did you stick it out?"

"Because I married you."

"Yes. Because you married Ichabod. You know, I wasn't in love with you when we were first married. You thought I was, but I wasn't. It was wonderful, being in bed with you and watching you walking around without any clothes on. Taking a bath. But it was too much for me and that's what started me making passes at everybody. And underneath it all I knew damn well why you married me and I hated you. You were making a fool of me and I kept waiting for you to say this farce was over. If you had, I'd have killed you."

"And I guess rightly."

"And all the later stuff. Running a poolroom and living on Mill Street. I blamed all of that on you. But things are better now since we moved here. Aren't they?"

"Yes, much better, as far as the way we live—"

"That's all I meant. If we didn't have Lantenengo Street and Princeton and those things to look back on, this wouldn't be a bad life for two ordinary people."

"It's not bad," she said.

"It's still pretty bad, but that's because we once had it better. Here's what I want to say. Any time you want to walk out on me, I won't make any fuss. You can have the children, and I won't fight about it. That's my birthday present to you, before it's too late. And I have no plans for myself. I'm not trying to get out of this marriage, but you're forty now and you're entitled to whatever is left."

"Thank you, Pete. I have nobody that wants to marry me."

"Well, maybe not. But you may have, sometime. I love you now, Bobbie, and I never used to. I guess you can't love anybody else while you have no self-respect. When the war was over I was sure I'd get the bounce at the plant, but they like me there, they've kept me on, and that one promotion. We'll never be back on Lantenengo Street, but I think I can count on a job here maybe the rest of my life. In a couple of years we can move to a nicer house."

"I'd rather buy this and fix it up a little. It's a better-built house than the ones they're putting up over on Fair Grounds Heights."

"Well, I'm glad you like it too," he said. "The other thing, that we hardly ever talk about. In fact never talk about. Only fight about sometimes. I'll try, Bobbie. I've been trying."

"I know you have."

"Well—how about you trying, too?"

"I did."

"But not lately. I'm not going to ask you who or when or any of that, but why is it you're faithful to me while I'm chasing after other women, and then when I'm faithful to you, you have somebody else? You're forty now and I'm forty-four. Let's see how long we can go without cheating?"

"You don't mean put a time limit on it, or put up a trophy, like an endurance contest? That's the way it sounds. We both have bad habits, Pete."

"Yes, and I'm the worst. But break it off, Bobbie, whoever it is. Will you please? If it's somebody you're not going to marry, and that's what you said, I've—well, it's a long time since I've cheated, and I like it much better this way. Will you stop seeing this other guy?"

"All right. As a matter of fact I *have* stopped, but don't ask me how long ago."

"I won't ask you anything. And if you fall in love with somebody and want to marry him—"

"And he wants to marry me."

"And he wants to marry you, I'll bow out." He leaned down and kissed her cheek. "I know you better than you think I do, Bobbie."

"That's an irritating statement to make to any woman."

"I guess it is, but not the way I meant it."

Now that is as far as I need go in the story of Pete and Bobbie McCrea. I promised a happy ending, which I shall come to in a moment. We have left Pete and Bobbie in 1947, on Bobbie's fortieth birthday. During the next thirteen years I saw them twice. On one occasion my wife and I spent the night with them in their house in Fair Grounds, which was painted, scrubbed and dusted like the Fair Grounds houses of old. My wife went to bed early, and Pete and Bobbie and I talked until past midnight, and then Pete retired and Bobbie and I continued our conversation until three in the morning. Twice she emptied our ash trays of cigarette butts, and we drank a drip-flask of coffee. It seemed to me that she was so thorough in her description of their life because she felt that the dinginess would vanish if she once succeeded in exposing it. But as we were leaving in the morning I was not so sure that it had vanished. My wife said to me: "Did she get it all out of her system?"

"Get what out of her system?"

"I don't know, but I don't think she did, entirely."

"That would be asking too much," I said. "But I guess she's happy."

"Content, but not happy," said my wife. "But the children are what interested me. The girl is going to be attractive in a few more

years, but that boy! You didn't talk to him, but do you know about
him? He's fourteen, and he's already passed his senior mathematics.
He's *finished* the work that the high school seniors are supposed to
be taking. The principal is trying to arrange correspondence courses
for him. He's the brightest student they ever had in Fair Grounds
High School, ever, and all the scientific men at the aluminum plant
know about him. And he's a good-looking boy, too."

"Bobbie didn't tell me any of this."

"And I'll bet I know why. He's their future. With you she wanted
to get rid of the past. She adores this boy, adores him. That part's
almost terrifying."

"Not to me," I said. "It's the best thing that could have happened
to her, and to Pete. The only thing that's terrifying is that they could
have ruined it. And believe me, they could have."

In 1960, then, I saw Pete and Bobbie again. They invited me, of all
their old friends, to go with them to the Princeton commencement.
Angus McCrea, Junior, led his class, was awarded the mathematics
prize, the physics prize, the Eubank Prize for scholarship, and some
other honors that I am sure are listed in the program. I could not
read the program because I was crying most of the time. Pete would
lean forward in his chair, listening to the things that were being said
about his son, but in an attitude that would have been more suitable
to a man who was listening to a pronouncement of sentence. Bobbie
sat erect and smiling, but every once in a while I could hear her
whisper, "Oh, God. Oh, God."

There, I guess, is our happy ending.

The Cellar Domain

Not just anyone and everyone got their hair cut and their faces shaved at Peter Durant's shop. Peter had a system to discourage new customers who in his opinion had not earned the right to join his clientele. Peter had, of course, the first chair, but he kept his eye on the other six chairs in his shop and on the order in which his customers arrived and should be attended to. A barber would finish with a customer, and Peter, almost without missing a snip at his own customer's hair, would call out: "You're next, Judge. Bobby, take Judge Buckhouse." Customers and barbers alike accepted Peter's decisions without argument, and an unwelcome newcomer would sometimes find that he had been passed over in favor of five or six men who had not been in the shop when he arrived. Once in a while there would be one who would say: "I think I was next."

"Can't help that," Peter would say, and that settled it. If the customer didn't like it, he was free to go elsewhere, which was exactly what Peter Durant intended. A young businessman, a young lawyer or doctor making his first appearance at Durant's, would know better than to risk a scene in the presence of Peter's established customers, who were the county's most prominent professional and financial men and some others who had received Peter's approval. In those long-gone days it was an important occasion when Peter Durant would say to a customer: "I'm ordering you a mug. Do you want your name on it or just your initials?" No one had ever declined the honor of a mug at Peter Durant's or hesitated to pay the two dollars for the mug and its gilt lettering. It was a diploma, the acceptance of a man's racing colors, membership in a club like the Philadelphia Union League, a rating in Bradstreet's, a commission on the Governor's military staff. It was all these things, because there were men in the county who had achieved one or another of these things but had not been invited to pay two dollars for a mug at Peter Durant's.

New Yorker (11 February 1961); *Assembly*

Although the shop was in the cellar of the hotel, it was not a convenience for hotel guests. Traveling salesmen were accommodated at Durant's only in the less busy hours of mid-afternoon, and even though some of his barbers might be shaving themselves, or sitting on the customers' bench and reading the Philadelphia *North American* or the London *Illustrated News,* Peter sometimes would take a quick look at a stranger and say: "Be an hour's wait."

"What about those men?" the stranger would say, nodding toward the idle barbers.

"That's my business. Better go down the street. You got a good barber down towards the railroad station."

The stranger would glare at Peter, but depart, and Peter would say: "That's the kind of a son of a bitch would ask for a manicure." Peter's barbers would laugh. They liked Peter; he paid them well, he did their thinking for them, and he backed them up in any dispute with a customer. There were only two rules they had to obey: a barber was not supposed to work if he had liquor on his breath; if he wanted to go on a drunk he could take the day off; and the other rule was that no barber, no customer for that matter, was permitted to address him as Pete. He was not deceived by the obsequious newcomer who called him Mr. Durant; but no judge, no doctor, no clergyman, no bank cashier, no retired millionaire got an answer when he said Pete instead of Peter. But then they never made that mistake; they knew better. Casual use of the diminutive had kept some men from getting a mug.

The shop sold nothing but shaves, haircuts, and facial and scalp massages. No tonics, no combs or brushes, no cigars or cigarettes, and only one special service: some men who shaved themselves would bring their razors to Peter for honing. A great deal of betting went on among the customers, especially during political campaigns, but Peter Durant participated only to the extent that bets made in his shop were recorded in a notebook he kept in his cash register. Both parties to a bet would see what he wrote in the notebook, sign their initials, and Peter would say: "Now nobody has to ask me do I remember who bet what." But Peter thus became the repository of valuable information that he kept confidential, and inevitably his customers' trust in his discretion got him in on some good things. He went on shaving men whom he could buy and sell, even though they might not know it.

Generally Peter Durant discouraged the favorite-barber custom, and among the newer customers it was not permitted. "One's as good as another in this shop," he would say. "Harry's as good a barber as me, and Elmer's as good as Harry." But Peter had his own favorite customers, and he would linger over a haircut, or speed it up, so that one of his favorites would get in his chair. Peter's chair, the first, was nearest the street window, and certain customers would stand on the sidewalk and look down into the shop until they had attracted his attention. If he nodded, they knew he would fit them into the order so that he would cut their hair; if he shook his head and make a face, they knew it to mean that they would have to take another barber. The other barbers, who were not fools, made every cooperative effort to see that Peter's favorites got to his chair, but it was a different matter altogether for them to understand why Peter Durant preferred some customers to others. They could understand why Edwin E. Patterson was entitled to the first chair, but most of the barbers could not understand why Andy Keever got in the shop at all.

Ned Patterson was in town a lot because he had business at the court house; not a large amount of business, and obviously not highly profitable, what there was. He usually got off the trolley-car from Swedish Haven at the corner across the street from the barber shop on mornings when he was to be in court. On court days he liked to be shaved by Peter Durant, and it did not escape the notice of the barbers that Peter often trimmed Ned's hair—"neatened it up," he called it—without charging him for a regular cut. "Now I guess you look all right," Peter would say.

"Thank you, Peter. Thank you very much," Ned would say, and lay down the same quarter and nickel—twenty cents for the shave, and ten-cent tip—and be off to the court house. At this time, shortly after the First World War, Ned Patterson was in his sixties, a good ten years older than Peter Durant, but nearly everyone still called him Ned. On court days he wore a black suit, black necktie and shoes, and starched collar and cuffs and shirt-bosom. Walter, the bootblack-porter at Durant's shop, could not have improved on the shine Ned had already given his shoes. Ned Patterson seldom encountered other lawyers in the shop; he was there too early in the day. But Judge Buckhouse sometimes arrived for a shave as Ned was leaving, and Ned would say: "Good morning to you, sir."

"Good morning, Ned. If you're not in too much of a hurry I can give you a lift."

"Very kind of you, Judge, but I've got a man waiting." He was fifteen years older than Judge Buckhouse, and the last two blocks to the court house were a steep climb, but he never accepted the judge's offer. Always, when the offers were made, Ned would explain that he had a man waiting, presumably a client, but Buckhouse knew that Ned Patterson sometimes came to the court house; wandered up and down the corridors, listened to trials, mingled with colleagues in the lawyers' room, and represented no client. Just by being there at every session of every term, Ned sometimes would be appointed by the court to defend a case and receive a fee that he would not get by staying in Swedish Haven. Sometimes a colleague would put something his way—a dreary job of searching in the prothonotary's records—that would be worth twenty-five dollars. Ned Patterson rarely went home empty-handed at the end of a term of court, but the juicy receiverships went to other lawyers, more aggressive or younger or more learned in the law. "In a jury trial," a lawyer once said, "it ought to be worth a few dollars to have Ned sitting with you at counsel table. That white hair and smooth skin, and that under-taker outfit he wears. He's the next thing to having a bishop on your side. But I don't know how often it would work. The jury might start wondering why God didn't examine the witnesses, or why He didn't make the closing address. Some juries would begin to think that maybe Ned didn't—quite—go along with you, and they'd smell a rat. And as for letting him examine a witness, you'd be taking a chance of ruining your case then and there. I like old Ned, but to tell you the truth he doesn't even copy things right. He knows his law, and loves it, and in some respects he'd have made a good judge. But not for the County. He'd never send anybody to prison." And so, in his late-middle sixties, Edwin E. Patterson, Esq., attorney-at-law, sole surviving member of the firm of Patterson & Patterson, was still waiting for the success that had seemed to come so easily to his father many years ago, the success without which Ned could not have continued his own unprofitable practice of law. For the truth was that Ned and his wife subsisted on the small income from his father's estate, and his professional fees provided him with the luxury of being a lawyer. He was a gentleman-at-law, an amateur of the law, who went to the court house as some men, old friends in Philadelphia, went to the opera. Some of *them* could not sing a note, but they loved Verdi. In much the same way, on court days, Ned Patterson would come to town, humming, as it were, the Rule in Shelley's Case.

In a sense, then, Ned Patterson's visits to Peter Durant's barber shop were time spent in the dressing-room, before the performances at the court house in which he might or might not take active part. The quiet dignity he maintained while covered with lather was genu-ine enough, lifelong and natural, but Peter Durant had no way of knowing that Ned at such times was especially content because he was already enjoying the promise of the day's later developments. "Never seen that man when he wasn't at peace with the world," Peter Durant would say. "Shaving him's a good way to start the day."

The more remarkable, then, that Peter Durant's other favorite customer should be Andy Keever.

Andy Keever's membership in the Durant clientele was offensive to more than one of the regulars. He knew everyone by name, and as he made an entrance in the shop he would walk past the waiting customers on the bench, speaking to each—"Mr. Hofman . . . Dr. English . . . Mr. Chapin . . ."—and shedding his outer clothing, removing collar and tie, and apparently not noticing that there would be a closing of ranks so that the men of substance would not have to make a place for him. He would stand at the far end of the shop, hanging his clothing on the rack, and call to the owner: "Hey, Peter, you coming to the hose company picnic?"

"Oh, sure," Peter Durant would say, smiling because everyone knew that he never went to hose company picnics. "I'll be there with bells on."

"Never mind the bells, we'll bring them." Andy would stand at the clothes rack, surveying the room and waiting for the exactly right moment, and then he would move quietly forward until he reached Elmer Bitzer's chair, without being seen by Elmer. He would goose Bitzer and simultaneously whistle through his teeth, a loud, piercing whistle, and Bitzer would jump. Everybody would laugh, but the hardest laughter was Peter Durant, who would drop his hands to his sides and bend over, weak with giggles. "That fellow, he kills me," he would say to the customer in the chair. "I can't help it, he makes me laugh." Even Bitzer, the perennial victim, would grin.

Andy Keever would find a place on the bench, look about him, stand up and say: "Any reverends here?"

"No," one of the barbers would say.

"Who's that under the hot towel? Not a reverend, sure?"

"Mr. Miller."

"Then I got a good one for you. Hey, Peter, I got a good one for you. There was this railroader come home and found his wife in bed with a Chinaman. You know, a Chinaman . . ."

Andy Keever never laughed at his own stories. When he finished one he would look around at all the men, and if one of the men had not been listening, was reading a newspaper, Andy would make a face at him and raise his voice and tell a dirtier story. Sometimes he would have French postcards and phallic toys that he would hold out to a barber, and then as the barber reached out his hand, Andy would quickly pull away. "Naughtee, naugh-tee. You're too eager," he would say. "I'm saving this for Walter. Hey, Walter, I bought you something in Philly."

Andy Keever was new in town, had come there after being mustered out of the Army early in 1919. One of the breweries, resigned to what was about to happen, was making the change from beer to ice cream, and Andy Keever was put in charge of a crew that canvassed candy stores and poolrooms and the like, signing up customers for the new product. Andy Keever was a live wire, a hard worker, and in a few short months it was understood that the brewery family were so pleased with him that it was only a question of time before he would be made general manager of the ice cream plant. He was a charter member of the Legion post, a sports fan, a founder of the Lions Club, a forward on one of the businessmen's basketball teams at the Y.M.C.A., and, within a year, one of the leaders of the small group who got things done. They were virtually a standing committee of Rotarians, Merchants Association members and Masons who ran the drives and campaigns that represented community activity, and Andy Keever was the first new face in that group in five years. Some of these men were patrons of Peter Durant's shop, which was the only place where they would frequently encounter those other men, men who were known as the Lantenengo Street crowd, the Gibbsville Club crowd, the plutocrats and "our would-be aristocrats." As individuals, in man-to-man relations, the members of the two leading groups got along nicely; but as group members they kept to themselves, recognizably different in clothes and manners. At Peter Durant's shop, there never was any doubt as to the proprietor's preference, and after waiting in vain to be sold a mug, some of the Rotarians would take their business elsewhere, invariably complaining of the service at Peter Durant's and omitting mention of the fact that a Ned Patterson got more cordial treatment than a director of the Building & Loan Society.

"I think Mr. Keever goes a bit too far," said one of Peter Durant's favorites one day.

"Fresh as paint, but he puts me in stitches," said Peter. "I don't know what there is about that fellow."

"Well, if *you* can put up with him," said the customer. "But I wouldn't like to be in Elmer Bitzer's chair, with Elmer holding a razor at my throat."

"Oh, you take notice sometime. Keever don't do that to Elmer when Elmer's shaving. Keever has more sense than that."

"Good. Glad to hear that, anyway."

"Oh, sure. That's something I never *would* put up with. In this business you learn to have an awful lot of respect for a razor."

"I should think so," said the customer.

"When I was learning the barber trade, if I nicked a customer my old man would fine me a week's pay, even if it wasn't my fault."

The customer closed his eyes, the signal to end conversation that was always respected by Peter Durant. There were other men who in other conversations revealed a distaste for the presence of Andy Keever, and Peter thought about the matter; but Keever's jokes and little pranks went on, and Keever remained a customer. Peter began to feel that criticism of Keever was by way of being criticism of himself, and he had had little experience of that. He ran his shop to suit himself, a first-class shop with first-class barbers, where the best men in the county sat with their collars and ties off, and one man— Peter Durant—was the only boss.

"You don't know a fellow named Andy Keever, do you, Ned?"

"Andy Keever. Keever? That's a new name to me," said Ned Patterson. "What does he do?"

"He's up there at the new ice cream plant. They got him in charge of the salesmen," said Peter Durant. "He's a customer, but never this early in the morning. Ha' past ten or eleven he usually comes in."

"Don't know him, but why do you ask?"

"Well, he rubs some people the wrong way. Other customers, and I kind of wondered did you ever hear them say anything."

"No, but you've always been able to get rid of men like him. True, you have to serve him, legally, but you have your methods."

"I don't want to get rid of him."

"Then by all means, don't. I've seen men in this shop that despise each other, but they behave themselves here. You have a gentlemen's institution here, Peter, and you've made it that and kept it that."

"Keever isn't what you'd call a gentleman."

"Well, I didn't mean that they're all the cream of the crop, but they behave like gentlemen."

"Not Keever."

"*Not* Keever? Then I don't see what your problem is, Peter. Very few places that men gather together and conduct themselves as well as they do here, but this is one of them. If this Keever man—what sort of thing does he do that annoys the other patrons?"

"Oh, jokes, and stuff like that."

"Well, if you mean dirty jokes, I've never heard you tell one, or enjoy one. I don't mind them myself, if they're really funny and well told. Abraham Lincoln. Mark Twain. John Kendrik Bangs. Arthur Twining Hadley. An off-color story didn't bother them, and I certainly wouldn't condemn your man Keever on *that* evidence. Unless, of course, you're referring to the reverend clergy. I know you have two ministers and I believe Monsignor What's His Name comes in here."

"He don't tell them in front of them."

"Then what's troubling you, Peter?"

"I don't know whose side I'm on, that's my trouble. Andy Keever makes me laugh till I'm weak, but a lot of my best customers—you can tell by the way they look at him. But on the other hand, is it my shop or does it belong to the customers?"

"I begin to see your problem, yes," said Ned Patterson.

"You see my problem."

"I do. One: does the proprietor claim the right to select his customers? Two: having selected his customers, have they in turn any inherent rights? Three: do those inherent rights include that of rejecting a new customer?"

"I follow you."

"I'm trying to see it as a lawyer might when he prepares a case for a judge's opinion. But now I have to follow a different procedure. The question really comes down to a matter that isn't governed by set rules. In other words, it becomes a matter of personal preference, Peter. Taste, on the one hand, and business expediency. Do you want this man around, and do you want him around enough to jeopardize your business? From what you've told me, and from what I know of your clientele, you may be running a real risk."

"That's what I've been thinking about."

"And now that you've told me as much as you have, you've suddenly shed some light on something else."

"What's that, Ned?"

"Well, you and I've been friends for a long time."

"Close on to thirty years," said Peter Durant.

"When court's in session I make it a habit to have my lunch at the club."

"The Gibbsville Club."

"Yes. Otherwise I never go near the place, and I hardly ever know what's going on up there, although I've been a member since my twenty-fifth birthday. But I *have* heard some talk, let me see, during the present term and during the May term—of putting in a barber chair. Putting in a chair and hiring a barber. I paid very little attention, but it's just possible, Peter, that some of your customers may be deciding to act."

"Oh, they are, eh?"

"It's a possibility. It's a probability. Most of the men at the club are customers of yours, and it may be more than a coincidence that there's been this talk of hiring a barber."

"You didn't hear who they were thinking of hiring, did you?"

"No, but there I'd draw the line at confiding in you. You understand that, of course."

"You wouldn't tell me if it was one of my men they were hiring?"

"No, I wouldn't. I don't mind passing this information on to you, since it may help you to decide your problem. But it would be quite another matter, Peter, to reveal any names. Either names of customers or the name of the barber, if I knew it. So, this conversation may only have added to your dilemma, but you've been warned."

"Well, I wouldn't expect you to name names, Ned. Just to tell me if it was one of my men."

"No, I wouldn't tell you that, either. Out of six men that you've had with you for a long time, you wouldn't have much trouble narrowing it down."

"You bet I wouldn't," said Peter Durant. "And I got a pretty good idea already."

"A word of caution. Better think about Mr. Keever and how much you like to have him as a customer. Don't spend your time wondering if one of your men has been offered another job. I don't think *I'd* like Mr. Keever, but I'm just throwing that in, free gratis."

Two days later Peter Durant fired Bobby Little, the second-chair barber who had been in the shop for more than twenty years. Bobby denied having had business conversations with Gibbsville Club men, but Peter Durant called him a liar. The firing took place in the evening, after the last customer had gone and the shades were drawn. "You think I'm stupid, you think I don't know what's going on behind my back?" said Peter to Bobby and to the other five barbers.

"You're gonna find out you were wrong, Peter," said Bobby Little. "But don't ask me to come back. I don't work for no man calls me a liar." He went to his post, wrapped his razors and scissors in the black leather case that he used on visits to sick customers, and held out his hand. "Give me me time."

"I'm giving you two weeks' pay."

"Give me me time, up till tonight. I don't want no favors from you. Two weeks' pay after twenty-one years. Calling me a liar. Pay me up till tonight and that's all. But believe me, Peter Durant, you got some things to learn."

Peter Durant handed Bobby three five-dollar bills and Bobby turned to the others. "Goodnight, fellows." The others said goodnight to him and stared at the curtained door after he left.

"I hope you're sure, Peter," said Harry Slazenger. "As far as I'm concerned, Bobby never said nothin' to me about no Gibbsville Club offer."

"That's a bright one," said Peter Durant. "Why the hell would he want to tell you? He'd be afraid you'd tell me."

"Well then he'd of been wrong, because I wouldn't of told you," said Harry Slazenger.

"No? Maybe you're in it, too. Maybe they're gonna have *two* chairs up there."

"I don't know. This is the first I heard about it that they were gonna have *one,* but if you don't believe me, Peter, why don't you come out and say it?"

"All right, I will say it," said Peter Durant. "I think you knew about this. Bobby's your brother-in-law."

"Are you calling me a liar?"

"Yes, I'm calling you a liar," said Peter Durant.

"Give me me time."

"With pleasure," said Peter Durant. "You want to be proud, like your brother-in-law, or will you take the full two weeks?"

"I'll take the two weeks. I'll take all I can get. If you want to give me two months I'll take it." Slazenger turned to the other barbers. "How many you fellows gonna show up for work tomorrow?"

"Leave me out of it, Harry," said Elmer Bitzer. "You and Bobby have your fight, but that don't say we gotta go without work."

"You trying to call a strike?" said Peter Durant. "This aint a union shop."

"Too bad it isn't," said Slazenger.

"You'll get three days and not another nickel," said Peter Durant. He opened the cash register, took out the money and slapped it on the shelf in front of Harry Slazenger's chair. Slazenger packed his equipment in a case similar to Bobby Little's.

"Something got into you, Peter. We all been noticing it. *They* won't admit it, but you got something festering inside of you."

"Take your God damn stuff and get out of here," said Peter Durant.

"You want me to tell you something?" said Slazenger. "Pretty soon you won't need six barbers. You'll be able to do it all yourself. Ned Patterson and that fellow Keever, that's who you'll have for customers."

"You worried about if I'm gonna have enough to eat?" said Peter.

"Oh, you got money, Peter. We know that. But you lose Bobby and now me, and even so you didn't find out who's going to the Gibbsville Club. One of those four, maybe. But which one, eh, Peter? Which one?"

"I got the right ones," said Peter Durant.

"No. But it's one of these four," said Slazenger. He laughed and departed.

Peter Durant looked at the remaining four barbers, but decided against making a speech. "Whose turn is it to open up tomorrow?"

"Bobby's," said one of the barbers.

"Well, I'll take his turn tomorrow," said Peter Durant. He locked the cash register and went about pulling the cords of the ceiling lamps, and the men said goodnight and departed.

The news that Peter Durant had fired two of his oldest employees got about very quickly, but during the first few days most of the regular customers were too tactful to inquire for details. On the Friday morning, however, Judge Buckhouse, who was president of the Gibbsville Club, asked Peter to join him in a corner of the hotel lobby upstairs.

"You made a mistake, Peter. You shouldn't have discharged those men. There *was* some talk about putting in a chair at the club, but I don't think it's going to come to anything."

"You'd say that now."

"I beg your pardon?"

"Maybe you decided you wouldn't put a chair in, but how do I know you didn't dicker with Bobby Little?"

"You don't know, but you can take my word for it," said the judge. "We never got to that stage."

"You didn't talk to any of my men?"

"The whole idea never got beyond the discussion stage."

"I don't know," said Peter Durant. "He acted very suspicious. And that Harry Slazenger! That son of a bitch."

"*What* don't you know? I said that the idea never got beyond the discussion stage, and you said 'I don't know.' Are you doubting my word?"

"I doubt everybody's word."

"Then there's nothing more to be said. That's all, Peter. Good day."

"Good day? What do you mean by that?"

"Goodbye, is what I mean."

"You're not coming in any more?"

"Certainly not. I wouldn't think of it."

"Well, I guess I'll have to get along without you, then. Where do you want me to send your mug? You paid two dollars for it, so it belongs to you."

"Oh, I don't care what you do with it, Peter."

"Your mug?"

"Throw it in the wastebasket. Now I have to be getting along." The judge crossed the lobby to the revolving door and entered his waiting limousine. Peter Durant slowly walked through the door marked Barber Shop—Gentlemen and down the steps to his shop. He removed his suit coat and put on his white jacket and took his place at his chair.

"All right. Who's next?" he called.

"Hey, Peter, you didn't say hello to me. Am I fired, too?" Andy Keever, from his place on the bench, was pleased with the big laugh he got.

"Oh, go to hell," said Peter Durant.

A Case History

For ten months at the outset of his professional career Dr. Drummond had served as ship's surgeon in various liners that called at South American, Australian, and Asiatic ports. In his front office hung framed photographs taken on some of his voyages, pictures of himself in tropical whites posed with men whom he would identify as presidents of banana republics, opera and concert performers on tour, forgotten financiers, the inevitable Englishmen of title, and Orientals in native costume or western dress. At home, his den was furnished with drums and spears, shrunken skulls, lovely brassbound boxes, Chinese gongs, and more photographs. The brass was now tarnished, the wooden objects now brittle dry, the drumheads crinkly and the photographs fading after nearly forty years of sunlight, but almost nothing had been moved from its original resting place. Dr. Drummond had always been delighted when a new patient commented on the photographs in the office or a visitor to his house showed curiosity about the primitive weapons. "Yes, that's me, if you can believe it," he would say. "On my right is Sir John Humberland. He wasn't Sir John then. That's when he was Leftenant Humberland, of the Yorkshire, uh, Yorkshire some regiment, but of course you probably read about him at Tobruk. On my left, that's a friend of mine named On Ling, he was a financial adviser to one of the famous war lords. An Oxford graduate, spoke beautiful English, of course. That was on a voyage from Auckland, New Zealand, to Hong Kong, and an interesting thing about that picture, it was the only time those two got that close together. Jack Humberland was thought to be a British intelligence agent, but if he was he never got anything out of On Ling. On Ling would bow to him very politely, but he'd never sit down with him, never engage in conversation. I finally got the two of them together long enough to pose for a photograph, but On Ling didn't like it very much. You can tell by his expression.

Assembly (1961)

"Now this is a young lady that we had with us on a trip from Havana to Santiago, Chile. Through the Panama Canal. Very attractive. Her husband was a chemist, worked for one of the big chemical companies . . . The man on her left. An American. I don't know what he did, if he did anything. He was three sheets to the wind all the time he was aboard. Glad to see him go, I can tell you . . . These, of course, you can guess where this was taken. Bali. That was before the Dutch made them cover up. I always manage to stand in front of this picture when the Reverend Hostetter's here for dinner, but I guess he must have seen it by this time . . . I bought this in Sydney. It's an authentic boomerang. Needs a bit of waxing, but I keep putting it off. My housekeeper before I had Mrs. Brophy took it upon herself to do a job on my collection, and she put her thumb through one of my drumheads, so I don't let anybody touch any of my souvenirs . . . That, that's a blowgun. You've heard of them. They use them to blow poison-tipped darts. Some of the tribes use curare, others have their own particular poison that you won't find listed in the U.S.P. United States Pharmacopoeia . . . I shot that tiger from the back of an elephant, but I didn't have enough money to bring the skin home with me so all I have is this snapshot. Oh, it's all a long, long way from Gibbsville, PA, in miles and in years . . . These teacups, aren't they delicate little things? The last ones I have left out of a set. Lucky to have these two, after forty years and the clumsy women I've had working for me."

The doctor was a widower, childless, whose wife had died of liver trouble during the Second World War. The late Mrs. Drummond had money, some of it her own, most of it the income from a trust fund established by her first husband. When she died everyone agreed that Buz Drummond had fully earned the money he inherited; he had been nice to Sadie, done all he could to make her stop drinking though knowing it to be a hopeless task, and for a time he had practically given up his practice to take care of her so that she could have her wish, which was that she not be sent to a hospital. Sadie loathed hospitals; her father and mother and first husband had all died in the same hospital, on the same floor, in the same year, and she was bounden determined that the only way they would get her into a hospital was if they put her in a straitjacket. That, as a matter of fact, was done, but Buz honored her wish and did not take her to a hospital. As soon as she died he again became more active in his practice, and he kept busy until the younger men returned from the war; then he announced that he was taking no new patients, and during the late Forties and the Fifties he more or less retired to play golf and bridge and to devote his time to writing. He had missed out on two great wars, but he had seen a great deal of the world and he had a lot of good stories to tell.

The news that Buz Drummond was writing a book immediately caused some alarm, since the town had not fully recovered from the notoriety that followed the publication of several novels by a former resident. But on second thought Buz Drummond's friends were able to reassure themselves with the knowledge that first of all Buz was a gentleman, and in the second place, he intended to live out his life in Gibbsville. He was, moreover, an M.D., and there certainly were some written or unwritten rules to govern the degree and kind of revelations a doctor could make, even in the guise of fiction. After the early alarm Buz Drummond's friends, with few exceptions, began to take a friendly interest in his new writing career. Most of his friends would ask him how his book was coming, and he would reply that there was a lot more work to it than he had anticipated but it was *fascinating* work. Those acquaintances who were inclined to be apprehensive or suspicious—other doctors and former patients— were in accord on one thing: they knew a thing or two about Buz. But most people relied on his good sense, his good taste, his professional ethics, his decision to remain a resident of the town, and the now comforting knowledge that he had never really completed anything he had set out to accomplish.

His contemporaries recalled that after serving his internship in a Philadelphia hospital, Buz had come home for a round of farewell parties. According to his announced intention he was about to take off for South America on the first leg of a journey to last five years, during which he hoped to make a special study of tropical diseases and their cure. The high point of the bon voyage festivities was a dinner dance at the brand-new country club, for which two hundred were invited and Markel's orchestra played. The dance went off without unpleasant incident, other than the too-frequent repetition of a song called "Tell Me Little Gipsy," which had to do with fortune telling and an obvious connection with the adventurous young doctor's future. Buz got moderately tight, and the next day departed for Baltimore and his first berth in a fruit boat bound for Honduras. His closer friends had chipped in for a farewell gift—a doctor's emergency kit in an alligator-hide satchel—but he accidentally left it on the train.

When he returned to Gibbsville in less than a year his friends supposed that he was merely on a holiday between voyages, and they said so, thus supplying him with an explanation of his return. "Waiting to hear from the Dollar Line," he would say. Then, as the weeks passed: "Oh, that Dollar Line proposition fell through." Meanwhile his friends were getting postcards and little gifts he had sent them before his return, and several boxes of stuff arrived at his mother's house on Frederick Street. Then, in the autumn of '21 he opened an office on lower Lantenengo Street, in a neighborhood nicknamed Pill Row. He bought a Dodge coupe—one of the standard doctors' cars—and became a regular attendant at the meetings of the County Medical Society until he noticed that the only men who seemed to find time for the meetings were the young fellows just starting out, the arthritic old men, and the mediocrities of the profession. His own practice at first surprised him. His office hours were from one to three in the afternoon and six to eight in the evening, and he always had one or two patients, at least, in the waiting-room. Some of them were deadbeats, but they were patients; quite a few of them were the servants of his well-to-do friends; high school boys with their first gonorrhea; consumptives from the Negro section; old men and old women with real or imaginary illnesses to talk about; schoolteachers who, in the vernacular, doctored with him because he did not charge too much.

He lived at home with his mother, who was financially secure but not rich, and he watched his expenses, but at the end of two years he owed money at the bank. Like every other doctor in Pill Row he was offered a substantial sum by one of the local bootleggers in return for his liquor prescriptions, but professional gossip had immediately identified those physicians who dealt with the bootleggers, and Buz declined their offer even though it would have got him out of debt and with money to spare. The solution to that problem, the respectable solution, was to marry a girl with money. There were of course other solutions less respectable, and still others that were respectable enough but, for a young man, a too-early admission of failure. He could sign up with one of the coal or iron operators, he could be the official examiner and physician for the middle-class lodges that provided insurance benefits. But one of the older men advised against either arrangement. "You'll find out that for their God damn fifty-cent fees they think they own you, and as far as the big companies—the surgeons are the only ones make any money out of them. The lodges and the coal companies will crowd the other patients out of your office." A nice girl with money would also complete the picture of the up-and-coming young physician that Buz Drummond wanted very much to impress on the public mind; he was anxious to have the townsfolk think of him as a well-traveled man, but he wanted them to believe that the curtailment of his five-year trip had been a decision of his own, a desire to settle down to something constructive.

He found that his mother had been proceeding along the same line of thought, was just as far along as he. "You'll be thirty any day now," she said. "That's not old for a man, but it's not young either. And there are two or three nice Gibbsville girls that aren't getting any younger either. Well situated financially. Mary Bowen, but unfortunately she's a Catholic. But there's Minnie Stokes, you've always liked Minnie. And you'd go a long way before you'd find a nicer girl than Josie Entwhistle. All the right age to get married, and just waiting to be asked."

"You can rule out Mary and Josie."

"Well, then, Minnie."

"Minnie's the only one of those three. I've already had too many arguments with Mary, about her religion. And Josie has you fooled, Mother."

"Well, I'm not insisting on either one of them, but find *some*body. Doesn't have to be a Gibbsville girl necessarily, but people would be that much more pleased if you married a town girl. And she doesn't have to be one of our friends. This town has a lot of money and it isn't all on Lantenengo Street."

"Oh, I know that."

"Look at some of the names of the directors of the banks."

"I have."

"Well, don't let the grass grow under your feet," said Mrs. Drummond.

Henrietta Moore chose this inopportune moment to inform Buz Drummond that she was pregnant and was taking her name off the nurses' registry. "I can go to Philly and have it taken care of, but, honey, I'm going to lose a couple months' work and I don't have much saved up."

"How the hell—"

"Oh, what's the use of complaining about it? I should of known better and you should of known better, but we took our chances, so I'm not taking any calls till maybe January or February. That's thirty-five dollars a week I'm out, times twelve weeks. Twelve fives sixty, twelve threes thirty-six and six to carry is four hundred twenty dollars."

"You're better at arithmetic than you are at some other things."

"You be careful I'm not too good at multiplication. Or addition. Catch wise?"

"Very witty, I'm sure. Well, you want me to raise five hundred dollars."

"I didn't say that. Five hundred is only what I'm out. Don't you expect to pay for the abortion and while I'm in the hospital? I need a thousand, Buz."

"A thousand dollars?"

"Do you want to do it yourself? You'll still have expenses. I want to be in a hospital. I don't want to start hemorrhaging in a boarding house. Listen, Buz, I'm not holding you up for anything, but I want to go to Philly and be in a hospital. I'd have a hard time getting it done here, in the hospital. I had my appendix out five years ago, so I can't use that old excuse."

"When do you have to have the money?"

"I have to let them know I'm coming at the hospital, two or three days' notice. A girl I trained with is the head nurse there."

"What hospital is it?"

"As if you didn't know. Every intern in Philly knows, and most nurses. And those society bimboes."

"All right, I'll get the money."

"You certainly are good-natured about it, I must say. *God!*"

Mrs. Drummond handed over a bond. "I'm not giving you this," she said. "This is a loan, and you must pay me back. I don't object to helping you when I know what the money's for, but you've told me two versions of why you need a thousand dollars and frankly I don't believe either one of them. I want the money back and forty-five dollars interest. I mean it, this time I do."

"You'll get it back, and I'm no child, Mother. I don't see why I have to account for every nickel I spend."

"There are a lot of nickels in a thousand dollars. And I'm no child, either, by the way. I think you're ashamed to tell me what you want the money for."

"Have it your own way," he said.

Henrietta Moore did not go back to work as soon as she had said she would, but when she did go back, Drummond's first knowledge of it was through the nurses' registry. He telephoned to find out what nurses were taking calls and Miss Moore's name was mentioned. "Tell her to call Dr. Drummond," he said.

She telephoned him. "Good evening, Dr. Drummond. This is Miss Moore."

He was alone in his office. "So you're back at work?"

"Yes, I'm going on a case for Dr. English, starting night duty tomorrow. Why?"

"Are you calling from some place where you can't talk?"

"No, I'm in a booth at the drug store. I stopped in after the movies and I saw you phoned. I can talk all right—if I want to. Only I don't want to. The least you could do was send me some flowers, all the time I was in Philly. I could of had a septicemia for all you cared."

"But you didn't have. And I take it you're all right again."

"You asking for a date?"

"No, I'm not, Henrietta."

"That's good, because you wouldn't of got one. Goodnight, Dr. Drummond."

She was a good nurse, was asked for by the leading physicians of the county, and if they guessed among themselves which of their number had gone to bed with her, they got no confirmation from her. She was equally discreet in the matter of passing professional opinions of the doctors. She had never been known to commit the unforgivable sin of expressing any but the most impersonal, complimentary comment on a member of the medical profession. Nevertheless she managed to convey favorable and unfavorable impressions of doctors without uttering a word, without making a face, and men like Malloy, English, and the Woodman brothers easily guessed that Henrietta Moore's opinion of young Buz Drummond was not very high. Oddly enough it was her non-professional opinion of Dr. Drummond that had the greater influence on the leading men. They could make up their own minds about Drummond as a physician, but if he could not stay out of trouble with Moore, if he antagonized such a good-natured old war horse—she was thirty-two—he could not be much of a fellow. They had been through too many vigils with her, been awakened by her from too many naps in too many Morris chairs, had drunk too many cups of her coffee and glasses of her iced tea, not to feel something that was part comradeship, part affection, part gratitude. She had helped them put chains on tires and taken the reins when they fell asleep in zero weather, and all of them knew that when she got them out of bed at four o'clock in the morning the patient had taken a turn for the worse. In her career as a nurse she had even seen one or two doctors cry.

She took herself out of Buz Drummond's life and was soon enjoying the company of a jovial cigar salesman from Reading, but Drummond's coldness during her brief pregnancy and the let-down after the abortion had done something to her spirits. The cigar salesman was new and therefore did not know that it was unusual for Henrietta to need a shot of rye to pep her up. But then one day, on a confinement case, Dr. Malloy said to her: "Did I smell whiskey on you?"

"Yes, Doctor. For cramps."

"Pack your bag and go home."

"Are you going to report me?"

"Not this time, but believe me if you'd lied to me I would have. What's the matter with you, Moore?"

"I don't know."

"Come and see me at my office tonight."

"I'm not sick."

"Then whatever's the matter, drinking on a case won't do you any good. You know how I feel about whiskey. You've been taking Sen-Sens, but I could smell that booze the minute I went in the room. God damn it, Moore, I'm giving you fair warning. Do you need money?"

"No thank you, Doctor."

"Maybe you'd better get married. I'm going to tell this patient I need you on another case. But this is the last time. God damn it to hell. Whiskey!"

On Malloy's word alone her name could have been stricken from the nurses' registry (nurses who detected whiskey on doctors' breaths kept silent), and the threat to her livelihood and to the work she loved was effective for a few weeks, but the cigar salesman complained of her lack of pep and she had a few shots of rye with him. When she turned up on her case to relieve the night nurse she was so badly hung over that the night nurse had to stay with the patient. "Any doctor could tell what you've been doing, Moore," said the night nurse. "I'll do a double trick, but you're gonna get caught."

"Oh, don't sermonize to me."

"Listen, if that's the thanks I get for protecting you, I'm supposed to report you anyway. You're drunk."

"Mind your own business and leave me alone," said Henrietta Moore.

The nurses had been raising their voices during the altercation and the patient's household later in the day reported to the attending physician, who quickly discovered that the night nurse was shielding Henrietta Moore. He telephoned her at her boarding house and there could be no doubt as to what had kept her off duty that day. She was incoherent, coddling, insulting. "Lay off me, Dr. Fabrikant. You lay off me and I'll lay off you," she said. Within the hour he had reported her to the Medical Society, and her nursing career was ended. In a couple of weeks she had vanished and no one in Gibbsville ever saw her or heard from her again.

Buz Drummond made an effort in the direction of Minnie Stokes. He took her to two programs of the cultural series—the Philadelphia Orchestra and the Denishawn Dancers—and to the Lions Club Ball. If it had been the summer season he could have played tennis or golf with her, and the conversational gaps would not have been so painfully noticeable; but Minnie Stokes was not deceived, no one was deceived. It was apparent that Buz Drummond had decided that Minnie Stokes would make him a suitable wife, and he was going through the perfunctory motions of courtship. Everybody was all for it: home town young doctor, home town rich girl. The only one who was not all for it was Minnie Stokes, whose self-respect and sense of humor caused her to vacillate from annoyance to laughter, and when he proposed to her she said, "No, Buz."

"I admit I haven't been very romantic, Minnie, but we've known each other all our lives. To suddenly act like Romeo . . ."

"Oh, it isn't that."

"Well then think it over. Don't say no right away."

"It'll always be no, Buz. At least *my* answer will always be no. I'm looking for a husband, but if we can't have love at least we ought to have some fun."

"What kind of fun?"

"Any kind. But you seemed to think the whole thing was cut and dried. Take Minnie to the concerts and a few dances, and then propose and get married. I know doctors are always thinking about their cases, but is that what you were so preoccupied with?"

"I suppose I was. It's my life work."

"Well, it's not going to be mine. That's what you can tell people if you want to. Tell them I wouldn't have made a good doctor's wife. As a matter of fact I probably wouldn't. Why don't you transfer your attentions to Mary Bowen? She's very serious, and she's free. And—well, why don't you?"

"What was the third thing about Mary?"

"She's well off. I somehow don't see you marrying a poor girl, Buz."

"That has nothing—well, why should I?"

"That's better. We couldn't even be frank until now, when it's too late. Shall I say something awful? This is the first time I've liked you since our first date. Buz, we're such old friends—why don't you marry Mrs. Loffler?"

"Mrs. *Loffler?*"

"She's only about thirty-five, and she has all that money from Mr. Loffler. Go on, marry Mrs. Loffler, and make her spend some of that money on someone besides herself. She's dying to, you know. She'd love to give parties and travel, and you like to travel, don't you?"

"How do you know she's only thirty-five?"

"Her class in high school."

"Seems older than that to me."

"That's because she's been wearing black since Mr. Loffler died, and you think of her as older because Mr. Loffler was older."

"Do you know her?"

"Worked with her at the Red Cross during the war. She's gained a little weight since then, but not too much. Love to hear her laugh. Daddy says she's worth over four hundred thousand dollars."

"From that musty old store?"

"And buildings. He owns most of the 300-block, or did. She's not afraid to spend money but she doesn't know how. She did over the Norton house when they bought it and she has very good taste. Well, *quite* good."

"I don't even know who she was."

"Sadie Gardner. Her father was Squire Gardner, where they used to take people when they were arrested."

"Of course, I remember her now. I had trouble placing her. Didn't she work in the telegraph office?"

"I don't know. I didn't get to know her till the Red Cross, during the war."

"She doesn't play golf or tennis, I imagine."

"No, she isn't in the club, and I doubt if she'd play if she were. But if you want me to I can have her here some afternoon and you can drop in, accidentally on purpose." Minnie put her hand on his arm. "Aren't you pleased, the way this is working out?"

"The way you're working it out. You're the one that should be pleased, Minnie."

"I am. I know you have to marry someone with money, but as long as it isn't me I'm in favor of it."

He put his arm around her. "I want to kiss you."

"All right," she said. She gave him a full kiss, then stopped. "That's the way we should have started, Buz. You should have taken me out in your coupe and parked."

"I didn't know that that's what you wanted."

"Oh, yes," she said.

"Do you now?"

She nodded. "If you'll take precautions."

"I haven't got any with me, but I could go downtown."

"No, then just let's be like this."

They were not long in advancing from lazy kisses to ardent demands on each other, and she amazed him with how much, how desperately she seemed to center her very will to live in the motions of her hips. She was going to be hard to give up now, with what he knew about her. It was not going to be easy to let her go.

Minnie's plan to effect a proper meeting between Drummond and

Mrs. Loffler was dropped. He was evasive because he did not want Minnie in on his conquest of the widow, for no other reason than a kind of squeamishness; it would embarrass him to have Minnie see him polite and attentive—and crafty. Instead he made a habit of driving past the old Norton house, now the Loffler house, when he was out on calls, and as he intended, his opportunity came. On some days he passed her house a dozen times, and finally he saw her hurrying home during a shower. He stopped his car at the curb, opened the door, tipped his hat, and said, "Jump in, I'll take you home."

"Oh, it's Buz Drummond? I mean Doctor. How nice."

She got in. "You sure you know who I am? You don't think I'm someone else? I'm Mrs. Loffler."

"Oh, come on, Sadie. Gibbsville isn't that big. We've both lived here all our lives."

"You never spoke to me before."

"The other way around. I've spoken to you, but you've never spoken to me."

They were only a couple of blocks from her house, and they reached it in a minute.

"Have a cigarette till the rain stops," he said.

"Shouldn't you be taking care of your sick people?"

"They'll wait till this clears up." He gave her a cigarette and lit it for her.

"I was never allowed to smoke while Mister was alive. He said a cigarette was the sign of a fast woman. Maybe he was right."

"Then there are a lot of fast women."

"Yes, and I'll bet *you* know a lot of them."

"Me? I'm a hard-working country doctor."

"Oh, yeah? That's what they *all* say."

"Too busy for that sort of thing, I'm afraid."

"Oh, sure. Oh, of course. Mr. Innocent talking. How come you're still single?"

"I just told you. Too busy."

"Oh, yeah? Too busy with what? I'll bet all those lady patients, not to mention those pretty young nurses."

"Neither men nor women are at their best when they're sick, and nurses only lead to trouble, so I'm told."

"That's not what I heard. A young doctor with S.A. Sex Appeal. How many of those lady patients really have something the matter?"

"Well, take yourself, for instance. You're an attractive young widow, but you never sent for me."

"I doctor with English when I have to have a doctor, which is very seldom."

"There's none better."

"But you wouldn't call him loaded with S.A. . . . Rain's stopped. Come on in and have a cup of tea, or something stronger if you wish. Or do you have to go?"

"I'll have a cup of tea, just to prove you're wrong about the medical profession."

"I wasn't talking about the medical profession. I was talking about Buz Drummond."

"And you're not afraid of me?"

"What's there to be afraid of?"

She went upstairs to take off her wet shoes, but she came down in a complete change of attire, a flowery print dress with a short skirt that revealed her pretty legs.

"I like your dress, or do you call it a frock?"

"You could call it a frock. It's old. I didn't have it on since Mister passed away. Just been hanging there waiting for me to wear it. You want tea, or liquor?"

"What are you having?"

"Tea. Liquor's supposed to be fattening, and I'm trying to reduce. Do you know anything I can take to reduce?"

"Yes."

"What?"

"Take in your belt a few notches, and when it fits you, that's how much you ought to eat every day."

"I don't wear a belt. You should see what I wear. I'm too stout. I'd give anything to take off ten pounds. Do you know what I weigh? I weigh a hundred and thirty-four in my birthday suit. That's too much for five foot three, don't you think so? A hundred and thirty-four with nothing on?"

"You wouldn't have any trouble losing ten pounds if you put your mind to it."

"The trouble is, the extra weight always goes to the wrong places, if you know what I mean. Well, I guess you do know, being a doctor. If I ask you a question—maybe I better not."

"Go ahead."

"Well I always wanted to ask it but Dr. English isn't—well, are you sure you don't mind? It's a personal kind of a question."

"I ask a thousand of them a day."

"Well, how do you feel when you have a lady patient, and you have to examine her, and she's somebody you know socially?"

"When you say examine her I presume you mean her Eustachian tube?"

"Like that."

He stood up. "Well, if I were going to examine your Eustachian tube—"

She held up her hands. "Go away, go away! I didn't ask you to examine me."

"Hold still!" he said, in the voice of command. She obeyed, though she was apprehensive.

"Now if I wanted to examine your Eustachian tube, Mrs. Loffler, what is the first thing I would say to you?"

"Well—I don't know, but something like 'Take off your dress,' or something like that."

"Why should I?"

"Well, because it's customary."

"Not in my office."

"It was when Dr. English examined me."

"Made you take your clothes off to examine your Eustachian tube? That old rascal, Billy English."

"He was a perfect gentleman. I wasn't a bit embarrassed."

"Mrs. Loffler, I might as well stop kidding you. The Eustachian tube is here, in your ear." He tapped his ear.

"Oh, *you!* And all the time I thought—I really thought there for a minute you were going to—well I wasn't sure exactly what I thought. You have a sense of humor. I must say I like a person with a sense of humor. You wouldn't think it, but Mister said a lot of funny things. He had that *dry* humor, you know. If some of the people in this town ever heard what he used to say about them."

"Do you miss him?"

"Well, I do. Not as much as I did, but I would have if we'd kept on living in the other house. This house he never lived long enough to get used to. But I miss him. After all I was married to him for eight years and you get used to a person. A lot of people criticized me for marrying a man so much older, but when two people get along, you forget about the age. And no woman could ask for a better husband. He lavished presents on me, really lavished them. I could go to Philadelphia and go hog wild in Wanamaker's, Strawbridge's, but it seemed to give him as much pleasure as me. Of course I didn't take advantage, too much, and in a business deal I guess Mister was one of the smartest men in town, if not *the* smartest. Starting out clerking in Boyle's dry goods store for four dollars a week. That's all he got. Four dollars. He had to open up in the morning and lock up at night. Twelve hours a day, six days a week, and no vacation the first two

years. Old Terence Boyle liked him so much he wanted him to marry
one of his daughters, but Mister wouldn't turn Catholic, and that was
how he happened to go in business for himself. You know, it isn't
generally known around town, but Mister was never very fond of the
dry goods end. People thought he was, but he wasn't. He was more
interested in buying and selling properties, real estate. But he kept
store because—to show you how clever he was, he didn't want people to think he was a real estate man. A dry goods and notions man,
people wouldn't think he was as smart as a real estate man when it
came to buying or selling a property. Oh, he was very good to me. I
never would of ended up in a house like this if it wasn't for Mister."

"Well, obviously you made him happy, too."

"If we'd of had children. But he ruptured himself when he was
younger and he blamed that on why we never had children. It's a big
house for just one person. I miss the war."

"The war?"

"Well, I don't mean the bloodshed and all those boys going away,
but the Red Cross. During the war I used to go to the Red Cross
four-five days a week and I made a lot of friends, but after the
Armistice they didn't have the Red Cross any more and I didn't see
as much of them. I'm thinking of learning to drive a car. A lot of
women do now. Mister didn't like a woman to drive a car, but he
never said I *shouldn't*. They're trying to sell me a Pierce-Arrow, but I
want to start out with something smaller. The Fierce-Sparrow. Imagine me driving a Fierce-Sparrow? What make is that little car you
brought me home in?"

"That's a Dodge."

"Are they hard to drive? Mary Bowen has that Paige, but that's
more of a big car. Minnie Stokes gave me a ride in her car and I
watched her manipulating all the things. She says it's much easier
than it looks. You get so it becomes second nature, she says."

"Minnie has a Templar."

"Oh, I wouldn't want anything as sporty as that, but I like that size
car. The Dodge sedan is a nice car. I noticed a lot of them around
with women driving. Everybody says don't buy a Ford, because it has
no gear shift."

"It has a gear shift, but you operate it with your feet."

"Well, you see how much I know about it. I'm pretty sure I won't
buy a Fierce-Sparrow, because then I'd have to hire a man to drive
it, and a woman my age driving around with a man all the time. It's
all right for Minnie's mother and ladies that age, but I wouldn't feel
right about it."

"Why don't you let me teach you to drive?"

"Oh—but how long would it take for that to get around? Can't you just hear them?"

"It would probably get around in two days, but do you care? I'm sure I don't."

"Well, will you give me a couple days to think about it? I'm not worried what they say about me, but—"

"Don't worry what they say about me."

"I was thinking of Mister. It's all his money. Or it was."

"You smoked a cigarette."

"I guess you're right. I'll ring you up, if you really mean it."

The estimate for the circulation of the news that Buz Drummond was giving Sadie Loffler driving lessons was fairly accurate. "Well, I just heard the latest," said his mother. "You and Sadie Gardner."

"Did you?"

"I did, and I guess everybody else has too if it's got to me."

"Have you any objections?"

"Depends on which way you look at it, I guess. But I guess you're looking at it financially."

"Your idea wasn't so good. Minnie turned me down."

"I know, but Sadie Gardner won't. She's older than you are, a good five years. She hasn't long to go before she's forty, and you're not going to get any children out of her."

"There's no proof of that, but anyway I've never longed to have children."

"Every man wants children, sooner or later."

"No, not every man. Not every man wants a wife, either. What's the matter with Sadie? Because her father was Squire Gardner?"

"If I have any objections to Sadie they're the same ones you'd make. Don't try to make me feel like a snob, when you're one yourself. A Frederick Street snob is worse than a Lantenengo. You and Joe Chapin, very much alike."

"I wish I had his money."

"Well, you won't have as much marrying Sadie Gardner, but it's a nice nest egg. You gave up very easily with Minnie, and she has more than Sadie Gardner Loffler, or will have."

"Minnie and I will always be very good friends, but I'd never propose twice to the same woman."

"You'd be making a lot more money if you'd become a surgeon. Why didn't you?"

"Can't stand the sight of blood."

"Don't be impertinent, Buz. A man that's rude to his own mother."

"All the rudeness has to be on the one side, eh, Mother? Is there anything else you want to say before I retire?"

"No. Yes. But you're so thin-skinned you might just as well go to bed."

"You pique my curiosity. What is it?"

"Did you ever have anything to do with a nurse named Henrietta Moore?"

"I had her on a lot of cases. Why?"

"If you're planning to marry Sadie Gardner, Sadie Gardner Loffler, make it quick. A story reached me that you paid this nurse a thousand dollars to leave town. And thinking back, you borrowed a thousand dollars from me just about that time."

"Jesus."

"There's something to it, isn't there?"

"What do you do when people come to you with stories like that about me?"

"I brazen it out, deny everything or else say I know nothing about your affairs, personal or professional. But alone, I think a good deal."

"Have you any more juicy tidbits?"

"Well, two in one evening. That seems to me a lot."

"Yes. Well, I guess I'd better get married before I get into more trouble. Isn't that what you'd suggest?"

"I suggested it a long while ago. Now I suggest you get married before it's too late. Squire Gardner's daughter probably has very old-fashioned, conventional ideas. They're great ones for respectability, people like Sadie. They're the ones that don't tolerate certain things that you and I might overlook."

"*You* might overlook, Mother?"

"Only because I have to, sometimes. My ancestors were among the people that made those rules, those ideas. Pity we didn't all live up to them."

"Didn't Father?"

"Well, he tried. Goodnight, son. I'm going to read a while."

"What are you reading, that has you in this mood?"

She held up her book, the spine toward him. "It's a library book, Miss Williams recommended it. Called *Winesburg, Ohio,* by a Sherwin Anderson. Sherwood Anderson. It's not for young people like you. It's for the old, like me. Full of plain, unpleasant truths. Very gloomy little stories that could have happened right here in Gibbsville. And did, some of them. Don't read it."

"I won't. I was just wondering what you were reading."

The book was in her lap when he came down in the morning and saw her sitting there, one side of her face contorted, but her appearance otherwise that of an aging lady who had stopped rocking her chair to let herself be overcome by a deep sleep.

II

Dr. Drummond's reappearances at the meetings of the County Medical Society were welcomed, since what he may have lacked in purely professional standing he possessed in civic prominence. He had money now, was not dependent on his practice to meet his bills. He was a doctor, he treated sick people, but as he said, he had time for other things. The more skillful members of the profession were perfectly willing to have Dr. Wallace P. Drummond represent the medical art at luncheons and banquets, and they conceded that he represented them well. Some of the ugliest men in town were among the most successful healers, but Buz Drummond's appearance on a dais was a great asset to the profession, to the enterprise of the moment, to the community, and to Buz Drummond. His light brown hair had grown darker, then patches of grey had appeared. He was clean shaven at a time when most doctors still grew moustaches. He was nearly six feet tall and flat-bellied. And since his marriage he had been going to a Philadelphia tailor. In this new phase of his life he discovered that he could talk on his feet, but no matter what he said or did not say, people liked to look at him while he told his introductory funny story, waxed persuasive in the inevitable appeal for funds, and ended with a winning smile and a modest disclaimer in advance of the applause that would follow. If most of this was directly or indirectly the result of marrying Sadie Loffler for her money, then it was worth it. There was no doubt that it was worth it to Sadie, to whom he was courteous in public to a degree that was a lesson to other husbands. She took pride in his new popularity and in being half of Dr. and Mrs. Wallace P. Drummond of Lantenengo Street. When he invaded the meetings of the County Medical Society he did so with a purpose. He wanted to be elected president of the Society, he was so elected, and he handed the honor to Sadie like a present. Thenceforth in print he was not merely Dr. Wallace P. Drummond, but Dr. Wallace P. Drummond, president of the Medical Society of Lantenengo County, his full style and title. He took care to remind the editors of the newspapers that the correct usage was Medical Society of Lantenengo County, and not the more abrupt Lantenengo County Medical Society.

No layman, of course, could successfully challenge Buz Drummond's authenticity as a doctor. There were those citizens who were

inclined to be cynical about the well-barbered, well-tailored personality, but Buz Drummond could smell their hostility and in their
presence he made a point of using medical language they could not
possibly understand, a protective device employed by doctors everywhere to defeat lay criticism. Buz Drummond had few occasions to
use it. In two or three years of the new prosperity he had made a
remarkable advance from his earlier mediocrity, and some of the
admiration for him that counted most came from other doctors. "Put
Buz Drummond on it, he gets things done," they would say. He
could telephone the mayor, the chief of police, the county judges,
and even the governor and get an audience. He did not deal with
lieutenants of local industry but captains only, and possibly because
he looked like the canon of a cathedral, he was influential with the
clergy of all denominations. Not one paused to consider what the
consequences might be for opposing Buz Drummond. In the beginning of his civic career no one said, "What if I don't?" The original
power was all persuasion, when Buz Drummond had no latent power
of reprisal against those who could have refused him. Then in a few
years it was too late; too many men had yielded too many favors
gracefully or unquestionably, and now the power was real. He had
prestige. Now he could quickly summon the support of the men who
had inadvertently given him his power, and since it was true that he
seemed to want nothing for himself, he usually got what he asked
for.

Politicians so thoroughly convinced themselves that he was an
ideal candidate for public office that they could not understand his
refusal to run. The smartest politician in the county, Mike Slattery,
said to his wife Peg Slattery, "I keep asking myself, what does this
fellow want? I have a hard time understanding a man like that.
Everybody wants something, and he was about ready to tip his mitt a
year ago, but it's nothing in my line."

"Ready to tip his mitt, how?" said Peg Slattery.

"I mean he was ripe. All these good works and civic activity. Usually I can tell when they're ready to announce. With him it was about
a year or so ago. But I asked him did he have his eye on anything,
and he said yes. He had his eye on a big new wing for the county
hospital. That was in the machinery, I told him. What about for him,
what did he want? To stay out of politics, he said. To stay out of
politics? That fellow's in politics up to his ears, every day of his life.
I'm not afraid of him, but I sure as Satan want him working for me.
The one thought did occur to me."

"What's that?"

"The man may just be stupid."

She shook her head. "No. That you can't say about him."

"Yes I can, and I do. The only man I came across in my reading that doesn't seem to want anything for himself is that little fellow in India. Mahatma Gandhi. And we can forget about him. He's not coming to this country, and if he did they'd lock him up."

"The little man with the goats, wears a shroud?"

"That's the man. I'd put Buz Drummond up against him and Buz would win every precinct. Here. Not in India, mind you. Oh, no. But those Hindus, they're a hundred and fifty years behind us, woman. We got free of England a hundred and fifty years ago, and that's all the farther they are now. When they get their independence that's when they start being like us, the way we started to be back in 1776. They won't need their little man then. They can start fighting amongst themselves, as we did. And do. You need a little fellow like Mahatma to lead the fight for independence, or a great fellow like George Washington with Jefferson's brains behind him. Men that don't want anything for themselves. But this is 1925, and we have our independence for a hundred and fifty years, and everybody's out for themselves. Those that don't are stupid, because this country is a nation of competition. Either Buz Drummond wants to be Mahatma, or he's stupid. Politically, I'm speaking now. And financially. Politically and financially he's stupid not to strike while the iron's hot. What else does a man like him want? Well, we have a dirty file on Buz. I started collecting items for it about two years ago."

"There was some story, but I don't remember it."

"Yes. There was one story got out. He knocked up a nurse, back a few years ago, and he gave her money to leave town. He sold a bond he got from his mother. A thousand-dollar bond. The nurse disappeared from the face of the earth. If she's alive or dead we don't know. The tip on that story came from Billy English. It isn't much of a story till we find out more what happened to the nurse, and that seems hopeless. Then I began delving into a trip he took, working as a ship's doctor. He was supposed to be gone five years, but he was home in less than one. Why? Well, he met some young woman that fell for him and they had a romance on the boat. She was supposed to get off some place in South America, but when the boat sailed she was on it. Left her husband because she was stuck on Drummond. Some place in Australia the American consul came and took her off the boat and they shipped her back to South America with a nurse. She went out of her head."

"Over him? Over Buz Drummond? She must have been *crazy.*"

"She was. That's what I said. That's what I just got finished telling you."

"I meant it differently."

"Then as I understand it he was on two other boats over in that part of the world, and on the second one an Englishman with a name like Cumberland took a shot at him."

"At Buz?"

"Yes, woman. Who're we talking about? Shot him in the arm. The official report says that Buz accidentally shot himself, but I don't always go by official reports. Buz had to stay in China or some place till the arm got better, and then he was quietly given the sack and shipped back home. How's that for Mr. Dr. Buz Drummond?"

"He doesn't know you have any of this?"

"Oh, good heavens, no. We spent a lot of money collecting this data. Most of the dirty files the data doesn't cost you a cent. But I had to know a few things about Buz when he began getting strong a year ago. What I told you cost us about eighteen hundred dollars. But wait. I'm not finished. The prize data didn't cost us anything at all, and it isn't a lot of stuff that happened when he was a young fellow, way out on the other side of the world. The prize is what's going on now, here in town."

"Wuddia want me to do? Say please? You're going to tell me, so go ahead. The prize data."

"*Who*—is Buz Drummond's girl friend?"

"Don't know, and didn't know he had one."

"None other than Miss, Minerva, Stokes, alias Minnie Stokes."

"That's old. She jilted him, oh, four-five years ago."

"Did she now? Peg, sometimes you're not as smart as I give you credit for. Dr. Wallace P. Drummond, alias Buz, and Miss Minnie Stokes have been carrying on together since before he got married, and right under Sadie's nose. Whenever Minnie jilted him, she turned right around and began having a passionate love affair with him that if this town ever finds out about it, I wouldn't be surprised if they stoned her. And what they'd do to him I can't in my wildest dreams imagine. Pillars of society, eminent practitioner of the medical profession. And underneath it all they're like a couple of alley cats. He puts his car in the garage at night, and there she is, waiting for him. The carriage-house, the old Norton place? Going on now for I guess five years. Just in the past year they stayed together as man and wife twice in New York and three times in Philadelphia. Dr. and Mrs. W. P. Drum, they go as. Oh, the sinning that goes on, Peg."

"You don't have to make a joke of it. I suppose it's useless to ask how you found out, and if you're sure."

"The meetings in the carriage-house, how that was discovered—well, not to make a joke of it but it was funny. Sadie Loffler had a maid, and *she* was using the room in the carriage-house to meet *her* boy friend. And one night she went up there and heard voices. Sneaked up the stairs in her bare feet and guess who she saw, using her hideout."

"Is that the Chapman woman, that works for Sadie?"

"Correct. She puzzled over whether to blackmail him or not but she asked the priest in confession, as if it was happening to a friend of hers, and the priest said he couldn't give absolution to a black-mailer. So she never said anything to Buz. But when I began making some inquiries she said she'd talk to me but no one else. I offered her some money, but she said she was afraid she wouldn't get absolution if she took money."

"Huh."

"Now don't start complaining about the dirty files. You couldn't run politics without them."

"I didn't say anything."

"You grunted. But I notice you always listen to every story I tell you."

"Well, I agree with you he is stupid."

"Sure he is. I could *make* him run for office if I had to. Usually the dirty files are used for the opposite effect, but if I ever need Buz Drummond, I've got him. And console yourself, Peg. I never used the dirty files to make a nickel in my insurance business. Not a nickel."

"Huh."

"There you go again," he said. "Can I get you a bottle of beer?"

"I'll have a bottle of beer."

"All right. But it's illegal. Ten years ago it wasn't illegal. Ten years from now it won't be. But now it is. That's law for you. And the Church changes its laws, too, Peg. What's your penance when you go to confession? Five Our Fathers and five Hail Marys. But you used to have to do sackcloth and ashes, in front of everybody. Think I'll have a Coke."

"You're a rascal. An old-time rascal."

"No, I'm not. I'm a man living in a world full of people, Peg. And I must be fond of them or I wouldn't study them so much. I'll bet you Lincoln and I would have a great time swapping stories together."

"Oh, tonight it's Lincoln. Who was it the other night, the Italian fellow?"

"Niccolò Machiavelli. Him, too. This is the most fascinating work there is, Peg. I wish I knew all those ones in the past, and the ones to come."

"Get the beer, will you, please? We can talk then."

III

Happy Sadie Drummond, fetching and carrying for people, giving of her money and her time, had wanted to go back to the days of the Red Cross, but the early years of her marriage to Buz Drummond made the Red Cross days (and marriage to Mister Loffler) seem like some sort of rehearsal. Every day she had something to do, somewhere to go, or new plans to engage her attention, Buz, she said, kept her busy. She had automatically become a member of the country club on her marriage to Buz, and she dutifully took some golf lessons, but she gave them up and did not even try to play tennis.

In the third year of her marriage her feelings were hurt, and she sulked and brooded until Buz had to give her a good talking-to. Minnie Stokes had invited Sadie to attend the meetings of the Wednesday Afternoon Bridge Club, not, at first, as a player but as one of the learners, along with a few younger girls who were just starting the game. In the second year Sadie had picked up enough of the rules and basic mechanics of the game to become a playing member, and one of her happiest times was in making preparations for the day when it was her turn to entertain the ladies. Her chicken à la king was all white meat; her dessert was not just ice cream but ice cream in molds, George and Martha Washington, cherry trees, hatchets, drums, stacked muskets, all appropriate to the third Wednesday in February; and she had not only a first prize and a booby prize, but favors for everyone. She completely ignored the custom of a five-dollar limit for first prize and two dollars for the booby. Her first prize was a silk-and-hand-embroidered-lace camisole from Bonwit's, Philadelphia; her booby prize, a pair of hand-painted salt and pepper shakers; and each lady received a cute little sterling silver bridge pencil with her initials engraved on it. "Oh, Sadie, you *shouldn't* have," said Minnie Stokes, the first-prize winner.

"Oh, I know, but after all why not? When a person has as much fun as I did selecting the things. And everybody *came*. I didn't have to ask anyone to substitute." She had dreaded the prospect of having to ask a non-member to fill in, since any acceptable substitute was probably more truly eligible than she.

In the third year, as October came and went and November was half over, and Sadie had not been notified of the resumption of the meetings, she said to Minnie Stokes: "When are you going to start the Wednesdays again, Minnie?"

"Well, we still have the Wednesdays but with a different bunch of girls. More serious bridge players, you know. They all play for blood."

"Oh."

"Not as much fun, of course, but some of the girls thought we had too much conversation and not enough bridge. After Christmas we may decide to have another club, more like the old one."

"I see," said Sadie. She saw plainly when she saw a group of cars parked at Josie Entwhistle's house. Josie Entwhistle was one of the girls whose bridge game was of a caliber to give Sadie confidence in herself.

"Mean, nasty stuck-up things," said Sadie to Buz. "And I don't trust that Minnie Stokes. I think she kept me out. She always looks at me funny."

"Now you listen to me, Sadie," said Buz. "You told me over and over again you were never going to learn the game. And there's nothing worse than playing bridge with somebody that doesn't *care* about the game. Spoils it for everybody. Minnie's a very good player. She plays with men."

"Maybe that's her trouble. If she played with them in other ways maybe she'd find herself a husband, before it's too late. Her and her golf and her tennis and playing cards."

"Well, perhaps so. But you like Minnie and she's never been stuck up with you, you *have* to admit that."

"She didn't used to," said Sadie. "But now she looks at me funny."

"Something you imagine."

Happy Sadie Drummond could not long sulk over a snub by other women when her intimate life with Buz was so exciting, full of things that were so exciting that she could not tell them to any of her friends. Sometimes he would stay away from her for weeks at a stretch, but she knew, because he told her so, that abstinence so deliberate stored up desire. He introduced her to methods of pleasure that he himself had not heard of until his voyages to the Orient, and he assured her that periods of abstinence were essential to the creation of a desire strong enough to conquer her feeling of wickedness. "I guess I ought to feel more wicked than I do," she once told him. But instead she only felt a superior pity over the girl she had been as Mrs. Sadie Loffler. Most of the time she could hardly remember that side of her life with Mister Loffler, and she was glad that Buz had no jealousy of her first husband. It would have embarrassed her to reveal now the unrefined pleasures of her first marriage. Sometimes at a banquet, when Buz was making a speech, she would steal a look at the faces of the women in the audience and think of them with their Lofflers and of herself with this man who was her husband, and her sense of possession would become almost unbearable. It was especially lovely torture when she had reason to guess that a period of abstinence might end that night.

IV

"One of these days," said Buz Drummond, "I'm going to have to do away with her."

"Why do you say that?" said Minnie Stokes.

"You'll see why," said Drummond.

"No I won't, so tell me," said Minnie. "You'll never do away with anybody, darling, but why do you think you have to say it? About once a year you say something like that."

"Some day, some year I won't say it, but just do it."

She shook her head. "Never," she said.

"Don't be so know-it-all. It's very exasperating," he said. They were lying on a bed in a hotel in Newark, New Jersey, a city in which neither of them knew a single human being.

"You're more apt to do away with *me*, as a matter of fact."

"Why?"

"Well, I can make you very cross. You lose your temper with me, but she only bores you. You might push me out of a window, but in anger. Or want to kill me when I can't go away with you, but then I wouldn't be there, when you lost your temper. But the only way you'd ever do away with her would be like giving her small doses of arsenic or something like that."

"I've thought of that."

"I'm sure you have."

"But that isn't the way. There are doctors in this town—I don't mean here, I mean Gibbsville—that are going to want to be damn sure there's nothing suspicious about the way she checks out, when she does check out."

"Yes."

"If she fell from the court house tower, in full view of everybody, there'd be doctors ready to do a post-mortem. If she ever gets sick I'm not even going to give her an aspirin tablet. I'll call in Billy English or somebody equally respectable, let him be responsible from the word go. Of course I wouldn't have these murderous thoughts if you'd marry me."

"Well, I don't intend to."

"She'd give me a divorce. I know she would."

"Yes, she probably would. If you told her that you were in love with me, she would."

"What kind of a life is this for you, Minnie?"

"Hmm." She smiled faintly.

"No, really?"

"Oh—it's all right I guess." She knelt on the bed and kissed his mouth.

"Well, it isn't," he said.

"No, of course it isn't. But you love me, and I love you. You love me as much as you can love anybody, and I love you the same way, which is more. You haven't got much love to offer, have you, Buz?"

"Well, that's what you keep telling me."

"But what there is is for me, isn't it?"

"Yes. All of it. A nasty little eyecupful of love, according to you."

"You're sweet," she said.

"But let me tell you something. An eyecup full of arsenic is a fatal dose, and the same amount of love has just as big an effect on me."

"How do you mean?"

"I mean, well, don't you get it? Whatever love I have to offer is yours, whether it's enough to fill a bathtub or an eyecup."

"Oh, yes. I see. I guess I see."

"Why don't you marry me? I'll make you happy."

"Maybe you could. You make *her* happy."

"Oh, Christ."

"But maybe the trouble is—I don't know—I love you, and never, never anyone else. But I've always shied away from you."

"I wouldn't say that, exactly."

"Oh, heavens. This? If you asked me to I'd do this in the middle of the floor at a club dance. Not really, of course, but I've often wanted to."

"Yes, I can think of times."

"There were other times that you didn't know about, too. Other boys I've danced with have got the benefit of what I was thinking about you."

"Who?"

"Oh, I don't know. Ever since I stopped thinking like a nice girl I had some such thoughts about you. But then you were so *dull* when you came a-courting. Fate protected me."

"Oh, shit."

"Don't say that. I don't like that word. You can say anything else."

"Well, to go on. You've told me this before, that if I hadn't been so considerate of your virginity we'd be married today."

"Yes. I expected to be swept off my feet, and was ready and willing. The second time I went out with you I even wore underclothes that wouldn't interfere. But you brought me home from the concert and didn't even try to kiss me."

"I know, I know. But why was that a mistake? You've never been able to tell me why. Do you know why?"

"Oh, I do now."

"Money-proud?"

"Not exactly. It was just that—as if I'd been looking forward to an affair with Don Juan and he spent the evening discussing iambic pentameter."

"I didn't discuss iambic pentameter."

"Or anything else. You just put in the time with Minnie Stokes, making a cold-blooded, calculating effort. And that made me realize that you could be cold-blooded and calculating. Gave me time to get my breath. I wasn't in awe of you any more."

"I see. Should have taken it right out and given you a jab with it."

"Well, something like that. Anything would have been better than yawning through Mendelssohn's Scotch Symphony. That's what they played."

"How do you remember that, or do you?"

"Oh, I do, Buz. I remember everything about us, things you've forgotten or never knew."

"The question is, when are you going to be a mature woman and marry me? You're over thirty, and people aren't going to say nasty little Minnie broke up Dr. Drummond's marriage. Everybody's grown up—except you. There are no young kids in this triangle."

"Do you know what people can do?"

"What?"

"Well, I won't say it, but you know what they can do."

"You mean they can go fuck themselves?"

"Yes. Thank you for saying it for me."

"It's a word that occasionally passes your lips. Minnie, do you *want* to stay single all your life?"

"I'm not single now, to my way of thinking. I couldn't be more double than I am with you."

"But I'll be forty before very long, Sadie's past it now. The longer you delay, the worse it's going to be for her, if that's what you're thinking about."

"Partly."

"The question of children. You've been very careful, but you've never said you didn't want to have children."

"I'm resigned to not having them. And you *don't* want them."

"Is that why you're resigned?"

"Partly. Principally."

"What is life going to be for you when you're, say, fifty? Do you think now that you and I will still want to go on like this? You won't be able to stand it. Love won't last that long, Minnie."

"Maybe not."

"Well, what will you have then?"

"When I'm fifty? Oh—I'll have you. By that time this won't be so important."

"You don't know much about biology if you believe that. Are you aware of the fact that after the climacteric, the menopause, many women get more pleasure out of sex than they ever did?"

"I don't believe it. I've heard it, but I doubt it very much."

"Take my word for it, free. No charge. See, I'm not just after your money."

"Ah, Buz, don't say that. Sweetheart."

"Well, Christ, what else is there for me to think? The fact of the matter is that I don't need Sadie's money any more. Or yours. If I wanted to I could make fifty thousand a year, in perfectly legitimate business. If I wanted to go into politics I could make a lot more. A *lot* more. But I won't do it as long as I'm married to Sadie. Why should I? I'm respectable and respected now. I carry a lot of influence, and incidentally I've given Sadie a good run for her money."

"Yes, you have. Nobody can take that away from you."

"The squire's daughter has gone as far as she'll ever go, and much farther than she had any right to expect. She's not on my conscience, even if she is on yours. She is, isn't she?"

"On my conscience? Yes, I guess so."

"You know so. That's the whole damn trouble."

"No it isn't. The truth is she bores me, too, intensely. I have to put up with her friendship, which I don't want. You have no idea how many times I've been tempted to describe a night with you, in vivid detail."

"Why don't you sometime?"

"That would do away with her, more quickly than arsenic. But why don't *you?*"

"Describe a night with you?"

"Yes."

"I don't know, I never thought of it. I guess I couldn't do that."

"You couldn't do it to her, or couldn't do it to me?"

"I don't think I could do it to her, because I know how she'd look. And I couldn't do it to you, because I couldn't tell anybody about you. I used to talk about girls and everything about them, everything. Naming names. But I wouldn't even admit that you have nipples on your breasts. You and I are—us."

She put her hand on his cheekbone. "The eyecup turns into a bathtub," she said.

"Yes, and I still don't get my answer."

"My darling, whatever answer I gave you would be a thinking answer, and false. The real answer is a feeling one, and I don't know what it is."

"All right," he said. "What would you like to do? I have another pint of Four Roses, bottled in bond. Shall I send down for some ginger ale? Or do you want to take the next train back to Philadelphia? Or do you want to just lie here and see what happens?"

"I certainly don't want to take the next train back to Philadelphia."

"One of these days you will," he said.

V

It was the day after Thanksgiving and the year was 1939, in which there were two Thanksgiving Days: the officially proclaimed, or FDR holiday, and the second a week later on the traditional fourth Thursday. Sadie and Buz were in a Chestnut Street jeweler's, doing their Christmas shopping.

The clerk stood patiently while Sadie contemplated a silver dish. "I tell you what you do," she said. "You take it over and ask my husband what he thinks of it. That's him over at the leather-goods counter. And while you're gone I'll have a look at these other things."

The clerk said, "Thank you, Mrs. Drummond," and departed. He always waited on her for silver articles. She busied herself for a moment, then turned to look at Buz and the clerk. But the clerk was talking to another customer, paying no attention to Buz, and the other man was shaking his head. The man was at least sixty-five years old and did not have the look of a regular customer of the shop. The clerk shrugged his shoulders and returned to his post. "I guess your husband must have moved to another counter," he said.

"He did not. He's still there. The tall man wearing the brown overcoat."

"Oh, I beg your pardon. Oh, *that's* Mr. Drummond?"

"Dr. Drummond."

"My mistake," said the clerk.

It was only one of several incidents that did not seem to annoy Buz as much as they annoyed her. In this instance Buz had been unaware of the incident, but she was unable to keep it to herself. "Are you ever sorry you married me?" she said, back at the hotel.

"When you make a mountain out of a molehill. You could have pointed me out and prevented that mistake."

"Then you'd have seen me point and thought I didn't have any manners."

"Oh, what balls, Sadie. You're forty-nine years old, and I'm forty-four. We're neither of us young people."

"But you should of seen what he picked out to be my husband. And not only the age. Practically an old tramp, in off the streets."

"Well, what do you want me to do? Try to look older? Let my appearance go to hell? Well, I refuse to. And I also refuse to pamper you. Every woman has to go through change of life and you're just being selfish. I won't put up with it. You over-tire yourself with this damned Christmas shopping and you take offense at the least little thing. I'll give you something now to put you to sleep and I'll go over and have dinner at the Union League."

"Anything to get away from me, that's what it is."

"Right. I don't care for your company, and I'm sure you don't care for mine."

"One of these days I'll kill myself. You mind. I will."

"Will you indeed? Here, take this and go to sleep."

"What is it?"

"It's something to put you to sleep, and I hope you'll wake up not feeling so sorry for yourself."

"Why shouldn't I feel sorry for myself? Nobody else does."

"Now listen to me, Sadie—"

"I don't want to listen."

"If you don't listen I'm going to pack my bag and leave you, this minute."

"If you do I'll jump out that window."

"No you won't, so just listen to what I have to tell you. Are you going to listen?"

"All right."

"You promised me a month ago that you weren't going to drink except before meals. Did you have something at the hairdresser's this afternoon?"

"No."

"Yes you did, or if not at the hairdresser's, somewhere. Now don't lie to me."

"I had a cocktail downstairs."

"You had three cocktails downstairs, or four."

"I had three, not four. And they were small ones, not doubles. They only give you a half a cocktail here anyhow. This place is a gyp."

"When we get home you're going to go see English."

"I am not, and anyway he's too old."

"Then somebody else, but you're going to make an appointment to see a doctor next week. So you decide which one you want to see."

"There's nothing the matter with me. You said so yourself, every woman goes through the change."

"Sadie, you *know* what else is wrong with you. I'm a doctor, remember. And even if I weren't, you couldn't keep it from me forever. You never used to take a drink unless I was there."

"Yes, but you're never there when I want one."

"I'd have to be there pretty much of the time, it seems to me."

"Are you calling me a drunkard?"

"I'm telling you that you're on the verge of becoming an alcoholic, and I'm telling you that your liver isn't going to be able to stand what you've been doing to it."

"It's the only pleasure I get out of life any more."

"Do you call it pleasure, sitting with Josie Entwhistle and getting drunk every afternoon?"

"I didn't see Josie all week, and what's the matter with Josie? She's one of *your* friends, the only one that's nice to me. The only one that ever shows any appreciation."

"You can't buy people's friendship." As soon as he said it he realized it was a mistake. Josie Entwhistle was the last of the Wednesday bridge players who continued to be companionable with Sadie.

"That was a nasty mean thing to say, and you said it to hurt me. You took all the pleasure out of my Christmas shopping. I wish I never would of married you. If I hadn't of been rich you never would of looked at me."

"That's insulting."

"Minnie Stokes wouldn't have you, that's why you married me."

The harm was done, and so he continued. "Well, I married you and I didn't marry Josie Entwhistle, if she's the one that gave you that idea. And she is." He had now spoiled her only companionship.

"I notice you don't deny it about Minnie Stokes."

"Josie Entwhistle has been jealous of Minnie all her life, long before you ever knew Josie or Minnie, and I'm not here to discuss Minnie."

"What are you here for?"

"To watch you go to sleep, and then have a few minutes' peace by myself."

At the word sleep she tried to fight it, but almost immediately her eyes closed. He watched her for five minutes and then went out. He walked over to South Broad Street and at the club he telephoned Minnie.

"I just wanted to hear your voice," he said.

"Is something wrong?"

"Yes. You're ninety-five miles away, and you always are."

"Yes, most of the time. I'm sorry, darling, but you caught me at a bad time. I'm going to dinner."

"Who's taking you out to dinner?"

"Mr. McHenry."

"Haven't you started to call him Arthur yet?"

"Well, yes I have, but it doesn't come naturally."

"It will."

"I don't know. Darling, I have to hang up. Shall I see you next week?"

"Come to the office, tomorrow evening?"

"No, I don't like that. You know I don't."

"All right. Next week. Monday night?"

"Tuesday night."

"Not Sunday night?"

"No, it'll have to be Tuesday at the earliest. Goodbye, darling. Sorry I couldn't be more help."

After Pearl Harbor he tried to get a commission, but he was not wanted. He was younger than some of the new majors and lieutenant commanders, lieutenant colonels and commanders, colonels and captains, but he was neither young enough nor good enough to overcome the Army's and Navy's indifference. There was a vague irony too to the fact that Sadie, with her fond recollections of the Red Cross of the First War, was asked to contribute money but not her services. The only people who knew her now were also tolerantly aware of her addiction to the bottle. "No, Buz," said Minnie Stokes McHenry. "We simply couldn't have her disrupting things."

"It might help her. It really might," he said.

"It might for a while, but what if she turned up drunk? Or had to be taken home? Then everybody in town would know, instead of just a few. No, I'm sorry."

"You've done a pretty thorough job of getting the Drummonds out of your life. Drummonds. It almost sounds like gremlins."

"She was never in my life, and you'll always be in it."

"What do you tell Arthur?"

"He has never asked."

"Can any man be that incurious?"

"He isn't incurious, but I told him I'd only marry him on condition that he not ask. I told him I'd had love affairs, but I wouldn't tell him how many or with whom."

"Some day you *will* tell him."

"Yes, some day I probably will, when I want to get some comfort out of my past, when I have to think back on how attractive I used to be. But I don't need that quite yet. A few years from now, probably."

"I hate Arthur McHenry."

"Well, I guess I hated Sadie but wouldn't admit it. If I'd given in to it I'd have been miserable, all those years."

"And might have married me. Do you remember one time I wanted to kill her?"

"I do. We were in Newark, New Jersey. You talked about it other times, too, but I remember that because there was something in your voice that day that—it was the one time I was afraid. You weren't angry. You were bored and weary, and I had a feeling it was getting you. You used to have a habit, you know, or you don't know but you did have a habit, when something bothered you."

"I'd lower my voice, speak more softly."

"No. This was completely unconscious. You'd start rubbing your scar, where the Englishman shot you. You were completely oblivious of it, but I noticed it."

"I'm sure Arthur McHenry has no such scars."

"He has no scars of any kind, that I've been able to find."

"Have you discovered any of your own?"

"Oh, a deep one, yes." She laughed. "But I can rub it, and I can't blame anybody for it but myself."

"Tell your physician."

"I'll tell you. It's what hurts when I think of how much I loved you and how happy we could have been. But every time I have my palm read they always say my head rules my heart. You've never read much. Did you ever read anything by Joseph Conrad?"

"No, I don't think I did."

"He said a very strange thing for an author to say. He said that thinking is the great enemy of perfection."

"That's why I don't read novels. Statements like that. But he has a point, at least in love affairs."

"Well, he included love affairs, as I remember it."

"And so you have a scar, too, Minnie?"

"Uh-huh. But it doesn't show. It doesn't show."

"When it does what's McHenry going to do?"

"Oh, he knows what love is. He loved his other wife, too. You never really loved anyone but me, did you? Or I anyone but you. What did that prizefighter say? We were robbed."

"We wuz robbed. Don't be so prissy."

"And don't you be so bossy, I'm a married woman now."

"Yes. That's what you are, Minnie. A married woman. And you have the scar to prove it."

"Don't make it hurt, please. That's not what a doctor's supposed to do."

"Well, you tell me a good anesthetic to use on myself."

"If I knew of one I would."

"I guess the best is what I tell some patients. Those that haven't got very long. 'Keep busy. Don't overdo, but keep yourself occupied.' It never made a one of them live a day longer than he should have, but at least some of them felt useful for a few months."

"You're useful."

"At the moment, I am."

"That isn't what I meant, Buz, but there are lots of ways, aren't there?"

"Oh, sure. As a matter of fact, what *did* you mean?"

"You thought I meant your practice, but I meant Sadie and myself. I don't know what either of us would do without you."

"You seem to be doing very well without me. Sadie is another story, one that we'll see the end of fairly soon. Two years, three years."

"Two or three years? I could almost laugh, couldn't you?"

"Sure. Often. But only almost. And in a way I'm glad you didn't wait."

"Why?"

"Well, my ethical problem is bad enough as it is, and if you were still single it would be much worse. Sadie is drinking herself to death, literally, and I know as her husband that she's doing it deliberately. Not in any mean or vindictive way, but because she has nothing to live for. Nothing. Sex is no pleasure for her any more. Dressing up. Giving parties. None of the things she enjoyed for a while. She doesn't want to look at herself in the mirror, and she doesn't, or when she does she cries. So she drinks. She gets what she calls soz-zled. For about two hours a day, in the middle of the afternoon, she makes a little sense and I try to go home and see her then. But the rest of the time she's intoxicated, or sozzled. I could probably have her committed, but she's not going to respond to any treatment that I know of, including psychiatry. I could compel her to go to a hospi-tal, but she has a genuine terror of hospitals, and in these times I have no right to put her in a hospital, with the shortage of nurses, and sick people sleeping in corridors. Can you imagine Sadie in a corridor? And would you put her in a private room when the demand is what it is today? Have you been to either of the hospitals lately?"

"Yes."

"Then you know. So I have Mrs. Brophy in the house. She's not a nurse and she's not young, but she's pretty strong and conscientious, and at least I know that Sadie isn't going to set fire to the house with a cigarette she left burning, or fall asleep in the bathtub. And if she has a bad fall, Mrs. Brophy always knows where she can reach me."

"What about Sadie herself?"

"Most of the time she doesn't know what's going on."

"Have you had any other doctors in to see her?"

"No, not yet. I know what they'll say. The younger men will say psychiatry, and pass the buck that way. One or two might recommend surgery, but why subject her to that ordeal when I know damn well that as soon as she comes home from the hospital she's going to start drinking again? I'm not giving her little doses of arsenic. My wife is a hopeless case. She's going to die from the things that are wrong with her organically, and even if they could be cured, she'd still die. There's a thing I've noticed about Sadie and others as well. There are some people that don't seem to be interested in themselves, seem to be more interested in other people. And we tend to think of them as unselfish and so on. But I wonder. Sadie, for instance, has always been outwardly generous and so forth, but I don't believe that she ever spent much time thinking about herself, about her own mind, her motives, her limitations. And if she did, possibly she didn't like what she learned, and therefore stopped. She was safe, comfortable, as long as she didn't do any thinking about herself."

"Escapism."

"Of course. But a case of escapism like Sadie's is a form of death. Not suicide, but death. Sadie probably died of shock years ago, when she got a good look at herself and didn't like what she saw."

"I never thought of it that way."

"Well, I never would have if I hadn't been married to a case of it. I think Sadie murdered Loffler."

"Oh, come on, Buz. He died in the hospital. That's why she hates hospitals."

"He not only died in the hospital. I also went to the trouble of looking up his death certificate. He died of normal causes. A heart condition. Billy English signed the death certificate. No postmortem. No suspicious element in the whole business. But I think she hoped so much for his death that she got her wish."

"Oh, well that's a different matter."

"Is it? I think that's what she saw that she didn't like. I think that after Loffler died she took the one and only look inside herself and was horrified by what she saw. Horrified. Admitted to herself that she had wanted him dead."

"Is she a witch? Is that what you're implying?"

"A kind of one, yes. Fat, and not very bright, not skinny and clever, the way witches are supposed to be. You said something a few minutes ago about fortune-tellers. Were they skinny?"

"No, as a matter of fact the fortune-tellers I went to were both stout women. I only went to two. One in New York and one in Collieryville, but they were both heavy-set."

"Well, I saw them in China, the Hawaiian Islands and several other places when I was out there years ago, and they were all fat women. Rather jolly fat women, except when they were fat men."

"Are you making this up?"

"No. If it sounds that way it's because I've never put it into words before. Even now I'm not going to tell you everything."

"What is there to keep back?"

"Things I don't like to tell, and that you wouldn't like to listen to."

"Oh, in the sexual line?"

"Yes."

"Well, without going into detail, what kind of thing? Be objective."

"Well, medically objective, which is to say things she didn't know herself, she was a sadist. But not in the obvious ways. With a man like Loffler, a man that couldn't have known there was such a word and was probably frustrated anyhow, she could have been very dangerous."

"How?"

"Well, I don't think he'd had much sex life before he married Sadie, and he was fifteen years older than she when they got married. He was always fifteen years older, of course. When I married Sadie I discovered that I was expected to function every night of the week."

"But you didn't."

"No, I didn't, but apparently she had Loffler trying every night. When it got dark, you went to bed, and when you went to bed you had sex. That must have been quite a strain on Loffler, who wasn't accustomed to any at all during the first forty years of his life. I can see how this conversation could become embarrassing to you, Mrs. McHenry."

"Well, yes, it could. But I'm fascinated by the witch theory. Since it's come up, I admit I always thought Sadie was—strange. I remember one time at a dinner at the hotel. You were making a speech for the Community Chest, I think it was, and I happened to notice Sadie. She wasn't looking at you at all. She was studying all the women, one after another. Pride, I thought it was at first, but that wasn't it. I decided it was more like jealousy, trying to guess which of the women wanted to go to bed with you. Why wasn't she more jealous of me? Why didn't her instinct tell her about us?"

"Who knows? She wasn't jealous of women patients, either. She once asked me what a doctor thought when a woman patient also happened to be a friend of his. I told her that sick women were completely devoid of any attraction for a doctor. She accepted that. She also accepted my statement that doctors never fool around with nurses. Those were the days when she accepted everything I told her. These past few years she doesn't believe anything, but that's not only directed against me. She doesn't believe anybody. Mrs. Brophy, me, anybody. Oh, if I were just out of medical school I wouldn't say this, but Sadie is crazy. Take away all the language of anatomy and diagnosis and therapy and prognosis—and I'm married to a crazy woman."

"Then she's not a witch, Buz," said Minnie, smiling.

"No? In the tropics the chief conversational topic after sex and money is witchcraft, whether you're in Port-au-Prince or Honolulu. I never knew a ship's officer that didn't have some favorite witchcraft story. But you have a word like poltergeist, which comes from the German, meaning a noisy ghost. Those things aren't confined to the dark-skinned people. The banshees. *Macbeth.* And I know this much about my wife. When Mrs. Brophy has to sit with her at night, she won't do it without her rosary beads. Don't ask me why, but I guess Mrs. Brophy has heard her say things in her sleep."

"What are you grinning at?" said Minnie.

"Something that might amuse you. Should, if you haven't lost your sense of humor."

"What?"

"Mrs. Brophy told me that Sadie thinks there's a ghost in the garage."

"*Us?* You mean to say she knew about us?"

"No, positively not. This ghost has only been there in the past year or so. It's over three years since you and I've been up there. This is completely imaginary."

"Unless one of your maids is going in for hanky-panky."

"Which one? Agnes, the cook? Or Mary Chapman? Agnes couldn't walk that far, and Mary could walk that far but who'd want her to?"

"I guess Sadie has nightmares."

"Of course she has. Delirium tremens nightmares. But I thought it would amuse you, ghosts in the garage."

"What if that had ever got out about us? Think what a sensation we'd have caused."

"I often think of the sensations we caused, Minnie."

"Never mind, never mind," she said. "Well, this is the first good talk we've had in three years."

"Yes, and think how many years since we had such a good talk fully dressed."

"I won't think about that, Buz, and don't you." She got up and left him as the crowd began to gather for the meeting of the Lantenengo County Red Cross Executive Committee, Dr. Wallace P. Drummond, chairman.

VI

A new doctor, wholly new to the town, created a place for himself that was made up in part of Buz Drummond's former position and in part his own. "I've only been practicing a little over thirty years," Buz said one evening at the Gibbsville Club. "Well, not quite forty. But already I'm obsolete, thanks to three things. Psychiatry. The wonder drugs. And the New Deal. If I were just getting out of medical school, knowing all I was supposed to know in 1921, I couldn't get a license to practice today. Not in this State. Most of us my age won't admit that, but it's true. You take thoracic surgery. I watched a man do an operation the other day that in my early days, if he'd have attempted it he'd have been expelled from the Gibbsville Hospital, kicked out of the Medical Society. It was a heart operation. Oh, our men operated on the heart, true, but this man went in and took care of the obstruction and then put a sleeve over the aorta—too complicated to explain to a layman—but the patient will live ten more years. In my day we'd have let him die, without any surgery. I started out with a Dodge coupe, but in reality I was one of the last of the horse-and-buggy doctors. Nowadays if a patient is too sick for an office call they send him to the hospital. Doctors are just too damn busy to make house calls, not to mention the fact that there aren't enough nurses to take care of private patients at home. Not to mention the bloody awful expense, and the fact that the hospitals have the facilities that aren't available at home. When I was starting out, though, if I sent a patient to the hospital the family would begin to wonder whether Pop had made a will."

"You mentioned the New Deal. Where does that come in?"

"Socialized medicine."

"But you're holding the line against that, you and the County Medical Society."

"Every two years we elect a new president—the same old new president. Me. But this year I'm not running again. I'd get licked, and I want to retire undefeated, bow out gracefully, if not graciously. You see, Arthur, the Society is still made up of men like me, who can outvote the new men, but every two years the new fellows are a little stronger. Officially the Society is opposed to socialized medicine, but the new young men are just waiting for a form of it that will be acceptable to them. And it won't be acceptable to me. The monthly meetings aren't what they used to be, a few nonentities getting together to talk shop, swap a few dirty stories and adjourn to the Elks for beer. We get a bigger attendance these days and some of the best men. And they're so damned serious. Oh, hell, Arthur, I'm on the shelf. Do you know that two doctors in this town have telephones in their cars?"

"No, but I'm not surprised."

"It doesn't surprise me either, except that I came across a discussion in the minutes of a meeting back around 1902, 1903. Old Dr. Wainwright, long since dead, led the discussion. The question was should doctors charge a fifty-cent fee for talking to patients over the phone. The vote was thirty-five to one against charging them. Today we charge two dollars, to those who can afford it. Wainwright brought up the point because he hadn't decided whether to put in a phone or not, and he wanted to be sure it would pay for itself. He was outvoted on the fifty-cent fee, so he didn't put in a phone. Now nearly every doctor in town has an office phone, a residence phone, an unlisted residence phone, and the answering service. And two of them, phones in their cars. How things have changed!"

"Yes."

"I was never very fond of Malloy. Too brusque, too domineering. But he was nice to me when I first started out, and I remember him trying to get me to stop smoking. A doctor must rely on all his senses, he said, and one of the most important is the sense of smell. Smoking ruins your sense of smell, he said. The reason I bring him up is how can you smell a patient over the phone, sitting in your car? I'm older now than Malloy was when he died, but he practically belongs in the Dark Ages, and where does that leave me? Sitting here in this club, waiting for our bridge partners. Standing on the first tee, waiting for the other members of a foursome. I have an M.D. on my automobile license plate, and sometimes I think I get it under false pretenses. However, last Sunday coming up from the club a state policeman pulled me out of a traffic tie-up. He saw my license plate and escorted me to an auto accident. I was too late for one poor son of a bitch, but I stopped another from bleeding to death. Not that a chiropractor couldn't have done the same. Or a first-class Boy Scout."

"How are you coming along with your book?"

"Oh, you've heard about my book? Well, I've been making a lot of notes. I have a dozen school tablets filled with them, and I could go on filling them with the things I remember. The trouble is I'm not sure what kind of a book I want to write."

"At least you know what kind you don't want to write."

"What kind is that?" said Buz Drummond.

"Like that piece of tripe Dr. Malloy's son wrote a few years ago," said McHenry.

"Oh, but that was a novel. Fiction. He made all that up."

"But he certainly gave this town a black eye."

"That's what I don't understand, Arthur. If it was all made up, what were people so sore about?"

"He gave the town a black eye, that's why. And not one damn thing he wrote about actually happened."

"That's what I said. But you as a lawyer, and I as a physician, we know that things *like* them happened."

"Oh, hell, as far as that goes, I know some things that if young Malloy ever heard about them . . ."

"So do I, Arthur," said Dr. Drummond.

The Pioneer Hep-Cat

Every time I come here you all seem to want to hear some more about Red Watson. I declare, if I ever thought there would have been such a demand for stories about Red Watson I would have sat down and written a book about him. I've told you story after story about people that I thought were much more interesting than Reds. Big people. People that made something of themselves instead of a man that nobody ever heard of outside of two or three counties in Pennsylvania, and even here the name Red Watson never meant a thing to the people generally considered worthwhile. You young people nowadays, I'd much rather tell you about a mine-boy, a young lad that worked in a breaker but was rescued from that and went away to a seminary and became a cardinal. We had one young fellow in this town that most of you don't even know he was born here, but he was. I'm talking about General Henry T. Corrigan. Lieutenant-General Corrigan was born right here in this town and sold papers here till his family moved away. I used to play ball with Henny Corrigan, out at the old Fourteenth Street schoolyard. He caught, and I played shortstop on a team we used to have, called the Athletics. I guess *some* of you would be able to guess where we got that name. Those of you that can't guess, we didn't get the name from Kansas City, if that's any hint. And I might mention that a few years ago, when I was attending the newspaper editors' convention in New York City, the principal speaker was none other than Lieutenant-General Henry T. Corrigan, all decorated with a chestful of ribbons and surrounded by famous editors and publishers from all over the country, all wanting to ask him questions about the Strategic Air Command. And there I was, not a very important person I must admit, but when it came my turn to meet the general he looked at me and then he looked at my name on the convention badge we were all wearing and he burst into a big smile. "Winky Breslin!" he said. That was my nickname when I was

Assembly (1961)

young. "Winky, you old son of a gun," and with that he took me by the arm and the two of us went over and sat down and you'd be surprised how many local people he remembered, some now dead and gone, but quite a few still living. Some of them the parents and grandparents of you here today. I ran a little story about it at the time, but I guess not many of you saw it. In any case, that's the kind of man I'd rather talk about, but every time I'm asked to speak at one of your Press Club suppers your representative either asks me outright or gives me a strong hint to the effect that the person you'd like me to talk about is Red Watson. I don't understand it.

I'd understand it a lot better if Reds were still alive, and some rock-and-roll idol. But he passed away before you even had swing, let alone rock-and-roll. And it isn't as if there were any of his old records floating around. Reds never made a record in his life. I don't say he wouldn't have been good, or popular. He would have been. If they'd ever heard of him outside of this section of the country, he might have been, well, not as popular as Gene Austin, or the early Crosby. He had a totally different style. As I've told you before, or your predecessors, there's nobody around today to compare him with. The styles of singing have changed so much from when Reds was around. Beginning I'd say with Rudy Vallee and then on to Russ Columbo and Bing, the crooners came in. All toned down as far as the volume was concerned and running ahead of or behind the beat. Not Reds. When Red Watson let go, he belted out a song in a way that you'd think was going to break every window in the place. And on the beat. Perfectly on the beat. And he was a tenor. The singers nowadays, if you can classify them at all, you'd have to call them baritones. But Reds was a tenor, a high tenor.

I was thinking the other evening, I happened to be watching a show on TV and one of your Tommy Sandses or Bobby Darins came on and those squealing girls, that I suspect are paid, began screeching. And I thought to myself, Red Watson hit a higher note than any of those bobby-soxers, but when he did it it was music. Yes, it was. That's the sad part about it that there aren't any records around to prove it.

When I was the age of some of you, or a little older, the name bands used to come through this region, playing the parks in the summer and the ballrooms in the winter. I notice you don't get many big bands any more. In fact, I'm told there aren't any, to speak of. But when I was a young fellow there wasn't a name band in the country that didn't play here and all around here. And over and over again. It won't mean anything to you, but I can remember one night when Paul Whiteman, with a thirty-five-piece band, was playing a one-nighter and only two miles away was Vincent Lopez, with *his* big band. How to compare it nowadays, it would be like—I don't know the names of the bands any more. Ray Conniff and Neal Hefti, I guess. But I can tell you this much, one of the singers with Whiteman was a young practically unknown singer with a trio, named Bing Crosby. And if memory serves, the famous Bix Beiderbecke was also with Whiteman around that time. Those of you that collect records will recognize the name Bix Beiderbecke. First name, Leon. Played cornet. Also piano. You have a musician today, Bushkin, he plays piano and horn, but Bushkin was never idolized the way Bix was. They even wrote a novel about him, and if I'm not mistaken, it was turned into a New York play.

Well, what I don't understand is your interest in Red Watson, because Red died around the time I've been speaking of. He was popular *before* Whiteman and Lopez started playing the parks and the ballrooms in this section. The big band then was the Sirens. The Scranton Sirens. Of course you've heard about the Sirens. Both Dorseys played with the Sirens. We had that in our paper when Tommy and Jimmy passed on there a little while ago, and I got a lot of letters from some of your mothers and fathers and I guess your grandparents, that still loved the Scranton Sirens. But with all due credit to the Dorsey boys, the real attraction was Red Watson. Mind you, it was a fine band. None better in the whole United States, because I heard them all. All the big ones of that day. Fletcher Henderson. Earl Fuller. The Barbary Coast. Art Hickman. Oh, my, just saying the names takes me back. Ted Weems. The Original Dixieland. Goldkette. Paul Biese. The Coon-Sanders Kansas City Nighthawks. Jack Chapman. I can remember more than once driving all the way to Atlantic City in a friend of mine's flivver, just to hear a band at the Steel Pier, and then *driving back the same night* so I'd be at work in the morning. That was a long trip then. It's still a long trip, but when we made it—I guess there isn't one of you here that would know how to vulcanize an inner tube. I can see you don't even know what I'm talking about. In those days you could go in any five-and-ten and buy an ignition key for your Ford, and it had a square hole cut in the key to turn on the tank for your headlights. No, you don't register, I might as well be talking about whip-sockets.

You must bear in mind, when I graduated from this school, in other words the same age as some of you within sound of my voice, jazz was such a new thing that they weren't even sure how to spell it. Some spelt it j, a, s, s, and I've seen Victrola records with Jass Band instead of Jazz Band printed on the label. But I'll tell you one thing. If you ever heard Red Watson sing "Jazz Me" you knew it was spelt with two z's. To be quite frank with you, I'm always hesitant about coming here and speaking about Red Watson, because as the I hope respectable editor of a family newspaper, I don't consider Reds a proper subject for a talk before a group of young high school students. If I weren't so convinced that you know as much about some things as I do, I'd have to decline your invitations. Or at least I'd choose another subject. But then I always say to myself, "These young people today, they know a lot more than I did when I was their age, about certain things, and maybe I can sneak over a moral lesson somehow or other." And I can. You see, boys and girls, or young ladies and gentlemen, Red Watson was an example of great talent wasted. He had a God-given voice, completely untrained, but I was told that he was given many offers to go away and take singing lessons. He came from a little town outside of Scranton and several rich people up there wanted to pay for his vocal training, but he'd have no part of it.

The story was—and those of you that were here two years ago must excuse me for repeating it—but according to the story that I always heard, and I could never summon up the courage to ask Reds to verify it—Reds was a breaker-boy, too. Like that cardinal. But when he was about thirteen years old, working in the breaker, his arm got caught in the conveyor and was so badly mangled that they had to amputate above the elbow. Thirteen, maybe fourteen years old. You can imagine what dreadful torture he must have gone through. The accident itself, and then the amputation which left him with a stump about, well, he used to fold up his left sleeve and pin it with a safety pin just under the shoulder. He was an orphan, living with relatives, and after he got out of the hospital he tried selling papers, but that wasn't as easy as you might think. A paper route was just about impossible to get, and selling papers on street corners was just as hard. You had to fight for the busy corners, and Reds only had one arm. So he used to get a few papers and go around to the saloons and try to sell them there, but somehow or other they found out that he could sing, and he began to make as much money singing for nickels and dimes, and pennies, as he could selling papers. At the age of fourteen he was known in all the saloons, and sometimes the miners used to get him liquored up, even though he was hardly more than a child. They'd give him whiskey and get him singing, and he told me himself that by the time he was sixteen years of age, he could drink beer all night long without getting intoxicated. Whiskey was another matter, but beer he could drink till the cows came home, and it wouldn't affect him. That much of the story is true, because Reds told me himself.

This part I can't vouch for, but you can take it for whatever you think it's worth. I've never been able to make up my mind one way or the other whether it's just imagination on someone's part, or based on the truth, and I never asked Reds. But according to the story that a lot of people believed, when Reds wanted to hit his high note, he'd think back on the time he lost his arm and the pain would come back to him and he'd scream. I don't know. It wasn't the kind of question I could ever ask Reds, although I got to know him pretty well. But I remember hearing a story about Caruso, too. He was supposed to be the greatest tenor that ever lived, and they say he hit his highest note when he was in pain from an abscess in his lung. Who knows? I have a hard time believing it, but I think Caruso died of an abscessed lung, or the effects of it, so there may be some connection between the pain and the high note. I know that Red Watson's stump always bothered him, and he became a heavy drinker to take his mind off the pain. But he wouldn't see a doctor. Oh, no. He said another operation—well, not to be squeamish about it, the stump was so short that there was hardly anything left of the arm, and where would they go after that? He said to me once that he wasn't like most people, because he knew exactly how long he had to live. He said he didn't have to measure it in years, like most people, but in a few inches of bone.

People ask me what Reds was like, because when I was a young fellow, I confess that it wasn't only my duty as a reporter that took me into the various places where alcoholic beverages were for sale. And I guess I was one of the pioneer hep-cats, although they didn't use that expression, and in fact I'm told by the modern generation that you don't even say hep any more. Hip? Or is that passé, too? Well, anyway, I know that the musicians used to call us alligators, because we'd stand in front of a band with our mouths open like alligators, so if you ever heard the expression, "Greetings, 'Gate," that's where it came from. The alligators. And I was one back in the early Twenties, just after the first World War. When we wanted to hear a good jazz band, an orchestra that didn't play waltzes all night, we had to go to the public dances on Saturday nights at the Armory, and whenever I hear you young people being called juvenile delinquents, I have to remind myself that there was plenty of it when I was about your age. Those dances at the Armory, I think the admission was fifty cents for ladies and seventy-five for gents. It may have been less. Fifty for gents and twenty-five for ladies. We had a name for those dances. We called them rock fights. In fact, we didn't even bother to call them by the full name, rock fights. We used to say, "Are you going out to the rocky tonight?" And out of that grew another nickname, the quarry. We used to speak of the rock fights as the quarry. In front of our parents we could say, "I'll see you at the quarry," and our fathers and mothers would think we were talking about going for a swim in the quarry dam. Oh, we were just as wild as you think you are, or almost.

You know, I don't often get to see TV in the daytime, but last year when I was laid up with arthritis I watched you kids, or young people of your generation, dancing on an afternoon program. And one great difference between you and us, *you* don't seem to be having a good time. You hardly even smile at each other. It wasn't that way in my youth. Good Lord, everybody was laughing and jumping around, racing all over the floor when they played a one-step. Now you just glare at your partner and she spins around and you pull her towards you. You don't have any fun. Incidentally, I don't think you dance very well, either, but that's a matter of opinion. I remember a fast tune called "Taxi!" When they played that you moved fast or you got out of the way. That was good exercise, and fun. There'd always be a few fellows pretty well liquored up and they'd take a spill, but that was part of the fun. And there was always at least one fist fight at the rockies. At least one. You see, most of the girls at those dances, they were high school age, but they weren't going to school. They had working permits and a lot of them worked in the silk mill, the box factories, and some of them were servant girls. You hear the expression, going steady, and you think it's new. Well, it isn't. Girls and boys went steady then, and what that meant was that a girl would go to a rock fight and pay her own way in, dance with as many fellows as she wanted to, but she always went home with the boy she was going steady with, and if she tried to go home with somebody else, there'd be a fist fight. That's really where those dances got the name, rock fights. They didn't throw rocks, and they wouldn't have called them rocks anyway. They called them goonies. A gooney was a piece of stone that boys would throw at each other on the way home from school. In some sections of town the boys used to in the winter take a gooney and wrap it up in snow. A snowball with a gooney in it could inflict a lot of damage. See this scar here in back of my ear? That was a gooney wrapped in snow. I never knew who or what hit me at the time, but a bunch of boys from Third Street school were waiting for us boys from Fourteenth Street one afternoon, and I was one of the casualties. My poor mother when they brought me home!

Well, you're very patient with me and I don't know why it is that the mere mention of Red Watson opens up the floodgates of reminiscence, only it's more about me than about Reds. I started to answer the question, what was he like? Well, in spite of his name being Watson, he had a real Irish face, no doubt about it. He wasn't a very big fellow. In fact he was on the short side. But he looked a lot older than his real age. When I first knew him he was only about twenty years of age, but he looked easily thirty. Face was almost purple from drink and he was already starting to get bald. He was usually smiling and he was *always* smiling when he got up to sing. He'd flirt with all the girls around the bandstand that gathered around when he took his place to sing. He was a cake-eater. That was slang for fellows that dressed a certain way. They were also called sharpies. A sharpie, or a cake-eater, wore a suit that was padded at the shoulders and tight at the waist, then flared out. It had exaggerated peaked lapels that went all the way up to the shoulders, hence the name sharpie. The coat was buttoned at the waist with link buttons, sometimes three pairs of link buttons. The cuffs flared out and they were divided, The trousers were very wide at the bottom, and if you were really sharp, they were laced at the sides, like Spanish bullfighters'. The sharpies wore either tiny bow ties, on an elastic, or very narrow four-in-hands. And they wore low-cut vests so that the whole shirt-front was exposed. Tiny little collars. Hair was plastered down with vaseline, and the cake-eaters wore side-burns. And that was the way Reds dressed, with one sleeve pinned up to his shoulder. You boys and girls are even too young to remember the zoot suit of twenty years ago, which was different from the cake-eater's outfit, but if Reds had lived in a later era, he'd have worn a zoot suit, I think.

As to his personality, he had two. One when he was singing, and the other when he wasn't. When he wasn't singing he wasn't a very remarkable young fellow. Good-natured as a rule, although quick-tempered at times. He liked the girls, and they certainly liked him, not because of his looks, you can be sure of that. And not only because of his singing. He had a car, a yellow Marmon roadster it was, and I went on a couple of rides with him after we became friendly, and we'd drive to Reading and Philadelphia, places where they didn't know him at all, and we'd stop some place to get a sandwich. If they had a waitress that was halfway good-looking Reds would start to kid her a little, and always end up with a date. Sometimes he had no intention of keeping the date, but he just had to convince himself that he was irresistible. And he usually was. In fact, too much so. I guess I knew him two or three years before he happened to mention that he was married when he was eighteen and had a baby daughter. He supported his wife and child, but he wasn't a good husband or father by any stretch of the imagination. I could understand his not getting along with his wife, but I've never been able to understand why he didn't seem to take the slightest interest in his daughter. But that was a closed subject, and I decided it was none of my business. In my opinion Reds was one of those people that seem to have a talent for certain things, such as music, writing, art, but they're deficient in the common-ordinary, everyday things that you don't hear so much about, but they're an accomplishment nevertheless. I mean the simple, ordinary things like the sacrifices that some of your mothers and fathers make for you boys and girls, that you may not even know of unless you stop to think about it. Forty boys and girls in this room. How many of you girls had a new dress this year? Don't raise your hands, because my next question is, how many of you girls got a new dress this year because your mother got one for you instead of for herself? And you boys. How many of you have cars—and don't *you* raise your hands, either. Because some of you must know, if you stop to think, that you wouldn't have a car if your fathers didn't decide to spend that money on you instead of on themselves. This isn't a lecture. I'm not at all sure what it is except an informal talk by a newspaper editor to some young people that are interested in the field of journalism. And you don't especially want me to talk about the newspaper business. But in fairness to you, if I'm invited to talk about a colorful character whose example I wouldn't want you to follow, in fairness to you I have to call your attention to the fact that you all have fathers and mothers that do set a good example in love and kindness, and patience and understanding. My conscience won't let me talk about Red Watson, and glamorize him, unless I point out to you that Reds only lived to be twenty-five years of age, and as far as I know—and I knew him pretty well—he never did anything for anybody but himself. With that understanding, I'll continue talking about him. But I had to make that clear. He never did anything for anybody but himself, and he died— well, I'll save that till later, inasmuch as half the members of your Press Club probably are hearing about Reds for the first time. The seniors and juniors were here when I spoke two years ago, but the sophomores and freshmen weren't.

So to continue about his two personalities. The one, he was fun to be with, but I only saw him on his visits to town, maybe four times a year. I don't know how he'd have been as a steady diet. Selfish, and no respect for girls whatsoever, and as I said before, he seemed good-natured, but he had a quick temper, too. I guess if I had to be completely frank about it, I was flattered because he wanted me for a friend. I was just a young fellow starting out in the newspaper business, and I used to enjoy it when some of our local prizefighters and celebrities would call me by my nickname. And in that little world, Red Watson was as big a celebrity as Kid Lefty Williams or Young Packy Corbett, two fighters we had at the time, both since passed on. Made me feel big, even though I had some misgivings about Reds.

But I'll tell you this, you always forgot what he was like when he got up to sing. I mean the things about him that I didn't go along with. It'd come his turn to sing a number and he'd go behind the piano and take a swig out of a pint bottle of whiskey, and a couple of fast drags on his cigarette, and then he'd go to the middle of the bandstand and stand there grinning at the people gathering around while the orchestra played a full chorus. And then he'd close his eyes and put his head back and start singing. It didn't make any difference what the number was. It might be a sort of a risqué song like "Jazz Me" or it might be a ballad. But the dancing would stop and everybody would stand still, as close to the bandstand as they could get, and you'd look at their faces and they were hypnotized. They'd be moving in time to the rhythm, but not dancing, and it was almost as though he were singing for them. Not only to them, but for them. I can remember thinking of him as a misplaced choir boy, and the crowd around him some of the toughest characters in the county. The girls just as tough as the young fellows. They'd all stop chewing gum while he was singing, and even when he happened to be singing a dirty song, they'd smile, but they didn't laugh. And if it was a ballad, he could make them cry. There's a high note in "Poor Butterfly"—"but if he don't come *back*"—that *always* made them cry. Then he'd finish his song and open his eyes and smile at them while they yelled and applauded, and he'd wink at them, and they'd start dancing again. One chorus. No encores, one song every half an hour. That was his agreement. He was paid fifty dollars a night with the band. But then after the dance was over we'd all meet at some saloon and after he had enough to drink you couldn't stop him. He'd get up on the bar and sing whatever you asked him, till the joint closed. The next night it'd be the same thing in some other town, six nights a week.

How he kept it up as long as he did, I don't know. He slept all day, but when he had his breakfast, at seven o'clock in the evening, that was often the only meal he ate all day. By eight o'clock he was hitting the bottle, and usually at half past eight, sometimes nine, he'd be with the band, ready to sing his first number. Naturally he couldn't keep that up, and he began failing to show up with the band. The first few times that happened, he got away with it, but then the crowds were disappointed and the managers of the dance-halls were afraid to advertise that he was coming. Then the band broke up and for about a year I didn't see Reds at all. I heard he was forming his own band, Red Watson's Syncopators. And he was leading the band, himself. But that didn't last long. Two or three months of that was all he could stand. And all the musicians could stand. He'd order special arrangements, but then he wouldn't pay for them, and he got in trouble with the union about paying his musicians, and the first thing he knew he was put on the unfair list. After that he just disappeared, and whenever I'd ask about him from people around Wilkes-Barre and Scranton they had conflicting reports, probably all true. I heard he'd opened a speakeasy in Wilkes-Barre and someone else told me he was in prison for non-support of his wife and child. The last time I saw him I was in Scranton, covering a United Mine Workers meeting, and I asked around and finally tracked him down. I asked him how things were, and not knowing I knew anything about him, he put on a great show. He said he'd got rid of the yellow Marmon and was buying a Wills Sainte-Clare. That was an expensive car. He had offers to go in vaudeville, et cetera, et cetera. And he wouldn't let me pay the check. We were in a speakeasy where his credit must have been good, because he told the bartender to put it on his tab and the bartender made a face, but said okay, Reds. I had a feeling that the bartender would have much preferred my cash. So I said to Reds, approaching the subject in a roundabout way, I said I was glad things were better. And he asked me what I meant by better, and I said I'd heard he'd a little trouble. Well, such vituperation! Such invective! And all directed at me. I was a cheap newspaper reporter that never made more than thirty dollars a week in my life, which was true, but I was also a snooping so-and-so, probably sent there by his wife's lawyer to find out all I could. He took a beer bottle off the bar and smashed the neck off it. That was a weapon known as a Glasgie Slasher, and he held it up to my face and said I deserved to have my eyes gouged out, snooping around and asking questions. I didn't dare move, for fear I'd get that thing in my face. And then I guess because I hadn't made any move he dropped the broken bottle in the gutter in front of the bar, and ran out.

I was given a drink by the bartender, and I needed it after that experience. "He'll murder somebody yet," the bartender said. "He's suspicious of everybody." I asked the bartender how Reds lived, and the man told me. I don't have to go into that here, but Reds was about as low as a man can get to make a living. Any real man would rather dig ditches, but Reds only had one arm and all he ever did was sing. Anyway, he had a place to live and a little cash. And then the bartender, a nice fellow, asked me how well I'd known Reds. Had Reds ever told me that he didn't measure his life by years, but inches of bone? And I said yes, he'd said that to me some years back. And the bartender said, "Well, he's heard the bad news. No more inches, and no more years. Months, and more likely weeks." Then he said he just hoped Reds got through the next couple of months without killing somebody.

Well, he did, boys and girls. The next I heard of Reds was a few weeks later at the office, the city editor handed me a little squib that came in over the U.P. wire. Patrick Watson, known throughout the coal region as Red Watson, the popular tenor, was found dead on the bandstand of the Alhambra dance-hall in Scranton. It was summer, the wrong time of the year for a dance at the Alhambra. So I got Scranton on the phone and checked. Yes, they found Reds at the Alhambra. Nobody else in the place, which was closed for the summer, and the watchman had no idea what Reds had gone there for. There was nothing worth stealing.

But you and I know why he went there, don't we? Yes, I think as I look at you, you know.

Thank you.

Money

The money was divided three ways: Ellen Brosnan got her widow's share, and as soon as possible she left town and went back to Buffalo, New York, where she had originally come from; the remaining two-thirds was split between Nan Brosnan and her sister Marietta Brosnan Kelly. The whole thing amounted to about two hundred thousand dollars, quite a sum in those days, but the distribution did not cause much talk in the town. A few said Ellen Brosnan was lucky to get anything, but they were quickly reminded by the knowledgeable that under the law it was almost impossible to cut Ellen off. It could be done, they said, but she would have had to agree and it would have had to be so stated in Clete Brosnan's will. He would have had to say that Ellen had been provided for during his lifetime (and God knows that would have been the truth) and consequently consented to accept the nominal sum of one dollar in exchange for waiving her dower rights. All were unanimous that the way Clete disposed of his estate was the best way: give Ellen her third and let her go back to her Buffalo, New York, without any excuse for making a fuss, and let the Brosnan girls enjoy life in peace and quiet, gratefully remembering their brother with Month's Mind and Anniversary Masses said for him and a simple urn of Indiana limestone to mark his grave. He had not had much peace and quiet during the latter portion of his life, but at least he could rest in peace now—that was what *"requiescat in pace"* meant, wasn't it, after all?—with Ellen back in Buffalo and Nan and Marietta home and keeping the name up. All were unanimous that Clete had managed to bring about in death the kind of order and dignity that he had so longed for in life.

They got a good price for the house in Oak Road. The house was only five years old, well built of the best materials and with all the latest modern conveniences. Electricity everywhere, and two full-sized bathrooms. A high antenna for the Stromberg-Carlson so that

New Yorker (24 March 1962); *The Cape Cod Lighter*

Ellen could get Kansas City and Chicago as clearly as other people
could get Pittsburgh and Schenectady. The garage door lifted easily
with one hand instead of being a swinging door that had to be swung
outward into the driveway. The Vic was an Orthophonic, and Ellen
was the only housewife on Oak Road who had a telephone extension
in her kitchen—although for the time she spent in her kitchen it
seemed like a waste of money. Ellen even had an electric contraption for polishing the hardwood floors, although no one thought for
a minute that Ellen was the one who pushed the contraption around.
That was a job for her maid. A maid—for a house containing eight
rooms and no children, where there were seldom any visitors to take
care of but always fresh candy in the cut-glass jars, where there was a
baby grand piano with no one who could play a note. Completely
furnished, rugs and all, the house brought twenty-eight thousand
dollars, which had to be divided up three ways under the terms of
Clete's will. "I'd as soon let her have the whole thing," said Nan
Brosnan.

"Well, not me. I wouldn't. I'd as soon she got none of it," said
Marietta Kelly. "She already got more than she's ever entitled to."

"Yes, but she's going to get all's coming to her or we'll have some
shyster lawyer hauling us into court."

"I didn't mean we should try any funny business. What Clete
wanted we have to conform with. But if she got what she was entitled
to, a roll of toilet paper'd be sufficient."

"It doesn't come by the roll in that house," said Nan Brosnan.

"Just a figure of speech," said Marietta.

"I know. And don't think I was having generous thoughts, lamb. If
I let her have the whole thing, it'd only be to get rid of her, to have
nothing more to do with her whatsoever . . . I'll say this for her.
You'll hardly find a mark on any of the furniture, not a scratch, and
in some ways the stuff is better than new."

"Why shouldn't it? At our place it's just the opposite, but I
brought up my three children in our place. Why shouldn't her stuff
look new? A hired girl with nothing to do but clean and dust—and
run that electric floor polisher. You'd think she was getting ready to
give a ball."

"And it's what killed Clete, too. Those slippery floors," said Nan
Brosnan. "That spill he took the summer before last, Clete was an
old man after that. Never the same."

"Oh, we can't blame her for that, Nan. Clete was delicate from as
far back as I can remember. True, he got a bad shaking up, but when
was Cletus Brosnan ever a Gene Tunney? You or I could always put
him down, as children."

"He wasn't a muscular man, but he made up for it in brains," said Nan.

"With only the one blind spot, but men are easily swayed. I ought to know, with a husband and three sons."

"You don't have to be married to know that," said Nan. "I didn't enter the convent at some tender age."

"I wasn't inferring anything, Nan. Don't always have a kind of a chip on your shoulder when the subject comes up about men."

"I didn't think you were inferring, lamb. But it's you with your husband and three sons that sometimes you act a *little* superior. I see all kinds of men at the office, away from their women, and many's the time I'm glad I never married. A woman in an office sees an entirely different side of things. I know I wouldn't want to be talked about the way some men talk about their wives, or have my husband say the things I've had married men say to me."

"Well, the more credit to you, Nan."

"Thanks. Just don't feel sorry for me."

"I don't. There've been times I envied you, and you know that."

"Well, we're not dependent on anyone now, you or I," said Nan Brosnan. "We can do as we please now, if we want to."

"Yes, and I hope you stick to it, your decision."

"To quit my job? Nothing'll shake me now, lamb."

"Oh, that I'm sure you'll do. I was thinking of your other decision."

"To give up my room? Well, if you still want me."

"Still *want* you?"

"You didn't say anything these last couple of weeks. I thought maybe you talked it over with Luke and he was against it."

"Good heavens, no. We got all that extra room, what's the use of paying room rent when we have all that extra room?"

"Well, I was thinking it over."

"Oh, Nan, there you go again with that chip on your shoulder. In other words, why didn't we ask you to stay with us before? Well, the only answer I could give to that question is the truthful one. We never thought of it before. You seemed content boarding at Bess Stauffer's, a few minutes' walk to your office. Me asking you to come live with us has nothing to do with your legacy, Nan, if that's what worried you."

"I'm not saying it did."

"No, but it stands to reason that's what you were thinking, your remark about thinking it over. After all, Nan, I have as much as you have from Clete, so don't start conjuring up some ulterior motive. It never would have occurred to me to ask you to live with us, only you said you were giving up your job, and then I thought why does Nan go on living at Bess Stauffer's, downtown? It was too far a walk from our place as long as you had your job, but if you're not going to an office every day, why not keep me company? I get lonesome for someone to talk to. I sound like another Ellen but it's true. You devote your whole life to making a home for a husband and three boys and then the boys all go off and get married and all those years you didn't make any friends of your own."

"You? You have a lot of friends, friends by the dozen."

"No. I have neighbors and acquaintances but not a single close friend. Don't confuse me with Luke, Nan. Luke has the Knights and the Legion he goes to and always some kind of political thing, but I never could join the Daughters or the Auxiliary when they wanted me to, and now I don't want to."

"They want you now, surely."

"Since the news of Clete's will, indeed they do. But I was always careful who I made friends with, and this is the time to be more careful than ever. That's a good thing for you to keep in mind, too, Nan."

"Oh-ho! Don't think I won't."

"Especially look out for men, Nan."

"The fortune-hunter type of man I can see through a mile away."

"I'm glad to hear that, Nan. Very glad to hear it. There's no more pitiful a figure than a woman suddenly come into money and no one to ward off the leeches and sponges."

"I can spot one of them a mile off. Don't forget, I've been a bookkeeper since I was seventeen years of age."

"I know, but with we Brosnans the heart often rules the head. Look at Clete and Ellen. Suddenly at almost forty-five years of age one of the cleverest businessmen in the county, Cletus Brosnan, J. Cletus Brosnan, what does he do but become infatuated with a pretty face in a nurse's uniform. If he could have seen her the first time dressed in something else there might be a different story to tell. But I had to sit there one day and listen while he told me about this angel of purity."

"Angel of purity is what he said to me, too. Did you ever think she was that?"

"Her? You're not seriously asking me that question, Nan. That kind of a bust development, I was sure she had one or two children."

"Oh, you can't tell anything by that. Remember Sister Mary Alexander?"

"I do. But in a black habit she still looked more like an angel of purity than Ellen in her white nurse's uniform. Could you ever picture Ellen in a nun's habit?"

Nan laughed. "No, that I couldn't."

"We have fun together, Nan. You come and stay with us. You'll get used to Luke, if that's worrying you. Once in a month of Sundays he comes home stewed to the gills, but he always has enough sense to sleep in the cellar those nights. 'If you come home in that condition,' I tell him, 'you don't deserve better than the dog. Sleep it off in the cellar,' I tell him. But that's only maybe once or twice a year."

"I've never seen Luke with one too many."

"That's the Legion. The brewery sends them good beer, a couple halves at a time, and they don't stop drinking till the barrels are empty. At that I'd rather have him get drunk on good beer than take a chance on going blind from bootleg hootch."

"Oh, any day. And if not blind, I heard of some that died of convulsions."

"Luke won't often take a drink of whiskey. He likes his beer, but the hard liquor he leaves for the younger fellows. He has that much sense, and that's something to be thankful for."

"You got the best of the Kelly boys. Clete always had only the nicest things to say about Luke. And I remember during the war people saying Luke didn't have to go, but he went."

"Well, there'd always been a Kelly in the Civil War and the Spanish-American, and our boys weren't old enough, so he went. He couldn't have gone if we didn't have Clete to help out, but Clete was glad to. You remember."

"I do. Clete was mortified when they wouldn't take him, but at least he could make some contribution."

"Mind you, it wasn't much. Two thousand, and Luke paid it all back. It took him five years, but he paid back every cent. Oh, yes. Every red cent. Luke was bounden determined he wouldn't go through life owing money to his brother-in-law."

"I never knew that. I never knew that at all."

"See? Here we are, sisters, living in the same town all our lives, and there's so many things we don't know about one another." Marietta Kelly was abruptly silent.

"What, lamb?" said Nan Brosnan.

"Please come and live with us, Nan."

"What's the matter? Is there something wrong? Tell me."

Marietta nodded. "I'd tell you, but I took my oath. You'll find out soon enough, God help us."

* * *

Nan Brosnan, in the weeks of accustoming herself to her new surroundings and leisure and to the constant close company of her sister, respected the mysterious oath Marietta had given. There were times when she had the guilty suspicion that Marietta had invented a crisis in order to persuade her to become a member of the Kelly household. But against that was the genuineness of Marietta's entreaty; it was not like Marietta to show any sign of weakness. In years gone by Marietta had taken things from her older sister, taken them without permission, stolen them on occasion; and when she asked favors she had always managed not to say please. Nan Brosnan could not remember ever hearing Marietta say please, and if she had actually uttered the word, the implication that the word carried was never in her tone. The word "please," and its significance as a sign of weakness, convinced Nan that Marietta had taken an oath and that the oath was necessary to hide a real, a desperate secret. Marietta was cheerful and chatty, sarcastic and revealing, but in those early weeks she did not again refer to the oath. It took weeks, but Nan Brosnan discovered that among all the persons and things that Marietta was so eager to talk about, one topic was omitted: not once, not ever, did Marietta tell a story that had Luke Kelly for the principal character. She told wonderfully funny stories about school days and the eccentricities of some of the nuns; stories about departed curates that she would never have told in front of a third person; anecdotes about her three sons growing up, and hearsay gossip about the inside maneuverings and machinations in the Legion Post and the Knights of Columbus Council. But Luke Kelly was never made the principal character of these reminiscences, and once Nan Brosnan discovered this omission she realized that the thing that troubled Marietta surely concerned Luke. Her mind leaped to a suspicion that it concerned Luke and Ellen, but as she listened further to Marietta's criticisms of Ellen, Nan Brosnan dismissed the suspicion: Marietta despised Ellen, but she was not jealous of her for any reason that had to do with Luke.

Nan grew fonder of Luke. Living in the same house with him she surprised herself with her quick acceptance of Luke as a sort of living substitute for Clete. He would never be Clete; he was too jolly and careless about every thing; his manners, his appearance, his outlook on life made him totally unlike Clete. Clete was hardly out of bed in the morning before he was shaved and wearing collar and tie, and if you ever saw Clete in his shirtsleeves it was only because he was doing some handyman chore about the house. His coat went back on the minute he finished the chore. But Luke would come down in the morning needing a shave, carrying his coat and vest and collar and tie, rubbing his whiskers, scratching himself wherever he felt the need and without regard for Nan's presence. "Hello, girls. You got the old man's breakfast ready?" he would say. "Nan, what are you doing up at this hour? You're supposed to be a lady of leisure. Go on back to bed." He would put an elbow on the table and rest his head on his hand as he spooned up big globs of Cream of Wheat, and while waiting for his eggs and bacon he would sit and smile sadly at Nan. "No rest for the weary, Nan," he would say. Sometimes in the interval between cereal and eggs he would stand up and put on his collar and tie. He would finish his breakfast and say, "Goodbye, girls. Anybody phones, I'll be at the barbershop." He was a collector for a furniture company, which allowed him to bring a Dodge coupé home at night, and he would be out of the house by half past eight, although he seemed to be dawdling and delaying. It was just that his way of doing things, unlike Clete's way, made him seem to be wasting time when he really wasn't. One morning the sisters were in the kitchen, and at eight-fifteen he had not made his appearance. "Will you go up and see if he went back to bed? He wasn't up when I came down."

"I thought I heard him moving around," said Nan. "I'll call him. I don't feel right about going up."

"If he went back to bed, calling won't waken him."

"Then you go up. I'll fry the eggs," said Nan.

Marietta was gone about five minutes. She returned to the kitchen and looked at her sister. "I can't move him. He's lying on the floor in the bathroom."

"Who do you doctor with?" said Nan.

"Young Michaels. The number's one-three-five-oh. But I think it's too late."

"They'll know where he is."

"Too late for Luke, I mean. I think he's gone."

"*No*, lamb. I'll phone Michaels and maybe he'll bring a pulmotor. You go on up with Luke."

Nan admired Marietta's calm without understanding it, but she understood it better when Marietta said, "It's what I've been expecting. What we both been dreading."

"The oath you took?"

"He had the one stroke, but he made me swear to keep it secret. He wanted to be Post commander and he was afraid they wouldn't vote for a man'd had a stroke."

"Go on up with him, lamb."

Marietta shook her head. "I can't, Nan. It isn't him," she said. "You can put the eggs back in the icebox, unless *you* want them."

"Oughtn't somebody to be up there with him? You phone Michaels and I'll go upstairs."

"Will you, then? You can wait out in the hall. But I just can't go up there, Nan."

Everyone said what a brave woman Marietta was throughout her ordeal of the next few days. When they compared notes they found that no one had seen her break, although some noticed that at the requiem Mass, while Joe Denny was singing "Beautiful Isle of Somewhere," she put her handkerchief to her eyes under her heavy veil. But that was the closest to a display of emotion that anyone saw during those days. "A brother and a husband in less than a year's time," they said. "It's lucky she's got her three boys."

"And Nan. It isn't as if she was all alone in the house."

"And at least they won't have any money worries."

Luke's insurance and the house and his savings came to nowhere near the size of Clete's legacy, but Marietta for the first time in her life could be considered comfortably well off. The boys were all self-supporting in more or less distant cities, and before they returned to their homes Marietta spoke to them about money. "Thanks to your Uncle Clete and your father, you won't have me to worry about. Aunt Nan and I'll be living here and sharing expenses. So you don't have to support me. Use your money to raise your own families."

The two older boys nodded silently, but the youngest, Bob, spoke up. "I was counting on a thousand dollars from Dad," he said. "I was *counting* on it, Mom. He as much as promised it to me."

"He didn't say anything in his will," said Marietta.

"I know, but when I married Polly, Dad said he was sorry he could only give me a hundred bucks for a wedding present. He told me he was paying off Uncle Clete and a hundred was all he could spare. He said he'd make up for it some day."

"I don't hear the others claiming a thousand dollars," said Marietta. "And as far as that goes, I don't hear *anybody* offering to chip in for the funeral expenses."

"Oh, wait a minute, Mom," said Gerald, the oldest brother. "The funeral expenses come out of his benefits from the Knights."

"Partially only," said Marietta. "If you want to see the bills, I'll show them to you when they come in. Are you going to say Dad promised you a thousand, too?"

"Well, he told me the same as he told Bob," said Gerald.

"And me," said Ray, the middle son.

"It's funny I never heard about any of these big promises, although Dad and I never had any secrets from one another. Especially about financial matters. And you, Robert, you're a strange one to bring it up, considering how we scraped and pinched to send you to pharmacy school."

"If I had a thousand dollars I could use it for downer money to open my own drugstore," said Bob.

"A thousand dollars to open a drugstore?" said Marietta.

"And Polly's father willing to go on my note, and the little I managed to save."

"If it wasn't for your Uncle Clete I'd have to sell this house and you'd all have to chip in to support me. Or I hope you would. It certainly would look nice if I had a son owner of a drugstore and another son a telegraph operator for the United Press and another son making carpenter's wages, and not enough from the three of them to keep me out of the poorhouse."

"Poorhouse? Bushwah!" said Bob. He stood up. "Dad made me a promise, and Jerry and Ray, too, and Dad always kept his promises. But I promise *you* something, Mom. This is the last time you'll see me in *this* house."

"Sit down, Bob," said Gerald.

"Don't have a fight over money with Dad hardly—" said Ray.

"Oh, go to hell," said Bob. "Stick around, maybe she'll give you my share."

"That calls for a—" Gerald began, but Bob went out.

"Sit down, Gerald," said Marietta. "I won't have any rough stuff in the house of the dead. Let him go, and I hope he keeps his promise, because I don't want any son of mine in my house that talks that way to his mother."

"He was telling the truth, though, Mom," said Ray. "Dad said the same thing to me he said to Bob."

"I don't doubt it for a minute, that Dad would say those things. But where the money was going to come from, that was another matter entirely. All the years we were married he used to say he was going to take me on a trip to Ireland. Five years from now, ten years from now, he used to say we'll go back and pay a visit to Roscommon and Waterford and look up the Kellys and the Brosnans and the Dooleys. But the only trips anybody ever made was when Dad was delegate to the Legion conventions. I never held him to any of those promises, although dear knows I'd of welcomed a trip anywhere. You'd a wonderful father, you boys, but he had a forgetful habit of saying we were going to do this and going to do that and then the whole thing would completely pass from his mind. He'd mean it at the time, but I soon found out it was like playing some kind of a game. 'Sure,' I'd say, 'we'll visit Ireland five years from now,' but when the five years were up I had more sense than to remind him.

I'm surprised he didn't promise you *five* thousand, but it shows how little you understood your father if you took those things seriously. Paying back your uncle, getting rid of the mortgage on this property —it cut him to the quick that the only money I ever had of my own had to come from my brother, not from him."

"Oh, let's drop the subject of money," said Gerald.

"Well, if you two honestly believe I'm holding on to money that rightfully belongs to you—if you honestly believe that? I'll give each of you five hundred as soon as Lawyer Phillips finishes with the legal end, and five hundred apiece next year or the year after. But not Robert. Robert's behavior in this house today puts him beyond the pale. Let him and his Polly and her father start their drugstore, and luck to them. Is that agreeable to you?"

"Whatever suits you, Mom," said Gerald.

"You, Ray?" said Marietta.

"The same for me," said Ray.

"I'll do the best I can for the two of you," said Marietta. "And don't forget, I'm not going to live forever, either. Just remember, no man knows the day or the hour."

Nan Brosnan joined her sister in double mourning. "As long as you wear black I'll wear it too," said Nan.

"Not you," said Marietta. "I'll always wear black, but a year's plenty long enough for you. You won't be criticized."

"I wasn't afraid of that. It's the way I felt about Luke. The next thing to a brother."

"Well, when the year's up for Luke I'll wear a little white in my hats, and you can start wearing colors."

"Well, we'll see," said Nan.

"I'm sure if you took a trip to Buffalo, New York, you wouldn't find a certain Mrs. J. Cletus Brosnan in widow's weeds. Oh, did I tell you? She sent Monsignor fifteen dollars for Masses for Luke. Imagine the gall! Never a word to me, never as much as a bunch of forget-me-nots for the funeral. But fifteen dollars for Masses."

"Well, it's one way of showing spite, if you want to look at it that way. Or maybe something's come over her since Clete passed on. Maybe she's finally learning to appreciate him, now that it's too late."

"Yes, and maybe she's having a high old time with poor Clete's money and what's fifteen dollars?"

"For me it's a lot of money when I think of how much you have to have in capital to get fifteen dollars' income."

"How much?" said Marietta.

"Well, fifteen dollars is three hundred dollars at five per cent."

"Yes, I guess it is," said Marietta. "It doesn't seem like much, does it, to only get fifteen dollars from three hundred."

"You don't get anywhere near that much from the bank."

"You hear about so many that are making money hand over fist in the stock market. Oughtn't we to go in the stock market, Nan?"

"I've been thinking about it. I was always afraid to when I only had my salary and my building-and-loan."

"Well, find out more about it. You're better at business than I am. Who do you go to for advice on such matters? Who did Clete go to?"

"A fellow named Ralph Fexler."

"Who's he? I never heard of him."

"He manages the local office for Westmore & Company. That's a New York stockbroker firm. Fexler goes around with the country-club outfit. He's a young fellow in his early thirties, I'd say."

"Oh, you know him?"

"I know him to say hello to, from coming in the office. He knew me as Clete's sister. Don't worry, you'll be hearing from him."

"Clete trusted him?"

"Oh, he's honest. Westmore & Company's a big firm, and a lot of the country-club outfit buy their stocks through Fexler. He'll be around to see us one of these days."

"Maybe we're losing money by not going to see him," said Marietta.

"Well, I had the same thought, but I didn't want to say anything till things got more settled. But now don't get the idea that everything you put money in guarantees a hundred-per-cent profit. You don't hear as much about the ones that lose money in the stock market."

"Oh, I know that much."

"Well, as long as you do. It's taking a chance when you buy a stock, lamb. If I lost all my money I'm pretty sure I could get a job, but I was a head bookkeeper. I wouldn't go in too deep if I were you. A little at a time. Risk five hundred or a thousand, and if you make a profit reinvest it. If you lose it, well, you learn by experience."

"That sounds like a very sensible idea, Nan. But don't you think maybe we ought to get started? Couldn't you go to see this Fexler man?"

"Not go to see him. He has a big office all full of men smoking cigars and watching the stock market."

"Watching the stock market?"

"A blackboard with the names of the stocks, and young Jimmy Shevlin—"

"Jule Shevlin's boy?"

"Uh-huh. Young Jimmy up there marking down the latest prices with a piece of chalk. I was never inside the place, but I often had to pass it and I could see in."

"Jule Shevlin'd never let her Jimmy work in a place if it wasn't reliable."

"Oh, I said it was reliable, and Clete did business with them for years, years. But I wouldn't just walk in and ask for Fexler. I'll write him a little note and tell him we were interested. If I put up five hundred and you put up five hundred it'd only be a thousand, small potatoes to Fexler, but he knows there's more. And remember this, lamb. He's a broker, and makes a little every time whether we buy or sell. He knows that between us there's over a hundred thousand dollars, and he'd love to have us for customers. You watch. When I tell him we're interested he'll come running, even if it's only a thousand to start with."

Marietta Kelly was quite taken with Ralph Fexler. "Did you notice his complexion?" she said to Nan. "Skin like a baby's. And isn't it nice to see a young fellow wear a stiff collar these days? I noticed his hands, too. He'd hands like Monsignor's. Clete had hands like that."

"And Ray, and Bob. Maybe Jerry would have, too, but a carpenter gets his hands banged up with a hammer, I guess," said Nan. "Anyway, we're in the stock market, lamb. Is it a thrill for you? It is for me."

"I feel as if it was the first day of school and Mom bought me a new dress," said Marietta.

They made money: their thousand-dollar investment grew to fifteen hundred in a year's time—"Makes bank interest look sick," said Nan—and along the way they learned about margin trading. They also overcame their shyness about sitting in the big room surrounded by men smoking cigars watching Jimmy Shevlin. One day Marietta was offered a cigarette by a man sitting in the next chair. "I believe I will," she said and grinned at Nan.

"So will I," said Nan Brosnan.

They added another fifteen hundred to their fund. Although their accounts were kept separate, they bought and sold the same shares in the same amounts, and calculated their winnings and losses in terms of a joint account. They were at the office of Westmore & Company nearly every day, all day, and when the market was being particularly active they had sandwiches and coffee sent in, just like the big traders among the men. They were at the Westmore office one day and heard the town fire whistle blow five times. "Five times," said Marietta. "That's the Fourth Ward, our Ward."

"Oh, good Lord," said Nan.

"What?"

"I'll be back in a minute," said Nan. She went to a telephone booth, and when she came back she was holding her hand over her breast and shaking her head. "It's our house, lamb. It's my fault. I'll pay you back, every cent."

"The fire? My house?"

"Maybe Mr. Fexler'd drive us there in his car," said Nan.

On the way to the house in Fexler's car she explained. As soon as she heard the alarm she remembered that on the way down to the office she was almost sure she'd left a cigarette burning in the kitchen. "I couldn't be altogether sure," she said. Marietta was very angry, but she did not want to say anything in front of Mr. Fexler.

"Fire must be out," said Fexler. "Here come two of the engines. The hook and ladder and the chemical."

The chief's car and another engine were standing at the curb. The house showed no damage, looked the same as usual except that the front door was open and a hose line ran from the fire plug, through the doorway, to somewhere inside the house. "Thank God," said Nan.

"Wait'll we have a look inside before thanking God," said Marietta.

"I'd be glad to wait for you ladies," said Mr. Fexler.

"No, no, that's all right. Thank you very much for being so accommodating," said Marietta.

"Well, let me know if I can be of any assistance," said Mr. Fexler.

Ed Sharp, the fire chief, was in the hall when the sisters entered. He shook his head. "Don't you know better than to leave a curling iron attached? For God's sake, if you're going to curl your hair, at least disconnect the thing when you're done with it. You got off easy this time, but—"

"How do you know it was the curling iron started it?" said Marietta.

"It's my job to know, that's how," said Ed Sharp. "Your God damn fire started in the bathroom and your God damn curling iron was the only thing hooked up. That was a dumb thing to do. Who do you insure with?"

"Joe Denny," said Marietta.

"Well, lucky he's a friend of yours."

"Do we get the insurance?"

"If it was up to me you wouldn't, anybody that would do a dumb thing like that. You got all that money, why don't you spend some of it on a permanent wave? Yeah, you'll get your insurance, this time. But I hope they make you pay double after this."

"Who discovered the fire, Ed?" said Nan Brosnan.

"The woman next door. Schrope. She noticed the smoke coming out the bathroom window, and she knew there was nobody home. Nobody home, I'll say. Nobody home." He made a revolving-wheel gesture with his finger over his ear. "Ten more minutes and this house would have been a vacant lot."

In her total humiliation Marietta could extract some consolation from the fact that even if the insurance company refused to pay, she had made enough money in the stock market to cover the damage. It was not as easy as that to take the blame away from Nan and assume it herself. "Well, why don't you say it? Say it was my fault," said Marietta.

"It could have been mine," said Nan. "I feel just as guilty."

"Like hell you do. You're standing there telling yourself I blamed you and all along it was my fault. Well, what if it was my fault? What's to stop me from putting a match to my own house if that's what I wanted to do?" Aloud, but to herself she added: "We ought to had the whole house rewired years ago. Luke was right." Then, to Nan she said: "Would you be willing to chip in to have the whole house rewired?"

"Well, being's you don't charge me any rent, sure. But why do we put money in this house? Why don't you sell it instead of putting good money in it?"

"And live where?"

Nan shrugged her shoulders. "Depends. An apartment is big enough for just the two of us. Or, if you want to splurge, we could buy a house on Oak Road."

"Oak Road," said Marietta. "Oh, if we could get back Clete's house, wouldn't that be delicious, Nan? Nan, we're rich. The two of us worked hard all our lives. Aren't we entitled to enjoy ourselves with the time we got left?"

"Clete's house has gone up since we sold it. But we might be able to get it back, if we offered that young couple a quick two or three thousand profit. How high would you want to go? They paid twenty-eight thousand. We could offer them thirty."

"I'll go to thirty-five! It's an investment, isn't it?"

"Well—nobody's going to refuse a seven-thousand-dollar profit on a twenty-eight-thousand investment. That comes to a twenty-five-per-cent profit in less than two years. If you want it that much, it's all right with me. But there we get into a legal problem. Who takes title to it? You, or me?"

"I will. I have more money than you have."

"Oh. You want to buy the whole thing yourself?"

"As I think it over, yes. I'm not crowding you out, Nan, but I think I ought to be the one to own the house, and maybe you wouldn't object to paying me a little rent."

"Like for instance, how much?"

"What did you pay at Bess Stauffer's?"

"I paid Bess fifteen a week for my room and breakfast and supper. That's sixty a month, seven-twenty a year. You wouldn't have any trouble getting a mortgage."

"Well, what do you think of the idea?"

"Well, it isn't what I started out thinking about, but maybe it's better for all concerned," said Nan.

"You'll always have a home with me, Nan. You know that," said Marietta.

Lawyer Phillips strongly advised against it, but within two months the purchase had been made and the sisters took up residence in the house their brother had built. "They must be crazy," their friends said. But even Lawyer Phillips was forced to admit that luck was on their side. A woman paid ten thousand dollars for Luke Kelly's old house and immediately converted it into six apartments. "Maybe that's what you should of done," said Nan. "She's going to have between two and three hundred a month from Luke's house."

"I'm satisfied," said Marietta. "I'm not out of pocket, and I own Clete's house. That's the real satisfaction, us living in Clete's house. Wait till Ellen hears that. Us sitting in her chairs. Can you still play the piano, Nan?"

"I guess I could pick it up again if I practiced."

"Have a few lessons. I'll make you a present of them," said Marietta.

"No, I wouldn't take lessons at my age, but I'll practice and see if it comes back to me. I'll buy some music at the five-and-ten."

"You practice your piano, and do you know what I'm going to do? I'm going to practice how to drive a car."

"Are you going to buy a car?"

"I am. An Essex coop. I told Jim Denny if I could learn to drive inside of a month, I'd buy one. I start tomorrow. Living out here one of us has to learn to drive a car, and I know you wouldn't care to."

"I might. I'm not as afraid of them as I used to be."

"Then so much the better. When Jim takes me for my lesson, you come along."

"No, you learn and I'll watch you."

"Yes, I can practically drive now, from watching Luke. He wouldn't let me drive, because the Dodge belonged to the store, but he showed me how everything worked. I understand the gearshift is different in an Essex, but the general idea is the same."

"You'll learn in no time," said Nan.

She began to feel deserted already. She would never learn to drive a car, and her eyesight was so bad that if anything happened to her glasses she would not be able to see the radiator cap. No matter what Marietta said to reassure her, Nan Brosnan felt far less at home in Clete's house than she had in Luke's. It was not only the mere act of paying rent in Clete's house—which she had not done while living at Luke's. Nan enjoyed spending money when she had it to spend. But her first mention of a house on Oak Road was a chance remark, not intended to interest Marietta specifically in Clete's house. She had not gone to the house very often while Clete was alive, not nearly as often as Marietta and Luke had been. The married couples had made a pretense of conviviality in the early years of Clete's marriage, partly because it was the right thing to do, and partly because Ellen had bought some, but not all, of her furniture through Luke, which meant a small commission for Luke even at reduced prices. In a sense every article of furniture in the house meant something to Marietta, either as a chair that had been bought through Luke, or a rug that Ellen had bought at Wanamaker's, and thus an item that contributed to Marietta's hatred of Clete's wife. There was little in the house that Marietta did not, as it were, know personally. In the final two years of Clete's life, when Ellen was supposed to be carrying on with the manager of the hotel, nothing new was added to the house furnishings. But Nan was accustomed to living in surroundings that had been chosen by other women: her mother, Bess Stauffer, Marietta, and now Ellen Brosnan. In what would soon be fifty years she had never bought so much as a footstool for herself, and now that she could afford to furnish a whole house she had neither the inclination nor an established taste to express in purchases of sofas and tables and draperies. For more than thirty years she had been making her neat little figures in ledgers, under lighting conditions that were not of the best, and now if she took off her glasses a picture on the wall was only a blurred square outline.

"Jim Denny says I'll be driving in a week," said Marietta, returning from her first lesson.

"Then we can start going to Westmore's again," said Nan.

"Well, I don't know about that, Nan," said Marietta. "Do you want to?"

"Don't you?"

"Well, we don't have to, you know. And I don't think it looks right, two women going there every day."

"We've been doing it, and we weren't the only women there."

"No, we weren't, but I don't have to tell you who one of the women was."

"But we never had to sit near her, and she never tried to get friendly or anything."

"No, and a good thing she didn't. But she was there every day and for a long time we didn't even know who she was. But believe you me, all the men knew. The worst madam in the county."

"Well, there was old Mrs. Lucas, she went every day."

"As queer as Dick's hatband," said Marietta.

"And Sylvia Levy."

"Yes, but always with her husband. Levy was there most of the time, but she only came up a little while in the morning and just before the market closed. I don't want to start going every day."

"Why? Since we're living on Oak Road?"

"All right, yes. Since we're living on Oak Road. We're not on a party line here, Nan. If Ralph has anything to tell us, like for instance a margin call, he can get us here almost as quick as if we were there in the board room."

"We can't be watching the board from here."

"Well, if you miss it that much, I'll take you down every day, but I won't promise to stay."

"What are you going to do?"

"I don't know, but one sure thing I'm not going to spend the whole day sitting in Westmore's office."

"Why don't you join the country club and learn to play golf?"

"Well, I'll tell you this much, sitting around a board room all day isn't going to get us in any country club."

"You and I could sit on the *steps* of the country club and they wouldn't ask us in if it rained kangaroos. If that's what you're thinking."

"Nan, we don't have to have a fight over this. If you want to go, I'll take you down in my car. And I'll bring you back in the afternoon."

"I can walk down to Market Street and take the trolley, and I can take the trolley home, thanks just the same."

So it came about that for a few weeks Nan Brosnan every morning boarded the trolley, spent four or five hours at Westmore & Company's office, and took the trolley home. She went stubbornly, hop-

ing that with the renewal of the habit the zest would return. But
without Marietta it was not fun. It was only business. Work. And
often there were stretches of hours at a time when nothing happened
that was of interest to her financially. The men who once had made
casual conversation now no longer chatted with her in that way they
had of talking about the market while never taking their eyes off the
board. Now they would bid her the time of day, but without Marietta
she was left alone. Marietta was not very pretty; the most that could
be said for her was that she was vivacious and had good legs. But
whatever she had to offer, in the board room it was what had im-
pelled the men to stop for a chat.

On a Friday afternoon Nan Brosnan made up her mind to discon-
tinue her visits to Westmore & Company. She got off the trolley and
walked up the hill to Oak Road. The garage was empty, and she let
herself in the front door. She was tired, and some of her weariness
was caused by apprehension. Marietta had not stopped being cross
with her. Her decision to abandon the trips to Westmore's was a
victory for Marietta, but nothing pleased Marietta.

In the livingroom Nan took off her shoes and started to go to the
kitchen, but she made only one step and the rug slipped away. For
the briefest moment she had a sense of exhilaration while both feet
were in the air, and even at the very moment that her leg was breaking the pain was slower in coming than her understanding of what
was happening to her. The pain came fully and strong and she forced
herself to look at her leg, just above the ankle, where blood was
coming. "Mother Mary, Mother of Jesus, let me die," she said. "Get
me out of here." Her prayer was not answered.

The Bucket of Blood

The place had several nicknames before Jay bought it and it more or less permanently became Jay's. Once it had been known as the Bucket of Blood, a name that did not stick because it was not really all that tough, and because there already was another Bucket of Blood in another part of town that deserved that name. The original, genuine Bucket of Blood was in one of the Italian sections of town, a neighborhood known as the Gravel Hole, that was entirely populated by the families of day laborers who worked on the navvy gangs for the railroads. They were miserably poor, scorned by the Italian grocers and fruiterers and barbers and cobblers, and so feared by the town police that they ignored everything that went on in the Gravel Hole. "Let them settle it among themselves," was the attitude. When there was a Black Hand War, which would break out every two or three years, and word of a homicide would leak out of the Gravel Hole, the town police would notify the State Constabulary, who were good cops and among whom were men who spoke Italian, some of whom were themselves Italian. The staties would put on civilian clothes and drive to the Bucket of Blood, which was the first building at the north end of the Gravel Hole and considered to be the deadline for outsiders. In a couple of hours the staties would usually come out with a prisoner, and he was usually the murderer. If they did not get the right man it was because the guilty party had had time to hop a coal train and get out of town. The only outsiders who were tolerated in the Gravel Hole were Father Guglielmo, the pastor, and Dr. Malloy, who spoke Italian, but even Dr. Malloy carried a gun. Other outsiders who had business in the Gravel Hole would have to wait on the steps of the Bucket of Blood, and sometimes that was as far as they got.

That was the original Bucket of Blood, and to give the name to Jay's place was rather unfair, although not entirely so. Jay's offered

New Yorker (25 August 1962); *The Cape Cod Lighter*

whiskey, beer, and, in the winter, a place to come in out of the cold. You could not get a sandwich at Jay's; the only edibles were bowls of salted peanuts on the bar and on the tables in the two back rooms. Jay had an alarm clock on the back bar and on the wall a large Pennsylvania Railroad calendar, showing a passenger train coming out of the Horseshoe Curve. Otherwise the saloon was devoid of decoration; there was no name on the windows, not even a ladies' entrance sign on the side door.

The neighborhood was as rough as any in town except the Gravel Hole. Within two blocks were four whorehouses, all owned by the same unmarried couple but differing in price and clientele and in the youth and beauty and cleanliness of the staff. The tracks of the Reading Railway ran parallel with the street, behind a fence which was broken by gates opening for spurs of track that led into warehouses and lumber yards. There were two blacksmith shops and half a dozen garages in the neighborhood, an old factory that was used as a drop by the beer mob, and such small businesses as a welder's shop, the shop of a man who repaired band instruments, a tinsmith's, a plumber's, and the headquarters of other artisans who had to make a lot of noise by day and went home quietly at night. No one had any legitimate business in Jay's neighborhood after seven in the evening, and the municipality spent very little money in lighting up the area. When darkness came the visitors to the neighborhood were there to drink or hire a woman, or both, and if they could have paid for better whiskey or better women, they would have been some place else. Nevertheless Jay managed to keep out of serious trouble.

He began by letting it be quickly known that he gave good value. He would explain how he cut his booze to anyone who asked, and he made a point of calling it booze in the aggregate and an individual drink he called a steam. Alcohol, caramel, and water were the principal ingredients of his booze, and he charged twenty-five cents for a shot in a two-ounce glass that he filled to the brim. He drank it himself out of the same bottle he poured for the customers, and he drank moderately but steadily all night long. "The party I get my white from, my alcohol, he knows I drink it myself," he often said. "If he wants me to stay in business, he gotta give me good stuff." The house bought generously; if two men were drinking together, the house bought every third round; if there were six at a table in the back room, the house bought the seventh drink. Nearly everyone could establish credit after a third or fourth visit to Jay's, and he would carry a heavy drinker even though he knew the customer had exhausted his credit elsewhere. But he made no effort to hide his preference for booze drinkers over the customers who drank beer. "I can't help it if the beer comes to me with ether in it. That's the way it comes. I'd have to charge a man a half a check for a good glass of beer, supposing I could get it in the first place. I bet you if you went to every joint in town right now, this minute, you wouldn't be able to find a barrel of real beer. Maybe the Elks. I understand they get delivery, but you have to be an Elk or with an Elk. I'm talking about where an ordinary fellow can go in and order a glass of beer, pay ten, fifteen cents for it. What they do at the breweries, they make good beer, then they take the alcohol out of it to stay out of trouble with the law. Then they get word that it's okay to make a shipment, and they quick needle it with ether. So a man comes in my place and drinks ten or fifteen beers and he's putting away a lot of ether. Bad for the disposition. I get more trouble out of my beer drinkers than I do out of my booze drinkers. They get sleepy and they try to stay awake and all they get is disagreeable. I'll tell you something else. Nine times out of ten a man don't know the difference between near beer and good beer. Nine times out of ten. If they want the taste of beer, they ought to drink Bevo. If they want a belt out of it, they ought to drink a boilermaker. I don't make a nickel out of my beer drinkers, but I have to accommodate them. Most of them don't have no place else to go, and I can't be so choosy."

Jay was *formal* with his beer trade. He gave them no cause for complaint; he was polite to them, and he would listen, hear them out, when they tried to hold him with conversation; but when he bought them a beer he would not drink with them, and when they tried to buy him a beer he would say, "That's all right," or "No thanks, it bloats me." But he would drink steam after steam with his booze customers, and he was such a little man to have that capacity. He was in his middle thirties, but already the upper half of his thin little face was shaded blue and his eyes were teary. He would lift a shot glass, take a breath, knock back the liquor, stare straight ahead as it went down, take another breath, and plunge the glass in the rinsing tank. He never said so, but he wanted and needed every drink. He seemed grateful for the company of booze drinkers, and he was; he had a personal superstition against taking a drink by himself. He respected solitary drinking in others; that was how some men preferred to drink. But he knew that he was in control of his own drinking only so long as he could make a rule about it and stick to it. The booze was there, gallons of it, and one little nip more or less would not do him any harm, but if it meant breaking his rule it could be, would be, the sign that he had lost control, and no one had ever seen him in that condition. Well, no one in this town.

Jay's last name, Detweiler, was fairly common in the town. There

was a Detweiler a butcher in the west end of town; Detweiler Brothers had a furniture store and undertaking parlor on the main drag,
out of the high-rent district; Clara Detweiler taught French in the
public high school; Billy Detweiler had had half a season at third
base with Reading, in the International League, before breaking his
leg; Isaac Detweiler was janitor and night watchman of the Citizens
Bank, a former fifer with the Spanish-American War Veterans Fife &
Drum Corps. There had been Detweilers in the town for seventy-five
years, and they had paid their bills and minded their own business,
attended the Lutheran or the Reformed church, and they were respected. Jay had no idea of their existence when he arrived in town,
nor had he had any intention of getting off the train. He was on his
way to a county fair sixty miles away to join a carnival show in the fall
of 1919, when he was stricken with acute appendicitis. The conductor put him off the train at the first town that had a hospital, having
wired ahead to have an ambulance meet the train. The appendix
ruptured while Jay was riding to the hospital and he nearly died of
peritonitis. It was inferred from papers in his pockets that he was
some connection of the local Detweiler family, and he became temporarily the beneficiary of all those years of respectability. He was in
the surgical ward for three weeks, a free patient, and by the time he
was able to convince the hospital people that he was not a Detweiler
of Gibbsville and that the eighteen dollars in his pocket was all the
money he had in the world, he had also made a good impression
with his courage and appreciation for everything that was done for
him.

"What are you going to do when you get out of here? You're going
to have to wear a belt for six months, maybe a year," said the doctor.

"A belt? What kind of a belt?"

"A surgical belt. You won't be able to do any heavy work. Not that
you have been, judging by your muscles."

"No, I always stayed away from that, if I could."

"But you spent a lot of time outdoors."

"I sure did, Doc. I sure did."

"What *do* you do?"

Jay smiled. "Well, I didn't exactly lie to you, but I didn't exactly
tell you the truth either. I told you I was a salesman. Well, I sell, but
I don't sell carpet sweepers or kitchen cabinets. I'm a pitchman."

"A pitchman. Oh, yes, I've heard of that. With a side show, a
carnival."

"That's correct, sir."

"Three-card monte and that sort of thing?"

"Well—if necessary."

"Hasn't been very profitable for you. You didn't have very much money on you when you were admitted."

"I was on my way to Bloomsburg, to the Fair. I had a job waiting for me with a friend of mine, but he don't know where I am. But I'll get in touch with him. He has an address in New York City."

"How old are you, Detweiler?"

"I'm just turned thirty."

"Just turned thirty. Why don't you turn honest? You seem like an intelligent fellow, and I guess you have to be sharp-witted to make a living in your profession, if I can call it that."

"And quick on your feet."

"I'll bet. You're quick with the booze, too, aren't you?"

"It's a weakness of mine."

"Yes, and I know what the other one is, too."

"How could you tell that? I'm clean as a whistle."

"The tattooing."

"Oh, Norma. Christ, that was in Muncie, Indiana, a long time ago. I'll bet she weighs a ton by now. Undying love. Well, she got J.D. tattooed on her rump. Not very big, about a half an inch high. She wanted it, I didn't ask her. But she couldn't have it too big. She done the dance of the seven veils and she had to cover up my brand with makeup, working. Norma. I was twenty years of age and I guess if she leveled with me she was thirty. The first real woman I ever had. Gave me up for a knife thrower, Captain Jack Montague. Johnny Muntz was the real handle, but I let him be Jack Montague, he was awful handy with them shivs."

"You're going to need some money. What do you plan to do?"

"I'm going to pay back this hospital. And you."

"You don't owe me anything. I'm on surgical duty. But you're expected to pay the hospital for medicines. Your belt."

"That I intend to. I'll work here, an orderly, till I'm off the nut. Of course what I could do, you give me a deck of cards and let me go upstairs where the rich patients are."

"Wouldn't *that* be nice?"

"No, I wouldn't do that here. You people here saved my life. Just give me a cot to sleep on and my scoff, my three meals a day, and I'll work as long as they say till I'm in the clear. Meantime I can get in touch with my buddy through *Billboard* and maybe he has something lined up. I can put the arm on him for a little walking-around money, *if* he answers my letter."

"You can't be an orderly. Too much lifting, and a lot of things you'd have to learn. But maybe you could run an elevator, something of that sort."

"It's a funny thing. I want to get out of here, but all the same I got a feeling for this place. I was ready to cash in, wasn't I?"

"Yes, you were."

"I come to in the ambulance, heard that bell ringing and I got it through my head, that nurse, never seen me before, nobody ever seen me before, but they're doing all they can for me. Then I guess the thing popped, huh? And the next I remember I was in a bed with clean sheets. Thirsty! God, I was thirsty. For water, not booze. Water. And I hurt good . . . That conductor, *he* was a nice fellow. *He* went to a lot of trouble. You know, Doc, I had him pegged for a mark. I only had eighteen bucks in my kick, and we don't generally take a risk with railroad conductors, but this guy I was gonna make a pitch. And then what'd he do? He saved my life."

"Well, young fellow, think about it."

"I do."

"Because it's something to think about. These were all people that you call marks. Easy marks, I guess that means. But one after another they helped save your life. You should have seen the pus in your belly. So do think about it, Detweiler, and stop being a wisenheimer."

Jay, seated in a white enameled iron chair, ran the elevator, worked off his debt to the hospital and made himself agreeable to the staff and patients. They were sorry to see him leave, but he had located the crap game that is to be found in every town the size of Gibbsville. In his cake-eater clothes, now not fitting him too well, he was obviously neither a cop nor a muscle man, and he was admitted to the game. He quickly identified the professionals in the game, and he bet their way; right when they bet right, wrong when they bet wrong. He was not interested in handling the dice himself and he passed up his turn; but he nursed his $10 case money until he had won $100, and then quietly departed. He was followed into the alley, and he knew it. He suddenly stopped and turned. "Get any closer and I'll rip your gut," he said.

"I ain't after your dough. I want to talk with you."

"You can talk standing in front of the restrunt, around the corner."

"All right, I'll meet you there."

The stranger, whom Jay recognized from the crap table, led the way to the Greek's all-night restaurant, which lighted up the sidewalk. He offered Jay a cigarette, which Jay declined.

"I oughtn't to smoke either. I just got out of the hospital, too."

"I don't remember you," said Jay.

"I be surprised if you did. You want to make a couple dollars?"

"Always do, but first who *are* you?"

"My name is Bartlett. Red Bartlett. I live here in town."

"Doing what?"

"Well, this and that."

"Like time? You done a little time, I know that much."

"Yeah, I been in the cooler. Nothing big. Breaking and entering. Assault and battery. I guess you done a couple of bits yourself."

"Uh-huh. I was hung for murder, and I did twenty years for holding up a stagecoach. What do you want, fellow?"

"I seen the way you were playing them dice. You look to me like a fellow was trying to get enough to leave town."

"And you got a proposition that me and you go in it together, we cut it up, and I leave town."

"You're pretty cute," said Bartlett.

"I'm cuter than that. They don't pin it on you, but they pin it on me because I blow town. Mister, I just as soon they didn't see me talking to you, anybody as dumb as you are."

"Six or seven hundred dollars, your end. Five, anyway."

"Listen, God damn you, I wanted to blow this town tomorrow, and now I can't. A thick-headed son of a bitch like you, you're gonna go ahead with this, whatever it is, and now I gotta stay. I gotta stay, and I gotta be able to account for every minute. You son of a bitch, I wish I never saw you. Goodnight, mister." Jay entered the restaurant and sat at the counter, drinking coffee and eating the bland filler of custard pie, until daylight. He went to his rooming house, carefully reminding the landlady of the time in case questions should be asked later. The precaution was unnecessary: at four o'clock in the morning Bartlett had already been shot and killed while resisting arrest during the burglary of Detweiler Brothers furniture store-undertaking parlor. It was a Saturday night, the beginning of the month, when installment payments were due, and there was more than $4,000 in the strongbox to be banked on Monday morning. Bartlett had once worked as a helper on Detweilers' delivery van, and even then had been fired for clumsiness.

Jay went back to the crap game that afternoon and watched it for a while without playing. It was a different game. The night before it had been professionals and working men with the gambling itch; today it was high school kids, the easiest kind of marks but the worst kind of trouble makers, who rightly suspected each other of using the tees, the miss-outs and plain ordinary loaded dice. Bad news. The house collected a nickel a pass, and the professionals stayed out of the game, waiting while one or two of the kids became big winners and cleaned out the small bankrolls, Mom's money from the sugar bowl. The professionals sat against the wall, staring at the caps of their shoes until they heard a kid say, "I'm shooting five dollars. Five dollars open here." The professionals jumped down from their high wire chairs; the men had been separated from the boys.

Soon the game resembled that of the night before, with the appearance of the winners from the night before and the losers who had promoted new bankrolls.

"Two to one no six," said a man.

"He sixes," said Jay, and he was back in the game. It was a long evening, less profitable than the previous one, but when at last he was $50 ahead on the night, he quit. Once again he was followed into the alley, this time by two men who immediately took him by the arms. They were two of the men he had identified as professionals. "Where we going?" said Jay.

"Up the street."

"Where up the street?"

One man laughed. "They call it the Bucket of Blood."

"And what happens there?" said Jay.

"We have a couple of shots," said the man.

"Out of a gun, or a bottle?" said Jay.

"Oh, a bottle. Why did you say a gun?"

"My little joke," said Jay.

"Maybe we'll throw you in front of a train, but we don't carry a gun."

Immediately Jay broke loose. "Well, I carry this," he said. He backed away, and they could see his knife, which he held as though he were shaking hands with it. "One of you gets it for sure, right up the gut," he said.

"Cut it out, Detweiler. We got business to talk."

"Like throwing me in front of a train. Lousy bastards."

"That was kidding. We both got guns, if we'd of wanted to knock you off."

"And I'm a cop," said the less talkative of the men.

"A cop?"

"You should of known that."

"A town cop?"

"A town cop. Put away that sticker and we go have a drink. Go on back to the dice game and ask anybody if I'm not a cop. Chapman, my name is."

"What kind of cops do they have in this town?" said Jay. "You *are* a cop. I can tell it now, but I didn't before."

"You're a sick man, Detweiler," said Chapman. "The two of us could make a run for it and I could shoot you as quick as I gave it to Bartlett."

"You gave it to Bartlett?" said Jay.

"Yeah."

"Who's this other fellow?" said Jay.

"Me? You heard them say my name. Dave Bangs."

"I know both your names, but what do *you* do, Bangs?"

"I hustle a buck," said Bangs.

"This town is wider open than I thought," said Jay.

"This town ain't wide open, only a couple streets," said Chapman. "You satisfied now, or do we run and shoot?"

"I'll say one thing about this town. It got the coldest-blooded cop I ever run up against. All right, buy me a drink."

The whiskey was so bad that Jay was almost afraid to finish his drink even after he had diluted it with water. "My first since I got out of the hospital," he said.

"The beer's even worse," said Chapman. "I'll send you around a couple of pints of drug-store rye tomorrow."

"Make it the first thing in the morning," said Jay. "Tomorrow's get-away day for me."

"Well, maybe. Listen to us first," said Chapman.

"Listening," said Jay.

"I owe you a favor, Detweiler. When I seen you talking to Bartlett I figured he was ready for something. What, I didn't know, but it was pretty near time he needed money."

"Where were you when I was talking to Bartlett?"

"Across the street. I follied you out in the alley. I seen you pull the toe-jabber on him, too. You know how to use that thing, don't you?"

"Now that I'm talking to a cop I gotta watch what I say."

"All right," said Chapman.

"This here guy's the smartest detective on the force," said Bangs.

"Out of how many?" said Jay.

"Two," said Chapman. "But last night didn't take much brains. You gave Bartlett a no, and all I had to do was hang on to him. I no sooner saw which way he was headed than I knew where he was going to."

"Tell me some more about how smart you are, Chapman. How did you know I wouldn't go in with Bartlett?"

"Well, I heard you call him a son of a bitch. Your voice carries, for a little fellow. Secondly, why should a smart little guy like you go in with a dumbhead like Bartlett? What was the percentage for you?"

"Yeah. He said my take would be five or six hundred. I understand there was close to five thousand dollars at the furniture store. He was a muttonhead, all right."

"He sure was. I went to school with him till fifth grade, he never got no further. They had him in Glen Mills for a couple years—"

"What's Glen Mills?"

"Reformatory. He come out of there worse than he went in. Strong as an ox, but used to beat up his old lady, a scrubwoman over at the Pennsy station. Kids with paper routes. A hooker down the street, she had him arrested for a. and b. He broke into a couple stores and we sent him up on one. He was what you call a habitual criminal, and if he ever had a hundred dollars in his pocket, I doubt it. Maybe a hundred, but I'll bet he never had two."

"Never two," said Bangs.

"No, I don't think he did either," said Chapman. "He said to me, the time I put the collar on him, he said, 'I'm gonna excape outa here. Excape. And I'm gonna come down and kick your brains out.' You know what? The warden told me Bartlett was a model prisoner, so model that he *liked* it up on the hill, and I wanta tell you something. Our county jail ain't one of your model prisons. They got rats up there the size of a fox terrier. I was up there one day and I seen a rat this big right on top of the warden's desk. I shot it. The warden was sore as hell, but I don't want to be in the room with a rat that big."

"And Bartlett was even bigger," said Jay.

"Yeah, Red was bigger. But not as smart. How smart are you, Detweiler?"

"Ah, now comes the pitch," said Jay. "Well, I been known to have two hundred dollars in my pocket. Maybe three. Maybe four. But there's a lot of guys smarter than me. Maybe if I was a little smarter I would have been a detective."

"Uh-huh. It's gonna take a week or ten days, but we'll find out how smart you were."

"What's the capital of Michigan?" said Jay.

"Michigan? Detroit, I guess. Why?"

"Illinois?"

"Well, I know it ain't Chicago," said Chapman. "Springfield? Why?"

"The capital of Michigan is Lansing, and you're right about Springfield. That's where the records are kept, and that's what you want to do, isn't it? Find out if they have a sheet on me? They have. But why should I save you the trouble? That's what they pay them clerks for."

"Illinois we know about. You did a year and a day in Joliet, assault with deadly weapon or something like that. We got an answer from Illinois. That was where your sharpie suit came from, Illinois. Some little town. The hospital reported you to us. New York State you're in the clear. Pennsylvania you're in the clear. You had eighteen bucks on you when you went in the hospital, and you were headed for the Bloomsburg Fair. I could run you in now and fingerprint you if I wanted to."

"But you won't, because you want something."

"Yep. You know who owns that crap game, and the joint we were playing in?"

"Well, I thought it was Jerry, the house man. But you ask me the question like that, who does own it? You? You and Bangs?"

"I and Bangs, we both got our fifty percent," said Chapman.

"Nice," said Jay.

"Yeah, but it's all I get. I don't take another nickel. I don't get to collect from the hookers. The saloons. The ordinance violations. Carnivals. Circuses. Taxi companies. Fortune tellers. All the other poolrooms in town. If you started another dice room in town, I'd close you up inside of fifteen minutes. But if you wanted to open up a saloon you'd have to see someone else."

"Well, that's the way it should be. Nobody gets too greedy. And the mayor and them, I guess they cut themselves in on your take," said Jay.

"That's none of your business, Detweiler."

"Right, it isn't," said Jay. "Well, wuddia got in mind for me?"

"We're looking for a man to take Jerry's job, and we gotta have one right away. Jerry got consumption and they're sending him to the sanitarium. The way I see it, winter's coming. That's your worst time of the year, but it's our best. When it's cold weather we got fellows waiting for tables to shoot pool, eleven o'clock in the morning to midnight. We make good money off the pool tables. But the big money, naturally that's the dice room. Payday at the mines. Payday out at the steel mill. And you know who's good for a bundle every week?"

"No."

"These traveling orchestras. Every week beginning October to April they get a famous jazz orchestra, famous ones that make Victrola records, one right after the other. They all like to shoot dice."

"And what you don't get, the hookshops do. I know them traveling orchestras," said Jay. "Do you handle muggles?"

"Them marijuana cigarettes? No, that's handled by a fortune teller and one of the hack drivers. Or there's a doctor on Lantenengo Street, if you got the right send-in. Nose candy. The needle. That's pretty quiet around here. Not much call for it except the hookers."

"And Jerry."

"Yeah, Jerry. Cocaine."

"And Dave, here," said Jay.

"Not me," said Dave.

"Have it your own way," said Jay.

"How about you?" said Chapman.

"Not so far, but there's no telling. Is that why you're giving Jerry the boot?"

"Partly. But he has consumption, too," said Chapman.

"He looks it. In other words, he was stealing too much."

"A little too much, yeah. You don't mind a little, but Jerry all of a sudden began stealing ten-fifteen dollars a day."

"A broad," said Jay. "Most likely some broad he was paying for her dope."

"What makes you think I took it?" said Dave.

"Yeah, we're back to that," said Jay. "Well, I guess I knew over a hundred men and women that took it."

"Were you ever wrong?" said Chapman.

"I been wrong."

"And you could be lying, too. I mean about you not taking it," said Chapman.

"I could be lying, but I'm not. It'll come to that, maybe, but my weakness is the booze. That I admit. Even this lousy rat-gut, now I started, I want another. What's the job, and what does it pay?"

"Fifty a week. You're house man. The pool tables, we got a kid racking up and shooting for the house. The dice game, you don't handle the dice. That is, you don't play. You collect on every pass, and a guy craps out, you say who gets the dice. And you keep the game honest."

"How honest?"

"Well, the dice have to hit the board on every roll or it's no dice."

"That's not what I meant."

"I know what you meant. There's two guys you never take the dice away from."

"Dave is one," said Jay. "And a fellow named Sol Green."

"That's correct. Anybody else you get suspicious, you change the dice. But not Dave, and not Sol."

"What if there's trouble? A chump starts a fight?"

"Usually it's an out-of-town guy that starts a fight. If I ain't there, Dave and a couple our friends can handle it. I don't want you pulling that toe-jabber unless the guy goes for you. But the way we handle a squawker, the first thing we do is get him out in the alley. Stop the game, and get that guy out in the alley."

"What about them kids?"

"There's a kid named Lefty Permento, they're all scared of him. We give him ten bucks a week and he shoots pool for free. An ugly bastard, but he sure likes to fight."

"Fifty dollars a week," said Jay. "Should I have a talk with Jerry and see how much I can steal?"

"Don't steal too much. Remember, this is all I got except my hundred and twenty a month from the police department. And it's *all* Dave got."

"And I'm there all day and all night," said Dave.

"Yeah, what are *my* hours?" said Jay.

"You come on at six o'clock. Very seldom you're there after ha' past one, two o'clock in the morning. Saturday and Sunday afternoon, you come on around one. You get Mondays off."

"Who does the bookkeeping?"

"We do, in our head. The Greek owns the building, we pay the rent in cash. Everything is cash. Electricity. Everything. Dave pays that stuff."

"Well, we'll give it a try," said Jay. "Say, I want to ask you—why do they call this place the Bucket of Blood?"

"Search me," said Chapman. "They got a place the other end of town, down in Little Italy. They call it the Bucket of Blood, too, but there they got reason to. This joint, I don't see how he keeps going."

"Who's the owner?"

"The fellow tending bar, Matt Hostetter. He's on his last legs, too. And yet when I was a kid this place did business. My old man and all the guys from the car shops and the freight yards used to come in here. Why? You want to buy it?"

"You never can tell."

"Just don't buy it with our money," said Chapman.

"*Some* of your money," said Jay.

He ran an orderly game for Chapman and Bangs. The dice players made him prove that he knew what he was doing and what they were doing. He could be witheringly sarcastic, but generally he was good-natured and he talked continually. "The man's shooting twelve dollahs, five covered, seven dollahs open, now two dollahs open. Fi' dollahs he's right coming out, fi' dollahs he's wrong. Shoot the dice, and his point is eight. Eight's the point and it's two to one he eights for fi' dollahs and five to two no eight the hard way. And—crap it is. The dice go to Mulligan. Mulligan, your dice. The man shoots two dollahs and he's covered, and you watch Mulligan run that deuce up to sixteen thousand dollahs. Well, not this time, Mulligan, a pair of beady little eyes. But Mulligan's a dead game sport and it's two dollahs open. Two dollahs. He's wrong for five dollahs, five dollahs he's wrong coming out and—*no dice!* The money *got* to be on the table, not in the air. No ghost bets here, gentlemen. The money *got* to be on the table. That's better. All right, Mulligan, roll them."

Beginning with his first night, he held out five dollars that was due the house and on big nights he got away with ten. He ran a faster, more efficient game than Jerry had run, and he stole a great deal less. All winter he made between eighty and a hundred dollars a week; he paid his room rent punctually, subsisted largely on eggs, and kept a pint of fair whiskey always within reach. And he saved his money. When warm weather came and with it a slackening off of business, he persuaded Chapman and Bangs to close the dice game for a month except for the big paydays, and he and Chapman would make tours of the amusement parks. During intermission and after the dance was over they would get a crap game going among the touring musicians and the concessionaires, and Chapman was delighted to discover that he had not lost a nickel by closing down the indoor game. On this deal Jay and Chapman went halves, and Bangs was not in it at all. Jay encountered some old carnival acquaintances among the concessionaires, and he could always get a carnie friend to act as a shillaber. The shill would win a little money and make a noise about it, and the musicians and concessionaires and the roust-abouts would be ready to be taken. It was seldom necessary to sneak in the educated dice more than two or three times during a game, but it had to be done at precisely the right moment and under the suspicious eyes of the concessionaires. The smarter men among the concessionaires could tell when Jay and Chapman *ought* to throw in the educated dice, and they would drop out of the game temporarily, but even with this knowledge the concessionaires were never sure enough of their suspicions to risk a challenge. And most of them knew that Chapman was a cop, carrying a gun, and that Jay had done time out West for cutting up a fellow with a knife. At the end of the summer layoff, Jay had saved up nearly six thousand dollars.

"The parks all close Labor Day," said Chapman, one night when they were driving back to town.

"Yeah, nothing lasts forever," said Jay.

"You must have a pretty good little bundle."

"Pretty."

"Dave wants to get a new man," said Chapman.

"I'd be sore too, if I was Dave, but we didn't need him. He would have been a li'bility. Clumsy. If he'd of been with us I'd of spent all summer waiting for him to throw out three dice."

"He wouldn't throw out three dice. He's too good for that. But you're right, he's getting clumsy."

"Chappie?"

"What?"

"Have you got a new man?"

"Well, we talked to a fellow down at the shore. Bangs knew him before. I just as soon get rid of Bangs and go partners with you, but Bangs has the money and you don't. I don't either, you know. I ain't finished paying for my house and my wife's old lady has to have an operation."

"That's all right. A year ago this time I was almost dead. Now I'm alive and a little ahead. If I bought Matt Hostetter's would I get any help from you?"

"As long as you don't open up a dice game. And as long as you don't mean you want any money from me."

"Just a good word with the right people. Hostetter wants five thousand dollars. He's crazy, but if I offer him thirty-five hundred I think he'll sell."

"I could make him sell. Not me, but Schmidt. All I do is I say to Schmidt, put Hostetter out of business and put a real go-getter in there. You'd be better for Schmidt than old Matt is. Matt's on his last legs."

"I wouldn't want to muscle him out. That wouldn't be good for business."

"You'd be doing him a favor. You understand, though, you have to get your goods where Schmidt says."

"I'd have to talk to Schmidt about that. Hostetter's been taking anything they send him. It's a wonder they don't go blind, drinking the stuff he sells."

"Well, you work that out with Schmidt. I wish you and me could go in together, but right now Bangs has the bankroll. Why do you want to run a broken-down joint like Hostetter's?"

"I tell you why, Chappie. From Hostetter's the only way you can go is up. I'm in business for about as little money as it's possible. And the main reason, I got a place of my own. No partners, my own boss."

"Yeah, I wish I didn't have so many partners. I got Dave, I got the mayor, I got the chief of police, I got my wife, my wife's old lady, my two kids, a couple broads always asking for stocking money. Maybe you think I got it good, but if you want to know the truth of the matter, I'm in hock to Dave for over four thousand. I owe on this car, and it's two years old. My house ain't paid for. Where does it all go? I don't live high, but if I had to live on my hundred-and-twenty cop's pay, I couldn't do it. My wife says to me, quit. Quit running the dice game, she says. Where would she be if I quit? And her old lady with a private room in the hospital? Don't be surprised if one of these days I come around and put the arm on you."

"Wait till I get on my own two feet, though."

"You'll be all right. I got a feeling. I just got a feeling. Jay, I'm gonna let you off at the Greek's. I got a date with a broad. You don't have that trouble, do you? I never seen you with a broad. What do you do when you want to get your ashes hauled? Not that it's any my business."

"Sophie."

"Sophie? The waitress Sophie? At the Greek's?"

"Uh-huh."

"She's kind of big for you, ain't she?"

"You mean I'm kind of small for her? I always liked big broads, and *I* don't have to *feed* her."

"Sophie, huh? Well, wuddia know. You know who else is there, don't you?"

"Sure. Dave."

"Just so you know. He could get her fired from the Greek's, and he would in a minute. He don't like you, Jay."

"That's a pleasure. *I* don't like *him,* and I got a word of advice for you, Chappie. That's a fellow that carries his own deck. We all carry our own deck—you do, I do, we all do. But Dave is the kind of a guy, he lets you think he's Big Hearted Joe. Like you owe him that four thousand dollars. Yeah, but whose four thousand dollars? I guarantee you, that was never money he had his hands on. I'm willing to lay the odds it was money you held out on him and told him. Am I right?"

"Yeah, but I don't think you're guessing."

"That's all I am, is guessing. Nobody had to tell me that about Dave. If you ask Dave for the *loan* of a thousand dollars, watch him try to wriggle out of it. He wouldn't like to part with money once he has it."

"You're a hundred percent right. I held out on him, once for fifteen hundred, the other time for three thousand. I told him I had the money and I was ready to give it to him but would it be all right if I held on to it. So you're right, he never had the money in his hands."

"Yeah, I met all kinds, including a lot of Daves. If you ever get the chance to get rid of him, do it. Not that you'd do a favor for me, but a favor to yourself. Well, goodnight, Chappie."

"I'll talk to Schmidt. Goodnight, Jay."

During the first week of his ownership Jay had Matt Hostetter back of the bar with him. "The new owner," Matt would say, serving a customer. At the end of the week Jay handed Matt five ten-dollar bills. "That's for the good will, Matt. Now so long, and don't ever come in here again. It's my joint, and I don't even want you for a customer."

"No hard feelings, young fellow. You treated me all right," said Hostetter. Matt went home, sat in a rocking chair, and in three months died of an embolism. Jay was among the mourners at the service in the Lutheran church and among the contributors when the hat was passed by the undertaker. Jay held a folded five-dollar bill between thumb and forefinger, suspended over the hat, and before he dropped it he said: "Three months ago he had enough to bury him."

"I guess he did, yeah. Don't know where it all went to," said the undertaker.

"Wild women, probably," said Jay.

"Oh, no. He was too old for that." The man was deeply shocked, but he took the money.

Schmidt, the cop who exercised authority over the lower-grade speakeasies, was surprisingly tractable when Jay announced he wanted to change alcohol dealers. "I'm for it," he said. "They were palming off some terrible stuff on old Matt. If somebody went blind, it'd sooner or later come back to me and it'd be my rap. You go ahead and get your alcohol where you want to. But beer, beer you have to stick with the same people. That's over my head, *I* take *my* orders on who supplies beer. And you take your orders from me. If I see you putting in some other beer, I'll come down here and close your place. That's my orders, Detweiler, so no trouble, you understand?"

"Sure," said Jay.

There was a noticeable improvement in the class of people coming in. The old customers stayed, but now the place began to attract the low-salaried white collar men who could not do without their booze; the artisans who had to have cheap whiskey; the pensioners who had nothing much left in life but the conversations and long silences they could share with other pensioners. The word had got around that Jay Detweiler served the cheapest decent drink in town. Among the new customers were a few men who were fearful of patronizing Matt Hostetter's old place, which they had always heard to be a dive for cutthroats in a neighborhood that was occupied by the most lawless element in town. But when they went to Jay's on a trial visit they found it to be not nearly so bad as they expected. The badly dressed, unshaven derelicts were there, but the place itself, though bare of beautifying features, was scrubbed clean and smelt clean; in among the beer and whiskey smells was the smell of strong soap, and the smell of disinfectant in the toilet was almost overpowering, but reassuring. The new owner, Detweiler, appeared to be rather young to be the proprietor of such a place, and he was certainly not equipped by nature to handle a fracas. He was frail and polite, and though he had a blackjack hanging on the back bar in plain sight, he seemed too agreeable as well as too fragile to be effective if trouble broke out. He wore a collar and tie and a waistcoat in which he kept fountain pen, pencils, pocket comb and a notebook. His customers were not aware that Jay had changed his style of dressing; he no longer wore his cake-eater suit, with its low-cut vest, or a string tie or striped silken shirt with a tiny, too-tight collar. He could easily be taken for a ticket seller in a railway station, standing behind his bar and dispensing his goods. After a while the timid ones enjoyed the cheap thrill of patronizing a place that was nicknamed the Bucket of Blood but that was hardly more disorderly than any hose company on a Saturday night.

The new proprietor was there every day but Sunday, from nine o'clock in the morning till one or two the next morning. On Sundays he would not open up until dark, and his customers had to do the best they could to get through the day without booze. The rest of the time Jay was at his place of business from opening to closing. At lunch time and at supper time he would have his food brought in from the Greek's by a waiter known as Loving Cup because of the size of his ears. Jay would put the tray on one end of the bar and eat the food standing up. He never licked the platter clean; he ate only because he knew how important it was for a drinking man to get some food in him.

At the end of his first year his pocket notebook showed him that he had recovered nearly half his investment. His bookkeeping was simplicity itself: it had cost him just under five thousand dollars to get going; twelve months later, after paying all his bills, including the payments to Schmidt, he had about two thousand dollars in cash, and he owned the business to boot. He refused to complicate the bookkeeping; the first year had been a gamble. He had put five thousand dollars into a game, and he came out of that game with two thousand cash, a business, and his living expenses for a year all taken care of. He had never worked so steadily and so hard in all his life, and he had never enjoyed himself so much. He was strongly tempted to give a party on the first anniversary, but decided against it; instead, he waited until midnight and then announced that thereafter until closing, all drinks would be on the house. He gave no reason except, "I just happen to feel big-hearted tonight." His custom of buying free drinks was so well established that his explanation was accepted without curiosity.

It amused him to think back over his first year and to realize that in all that time he had lived in an area that was roughly four blocks by three—squares, the town people called them. He had never so much as taken a stroll two blocks to the north, two blocks to the south of the Greek's, one block to the east of his rooming house, or one block to the west of his doctor's office. He read the town papers thoroughly and he knew what was going on, but he had not had time to look around. The area in which he had confined himself was not much larger than the area to which he had once been confined by the State of Illinois—with the great difference that when he was in the pen he had not been free to wander. Twice in his lifetime—once by a judge's sentence and the other by his own preference—he had stayed put for a year.

He had run away from his uncle's farm at fourteen, and since that time he had wandered up and down and across every state east of the Dakotas, north of Tennessee, west of Massachusetts, and south of the Canadian border. He had stayed out of the South, where the small town cops and sheriffs were said to be mean; and he had stayed out of the West because of the distances between towns. Up and down, back and forth, with circuses, carnivals, medicine shows, Chautauquas, Tom shows, and working the county fairs alone or with a companion. He had put cardboard in his shoes and newspapers under his shirt to keep warm; ridden in the caboose with a too friendly brakeman and had two teeth knocked out by a special cop on the Nickel Plate; slept in a van with a dog and pony act, and driven his own Cole Eight after a highly successful week at the Columbus State Fair. He had seen all the awful things that can occur in a circus train wreck; and he had felt the dull, sickening hatred of a "committee" in a town in southern Indiana, where a man from a previous carnival had raped a little girl. He had comforted a tent-show girl whose six-hundred-dollar boa constrictor was shot by a drunken miner in Kentucky. He had been taken for his only aeroplane ride by an Army lieutenant in Rantoul, Illinois, whom he had taught the O'Leary belt trick. He had got crabs at a fraternity house in southern Illinois and gonorrhea from a corset demonstrator in Fort Wayne. He had run twenty dollars up to sixteen thousand in a crap game in Louisville on the eve of Derby Day and was about to drag his winnings when a friend almost imperceptibly shook his head, and Jay took the motion as a signal to make one more throw. But the friend was only being bothered by an insect on the back of his neck, and the dice came up a deuce and an ace. And now, after about twenty years of knocking around, he owned his own business in a town he had never heard of two years ago.

Jay had often pondered the mysterious ways of fate. Throughout his life accident and coincidence and luck had governed his actions with the unpredictability of a pair of honest dice. To some extent you could figure the percentages; they were known. It was easier to make an eight than a nine, harder to make a five than a six. You could shake the dice noisily in your fist—a pair of honest dice—and if you were very good you could improve your percentage by little tricks, like holding one die in the grip of your little finger. But in his study of the behavior of dice he had often given them an honest shake and an honest roll, and still come up with some strange sequences. Once he had rolled fourteen (or fifteen?) four-three sevens in a row, without manipulating the dice during the shake or the roll. And he had seen experts, using his dice, roll out numerical sequences in arithmetical order from two to twelve and downward from twelve to two. You could improve your chances legitimately or semi-legitimately. But you could not always explain accident and coincidence and luck; you just had to believe in it because it was there.

If he had not been put off that train, he would have died. But he *had* been put off the train, in a strange town that was full of people who had the same last name as his own. In all his wanderings he had never met another Detweiler, and in this town there were thirty or forty of them. He still had not met any of his namesakes; he was sure they would not like to claim kinship with him. And he knew so little about his parents that he would not be able to establish—or deny— any connection with the local Detweilers. He had no recollection whatever of his father and almost none of his mother. He had been raised by her brother, always with the reminder that he was another mouth to feed, with no credit for doing a man's work from the time he was able to lift a pitchfork, and to take a man's beating before that. His uncle was named Ben Russell, and he had always called him Mr. Russell, not Uncle Ben. He had never called Ben's wife aunt. She was, if possible, harder to get along with than Ben. Even now Jay hated to see a counterman cut into a fresh pie; it reminded him of the hundreds of times Mrs. Russell had sliced a pie into six wedges for the six Russells and nothing for Jay.

Now he could cut the pie the way he wanted it—all six wedges for Jay Detweiler. Unlike Chapman, the detective, he did not consider himself in reluctant partnership with people who were essential to his business, and, also unlike Chapman, he did not regard as partners the people who were essential to his pleasures or who were dependent on him for a living. He paid a scrubwoman to keep his place clean, he paid room rent to Sadie Tupper, graft to Sergeant Schmidt, so much to the beer mob, so much to the alcohol mob. He took what he needed out of his own till, and he gave Sophie George ten dollars every Sunday.

The first sign of discontentment in his new way of living was the discovery, on awakening one Sunday morning, that he had no desire to go to Sophie's room and spend the day with her. He had desire, but not for Sophie, and in a little while he was knocking on the door of the second best of the whorehouses. It was eleven o'clock in the morning, and the door was opened by the bouncer, a booze customer of Jay's, a man known as Sport. "The girls are all asleep," said Sport. "If that's what you came for." He was in a pair of pants pulled over a union suit and his hair was uncombed. "Come in, have a cup of coffee."

"Thanks," said Jay. "When do they start getting up?"

"Well, those with their regulars, they'll be getting up any time now. A couple the girls got Sunday regulars. You ever been here?"

"No."

"I thought you weren't. I didn't remember seeing you. I wasn't sure. You want cream and sugar? I make good coffee and I like it good and sweet. They say it spoils the taste, but I say it gives a different taste. My coffee you can drink black, and it's good that way, or you can put cream and sugar in it and it's just as good, only different. All the girls here say my coffee spoils it for them when they go to a restrunt."

"It has a nice aroma," said Jay.

"That's the tip-off. If it don't have a nice aroma, it ain't gonna have a good taste. You might as well start a new batch."

"I don't want to wake up any of the girls. Ain't any of them up yet? They all asleep?"

"I'll call upstairs," said Sport. He went to the hall. "Hey, anybody up?"

"Who is it?" a woman's voice replied.

"A friend of mine," said Sport.

"I'll be down," said the woman.

"That's a girl named Jenny," said Sport. "She come here from Fort Penn a month or so ago. Good-lookin' broad. She'd pass for respectable—if you didn't look too close. She don't dress like a hooker, is what I mean. Age, maybe thirty, maybe a little younger, a little older."

The woman, wrapped in a kimono, appeared. "I smelt that coffee and it woke me up. Hello, mister."

"Hello, Jenny," said Jay.

"You want me to take him on? Can I have a cup of coffee first?"

"Well, what do you think, Jay?" said Sport.

"Fine, fine," said Jay.

"A friend of yours?" said Jenny.

"Great pal of mine," said Sport.

"As soon as I have a cup of coffee, all right?" said Jenny.

"Sure, sure," said Jay. "There's no rush."

"Sport, you're gonna have to get the doctor for Beulah. She got a pain in her stomach and the sweats."

"That sounds to me like appendicitis. I had that," said Jay.

"Can she die from it?" said Sport.

"She sure as hell can," said Jay.

"I'll say she can. I had it too. I was operated four years ago," said Jenny. "I nearly died from it."

"So did I," said Jay. "Did yours rupture?"

"I thought only men got ruptures," said Jenny.

"That kind, but appendicitis can rupture," said Jay.

"They didn't tell me anything about that," said Jenny. "I just remember I had the gripes so bad, and the sweats. Did you have to wear a belt after? I had to wear a belt and I was out of work for over two months. Went back to work too soon anyway, the doctor told me. I got a thing they call adhesions, and had to be operated again. So you better get the doctor for Beulah, Sport."

"I will. I'll call him up on the phone," said Sport.

"And don't take all day about it, or you'll wheel her out of here to the undertaker's," said Jenny.

"Keep your shirt on," said Sport.

"If she keeps her shirt on I get a reduction," said Jay.

"You're a kidder, mister," said Jenny. "Anyway, I don't have a shirt. Well, any time you're ready, I am."

Jay became a Sunday regular of Jenny's, and she became a customer of his, as much, she told him, for the conversation as for the booze. He had never encouraged Sophie George to visit his saloon, and strictly speaking he had not extended a more than casual invitation to Jenny; but he was pleased with Jenny's visits. The other women among his customers were not much different from the men; drinkers in skirts, nothing to look at, and only too well aware that they had to stay out of trouble or be barred. Jenny was welcome—so long as she too behaved herself, and didn't come in too often. That she liked Jay personally was obvious to him.

Once in a while she would drop in of an afternoon, alone or with another girl, and take only a soft drink—a "temperance," she called it. She had been shopping for a bottle of perfume, a hat, a new kimono, and she felt like chatting before going to work. "It does a person good to get a breath of fresh air," she would say. Some of the girls in her house never left the place except to go to Dr. Traff's for their weekly examinations. "Which is a laugh, the inspection he gives you," said Jenny. "But if you don't go once a week, Sport won't let you work. He's under orders, just the same as the rest of us. Oh, I guess it's some protection, for a while. Sooner or later you're going to run into hard luck, but it's the same in your business. Sooner or later you're liable to get a bad shipment and they'll all go falling out of here with the blind staggers."

"It ain't the same thing, Jenny," said Jay. "I get a report on every shipment before I mix a batch of booze. Don't forget, I drink more of this than anybody."

"Yeah, and I don't see how you do it and stay on your feet."

"I don't let it get control over me."

"It will, though," she said.

"Yeah, the odds are it will, some day," said Jay.

He liked her friendly interest in him, and it was only old-time caution and not anything she said that put him on his guard with her. It was a long time coming, half a year or more, but he was ready when she made her pitch. "I want to get out of working in a house," she said, one afternoon.

"How do you mean? You'd have a hard time working independent. You couldn't rent a room, the cops'd make it tough for you. This is a small town, Jenny."

"I know. I was thinking if you and me, the two of us lived together."

"Married, you mean?"

"Well, either way. But I could make seventy-five to a hundred a week here."

"Hustling?"

"How else? And the two of us could stash away a nice buck."

"Not a chance, Jenny."

"You got that little room back there and I notice it has a sofa."

"That's for if a man and woman don't have no place else to go," said Jay. "And they gotta be people I know. Another thing, I don't charge them. If I charged them the cops'd raise their take. You got pipe dreams, Jenny. You wouldn't make any seventy-five, a hundred a week here. Not my customers."

"Let me go to work and I'd show you."

"No," said Jay. "Oh, I ain't saying you couldn't pick up a few dollars. Any place that sells booze, it don't take a very smart hustler to make coffee and cakes. Even the old men I got coming in here, you could hustle them, but they don't have the ten dollars to spare, and you're a ten-dollar girl. Some of my old guys make a sawbuck stretch out for a whole week, and you'd take it away from them in ten minutes. No."

"I could make twenty dollars a day, six days a week."

"No dice, Jenny. The whole place'd change."

"It's nothing much now," she said.

"Not to you, maybe."

"Well what the hell are you so stuck up about it? They call it the Bucket of Blood, for God's sake."

"Not any more. They used to, but not as much."

"Why don't you give *me* a break?" she said.

"A break, yeah, but I don't want to ruin a business I built up."

"I'll give you half, Jay. I tell you what I'll do. I'll bet you five dollars I can hustle the next guy comes in, I don't care who he is or how old or anything."

"Sure you can. You can hustle me, but that ain't saying you're gonna work here."

"You're a mean little bastard. Next Sunday go some place else."

"You don't have to take it personal."

"Well, I do, see? And next Sunday, stay away. We don't have to work Sunday if we don't want to. Sunday we can have anybody we want to, and I—don't—want—you, see?"

"That's your privilege. Have a steam?"

"The hell I will, now or any other time," she said.

He was sorry to break off with Jenny, and amidst his regret was deep appreciation of the compliment to himself and to his business in her willingness to marry him. It was easy to find a woman who would marry a man with a successful business, but Jenny had been willing to be a partner, to bring to the partnership her earning ability. It was a high compliment indeed, and it made little difference whether it flattered his business or himself, since one was the same as the other. He wondered how many other Detweilers in the town had had this satisfaction.

There was no one else in the saloon, and he was pleased that that was so. He poured himself a steam and raised his glass and faced the door. "Good luck, Jenny," he said.

Winter Dance

When the big Packard Twin-Six came rumbling into view it was an exciting sight to the boy. The radiator and hood had a leather cover that was streaked with ice. Strapped to the spare tires at the rear of the car was a long-handled shovel, crusted with snow. Icicles hung from the fenders, and the running-boards carried an extra thickness of frozen slush. All the side curtains were securely in place. The windshield was solid ice except for an arc, directly in front of the chauffeur, which the manually operated wiper had kept partially clear. The heavy car moved slowly as the tire chains bit into the snow. You could not see the spokes of the artillery wheels; they were hidden by a disc of ice and snow. But the big car had made it, as it nearly always made it in spite of the winter in the mountains. Now, moving slowly along South Main Street, the car made the boy think of those trains in the far West that were drawn by two and three locomotives up and through the mountain passes. There was something triumphant and majestic now in the way the big Packard eased its way along South Main. Here it was safe and sound, the dignified winner over fifteen miles of narrow, winding mountain roads and the hazards that winter could put in its way.

The boy watched the Packard until it came to a stop ten feet from the curb but as close as it could get to Winkleman, the furrier's.

"There goes your girl, Ted."

"Aw, shut up," said the boy.

"She's stopping at Winkleman's. Why don't you go in and price his coonskins? He has a coonskin in the window."

"And a card on it saying three hundred dollars," said the boy.

"Well, ask him if he's got any for less."

"In front of her?" said the boy.

"Okay. I was only trying to be helpful."

"We could take a walk down and have a *look* at the coat," said the boy.

"And wait till she comes out? She may be all day. Go on in and try it on."

"Winkleman knows I'm not in the market for a coonskin," said the boy.

"Listen, for Christ's sake, Ted. This is your best chance to talk to her. You know where she's probably going from there."

"I know."

"You want to talk to her, don't you?"

"Sure," said the boy.

"And not with the older crowd."

"Yes," said the boy.

"Well, you won't be able to get her away from the older crowd. Even if you cut in on her, they won't let you get two steps with her."

"Shall we take a walk down to Winkleman's?" said the boy.

"Give her a few seconds to get out of the car and inside of the store."

"That's a good idea. We'll wait till she gets inside," said the boy. "But then I don't know what to say."

"Just strike up a conversation."

"That's easier said than done," said the boy. "Think of something."

"Well, just casually sidle up to her and say, 'Oh, hello, Natalie. Going to the tea dance?' And she'll say, 'Yes, are you?' "

"End of conversation," said the boy.

"Not necessarily. Ask her where she's staying tonight."

"I know where she's staying, and anyway, she'll think it's kind of fresh. It's none of my business where she's staying," said the boy.

"Well, have you got some money with you?"

"Dollar and forty, forty-five cents."

"That's enough. Ask her if she wants a hot chocolate. She just had a cold ride, and I'll bet she'd welcome a hot chocolate."

"*I've* never asked her to have a hot chocolate."

"What if you haven't? You have to start sometime, you dumb bastard. I'll bet she'd give anything for a hot chocolate. That's a cold ride, believe you me. And even if she says no, at least she'll give you credit for being considerate. My sister Kit, I've heard her say a hundred times, next to a good dancer, if a boy's considerate."

"She's liable to think I'm too young to buy her a hot chocolate. She's at least twenty."

"You have a dollar and forty cents. A hot chocolate will set you back fifteen cents. She knows fifteen cents won't break you. Maybe she won't even think of that, if she *wants* a hot chocolate. She's probably half frozen."

"No. They have one of those charcoal heaters, and sixty-five robes. It's as warm in her car as Mrs. Hofman's limousine."

"How do you know?"

"Because last year she gave us all a ride home from tobogganing."

"Natalie?"

"Well, not Mrs. *Hofman.* Huh. Fancy that, Mrs. Hofman giving us a ride in her limousine. I'd like to see *that.*"

"Well, she's inside. Now's your chance."

"I wish it was some other store," said the boy. "I don't like to go barging in Winkleman's. That's a woman's store."

"He has a man's raccoon coat in the window. And who else is going to buy a raccoon if we don't? Not my *father.* Not *your* father. Maybe Winkleman will think you're getting one for a Christmas present. *I* am, but not this year."

"Oh, I'm getting one, next year or the year after," said the boy.

"Well, then you have a good excuse."

"The only trouble is, Winkleman will start waiting on us, and then how do I get to strike up a conversation with *her?* 'What can I do for you, boys?' And then I barge over and ask her if she wants a hot chocolate. Boy, will she see through that. She'll know we followed her in, and she'll be sore as hell."

"She'll be so busy she won't pay any attention till you speak to her. Didn't you ever go shopping with a woman?"

"Oh, you know so much about everything, you make me sick."

"You're the one that makes me sick. What's the worst she can do? Chop off your head and put it on a pikestaff? The positively worst she can do is say, 'No thank you, Ted. I do not wish a hot choco-late.'"

"If I thought for sure she wanted a hot chocolate," said the boy. "Maybe she's not going to stay in there very long. By the time we get there maybe she'll be just leaving. Nobody gets to the tea dance before six. She's spending the night at Margery Hill's. If they all left at half past five, they'll be at the club around six. If she has to change her dress, that'll take her at least a half an hour. Five o'clock. I'm trying to dope out whether she's going to be in Winkleman's long enough. And anyway, maybe she's going some place else besides Winkleman's. I don't think Winkleman's is such a good idea. I'll bet she has other places to go. No, she wouldn't have time for a hot chocolate."

"Well, you're right. She's leaving Winkleman's. Let's see where she goes."

The girl in her six-buckle arctics came out of the fur shop, stepped into the snowbank and got in her car. The boy and his friend watched the big Packard moving slowly southward and turning west into Lantenengo Street. They did not speak until the car was out of sight.

"Well, you're fifteen cents ahead. Buy *me* a hot chocolate."

"You just had one," said the boy.

"I could polish off another."

"Oh, all right. Then what? Shall we start for the club?"

"Christ, it's only twenty after four."

"I have to pick up the kid sister. The old man wouldn't let me have the car unless I dragged her. *They* want to get there *early*. They *always* want to get there early."

"Yeah, they don't want to miss anything. What's there to miss before six o'clock? But what do *you* want to get there early for?"

"Because my damn kid sister wants to, and my old man said I had to," said the boy. "And I have to dance the first dance with her, and if she's left in the lurch I have to dance with her, and when she's ready to go home *we* have to go home. God damn it I wish I had my own car."

"I'm getting one when I graduate. I don't know whether I want a Ford or a Dodge."

"New or second-hand?"

"Brand-new."

"The Dodge costs more, but around here you need a Ford for the hills," said the boy.

"Yeah, but I wouldn't use it much around here. I'd use it mostly in the summer, and the Vineyard's practically all flat."

"I never thought of that," said the boy. "Well, I guess we ought to get started."

"Where's your car?"

"Henderson's Garage. The old man left it there to get new chains put on. Finish your hot chocolate. You'll get plenty at the club, free."

"It'll have skin on it. Christ, I hate skin on hot chocolate. It makes me puke."

"You're so delicate," said the boy.

"Well, do you like it?"

"No," said the boy. "But I have sense enough to drink tea."

The orchestra was playing "Rose of the Rio Grande," a fine fox trot with a melody that could just as easily have had a lyric about China, and the next tune *was* about Chinese—"Limehouse Blues." The band was just getting started, and trying to fill the dance floor.

"Stop trying to lead," said the boy.

"Oh, you stop being so bossy," said his sister. "Why are you so grouchy? Because your girl isn't here? Well, here she comes."

"Where?"

"In the vestibule. All the older crowd. Margery Hill has a new hat. Oh, isn't that becoming?"

" 'Oh, isn't that becoming?' You sound like Mother."

"And you sound like the Terrible-Tempered Mr. Bangs. Oh, hello, Ralph. Are you cutting in on my adorable brother? Teddy, dear, will you relinquish me?"

"Thanks for the dance," said the boy. He joined the stag line and lit a cigarette.

"Got a butt?"

"Hello, Jonesy. Sure," said the boy, offering a pack.

"Your girl's here. Just got here a minute ago."

"Oh, crack wise," said the boy, and turned away. Presently the fellows from the older crowd gathered in the vestibule, waiting for the girls to come downstairs from the ladies' dressing-room.

"Hello, Teddy," said Ross Dreiber.

"Hello, Ross," said the boy.

"Why aren't you out there tripping the light fantastic? Looking them over?"

"Just looking them over."

"Any new talent? I see your sister. She fourteen?"

"Fifteen."

"Fifteen. Well, I'll be out of college by the time she's allowed to go to proms. But she certainly has sprung up since last summer."

"Sure has."

"What have you got? Two more years?"

"One more after this," said the boy.

"Then where?"

"Lafayette, I guess. Maybe Princeton."

"Well, when you get ready to go, if you decide on Lafayette, I'd be glad to write a letter to our chapter there. You know you can't go wrong with Deke, anywhere. What was your father?"

"Theta Delt."

"Well, I have nothing to say against Theta Delt. They're a keen organization. But take a look at Deke before you shake hands. And think twice about Princeton, boy. I know a lot of good eggs were awfully disappointed they went to Princeton. Take my word for it. But of course it all depends on the man."

"Yeah. Sure."

"Have you got another butt on you? . . . Omars! My brand! Deke for you, boy. You even smoke the right cigarettes."

The boy held a match to Dreiber's cigarette.

"Hello, Teddy."

He turned. "Hello, Nat," he said.

"Finish your cigarette, Ross. I'll dance with Teddy. Or are you waiting for somebody?"

"No, I'm not waiting for anybody. But do you mean it?"

"Of course I do. Come on," she said.

"Probably get about two steps," said the boy.

"Well, then let's walk down to the other end of the room and start from there. Shall we?"

"Fine," said the boy.

She took his arm and they marched to the far end of the room. She greeted friends along the way, but said nothing to the boy. Then she held up her arms and said, "All right?" and they began to dance. He was good, and he had self-confidence because he was good. She was good, and she liked dancing with him. There was no need to talk, and at this end of the room people got out of their way. They got all through two choruses of "Stumbling" before the music stopped. "Oh, that was grand," she said. She applauded with him.

"Shall we sit down?" said the boy.

"Well, I think I'd better find our crowd."

"Don't do that, Nat. Please?" said the boy.

"No, Teddy. I must, really," she said. "Cut in later."

"Couldn't we just sit down a minute?"

She shook her head. "You know they'll only kid you."

"Oh, you know that?"

"Uh-huh. They kid me too, don't forget."

"They do? Who does?"

"Oh, my crowd. Same as your crowd kids you."

"You're not sore at me because they kid you?"

"Of course not. And don't you be embarrassed, either."

"You know it's all my fault, Nat," said the boy.

She hesitated. "You mean on account of the postcard?"

"I showed it to everybody. I shouldn't have."

"Well, if I felt like sending a friend of mine a postcard," she said.

"But I went around bragging about it, and showing it to everybody."

"Well, if you wanted to. I don't even remember what I said on the card."

" 'You would love it here. Lots of good trout fishing. Have gone on two pack trips. See you at Christmas. Natalie.' And a picture of the ranch."

"I remember," she said. "Not very incriminating, was it? Will you take me over to their table now, Teddy?"

"And your word of honor you're not annoyed with me."

"Only if you let them embarrass you," she said.

"Nat?"

"What?"

"I don't have to say it, do I? You know, don't you? You do know?"

She nodded. "Give me your arm," she said.

Claude Emerson, Reporter

For thirty years Claude Emerson got up every morning at six o'clock, put the coffee on, shaved himself with one of his two straight razors, took a cup of coffee in to his wife, and then went back to the kitchen and sat at the table and drank two cups by himself. He would sit there, staring straight ahead, slowly stirring the coffee between sips, and when he had finished the second cup he would put on his glasses. There was a small mirror on the kitchen wall, and he would stand in front of it while putting on his collar, in which his necktie was already inserted. He would knot the tie and pull it a little to one side, a little to the other, until he was satisfied that it was in the right place, then he would smooth it down with the palm of his hand, throw back his shoulders until the tie bulged the right amount, and *then* he would insert his stickpin at the right place, slide the safety catch over the pin, and draw away to inspect his work. His next move would be to put on his toupee, which took less time but no less care than the tying of his tie. In thirty years and more Claude Emerson's toupee had deceived no one. It had never quite matched the color of his own hair, which went gradually from an orangey red to a reddish grey. Claude Emerson was always a little behind the natural color changes. He bought a new toupee every five or six years, but he could not afford to keep up with nature. Indeed, he had never been able to afford even one first-class matching job. His friends, his wife, and Peter Durant, his barber, urged him to abandon his toupees, but Claude Emerson refused because, he said, he always caught cold when he went without one.

And so, every morning, there was that part of his personal ritual; putting the toupee in place, smoothing it down gently with the palms of both hands, the final adjusting pull over one ear. After that, his coat and waistcoat, which he put on together, and the business of his watch and chain, which he could do while on his way to the clothes-tree in the front hall. He would put on his seasonal hat and the outer

The Cape Cod Lighter (1962)

wear appropriate to the weather—rubber coat, gum-shoes, umbrella —and he was ready for the street.

On very few mornings he failed to find someone to walk with, and he tried not to walk with the same man on successive mornings. His companions were the bookkeepers and store clerks and men who worked in the offices of the railroads and the coal companies, white-collar men like himself, but whose jobs were nowhere near as exciting as Claude Emerson's. "I'd like to have gone in the writing game," they would often say. "But I was never much of a speller."

Claude Emerson would reply consolingly: "Well, with me it was always arithmetic. When I was in High they tried to teach me book-keeping, but I could never strike a trial balance."

Most of his morning companions were men who *had* learned bookkeeping, but their work did not furnish much of a topic for conversation. Claude's work, on the other hand, was of the stuff that conversations are made on: last night's meeting of the Borough Council; yesterday's burglary; the untimely passing of a Civil War veteran; a two-alarm fire in the Sixth Ward; tax millages; church picnics; a new movie theater; the Burton Holmes lecture; the gilding of a church steeple; the birth of twins; the price of strawberries; the new uniforms for the band. To the man who spent his days perched on a bookkeeper's high stool, the life of Claude Emerson seemed full of variety and stimulation; and Claude Emerson thought so too, for he loved his work.

He was a big man: six foot two, never less than two hundred twenty pounds. In High he had not liked football, but because of his size he had had no choice but to play. He lacked aggressiveness, but he stood head and shoulders over most high school players, and in helmet and noseguard, shoulder harness and kidney pads, he was valuable to the team even before the game began. For four years he heard opposing players say, "Get a look at that big son of a bee. I'll bet he's a ringer." Claude's own coach would say to him: "Just watch the center, Emerson, and as soon as the ball's snapped back, fall forward, *fall forward!*" In Claude Emerson's football days there was no forward passing and not much running around the ends; the principal play was the center rush, and Claude's bulk made him worth two line players, leaving, as it did, one extra guard free to engage the opposing line players on every scrimmage. In spite of the hard-rubber noseguard-mouthpiece, Claude lost four front teeth during his playing career, but he gained a reputation as a stalwart son of Old High which lasted all his life, and, better yet, football introduced him to his lifework; he was paid $1.50 for his reporting of the out-of-town games in which he played.

The paper had no sports section or regular sports writer in those days. Claude Emerson's account of the previous Saturday's game seldom appeared before Tuesday, and often did not appear until Wednesday. Nevertheless his stories usually ran a full column in length, and when he was ready to graduate from High he was taken on as a general news reporter at $1.50 a week. At the end of two years, when his salary had reached $3.50 a week, he asked to be raised to $10; he was keeping company with Clara Stahlnecker, a high school classmate, and her father would not give his consent to Clara's engagement until Claude was earning $60 a month and had at least $200 in the bank. The editor of the paper, though heartily approving of marriage, could not see his way clear to a salary jump from $3.50 to $10, and took the opportunity to caution Claude against such an impulsive step as matrimony at the age of twenty or twenty-one. "Think these things over, Emerson," said Bob Hooker, the editor.

"I did think it over, Mr. Hooker," said Claude Emerson. "And I guess I have to tell you, I can get ten dollars at the *Telegraph.*"

"I don't believe you," said Hooker. "When did they tell you that?"

"Four or five months ago."

"Bosh! If that was true you would have said something then."

"I almost did, but I was hoping I'd get a bigger raise this time."

"Even if you're telling the truth, which I doubt, you realize that the *Telegraph* is on its last legs? So go on over to them, but don't come back looking for work here when the *Telegraph* shuts down," said Hooker. "I'll give you six dollars a week and a dollar-a-week raise every six months."

"Two years before I get ten? No sir, I can't wait that long."

"You haven't got the Stahlnecker girl in some kind of trouble?"

"I don't have to stand for that kind of talk," said Claude. "Now I quit!"

From time to time during the next dozen years Bob Hooker would try to re-hire Claude Emerson. To more and more citizens of the town Claude Emerson was becoming a symbol, the only symbol, of newspaper reporting. They saved their news items for him and would give them to no one else. They would stop him in the midst of his morning rounds and shyly hand him articles they had written. "You fix it up so it reads right, Claude," they would say, and he would do so. They were fascinated and not antagonized by the changes he would make, and when they saw their items in print, written in Claude Emerson's ornate style—"the festive board groaned under the weight of delicious viands"—they became members of Claude's small army of volunteer reporters. Nor was it only the humble who relied on Claude Emerson for the proper presentation of news items; doctors and bankers trusted him; lawyers and clergymen had confidence in him; rich old ladies, who had heard of him through their medical and spiritual and financial advisers, would make their rare announcements only to Emerson, that nice young man at the *Telegraph*. He was summoned to the homes of certain citizens who had never spoken to Bob Hooker, homes to which Mrs. Hooker had never been invited. In such surroundings Claude Emerson was awkward and perhaps over-polite, but he also had the big man's dignity, and he confined his questions to the matter in hand. He seemed to know instinctively that these ladies felt it their duty to make public the information they gave, while wishing to keep out of the papers themselves. "I don't want this to look as if it came from me," they would say, and so Claude Emerson would begin his story: "Word has been received here of the untimely passing of John W. Blank, former town resident, who for the past forty years has made his home in St. Paul, Minnesota," or, "Through the generosity of a donor who wishes to remain anonymous, a handsome, new, mahogany Chickering piano has been installed in the Parish House of Trinity Church." Claude Emerson's stories appeared without a byline, but Bob Hooker recognized the Claude Emerson touches. In an Emerson story an oyster was always a succulent bivalve and every funeral had a cortege, but all the names and the middle initials were always there and invariably correct.

"Claude, I'd like you to come in and see me one of these days," said Bob Hooker, in his first attempt to re-hire him.

"I don't know if that would look right, Mr. Hooker," said Claude.

"Then I'll say it now, here. I'll pay you twenty a week," said Hooker.

"I'm getting better than that at the *Telegraph*."

"I don't believe you, but if you are, you won't be getting it for long. That rag is on its last legs."

Several times in the next seven years Claude Emerson had reason to know that the *Telegraph* was having financial difficulties. His pay envelope contained $12.50 and not the full $25. "That's as much as I could scrape together, Claude," said George Lauder, the editor and publisher. "I'll give you my note, but right now things are slow. They should pick up after Labor Day. I'll give you my note, or I'll give you some stock, but I advise you to take my note. Gives you a better claim in case things don't get better around here." Things never got much better at the *Telegraph*, and they would have been much worse without Claude Emerson, who, as in his football days, did the work of two men. The difference now was that he liked what he was doing, and George Lauder was not a coach who failed to appreciate him. It was a sad day for Claude Emerson when George Lauder, unable to face another slow summer, drank a pint of cheap whiskey and put a bullet through his heart. He owed Claude Emerson $412.50 in back wages. The money was uncollectible, since Claude Emerson had never taken one of George's notes and for more than a year George had failed to keep any books. The bank realized as much as it could on the sale of the equipment, and Claude Emerson, literally with hat in hand, went to call on Bob Hooker.

"Well, you see, Claude," said Hooker. "I've got this young lady, a college graduate, that does all the social-and-personals. I don't pay her anything. She's doing it for the experience, and she works like a mule. When she leaves I'll get another like her."

"I didn't want to apply for social-and-personals," said Claude Emerson.

"All you have to do is look at the paper to realize I have no other place for you. The other jobs are filled by fellows you know."

"Well, if you hear of anything elsewhere in the county—"

"Why don't you put an ad in Fernald's Exchange, Springfield, Mass.?"

"No, that'd be a waste of money for me. I'll have to look for something else, maybe up at the court house."

"You mean give up reporting?"

"I guess I'm going to have to," said Claude Emerson.

The threat of this waste of a good reporter was too much even for Bob Hooker. "I wouldn't want to see you do that, Claude," he said. "I'll tell you. I can pay you twenty dollars a week and a commission on any new advertising you bring in."

"Couldn't you make it twenty-five? I have the two children starting school. I tried to sell ads for George Lauder, but I was never any good at it."

"Well, you're a family man, and you're not a drinker," said Bob Hooker.

"No, Mr. Hooker! That's not it. I'm good at my job! I get more news than any two reporters in town. You know that. I could go uptown this minute and get five or six items that won't be in your paper tonight."

"Say, you're pretty sure of yourself."

"About that I am. I didn't use to be, but think how many times I had items in the *Telegraph* that you never had. Or maybe had them a day late."

"I never expected you to get conceited," said Hooker.

"Let me say this, will you, please? The *Telegraph* stopped printing three weeks ago tomorrow, but I made my rounds every day, just the same as usual, just as if the paper was coming out that afternoon. And every day I got at least one story that you would have run on Page One. Let me show you some, here in my pocket. I'm not conceited, but when it comes to getting the news, I don't have to take a back seat for anybody. No, Mr. Hooker, I have to start at twenty-five, and no selling ads." He rose, and the sweat ran down from beneath his toupee. He wiped his forehead with a bandana handkerchief and blew his nose loudly. His speech to Hooker had left him momentarily without a sense of direction, and he made for the wrong door.

"That's the toilet," said Hooker.

"Oh, excuse me," said Claude Emerson. "Well, good day."

"All right, Emerson. I'll start you Monday. Twenty-five a week."

"Is it all right if I start today? I have a story."

"What is it?"

"The Second National bought the Eisenhauer property at Main and Scandinavian. They're going to move there and put up a five-story office building over the bank."

"That's just a rumor."

"The papers were signed last night. I got that from J. Edward Stokes himself."

"I saw him this morning. He didn't say anything to me about it."

"I saw him this morning, too, and he gave me the whole story. I asked him if he'd keep it quiet for a few days, and he kept his promise . . . Do you want a few lines on Dr. and Mrs. English getting back from their trip to Egypt?"

"When they get back."

"They're back. I was with him earlier this afternoon. He has some very clear pictures of him and the missus in front of the Pyramids. Both riding camels. I talked to Father McCloskey. He has his silver jubilee on the twenty-fourth day of next June, and plans are under way—"

"All right, Emerson. Go on upstairs and go to work," said Hooker. "The other door."

That was in 1908, a year that could be said to mark the beginning of the golden era in the career of Claude Emerson. He was thirty-three years old, an age at which he had grown up to his size. His face had lost the last of the baby-fat look that remained with him through the mid-twenties. He had become, in more than one sense of the word, a prominent figure, instantly recognizable at council meetings, fires, parades, and his volunteers could easily find him. For the same reason it was easier for those who wished to avoid him to keep out of his sight; but few citizens had anything to fear from Claude Emerson. What he knew, he knew, and his inside information was considerable, but the paper he worked for was not a scandal sheet. Even in the heat of the primary election campaigns, when the rules of fair play and reticence were suspended, the paper refrained from publishing the dirtier truths about the opposition candidates. A candidate for the Republican nomination could expect to be called a grafter and an incompetent, and the paper would ask, in large type, what this faithless public servant had done with his share of the looting of the public treasury; but it was never hinted that the man had spent any of the money on women or booze. That sort of accusation was harder to take back when and if the man under attack happened to win the nomination. If there had ever been a threatening Democrat the paper would have used—invented, if necessary—anything it had on the man. Democrats, however, were so few in number that they could not present a formidable candidate. Some Democrats registered as Republicans in order to vote Republican in the primaries, in the fantastic hope that the weaker Republican would be nominated and thus give the Democratic candidate a tiny chance in the November elections. There were some spiritual Democrats who had never voted for a Democrat in the primaries. There were, to be sure, a few Democrats who had never voted for a Republican at any time.

Within two weeks of Claude Emerson's return to the *Standard,* Bob Hooker's paper, there was a noticeable increase in the paper's circulation. It was the custom to place a pile of papers just inside the front door, where workmen could pay their pennies and pick up a copy on the way home.

"We're getting new readers," said Bob Hooker to Claude Emerson, late one afternoon. "We're selling fifty to sixty more papers off the pile, every evening."

Claude Emerson smiled. "Oh, yes. Yes indeed."

"A lot of them I don't recognize," said Hooker. "Who are they? Friends of yours that followed you from the *Telegraph?*"

"I'll tell you who most of them are. They're Democrats. They used to read the *Telegraph.* Now they read the *Standard.*"

"Then they *did* follow you? I knew George Lauder was a Democrat, but don't tell me you're one."

"No sir, but I know most of them. Most of those men, you can tell by looking at them, they work in the car shops. I cultivated them. They didn't read the *Standard* when I worked here before, but these past years when I worked for the *Telegraph* I made a practice of chatting with them during lunch hour. It wouldn't surprise me if you got another fifty or seventy-five taking the paper on home delivery."

"Maybe we could get them to vote the right way, in time."

"I don't know about that. Not these fellows," said Claude Emerson.

It was a poorly kept, impossible to keep, secret that the *Standard* was subsidized by the Coal & Iron Company. It was known as a scab rag, a company sheet, anti-labor, anti-union. It had no circulation in the mining patches, and even in the town its circulation was smaller than the opposition paper's. But the Coal & Iron Company subsidy was one of the two factors that made the *Standard* a superior paper. In losing years the deficits were covered, and in profitable years improvements were made. The other factor in the *Standard*'s favor was Bob Hooker himself, who was actuated by greed and inspired by his love for the newspaper business. The greedy man had begun life as a poor boy, whose formal education ended with grammar school. He was of Yankee and Pennsylvania Dutch stock, a common enough combination in the anthracite region. Among his ancestors was an early president of Yale, and on his mother's side there were numerous Lutheran clergymen. His father, however, was a drunkard who died young, and Hooker's mother supported herself and her son with work as a seamstress until her eyesight gave out and she had to take in washing and ironing. She died of consumption in the year that her son finished grammar school. He was a frail boy with an outsize head, and the only job he could find seemed cruelly unsuitable inasmuch as he suffered from defective vision. The job was printer's devil, paid him a dollar a week and a cot to sleep on in the back of the shop. In spite of his bad eyesight he learned his trade quickly and well, and he read his mother's Bible from habit every day, learned three new words out of the dictionary every day, and on Sundays he read every line of all the out-of-town newspapers that he was able to store up during the week. At sixteen he got a job as printer on the *Standard,* and at nineteen he owned it.

As the new owner of the paper he wrote his own editorials in a day when small-town newspapers ran no editorials or meekly reprinted the political opinions of the metropolitan dailies. The small-town public was usually startled to find a local reference in an editorial, and the *Standard,* and its youthful publisher, attracted the attention of the educated citizens. Under the influence of Henry Wadsworth Longfellow and William Cullen Bryant the young editor wrote a weekly poem in which he introduced the local place-names of Indian origin—Lantenengo, Nesquehela, Taqua, Swatara, Mauch Chunk— and on other days he wrote short paragraphs with the standing head, This & That, which failed as humor but were of local, topical interest.

Bob Hooker was only five years older than Claude Emerson, and had had four years' less schooling, and yet there never was any question as to who was in command. The power rested in something other than the authority to hire and fire, although both men were continually conscious of that authority. The two men had remarkably similar backgrounds. Claude Emerson was a Mayflower descendant, a genealogical fact that was passed down to him by his father and mother and almost never mentioned outside the family. (Once in a great while someone would ask Claude: "Is that a baby ring?" and he would touch the smooth-worn gold ring on his little finger: "No, it belonged to my father," he would say.) Alexander Emerson, though not a drunkard, had died at a fairly early age, leaving a wife and fourteen-year-old son Claude. Alexander's widow had a mortgage-free house on Scandinavia Street and her husband's life savings from his job as cashier-bookkeeper with a dry-goods concern. She did not touch her inheritance. She returned to her old job of teaching seventh and eighth grades in the public school, and continued to teach until Claude married the Stahlnecker girl. The then newlyweds lived with her in the Scandinavia Street house for the first eighteen months of their marriage, at which time the senior Mrs. Emerson suffered her third stroke and passed on. She was very tall for a woman—slightly taller than her husband—and everyone said she tried to do too much; coming home tired after the long hours in the classroom, and pitching in to do a lot more than her share of the housework. She had never got used to letting Clara Stahlnecker sweep and scrub and cook, and possibly Clara should have taken a firmer stand, but Clara was so tiny compared to Mrs. Emerson, and Mrs. Emerson all her life was accustomed to giving orders, not taking them. No one could possibly blame Clara, and, after a time, no one did. Some of the neighbors thought Claude could have been firmer with his mother.

The obvious differences in the respective backgrounds of Bob Hooker and Claude Emerson were inherent in the similarities, the principal difference, of course, being the considerable fact that Bob Hooker was practically a homeless waif while Claude Emerson, at the same period in his life, enjoyed the love and protection of his mother. And yet Claude, compelled by the accident of his size to play a brutal game in which he took no pleasure, may have been no better off than Bob Hooker, who at least was no more uncomfortable than the child Mozart. One thing was certain: that Claude Emerson, protected and loved throughout his boyhood, inspired affection in later life, even or perhaps especially among men who treated him with something less than complete respect. No one, on the other hand, was ever known to speak with affection of Bob Hooker, even those men who treated him with respect. Claude was not particularly conscious of inspiring affection, but Bob Hooker was aware of it and mystified by it. Why was that overgrown clod so popular? He was almost a clown, with his ridiculous unmatching toupee, his squarish derby from September to May and his planter's Panama from May to September; his big, pigeon-toed feet and his dainty short steps: his black undertaker's suit with its pockets bulging with wads of copypaper. Claude Emerson's popularity was particularly galling after such incidents as the visit of old Mrs. W. S. Hofman. Her barouche and sorrel pair stopped one morning in front of the *Standard* office, and Bob Hooker rushed out to greet her.

"Good morning, Mr. Hooker," she said. "I have something for Mr. Emerson. A little item that I think might be of some interest."

"Emerson's uptown on his morning rounds, but I'll be pleased to take it," said Hooker.

"Oh, he is? Do you expect him back soon?"

"No, not for another hour or so," said Hooker. "But I'll be glad to see that it's taken care of. Would you care to come in my office?"

"Thank you very much, but it'll keep. Mr. Emerson knows how I— he usually comes to my house, but since I was in the neighborhood. If it's convenient I'd like him to stop in this afternoon. Half past five, we usually meet. But thank you, Mr. Hooker. All right, Clancy. We'll go to the bank, now, please."

It was no consolation to Bob Hooker that Claude Emerson not only would be treated almost as a servant but that he would conduct himself almost as a servant. It was no comfort, either, that Mrs. W. S. Hofman saved her news for the *Standard*. The irritating fact was that Claude Emerson had a place in Mrs. W. S. Hofman's scheme of things while Bob Hooker had not. The old lady had not even been rude; she had treated him with automatic, impersonal, infuriating politeness, and closed the door of her barouche in his face.

The power, the strength, that Bob Hooker exerted over Claude Emerson was the strength of envy, and it endured because Bob Hooker refused to acknowledge its existence. Instead he kept Claude Emerson on his payroll year after year, raising his salary when necessary, working him hard, diluting his compliments on Emerson's industry with humorously tolerant remarks about his cliché-ridden literary style. Claude Emerson had never pretended to be a writer. He learned early that there was a set journalese phrase for nearly every detail of every event that made a news item, and when he had acquired them all he saw no reason to originate another batch. The people read what he wrote, they understood what he was saying, and they were subtly complimented by his frequent use of elegant expressions. It was nicer to have your daughter united in the bonds of holy matrimony than merely married; the last sad rites were so much more appropriate than a funeral; and Jupiter Pluvius, with his torrential downpours, was more exciting than a two-inch rainfall. It was supposed to be a private, mild, office joke when Bob Hooker would say, in the presence of the other reporters, "Well, I noticed in yesterday's paper that that robber brandished a wicked-looking blue steel automatic." He would not mention Claude Emerson; he did not have to. "Anybody here ever see a holy-looking black automatic?" The city editor and the other reporters would laugh, and so would Claude Emerson. No one, not even Claude, thought Bob Hooker was being cruel. "Emerson's an excellent reporter," Hooker would say privately to the city editor, "but I have to jack him up once in a while. Inclined to get a swelled head."

In spite of Bob Hooker's criticisms in the office Claude Emerson retained his self-confidence "on the street." Again and again he was paid the ultimate compliment by a civic organization to a reporter: they would hold up the start of a meeting until he made his appearance. It was almost as high a compliment as its corollary: "Don't let Claude Emerson find out we're having this meeting." It was finally through a compliment, the second-grade kind, that Claude Emerson became vulnerable to an act of revenge by Bob Hooker.

It was now 1926. Claude Emerson's silver anniversary as a member of the Fourth Estate had passed unnoticed. His son and daughter were married, his wife was content with a daily box of Lowney's, Samoset, Page & Shaw's or Whitman's to assuage her craving for candy, and at $40 a week Claude Emerson was the best-paid reporter in town. He was fifty-one years old and without realizing it he had written the history of the town for all there was of the Twentieth Century and a few years beyond. He had recorded marriages of a hundred young persons whose births he had written up for one paper or another. He had covered all the details of the rebirth of the town from a borough to a third-class city, and he had written the story of the passing of the last horse-drawn fire-fighting equipment. He had seen the vanishing of news value in items concerning local reception of radio programs from Kansas City, Missouri. An Old High teammate had a Princeton son who was on Walter Camp's Second All-America team, and the *Standard* not only had a regular sports department but carried accounts of golf tournaments at the country club. The new hotel was no longer a novelty, and three Philadelphia brokerages had branch offices, complete with stock quotation boards, competing for local investors' business. Two county judges posed for photographs in white linen knickerbockers, and four state troopers went to prison for accepting bribes from bootleggers. The largest and oldest brewery was now an ice cream plant. Bob Hooker was one of the newest members of the Union League in Philadelphia. War was so much a thing of the past that there were only two officers left in the National Guard companies who had seen service on the Mexican Border and in France. A sound Yankee was President of the United States and a sound Pennsylvanian was Secretary of the Treasury . . . The town had no archivist, but it did have Claude Emerson, and his word was accepted as final in the settling of bets. ("I say it was 1911, you say it was 1910. We'll ask Claude Emerson.") In a peculiar, intangible sense he owned the town, the town was his, because he possessed so many of the facts of its life.

Then one morning in 1926, having given Clara her eye-opener cup of coffee, and adjusted his toupee, and taken his bumbershoot out of the hall stand, he fell in step with Marvin F-for-Frederick Nerdlinger, a friend who lived two squares west on Scandinavia Street. Marvin worked in the laboratory of the Coal & Iron Company. He and Claude Emerson had been classmates at Old High, and the Coal & Iron gave Marvin a job as soon as he graduated. There was even some talk of sending Marvin to Lehigh for college chemistry and physics, but Marvin did not want to waste a lot of time on English and history and the other stuff they made you take in college. Now, at fifty-one, he had college graduates working under him at the lab, although they did not as a rule stay with the company after two years.

"Morning, Marvin," said Claude.

"Claude," said Marvin Nerdlinger, without breaking stride.

"A light precipitation," said Claude, holding his umbrella over his shorter friend.

"Thanks, I don't mind a little rain," said Marvin. "You weren't around yesterday."

"Should I have been?"

"Might have been worth your while, I expected you," said Marvin.

"You had a story for me?"

"No, I didn't, but I thought you'd be around trying to get one."

"Come on, now, Marvin. Don't tantalize me. Something happened. What was it?"

"Fourth of July came early this year."

"Fourth of July? You had an explosion? Anybody hurt?"

"Not hurting any more. Never have another moment of pain."

"Who? You mean someone was killed?"

"All I said was the Fourth came early this year. The rest you'll have to find out for yourself."

"That's what I'm trying to do."

"Oh, no. Not me. I said as much as I'm going to."

They parted company at the corner of Main and Scandinavia, and Claude Emerson hurried to his office and the telephone. After calls to the hospitals, the Coal & Iron doctor, the coroner's office, and the fire chief, Claude Emerson said to Frank Carter, the new city editor: "I'm up against a stone wall."

"I wasn't listening," said Carter. "What stone wall?"

"I understand there was an explosion yesterday over at the C. & I. lab. That's over on Coal Street. They keep it separate from the main building."

"What do they do there?"

"Well, a lot of things. Chemical things. I don't understand much of it, but one thing I know they do do, they analyze dynamite and caps. The lab is a little stone building near the car shops. Built of stone and brick. Walls two feet thick. Looks like a guardhouse. They're not allowed to have it in a residential or business area."

"Then why don't you go there and have a look?"

"I will, but the way I always work, on a story like this I don't go and ask them if the thing happened. We know it happened."

"You're sure of that?" said Carter.

"I'm sure. And I'm sure a man was killed. I'd like to have the man's name and some of the details before I go there. The more I have, the less they can deny."

"They can't deny it if a man was killed."

"Oh, can't they?" Claude chuckled. "Wait till you're here a few months. You'll find out they can deny anything. Do me a favor, don't tell the boss I'm working on this."

"If he asks me, I'll have to tell him."

"I understand that, sure. But wait till he asks you. He won't be in for another hour or so, but when he comes in just don't say anything. By that time I may have some facts."

"Are you going to get me into trouble?" said Carter.

"Just stay out of it and you won't get in any trouble."

"Why do they want to be so secretive? Accidents happen all the time. Miners get killed every day, it seems to me."

"This is a different matter. They never had a man killed at the lab, to my recollection, and when this gets out it's going to make people nervous. You're not supposed to keep any dynamite in the city limits. That's an old ordinance from the borough days. Gibbsville Supply Company had an explosion back around 1892, two men killed and a conflagration that gutted three buildings. There was hell to pay, and they passed an ordinance. No more dynamite in borough limits. It's right down there in black and white."

"Well, get after it."

"I'll do that little thing," said Claude Emerson.

Police Sergeant Biddle said there was nothing on the blotter, but he avoided looking at his old friend. "Anyway, it's not a police matter, Claude."

"I know. The fire chief. But Billy McGrew is making himself scarce. I've been after him all morning."

"Go have a look in his book. If there was an alarm turned in, he has to keep a record of it. What time was this supposed to happen?"

"You know darn well when it happened."

"Not a police matter, I told you. You start calling me a liar and I'll kick your big ass out of here."

"I don't have a big ass, and you didn't use to, before you were promoted to sergeant."

At the word sergeant, Biddle looked up. As much as to any politician he owed his chevrons to the daily favorable mentions he had got from Claude Emerson. "Is there anybody out there?"

"No," said Claude Emerson, peeking out in the hallway.

"This didn't come from me, mind you?"

"Hell, you know me better than that," said Claude.

"Somewhere between four P.M. and a quarter after, we got a still alarm. Fire reported at 220 South Coal. Billy McGrew answered it in the chief's car, and the combination truck from Perseverance and some other apparatus in the First and Second Ward. The usual still alarm equipment. When they got there the fire was out, or under control. But there was some scraps of a human body, what was left of it, scattered all over the lab. Name of the man, Kenneth W. Cameron. Age twenty-seven. Married. No children. Employed as chemist by the C. & I. Home address, 22 North Frederick. Moved here from Wilkes-Barre about six months ago. Cause of death, accidental explosion of unknown chemicals. The rest you're gonna have to find out for yourself. Now don't say I never gave you anything."

"I won't say anything, not about you, anyway. What did you say your name was? John J. Jones?"

"Huh? . . . Oh, I catch on. Well, you better not," said Sergeant Biddle.

The deputy coroner was an undertaker, Miles T. Wassell, and Claude Emerson found him in his office in back of the funeral parlor. "Morning, Miles. I hear you won't have much to work with, that young fellow yesterday."

"What young fellow was that, Claude?"

"Oh, I thought the deputy coroner was supposed to know all these things. Well, that'll have to go in my story. 'Deputy Coroner Miles T. Wassell was not informed of the fatal accident to Mr. Cameron.' "

"You better not print that or I'll sue you."

"Then you better tell me what you know—that I didn't find out already, and without any help from you, Miles. I don't have to tell you, the coroner's records are public property. How much dynamite did they have at the lab?"

"I didn't say they had any."

"Then what caused the explosion? Maybe he was making tea and put too much sugar in it."

"I don't know anything about any dynamite."

"Or anything else, so it appears. But remember, if you want to try to make a fool out of me, it'll be tit for tat."

"The man was killed by some unknown chemicals exploding."

"You don't have enough of him for an autopsy. When is the inquest?"

"I'm waiting to hear from the Coroner."

"Yes, I'm waiting to hear from him, too. You can tell him that when you talk to him. Is he taking personal charge?"

"Yes."

"I see. You're under orders to him, then. Well, you just tell him I tried to reach him this morning, and I'm not going to try again. I can be reached at the *Standard* after twelve noon."

The windows of the laboratory were boarded over and a Company policeman stood in the doorway. He was a stranger. "You can't go in there," he said.

"Why not? I'm going to see Mr. Nerdlinger."

"You work for the Company?" said the policeman.

"No, I didn't say I did."

"Then you're not allowed in. I got orders to keep everybody out. Does Nerdlinger know you're coming?"

"He was expecting me yesterday."

"Well, that was yesterday. I wasn't here yesterday, all I got is my orders for today. What are you, a salesman?"

"Tell Mr. Nerdlinger that Mr. Emerson is here. And tell him I don't enjoy standing out here in the rain."

"Well, I guess you can stand here in the doorway. Wait here a minute, but don't go inside. You're not allowed inside till Nerdlinger says it's okay. Emerson?"

"Claude Emerson."

"Claude. Huh. Claude. All right, Claude, stand here, but don't go any farther, or as big as you are I'll throw you out in the gutter."

"Don't talk that way. Captain Wingfield wouldn't like it."

"You know Captain Wingfield? Are you a friend of Captain Wingfield?"

"I'm a friend of everybody's, unless they try to throw me in the gutter. Yes, I know Cap Wingfield, very well indeed. I knew him before he worked for the Company."

"Are you a lawyer?"

"Listen, go on in and tell Mr. Nerdlinger I'm here, and stop asking me questions, will you?"

Still in doubt, the policeman went inside, and as he opened the door Claude got a strong whiff of the odor of chemicals and stale smoke, but the policeman closed the door too quickly for a good look at the laboratory. Claude tried the door; it was locked.

The policeman returned. "He can't see you. He's busy," he said.

"Well, I'm willing to wait, but not long," said Claude. He made a sniffing noise. "Sure is some smell."

"It's a hell of a lot worse in there," said the policeman.

"Would you mind going back in and ask Marvin—that's Nerdlinger—ask him when he can see me?"

"He didn't sound like he was going to see you. He just said to tell you he was busy."

"Nonsense. What is there to do in there today? Clean up, but he can do that any time."

"No, they have to do it today. They found a piece of the fellow's jaw this morning."

"I didn't think there was that much of him left."

"Oh, that was just talk," said the policeman.

"I thought he was blown into a thousand pieces."

"Nah. From his waist down you wouldn't know he was hurt. The trunk and the head were all blown apart."

"Did you have to look at him?"

"Hell, I seen worse in the army. I dug a grave for worse. Yeah, I saw him. The undertaker put him in a canvas bag last night, the bottom half of him and the big hunks. The piece from his jaw, they found that up on the top shelf where they keep them glass jars, look like Mason jars."

"Oh, I understood all the glass was broken."

"Nah. Dynamite acts funny. You take now for instance a Mills grenade. That goes off and all those little squares, they go in all directions, every which way. But there's a lot of stuff in that labbatory, it wasn't even touched. Smoky, from the fire, but all in one piece."

"There was one report that it was nitro-glycerin."

"Dynamite. This poor son of a bitch was making some kind of a test, and—hyuh, Captain. Friend of yours here."

Captain Thomas L. Wingfield, chief of the Coal & Iron Police Division, stood in the rain and stared at Claude Emerson. "What are you doing here, Emerson?"

"Trying to get in to see Marvin Nerdlinger," said Claude.

"Have you been gabbing to this man?" said Wingfield to the policeman.

"No, I just got here," said Claude.

"You shut up, Emerson. You, Chapman. What was that about some son of a bitch making a test? What have you been telling this fellow?"

"Now wait a minute, Cap," said Claude.

"You didn't let this fellow get inside, did you?" said Wingfield, ignoring Claude.

"Who is he, this fellow?" said Chapman.

"He's a God damn reporter."

"You God damn son of a bitch!" said Chapman. He went at Claude Emerson with both fists driving into Claude's belly. One punch was enough; Claude Emerson had not been physically attacked since high school days, and he was fifty-one years old.

"Cut that out," said Wingfield, and the beating stopped. "Emerson, you're sticking your nose in where you ought to know better. Go on, get out of here."

"I have to sit down a minute," said Claude. "Can't get my breath." He lowered himself to the stone stoop.

"Let him sit there," said Wingfield.

"Solar plexus," said Claude Emerson.

"You ought to know better," said Wingfield. "Get up and walk around. It'll do you good."

"I don't know if I can."

"Go on in and bring him a drink of water," said Wingfield.

"Yes sir," said Chapman, and went inside.

"What the hell is the matter with you, Claude? Bob Hooker isn't going to print anything about the accident. He's on the Company payroll the same as me."

"I know."

"This Chapman is a bully-boy, as tough as they come. The next thing would have been the boot for you. One of the toughest men I have."

"Could you send around and get me a taxi?"

"Where do you want to go? Home? I'll drive you there."

"The office."

"I advise you to go home and go to bed, and stay there. You took a couple of mean punches. He goes in there like a pile-driver, with both hands. Come on, I'll drive you home."

"No, I have to go to the office, Cap. I'm getting my breath back."

"I wish this wouldn't have happened," said Wingfield. "Fellows our age, that's real punishment." He helped Claude to his feet and they got in Wingfield's car. It was only about seven blocks to the *Standard* office, and the cold rainy air helped to revive Claude, but he and Wingfield maintained silence until the car stopped at the office. "I wouldn't have had this happen for the world, Claude. You know that. But you should have known better."

"Both doing our jobs, Cap. Thanks for the ride."

"I wish I could fire Chapman, but the trouble is I need him."

"Doing his job, too. So long, Cap," said Claude.

He had to stop and rest a couple of times on his way up the stairs, and when he reached the newsroom it was immediately apparent to Frank Carter and the others that he was not well. "Are you all right?" said Carter.

"Had a kind of an accident, you might call it. I'll be all right after I had a little rest." He hung his hat and raincoat and umbrella on the clothes-tree, and made his way to his desk. "I got a lot on the explosion, but I need more. Did you get anything on it?"

Carter reached in the wire basket and took out two pieces of paper, one typewritten, one in pencil. "I got this," he said, handing it to Claude. "The Boss wrote the story *and* the head."

"A Number 30 head? For this story?" said Claude.

"Read the story. A 30-head is all it's worth," said Carter.

Claude read aloud:

"Kenneth W. Cameron, age 27, of 22 North Frederick Street, was fatally injured yesterday while conducting an experiment in the laboratory at 220 South Coal Street. The accident occurred, according to eyewitnesses, when Cameron apparently misjudged the proportions of chemicals in a test he was conducting as part of a safety program.

"Cameron, who recently came here from Wilkes-Barre, was the son of Mr. and Mrs. James D. Cameron, of that city. He was a graduate of the Rensselaer Polytechnic Institute, at Troy, N.Y. He was a member of Sigma Chi and Sigma Xi, the latter an honorary fraternity. In addition to his parents, his wife, formerly Miss Nancy

Benz, of Nanticoke, survives. Funeral arrangements have not yet been completed. Burial is expected to be in Wilkes-Barre."

"And that's all? That's it?" said Claude Emerson.

"And the head. 'Chemist Dies in Safety Test,' " said Carter.

"And the Boss wrote it all himself," said Claude. "Where are you going to run it?"

"Page three."

Claude Emerson handed the story and headline back to Carter. "I had a little more than that," he said.

"I'll bet you did," said Carter.

"I even had the name of the company Cameron was working for. I see the Boss doesn't mention that."

"I noticed that, too, Claude," said Carter.

"I hope the Boss didn't have as much trouble getting his story as I did mine," said Claude.

"What happened?"

"Ran up against a stone wall. Not the same one I mentioned earlier. Although it was, in a way," said Claude. "Frank, I don't want to leave you short-handed, but I'm going to have to take the rest of the day off. Would you do me a favor and call the cab company? I don't feel much like walking. Or anything else."

"Listen, I'll get one of the boys to drive you home. The circulation department has a car."

"Any other time, but today I'd rather take a taxi. This is the first time in thirty-two years I wished I'd been a bookkeeper."

"Not you, Claude," said the city editor.

Jurge Dulrumple

On long trips—to see the cherry blossoms in Washington, to hear the music in the Berkshires, to visit relatives at distant points—Miss Ivy Heinz and her friend Miss Muriel Hamilton sang two-part harmony, not only because they loved to sing but as a safety measure. Muriel Hamilton had never learned to drive, and their singing kept Ivy Heinz from getting too drowsy. They sang well together, especially considering that both were natural altos. Muriel Hamilton carried the melody, since it was a little easier for her to get out of the lower register and also because she was more likely to know the words. Ivy Heinz could go awfully low, and sometimes for a joke she would drop down in imitation of a man's bass, and whenever she did that, just about *every* time she had done it, Muriel Hamilton would say, quickly, without a pause in the singing, "George Dalrymple."

"No, *no!*" Ivy would say, and they would laugh.

Any mention of George Dalrymple was good for a laugh when Ivy Heinz and Muriel Hamilton got together. It was an extremely private source of amusement, sure-fire or not. Shared with a third party it would have been an act of cruelty to George because an explanation of the laughter would have involved revealing a secret that concerned only George and the two women. It went back to a time when all three were in their middle twenties, the summer in which George Dalrymple proposed first to Muriel Hamilton and then, a month later, proposed to Ivy Heinz. Neither girl had been enormously complimented by a proposal from George Dalrymple, but they knew that from George's point of view it was a compliment, a terribly serious one that was no less serious or sincere because he had gone so soon from Muriel to Ivy. George Dalrymple was a serious man, a fact that made it fun to have a private joke about him, but in public you had to treat such seriousness seriously.

Other people, in discussing George Dalrymple or even in merely

The Cape Cod Lighter (1962)

mentioning his name, would often lower the pitch as far down as they could get. They would pull their chins back against their necks, and the name would come out, "Jurge Dulrumple." His speaking voice was so deep, his enunciation so economical, that his vocal delivery was his outstanding characteristic, more distinctively his than those details of appearance and carriage and manners that he might share with other men. There were, for example, other men just as tall and thin; others who swayed their heads from side to side independently of their bodies when they walked; and others who were as quickly, instantly polite in such things as standing up when a lady entered the room, lighting a girl's cigarette, opening doors. George did all these things, but what set him apart was his way of talking, his words coming from down deep in his mouth and expelled with a minimal motion of his lips. His friends, such as Ivy Heinz and Muriel Hamilton, knew that he was not self-conscious about his teeth, which were nothing special but all right; and it was not in George Dalrymple's character to go around talking like a jailbird or a ventriloquist. George Dalrymple talked that way because he was serious and wanted people to realize that everything he said was serious.

When George came back from his army duties in the winter of 1919 he was twenty-three years old. His military service had largely consisted of guarding railroad bridges along the Atlantic Seaboard, a task he performed conscientiously with the result that he was discharged a corporal. If the woor—the war—had lasted six months longer he would have been a second lieutenant and probably sent to Brest, France, or some such point of debarkation; his congressman had been practically promised the commission by the War Department. But once the Armistice was signed George was anxious to get out of the Urmy and resume work at the bank. He had already lost practically two years, and in the banking business it was wise to start early and stick to it. The time he had put in at the bank before he was drafted was now just about matched by the fifteen months he had spent protecting the railway systems from German spies. The bank took him back at a slight raise in pay and with full credit in seniority for the time he had been in the service of his country. It was a pleasant surprise to find that one of the newer bookkeepers at the bank was none other than his high school classmate, Muriel Hamilton.

Two of the women who had been hired during the hostilities were let go, as they had been warned they would be, but Muriel Hamilton was kept on. The recently inaugurated school savings plan, for children in the public and parochial schools, owed at least some of its success to Muriel Hamilton and her ability to get along with children. She was painstaking and patient, and the bank officials put her in complete charge. Once a year she went around and gave a talk to all the classes from seventh grade to senior high, and the bank could see the results immediately. No one was more surprised than Muriel herself.

In her four years at High she had been so near to failing in Public Speaking—which almost no one ever failed—that it had pulled down her general average and kept her out of the first third of her class. George Dalrymple's marks in Public Speaking were as bad as Muriel's, but his other subjects kept him in the first ten in a class of eighty-five boys and girls, the largest class in the history of G.H.S. It surprised no one that George Dalrymple, on graduation, had a job waiting for him at the Citizens Bank & Trust. His high school record merited the distinction, a fact that delighted his father, the assistant cashier. John K. Dalrymple was not a man who would have forced his son on the bank.

In his pre-army days as a runner at the bank George Dalrymple and his father always walked home together for noonday dinner. Each day John K. Dalrymple would take the opportunity to review George's morning activities in detail. The father had George repeat all the conversations he had had with the tellers at the other banks, and he would suggest ways of improving the impression he created in the banking community. "It's all very well to have the light touch," John Dalrymple would say. "But it can be carried too far. It's better to be all business at your age. Time enough for ordinary conversation later on." There was no actual danger that George might get a reputation for frivolity, but he was young and did not know all the ropes, and his father did not want George's natural gravity to be affected by nervous unfamiliarity with the work.

John Dalrymple, as assistant cashier, did not have to stay as late as his son, and they did not walk home together at the close of business. But as soon as George got home he would get into his overalls and join his father in the flower garden, or, during the cold months, in the odd jobs about the house that John Dalrymple claimed kept him from getting stale. Father and son had very little time together in the evenings; John Dalrymple liked to stay home and read, while George had choir practice one night, calisthenics and basketball at the "Y" two nights, stamp club another, Sunday evening services at the Second Presbyterian Church, and the remaining evenings he spent with his friend Carl Yoder. Sometimes the boys would be at the Yoders' house, sometimes at the Dalrymples', and once in a while they would take in a picture show if it was Douglas Fairbanks or a good comedy.

It was a terrible thing when Carl passed on during the influenza epidemic. George could not even get leave to come home for the funeral. In fact, there was no real funeral; the churches and theaters and all such public gatherings were prohibited during the epidemic; the schools were closed, and you could not even buy a soda at a soda fountain. The death rate was shockingly high in the mining villages, but death by the wholesale did not affect George Dalrymple nearly so much as the passing of funny little Carl, the Jeff of the Mutt-and-Jeff team of Dalrymple and Yoder in the Annual Entertainment at G.H.S., senior year. George Dalrymple knew that things would not be the same at home without Carl trotting along after him everywhere they went.

One of the first conversations he had with Muriel Hamilton at the bank was about Carl Yoder, their classmate, and George was quite surprised to discover how fond she had been of Carl. "I always thought it was mean to call him The Shrimp," she said. "He didn't like it, did he?"

"No, he certainly did not," said George. "But he wouldn't let on to anybody but me."

"I didn't like it either, because remember in the Annual Entertainment when he wore girl's clothes? I loaned him that dress. And if Carlie was a shrimp, then that made me one too."

"Oh, yes. I remember that dress. That's right, it was yours. But that wouldn't make you a shrimp, Mure. Girls aren't as tall. I never think of you as a short girl."

"Five feet two inches."

"That makes me ten inches taller than you and ten inches taller than Carl."

"Oh, I thought you were taller."

"No, it's because I'm skinny, and so much taller than Carl. Just six feet and maybe an eighth of an inch."

"I never saw you in your uniform."

"Well, you have that treat in store for you. I'm going to be marching in the parade, Decoration Day."

She was a girl, not a short girl, and soon after that first conversation he formed the habit of walking part way home with her after the bank closed for the day. He would say goodnight to her at Eighth and Market, slowing down but not stopping when she entered her house. His new duties at the bank included opening up in the morning, a full half hour before Muriel reported for work, and he did not see her in the evening after supper except by accident. His schedule also had been rearranged so that his and his father's lunch hours did not coincide, and George was not entirely displeased. His father's questions about army life indicated a belief that it had been far more exciting and sinful than was actually the case. Some aspects of army life had disgusted George and he hoped never again to see some of the men in his company; the bullies, the drunkards, the dirty talkers, the physically unclean. George Dalrymple had come out of the army a somewhat coarsened but still innocent young man; he had lived closely with men who really did so many of the things that George and Carl Yoder had only heard about. He had heard men tell stories that they could not possibly have made up, and some of the stories were told by men about their own wives. Nevertheless George Dalrymple had no inclination to discuss that sort of thing with his father. It would have been almost as bad as discussing them with his mother. The war was over, he was through with the army, he had not liked being a soldier, but the whole experience was his own, a part of him, and to speak of it to his father would be an act of disloyalty to himself and the army that he could not explain to himself but that he felt deeply. It was private.

The time would come, he knew, when it would be no more than the right thing to invite Muriel Hamilton to a picture show and a soda afterward. If, in those circumstances, she showed another side of her, he would start keeping company with her and, eventually, ask her to marry him. She was exactly his own age, but he did not know any younger girls. She was what some people called mousy, but she was very well thought of at the bank, and he liked her femininity and her neatness. As soon as there was a tiny daub of ink on her finger she would scrub it off; she never had a hair out of place; and he was sure she used perfume, although that may have been perfumed soap. He had watched carefully the tightening of her shirtwaists over her bosom, and concluded unmistakably that marriage to her would be a pleasure. She had not been one of the prettier girls at G.H.S., and yet she was not by any means homely, and it was remarkable that she was still single while other girls, less attractive, were already married. She belonged to a group that called themselves the H.T.P.'s, who went to the pictures and had sodas together and had been doing so since senior year. One of the group dropped out to get married, and shortly thereafter it became common knowledge that H.T.P. stood for Hard To Please. Now the only ones left of the original H.T.P.'s were Muriel Hamilton and Ivy Heinz.

Muriel so readily accepted George Dalrymple's first invitation to take in a show that he felt sorry for her. She was not really an H.T.P.; she was merely waiting to be asked. They went to the movies, they had a soda. "There'll be a trolley in about seven minutes," said George.

"A trolley, to go eight squares?"

"I forgot to ask you before," he said.

"The only time I ever take the trolley is if it's pouring rain and I'm going to be late to work," she said. "I like walking. It's good exercise."

"So do I, now. I got pretty tired of it in the army, but that was different."

Watching the movie, they had not had any conversation, and now, walking her home, he began a story, about his army duties, that he had not finished when they reached her house. She stood on the bottom of their front steps while he hurried the story to an ending. "Well, thank you for taking me to the movies, George. I enjoyed it very much," she said.

"The pleasure was all mine," he said.

"See you tomorrow," she said.

"Bright and early," he said. "Goodnight."

He said no more than good morning to her the next day. He was determined not to let their outside relationship alter their conduct at the bank. Nevertheless he waited for her when the bank closed, and he soon discovered that their relationship had been altered. "George, I, uh, maybe I ought to wait until you ask me again, but if you have any *intention* of asking me—to go to the movies, that is— then maybe we oughtn't to walk home together every day. Walking home from work, that's one thing. But having a date, that's another. And I don't think we ought to do both. Maybe that's rather forward of me, but if you had any intention of asking me for a date?"

"Yes. Yes, I see."

"Half the people at the bank knew we had a date last night."

"Oh, they did?"

"You can't do anything here without everybody finding out about it."

"Well, personally I don't mind if they find out about that."

"But I do, George. Walking home from work, that's just politeness, but when a fellow and a girl have dates at night in addition, then that's giving them something to talk about."

"I'd be willing to give them something to talk about, but that's up to you, Mure."

"It is and it isn't, if you know what I mean. It all depends on whether you were going to ask me to go out with you in the evening. But if you were, I'd have to say no. And I don't want to say no."

"On the other hand, I don't want to give up walking home with you."

"Then we haven't solved anything, have we?"

"Not exactly," he said. "But maybe I can solve it. How would it be if we kept on walking home every day, but didn't have *regular* dates? Most fellows and girls have date-night on Wednesday, and when they start going real steady, he goes to her house on Sunday."

"We're a long way from that," she said. "All right. We'll walk home after work, as usual, and if you want to take me to a picture, you say so and sometimes I'll say yes and sometimes I'll say no. Is that all right with you?"

"Anything's all right that you agree to."

They violated the agreement immediately. He saw her every Wednesday night, and on Sunday evenings he walked home with her and Ivy Heinz. He and Ivy would say goodnight to Muriel, and he would then walk home with Ivy. But though Muriel had never invited him inside her house, Ivy simply opened the door and expected him to follow her, which he did, on the very first night he walked home with her. She called upstairs: "It's me, Momma. I have company."

"All right, but if you're going to play the Vic don't play it too loud. It's Sunday. And don't forget, tomorrow's Monday morning."

Ivy wound up the Victrola and put on Zez Confrey's "Kitten on the Keys."

"Do you still dance, George?"

"Oh, I'm terrible."

"Well, we can try," said Ivy.

He knew as soon as he put his arm around her waist that the dancing was only an excuse. She stood absolutely still and waited for him to kiss her. They kissed through three records, one of them a non-dance record of Vernon Dalhart's, and at the end of the third she stopped the machine and led George to the sofa, stretched out and let him lie beside her. She seemed to be able to tell exactly when he would be about to get fresh, and her hand would anticipate his, but she kissed him freely until the court house clock struck eleven.

"I-vee-ee? Eleven o'clock," her mother called.

"You have to go now," said Ivy.

Sunday after Sunday he got from Ivy the kisses he wanted from Muriel, and after several months it was more than kisses. "Next Sunday you come prepared, huh?" said Ivy, when their necking reached that stage.

"I am prepared, now," he said.

"No. But next Sunday Momma's going to be away and I'll be all alone. We won't have to stay down here."

He had grown fond of Ivy. From the very beginning she had understood that he was in love with Muriel and had never brought her into their conversations in any way that would touch upon her disloyalty to her friend or his weakness of character. Nor was she jealous of his feeling for Muriel. Nor was Muriel so much as curious about what might go on after they said goodnight to her on Sunday evenings. But fond as he was of Ivy, it was her taking him to bed with her—his first time with any woman—that compelled him to propose marriage to Muriel. He had no doubts about himself now, and among the doubts that vanished was the one that concerned his marital relations with Muriel. As husband he would be expected to know what to do, but before the night in Ivy's bed he had not been sure himself.

He took Muriel to the picture show on the Wednesday following the Sunday in Ivy's room, and when they got to Muriel's house he said, "Can we go inside a minute?"

"It's after eleven, George."

"I know, but I didn't have much chance to talk to you. I wish you would, Mure."

"Well, I guess they won't object, a few minutes. But you can't stay after half past eleven."

His manner did not show it, but he had never been so sure of himself or wanted Muriel so fiercely. He stood behind her as she was hanging up her things on the clothes-stand, and when she turned and faced him he did not get out of the way. "I want to kiss you, Muriel."

"Oh, George, no. I noticed all evening—is that what you were thinking about?"

"Much more, Muriel. I want you to marry me."

"Oh—goodness. You're standing in my way. Let's go in the parlor."

She switched on the parlor chandelier and took a seat on the sofa, where he could sit beside her. She let him take her hand. "Did you just think of this?"

"Of course not. I've been thinking about it for over a year," he said. "Maybe longer than that, to tell you the truth. You're an intelligent girl, and you know I've never dated anyone else."

"As far as I know, you didn't. But I never asked you and you never told me. You could have been having dates with other girls."

"Maybe I could have, but I never did. Ever since I got out of the army the only girl I wanted to be with was you. And that's the way I want it to be the rest of my life. I love you, Muriel."

"Oh, George. Love. I'm afraid of that word."

"You? Afraid of the word love? Why, you, you're so feminine and all, love ought to be—I don't know."

"Well, marriage, I guess. I guess it's marriage I'm afraid of."

"I guess a lot of girls are, but they get over it. Your mother did, my mother did, and look at them."

"You have so many wonderful qualities, George, but I don't think I could ever love you the way Mama loves Father. And your parents. It's nothing against you, personally, it's just me. And any fellow."

"My goodness, you love children."

"You mean when they come in the bank? But that's what they are. Children. You're a man, George."

"Don't tell me you're a man-hater."

"No, not a man-hater. Heavens. But I could never—I never want to get married! Why don't you help me? You know what I'm trying to say. I wouldn't like a man to—I was afraid you were going to kiss me, in the hallway. *That.* That's what I'm trying to tell you. I could never have children. When we were in High didn't you use to feel the same way about girls? I used to think you did. You never went out with girls, George. You and Carlie had more fun than anybody."

"But I always liked girls."

"Well, I liked boys, too, but I never wanted to be alone with a boy. You know how old I am, and I've never kissed a boy in my whole life. And I never will."

"You're wrong, Muriel. You'll fall in love with one some day. I wish it was going to be me."

"How wrong *you* are. I wouldn't let you sit here if I thought you were like the others." In the conversation she had taken away her hand, and now she put it back on his. "I want a man for a friend, George, but that's all. When I was little I read a story about a princess. She was forced to marry this king or else he'd declare war on her father. I couldn't do that. I'd sooner kill myself."

"Why?"

"Don't ask me why. I think all girls feel that way, underneath. I don't think they ever get used to some things, but they pretend to because they love their husbands for other reasons. I could love you that way, George, but you wouldn't love me. You wouldn't be satisfied with just being nice. You'd have to be a man and do those things that are so ugly to my way of thinking."

"But girls have desires, Mure."

She shook her head. "No. They only pretend. Most girls have to have a man to support them, but if they had a job they'd never get married. I have a job and Ivy has a job, so we didn't have to have a man to support us."

"The rich girls on Lantenengo Street, they don't need a man to support them."

"Not to support them, but that's the way they stay rich. The rich girls marry the rich boys and the money all stays together."

"I hear some pretty funny stories about some of those girls."

"Yes, but most of them drink, and the men take advantage of them. The girls are nice, but when they take too much to drink they're not responsible. That's why the men up there encourage them to drink."

"Well, I know very little about what goes on up there, but at the rate they're spending it, some of them won't have it very long."

"I feel sorry for the women. I don't really care what happens to the men, especially one of them."

"Did something to you?"

"Not to me, but to a girl I know. One of the H.T.P.'s. One night at the picture show, he did something. Don't ask me any more about it because I won't tell you. But they're all alike, up there."

"You'd better not say that at the bank."

"Oh, I should say not. But whenever that man comes in I think of what his wife has to put up with. And they're supposed to be the people everybody looks up to. Rich, and educated, the privileged class."

"I wouldn't be like that, Muriel."

"I know you wouldn't, George. But maybe men can't help themselves."

"It's a good thing we talked about this."

"Oh, I wouldn't have married you, George. Or anybody else."

"I was thinking of something else. You make me wonder about women, how they really feel. You're a woman, and I guess you ought to know."

"We just don't have the same feelings men do."

"Then if women all had jobs the whole race would die out."

"Yes, except that don't forget women love children and they'd still go through it all to have them."

"Would you?"

"No, I don't love children that much."

"What do you love, Mure?"

"What do I love? Oh, lots of things. And people. My parents. Some of my friends. The music in church. Singing with our old bunch. Nature. I love nature. I love scenery, a good view. Flowers. Nearly all flowers I love, and trees on the mountains. The touch of velvet, like this cushion. And I love to swim, not at the shore, but in a dam if the water's not too cold. And my one bad habit. Smoking cigarettes."

"Now I never knew you smoked."

"I don't get much chance to, except when I go to Ivy's. Mrs. Heinz has something the matter with her nose, some condition, and we can smoke one right after the other and she never catches on. If my parents knew I smoked they'd disown me."

He looked at her hand. "Muriel, some day the right fellow will come along, and all these things you said tonight, you won't even remember thinking them."

"Don't say things like that, George. You don't know me at all, what I really feel. Nobody does, not even Ivy."

"Your trouble is, you're just too good, too innocent."

"Oh, I don't like that, either. You meant it as a compliment, but it shows a great lack of understanding. Of me, that is. You think that some fellow with wavy hair—"

"Maurice Costello."

"Or Thomas Meighan. I'll meet somebody like that and forget the things I believe. But you're wrong. I'd love to have Thomas Meighan for a friend, but honestly, George, I'd just as soon have you. At least I know you better, and I don't know what I'd ever find to talk about with Thomas Meighan." She looked at him intently. "George, I don't want to put you off proposing to someone else. You'll make some girl a good husband. But when you do find the right girl, if you want to make her happy, don't be disappointed if she doesn't like the kissing part of married life. You know what I mean, and it isn't just kissing."

"I know."

"A friend of mine, a girl you know too, she got married, and now she comes to me and cries her heart out. 'You were right, Muriel,' she says. 'I hate the kissing.' I used to try to tell her that she wasn't going to like it, but she wouldn't believe me. She said if you love a person, you don't mind. Well, she loved the fellow she married but now he hates her. Isn't that awful? And I feel just as sorry for the fellow, George. He can't help it that he has those animal instincts. All men have them, I suppose. I guess even you, because I admit it, I had that feeling earlier that you were going to want to kiss me, and that's the first step. I've always known that about boys, and that's why I've never let one kiss me."

"Well, I guess we'd better not have any more dates."

"Oh, we couldn't now. And maybe you'd better not wait for me after work tomorrow. I've told you so much about myself, I don't know how I'm going to look at you in the morning."

"Do you feel naked?"

"George! Oh, why did you say that? Go home, go home. Please

go, this minute." She was in angry tears, and he left her sitting on the sofa.

At the bank in the morning she seemed cool and serene, but he was not deceived. At moments when once she would have given him a bright, quick smile, she would not look at him. In the afternoon he stayed behind longer than usual, to give her a chance to leave well ahead of him. On Sunday night she was not at church, and he walked home with Ivy.

"You can't come in," said Ivy. "My mother's still downstairs."

"Then she must be sitting in the dark," he said.

"All right, you can come in, but it won't be any use," she said.

He put a record on the Victrola, but she braked the turntable. He put his arms around her, but she turned her face away and sat in a chair where there was not room for him. She lit a cigarette before he could get out his matches. "Muriel told you, huh?" he said.

"Sure. She tells me everything. I don't tell her everything, but she tells me. Now you'd better leave her alone."

"Oh, I will. She's a man-hater."

"Just finding that out? And what if she is?"

"At least you're not."

"Maybe I should be."

"Oh, she handed you some of her propaganda," said George.

"Think back to one week ago tonight, George Dalrymple. Then Monday, Tuesday, and Wednesday you proposed to Muriel."

"Ivy, you knew all along that some day I was going to ask Muriel to marry me."

"No I didn't. I thought you'd find out that she was never going to marry anybody. You had a lot of talks with her."

"Not about that subject. What's the matter with her?"

"Does there have to be something the matter with her?"

"Well, there's nothing the matter with you. You want to get married some day."

"Maybe I do and maybe I don't."

"Yes you do. What if I asked you to marry me?"

"You didn't ask me."

"Then I do ask you. Will you marry me?"

"No."

"Well, maybe that's because you're sore at *me*. But you're going to marry somebody."

"There you're wrong."

"You'll have to have somebody."

"I have somebody—now."

"Who?"

"Wouldn't you like to know?"

"That's why I'm asking you. Harry Brenner?"

"No, not Harry Brenner."

"Chick Charles?"

"Not him, either."

"Oh, that new fellow in the jewelry store."

"Wrong again."

"I can't think of anybody else you had a date with. Is it a married man?"

"Give up, stop trying."

"All right, I give up. Who is it?"

"That's for me to know and you to find out."

"Don't be sore at me, Ivy."

"I'm not really sore at you, George."

"Yes you are, but when you get over it, let's take in a movie next week?"

"No. Thanks for asking me, but I'm not going to see you any more."

"You're sore about Muriel. Well, I couldn't help it."

"Honestly, George, I'm not sore about Muriel. Not one bit."

"Well, I'm going to keep my eye on you. I want to find out about this mystery man."

"It's a free country, George."

On the next Wednesday night he happened to be at the movies with Harry Brenner's brother Paul, and sitting two rows in front of them were Ivy Heinz and Muriel Hamilton. Later, at the soda fountain, George walked over and reached down and picked up the girls' check. "Allow me, ladies?" he said.

"Oh, no, George, you mustn't," said Muriel.

"My treat," he said. "I guess thirty-two cents won't break me." He paid the cashier on the way out, and stood on the sidewalk. The girls stopped to thank him again, and Muriel, somewhat ill at ease, made some polite conversation with Paul Brenner. George, in his muttering way, spoke to Ivy. "Using Muriel as a disguise, eh?"

"Curiosity killed the cat," said Ivy.

It was a long time, many Wednesdays, before George Dalrymple allowed himself to believe that Ivy was not using Muriel as a disguise. But they were just as nice about his secrets, too.

The Engineer

Work on the big dam had been suspended in 1917 and '18, but after the War the engineers began to arrive in considerable numbers. They were all sorts, running in age between the middle twenties and the early fifties; college men and practical men; married and single; brilliant and barely competent; construction men, electrical men, supervisory men, financial men; men who had worked together in far corners of the world, men who were meeting for the first time; the ambitious, the washed-up, the healthy, the drunkards, the womanizers, the cheats, the gipsies, the dedicated, the dullards, the mysterious, the dependable. Some came and did their jobs and were off and gone in a month or two; others, on jobs that took longer, brought their families; and a few stayed on and became residents of the town, usually because they had had some mining experience and found work in one of the independent coal operations. But whether they left in a month or stayed forever, as a class they were a positive addition to the life of the town. They were educated, well-traveled men; scoundrels or worthy citizens, they were The New Engineers in Town, and no other group of men ever enjoyed quite the same welcome. If some of them abused the welcome, they were usually punished by their confreres' ostracism or efficiently banished by the Company. They all came to a town already respectful of engineers as a class—the successful and the mediocrities among the native-born mining engineers prepared the way for the new men. And except for the gipsies, the chronically footloose, they could look around and see that for an engineer it was not a bad place to be. Indeed, several of them partnered up to form small engineering firms of their own, with the town as home base, and a couple of those firms are now in the hands of the second generation, not getting rich but getting by.

But in the early Twenties the New Engineers were all strangers in the town, fresh or not so fresh from Cornell and Case and M.I.T.,

The Cape Cod Lighter (1962)

from Wyoming and Montana and Alabama universities, and from Sweden and Scotland and Turkey and France. They took rooms in the Gibbsville Club and the Y.M.C.A., in the hotels and boarding houses, whatever they could get that was appropriate to their position and pay. A man who had had five servants in China was lucky when his bed got made in his boardinghouse on North Frederick Street; and another man who as a colonel had rated his own batman now had to polish his own shoes. But as a group they were adaptable.

Chester L. Weeks arrived in town in 1921, after most of the first wave had gone on to other jobs, and the big generators were in. He checked in at the American House, the oldest and largest hotel, but not the best and by no means the worst. "You understand," he told the desk clerk, "as soon as there's a room with a private bath, I want it. I'm going to be here for some time."

"We understand that, Mr. Weeks," said the clerk. "As soon as Judge Boxmiller checks out."

"How soon do you think that'll be?"

"Well, that's hard to say. Another two-three weeks. He's an out-of-town judge, from over Nesquehela County. There's some special case he's hearing, I don't exactly know what."

"But when he leaves, I can have the room with bath—and hold on to it? I don't want to give up my private bath every time a judge hears some special case."

"No, this don't happen but once every two-three years."

"Good. Now I have a lot of pressing, and laundry."

"You can give all that to Jimmy, he'll take care of it for you. You can have your laundry back the day after tomorrow."

"Not before then?"

"Well, if Jimmy wants to take it home, his wife can do it special if you're in a hurry."

Chester L. Weeks turned to the colored man beside him. "Are you Jimmy?"

"Yes sir, that's me. Jimmy."

"Is your wife a good laundress?"

"Don't like to brag, but she does the best work I know. All hand work, fifteen cents a shirt."

"And how late is the barber shop open?"

"Oh, ha' past eight, nine o'clock, depending," said Jimmy.

"What time do they open in the morning?"

"In the morning?" said Jimmy.

"They're open around eight o'clock in the morning," said the clerk.

"Fifteen cents for a shirt, eh?" said Weeks.

"Maybe she do it for—twelve?"

"Or maybe she'll never do it again, if she doesn't do good work this time," said Chester Weeks.

"She do good work, that I guarantee you," said Jimmy.

"Do you know what I've been accustomed to paying for a shirt?"

"No sir."

"One cent."

"One cent! A penny! You couldn't even get that low a price from the Chinaman."

"This *was* a Chinaman. In China."

"Oh, in China. That's different. Everything cheaper over there, so I'm told. Them Chinamen, they eat rats and rice. I wouldn't like that. Who'd ever want to eat rats and rice?"

"I have. It can be quite a delicacy."

"Not me. Rice I don't mind. I eat lots of rice, but don't give me no rats with it."

"You probably wouldn't like sheep's eyes."

"Sheep's eyes. You mean eyes out of a regular sheep? Ha ha ha ha. Listen to you talk. Sheep's eyes. Mister, now I *know* you joking me. Mister?"

"What?"

"What else you eat?"

"Oh—fried grasshoppers."

"Fried grasshoppers. Ha ha ha ha ha. What else?"

"Bamboo shoots."

"Bamboo shoots. Ha ha ha. You ever eat any—any—I don't know."

"Thigh meat. I got sick from it."

"What that, thigh meat?"

"Thigh meat, from a man's thigh. They said it was pork, but it wasn't pork."

"Huh? You ate a man?"

"I ate part of a man."

Jimmy was disturbed, and very near to anger.

"Some of the places I've been, and the things I've eaten, it was better not to ask what they were. What are we waiting for? Oh, the rest of my luggage."

"It's coming by Penn Transfer, Mr. Weeks. You don't have to wait. I'll send it up as soon as it gets here. One trunk and one large suitcase?"

"All right, send it up."

In the silent ride up the elevator and the walk to Chester Weeks's room Jimmy decided that no disparagement of his color had been intended by the newcomer, and his anger subsided.

"I'll unpack these bags," said Weeks. "You can take the dirty linen with you, then come back and get the rest when my trunk arrives. Do you send my suits out or are they done here in the hotel?"

"We got a tailor in the basement, he does them."

"No creases in the sleeves, will you tell him?"

"Yes sir. No creases in the sleeves."

"Does your wife know how to wash a linen suit?"

"Yes sir. Sir?"

"Yes?"

"What that sign there, say Raffles?"

"That's the name of a hotel. Singapore. Asia."

"You was in Asia?"

"China's in Asia."

"Oh, yeah. Yeah. Raffles. Some name for a *ho*tel, hey?"

"Some hotel, too."

"Man!"

"What?"

"Look at them guns. Mister, how many guns you got?"

"Three. Just these. This one's a Webley. English. This one is French, and this one's American."

"All countries."

"Well, three. That's so it would be easier for me to get ammunition. Couldn't always get American cartridges everywhere I went. And some places I couldn't get British, and so on. But I could usually get one of the three."

"Was you in the War?"

"Yes. At least I was in the army. Were you in the army?"

"Yes sir, I was a lance corporal. Orderly in the Quartermaster Corps. Served ten months at Frankford Arsenal. Honorable *dis*charge."

"Frankford Arsenal? Where's that?"

"Philadelphia, P A, sir."

"Oh, yes. Here, will you hang these up, please?"

"Hmm. Silk. I never saw a suit made out of silk."

"They won't do me much good when winter comes. How cold does it get here?"

"Oho. Cold. Hot in summer, cold in winter. In the mountains, here. Trolleys don't run. Snow plows get stuck. River gets froze. Poor people don't get enough heat. Children take sick and die. Men got no work. Get drunk and fight, every night, not only Saturday. Folks stay home, ain't got shoes, can't even *look* for work. Men like me, got a steady job in a *ho*tel, they let us take home stale bread for our neighbors. But winter's no good for us, no good at all."

"Why do you come North?"

"Sir, I didn't come North, I was born North. My pappy was born North, *his* pappy born North. We's always here in town, since *I* can remember."

"Then why don't you go South?"

"Huh. South. You can freeze there, too. Wintertime ain't no good anywhere if you don't have wood in the stove and bread in the box. It don't get cold in China?"

"You bet it does. And hot."

"Huh. Guess I'll stay here."

"You might as well. Who polishes the shoes?"

"Me. They got another boy in the barber shop, but the people in the rooms, I shine them."

"Do you take the laces out?"

"When they ask. I run them under the tap and rinse 'em out to look nice and fresh. I do it right. But some don't ask."

"Well, I ask."

"Yes sir, I seen that."

"I like to have my things just so. If I gave you a fixed sum every week would you see to it that my shoes are always polished, and my clothes in order? My hats brushed and so on?"

"Like a valley?"

"Yes."

"A fixed sum? How much is that, a fixed sum?"

"Two dollars a week?"

"Two dollars—I don't know. I got a lot of work to do."

"Five dollars."

"Five? Yes sir, I can do it for five. I come in early or stay late for five. I tend to your shoes, take your suits down when you need a press. Brush your hat. Brush it with a brush, no whisk broom."

"All right, five dollars a week. Here."

"Six dollars?"

"Five dollars for your first week, the other dollar is for today. And don't think I always tip a dollar, because I don't."

"No sir. Thank *you*, sir."

The hotel staff and, very soon, the friends of the hotel staff were fascinated by the latest member of the corps of engineers. There had been other strange ones, nutty ones, but this Weeks man was the first they ever heard of who had eaten human flesh; a white cannibal. Chester L. Weeks in a week's time attained a celebrity among the hotel and domestic servants and their friends in advance of his first invitations from the resident engineers and non-engineers of the town. But that is not to say he went unnoticed. It was summer, and the business and professional men of the town wore their Palm Beaches and mohairs, and a few of the rich wore linen suits; but Chester L. Weeks had a tropical wardrobe that was just different enough to attract attention every day, everywhere he went. He changed his suit every day, from spruce, crisp linen to luxurious silk; from Panama to Leghorn to Bangkok to sailor, with puggree bands and the colors of remote clubs to add brightness to his headgear. The stuff was not new, but the style and the variety were new to the town, and in those first days the men with whom Chester L. Weeks had to do business were so bedazzled by his wardrobe that they were slow in realizing that he was no mere dude. He was quick, sharp, and knew his business. The other engineers had dressed very conservatively, casually, or even shabbily; but then Chester L. Weeks was not, strictly speaking, an engineer. He had an engineering degree, and he worked for an engineering firm, but he was essentially a financial man. He was not exactly an accountant, although he discussed accounts; he was not a purchasing agent, although he was keenly interested in prices; he was certainly not a lawyer, but he knew the language of contracts. Nor did he come under the head of the fairly new and somewhat suspect designation of efficiency engineer. One thing was certain: he was not the kind of engineer who put on hobnailed boots and carried a transit on his shoulder.

Whatever the precise nature of his job, he seemed to rate on equal terms with the supervising engineer of the entire hydroelectric project, J. B. Wilcey, who had been in charge of the dam building and the plant construction since the earliest blueprint stage, and who was now something of a fixture in the town, with a good-sized house, a wife who played bridge and tennis, and two children in private schools. Jess Wilcey took Chester L. Weeks around and introduced him to the top men of the business and financial community, who did not fail to notice that Wilcey's manner indicated a willingness to please Weeks. "Thank you, Jess," Weeks would say, politely but unmistakably telling him to go and leave him with the new contact. It did not take long for the business men to get it through their heads that this new fellow, with his blue shirts and linen neckties and highly polished oxfords, was very well thought of in the home office back in New York. The concurrent stories that had somehow got around, to the effect that Weeks had once escaped from Chinese bandits and had seen a companion slaughtered to provide food, probably had enough basis in fact, the business men believed, to prove that dude or not, his manhood could not be questioned. It was hard not to question the manhood of an American who carried his handkerchief in his sleeve.

He was a rather small man, with no extra fat on him anywhere, the skin drawn tight over his cheekbones and a mouthful of large, even teeth. He was nearly bald, and on his face and pate and hands, in a fading suntan, were numerous large freckles or liver spots. He had a sharp nose and thin lips that he had a habit of moistening while he studied a business paper. His concentration was intense and he was liable to be impatient when it was interrupted, but his memory, especially for figures, was remarkable. "Thirty-two cents a foot, I think you said," he would say to a business man, referring to a minor detail of a large sheet of figures.

"I can easily look it up," the business man would say.

"Never mind. It was thirty-two," Weeks would say. "But couldn't you have saved us money on those shipping costs? Why the Lehigh Valley instead of the Pennsylvania? We had our own trucks, and the Pennsylvania railhead is only four miles farther than the Lehigh Valley. But you took this roundabout way because the Lehigh Valley was four miles closer to the dam. Just at a guess I'd say that made a difference of between eight and ten thousand dollars, without having a table of freight rates at hand."

"You're right except for one thing."

"Where am I wrong?"

"You weren't here, so you don't happen to know that the Pennsy was having a strike. A rump strike."

"Then I apologize. It must be very annoying to have me come here, a total stranger, and start right in by questioning your judgment. I'll be more careful in the future. Next time I won't go off half-cocked. But that doesn't say there won't *be* a next time."

He was as unconcerned over the obvious fact that he antagonized some reputable business men as he was by the admiration of others. ("Show the son of a bitch whatever he's entitled to see, but keep him away from me.") The respect that was shown him automatically by virtue of his position in Wadsworth & Valentine was followed by respect he quickly earned on his own, in his relentless preoccupation with facts and figures and his apparent passion for work. "Don't you ever take time off to relax?" said Jess Wilcey, after two weeks of Chester L. Weeks and his zeal.

"Am I going too fast for you, Wilcey?" said Weeks.

"No, but there's no use killing yourself. You don't have to do it all in a month. In fact, you can't. And my wife's waiting for you to say the word, when we can entertain for you."

"That's very nice of her. Tell her any time from now on. The usual Company dinner?"

"Yes, I guess that's what it'll have to be, the first one. You haven't met any of the wives, have you?"

"No. How many are there?"

"Six," said Wilcey. "Seven couples and you."

"All right, tell Mrs. Wilcey she can get that over with any time next week or the week after."

"Do you want to join the clubs? You almost have to join the Gibbsville Club, but what about the country club?"

"I'll join it. Company pays for it."

"I don't imagine you want to rent a house, but any time you want to move out of the American House you can probably live at the Gibbsville Club, or my secretary will find you an apartment."

"I like the American House. It's a bit broken down, but I like the atmosphere. How many Company dinners do I have to go to?"

"Just ours. The other wives will ask you to Sunday afternoon tea, but you know which ones you have to go to. Then whenever you're ready, Maria—"

"I know. The dinner to meet the natives. You seem to like it here."

"Yes, I do. We both do."

"Have you had any good offers to stay?"

"Yes, although you have a hell of a nerve to ask that question."

"Well, I *have* a hell of a nerve. That's no news to you, Wilcey. Don't tell me you haven't had a half a dozen letters telling all about me. I've had to play Company politics, too, don't forget. I found out all I could about *you* before I came here. That's part of the fun of working for a big company."

"I don't consider it fun. I stay out of Company politics as much as I can."

"Then you'd better seriously consider that local offer, because when you get to where you are and I am, that's when the Company politics is playing for high stakes."

"I'm a construction man."

"Then I don't have to worry about *you*, since you're planning to settle down here."

"I didn't say that."

"You didn't have to, and I could almost tell you what your next job'll be. But that's fine with me, Wilcey. You and I make about the same money, and the next step up is for you, or me, or McDonald, in Manila. You've eliminated yourself, so it's between McDonald and I.

That ought to make for harmonious relations between you and I. Fine. Excellent."

Wilcey smiled. "Where did you learn your politics? In China? I was only out there for one year. Maybe I should have stayed longer."

"You're a construction man, Wilcey. And a good one. You stick to that. Ten years from now we may be able to do business."

"When you're president of Wadsworth & Valentine?"

"Chairman of the board. You're the type of man they make presi-dent. I don't want it. I want to settle down in New York. Well, now we understand each other perfectly. I thought we'd be six months getting around to this conversation. I hope you're as relieved as I am."

"I wouldn't say we understand each other perfectly, Weeks. But we made progress."

"I stand corrected. Let's say we understand each other as well as we ever have to. And you're a little keener than I gave you credit for."

"Thanks."

Maria Wilcey's Company dinner for Chester L. Weeks went according to protocol except that the guest of honor was the last to leave.

"Where do you get Scotch around here?" said Weeks.

"I got this through the Gibbsville Club."

"Pretty good. It actually tastes like Scotch. Mrs. Wilcey, may I congratulate you on a very nice dinner party? I hope it wasn't too dull for you."

"No, it went off pretty well, I thought. I'm sorry we couldn't have a young lady for you, but next time there'll be all local people and the town is full of attractive girls. Withering on the vine, I may say."

"I look forward to that."

"So are they," said Maria Wilcey. "They've all been wondering who you were, and by the way they've heard the most awful stories about you."

"I have a spotless reputation."

"No you haven't. Morally, yes, but did you know that you're supposed to be a cannibal?"

"A cannibal, did you say?"

"It isn't a subject I cared to bring up at a dinner party, especially a Company dinner party. But I've been asked whether it was true."

Weeks smiled. "Well—I once partook of human flesh. It was fed to me as pork, but I knew damn well it wasn't. That was in Borneo, when a party of us were sent looking for oil. But how did that get all the way back here? Oh, of course. I know. The bellboy at my hotel. What other damage to my reputation?"

"Do you carry a revolver?"

"No, but I know where that started, too. Same source."

"And you never were a spy," said Maria Wilcey.

"I was a military intelligence officer."

"But not a spy, running from one country to another."

"I've run from one country to another, but always for the greater honor and glory of Wadsworth & Valentine, Incorporated."

"Isn't that a military ribbon you wear?"

"It's the Croix de Guerre, but I got that in France three years ago. I think I'll stop wearing it, now that I'm back in the States."

"You didn't get it for spying?"

"No. My company happened to be next-door neighbors to a French outfit, and they gave all the American officers the Croix de Guerre. Our colonel got the Legion of Honor, and their colonel got the D. S. M. The French outdid us in courtesy, but of course they always do."

"He's lying to you, Maria. He got the Distinguished Service Cross," said Jess Wilcey.

"But not for spying, and that's what Mrs. Wilcey wanted to know about. I wouldn't have made a good spy. Too obvious. Too secretive."

"You had a very good war record. One of the best," said Wilcey.

"Well, all right, I did, but I'm not trading on it," said Chester L. Weeks. "Although of course I always wore my medals whenever the British wore theirs, in China. I have the Military Cross, and that did me no harm—or the Company."

"You're all for the Company, aren't you?" said Wilcey.

"I'm all for Chester L. Weeks, just as you're all for J. B. Wilcey."

"If the truth be told," said Wilcey.

"How long have you been with the Company?" said Maria Wilcey.

"Twelve years, with time out for the army. Do you want to know my age, Mrs. Wilcey? Thirty-seven. Your husband could have told you that."

"He didn't tell me anything about you, except that you were coming, and that you were here." Maria Wilcey was annoyed. "I heard much more about you from outside sources."

"A full description of me—or pretty full—was sent to your husband at least a month before I got here. It always is. You know how the Company works."

"Yes, but you obviously don't know how Jess works."

"Mrs. Wilcey, my job here is going to take about two years, then I'll be sent somewhere else. Maybe back to China. Mexico. We're going to have to see a lot of each other these next two years, and suddenly I seem to have gotten off on the wrong foot with you. Was it that remark about my age?"

"Yes."

"Well, I apologize. You see, I'm accustomed to wherever I go, the Company wives take it upon themselves to play Company politics with me, as happened several times this evening. Then they want to marry me off to their sisters. Well, I don't want to play Company politics with the wives. And I'll be damned if I want to marry their sisters. So I'm on my guard at all times, and if I was rude to you, I'm sorry."

"Well, let's have another Scotch-and-soda and forget about it," said Wilcey.

"First I want to know where I stand with Mrs. Wilcey. Do you accept my apology?"

"Of course," said Maria Wilcey.

"Thank you. Now I'll tell you something. I think you are the most charming, and probably the most intelligent Company wife I've met in many years. I would have thought so anyway, but I might not have told you so if we weren't going to be friends. Wilcey, think twice about taking that other job. I hate to see this charming lady wasted on this town."

"She likes it here," said Wilcey.

"You will too, when you've been here a while, Mr. Weeks."

"Not if I can help it. Your husband knows which way I'm headed."

He refused a lift home, and when the Wilceys had turned off the porch light they could hear the precise tapping of his heels on the sidewalk as he marched homeward. "Listen," said Maria Wilcey. "He even walks like a pouter pigeon."

"A pouter pigeon—"

"I know. Hasn't got leather heels. But isn't he a strutting little man?"

"Oh, I guess he's all right."

"I'll turn Mary Beth Huber on him. She's the last thing he'd expect to encounter here."

"Why do you want to do that?"

"Because he's so darn patronizing about this town."

"So were you, at first."

"So I was."

Mary Beth Huber, the most widely traveled young woman in the town, and soon to be off on another trip, sat next to Chester L. Weeks at Maria Wilcey's second dinner party. At the meat course she announced: "I refuse to apologize for monopolizing this man, but he has news of friends of mine I haven't seen in aeons. Now, Mr. Weeks, tell me about Jack and Lydia Banning-Douglass. Did they ever patch it up?"

"No. She went home, and he stayed in Hong Kong."

"And married the Russian? I can't believe *that.*"

"No, she was around Shanghai for a while, then she disappeared."

"I didn't think that would come to anything," said Mary Beth. "Did you ever know Hans van Blankers?"

"Van Blankers? Was he with Shell?"

"I don't think so."

"Where would I have known him?"

"In Bangkok."

"Oh, well you see I haven't been there since before the War."

"No, he was there after the War."

"My particular friends in Bangkok were the Van Egmonds."

"Still there. I had a Christmas card from them last year."

"So did I. Picture of a Dutch boy and Dutch girl skating on the canal."

"And the windmills in the background. Homesick, and afraid to go home after so many years. Just like so many of our friends out there. Did you find that to be the case?"

"Almost invariably, if they stayed in one place. The people that shifted around, or got home every two or three years, they didn't want to stay put. But some of the others you couldn't budge."

"And no wonder. I don't imagine they could live on the same scale back in England, or Holland."

"Although it was the women that usually wanted to go home."

"Well, that's understandable, too. Nobody ages very well in the tropics, but it tells more on the women. Physically, I mean. Are you going back?"

"I just got here, don't send me back so soon. I've just unpacked. Truthfully, I don't know. I'll be here about two years, then I don't know what comes next. We never do, especially we bachelors."

"If you had your way what would you do?"

"Oh, I have my way, Miss Huber. I'm not doing anything I don't want to do. But I suppose you mean if I had the money to do everything I want to do?"

"Yes."

"I'd go on working. I'd be doing more important things than I'm doing now, but working just as hard, using the same brains."

"The tropics haven't affected your ambition."

"I haven't spent all my time in the tropics, and in any case I wouldn't use that as an excuse for laziness. My offices in Hong Kong and Shanghai were no more uncomfortable than my office here. The electric fan was a great invention. The electric fan, used in conjunction with the paperweight."

"I'm going abroad next week. I'll be very much interested to see how you like Gibbsville when I get back."

"Where are you off to?"

"I'm taking my mother to the French Riviera. We'll take trips to North Africa, but I don't expect to see any of our mutual friends. I might go out that way again next year. It would be fun to. Did you play polo in China?"

"Yes, some."

"Then you must have known a man called Pat Dinsmore."

"I was wondering how you happened to miss Pat."

"Oh, I know, Mr. Weeks. But you must admit he has charm."

"Carloads of it."

"I fell for it, just like all the others, before and since. Was he a friend of yours? Do you hear from him?"

"Hear from him? He can barely read and write. No. I don't expect to hear from him. As for his being a friend of mine, he doesn't need friends. He has charm. But I suppose if I wrote to him I'd get an answer, some time in the next year."

"Don't on my account. But how is he?"

"Well, I saw him in June. He came to a stag farewell party for me, and that was one night he left his charm at home."

"And I guess that wasn't the first time. But you forgave him. Why *do* we, people like that? We're so intolerant of little faults in nice people, and yet we're prone to overlook big faults in people like Pat Dinsmore."

"Since you honor me with your confidence, I'll tell you that I never did forgive Pat Dinsmore. And if you ever do see him again, please don't mention my name, when I'm not there to defend myself. Will you promise me that?"

"Of course. Not that I ever expect to see him."

In her remaining days at home Mary Beth Huber did more than dispel some early suspicions that Chester L. Weeks was somehow phony. Especially among the younger men of the town, and particularly among those who had gone to good prep schools and colleges, the social judgment on him was severe. They conceded that his engineering degree from a Western Conference university was probably authentic; Wadsworth & Valentine would have checked on that. They accepted the Wadsworth & Valentine opinion of his professional ability. But his manners and his taste in clothes were a little wrong—and therefore all wrong. The word of Mary Beth Huber,

world traveler, was indisputable in fixing Chester L. Weeks's previous social position in the Far Eastern polo and gin sling world. And
yet he was not right. He made no claims that were probably false; he
made few claims at all, and in two spheres of admirable activity—his
work, and his war record—he did not take the credit he was entitled
to. The same kind, and a lesser degree, of offense had been given
when the leading bootlegger's younger brother had blossomed forth
in a five-hundred-dollar raccoon coat. The fact that Chess-turr (they
dragged out his name derisively) did not lie and that his credentials
were valid was frustratingly infuriating, and it was not particularly
pacifying to call him a wet smack and let it go at that.

He was at his most offensive at the bridge table. He was exceptionally good in a community where the standard of bridge was high.
He would sometimes, after the fourth or fifth trick, lay down his
hand and say, "I'll give you the king of clubs and a diamond trick.
The rest are mine," and pick up a pencil to mark the score.

"Let's play it out," someone would say.

"Why? If you insist, all right, but I assume you're going to follow
suit. All right, *let's* play it out." He was, of course, always right in
such cases, and he was annoyingly over-patient with slow players.

"Is that your lead, Mrs. Walker?" he would say.

"Yes. The ten of hearts."

"I see the ten of hearts, but I want to make sure it's your final
decision. Mrs. Walker has led the ten of hearts. From dummy, Mr.
Weeks plays the queen. The queen of hearts, Mr. Forbes. Your king,
Mr. Forbes? My ace. And now I lead my jack in the same suit. The
jack of hearts, led. Mrs. Walker. The knave."

"Oh, dear."

"Why don't you play your four of hearts, Mrs. Walker? *Or* your
five. I'm almost sure you have one or the other, because I see that
little deuce and that little trey sitting over there in dummy. Ah, the
four! Thank you, Mrs. Walker. From dummy I shall play the little
deuce. And Mr. Forbes, I count on you to have the six-spot. Yes, the
six. Nice distribution, isn't it? But I don't think we'll try that again.
What's that they say about the children of London?"

"The children of London are starving because their fathers
wouldn't lead trumps."

"I *thought* you'd know that, Mrs. Walker."

At least once a week he would play at a dinner-and-bridge or a
bridge-and-supper, and if in the course of the evening there was
always someone to feel the sting of his sarcasm for a wrong bid or an
unreturned lead, no one could deny that Chester L. Weeks had the
game to back it up. He played regularly in another foursome of two

other men and a woman who were generally conceded to be the bridge sharks of the town, and he was equally tyrannical with them, although in this foursome the others fought back. The game was never played for high stakes; a quarter of a cent a point, in stag games at the Gibbsville Club, was the limit. But social prestige and the entree to certain formidable houses were reward enough for a man in his first winter in the town. And as he improved his position it seemed foolish and futile to maintain a hostility toward him that was based on little more than a hunch that he was somehow a faker. At the end of his first year in the town he had demonstrated his superiority in bridge, which could not have been faked; he was respected by the men of business and, obviously, by the Company that employed him; he really had played some polo in China; he had some first-class military decorations for bravery under fire. It was ridiculous to say that no one knew anything about him; no one knew very much about any of the new engineers' pre-Gibbsville history, and because of the special animosity toward him, more questions had been asked about his background than about any other man's in the Company. In a year's time the active animosity toward him practically vanished because it had become a bore, and it disappeared without having done anything to mollify or appease the young men who condemned him. They could have beaten him at golf and tennis, but he not only declined their invitations to play; he wondered aloud why presumably grown men wasted their energies on such silly pastimes. Then, to prove that he was not merely anti-sports, he won a mile race against a recent captain of the Penn swimming team.

All this was observed and duly noted by the mothers of nubile young women, most keenly by those mothers whose husbands had accurate information on Chester L. Weeks's personal finances. He was a long way from wealthy, but he was making fifteen thousand a year and his capital was somewhere around a hundred thousand. He was, moreover, thirty-eight years old, and according to Maria Wilcey, next in line for an important position in the home office in New York. He had distributed his attentions evenly among the young women of good family, and he had been classified as elusive; but no conscientious mother believed that an elusive bachelor was a confirmed one, and Blanchette Moseley was the conscientious mother of Ida Moseley, age twenty-five, graduate of Miss Harper's School for Girls, near Ardmore, and of Wellesley College. Blanchette Moseley was convinced that her Ida was just the kind of girl who ought to appeal to a man like Chester L. Weeks. *"You've* got to do something about it, Adam," she admonished her husband.

"All right, but what?" said Adam Moseley. "We've had him here for dinner a couple of times."

"Oh, *that.* So has everybody else. Get him interested in the bank."

"Oh, positively. I can just see the expression on certain faces when I say we ought to put this new fellow on the board. Apart from the fact that Weeks doesn't own a single share of bank stock."

"Wedding present."

"Well, if you want to give him your stock, that's all right with me."

"You don't have to give it to *him,* do you? We can give it to Ida."

"Bee, we don't want to get in any money competition to buy a husband for Ida. She'd hate that, and anyhow, we wouldn't necessarily win that kind of a competition."

"Have a talk with Ida and see how much she'd hate it. She thinks Chester's the most interesting man that ever came to town."

"In some ways he is, but how does he feel about Ida?"

"He has to be prodded, that's all. They have a lot in common. Don't forget Mary Ku."

"Mary Ku? Oh, that Chinese girl."

"Ida's best friend at Wellesley. Through her Ida knows a lot about China. And Ida loves to travel."

"I know that, all right. But so does Mary Beth. I'll do anything and everything I can, but first Weeks has to show some interest."

"He does not! That's exactly where you're wrong. He's so set in his ways that he'll never marry anybody if somebody doesn't prod him."

"You keep saying prod him. I don't quite know what you mean."

"Let's invite him on a trip, away from here."

"Just the four of us? You can't just up and invite him to go along on a trip with us and Ida."

"You don't have to do it that way. Take him up to the camp and Ida and I'll come along later."

"Well, that might work out. If he'll go."

"Ask him. He's not going to hear it by Ouija board."

"It won't look right if it's just he and I. I don't know him that well. I ought to ask a couple other men."

"Ask as many as you please, but not their wives and daughters."

An invitation to spend three or four days at Adam Moseley's camp with two or three men of equal substance would not be taken as a black mark on Chester L. Weeks's record at the home office. Jess Wilcey, for example, had not been given such an invitation until he had lived in Gibbsville three years. "I can guarantee you a buck if you know which way to point a rifle, and there's some trout fishing. In the evening we usually get up a game of bridge or poker. What size shoe do you wear?"

"Eight-B," said Chester L. Weeks.

"Then I guess I can fix you up with all the clothes you'll need. Not very dressy up there, you know. But plenty of hot water. You'll want a hot bath, especially after that first day in the woods. I notice you're a Scotch drinker, and we also have plenty of Canadian ale. We can leave here the afternoon of the fourteenth, about three hours' drive. Have a good dinner and turn in early so we can be up first thing in the morning. You familiar with the Thirty-O-Six? That's the rifle most of us use."

"Know the rifle very well."

"Good. I have four of them, and you can take your pick. Or you can use a different one every day till you get the limit. Our limit, that is. Our limit's one buck to a man. That's over the legal limit, but it's fair. The game wardens use common sense."

"I haven't brought down a deer since I left Michigan."

Here, at this precise point, by naïvely accepting an invitation he considered a simple compliment, Chester L. Weeks had made a decision he would regret throughout the rest of his life. On Wednesday afternoon Adam Moseley picked him up in his Dodge coupe. They arrived at the camp approximately three hours later, to be greeted by the other hunters, Samuel D. Lafflin, a Wilkes-Barre coal operator, and Malcolm Macleod, division superintendent of the Pennsylvania Railroad, both good shots and good bridge players. They had a steak dinner, cooked by Moseley's guide and caretaker; three rubbers of bridge after dinner, and a good night's sleep. They left the cabin at five-thirty in the morning, and were back at eleven, Lafflin having got his buck in the first hour. Toward dusk MacLeod, Moseley, Weeks, and the guide went out again, and Weeks shot his buck while there was still enough light for a good photograph of the animal and the overjoyed hunter. "Another fifteen minutes and you wouldn't have gotten him," said Moseley. "I'm going to make you a present of his head, mounted. I know a good taxidermist in Allentown."

"Why wouldn't I have gotten him fifteen minutes later? Too dark?"

"Yes. You could have still seen him, all right, but I wouldn't have let you shoot. If you'd missed, you know. Buck fever. A spent bullet from a Thirty-O-Six could kill a man a mile away and you'd never know it."

"But I didn't miss, and anyway I don't get buck fever."

"No, you certainly don't," said Moseley.

"We have two more days," said Weeks. "If you and MacLeod don't get your deer by Saturday afternoon, is it permissible for me to take another shot?"

"Well, yes. But you have to let MacLeod have first shot. That's the usual understanding."

"And what about you?"

"You can have my shot."

"Thank you."

In spite of Moseley's guarantee, no more deer were shot, but Weeks remained keyed up until late Saturday afternoon. His disappointment at not getting a second kill was offset by his being, with Lafflin, one of the two lucky hunters, and the arrival of Mrs. Moseley and her daughter in the middle of the afternoon furnished him with a new audience. "Do you shoot, Mrs. Moseley?" he said, at dinner.

"Only with my camera. Ida has. Ida got her first deer when she was fourteen."

"Fifteen, Mother," said Ida Moseley.

"Your first? And how many have you shot since then?"

"Six, here. Two years ago, in Maine, I shot a moose." She pointed to a head over the fireplace. "That one. Everybody thinks that was Daddy's, but it wasn't. It was mine. Daddy *wishes* it was his, but it isn't."

"I don't wish it was mine," said Moseley. "I just wish it had been T.R., instead of a poor inoffensive moose."

Blanchette Moseley's apprehension that Weeks might resent the feminine invasion of the stag party was unfounded. Rather, he seemed to be stimulated by the presence of women, and he was gracious and entertaining until after lunch on Sunday, when they were all ready to leave for home. "I wish I could spend a month up here," he said.

"It's all yours, if you can persuade Wadsworth & Valentine to give you a vacation," said Moseley. "But it'd probably get pretty lonely up here with only Joe Mossbacher to talk to. He doesn't have much to say."

"The less he said the better. Maybe I might even send him away."

"I don't know," said Moseley. "It'd be quite a change for you, you keep pretty busy."

"Isn't that what I want? A change?"

Blanchette Moseley easily maneuvered Weeks into Ida's car for the homeward journey, and herself into Adam Moseley's Dodge. "It went off very well," she said. "Nothing forced, nobody got self-conscious."

"No, but don't count on me for any more cooperation. I don't like this fellow."

"Oh, now what? I knew you had something plaguing you."

"I don't want him for a son-in-law. No, it's not that. I don't want Ida to be his wife, that's what I don't want."

"I hope you'll respect Ida's wishes in the matter. You'll get a very different story from her. What terrible thing did you find out about him?"

"It's nothing you'd understand."

"Irritating. What is there that you'd understand that I wouldn't, pray tell?"

"The effect it had on him when he killed his buck. Right away he wanted to go on a killing rampage. He wanted to kill Mac's buck and mine."

"You didn't get one, neither did Mac."

"No, you wouldn't understand it at all. He's the kind of a fellow that comes up here and kills three or four deer, as many as he can kill, and leaves them to rot. Doesn't even bother to skin them out."

"You were willing to let him stay here a month."

"That was a safe invitation. There's something about this man's character, I don't pretend to know what it is, but I don't want to see him married to Ida."

"Well, I hope for Ida's sake that she can overlook these mysterious flaws in his character. And don't you help her go looking for them."

"We're going to have snow," said Moseley. "They're having a blizzard in Montana, I read."

"Oh, pish and tush, Adam Moseley."

Ida Moseley had her friends, and throughout that fall and winter Chester L. Weeks was so frequently asked to call for Ida—he would walk to her house, and they would proceed to parties in her car— that it began to be taken for granted that he would be her escort at the social functions of the younger set. She was not so beautiful that habitual propinquity to her was likely to turn a man's head; there was no compelling urgency in a friendship with Ida Moseley, and no unbearable suspense was created for her friends. With Ida it was said you could have a good time without getting serious, and plainly Chester Weeks had a good time with Ida, a jolly good time. But Ida was unable to confide in even her closest friends that Chester had misbehaved, made passes, got fresh, or stayed late at her house. He was of course an older man, a man of the world who had himself under control at all times and one who was more likely to protect a girl's reputation than some of the young bachelors and young husbands in Ida's set. It was somehow understood that he *probably* had secret affairs with some of the women in the town who were understood to have secret affairs with men like Chester L. Weeks; those well-dressed dressmakers and nurses and manicurists who went out with traveling salesmen but rarely were seen in public with town men. It would have been so easy for him to have just that kind of extremely private life while living at the American House. He had refused to take advantage of the vacancies at the Gibbsville Club when they occurred, and the American House was known to be lax about women visitors in men's rooms. And Chester himself, so secretive and so independent and self-sufficient, was just the kind of man who would be too discreet to patronize one of the whorehouses but would make elaborate, secret arrangements for his pleasure. Without a doubt he had had concubines in China, and on the word of Mary Beth Huber he had moved in a fast set on the other side of the world.

Among the older men and women, contemporaries of Adam and Blanchette Moseley, the belief in Chester Weeks's clandestine affairs was so fixed that they expressed some cautious concern for Ida's future: if, as seemed reasonable to suppose, he were eventually to marry Ida, would he give up his other women? Ida pretended to be a sophisticated girl, but did she know what she might be getting into? A man like that could ruin a nice girl's life, and for all her sophistication—reading books by Schnitzler, shooting crap with the young men, driving her Hudson Speedster at eighty miles an hour, and the black silk one-piece bathing suit that had got her a strongly worded note from the club—Ida was a nice girl. Friends of Adam and Blanchette Moseley hoped Ida would not make a fool of herself over this man, and they would be glad when his two years were up and he went away.

Not much was left of his two years at the end of that second winter, and Ida Moseley faced the spring in a mood that sickened her because she would not treat it as desperation. Every day was lost time, and the first of August less than four months away. Chester thought he knew where he was going next: the Company had already asked him how he would feel about being "loaned" to the Irish government.

"Would you like that?" said Ida.

"Hard to say," said Chester. "It could be a big step forward, or it could turn out to be a waste of time. One thing that would interest me."

"What?"

"Well, the language. In China we used to hear that Gaelic and one of the Chinese dialects—I forget which—had words in common. I'd know as soon as I heard them. And of course living in Ireland is much cheaper than living here. I'd save a lot of money there."

"You never worry about money."

"I don't worry about it, but I think about it."

"When would you go, if you went?"

"I get a month off in August, then I report to the home office. Probably the middle of September, late September."

"Won't you be at all sorry to leave Gibbsville?"

"No. I'm not like Jess Wilcey. He's staying here, you know."

"Yes, I know. Maria told me."

"And that's why he's staying. Because Maria likes it. And I guess he does too, although it's Maria that makes the decisions."

"You don't like Maria."

"No. A man as good as Jess shouldn't stop here. He should have made at least one more step upward."

"You've made a lot of friends here."

"Name two. You, but who else?"

"Oh—dozens. You've been one of the most popular men we've ever had. You could be going somewhere every evening if you wanted to."

"Only to escape another kind of boredom. If I had to, I could finish up my job here in four or five weeks. I'm 'way ahead of my schedule. As a matter of fact, I've thought about doing just that, finishing up and taking a leave of absence before the Irish job."

"What other kind of boredom did you mean?"

"Sitting in my room with no work to do."

"Before you go I want to see your room."

"Why? There's nothing to see. Half a dozen prints, and a mantelpiece full of photographs. But my own furniture's in storage in New York."

"I'd still like to see it, where you've lived for nearly two years."

"No. Can you imagine the buzzing if you were seen leaving the American House?"

"Well, naturally."

"If I had my own things it might be worth it. I have some really lovely pieces I picked up in China. Some jade, naturally. And some tapestries that date back to the twelfth century."

"Haven't you any of the jade here?"

"Four pieces, minor items in my collection because I know what hotel chambermaids can do. But the good stuff is stored in New York till I have a house there. Has to be a house. No apartment for me."

"I still want to see your room at the American House."

"It can't be done. Your mother would not approve."

"What if I went there with her?"

He smiled. "Sure, if your mother's interested in brass beds and Grand Rapids rockers."

"Tomorrow, after dinner?"

"Day after tomorrow. I'd offer you dinner, but they don't set a very good table at the American House. You and your mother come in any time after half past eight."

At nine o'clock on the second evening Ida Moseley appeared in the hotel lobby, went to the house telephone, and was connected with Chester's room. "We're downstairs," she said.

"Come right up," he said.

He stood in the hall outside his room, and said nothing when she walked past him through the doorway. He closed the door.

"This could get you in all sorts of trouble, Ida," he said.

"Well, I'm here, so it's too late to do anything about it now," she said. "Don't be cross, Chester. Give me a drink."

"I'll have to send downstairs for some ice. That means the bellboy, getting a good look."

"Jimmy Scott? I've seen him already. Jimmy used to work for us, in our garden. Just give me whiskey or gin and some water from the tap. And a match, please."

He lit her cigarette and made two Scotch-and-waters. She took off her hat and tossed it in a chair.

"What exactly did you have in mind, Ida?"

"I wanted to put you in a compromising position."

"Compromising positions are passé, but endangering your own reputation is just damn foolishness. And that's all you're doing."

"Well, let's have a drink on it."

"It won't be your first, either."

"No, I sneaked a few at home. Is it noticeable? I only had two. No, three. I had a brandy with Daddy, and two by myself."

"Where's your car?"

"Parked down the street in front of the bank. Why?"

"Finish your drink, and we'll go for a ride."

"No hurry."

"That's just the point, there is. If we go now, right this minute, you might be able to get away with it. Not even that evil-minded night clerk could accuse you of much in five minutes."

"Oh, you have a portable. Have you got any new records?"

"Ida, let's cut out the nonsense."

"Now, you've made your honorable gesture, honorable Chester. Honorable Chester with the honorable gesture. But having done so, your conscience is clear and I, for one, would like another Scotch. How about you?"

"No more, for me or you,"

"Don't be an Airedale. I'm not some sixteen-year-old virgin, unacquainted with the facts of life. Surely you don't think I'm so hopeless that I could reach the age of twenty-five without being seduced. I wouldn't call that a compliment, not a bit. Chester?"

"What?"

"Don't make me talk this way. I don't want to get tight. But I have to have something to get up my nerve. If you knew the times I wanted you to kiss me. And if you had, you could have gone the limit. Did you know that? Is that why you didn't kiss me? You could tell that, couldn't you?"

"I suppose so."

"You know so. I don't know whether I love you or not. I think I do. But whether I do or not, I'm sort of hypnotized by you. And that's just as good or just as bad as being in love. I don't care a *thing* about that other boy. He was just a—well, he was a *darling* boy. I won't say anything against him. And I admit it, I was crazy about him. But with you it was sex without being sex, if you know what I mean, and you probably don't. Or maybe you do. Do you?"

"Yes."

"Oh, you do? Then you knew about me, and you didn't want to start something. See, that's where Neddie was inexperienced. Neddie was the boy. He never would have understood that, but you do. That's where you're experienced. All those women, probably Chinese girls and heaven knows what all. You know we're a lot alike, you and I. You were probably seducing me all that time without even holding my hand, and I felt it. I knew what you were doing. You learned that in China, didn't you? I read it somewhere, something to that effect. Or India. It takes immense concentration. But I have a lot to learn, haven't I?"

"Yes, you have."

"I'll be with you in a minute," she said. She went to his bathroom, and came out in a few minutes, wearing her slip and shoes. "I'm still a bit shy," she said.

"So I see."

"You hurry, though, please? And while you're in there I hope you don't mind if I turn out the light."

"I'm not going in there, Ida."

"All right. Come here and kiss me, darling."

He sat on the edge of the bed, took her in his arms, and kissed her. "There," he said.

"No, I think the light's too strong," she said. "It's the light, it's much too strong. And take off your coat. Your coat and vest, take them off."

"No, Ida, I'm sorry."

"I'll take off this slip."

"No, don't."

"I have a nice shape, I really have."

"I know you have. It's quite lovely."

"One of the best in my class."

"I'm sure."

She smiled. "But you don't have to take my word for it."

"I'd rather," he said. "I'd really rather, Ida."

"Don't you want to *see* me?"

"I don't really want to see you."

"You want to wait a while?"

"It isn't that. Seeing you won't make the slightest difference. Nothing will."

She was silent. She gazed thoughtfully at the brass posts at the foot of the bed, and she frowned. Then she remembered that her hand was on his shoulder, and she took it away.

"You mean you can't?" she said.

"I can't because I don't want to."

"Oh."

"It isn't you, Ida. You're very sweet. Very sweet. And I'm sorry."

"Wouldn't you just like to lie here with me, gently?"

"It wouldn't be any use, and I wouldn't like it. No, I don't want to."

"Is it men?"

"When it's anything, yes."

"But that's terrible, Chester. I feel so sorry for you."

He smiled. "That's because you're nice. You are nice, you know."

"I never guessed. You know—I'm supposed to be pretty blasé."

"Well, now I guess you will be. When you've had time to think it over."

"I don't need time. And I don't like being blasé."

"No, it isn't much."

"It's nothing. Really nothing."

"And now I'm nothing, am I?"

"I don't know. Kiss me again."

He kissed her cheek. She shook her head. "It's much too much for me to understand. I'll have a drink, please."

He went to the table, and while his back was turned she slipped past him to the bathroom. She came out fully dressed, and accepted the glass he held out for her. She sat down and gave him a quick smile, but looked away from him.

"Is this one of the jades you brought from China?"

"Yes, not a very good one."

She put it down without examining it very carefully. "I don't know anything about jade. I have one in my room at home that's supposed to be pretty good. Given to me by a Chinese friend of mine."

"Mary Ku," he said.

"Yes, you've heard me speak of her. She's been here. Everybody adored her."

"Go on home, Ida. Don't make talk-talk."

She finished her drink quickly. "I think I will. Are you coming for dinner Friday?"

"No, I don't think so."

"You can if you want to."

"No."

"I guess you're right, really."

"If I sent you one of my good jades would you keep it?"

"Oh, you know I'd like to, but—"

"Say no more."

"I need a little time to straighten things out in my mind. Oh, heavens, Chester. *You* know."

"Of course."

"Goodnight," she said.

Her car went off the road at a turn about five miles north of Reading, some time around half past ten. It was quite possible that she was blinded by the headlights of a bootlegger's truck, but no one knew why she was so far from home, and alone, at that hour of the night. But they found a considerable amount of alcohol in her stomach, and that was when the questions led back to the American House. Dr. Mary Ku came all the way from Massachusetts General to attend the funeral.

Pat Collins

Now they are both getting close to seventy, and when they see each other on the street Whit Hofman and Pat Collins bid each other the time of day and pass on without stopping for conversation. It may be that in Whit Hofman's greeting there is a little more hearty cordiality than in Pat Collins's greeting to him; it may be that in Pat Collins's words and smile there is a wistfulness that is all he has left of thirty years of a dwindling hope.

The town is full of young people who never knew that for about three years—1925, 1926, 1927—Whit Hofman's favorite companion was none other than Pat Collins. Not only do they not know of the once close relationship; today they would not believe it. But then it is hard to believe, with only the present evidence to go on. Today Pat Collins still has his own garage, but it is hardly more than a filling station and tire repair business on the edge of town, patronized by the people of the neighborhood and not situated on a traffic artery of any importance. He always has some young man helping out, but he does most of the work himself. Hard work it is, too. He hires young men out of high school—out of prison, sometimes—but the young men don't stay. They never stay. They like Pat Collins, and they say so, but they don't want to work at night, and Pat Collins's twenty-four-hour service is what keeps him going. Twenty-four hours, seven days a week, the only garage in town that says it and means it. A man stuck for gas, a man with a flat and no spare, a man skidded into a ditch—they all know that if they phone Pat Collins he will get there in his truck and if necessary tow them away. Some of the motorists are embarrassed: people who never patronize Pat Collins except in emergencies; people who knew him back in the days when he was Whit Hofman's favorite companion. They embarrass themselves; he does not say or do anything to embarrass them except one thing: he charges them fair prices when he could hold them up, and to some of those people who knew him long ago that is the most

The Cape Cod Lighter (1962)

embarrassing thing he could do. "Twelve dollars, Pat? You could have charged me more than that."

"Twelve dollars," he says. And there were plenty of times when he could have asked fifty dollars for twelve dollars' worth of service—when the woman in the stalled car was not the wife of the driver.

Now, to the younger ones, he has become a local symbol of misfortune ("All I could do was call Pat Collins") and at the same time a symbol of dependability ("Luckily I thought of Pat Collins"). It is mean work; the interrupted sleep, the frequently bad weather, the drunks and the shocked and the guilty-minded. But it is the one service he offers that makes the difference between a profit and breaking even.

"Hello, Pat," Whit Hofman will say, when they meet on Main Street.

"Hyuh, Whit," Pat Collins will say.

Never more than that, but never less . . .

Aloysius Aquinas Collins came to town in 1923 because he had heard it was a good place to be, a rich town for its size. Big coal interests to start with, but good diversification as well: a steel mill, a couple of iron foundries, the railway car shops, shoe factories, silk mills, half a dozen breweries, four meat packing plants and, to the south, prosperous farmers. Among the rich there were two Rolls-Royces, a dozen or more Pierce-Arrows, a couple of dozen Cadillacs, and maybe a dozen each of Lincolns, Marmons, Packards. It was a spending town; the Pierce-Arrow families bought small roadsters for their children and the women were beginning to drive their own cars. The Rolls-Royces and Pierce-Arrows were in Philadelphia territory, and the franchises for the other big cars were already spoken for, but Pat Collins was willing to start as a dealer for one of the many makes in the large field between Ford-Dodge and Cadillac-Packard, one of the newer, lesser known makes. It was easy to get a franchise for one of those makes, and he decided to take his time.

Of professional experience in the automobile game he had none. He was not yet thirty, and he had behind him two years at Villanova, fifteen months as a shore duty ensign, four years as a salesman of men's hats at which he made pretty good money but from which he got nothing else but stretches of boredom between days of remorse following salesmen's parties in hotels. His wife Madge had lost her early illusions, but she loved him and partly blamed life on the road for what was happening to him. "Get into something else," she would say, "or honest to God, Pat, I'm going to take the children and pull out."

"It's easy enough to talk about getting another job," he would say. "I don't care what it is, just as long as you're not away five days a week. Drive a taxi, if you have to."

When she happened to mention driving a taxi she touched upon the only major interest he had outside the routine of his life: from the early days of Dario Resta and the brothers Chevrolet he had been crazy about automobiles, all automobiles and everything about them. He would walk or take the "L" from home in West Philadelphia to the area near City Hall, and wander about, stopping in front of the hotels and clubs and private residences and theaters and the Academy of Music, staring at the limousines and town cars, engaging in conversation with the chauffeurs; and then he would walk up North Broad Street, Automobile Row, and because he was a nice-looking kid, the floor salesmen would sometimes let him sit in the cars on display. He collected all the manufacturers' brochures and read all the advertisements in the newspapers. Closer to home he would stand for hours, studying the sporty roadsters and phaetons outside the Penn fraternity houses; big Simplexes with searchlights on the running-boards, Fiats and Renaults and Hispanos and Blitzen-Benzes. He was nice-looking and he had nice manners, and when he would hold the door open for one of the fraternity men they would sometimes give him a nickel and say, "Will you keep your eye on my car, sonny?"

"Can I sit in it, please?"

"Well, if you promise not to blow the horn."

He passed the horn-blowing stage quickly. Sometimes the fraternity men would come out to put up the top when there was a sudden shower, and find that Aloysius Aquinas Collins had somehow done it alone. For this service he wanted no reward but a ride home, on the front seat. On his side of the room he shared with his older brother he had magazine and rotogravure pictures of fine cars pinned to the walls. The nuns at school complained that instead of paying attention, he was continually drawing pictures of automobiles, automobiles. The nuns did not know how good the drawings were; they only cared that one so bright could waste so much time, and their complaints to his parents made it impossible for Aloysius to convince Mr. and Mrs. Collins that after he got his high school diploma, he wanted to get a job on Automobile Row. The parents sent him to Villanova, and after sophomore year took him out because the priests told them they were wasting their money, but out of spite his father refused to let him take a job in the auto business. Collins got him a job in the shipyards, and when the country entered the war, Aloysius joined the Navy and eventually was commissioned. He married Madge Ruddy, became a hat salesman, and rented half of a two-family house in Upper Darby.

Gibbsville was on his sales route, and it first came to his special notice because his Gibbsville customer bought more hats in his high-priced line than any other store of comparable size. He thus discovered that it was a spending town, and that the actual population figures were deceptive; it was surrounded by a lot of much smaller towns whose citizens shopped in Gibbsville. He began to add a day to his normal visits to Gibbsville, to make a study of the automobile business there, and when he came into a small legacy from his aunt, he easily persuaded Madge to put in her own five thousand dollars, and he bought Cunningham's Garage, on Railroad Avenue, Gibbsville.

Cunningham's was badly run down and had lost money for its previous two owners, but it was the oldest garage in town. The established automobile men were not afraid of competition from the newcomer, Collins, who knew nobody to speak of and did not even have a dealer's franchise. They thought he was out of his mind when he began spending money in sprucing up the place. They also thought, and said, that he was getting pretty big for his britches in choosing to rent a house on Lantenengo Street. The proprietor of Cunningham's old garage then proceeded to outrage the established dealers by stealing Walt Michaels' best mechanic, Joe Ricci. Regardless of what the dealers might do to each other in the competition to clinch a sale, one thing you did not do was entice away a man's best mechanic. Walt Michaels, who had the Oldsmobile franchise, paid a call on the new fellow.

A. A. Collins, owner and proprietor, as his sign said, of Collins Motor Company, was in his office when he saw Michaels get out of his car. He went out to greet Michaels, his hand outstretched. "Hello, Mr. Michaels, I'm Pat Collins," he said.

"I know who you are. I just came down to tell you what I think of you."

"Not much, I guess, judging by—"

"Not much is right."

"Smoke a cigar?" said Pat Collins.

Michaels slapped at the cigar and knocked it to the ground. Pat Collins picked it up and looked at it. "I guess that's why they wrap them in tinfoil." He rubbed the dirt off the cigar and put it back in his pocket.

"Don't you want to fight?" said Michaels.

"What for? You have a right to be sore at me, in a way. But when you have a good mechanic like Joe, you ought to be willing to pay him what he's worth."

"Well, I never thought I'd see an Irishman back out of a fight. But with you I guess that's typical. A sneaky Irish son of a bitch."

"Now just a minute, Michaels. Go easy."

"I said it. A sneaky Irish son of a bitch."

"Yeah, I was right the first time," said Collins. He hit Michaels in the stomach with his left hand, and as Michaels crumpled, Collins hit him on the chin with his right hand. Michaels went down, and Collins stood over him, waiting for him to get up. Michaels started to raise himself with both hands on the ground, calling obscene names, but while his hands were still on the ground Collins stuck the foil-wrapped cigar deep in his mouth. Three or four men who stopped to look at the fight burst into laughter, and Michaels, his breath shut off, fell back on the ground.

"Change your mind about the cigar, Michaels?" said Collins.

"I'll send my son down to see you," said Michaels, getting to his feet.

"All right. What does *he* smoke?"

"He's as big as you are."

"Then I'll use a tire iron on him. Now get out of here, and quick."

Michaels, dusting himself off, saw Joe Ricci among the spectators. He pointed at him with his hat. "You, you ginny bastard, you stole tools off of me."

Ricci, who had a screwdriver in his hand, rushed at Michaels and might have stabbed him, but Collins swung him away.

"Calling me a thief, the son of a bitch, I'll kill him," said Ricci. "I'll *kill* him."

"Go on, Michaels. Beat it," said Collins.

Michaels got in his car and put it in gear, and as he was about to drive away Collins called to him: "Hey, Michaels, shall I fill her up?"

The episode, the kind that men liked to embellish in the retelling, made Pat Collins universally unpopular among the dealers, but it made him known to a wider public. It brought him an important visitor.

The Mercer phaeton pulled up at Pat Collins's gas pump and Collins, in his office, jumped up from his desk, and without putting on his coat, went out to the curb. "Can I help you?" he said.

"Fill her up, will you, please?" said the driver. He was a handsome man, about Collins's age, wearing a brown Homburg and a coonskin coat. Pat Collins knew who he was—Whit Hofman, probably the richest young man in the town—because he knew the car. He was conscious of Hofman's curiosity, but he went on pumping the gasoline. He hung up the hose and said, "You didn't need much. That'll cost you thirty-six cents, Mr. Hofman. Wouldn't you rather I sent you a bill?"

"Well, all right. But don't I get a cigar, a new customer? At least that's what I hear."

The two men laughed. "Sure, have a cigar," said Collins, handing him one. Hofman looked at it.

"Tinfoil, all right. You sure this isn't the same one you gave Walt Michaels?"

"It might be. See if it has any teeth marks on it," said Collins.

"Well, I guess Walt had it coming to him. He's a kind of a sore-head."

"You know him?"

"Of course. Known him all my life, he's always lived here. He's not a bad fellow, Mr. Collins, but you took Joe away from him, and Joe's a hell of a good mechanic. I'd be sore, too, I guess."

"Well, when you come looking for a fight, you ought to be more sure of what you're up against. Either that, or be ready to take a beating. I only hit him twice."

"When I was a boy you wouldn't have knocked him down that easily. When I was a kid, Walt Michaels was a good athlete, but he's put away a lot of beer since then." Hofman looked at Collins. "Do you like beer?"

"I like the beer you get around here. It's better than we get in Philly."

"Put on your coat and let's drink some beer," said Hofman. "Or are you busy?"

"Not that busy," said Collins.

They drove to a saloon in one of the neighboring towns, and Collins was surprised to see that no one was surprised to see the young millionaire, with his Mercer and his coonskin coat. The men drinking at the bar—workingmen taking a day off, they appeared to be— were neither cordial nor hostile to Hofman. "Hello, Paul," said Hofman. "Brought you a new customer."

"I need all I can get," said the proprietor. "Where will you want to sit? In the back room?"

"I guess so. This is Mr. Collins, just opened a new garage. Mr. Collins, Mr. Paul Unitas, sometimes called Unitas States of America."

"Pleased to meet you," said Paul, shaking hands.

"Same here," said Collins.

"How's the beer?" said Hofman.

Paul shook his head. "They're around. They stopped two truck-loads this morning."

"Who stopped them? The state police?" said Hofman.

"No, this time it was enforcement agents. New ones."

Hofman laughed. "You don't have to worry about Mr. Collins. I'll vouch for him."

"Well, if you say so, Whit. What'll you have?"

"The beer's no good?"

"Slop. Have rye. It's pretty good. I cut it myself."

"Well, if you say rye, that's what we'll have. Okay, Collins?"

"Sure."

Hofman was an affable man, an interested listener and a hearty laugher. It was dark when they left the saloon; Collins had told Hofman a great deal about himself, and Hofman drove Collins home in the Mercer. "I can offer you some Canadian Club," said Collins.

"Thanks just the same, but we're going out to dinner and I have to change. Ask me again sometime. Nice to've seen you, Pat."

"Same to you, Whit. Enjoyable afternoon," said Collins.

In the house Collins kissed Madge's cheek. "Whew! Out drinking with college boys?" she said.

"I'll drink with that college boy any time. That's Whit Hofman."

"How on earth—"

She listened with increasing eagerness while he told her the events of the afternoon. "Maybe you could sell him a car, if you had a good franchise," she said.

"I'm not going to try to sell him anything but Aloysius Aquinas Collins, Esquire. And anyway, I like him."

"You can like people and still sell them a car."

"Well, I'm never going to try to make a sale there. He came to see me out of curiosity, but we hit it off right away. He's a swell fellow."

"Pat?"

"What?"

"Remember why we moved here."

"Listen, it's only ha' past six and I'm home. This guy came to see me, Madge."

"A rich fellow with nothing better to do," she said.

"Oh, for God's sake. You say remember why we moved here. To have a home. But *you* remember why I wanted to live on this street. To meet people like Whit Hofman."

"But not to spend the whole afternoon in some hunky saloon. Were there any women there?"

"A dozen of them, all walking around naked. What have you got for supper?"

"For *dinner,* we have veal cutlets. But Pat, remember what we are. We're not society people. What's she like, his wife?"

"How would I know? I wouldn't know her if I saw her. Unless she was driving that car."

They had a two weeks' wait before Whit Hofman again had the urge for Pat Collins's company. This time Hofman took him to the country club, and they sat in the smoking-room with a bottle of Scotch on the table. "Do you play squash?" said Hofman.

"Play it? I thought you ate it. No, I used to play handball."

"Well, it's kind of handball with a racquet. It's damn near the only exercise I get in the winter, at least until we go South. If you were a good handball player, you'd learn squash in no time."

"Where? At the Y.M.?"

"Here. We have a court here," said Hofman. He got up and pointed through the French window. "See that little house down there, to the right of the first fairway? That's the squash court."

"I was a caddy one summer."

"Oh, you play golf?"

"I've never had a club in my hand since then."

"How would you like to join here? I'll be glad to put you up and we'll find somebody to second you. Does your wife play tennis or golf?"

"No, she's not an athlete. How much would it cost to join?"

"Uh, family membership, you and your wife and children under twenty-one. They just raised it. Initiation, seventy-five dollars. Annual dues, thirty-five for a family membership."

"Do you think I could get in? We don't know many people that belong."

"Well, Walt Michaels doesn't belong. Can you think of anyone else that might blackball you? Because if you can't, I think I could probably get you in at the next meeting. Technically, I'm not supposed to put you up, because I'm on the admissions committee, but that's no problem."

Any hesitancy Pat Collins might have had immediately vanished at mention of the name Walt Michaels. "Well, I'd sure like to belong."

"I'll take care of it. Let's have a drink on it," said Whit Hofman.

"We're Catholics, you know."

"That's all right. We take Catholics. Not all, but some. And those we don't take wouldn't get in if they were Presbyterian or anything else."

"Jews?"

"We have two. One is a doctor, married to a Gentile. He claims he isn't a Jew, but he is. The other is the wife of a Gentile. Otherwise, no. I understand they're starting their own club, I'm not sure where it'll be."

"Well, as long as you know we're Catholics."

"I knew that, Pat," said Hofman. "But I respect you for bringing it up."

Madge Collins was upset about the country club. "It isn't only what you have to pay to get in. It's meals, and spending money on clothes. I haven't bought anything new since we moved here."

"As the Dodge people say, 'It isn't the initial cost, it's the upkeep.' But Madge, I told you before, those are the kind of people that're gonna be worth our while. I'll make a lot of connections at the country club, and in the meantime, I'll get a franchise. So far I didn't spend a nickel on advertising. Well, this is gonna be the best kind of advertising. The Cadillac dealer is the only other dealer in the country club, and I won't compete with him."

"Everything going out, very little coming in," she said.

"Stop worrying, everything's gonna be hunky-dory."

On the morning after the next meeting of the club admissions committee Whit Hofman telephoned Pat Collins. "Congratulations to the newest member of the Lantenengo Country Club. It was a cinch. You'll get a notice and a bill, and as soon as you send your cheque you and Mrs. Collins can start using the club, although there's no golf or tennis now. However, there's a dance next Friday, and we'd like you and your wife to have dinner with us. Wear your Tuck. My wife is going to phone Mrs. Collins some time today."

In her two years as stock girl and saleslady at Oppenheim, Collins —"my cousins," Pat called them—Madge had learned a thing or two about values, and she had style sense. The evening dress she bought for the Hofman dinner and club dance was severely simple, black, and Pat thought it looked too old for her. "Wait till you see it on," she said. She changed the shoulder straps and substituted thin black cord, making her shoulders, chest, and back completely bare and giving an illusion of a deeper décolletage than was actually the case. She had a good figure and a lovely complexion, and when he saw her ready to leave for the party, he was startled. "It's not too old for you any more. Maybe it's too young."

"I wish I had some jewelry," she said.

"You have. I can see them."

"Oh—oh, stop. It's not immodest. You can't see anything unless you stoop over and look down."

"Unless you happen to be over five foot five, and most men are."

"Do you want me to wear a shawl? I have a nice old shawl of

Grandma's. As soon as we start making money the one thing I want is a good fur coat. That's all I want, and I can get one wholesale."

"Get one for me, while you're at it. But for now, let's get a move on. Dinner is eight-thirty and we're the guests of honor."

"Guests of honor! Just think of it, Pat. I haven't been so excited since our wedding. I hope I don't do anything wrong."

"Just watch Mrs. Hofman. I don't even know who else'll be there, but it's time we were finding out."

"Per-*fume!* I didn't put on any per*fume*. I'll be right down."

She was excited and she had youth and health, but she also had a squarish face with a strong jawline that gave her a look of maturity and dignity. Her hair was reddish brown, her eyes grey-green. It was a face full of contrasts, especially from repose to animation, and with the men—beginning with Whit Hofman—she was an instant success.

The Hofmans had invited three other couples besides the Collinses. Custom forbade having liquor bottles or cocktail shakers on the table at club dances, and Whit Hofman kept a shaker and a bottle on the floor beside him. The men were drinking straight whiskey, the women drank orange blossoms. There was no bar, and the Hofman party sat at the table and had their drinks until nine o'clock, when Hofman's wife signalled the steward to start serving. Chincoteagues were served first, and before the soup, Whit Hofman asked Madge Collins to dance. He was feeling good, and here he was king. His fortune was respected by men twice his age, and among the men and women who were more nearly his contemporaries he was genuinely well liked for a number of reasons: his unfailingly good manners, no matter how far in drink he might get; his affability, which drew upon his good manners when bores and toadies and the envious and the weak made their assaults; his emanations of strength, which were physically and tangibly demonstrated in his expertness at games as well as in the slightly more subtle self-reminders of his friends that he *was* Whit Hofman and *did have* all that money. He had a good war record, beginning with enlistment as a private in the National Guard for Mexican Border service, and including a field commission, a wound chevron, and a Croix de Guerre with palm during his A.E.F. service. He was overweight, but he could afford bespoke tailors and he cared about clothes; tonight he was wearing a dinner jacket with a white waistcoat and a satin butterfly tie. Madge Ruddy Collins had never known anyone quite like him, and her first mistake was to believe that his high spirits had something special to do with her. At this stage she had no way of knowing that later on, when he danced with his fat old second cousin, he would be just as much fun.

"Well, how do you like your club?" he said.

"My club? Oh—*this* club. Oh, it's beautiful. Pat and I certainly do thank you."

"Very glad to do it. I hope you're going to take up golf. More and more women are. Girl I just spoke to, Mrs. Dick Richards, she won the second flight this year, and she only started playing last spring."

"Does your wife play?"

"She plays pretty well, and could be a lot better. She's going to have a lot of lessons when we go South. That's the thing to do. As soon as you develop a fault, have a lesson right away, before it becomes a habit. I'm going to have Pat playing squash before we leave."

"Oh."

"He said he was a handball player, so squash ought to come easy to him. Of course it's a much more strenuous game than golf."

"It is?"

He said something in reply to a question from a man dancing by. The man laughed, and Whit Hofman laughed. "That's Johnny King," said Hofman. "You haven't met the Kings, have you?"

"No," said Madge. "She's pretty. Beautifully gowned."

"Oh, that's not his wife. She isn't here tonight. That's Mary-Louise Johnson, from Scranton. There's a whole delegation from Scranton here tonight. They all came down for Buz McKee's birthday party. That's the big table over in the corner. Well, I'm getting the high sign, I guess we'd better go back to our table. Thank you, Madge. A pleasure."

"Oh, to me, too," she said.

In due course every man in the Hofman party danced with every woman, the duty rounds. Pat Collins was the last to dance with Madge on the duty rounds. "You having a good time?" he said.

"Oh, *am* I?" she said.

"How do you like Whit?"

"He's a real gentleman, I'm crazy about him. I like him the best. Do you like her, his wife?"

"I guess so. In a way yes, and in a way no."

"Me too. She'd rather be with those people from Scranton."

"What people from Scranton?"

"At the big table. They're here to attend a birthday party for Buzzie McKee."

"Jesus, you're learning fast."

"I found that out from Whit. The blonde in the beaded white, that's Mary-Louise Johnson, dancing with Johnny King. They're dancing every dance together."

"Together is right. Take a can-opener to pry them apart."

"His wife is away," said Madge. "Where did Whit go?"

Pat turned to look at their table. "I don't know. Oh, there he is, dancing with some fat lady."

"I don't admire his taste."

"Say, you took a real shine to Whit," said Pat Collins.

"Well, he's a real gentleman, but he isn't a bit forward. Now where's he going? . . . Oh, I guess he wanted to wish Buzzie Mc-Kee a happy birthday. Well, let's sit down."

The chair at her left remained vacant while Hofman continued his visit to the McKee table. On Madge's right was a lawyer named Joe Chapin, who had something to do with the admissions committee; polite enough, but for Madge very hard to talk to. At the moment he was in conversation with the woman on his right, and Madge Collins felt completely alone. A minute passed, two minutes, and her solitude passed to uneasiness to anger. Whit Hofman made his way back to the table, and when he sat down she said, trying to keep the irritation out of her tone, "That wasn't very polite."

"I'm terribly sorry. I thought you and Joe—"

"Oh, *him*. Well, I'll forgive you if you dance this dance with me."

"Why of course," said Hofman.

They got up again, and as they danced she closed her eyes, pretending to an ecstasy she did not altogether feel. They got through eighteen bars of "Bambalina," and the music stopped. "Oh, hell," she said. "I'll let you have the next."

"Fine," he said. She took his arm, holding it so that her hand clenched his right biceps, and giving it a final squeeze as they sat down.

"Would you like some more coffee?" he said. "If not I'm afraid we're going to have to let them take the table away."

"Why?"

"That's what they do. Ten o'clock, tables have to be cleared out, to make room for the dancing. You know, quite a few people have dinner at home, then come to the dance."

"What are they? Cheap skates?"

"Oh, I don't know about that. No, hardly that."

"But if *you* wanted to keep the table, they'd let you."

"Oh, I wouldn't do that, Madge. They really need the room."

"Then where do we go?"

"Wherever we like. Probably the smoking-room. But from now on we just sort of—circulate."

"You mean your dinner is over?"

"Yes, that's about it. We're on our own."

"I don't want to go home. I want to dance with you some more."

"Who said anything about going home? The fun is just about to begin."

"I had fun before. I'm not very good with strangers."

"You're not a stranger. You're a member of the club, duly launched. Let's go out to the smoking-room and I'll get you a drink. How would you like a Stinger?"

"What is it? Never mind telling me. I'll have one."

"If you've never had one, be careful. It could be your downfall. Very cool to the taste, but packs a wallop. Sneaks up on you."

"Good. Let's have one." She rose and quickly took his unoffered arm, and they went to the smoking-room, which was already more than half filled.

At eleven o'clock she was drunk. She would dance with no one but Whit Hofman, and when she danced with him she tried to excite him, and succeeded. "You're hot stuff, Madge," he said.

"Why what do you *mean?*"

"The question is, what do *you* mean?"

"I don't know what you're *talking* about," she said, sing-song.

"The hell you don't," he said. "Shall we go for a stroll?"

"Where to?"

"My car's around back of the caddyhouse."

"Do you think we ought to?"

"No, but either that or let's sit down."

"All right, let's sit down. I'm getting kind of woozy, anyhow."

"Don't drink any more Stingers. I told you they were dangerous. Maybe you ought to have some coffee. Maybe I ought to, too. Come on, we'll get some coffee." He led her to a corner of the smoking-room, where she could prop herself against the wall. He left her, and in the hallway to the kitchen he encountered Pat Collins on his way from the locker-room.

"Say, Pat, if I were you—well, Madge had a couple of Stingers and I don't think they agree with her."

"Is she sick?"

"No, but I'm afraid she's quite tight."

"I better take her home?"

"*You* know. Your first night here. There'll be others much worse off, but she's the one they'll talk about. The maid'll get her wrap, and you can ease her out so nobody'll notice. I'll say your goodnights for you."

"Well, gee, Whit—I'm sorry. I certainly apologize."

"Perfectly all right, Pat. No harm done, but she's ready for beddy-bye. I'll call you in a day or two."

There was no confusing suggestion with command, and Pat obeyed Hofman. He got his own coat and Madge's, and when Madge saw her coat she likewise recognized authority.

They were less than a mile from the club when she said, "I'm gonna be sick."

He stopped the car. "All right, *be* sick."

When she got back in the car she said, "Leave the windows down, I need the fresh air."

He got her to bed. His anger was so great that he did not trust himself to speak to her, and she mistook his silence for pity. She kept muttering that she was sorry, sorry, and went to sleep. Much later he fell asleep, awoke before six, dressed and left the house before he had to speak to her. He had his breakfast in an all-night restaurant, bought the morning newspapers, and opened the garage. He needed to think, and not so much about punishing Madge as about restoring himself to good standing in the eyes of the Hofmans. He had caught Kitty Hofman's cold appraisal of Madge on the dance floor; he had known, too, that he had failed to make a good impression on Kitty, who was in a sour mood for having to give up the Buz McKee dinner. He rejected his first plan to send Kitty flowers and a humorous note. Tomorrow or the next day Madge could send the flowers and a thank-you note, which he would make sure contained no reference to her getting tight or any other apologetic implication. The important thing was to repair any damage to his relationship with Whit Hofman, and after a while he concluded that aside from Madge's thank-you note to both Hofmans, the wiser course was to wait for Whit to call him.

He had a long wait.

Immediately after Christmas the Hofmans went to Florida. They returned for two weeks in late March, closed their house, and took off on a trip around the world. Consequently the Collinses did not see the Hofmans for nearly a year. It was a year that was bad for the Collins marriage, but good for the Collins Motor Company. Pat Collins got the Chrysler franchise, and the car practically sold itself. Women and the young took to it from the start, and the Collins Motor Company had trouble keeping up with the orders. The bright new car and the bright new Irishman were interchangeably associated in the minds of the citizens, and Pat and Madge Collins were getting somewhere on their own, without the suspended sponsorship of Whit Hofman. But at home Pat and Madge had never quite got back to what they had been before she jeopardized his relationship with Whit Hofman. He had counted so much on Hofman's approval that the threat of losing it had given him a big scare, and it would not be far-fetched to say that the designers of the Chrysler "70" saved the Collins marriage.

Now they were busy, Pat with his golf when he could take the time off from his work—which he did frequently; and Madge with the game of bridge, which she learned adequately well. In the absence of the Whit Hofmans the social life of the country club was left without an outstanding couple to be the leaders, although several couples tried to fill the gap. In the locker-room one afternoon, drinking gin and ginger ale with the members of his foursome, Pat Collins heard one of the men say, "You know who we all miss? Whit. The club isn't the same without him." Pat looked up as at a newly discovered truth, and for the first time he realized that he liked Whit Hofman better than any man he had ever known. It had remained for someone else to put the thought into words, and casual enough words they were to express what Pat Collins had felt from the first day in Paul Unitas's saloon. Like nearly everyone else in the club the Collinses had had a postcard or two from the Hofmans; Honolulu, Shanghai, Bangkok, St. Andrew's, St. Cloud. The Hofmans' closer friends had had letters, but the Collinses were pleased to have had a postcard, signed "Kitty and Whit"—in Whit's handwriting.

"When does he get back, does anyone know?" said Pat.

"Middle of October," said the original speaker. "You know Whit. He wouldn't miss the football season, not the meat of it anyway."

"About a month away," said Pat Collins. "Well, I can thank him for the most enjoyable summer I ever had. He got me in here, you know. I was practically a stranger."

" 'A stranger in a strange land,' but not any more, Pat."

"Thank you. You fellows have been damn nice to me." He meant the sentiment, but the depth of it belonged to his affection for Whit Hofman. He had his shower and dressed, and joined Madge on the terrace. "Do you want to stay here for dinner?"

"We have nothing at home," she said.

"Then we'll eat here," he said. "Did you know the Hofmans are getting back about four weeks from now?"

"I knew it."

"Why didn't you tell me?"

"I didn't know you wanted to know, or I would have. Why, are you thinking of hiring a brass band? One postcard."

"What did you expect? As I remember, you didn't keep it any secret when we got it."

"You were the one that was more pleased than I was."

"Oh, all right. Let's go eat."

They failed to be invited to the smaller parties in honor of the

returning voyagers, but they went to a Dutch Treat dinner for the
Hofmans before the club dance. Two changes in the Hofmans were
instantly noticeable: Whit was as brown as a Hawaiian, and Kitty was
pregnant. She received the members of the dinner party sitting
down. She had lost one child through miscarriage. Whit stood beside
her, and when it came the Collinses' turn he greeted Pat and Madge
by nickname and first name. Not so Kitty. "Oh, he*llo*. Mrs. *Co*llins.
Nice of you to come. Hello, Mr. Collins." Then, seeing the man next
in line she called out: "Bob-bee! Bobby, where were you Tuesday?
You were supposed to be at the Ogdens', you false friend. I thought
you'd be at the boat."

The Collinses moved on, and Madge said, "We shouldn't have
come."

"Why not? She doesn't have to like us."

"She didn't have to be so snooty, either."

"Bobby Hermann is one of their best friends."

"I'm damn sure we're not."

"Oh, for God's sake."

"Oh, for God's sake yourself," she said.

The year had done a lot for Madge in such matters as her poise
and the widening of her acquaintance among club members. But it
was not until eleven or so that Whit Hofman cut in on her. "How've
you been?" he said.

"Lonely without you," she said.

"That's nice to hear. I wish you meant it."

"You're pretending to think I don't," she said. "But I thought of
you every day. And every night. Especially every night."

"How many Stingers have you had?"

"That's a nasty thing to say. I haven't had any. I've never had one
since that night. So we'll change the subject. Are you going to stay
home a while?"

"Looks that way. Kitty's having the baby in January."

"Sooner than that, I thought."

"No, the doctor says January."

"Which do you want? A boy, or a girl?"

"Both, but not at the same time."

"Well, you always get what you want, so I'm told."

"That's a new one on me."

"Well, you can *have* anything you want, put it that way."

"No, not even that."

"What do you want that you haven't got?"

"A son, or a daughter."

"Well, you're getting that, one or the other. What else?"

"Right now, nothing else."

"I don't believe anybody's ever that contented."

"Well, what do *you* want, for instance?"

"You," she said.

"Why? You have a nice guy. Kids. And I hear Pat's the busiest car dealer in town."

"Those are things I have. You asked me what I wanted."

"You don't beat about the bush, do you, Madge? You get right to the point."

"I've been in love with you for almost a year."

"Madge, you haven't been in love with me at all. Maybe you're not in love with Pat, but you're certainly not in love with me. You couldn't be."

"About a month ago I heard you were coming home, and I had it all planned out how I was going to be when I saw you. But I was wrong. I couldn't feel this way for a whole year and then start pretending I didn't. You asked me how I was, and I came right out with it, the truth."

"Well, Madge, I'm not in love with you. You're damn attractive and all that, but I'm not in *love* with you."

"I know that. But answer me one question, as truthful as I am with you. Are you in love with your wife?"

"Of course I am."

"I'll tell you something, Whit. You're not. With her. With me. Or maybe with anybody."

"Now really, that *is* a nasty thing to say."

"People love you, Whit, but you don't love them back."

"I'm afraid I don't like this conversation. Shall we go back and have a drink?"

"Yes."

They moved toward the smoking-room. "Why did you say that, Madge? What makes you think it?"

"You really want me to tell you? Remember, the truth hurts, and I had a whole year to think about this."

"What the hell, tell me."

"It's not you, it's the town. There's nobody here bigger than you. They all love you, but you don't love them."

"I love this town and the people in it and everything about it. Don't you think I could live anywhere I wanted to? Why do you think I came back here? I can live anywhere in the God damn world. Jesus, you certainly have that one figured wrong. For a minute you almost had me worried."

He danced with her no more that night, and if he could avoid speaking to her or getting close to her, he did so. When she got home, past three o'clock, she gave Pat Collins a very good time; loveless but exceedingly pleasurable. Then she lay in her bed until morning, unable to understand herself, puzzled by forces that had never been mysterious to her.

The Hofman baby was born on schedule, a six-pound boy, but the reports from the mother's bedside were not especially happy. Kitty had had a long and difficult time, and one report, corroborated only by constant repetition, was that she had thrown a clock, or a flower vase, or a water tumbler, or all of them, at Whit at the start of her labor. It was said, and perfunctorily denied, that a group of nurses and orderlies stood outside her hospital room, listening fascinatedly to the obscene names she called him, names that the gossips would not utter but knew how to spell. Whatever the basis in fact, the rumors of hurled bric-a-brac and invective seemed to be partially confirmed when Kitty Hofman came home from the hospital. The infant was left in the care of a nurse, and Kitty went to every party, drinking steadily and chain-smoking, saying little and watching everything. She had a look of determination, as though she had just made up her mind about something, but the look and decision were not followed up by action. She would stay at the parties until she had had enough, then she would get her wrap and say goodnight to her hostess, without any word or sign to Whit, and it would be up to him to discover she was leaving and follow her out.

Their friends wondered how long Whit Hofman would take that kind of behavior, but no one—least of all Pat Collins—was so tactless, or bold, as to suggest to Whit that there *was* any behavior. It was Whit, finally, who talked.

He was now seeing Pat Collins nearly every day, and on some days more than once. He knew as much about automobiles as Pat Collins, and he was comfortable in Pat's office. He had made the garage one of his ports of call in his daytime rounds—his office every morning at ten, the barber's, the bank, the broker's, his lawyer, lunch at the Gibbsville Club, a game of pool after lunch, a visit with Pat Collins that sometimes continued with a couple of games of squash at the country club. On a day some six weeks after the birth of his son Whit dropped in on Pat, hung up his coat and hat, and took a chair.

"Don't let me interrupt you," he said.

"Just signing some time-sheets," said Pat Collins.

Whit lit a cigarette and put his feet up on the windowsill. "It's about time you had those windows washed," he said.

"I know. Miss Muldowney says if I'm trying to save money, that's

the wrong way. Burns up more electricity. Well, there we are. Another day, another dollar. How's the stock market?"

"Stay out of it. Everything's too high."

"I'm not ready to go in it yet. Later. Little by little I'm paying back
Madge, the money she put in the business."

"You ought to incorporate and give her stock."

"First I want to give her back her money, with interest."

"Speaking of Madge, Pat. Do you remember when your children
were born?"

"Sure. That wasn't so long ago."

"What is Dennis, about six?"

"Dennis is six, and Peggy's four. I guess Dennis is the same in
years that your boy is in weeks. How is he, Pop?"

"He's fine. At least I guess he's fine. I wouldn't know how to tell,
this is all new to me."

"But you're not worried about him? You sound dubious."

"Not about him. The doctor says he's beginning to gain weight and
so forth. Kitty is something else again, and that's what I want to ask
you about. You knew she didn't have a very easy time of it."

"Yes, you told me that."

"How was Madge, with her children?"

"I'll have to think back," said Pat. "Let me see. With Dennis, the
first, we had a couple false alarms and had the doctor come to the
house one time at four o'clock in the morning. He was sore as hell. It
was only gas pains, and as soon as she got rid of the gas, okay. The
real time, she was in labor about three hours, I guess. About three.
Dennis weighed seven and a quarter. With Peggy, she took longer.
Started having pains around eight o'clock in the morning, but the
baby wasn't all the way out till three-four in the afternoon. She had a
much harder time with the second, although it was a smaller baby.
Six and a half, I think."

"What about her, uh, mental state? Was she depressed or anything
like that?"

"No, not a bit. Anything but."

"But you haven't had any more children, and I thought Catholics
didn't believe in birth control."

"Well, I'll tell you, Whit, although I wouldn't tell most Protestants.
I don't agree with the Church on that, and neither does Madge. If
that's the criterion, we're not very good Catholics, but I can't help
that. We had two children when we could only afford one, and now I
don't think we'll ever have any more. Two's enough."

"But for financial reasons, not because of the effect on Madge."

"Mainly financial reasons. Even if we could afford it, though,

Madge doesn't want any more. She wants to enjoy life while she's young."

"I see," said Whit Hofman. The conversation had reached a point where utter frankness or a change of the subject was inevitable, and Whit Hofman retreated from candor. It then was up to Pat Collins to break the silence.

"It's none of my business, Whit," he began. "But—"

"No, it isn't, Pat. I don't mean to be rude, but if I said any more about Kitty, I'd sound like a crybaby. Not to mention the fact that it goes against the grain. I've said too much already."

"I know how you feel. But nothing you say gets out of this office, so don't let that worry you. I don't tell Madge everything I know. Or do. She made some pretty good guesses, and we came close to busting up. When I was on the road, peddling hats and caps, I knew a sure lay in damn near every town between Philly and Binghamton, New York. Not that I got laid every night—but I didn't miss many Thursdays. Thursday nights we knew we were going home Friday, salesmen. You don't make any calls on Friday, the clients are all busy. So, somebody'd bring out a quart."

"Did you know a sure lay in this town?"

"Did I! Did you ever know a broad named Helene Holman?"

"I should say I did."

"Well, her," said Pat Collins.

"You don't see her now, though, do you?"

"Is that any of your business, Whit?"

"Touché. I wasn't really asking out of curiosity. More, uh, incredibility. *Incredulity*. In other words, I've always thought you behaved yourself here, since you've been living here."

"I have. And anyway, I understand the Holman dame is private property. At least I always see her riding around with the big bootlegger, Charney."

"Ed Charney. Yes, she's out of circulation for the present, so my friends tell me."

"Yes, and you couldn't get away with a God damn thing. You're too well known."

"So far I haven't tried to get away with anything," said Whit Hofman. "How would you feel about a little strenuous exercise?"

Pat Collins looked up at the clock. "I don't think any ripe prospect is coming in in the next twenty minutes. Two games?"

"Enough to get up a sweat."

They drove to the country club in two cars, obviating the continuance of conversation and giving each man the opportunity to think his own thoughts. They played squash for an hour or so, took long hot showers, and cooled out at the locker-room table with gin and ginger ale. "I could lie right down on that floor and go to sleep," said Whit. "You're getting better, or maybe I'm getting worse. Next year I'm not going to give you a handicap."

"I may get good enough to take you at golf, but not this game. You always know where the ball's going to be, and I have to lose time guessing." They were the only members in the locker-room. They could hear occasional sounds from the kitchen of the steward and his staff having supper, a few dozen feet and a whole generation of prosperity away. The walls of the room were lined with steel lockers, with two islands of lockers back-to-back in the center of the room, hempen matting in the passageways, a rather feeble ceiling lamp above the table where their drinks rested. It was an arcane atmosphere, like some goat-room in an odd lodge, with a lingering dankness traceable to their recent hot showers and to the dozens of golf shoes and plus-fours and last summer's shirts stored and forgotten in the lockers. Whit, in his shorts and shirt, and Pat, in his B.V.D.'s, pleasantly tired from their exercise and additionally numbed by the gin and ginger ales, were in that state of euphorious relaxation that a million men ten million times have called the best part of the game, any game. They were by no means drunk, nor were they exhausted, but once again they were back at the point of utter frankness or retreat from it that they had reached in Pat's office, only now the surrounding circumstances were different.

"Why don't you get it off your chest, Whit?"

Whit Hofman, without looking up, blew the ash off his cigarette. "Funny, I was just thinking the same thing," he said. He reached for the gin bottle and spiked Pat's and his own drinks. "I have too damn many cousins in this town. If I confided in any of them they'd call a family conference, which is the last thing I want." He scraped his cigarette against the ash tray, and with his eyes on the operation said, "Kitty hates me. She hates me, and I'm not sure why."

"Have you got a clear conscience?"

"No," said Whit. "That is, *I* haven't. When we were in Siam, on our trip, Kitty got an attack of dysentery and stayed in the hotel for a couple of days. I, uh, took advantage of that to slip off with an American newspaper fellow for some of the local nookie. So I haven't got a clear conscience, but Kitty doesn't know that. Positively. I don't think it's that. I *know* it isn't that. It's something—I don't know where it began, or when. We didn't have any fights or anything like that. Just one day it was there, and I hadn't noticed it before."

"Pregnant."

"Oh, yes. But past the stage where she was throwing up. Taking it very easy, because she didn't want to lose this baby. But a wall between us. No, not a wall. Just a way of looking at me, as if I'd changed appearance and she was fascinated, but not fascinated because she *liked* my new appearance. 'What's this strange animal?' That kind of look. No fights, though. Not even any serious arguments. Oh, I got sore at her for trying to smuggle in a ring I bought her in Cairo. I was filling out the customs declaration and I had the damn thing all filled out and signed, then I remembered the ring. I asked her what about it, and she said she wasn't going to declare it. She was going to wear it in with the stone turned around so that it'd look like a guard for her engagement ring. So pointless. The ring wasn't *that* valuable. The duty was about a hundred and fifty dollars. An amethyst, with a kind of a scarab design. Do you know that an amethyst is supposed to sober you up?"

"I never heard that."

"Yeah. The magical power, but it doesn't work, I can tell you. Anyway, I gave her hell because if you try to pull a fast one on the customs inspectors and they catch you, they make you wait, they confiscate your luggage, and I'm told that for the rest of your life, whenever you re-enter the country, they go through everything with a fine tooth comb. And incidentally, an uncle of Jimmy Malloy's was expediting our landing, and he would have got into trouble, no doubt. Dr. Malloy's brother-in-law, has something to do with the immigration people. So I had to get new forms and fill out the whole God damn thing all over again. But that was our only quarrel of any consequence. It did make me wonder a little, why she wanted to save a hundred and fifty when it wasn't even her money."

They sipped their drinks.

"The day she went to the hospital," Whit Hofman continued, "it was very cold, and I bundled her up warm. She laughed at me and said we weren't going to the North Pole. Not a nice laugh. Then when we got to the hospital the nurse helped her change into a hospital gown, but didn't put her to bed. She sat up in a chair, and I put a blanket over her feet, asked her if she wanted anything to read. She said she did. Could I get her a history of the Hofman family? Well, there *is* one, but I knew damn well she didn't want it. She was just being disagreeable, but that was understandable under the circumstances. Then I sat down, and she told me I didn't have to wait around. I said I knew I didn't have to, but was doing it because I wanted to. Then she said, 'God damn it, don't you know when I'm trying to get rid of you?' and threw her cigarette lighter at me. Unfortunately the nurse picked that exact moment to come in the room, and the lighter hit her in the teat. I don't know what came over Kitty. 'Get that son of a bitch out of here,' and a lot more on the same order. So the nurse told me I'd better go, and I did." He paused. "Kitty had an awful time, no doubt about it. I was there when they brought the baby in to show her. She looked at it, didn't register any feeling whatsoever, and then turned her face away and shut her eyes. I have never seen her look at the baby the way you'd expect a mother to. I've never seen her pick him up out of his crib just to hold him. Naturally she's never nursed him. She probably hasn't enough milk, so I have no objection to that, but along with hating me she seems to hate the baby. Dr. English says that will pass, but I know better. She has no damn use for me *or* the child." He paused again. "The Christ-awful thing is, I don't know what the hell I *did.*"

"I agree with Dr. English. It'll pass," said Pat Collins. "Women today, they aren't as simple as they used to be, fifty or a hundred years ago. They drive cars and play golf. Smoke and drink, do a lot of the same things men do."

"My mother rode horseback and played tennis. She didn't smoke that I know of, but she drank. Not to excess, but wine with dinner. She died when I was eight, so I don't really know an awful lot about her. My father died while I was still in prep school. From then on I guess you'd say I was brought up by my uncle and the housekeeper and my uncle's butler. I have an older brother in the foreign service, but he's too close to me in age to have had much to do with bringing me up. He was a freshman when our father died."

"I didn't know you had a brother."

"I saw him in Rome. He's in the embassy there. Both glad to see each other, but he thinks I'm a country bumpkin, which I am. And since I don't speak French or Italian, and he has a little bit of an English accent, you might say we don't even speak the same language. He married a Boston girl and you should have seen her with Kitty. Every time the Italian men flocked around Kitty, Howard's wife would act as an interpreter, although the Italians all spoke English. But I don't think that has anything to do with why Kitty developed this hatred for me. Howard's wife disapproved of me just as heartily as she did Kitty. We were all pretty glad to see the last of each other. Howard's wife has twice as much money as he has, so he doesn't exactly rule the roost, but in every marriage one of the two has more money than the other. That's not what's eating Kitty." He sipped his drink. "I've been thinking if we moved away from here. Someone told me that this town is wrong for me."

"They're crazy."

"Well, it's bothered me ever since. This, uh, person said that my friends liked me but I didn't like them back."

"That *is* crap."

"As a matter of fact, the person didn't say like. She said love. Meaning that as long as I lived here, I wouldn't be able to love anybody. But I've always loved Kitty, and I certainly love this town. I don't know what more I can do to prove it."

"As far as Kitty's concerned, you're going to have to wait a while. Some women take longer than others getting their machinery back in place after a baby."

Whit Hofman shook his head. "Dr. English tells me Kitty's machinery is okay. And whatever it is, it started before the machinery got out of place. It's me, but what in the name of Christ is it? It's getting late, Pat. Would you have dinner with me here?"

"If you'll square me with Madge. It *is* late. I'm due home now."

"You want me to speak to her, now?"

"We both can."

There was a telephone in the hall off the locker-room and Pat put in the call.

"I knew that's where you'd be," said Madge. "You could just as easily called two hours ago."

"I'm going to put Whit on," said Pat, and did so.

"Madge, I take all the blame, but it'll be at least an hour before Pat could be home. We're still in our underwear. So could you spare him for dinner?"

"Your wish is our command," said Madge.

Whit turned to Pat. "She hung up. What do you do now?"

"We call Heinie and order up a couple of steaks," said Pat.

It was not only that the two men saw each other so frequently; it was Pat's availability, to share meals, to take little trips, that annoyed Madge. "You don't have to suck up to Whit Hofman," she would say. "Not any more."

"I'm glad I don't."

This colloquy in the Collins household resembled one in the Hofmans'. "Not that it matters to me, but how can you spend so much time with that Pat Collins person?" said Kitty.

"What's wrong with Pat? He's good company."

"Because your other friends refuse to yes you."

"That shows how little you know about Pat Collins," he said. "You don't seem to realize that he had hard going for a while, but he never asked me for any help of any kind."

"Saving you for something big, probably."

"No. I doubt if he'll ever ask me for anything. When he needed money to expand, he didn't even go to our bank, let alone ask me for help. And I would have been glad to put money in his business. Would have been a good investment."

"Oh, I don't care. Do as you please. I'm just amused to watch this beautiful friendship between you two. And by the way, maybe he never asked you for anything, but did he ever refuse anything you offered him? For instance, the club."

"He would have made it."

"Has he made the Gibbsville Club?"

"As far as I know, he's not interested."

"Try him."

"Hell, if I ask him, he'll say yes."

"Exactly my point. His way is so much cagier. He's always there when you want him, and naturally you're going to feel obligated to him. You'll want to pay him back for always being there, so he gets more out of you that way than if he'd asked for favors. He knows that."

"It's funny how *you* know things like that, Kitty."

She fell angrily silent. He had met her at a party just after the war, when he was still in uniform and with two or three other officers was having a lengthy celebration in New York. Whit, a first lieutenant in the 103d Engineers, 28th Division, met a first lieutenant in the 102d Engineers, 27th Division, who had with him a girl from New Rochelle. She was not a beauty, but Whit was immediately attracted to her, and she to him. "This man is only the 102d and I'm the 103d. He's only the 27th and I'm the 28th," said Whit. "Why don't you move up a grade?"

She laughed. "Why not? I *want* to get up in the world."

He made frequent trips to New York to see her. She was going to a commercial art school, living at home with her family but able to spend many nights in New York. Her father was a perfectly respectable layout man in an advertising agency, who commuted from New Rochelle and escaped from his wife by spending all the time he could in sailing small boats. His wife was a fat and disagreeable woman who had tried but failed to dominate her husband and her daughter, and regarded her husband as a nincompoop and her daughter as a wild and wilful girl who was headed for no good. One spring day Kitty and Whit drove to Greenwich, Connecticut, and were married. They then drove to New Rochelle, the first and only time Whit Hofman ever saw his wife's parents. Two days later the newly married couple sailed for Europe, and they did not put in an appearance in Gibbsville, Pennsylvania, until the autumn. It was all very unconventional and it led to considerable speculation as to the kind of

person Whit Hofman had married, especially among the mothers of
nubile girls. But a *fait accompli* was a *fait accompli,* and Whit
Hofman was Whit Hofman, and the girls and their mothers had to
make the best of it, whatever that turned out to be.

In certain respects it turned out quite well. The town, and indeed
the entire nation, was ready to have some fun. There was a considerable amount of second-generation money around, and manners and
customs would never revert to those of 1914. Kitty Hofman and the
Lantenengo Country Club appeared almost simultaneously in Gibbsville; both were new and novel and had the backing of the Hofman
family. Kitty made herself agreeable to Whit's men friends and made
no effort in the direction of the young women. They had to make
themselves agreeable to her, and since their alternative was self-
inflicted ostracism, Kitty was established without getting entangled
in social debts to any of the young women. A less determined, less
independent young woman could not have achieved it, but Gibbsville
was full of less determined, less independent young women whom
Whit Hofman had not married. And at least Whit had not singled
out one of their number to the exclusion of all the others, a mildly
comforting and unifying thought. He had to marry somebody, so
better this nobody with her invisible family in a New York suburb
than a Gibbsville girl who would have to suffer as the object of
harmonious envy.

Kitty did nothing deliberately to antagonize the young women—
unless to outdress them could be so considered, and her taste in
clothes was far too individualistic for her new acquaintances. She
attended their ladies' luncheons, always leaving before the bridge
game began. She played in the Tuesday golf tournaments. She precisely returned all invitations. And she made no close friendships.
But she actively disliked Madge Collins.

From the beginning she knew, as women know better than men
know, that she was not going to like that woman. Even before
Madge got up to dance with Whit and made her extraordinary, possessive, off-in-dreamland impression with her closed eyes, Kitty
Hofman abandoned herself to the luxury of loathing another
woman. Madge's black dress was sound, so much so that Kitty accurately guessed that Madge had had some experience in women's
wear. But from there on every judgment Kitty made was unfavorable. Madge's prettiness was literally natural: her good figure was
natural, her amazing skin was natural, her reddish brown hair, her
teeth, her bright eyes, her inviting mouth were gifts of Nature. (Kitty
used a great deal of makeup and dyed her blond hair a lighter shade
of blond.) Kitty, in the first minutes of her first meeting with Madge,

ticketed her as a pretty parlor-maid; when she got up to dance with Whit she ticketed her as a whore, and with no evidence to the contrary, Madge so remained. Kitty's judgments were not based on facts or influenced by considerations of fairness, then or ever, although she could be extremely realistic in her observations. (Her father, she early knew, was an ineffectual man, a coward who worked hard to protect his job and fled to the waters of Long Island Sound to avoid the occasions of quarrels with her mother.) Kitty, with her firmly middle-class background, had no trouble in imagining the background of Madge and Pat Collins, and the Collinses provided her with her first opportunity to assert herself as a Hofman. (She had not been wasting her first years in Gibbsville; her indifferent manner masked a shrewd study of individuals and their standing in the community.) Kitty, who had not been able comfortably to integrate herself into the established order, now rapidly assumed her position as Whit's wife because as Mrs. Whit Hofman she could look down on and crack down on Madge Collins. (By a closely related coincidence she also became a harsher judge of her husband at the very moment that she began to exercise the privileges of her marital status.) Kitty's obsessive hatred of the hick from West Philadelphia, as she called Madge Collins, was quick in its onset and showed every sign of being chronic. The other young women of the country club set did not fail to notice, and it amused them to get a rise out of Kitty Hofman merely by mentioning Madge Collins's name.

But the former Madge Ruddy was at least as intuitive as Kitty Hofman. Parlor-maid, whore, saleslady at Oppenheim, Collins—the real and imagined things she was or that Kitty Hofman chose to think she was—Madge was only a trifle slower in placing Kitty. Madge knew a lady when she saw one, and Kitty Hofman was not it. In the first days of her acquaintance with Kitty she would willingly enough have suspended her judgments if Kitty had been moderately friendly, but since that was not to be the case, Madge cheerfully collected her private store of evidence that Kitty Hofman was a phony. She was a phony aristocrat, a synthetic woman, from her dyed hair to her boyish hips to her no doubt tinted toenails. Madge, accustomed all her life to the West Philadelphia twang, had never waited on a lady who pronounced third *thade* and idea *ideer*. "Get a look at her little titties," Madge would say, when Kitty appeared in an evening dress that had two unjoined panels down the front. "She looks like she forgot to take her hair out of the curlers," said Madge of one of Kitty's coiffures. And, of Kitty's slow gait, "She walks like she was constipated." The animosity left Madge free to love Kitty's husband without the restraint that loyalty to a friend might have invoked. As for disloyalty to Pat Collins, he was aware of none, and did he not all but love Whit too?

Thus it was that behind the friendly relationship of Pat Collins and Whit Hofman a more intense, unfriendly relationship flourished between Madge Collins and Kitty Hofman. The extremes of feeling were not unlike an individual's range of capacity for love and hate, or, as Madge put it, "I hate her as much as you like him, and that's going some." Madge Collins, of course, with equal accuracy could have said: "I hate her as much as I love him, and *that's* going some." The two men arrived at a pact of silence where their wives were concerned, a working protocol that was slightly more to Whit's advantage, since in avoiding mention of Madge he was guarding against a slip that would incriminate Madge. He wanted no such slip to occur; he needed Pat's friendship, and he neither needed nor wanted Madge's love. Indeed, as time passed and the pact of silence grew stronger, Whit Hofman's feeling for Madge was sterilized. By the end of 1925 he would not have offered to take her out to his parked car, and when circumstances had them briefly alone together they either did not speak at all or their conversation was so commonplace that a suspicious eavesdropper would have convicted them of adultery on the theory that two such vital persons could not be so indifferent to each other's physical presence. One evening at a picnic-swimming party at someone's farm—this, in the summer of '26—Madge had had enough of the cold water in the dam and was on her way to the tent that was being used as the ladies' dressing-room. In the darkness she collided with a man on his way from the men's tent. "Who is it? I'm sorry," she said.

"Whit Hofman. Who is this?"

"Madge."

"Hello. You giving up?"

"That water's too cold for me."

"Did Pat get back?"

"From Philly? No. He's spending the night. It's funny talking and I can't really see you. Where are you?"

"I'm right here."

She reached out a hand and touched him. "I'm not going to throw myself at you, but here we are."

"Don't start anything, Madge."

"I said I wasn't going to throw myself at you. You have to make the next move. But you're human."

"I'm human, but you picked a lousy place, and time."

"Is that all that's stopping you? I'll go home now and wait for you, if you say the word. Why don't you like me?"

"I do like you."

"Prove it. I'm all alone, the children are with Pat's mother. I have my car, and I'll leave now if you say."

"No. You know all the reasons."

"Sure I do. Sure I do."

"Can you get back to the tent all right? You can see where it is, can't you? Where the kerosene lamp is, on the pole."

"I can see it all right."

"Then you'd better go, Madge, because my good resolutions are weakening."

"Are they? Let me feel. Why, you are human!"

"Cut it out," he said, and walked away from her toward the lights and people at the dam.

She changed into her dress and rejoined the throng at the dam. It was a good-sized party, somewhat disorganized among smaller groups of swimmers, drinkers, eaters of corn on the cob, and a mixed quartet accompanied by a young man on banjo-uke. Heavy clouds hid the moon, and the only light came from a couple of small bonfires. When Madge returned to the party she moved from one group to another, eventually staying longest with the singers and the banjo-uke player. "Larry, do you know 'Ukulele Lady'?"

"Sure," he said. He began playing it, and Madge sang a solo of two choruses. Her thin true voice was just right for the sad, inconclusive little song, and when she finished singing she stood shyly smiling in the momentary total silence. But then there was a spontaneous, delayed burst of applause, and she sat down. The darkness, the fires, the previously disorganized character of the party, and Madge's voice and the words—"maybe she'll find somebody else/ bye and bye"—all contributed to a minor triumph and, quite accidentally, brought the party together in a sentimental climax. "More! More! . . . I didn't know you were a singer . . . Encore! Encore!" But Madge's instinct made her refuse to sing again.

For a minute or two the party was rather quiet, and Kitty had a whispered conversation with the ukulele player. He strummed a few introductory chords until the members of the party gave him their attention, whereupon he began to play "Yaaka hula hickey dula," and Kitty Hofman, in her bare feet and a Paisley print dress, went into the dance. It was a slow hula, done without words and with only the movements of her hips and the ritualistic language of her fingers and arms—only vaguely understood in this group—in synchronous motion with the music. The spectators put on the knowing smiles of the semi-sophisticated as Kitty moved her hips, but before the dance and the tune were halfway finished they stopped their nervous laughter and were caught by the performance. It hardly mattered that they could not understand the language of the physical gestures or that the women as much as the men were being seduced by the dance. The women could understand the movements because the movements were formal and native to themselves, but the element of seductiveness was as real for them as for the men because the men's responsiveness—taking the form of absolute quiet—was like a held breath, and throughout the group men and women felt the need to touch each other by the hand, hands reaching for the nearest hand. And apart from the physical spell produced by the circumstances and the dance, there was the comprehension by the women and by some of the men that the dance was a direct reply to Madge's small bid for popularity. As such the dance was an obliterating victory for Kitty. Madge's plaintive solo was completely forgotten. As the dance ended Kitty put her hands to her lips, kissed them and extended them to the audience as in a benediction, bowed low, and returned to the picnic bench that now became a throne. The applause was a mixture of hand clapping, of women's voices calling out "Lovely! Adorable!" and men shouting "Yowie! Some more, some more!" But Kitty, equally as well as Madge, knew when to quit. "I learned it when Whit and I were in Hawaii. Where else?" she said.

Madge Collins went to Kitty to congratulate her. "That was swell, Kitty."

"Oh, thanks. Did you think so? Of course *I* can't *sing,*" said Kitty.

"You—don't—have—to—when—you—can—shake—that—thing," said Bobby Hermann, whose hesitant enunciation became slower when he drank. "You—got—any—more—hidden—talents—like—that—one—up—your—sleeve?"

"Not up her sleeve," said Madge, and walked away.

"Hey—that's—a—good—one. Not—up—her—sleeve. Not—up—your—sleeve—eh—Kitty?"

In the continuing murmur of admiration for the dance no one—no one but Madge Collins—noticed that Whit Hofman had not added his compliments to those of the multitude. In that respect Kitty's victory was doubled, for Madge now knew that Kitty had intended the exhibition as a private gesture of contempt for Whit as well as a less subtle chastening of Madge herself. Madge sat on a circular grass-mat cushion beside Whit.

"She's a real expert," said Madge. "I didn't know she could do the hula."

"Uh-huh. Learned it in Honolulu."

"On the beach at Waikiki."

"On the beach at Waikiki," said Whit.

"Well, she didn't forget it," said Madge. "Is it hard to learn?"

"Pretty hard, I guess. It's something like the deaf-and-dumb language. One thing means the moon, another thing means home, another means lonesome, and so forth and so on."

"Maybe I could get her to teach me how to say what *I* want to say."

"What's that?" said Whit.

"Madge is going home, lonesome, and wishes Whit would be there."

"When are you leaving?"

"Just about now."

"Say in an hour or so? You're all alone?"

"Yes. What will you tell *her?*"

"Whatever I tell her, she'll guess where I am. She's a bitch, but she's not a fool."

"She's a bitch, all right. But maybe you're a fool," said Madge. "No, Whit. Not tonight. Any other time, but not tonight."

"Whatever you say, but you have nothing to fear from her. You or Pat. Take my word for it, you haven't. She's watching us now, and she knows we're talking about her. All right, I'll tell you what's behind this exhibition tonight."

"You don't have to."

"Well I hope you don't think I'd let you risk it if I weren't positive about her."

"I did wonder, but I'm so crazy about you."

"When we were in Honolulu that time, I caught her with another guy. I'd been out playing golf, and I came back to the hotel in time to see this guy leaving our room. She didn't deny it, and I guessed right away who it was. A naval officer. I hadn't got a good look at him, but I let her think I had and she admitted it. The question was, what was I going to do about it? Did I want to divorce her, and ruin the naval officer's career? Did I want to come back here without her? That was where she knew she had me. I *didn't* want to come back here without her. This is my town, you know. We've been here ever since there was a town, and it's the only place I ever want to live. I've told you that." He paused. "Well, you don't know her, the hold she had on me, and I don't fully understand it myself. There are a lot of damn nice girls in town I might have married, and you'd think that feeling that way about the town, I'd marry a Gibbsville girl. But how was I ever to know that I was marrying the girl and not her mother, and in some cases her father? And that the girl wasn't marrying me but my father's money and my uncle's money. Kitty didn't know any of that when I asked her to marry me. She'd never heard of Gibbsville. In fact she wasn't very sure where Pennsylvania was. And I was a guy just out of the army, liked a good time, and presumably enjoying myself before I seriously began looking for a job. The first time Kitty really knew I didn't have to work for a living was when I gave her her engagement ring. I remember what she said. She looked at it and then looked at me and said, 'Is there more where this came from?' So give her her due. She didn't marry me for my money, and that was somewhat of a novelty. Are you listening?"

"Sure," said Madge.

"That afternoon in the hotel she said, 'Look, you can kick me out and pay me off, but I tried to have a child for you, which I didn't want, and this is the first time I've gone to bed with another man, since we've been married.' It was a good argument, but of course the real point was that I didn't want to go home without a wife, and have everybody guessing why. I allowed myself the great pleasure of giving her a slap in the face, and she said she guessed she had it coming to her, and then I was so God damned ashamed of myself—I'd never hit a woman before—that I ended up apologizing to her. Oh, I told her we were taking the next boat out of Honolulu, and if she was ever unfaithful to me again I'd make it very tough for her. But the fact of the matter is, her only punishment was a slap in the face, and that was with my open hand. We went to various places—Australia, Japan, the Philippines, China—and I got her pregnant."

"Yes. But what was behind this hula tonight?"

"I'd forgotten she knew how to do it. The whole subject of Honolulu, and ukuleles, hulas—we've never mentioned any of it, neither of us. But when she stood up there tonight, partly it was to do something better than you—"

"And she did."

"Well, she tried. And partly it was to insult me in a way that only I would understand. Things have been going very badly between us, we hardly ever speak a civil word when we're alone. She's convinced herself that you and I are having an affair—"

"Well, let's."

"Yes, let's. But I wish we could do it without—well, what the hell? Pat's supposed to be able to take care of himself."

"I have a few scores to settle there, too."

"Not since I've known him."

"Maybe not, but there were enough before you knew him. I used to be sick with jealousy, Monday to Friday, Monday to Friday, knowing he was probably screwing some chippy in Allentown or Wilkes-Barre. I was still jealous, even after we moved here. But not after I met you. From then on I didn't care what he did, who he screwed.

Whenever I thought of him with another woman I'd think of me with you. But why isn't Kitty going to make any trouble? What have you got on her, besides the navy officer?"

"This is going to sound very cold-blooded."

"All right."

"And it's possible I could be wrong."

"Yes, but go on."

"Well—Kitty's gotten used to being Mrs. W. S. Hofman. She likes everything about it but me—and the baby. It's got her, Madge, and she can never have it anywhere else, or with anybody else."

"I could have told you that the first time I ever laid eyes on her."

"I had to find it out for myself."

There is one law for the rich, and another law for the richer. The frequent appearances of Whit Hofman with Madge Collins were treated not so much as a scandal as the exercise of a privilege of a man who was uniquely entitled to such privileges. To mollify their sense of good order the country club set could tell themselves that Whit was with Pat as often as he was with Madge, and that the three were often together as a congenial trio. The more kindly disposed made the excuse that Whit was putting up with a great deal from Kitty, and since Pat Collins obviously did not object to Whit's hours alone with Madge, what right had anyone else to complain? The excuse made by the less kindly was that if there was anything *wrong* in the Whit-Madge friendship, Kitty Hofman would be the first to kick up a fuss; therefore there was nothing scandalous in the relationship.

The thing most wrong in the relationship was the destructive effect on Madge Collins, who had been brought up in a strict Catholic atmosphere, who in nearly thirty years had had sexual intercourse with one man, and who now was having intercourse with two, often with both in the same day. The early excitement of a sexual feast continued through three or four months and a couple of narrow escapes; but the necessary lies to Pat and the secondary status of the man she preferred became inconvenient, then annoying, then irritating. She withheld nothing from Whit, she gave only what was necessary to Pat, but when she was in the company of both men—playing golf, at a movie, at a football game—she indulged in a nervous masquerade as the contented wife and the sympathetic friend, experiencing relief only when she could be alone with one of the men. Or with neither. The shame she suffered with her Catholic conscience was no greater than the shame of another sort: to be with both men and sit in self-enforced silence while the man she loved was so easily, coolly making a fool of the man to whom she was married. The amiable, totally unsuspecting fool would have had her sympathy in different circumstances, and she would have hated the character of the lover; but Pat's complacency was more hateful to her than Whit's arrogance. The complacency, she knew, was real; and Whit's arrogance vanished in the humility of his passion as soon as she would let him make love to her. There was proficiency of a selfish kind in Pat's lovemaking; he had never been so gentle or grateful as Whit. From what she could learn of Kitty Hofman it would have been neatly suitable if Pat had become Kitty's lover, but two such similar persons were never attracted to each other. They had, emotionally, everything in common; none of the essential friction of personality. Neither was equipped with the fear of losing the other.

It was this fear that helped produce the circumstances leading to the end of Madge's affair with Whit Hofman. "Every time I see you I love you again, even though I've been loving you all along," she told Whit. Only when she was alone with him—riding in his car, playing golf, sitting with him while waiting for Pat to join them, sitting with him after Pat had left them—could she forget the increasingly insistent irritations of her position. Publicly she was, as Whit told her, "carrying it off very well," but the nagging of her Catholic conscience and the rigidity of her middle-class training were with her more than she was with Whit, and when the stimulation of the early excitement had passed, she was left with that conscience, that training, and this new fear.

The affair, in terms of hours in a bed together, was a haphazard one, too dependent on Pat's unpredictable and impulsive absences. Sometimes he would telephone her from the garage late in the afternoon, and tell her he was driving to Philadelphia and would not be home until past midnight. On such occasions, if she could not get word to Whit at his office or at one of the two clubs, the free evening would be wasted. Other times they would make love on country roads, and three times they had gone to hotels in Philadelphia. It seldom happened that Whit, in a moment of urgently wanting to be with her, could be with her within the hour, and it was on just such occasions, when she was taking a foolish chance, that they had their two narrow escapes in her own house. "You can never get away when I want you to," said Whit—which was a truth and a lie.

"Be reasonable," she said, and knew that the first excitement had progressed to complaint. Any time, anywhere, anything had been exciting in the beginning; now it was a bed in a hotel and a whole night together, with a good leisurely breakfast, that he wanted. They were in a second phase, or he was; and for her, fear had begun. It told on her disposition, so that she was sometimes snappish when alone with Whit. Now it was her turn to say they could not be together when she wanted him, and again it was a truth and a lie of exaggeration. They began to have quarrels, and to Whit this was not only an annoyance but a sign that they were getting in much deeper than he intended. For he had not deceived her as to the depth or permanence of their relationship. It was true that he had permitted her to deceive herself, but she was no child. She had had to supply her own declarations of the love she wanted him to feel; they had not been forthcoming from him, and when there were opportunities that almost demanded a declaration of his love, he was silent or noncommittal. The nature of their affair—intimacy accompanied by intrigue —was such as to require extra opportunities for candor. They were closer than if they had been free and innocent, but Whit would not use their intimacy even to make casual pretense of love. "I can't even wring it out of you," she said.

"What?"

"That you love me. You never say it."

"You can't expect to *wring* it out of anyone."

"A woman wants to hear it, once in a while."

"Well, don't try to wring it out of me."

He knew—and she knew almost as soon as he—that his refusal to put their affair on a higher, romantic love plane was quite likely to force her to put an end to the affair. And now that she was becoming demanding and disagreeable, he could deliberately provoke her into final action or let his stubbornness get the same result. It could not be said that she bored him; she was too exciting for that. But the very fact that she could be exciting added to his annoyance and irritation. He began to dislike that hold she had on him, and the day arrived when he recognized in himself the same basic weakness for Madge that he had had for Kitty. And to a lesser degree the same thing had been true of all the women he had ever known. But pursuing that thought, he recalled that Madge was the only one who had ever charged him with the inability to love. Now he had the provocation that would end the affair, and he had it more or less in the words of her accusation.

"You still won't say it," she said to him one night.

"That I love you?"

"That you love me."

"No, I won't say it, and you ought to know why."

"That's plain as day. You won't say it because you don't."

"Not *don't*. *Can't*," he said. "You told me yourself, a long time ago. That people love me and I can't love them. I'm beginning to think that's true."

"It's true all right. I was hoping I could get you to change, but you didn't."

"I used to know a guy that could take a car apart and put it together again, but he couldn't drive. He never could learn to drive."

"What's that got to do with us?"

"Don't you see? Think a minute."

"I get it."

"So when you ask me to love you, you're asking the impossible. I'm just made that way, that's all."

"This sounds like a farewell speech. You got me to go to a hotel with you, have one last thing together, and then announce that we're through. Is that it?"

"No, not as long as you don't expect something you never expected in the first place."

"That's good, that is. You'll let me go on taking all the risks, but don't ask anything in return. I guess I don't love you *that* much, Mr. Hofman." She got out of bed.

"What are you going to do?"

"I'm getting out of this dump, I promise you that. I'm going home."

"I'm sorry, Madge."

"Whit, you're not even sorry for yourself. But I can make up for it. I'm sorry for you. Do you know what I'm going to do?"

"What?"

"I'm going home and tell Pat the whole story. If he wants to kick me out, all he has to do is say so."

"Why the hell do you want to do that?"

"You wouldn't understand it."

"Is it some Catholic thing?"

"Yes! I'm surprised you guessed it. I don't have to tell him. That's not it. But I'll confess it to him instead of a priest, and whatever he wants me to do, I'll do it. Penance."

"No, I don't understand it."

"No, I guess you don't."

"You're going to take a chance of wrecking your home, your marriage?"

"I'm not very brave. I don't think it is much of a chance, but if he kicks me out, I can go back to Oppenheim, Collins. I have a charge account there now." She laughed.

"Don't do it, Madge. Don't go."

"Whit, I've been watching you and waiting for something like this to happen. I didn't know what I was going to do, but when the time came I knew right away."

"Then you really loved Pat all along, not me."

"Nope. God help me, I love you and that's the one thing I won't tell Pat. There I'll have to lie."

It was assumed, when Pat Collins began neglecting his business and spending so much time in Dick Boylan's speakeasy, that Whit Hofman would come to his rescue. But whether or not Whit had offered to help Pat Collins, nobody could long go on helping a man who refused to help himself. He lost his two salesmen and his book-keeper, and his Chrysler franchise was taken over by Walt Michaels, who rehired Joe Ricci at decent wages. For a while Pat Collins had a fifty-dollar-a-week drawing account as a salesman at the Cadillac dealer's, but that stopped when people stopped buying Cadillacs, and Pat's next job, in charge of the hat department in a haberdash-ery, lasted only as long as the haberdashery. As a Cadillac salesman and head of the hat department Pat Collins paid less attention to business than to pill pool, playing a game called Harrigan from one o'clock in the afternoon till suppertime, but during those hours he was at least staying out of the speakeasy. At suppertime he would have a Western sandwich at the Greek's, then go to Dick Boylan's, a quiet back room on the second story of a business building, patron-ized by doctors and lawyers and merchants in the neighborhood and by recent Yale and Princeton graduates and near-graduates. It was all he saw, in those days, of his friends from the country club crowd.

Dick Boylan's speakeasy was unique in that it was the only place of its kind that sold nothing but hard liquor. When a man wanted a sandwich and beer, he had to send out for it; if he wanted beer without a sandwich, Boylan told him to go some place else for it; but such requests were made only by strangers and by them not more than once. Dick Boylan was the proprietor, and in no sense the bartender; there were tables and chairs, but no bar in his place, and Boylan wore a suit of clothes and a fedora hat at all times, and always seemed to be on the go. He would put a bottle on the table, and when the drinkers had taken what they wanted he would hold up the bottle and estimate the number of drinks that had been poured from it and announce how much was owed him. "This here table owes me eight and a half," he would say, leaving the bookkeeping to the customers. "Or I'll have one with you and make it an even nine." Sometimes he would not be around to open up for the morning customers, and they would get the key from under the stairway lino-leum, unlock the door, help themselves, and leave the money where

Dick would find it. They could also leave chits when they were short of cash. If a man cheated on his chits, or owed too much money, or drank badly, he was not told so in so many words; he would knock on the door, the peephole was opened, and Boylan would say, "We're closed," and the statement was intended and taken to mean that the man was forever barred, with no further discussion of the matter.

Pat Collins was at Dick Boylan's every night after Madge made her true confession. Until then he had visited the place infrequently, and then, as a rule, in the company of Whit Hofman. The shabby austerity of Dick Boylan's and Boylan's high-handed crudities did not detract from the stern respectability of the place. No woman was allowed to set foot in Boylan's, and among the brotherhood of hard drinkers it was believed—erroneously—that all conversations at Boylan's were privileged, not to be repeated outside. "What's said in here is Masonic," Boylan claimed. "I find a man blabbing what he hears—he's out." Boylan had been known to bar a customer for merely mentioning the names of fellow drinkers. "I run a san'tuary for men that need their booze," said Boylan. "If they was in that Gibbsville Club every time they needed a steam, the whole town'd know it." It was a profitable sanctuary, with almost no overhead and, because of the influence of the clientele, a minimum of police graft. Pat Collins's visits with Whit Hofman had occurred on occasions when one or the other had a hangover, and Boylan's was a quick walk from Pat's garage. At night Whit Hofman preferred to do his drinking in more elegant surroundings, and Pat Collins told himself that he was sure he would not run into Whit at Boylan's. But he lied to himself; he *wanted* to run into Whit.

At first he wanted a fight, even though he knew he would be the loser. He would be giving twenty pounds to a man who appeared soft but was in deceptively good shape, who managed to get in some physical exercise nearly every day of his life and whose eight years of prep school and college football, three years of army service, and a lifetime of good food and medical care had given him resources that would be valuable in a real fight. Pat Collins knew he did not have a quick punch that would keep Whit down; Whit Hofman was not Walt Michaels. Whit Hofman, in fact, was Whit Hofman, with more on his side than his physical strength. Although he had never seen Whit in a fight, Pat had gone with him to many football games and observed Whit's keen and knowing interest in the niceties of line play. ("Watch that son of a bitch, the right guard for Lehigh. He's spilling two men on every play.") And Whit Hofman's way of telling about a battle during one of his rare reminiscences of the War ("They were awful damn close, but I didn't lob the God damn pineapple. I *threw* it. The hell with what they taught us back in Hancock.") was evidence that he would play for keeps, and enjoy the playing. Pat admitted that if he had really wanted a fight with Whit Hofman, he could have it for the asking. Then what *did* he want? The question had a ready answer: he wanted the impossible, to confide his perplexed anger in the one man on earth who would least like to hear it. He refused to solidify his wish into words, but he tormented himself with the hope that he could be back on the same old terms of companionship with the man who was responsible for his misery. Every night he went to Dick Boylan's, and waited with a bottle on the table.

Dick Boylan was accustomed to the company of hard drinkers, and when a man suddenly became a nightly, hours-long customer, Boylan was not surprised. He had seen the same thing happen too often for his curiosity to be aroused, and sooner or later he would be given a hint of the reason for the customer's problem. At first he dismissed the notion that in Pat Collins's case the problem was money; Collins was selling cars as fast as he could get delivery. The problem, therefore, was probably a woman, and since Collins was a nightly visitor, the woman was at home—his wife. It all came down to one of two things: money, or a woman. It never occurred to Dick Boylan—or, for that matter, to Pat Collins—that Pat's problem was the loss of a friend. Consequently Dick Boylan looked for, and found, all the evidence he needed to support his theory that Collins was having wife troubles. For example, men who were having money troubles would get phone calls from their wives, telling them to get home for supper. But the men who were having wife trouble, although they sometimes got calls from women, seldom got calls from their wives. Pat Collins's wife never called him. Never. And he never called her.

It was confusing to Dick Boylan to hear that Pat Collins's business was on the rocks. Whit Hofman did not let his friends' businesses go on the rocks. And then Boylan understood it all. A long forgotten, overheard remark about Whit Hofman and Madge Collins came back to him, and it was all as plain as day. Thereafter he watched Pat Collins more carefully; the amount he drank, the cordiality of his relations with the country clubbers, the neatness of his appearance, and the state of his mind and legs when at last he would say goodnight. He had nothing against Pat Collins, but he did not like him. Dick Boylan was more comfortable with non-Irishmen; they were neither Irish-to-Irish over-friendly, nor Irish-to-Irish condescending, and when Pat Collins turned out to be so preoccupied with his problems that he failed to be over-friendly or condescending, Dick Boylan put him down for an unsociable fellow, hardly an Irishman at all, but certainly not one of the others. Pat Collins did not fit in anywhere, although he got on well enough with the rest of the customers. Indeed, the brotherhood of hard drinkers were more inclined to welcome his company than Collins was to seek theirs. Two or three men coming in together would go to Pat's table instead of starting a table of their own and inviting him to join them. It was a distinction that Dick Boylan noticed without comprehending it, possibly because as an Irishman he was immune to what the non-Irish called Irish charm.

But it was not Irish charm that made Pat Collins welcome in the brotherhood; it was their sense of kinship with a man who was slipping faster than they were slipping, and who in a manner of speaking was taking someone else's turn in the downward line, thus postponing by months or years the next man's ultimate, inevitable arrival at the bottom. They welcomed this volunteer, and they hoped he would be with them a long while. They were an odd lot, with little in common except an inability to stand success or the lack of it. There were the medical men, Brady and Williams; Brady, who one day in his early forties stopped in the middle of an operation and had to let his assistant take over, and never performed surgery again; Williams, who at thirty-two was already a better doctor than his father, but who was oppressed by his father's reputation. Lawyer Parsons, whose wife had made him run for Congress because her father had been a congressman, and who had then fallen hopelessly in love with the wife of a congressman from Montana. Lawyer Strickland, much in demand as a high school commencement speaker, but somewhat shaky on the Rules of Evidence. Jeweler Linklighter, chess player without a worthy opponent since the death of the local rabbi. Hardware Merchant Stump, Eastern Pennsylvania trapshooting champion until an overload exploded and blinded one eye. Teddy Stokes, Princeton '25, gymnast, Triangle Club heroine and solo dancer, whose father was paying blackmail to the father of an altar boy. Sterling Agnew, Yale ex-'22, Sheff, a remittance man from New York whose father owned coal lands, and who was a part-time lover of Kitty Hofman's. George W. Shuttleworth, Yale '91, well-to-do widower and gentleman author, currently at work on a biography of Nathaniel Hawthorne which was begun in 1892. Percy Keene, music teacher specializing in band instruments, and husband of a Christian Science practitioner. Lewis M. Rutledge, former captain of the Amherst golf team and assistant manager of the local branch of a New York brokerage house, who had passed on to Agnew the information that Kitty Hofman was accommodating if you caught her at the right moment. Miles Lassiter, ex-cavalry officer, ex-lieutenant of the State Constabulary, partner in the Schneider & Lassiter Detective & Protective Company, industrial patrolmen, payroll guards, private investigators, who was on his word of honor never again to bring a loaded revolver into Boylan's. Any and at some times all these gentlemen were to be found at Boylan's on any given night, and they constituted a clientele that Dick Boylan regarded as his regulars, quite apart from the daytime regulars who came in for a quick steam, drank it, paid, and quickly departed. Half a dozen of the real regulars were also daytime regulars, but Boylan said—over and over again—that in the daytime he ran a first-aid station; the sanctuary did not open till suppertime. (The sanctuary designation originated with George Shuttleworth; the first-aid station, with Dr. Calvin K. Brady, a Presbyterian and therefore excluded from Boylan's generalities regarding the Irish.)

For nearly three years these men sustained Pat Collins in his need for companionship, increasingly so as he came to know their problems. And know them he did, for in the stunned silence that followed Madge's true confession he took on the manner of the reliable listener, and little by little, bottle by bottle, the members of the brotherhood imparted their stories even as Whit Hofman had done on the afternoon of the first meeting of Whit and Pat. In exchange the members of the brotherhood helped Pat Collins with their tacit sympathy, that avoided mention of the latest indication of cumulative disaster. With a hesitant delicacy they would wait until he chose, if he chose, to speak of the loss of his business, the loss of his jobs, the changes of home address away from the western part of town to the northeastern, where the air was always a bit polluted from the steel mill, the gas house, the abattoir, and where there was always some noise, of which the worst was the squealing of hogs in the slaughterhouse.

"I hope you won't mind if I say this, Pat," said George Shuttleworth one night. "But it seems to me you take adversity very calmly, considering the first thing I ever heard about you."

"What was that, George?"

"I believe you administered a sound thrashing to Mr. Herb Michaels, shortly after you moved to town."

"Oh, that. Yes. Well, I'm laughing on the other side of my face now. I shouldn't have done that."

"But you're glad you did. I hope. Think of how you'd feel now if you hadn't. True, he owns the business you built up, but at least you have the memory of seeing him on the ground. And a cigar in his mouth, wasn't it? I always enjoyed that touch. I believe Nathaniel would have enjoyed it."

"Who?"

"Nathaniel Hawthorne. Most generally regarded as a gloomy writer, but where you find irony you'll find a sense of humor. I couldn't interest you in reading Hawthorne, could I?"

"Didn't he write *The Scarlet Letter?*"

"Indeed he did, indeed so."

"I think I read that in college."

"Oh, I hadn't realized you were a college man. Where?"

"Villanova."

"Oh, yes."

"It's a Catholic college near Philly."

"Yes, it must be on the Main Line."

"It is."

"Did you study for the priesthood?"

"No, just the regular college course. I flunked out sophomore year."

"How interesting that a Catholic college should include *The Scarlet Letter.* Did you have a good teacher? I wonder what his name was."

"Brother Callistus, I think. Maybe it was Brother Adrian."

"I must look them up. I thought I knew all the Hawthorne authorities. Callistus, and Adrian. No other names?"

"That's what they went by."

"I'm always on the lookout for new material on Nathaniel. One of these days I've just got to stop revising and pack my book off to a publisher, that's all there is to it. Stand or fall on what I've done— and then I suppose a week after I publish, along will come someone with conclusions that make me seem fearfully out of date. It's a terrifying decision for me to make after nearly thirty years. I don't see how I can face it."

"Why don't you call this Volume One?"

"Extraordinary. I thought of that very thing. In fact, in 1912 I made a new start with just that in mind, but after three years I went back to my earlier plan, a single volume. But perhaps I could publish in the next year or two, and later on bring out new editions, say every five years. Possibly ten. I'd hoped to be ready for the Hawthorne Centenary in 1904, but I got hopelessly bogged down in the allegories and I didn't dare rush into print with what I had then. It wouldn't have been fair to me or to Nathaniel, although I suppose it'd make precious little difference to him."

"You never know."

"That's just it, Pat. He's very real to me, you know, although he passed away on May eighteenth or nineteenth in 'sixty-four. There's some question as to whether it was the eighteenth or the nineteenth. But he's very real to me. Very."

This gentle fanatic, quietly drinking himself into a stupor three nights a week, driven home in a taxi with a standing order, and reappearing punctually at eight-thirty after a night's absence, became Pat Collins's favorite companion among the brotherhood. George was in his early fifties, childless, with a full head of snowy white hair brushed down tight on one side. As he spoke he moved his hand slowly across his thatch, as though still training it. Whatever he said seemed to be in answer to a question, a studied reply on which he would be marked as in an examination, and he consequently presented the manner, looking straight ahead and far away, of a conscientious student who was sure of his facts but anxious to present them with care. To Pat Collins the mystery was how had George Shuttleworth come to discover whiskey, until well along in their friendship he learned that George had begun drinking at Yale and had never stopped. Alcohol had killed his wife in her middle forties—she was the same age as George—and Boylan's brotherhood had taken the place of the drinking bouts George had previously indulged in with her. "The Gibbsville Club is no place for me in the evening," said George. "Games, games, games. If it isn't bridge in the card room, it's pool in the billiard room. Why do men feel they have to be so strenuous—and I include bridge. The veins stand out in their foreheads, and when they finish a hand there's always one of them to heave a great sigh of relief. That's what I mean by strenuous. And the worst of it is that with two or possibly three exceptions, I used to beat them all consistently, and I never had any veins stand out in *my* forehead."

As the unlikely friendship flourished, the older man, by the strength of his passivity, subtly influenced and then dominated Pat Collins's own behavior. George Shuttleworth never tried to advise or instruct his younger friend or anyone else; but he had made a life for himself that seemed attractive to the confused, disillusioned younger man. Ambition, aggressiveness seemed worthless to Pat Collins. They had got him nowhere; they had in fact tricked him as his wife and his most admired friend had tricked him, as though Madge and Whit had given him a garage to get him out of the way. He was in no condition for violent action, and George Shuttleworth, the least violent of men, became his guide in this latter-day acceptance of defeat. In spite of the friendship, George Shuttleworth remained on an impersonal basis with Pat Collins; they never discussed Madge at all, never mentioned her name, and as a consequence Pat's meetings with his friend did not become an opportunity for self-pity.

The time then came—no day, no night, no month, no dramatic moment but only a time—when George Shuttleworth had taken Whit's place in Pat Collins's need of a man to admire. And soon thereafter another time came when Pat Collins was healed, no longer harassed by the wish or the fear that he would encounter Whit. It was a small town, but the routines of lives in small towns can be restrictive. A woman can say, "I haven't been downtown since last month," although downtown may be no more than four or five blocks away. And there were dozens of men and women who had been born in the town, Pat's early acquaintances in the town, who never in their lives had seen the street in the northeastern section where Pat and Madge now lived. ("Broad Street? I never knew we had a Broad Street in Gibbsville.") There were men and women from Broad Street liberated by the cheap automobile, who would take a ride out Lantenengo Street on a Sunday afternoon, stare at the houses of the rich, but who could not say with certainty that one house belonged to a brewer and another to a coal operator. Who has to know the town as a whole? A physician. The driver of a meat-market delivery truck. A police officer. The fire chief. A newspaper reporter. A taxi driver. A town large enough to be called a town is a complex of neighborhoods, invariably within well-defined limits of economic character; and the men of the neighborhoods, freer to move outside, create or follow the boundaries of their working activities—and return to their neighborhoods for the nights of delight and anguish with their own. Nothing strange, then, but only abrupt, when Pat Collins ceased to see Whit Hofman; and nothing remarkable, either, that three years could be added to the life of Pat Collins, hiding all afternoon in a poolroom, clinging night after night to a glass.

"What did you want to tell me this for?" he had said.

"Because I thought it was right," she had said.

"Right, you say?"

"To tell you, yes," she said.

He stood up and pulled off his belt and folded it double.

"Is that what you're gonna do, Pat?"

"Something to show him the next time," he said.

"There'll be no next time. You're the only one'll see what you did to me."

"That's not what I'm doing it for."

"What for, then?"

"It's what you deserve. They used to stone women like you, stone them to death."

"Do that, then. Kill me, but not the strap. Really kill me, but don't do that, Pat. That's ugly. Have the courage to kill me, and I'll die. But don't do that with the strap, please."

"What a faker, what a bluffer you are."

"No," she said. She went to the bureau drawer and took out his revolver and handed it to him. "I made an act of contrition."

"An act of contrition."

"Yes, and there was enough talk, enough gossip. You'll get off," she said.

"Put the gun away," he said.

She dropped the revolver on a chair cushion. "You put it away. Put it in your pocket, Pat. I'll use it on you if you start beating me with the strap."

"Keep your voice down, the children'll hear," he said.

"They'll hear if you beat me."

"You and your act of contrition. Take off your clothes."

"You hit me with that strap and I'll scream."

"Take your clothes off, I said."

She removed her dress and slip, and stood in brassiere and girdle.

"Everything," he said.

She watched his eyes, took off the remaining garments, and folded her arms against her breasts.

He went to her, bent down, and spat on her belly.

"You're dirty," he said. "You're a dirty woman. Somebody spit on you, you dirty woman. The spit's rolling down your belly. No, I won't hit you."

She slowly reached down, picked up the slip and covered herself with it. "Are you through with me?"

He laughed. "Am I through with you? Am *I* through with you."

He left the house and was gone a week before she again heard from him. He stayed in town, but he ate only breakfast at home. "Is this the way it's going to be?" she said. "I have to make up a story for the children."

"You ought to be good at that."

"Just so I know," she said. "Do you want to see their report cards?"

"No."

"It's no use taking it out on them. What you do to me, I don't care, but they're not in this. They think you're cross with them."

"Don't tell me what to do. The children. You down here, with them sleeping upstairs. Don't you tell me what to do."

"All right, I won't," she said. "I'll tell them you're working nights, you can't come home for dinner. They'll see through it, but I have to give them some story."

"You'll make it a good one, of that I'm sure."

In calmer days he had maintained a balance between strict parenthood and good humor toward the children, but now he could not overcome the guilt of loathing their mother that plagued him whenever he saw the question behind their eyes. They were waiting to be told something, and all he could tell them was that it was time for them to be off to school, to be off to Mass, always time for them to go away and take their unanswerable, unphrased questions with them. Their mother told them that he was very busy at the garage, that he had things on his mind, but in a year he had lost them. There was more finality to the loss than would have been so if he had always treated them with indifference, and he hated Madge the more because she could not and he could not absolve him of his guilt.

One night in Boylan's speakeasy George Shuttleworth, out of a momentary silence, said: "What are you going to do now, Pat?"

"Nothing. I have no place to go."

"Oh, you misunderstood me. I'm sorry. I meant now that Overton's has closed."

"That was over a month ago. I don't know, George. I haven't found anything, but I guess something will turn up. I was thinking of going on the road again. I used to be a pretty good hat salesman, wholesale, and when I was with Overton I told the traveling men to let me know if they heard of anything."

"But you don't care anything about hats."

"Well, I don't, but I can't pick and choose. I can't support a family shooting pool."

"Isn't there something in the automobile line? A man ought to work at the job he likes best. We have only the one life, Pat. The one time in this vale of tears."

"Right now the automobile business is a vale of tears. I hear Herb Michaels isn't having it any too easy, and I could only move four new Cadillacs in fourteen months."

"Suppose you had your own garage today. Could you make money, knowing as much as you do?"

"Well, they say prosperity is just around the corner."

"I don't believe it for a minute."

"I don't either, not in the coal regions. A man to make a living in the automobile business today, in this part of the country, he'd be better off without a dealer's franchise. Second-hand cars, and service and repairs. New rubber. Accessories. Batteries. All that. The people that own cars have to get them serviced, but the people that need cars in their jobs, they're not buying new cars. Who is?"

"I don't know. I've never owned a car. Never learned to drive one."

"You ought to. Then when you go looking for material for your book, you'd save a lot of steps."

"Heavens no," said George Shuttleworth. "You're referring to trips to Salem? New England? Why it takes me two or three days of walking before I achieve the proper Nineteenth Century mood. My late lamented owned a car and employed a chauffeur. A huge, lumbering Pierce-Arrow she kept for twelve years. I got rid of it after she died. It had twelve thousand miles on the speedometer, a thousand miles for each year."

"Oh, they were lovely cars. Was it a limousine?"

"Yes, a limousine, although I believe they called it a Berliner. The driver was well protected. Windows on the front doors. I got rid of him, too. I got rid of him *first*. Good pay. Apartment over the garage. Free meals. New livery every second year. And a hundred dollars at Christmas. But my wife's gasoline bills, I happened to compare them with bills for the hospital ambulance when I was on the board. Just curiosity. Well, sir, if those bills were any indication, my wife's car used up more gasoline than the ambulance, although I don't suppose it all found its way into our tank. But she defended him. Said he always kept the car looking so nice. He did, at that. He had precious little else to occupy his time. I believe he's gone back to Belgium. He was the only Belgian in town, and my wife was very sympathetic toward the Belgians."

"Took his savings and—"

"His plunder," said George Shuttleworth. "Let's not waste any more time talking about him, Pat. You know, of course, that I'm quite rich."

"Yes, that wouldn't be hard to guess. That house and all."

"The house, yes, the house. Spotless, not a speck of dust anywhere. It's like a museum. I have a housekeeper, Mrs. Frazier. Scotch. Conscientious to a degree, but she's made a whole career of keeping my house antiseptically clean, like an operating surgery. So much so, that she makes me feel that I'm in the way. So I'm getting out of the way for a while. I'm going away."

"Going down South?"

"No, I'm not going South. I'm going abroad, Pat. I haven't been since before the War, and I'm not really running away from Mrs.

Frazier and her feather dusters. I have a serious purpose in taking this trip. It has to do with my book. You knew that Nathaniel spent seven years abroad. Perhaps you didn't. Seven years, from 1853 to 1860."

"You want to see what inspired him," said Pat.

"No, no! Quite the contrary. He'd done all his best work by then. I want to see how it spoiled him, living abroad. There were other distractions. The Civil War. His daughter's illness. But I must find out for myself whether European life spoiled Nathaniel *or* did he flee to Europe when he'd exhausted his talent. That may turn out to be my greatest contribution to the study of Hawthorne. I can see quite clearly how my discoveries might cause me to scrap everything I've done so far and have to start all over again. I've already written to a great many scholars, and they've expressed keen interest."

"Well, I'll be sorry to see you go, George. I'll miss our evenings. When do you leave?"

"In the *Mauretania,* the seventh of next month. Oh, when I decide to act, nothing stops me," said George Shuttleworth. "I want to give you a going-away present, Pat."

"It should be the other way around. You're the one that's leaving."

"If you wish to give me some memento, that's very kind of you. But what I have in mind, I've been thinking about it for some time. Not an impulse of the moment. How much would it cost to set you up in a business such as you describe?"

"Are you serious, George?"

"Dead serious."

"A small garage, repairing all makes. No dealership. Gas, oil, tires, accessories. There's an old stable near where I live. A neighbor of mine uses it to garage his car in. You want to go on my note, is that it?"

"No, I don't want to go on your note. I'll lend you the money myself, without interest."

"Using mostly second-hand equipment, which I know where to buy here and there, that kind of a setup would run anywhere from five to ten thousand dollars. Atlantic, Gulf, one of those companies put in the pump and help with the tank. Oil. Tools I'd have to buy myself. Air pump. Plumbing would be a big item, and I'd need a pit to work in. Anywhere between five and ten thousand. You can always pick up a light truck cheap and turn it into a tow-car."

George Shuttleworth was smiling. "That's the way I like to hear you talk, Pat. Show some enthusiasm for something. What's your bank?"

"The Citizens, it was. I don't have any at the moment."

"Tomorrow, sometime before three o'clock, I'll deposit ten thousand dollars in your name, and you can begin to draw on it immediately."

"There ought to be some papers drawn up."

"My cheque is all the papers we'll need."

"George?"

"Now, now! No speech, none of that. I spend that much every year, just to have a house with sparkling chandeliers."

"Well then, two words. Thank you."

"You're very welcome."

"George?"

"Yes, Pat."

"I'm sorry, but you'll have to excuse me. I—I can't sit here, George. You see why? Please excuse me."

"You go take a good long walk, Pat. That's what you do."

He walked through the two crowds of men and women leaving the movie houses at the end of the first show. He spoke to no one.

"You're home early," said Madge. "Are you all right?"

"I'm all right."

"You look sort of peak-ed."

"Where are the children?"

"They're out Halloweening. They finished their home work."

"I'm starting a new business."

"You are? What?"

"I'm opening a new garage."

"Where?"

"In the neighborhood."

"Well—that's good, I guess. Takes money, but it'd be a waste of time to ask you where you got it."

"It'd be a waste of time."

"Did you have your supper?"

"I ate something. I'm going to bed. I have to get up early. I have to go around and look for a lot of stuff."

"Can I do anything?"

"No. Just wake me up when the children get up."

"All right. Goodnight."

"Goodnight."

"And good luck, Pat."

"No. No, Madge. Don't, don't—"

"All right. I'm sorry," she said quietly. Then, uncontrolled, "Pat, for God's sake! Please?"

"No, Madge. I ask you."

She covered her face with her hands. "Please, please, please, please, please."

But he went upstairs without her. He could not let her spoil this, he could not let her spoil George Shuttleworth even by knowing about him.

"Hello, Pat."

"Hyuh, Whit."

Never more than that, but never less.

Exterior: with Figure

As the years, the decades, go by, it is not so remarkable that the most interesting member of the Armour family should turn out to be Harry Armour, Mr. Henry W. Armour, himself. His wife and his children all had a shot at being interesting, and they all did behave or misbehave in ways that had one or another member of the family always being talked about. If it wasn't Kevin, it was Mary Margaret; if it wasn't Mary Margaret, it was Rose Ann; and if it wasn't either of the children, it was Mrs. Armour, one of the first women in town to have her own car, and the first woman in the county to be involved in a fatal motor accident. It is strange, then, for me to say now that in my younger days my principal recollection of Harry Armour was of a man who was always going for walks, but whom I seldom saw walking. He would stand in front of someone's house, apparently admiring the rose bushes, or I would see him watching the telephone linemen at work, his hands clasped behind his back while he stood at a nonconversational distance from the workmen. As it happens, I often rode horseback with Harry Armour, but I do not think of him as a riding companion. I think of him as a man who could stand and look at nothing by the hour, and that, of course, is a visual record that I wish to correct.

I say it is not so remarkable that this man should turn out to be interesting. And why do I say that about a man who seemed almost lifeless? Well, in view of what has happened to his family, he becomes interesting either because of his influence on their lives—or because he had no influence whatever. One's first guess, and the once prevalent one, would be that Harry Armour had no influence.

He looked like a butler, or at least like a non-comic butler in a serious play. He was, of course, smooth-shaven, *clean*-shaven at all times. His skin had a polish rather than a shine, and though he was not a thin man, the skin was tight over the cheekbones and the bridge of his nose and the jaw-line. His lower lip protruded slightly

Saturday Evening Post (1 June 1963); *The Hat on the Bed*

because the upper lip was pulled in and down. He was fairly tall, perhaps five foot ten, and broad-shouldered, but he had the appearance of solidity rather than of muscular strength. His clothes were exquisitely tailored, of sombre materials, and you could be sure that he was not a man who put on his jacket and waistcoat in a single operation, and that he made sure his pocket flaps and lapels were lying flat before he put on his overcoat. He would have his gloves on before he left the house, and his hat on in the vestibule. He wore a starched linen collar that was called, I think, a Dorset; it was a turn-over, perhaps two inches high, showing none of the knot of the necktie. He went on wearing Dorsets long after even the oldest men gave them up.

Dressed for the street, he would go for one of those walks of his, but I cannot remember how he walked—short steps or long, fast or slow. The logical conclusion is that he walked very slowly, since I never saw him on foot more than five or six blocks from his house, and whenever I saw him he was standing still and *maybe* admiring a rose bush, *maybe* fascinated by the digging of a sewer, but more likely, I thought, totally unaware of the beauties of the petals or the efficiency of the laborers.

It is a curious thing about the old-fashioned small town, where everyone was supposed to know all about everyone else, that there were so many people whose privacy was impenetrable. It was known about Harry Armour, for instance, that he and a brother had owned some mineral rights which they sold to the big coal company for a great deal of money. Mrs. Armour, with money of her own, also got her money from coal mining. But having established themselves in their large new house on Lantenengo Street, the Armours made no further effort to get into society, and in my generation there were those who believed that the Armours got their money from meat-packing. Such was not the case, as I knew because my father was an usher at Harry Armour's wedding, had known Harry Armour all their lives, and hardly ever spoke to him. If I had had a little active curiosity I might have found out a lot of things about Harry Armour, but my father died when I was nineteen, and I never knew what went on between the two extremely reticent men. We were Catholics, and so were the Armours, and I guess that when Harry Armour was choosing his ushers, he picked my father because he was a doctor, handsome, a bit of a dude, a member of the Gibbsville Club and of the Gibbsville Assembly, and a North-of-the-Mountain boy like Armour himself. I do not believe that there was ever any feeling of friendship between the two; on the other hand, Mrs. Armour had a younger brother, who died before I was born, for whom my father expressed what amounted to affection. "Ray Reilly was the best of *that* lot," he said.

One day, when I was about twelve or thirteen, I was told that I was wanted on the telephone. I naturally expected that the call was from one of my contemporaries, but when I said "Hello," the voice at the other end of the wire said, "James, this is Mr. Armour. Would you like to go riding with me?"

The Armour son, Kevin, had a high-pitched, through-the-nose voice. His father had bought him a good saddle horse, but Kevin was afraid of horses and I knew it was not he calling. Nor was it the kind of practical joke that my friends would think up. "What did you say, Mr. Armour?" I said.

"Riding. Would you care to go riding with me tomorrow?" said Harry Armour. "You could stop for me at our house, four o'clock, after school."

"Yes, thank you," I said.

"Fine, fine. Goodbye," he said.

To my surprise, my father was not at all surprised. "You be polite to Mr. Armour," my father said. "He's not a very good rider. Don't show off."

"Why does he want *me* to ride with him?"

"Because his horse needs the exercise," was my father's oblique answer.

"And Kevin is afraid of horses," said my mother. "He dreads it."

The next day I arrived at the Armours' house around four o'clock. They had a combination stable and garage; one box stall, an open stall, and room for three cars. It was a handsome brick building, a simpler version of the main house, with a cupola and a golden horse for a weathervane. Mr. Armour, smoking a cigar, was looking up at the weathervane when I rode up the driveway. "Hello, James," he said. He turned and spoke to the chauffeur-groom. "Jerry, bring my horse out."

Jerry led the chestnut, already saddled, and stood at the horse's head while Mr. Armour mounted. He did two or three wrong things that revealed his lack of experience with horses, but once he was in the saddle he smiled, and I had never seen him smile. "All right, where shall we go?" he said.

"Anywhere," I said. "I don't care."

"Out to The Run?" he said.

"All right," I said.

"Where do you usually ride to?"

"Oh—all over," I said. "Sometimes out to The Run. But you haven't been riding much, have you, Mr. Armour?"

"Not lately, not since I used to ride with your father."

"Then maybe we'd better not go all the way to The Run," I said. "There and back is pretty far for the first day. You'll get sore."

"Sore? Oh, you mean in the seat," he said.

I was slightly embarrassed to be making any kind of reference to the rear end of a man who was the father of one of my contemporaries. "Maybe halfway would be better," I said.

"Yes, I think you're right," he said. "Thanks for reminding me."

He was not a good rider and never would be one. He asked me, on our rides during that winter and spring, to correct him when he did things wrong, and I made a lot of suggestions that he adopted. But you cannot be taught to ride well any more than you can be taught to dance well. It has to be there. Someone must have told him that a rider should fix his sight between the horse's ears, and it is true that when you are learning to jump horses, that is one of the things they tell you. But we were not jumping our horses—thank God!—and yet Mr. Armour always rode with his eyes staring at that point between his horse's ears. As soon as he was in the saddle he always tightened up and stayed that way throughout the ride. I never suspected that he was afraid of the horse; it was not the tension of fear. It was determination to stay on the horse's back for five or ten miles while he and the animal got their exercise. I taught him, for instance, to post to the trot, and watching him do it I was reminded of the pistons in an automobile engine. In the six or seven months that we rode together we never galloped and we seldom cantered, although the chestnut had a nice, free canter. I will say this for Mr. Armour: although he held a tight rein, he was not cruel with the curb or with his spurs. In the beginning he carried a bone-handle crop with a silver ferrule. It was brand-new, like his tweed jacket and checked breeches and boots and derby, all from Wanamaker's London Shop in Philadelphia, expensive and faultless. I knew to the dollar what he had paid for everything, because I had priced them all, hopefully. He wore a stock—so did I—which on him was a continuance of his Dorset collars. I tried to think of some way to get him to stop carrying the crop; four reins were enough in the hands of a man who rode so tight. Then one afternoon he dropped it and I rode back and picked it off the ground without dismounting. "It sure is a nice-looking crop," I said, overacting a little.

"Would you like to have it, James? I'll give it to you. It's yours."

"Honestly? You mean it?" I said.

"Make you a present of it," he said. "I don't see why I carry it anyway, I'd never use it."

"Well, thanks. Thank you very much," I said.

Our conversations, such as they were, always took place on the way home. My mare had a good fast walk, faster than the Armour chestnut, and sometimes Armour would have to go into a slow trot to keep up with me, a fact which did not help conversation. In the winter months we usually were riding in the dark on the homeward half and were safer riding single file, and that, too, was a conversation deterrent. But in the spring months we did a little talking. As a matter of loyalty we refrained from any mention of his son, the obvious person to talk about. The next logical person was my father, but what can a boy say about his father to a man whom the father sometimes cut dead, sometimes merely nodded to? But in the only conversation that I remember clearly we touched upon both his son and my father. "Are you going to study medicine?" said Mr. Armour.

"I don't know," I said. "I don't think so."

"But you ought to. Think how proud your father would be," he said. "He wants you to, doesn't he?"

"Oh, sure. But I'd rather be something else."

"What?"

"A writer," I said.

"A writer? Of what? Of stories? Books?"

"Yes."

"Well, I suppose there's good money in that, if you make the grade. But nobody in your family was ever a writer."

"Not that I know of."

"Then why do you think you could be one? How would you go about it?"

"Don't ask *me*," I said.

"Well, you'll probably change your mind."

"What does Kevin want to be?"

"Kevin? He never told me. He may turn out to be a gentleman of leisure, but I hope not. It's better to be doing something."

That was one of our last rides together. The Armours went away for the summer, to their cottage in Ventnor, and when the fall came I went away to school. So many new things entered my life, things and people, that I scarcely ever thought of Mr. Armour. It certainly never occurred to me to ask about him. I may have seen him at the late Mass when I was home on vacation, but we had no conversation. In fact it was two or maybe three years later, when the Armours had a birthday party for Kevin, that I next visited their house and learned that they had sold the chestnut. After I finished prep school, and my father died and I went to work on a newspaper, I would sometimes

see Mr. Armour on one of his walks, and by that time he had become, to our crowd, somewhat of a character.

We had various characters. The drinking judge. The drinking
mother of one of the girls in our crowd. The lecherous father of a
boy and girl. A retired army colonel who wrote unprintable—though
not obscene—insulting letters to the newspapers. A retired Navy
commander, another drinker, who suddenly appeared at my house
one day to give me all his old tennis balls, which were stamped with a
fouled anchor. A man who was related to quite a few of our crowd,
who had locomotor ataxia and was half blind, but attended most of
the club dances. An awesomely respectable lawyer, married, and his
schoolteacher lady friend. Among our group the first names or titles
or our nicknames for the characters became synonymous with special weaknesses, such as alcoholism and lechery or physical handi-
caps. The commander, for instance, never knew this, but when we
began to have drinking parties we always, at some point during the
evening, recited: "Here's to the commander, he's true blue/he's a
drunkard, through and through/so fill him up a bumper and celebrate the day/if he doesn't go to heaven, he'll go the other way/so it's
drink, chucka-chuck chucka-chuck, so it's drink, chucka-chuck,
chucka-chuck, so it's drink, chucka-chuck, chucka-chuck." He had
taught us the toast, and if we saw him on the street one of us was
sure to say, "Chucka-chuck." I don't think there was any meanness
in these criticisms of our elders, although there was plenty of scorn
in our laughter at the lecherous father of the boy and girl, and a
Goddard—the name of the pious lawyer—was in our code language
a hypocrite. Sometime during this period Mr. Armour became a
character, but his name did not become symbolic of anything. In an
extremely dull way he was unique.

Things were happening to members of his family. Mrs. Armour
had her automobile accident, skidding into a man on a motorcycle.
No charge was preferred against her, but it was generally believed
that some money changed hands. Then Kevin, practically in secret,
developed into an expert shot and from the age of sixteen he was
high gun at county and state matches. He had never displayed any
other signs of coordination, and this accomplishment astonished us.
He was sought after by older men, and he spent so much time in
their company that he grew bored with us, his contemporaries. He
was winning a lot of money on bets, and at eighteen he was a heavy
drinker. He managed to get admitted to the University of Virginia,
and there, with his guns and his Wills-Ste. Claire, he remained for
two full—very full, as we used to say—years. His family had no
control over him, although they did not try very hard or very long.

They threatened, but only threatened, to stop his allowance, and his reply was to win fifteen hundred dollars in a live bird match. If he had not been so stupid, so totally lacking in a sense of humor, he would have been insufferable; but when Bob Reynolds, the kidder in our group, asked Kevin who was buried in Grant's Tomb, Kevin thought a moment and caught on. "You trying to razz me?" he said. He was not easily distracted, and he therefore played a competent game of bridge and a safe game of poker. One of the girls in our crowd was madly in love with him and made no bones about it, but when Kevin was away on a shooting trip she would call the rest of us until she found someone to take her out. She was much higher than he in the social scheme, but he would not marry her because she was not a Catholic. I doubt that Kevin could have explained what was meant by the Immaculate Conception, but he was a staunch Catholic. At Mass he would take out his beads and I know he was saying his Hail Mary's because I could see his lips moving, but I do not think he prayed. He thought he was praying.

The praying one in the Armour family was Rose Ann, three years younger than Kevin and a colleen specimen; creamy white skin, blue eyes, black hair, a voluptuous little figure. She was ebullient, a laugher, at parties, but in church she read her Missal and was acutely attentive to the ritual on the altar, oblivious of the people in her pew and of the other worshipers. There could be no doubt that she was devout. Still it came as almost as big a surprise to me as to our Protestant friends when Rose Ann became a novice in a convent in upstate New York. Mrs. Armour wept on my mother's shoulder and I gathered that they were not tears of joy. Apparently Mrs. Armour would have been willing to donate her other daughter, Mary Margaret, who had the misfortune to look exactly like Mr. Armour, to the service of the Lord. Mary Margaret already had the appearance of a young mother superior, but Rose Ann was *pretty*. It was a scandal in reverse, so to speak, and the only really amusing thing about it for me was to listen to several of the Protestant girls who said they wished they could become nuns. "They cut off all your hair," I told them, thereby discouraging some vocations.

Then one day Mr. and Mrs. Armour quietly left town and nothing was heard from them for three or four weeks. Neither Mary Margaret nor Kevin volunteered any information, but it was reported that Mr. and Mrs. Armour had gone abroad and that they were accompanied by Rose Ann. My mother was in on the secret and I suppose my father was too, but not until the whole town had the story did my mother reveal any of it to me. Something—I was not told what—had occurred at the convent, a couple of weeks before Rose Ann was to take the veil. Mr. and Mrs. Armour were sent for, and they made their sudden arrangements to have Rose Ann go abroad with them.

Mr. Armour stayed in Europe a couple of months, then returned home alone. Mrs. Armour remained with Rose Ann for about a year, then she too returned alone. Meanwhile no one had had a word from Rose Ann, not even a post card to indicate her whereabouts. Meanwhile, too, Mr. Armour had resumed his walks, his starings at nothing, which for him were so normal that in this unusual situation he seemed to be hastening the restoration of usual, normal conditions. He had returned, and because of his unapproachability and the neighbors' tact during a delicate period, he had considerably reduced the inquisitiveness of the neighbors when Mrs. Armour came home. They had gotten used to seeing Mr. Armour around, and some of their curiosity was dispelled or simply evaporated.

Betty Allen, a friend of Rose Ann's, telephoned Mrs. Armour to say she was going abroad and would like to have Rose Ann's European address. It was a bold move, but Mrs. Armour gave her the address. "I'm sure she'd love to see you," said Mrs. Armour. "She had a nervous breakdown a year ago, you know, but she's fine now. Living with this French family about forty kilometres outside of Paris. Her appearance has changed. She's put on much too much weight, but there'll be time to do something about that after she gets her health back. I'll tell her to expect to hear from you."

Betty went to see Rose Ann, and her report was contained in a long letter which I read. Betty was genuinely fond of Rose Ann, and the accuracy and incompleteness of her account of her visit had to be judged on a basis of friendship. Nevertheless it was, I recall, a sad letter. Rose Ann had indeed changed in more ways than in her appearance. She was stout, said Betty, and during the three days of Betty's visit Rose Ann ate enormous meals and drank a great deal of wine—without, Betty added, getting tight. Rose Ann wanted to know all about the boys and girls in the old crowd, and she surprised Betty by recalling things that had happened to us when we were small children. But she was hazy or completely wrong on things that had happened more recently, even where they concerned members of her own family. She had Kevin, for instance, in love with a Philadelphia girl whom Kevin had never had a date with. Then when Rose Ann calmly spoke of Mary Margaret as her dead sister, Betty had to fight back the tears. On the last day of Betty's visit they went for a walk together, and at one point Rose Ann led Betty to a barn. "I didn't want to frighten you," said Rose Ann. "But we were being followed. It's all right now. He's gone."

Betty spoke good French and was able to form a judgment of the middle-aged couple at whose house Rose Ann was a paying guest. They were childless. The husband owned a garage, the wife had been a trained nurse, and Rose Ann was not the first paying guest that had been sent to them by Rose Ann's doctor. The doctor came out from Paris once a fortnight and had a meal with Rose Ann and the couple, then he would chat with Rose Ann while the couple were doing the dishes. They were a decent, hard-working couple, frankly pleased to have the extra money from their p.g., equally frank about their personal attitude toward Rose Ann as a commercial proposition. It was not for them, they told Betty, to provide anything but peace and quiet, a clean room, and good plain food. They referred to Rose Ann as a *malade à domicile.*

When Betty returned home she went to see Mrs. Armour, and I learned about their conversation from Betty herself. "You may have thought I should have told you about Rose Ann," said Mrs. Armour. "I didn't, for a reason. I wanted her to see you just as you are, and I didn't want you to go there all self-conscious, making forced conversation. I wanted you to be your natural self, or she'd have noticed the difference right away."

"It was a shock, though, Mrs. Armour."

"Yes, I'm sorry," said Mrs. Armour. "But I wouldn't have given her address to anyone but you."

"I hope my visit did some good."

Mrs. Armour shook her head. "Who knows? She never even mentioned your visit the next time the doctor went to see her."

"I met Dr. Claverie, you know," said Betty. "He was awfully nice."

"I know you did, and he said the same thing about you."

"It was amazing how much he knew. I mean, the questions he asked me, you might have thought he was there all the time I was with Rose Ann."

"Like her thinking she was being followed?"

"And the kind of things she remembered and didn't remember."

"He is an amazing man," said Mrs. Armour. "I just hope he's the right man. She never goes to church, and I should have thought he'd encourage her to go. Such a deeply religious girl. I know I always turn to the church when I have something troubling me."

Betty changed the subject. "When are you going to see Rose Ann again?"

"When Dr. Claverie lets me. Whenever he sends for me. I have no idea when that will be."

It was about a year later that the French psychiatrist sent for Mr. and Mrs. Armour. Rose Ann was dead, drowned in a canoeing accident in one of those narrow, swift, deep little streams that the

French call rivers. They brought her body home for burial, and my mother and I were kept busy explaining to our Protestant friends that the Church was satisfied that Rose Ann had not committed suicide, otherwise there would have been no requiem Mass. I was not exactly telling a lie, but I did not believe what I was saying. The church, which was large, was nearly half filled with the young and the no-longer young. What is sadder than the death of an unhappy young girl? I did not go along with those of my friends who said that Rose Ann was better off. Why, there is some hope even for a girl whose lungs are filled with water. I was an honorary pallbearer, and I cried all through the Mass and the blessing of the body. At our house, after the burial, my mother said to me, "Were you in love with Rose Ann?"

"No! God damn it, *no!*" I shouted.

There was something in my profane outburst that my mother took personally, and she slapped my face. Well, she was right. I was protesting against her lack of understanding. My mother was old enough to forget that Rose Ann was us, the young. "Don't you *dare* speak to me that way," said my mother.

"I'm sorry for swearing," I said.

I have no recollection of even *seeing* Mr. Armour at the church, at the cemetery, or at lunch at his house after the funeral. He was there, of course; it is just that I have no recollection of him, although I must have shaken hands with him at least once and probably muttered some words of condolence. This failure of my memory was not caused by my grief, but rather by his failure to say or do or look anything that would make me remember him. On the other hand, I do remember that on the very next afternoon I saw him standing at a street corner three blocks past his house. He appeared to be reading the collection sign on a mailbox—a box that he must have passed a thousand times. He was wearing overcoat and scarf, and he had no letter in his gloved hand.

Mary Margaret Armour, whom we sometimes referred to as Horse Face, kept her sister's death alive much too long. I, we, wanted to have Rose Ann as a secret sorrow. We would not forget her, but we did not want to be reminded of her whenever three or more of us got together. Mary Margaret refused to cooperate. At a bridge party, two months after Rose Ann's funeral, Mary Margaret announced that she had had the nicest letter from some teacher of Rose Ann's and wanted to read it to us all. "Very nice," a few of us said, when she finished reading it.

"Well, *I* thought so," said Mary Margaret, implying that we had failed to appreciate the letter. A few weeks later, at another party, she announced that she had had another letter, from someone else.

"Oh, for God's sake, Mary Margaret," said Betty Allen.

"What?" said Mary Margaret.

"Do you *have* to?"

"No, I don't have to. And I don't have to stay here, either. *You*, Betty Allen, I know all the horrible things you said about Rose Ann."

No one said a word. Sixteen young people at four bridge tables sat in indignant silence. It was a lot of silence. Mary Margaret looked around, saw no relief or assistance, and again turned on Betty Allen. "I could kill you."

The hostess, Nan Brown, stood up. "Mary Margaret, I'm terribly sorry, but I'm going to have to ask you to leave. You're being very unfair to Betty, and—"

"Ask me to leave? That's a laugh. I wouldn't stay in this house another minute. Kevin Armour, are you coming with me?"

"Nan, do you want me to go, too?" said Kevin.

"No, of course not," said Nan Brown.

"That's the kind of brother I have. Lily-livered son of a bitch. *Stay!*"

Betty Allen stood up. "I started this, Nan, and I'm very sorry. I'll apologize to Mary Margaret if she'll apologize to me. Then we can forget the whole damn—"

"I don't want your apology and I'm not going to forget one single word," said Mary Margaret. She left.

"I'm sorry, everybody," said Nan Brown. "Maybe I could get Mother to take her hand."

"Whoever is dummy at the other tables can sit in for Mary Margaret," someone suggested. "It'll slow things up, but . . ."

Play was resumed, and for the rest of the evening the score was kept for Mary Margaret, in her name, and on the final count it turned out that she had won second prize, a small silver ash tray with the figure of a Scottie in the center. I don't know if anyone else thought of it, but I wanted to inquire if the dog was supposed to be a bitch. However, I kept quiet.

"Will you give this to Mary Margaret?" said Nan Brown to Kevin.

"I will not. Give it to the third. Who was third?"

"Third? Why, third was none other than Mr. James Malloy," said Nan.

"I'll take it," I said. "I always wanted a Scottie."

"You knew it all along," someone said. "When you were my part-

ner you got set four tricks, doubled and redoubled, and that's part of
Mary Margaret's score."

"Well, I wanted that Scottie," I said. "Not to mention the fact that
you, you dumb bastard, you left me in that bid and never even mentioned your hearts."

Some rough kidding always took place in our bridge games, but on
this occasion it was urgent and nervous; we all knew that Mary Margaret Armour could be extremely unpleasant, in the best of circumstances.

She stayed away from the country club and declined all invitations
—which I must say were extended half-heartedly after her behavior
at Nan Brown's. Through political pull she got a very minor job in
the Court House, and I would occasionally see her in the speakeasies
and roadhouses, drinking with politicians and county detectives, and
semi-pro athletes, all men who considered two fifty-dollar bills a
fortune. More than once, when she spoke to me, I caught her making a face at me and whispering something to her companions. She
would have started trouble for me, but her companions happened to
be men who liked to see their names in print, favorably, and my job
had me covering some politics, some sports, and general assign-
ments. Often, very late at night, I would see her driving her Chrysler
convertible home alone, going like hell and unmistakably stewed.
She was sore at the world, and nobody liked her much either.

The Armours, mother and children, took turns in getting talked
about, but I moved to New York and the doings of Mrs. Armour and
Kevin and Mary Margaret were of no interest to me at that distance.
Mrs. Armour had an operation for cataracts. Mary Margaret eloped
with a county detective, then had the marriage annulled. Kevin was
sued for breach of promise by a switchboard operator in a Reading
hotel. The case was settled out of court for five hundred, a thousand,
maybe two thousand dollars. Such items were conveyed to me from
time to time, and between times I heard nothing. It became a custom, very nearly a tradition, that the only information concerning the
Armours that was passed on to the Gibbsville colony in New York
was bad news. To break the monotony I once asked how Kevin was
getting along with his shooting; had he won the State championship?
Oh? I hadn't heard about that? Hadn't anyone told me that Kevin
had had to give up shooting because of an abscess in his ear? And
that the real reason was not an abscess in his ear, but that he had
been barred from competition because he had grown careless with
guns? At a match near Allentown he had accidentally blown a hole
in the ground with a 16-gauge pump gun that had one live shell left

in the magazine; at another match he accidentally killed a valuable pointer.

If there was any good news of Mary Margaret it was not made known to me.

There are, most definitely, such things as hard-luck-people, hard-luck families; at least it is a working thesis that misfortune is repeatedly attracted to certain families like the Armours. At first the incidence of misfortune is looked upon as a phenomenon; then it becomes a wry joke; and then, self-protectively, we hesitate to bring up the family name for fear of hearing one more bit of evidence that bad luck begets bad luck, that we too, once started on a run of bad luck, may have to endure not only a single disaster but a lifetime of it. As something of a mystic and very much of an overprotesting enemy of superstition, I deliberately deprived myself of information about the Armours, and years went by, twenty years, thirty years, during which I created a practical non-curiosity about them. I did not know which of them were alive, which dead.

Then one day last winter I read a small item in a newspaper that I bought on the train from New York to Washington. It stated that Kevin Armour had been sentenced to prison for defrauding some woman who had entrusted him with fifteen thousand dollars' worth of securities. In Washington I was meeting a boyhood friend, and by this time I was so insulated against the Armour bad luck that I mentioned the newspaper article. "Yes, they finally caught up with Kevin," said my friend. "This time they really nailed him."

"Have they any money left?" I said.

"Who?"

"The Armours," I said.

"The Armours? There aren't any more Armours. Kevin's the last. Mrs. Armour died ten or fifteen years ago. Mary Margaret not long after. The sauce did it to her, although I will say it took a lot of it."

"And old Henry W.?" I said.

"Lived to be eighty-four. He died last year in a veterans' home."

"Veteran of what?"

"The Spanish-American War, I think. Yes, it must have been. Anyway, that's where he died."

My friend in those few sentences had wiped out the Armour family, and if I had once been afraid of them and their bad luck, I was afraid no longer. My friend and I talked a little about them, their individual personalities, their money, their scale of living, and we exchanged the usual commonplaces about the evanescence of wealth. I did not want to spend much time talking about the Armours; I wanted to think about them, and I have done so.

I had not seen any of them in more than thirty years, consequently had only an out-of-date recollection of the physical appearance of Mr. and Mrs. Armour and Kevin and Mary Margaret. They had traveled many miles—no matter where—and lived through three decades, more or less, and I had to invent the grossness that would have come into the faces of Kevin and Mary Margaret when youth was gone, the ravages to the faces of Harry Armour and his wife when old age set in. It was not much of a pastime; they refused to hold still for my fanciful portraits of them, kept returning to the mental photographs I retained from the days when I had known them well.

I discovered that I had learned, by 1930, all that I wanted to know about the Armours, perhaps all of value that there was to know. Mrs. Armour, a flighty, silly woman who had killed a man with her motor car, was no less flighty for having had bad eyesight. Mary Margaret, trying to trade on the tragic death of her pretty sister, was not much different from the self-indulgent lush that she made herself into. Kevin, submissive to a faith that his lazy mind would not accord the respect of curiosity, would at twenty-five have stolen from a woman if he had needed the money. And even poor Rose Ann, for whom I had once wept ("Weep not for me, but for yourselves and for your children"?), had got only as far as laughter would take her.

And Harry Armour. Henry W. Armour himself. Harry Armour. Henry W. Armour. Mr. Armour. He was—what? A man who stood and looked at nothing? I do not know. I wish I knew. I want to know, and I never can know. I wish, I wish I knew.

The Man on the Tractor

They were the fabulous Denisons, Pammie and George.
There was a time when Booth Tarkington and Louis Bromfield, who had never met the Denisons, were called upon to admit or deny that they had used the Denison family in certain novels. By letter and in person the novelists tried to make it clear that they had relied on invention, and though coming so close to the facts of the Denison family, they had not been assisted by a knowledge of the Denison history, past or present. A letter from a Gibbsville lady to F. Scott Fitzgerald went unanswered, and the lady and her friends agreed that Fitzgerald did not dare deny that the automobile accident in *This Side of Paradise* was right out of life. Why, even the car was the same as George Denison's old Locomobile. True, George Denison had run over a man on the Boston Post Road, but obviously Fitzgerald had made that change to confuse people. And if Daisy in *The Great Gatsby* was not patterned after Pammie Stribling Denison, the lady from Gibbsville would eat your hat. For instance, Pammie Stribling, as everyone knew, had been madly infatuated with Johnny Gruber, the qualified assistant pharmacist at Hudson's drugstore. Same initials as Jay Gatsby's; and wasn't Gatsby somehow mixed up in patent medicines or something? Fitzgerald would not have had a leg to stand on, and he was pretty smart not to answer those letters. He wouldn't have had a leg to stand on. How absurd of Booth Tarkington to pretend he had not patterned the Ambersons after the Denisons; how ridiculous of Louis Bromfield to protest that the Shaynes were not more or less based on the Denisons.

Regardless of the denials and the non-denial, the legend of the Denisons as literary source material went into the Gibbsville lore, along with the firmly held belief that Lichtenwalner's ice cream was famous the world over and that the town was the richest per capita of all third-class cities east of the Mississippi. As it happens,

New Yorker (22 June 1963); *The Hat on the Bed*

Lichtenwalner's has gone out of business, and little is said these days of per capita wealth in Gibbsville; but due in part to the Fitzgerald revival the Denison legend has persisted. Men and women of a certain age have told their children that not only Fitzgerald, but Booth Tarkington and Louis Bromfield too, wrote stories about the Denisons. It has been denied that Scott and Zelda ever visited Gibbsville, but the denials have grown weaker, and it is certainly true that Pammie and George did once have as house guests a screwy couple with an Irish name who could very well have been the Fitzgeralds. The man was short and good-looking and insisted on playing the drums at a club dance; the woman stayed in her room all the time she was at the Denisons'. Walter Spiker, the Denisons' best friend, would have been able to say for sure whether it had been the Fitzgeralds, but Walter, alas, was dead. Long dead, and during the last five years of his life had lost the power of speech. If Walter had had any literary ability *he* could have written about the Denisons— and how! He knew more about the Denisons than the Tarkingtons and Bromfields and Fitzgeralds all put together, and he would have got it right.

Pammie and George were in town not long ago, stopping at the John Gibb Hotel, but they saw only a very few people. Their reservation at the hotel was handled by a clerk who wrote out a slip for M & M Geo. Dennison; the name meant nothing to him, but the request for the reservation had come from a reputable travel agency in New York. When Mr. and Mrs. Denison arrived at the hotel the clerk saw only a man and woman who were pretty sure of themselves in a hotel lobby, with four pieces of expensive foreign luggage; the woman in a tweed suit with a little cape on the shoulders, the man in a striped gray flannel suit and a reversible tweed-and-gab topcoat over his arm. "Check-out time is three P.M.," said the clerk.

"Is it indeed?" said the man, signing the registration card.

"But an extra hour, I guess we won't charge you a full day," said the clerk.

"I'm sure of it," said Denison. "Maybe even two hours."

"I don't know about *two* hours. It's our—"

"*I* do," said Denison. "Will you see that my car's washed and serviced, high-test gas, and back here in an hour, please? It's the green Bentley. The bellboy knows. But I want *you* to see that I have it back in an hour."

"I'll try," said the clerk.

"You do a little better than try, won't you?" said Denison.

"Let's find out if there's a hairdresser in the hotel," said his wife.

"Is there?" said Denison.

"No sir, not in the hotel. There's one around the corner to the right, three doors to the right. Our switchboard will connect you."

"Dear, it's twenty of three," said Denison to his wife. "You go on upstairs. I'm going over and see Andy Stokes before the bank closes. I'll only be a few minutes, but I don't want to miss him."

The mention of the name Stokes had as much impact on the clerk as the name Bentley. "If there's anything I can do, sir."

"There is. Will you send up a bottle of Scotch, any good Scotch that you have, and a bottle of sherry. Bristol Cream. And the Gibbsville papers."

"There's only the one paper in the afternoon."

A man had come up behind Denison during the exchange with the clerk. The man fully recognized Denison, but he allowed himself the protection of a feigned uncertainty. "Isn't this George Denison?" said the man.

Denison turned. "Yes it is," said Denison.

"George, you don't remember me, it's such a long time and all," said the man. "Karl Isaminger? Used to drive for your Aunt Augusta, Mrs. Hamilton?"

"Why, I *didn't* recognize you, Karl," said Denison.

"Hello, Karl," said Pammie Denison.

"Hello, Mrs. Denison."

"What are you doing now, Karl?" said Denison.

"Oh, I'm the night man at Coleman's Garage."

"Coleman's? I don't know that name."

"Used to be Jimmy Brady's that had the Studebaker agency."

"Uh-huh. Aren't you up rather early for a night watchman?"

"Oh—I can't stay in bed more'n six hours at the most. I had this operation three years ago the twentieth of May. You remember Doc Robbins, or was he since you left town?"

"Must have been after my time. You living here at the hotel, Karl?"

"Ah, you, George. Living *here?* No, I come in here to buy a magazine. Gives me something to read at work, and when I get finished with it the wife likes to look through it. The print's a little small for her, but she says her glasses gives her a headache. Won't *wear* glasses. I said to her—"

"Dear, if you're going to get to the bank before it closes, I hate to interrupt but—" said Pammie Denison.

"Oh, ixcuse me, I didn't—"

"That's all right, Karl," said George Denison. "You can walk to the bank with me, if you like."

"No, I wouldn't do that, George. I just wanted to come up and say hello to you and Mrs. You're both looking fine. I'd of known you anywhere. Remember the old Pierce-Arrow, Mrs. Denison? 'Karl, go fetch Pammie Stribling,' Mrs. Hamilton used to say. Remember when you used to come and play the piano for the old lady? Rainy days, she used to like you to come play the piano for her."

"Oh, do I? Shades of 'Country Gardens.' Dum-dum tee dum-dum, dum-dum tee dum. But always followed by hot chocolate and *sand* tarts."

"*I* remember them sand tarts," said Karl Isaminger.

"So do I," said George Denison. "Mrs. Hamilton used to send them to me at school. But this isn't getting to the bank. Karl, nice to see you. Remember me to your wife. Dear, I'll see you in about an hour or less."

"Don't hurry, George," said Pammie.

"The sand tarts had little pieces of citron in the middle," said George Denison. "Some had pecans, but I preferred the citron." He left them.

Andy Stokes was expecting him. They had had correspondence over the years, and Andy Stokes was one of the few Gibbsville citizens who occasionally saw the Denisons. When the pleasantries were over Stokes rang for his secretary. "Miss Arbogast, will you bring me the papers on the Denison sale?" said Stokes.

"Certainly," said Miss Arbogast. She smiled at George Denison, who had already greeted her in the outer office.

Andy Stokes sat back in his chair. "It's kind of sad, George," he said. "I don't mean how little you're getting for the property. I guess your tax man has that all figured out for you. But this land is your last link with Gibbsville."

"Except for my stock in this bank," said George Denison.

"Well, that, of course. I hope you never part with that," said Stokes. "But that's not the same as actual land. That land's been in the Denison family close to a hundred years. I had a look at the title search, naturally, but I hadn't realized how long you'd held it. Do you know what I wish?"

"What do you wish, Andy?"

"Well, I wish you and your tax man could figure out some way to donate the land for a playground, a park, something on that order. And continue the Denison name."

"My tax man would much rather have me take the money," said George Denison.

Miss Arbogast came in with the papers, laid them on Stokes's desk, smiled again at Denison without looking at him, and departed.

"Yes, I suppose he would. That was just a sentimental thought I had," said Stokes. "Considering how little you're getting for the land. If it was a big deal I never would have thought of it, but what's eighteen thousand to you?"

"I don't know, but my tax man does. He said to unload it, and I'm unloading it."

"Well, I wouldn't give *him* an argument. From the correspondence I've had with him, I'd say he was as smart as a tack. Doesn't miss a trick."

"He's kept me out of prison, that's as much as *I* know," said George Denison.

"Okay, George. All you have to do now is sign your name on these papers, where you see the check-mark. Miss Arbogast will notarize them and I'll have one of our people witness them. Here's your cheque. It's made out to the Denison Land Company. Want me to forward that to Longstreet?"

"Yes, will you please?" said Denison, busy with Stokes's desk pen.

"The last transaction of the Denison Land Company," said Stokes. "In the old days an occasion like this would call for some kind of a celebration."

"Well, we're not exactly celebrating, Pammie and I, but we decided to make the trip. They sure have done a lot of things to the roads around here. The town is practically by-passed. What ever happened to South Main Street? We never did get on South Main. And these God damn one-way streets. I almost got a ticket. If I hadn't had a Connecticut license, the cop at Main and Scandinavian was going to slap me with a summons."

"That was Paul Keppler. He's tough."

"Oh, God, is that who that was? The big fat baby-faced guy? That would have been appropriate. His father arrested me back in 1920 or thereabouts. But he took a look at my driver's license and let me go. He never said who he was, or pretended to know me. 'Just watch the signs,' he said, and waved me on."

"You can be damn sure he knew who you were, though. We think he's the best cop on the force. He graduated from the FBI school, and he's the only one the kids pay any attention to."

"There," said George Denison, laying down the pen. "I guess that does it." He picked up the cheque, read it, and put it back on Andy Stokes's blotter. He found that Stokes was looking at him, half smiling, trying to read his mind. George Denison smiled back and shook his head. "No, Andy, I'm not going to cry," said George Denison.

"Maybe not, but for just a few seconds it hit you," said Andy Stokes.

"I suppose so," said George Denison.

"I'll tell you who we're having tonight," said Stokes. "Out of deference to your wishes we kept it small. We couldn't get Joe and Verna. Joe's in Philadelphia, having a big operation. Cancer. It doesn't sound so good, either. Verna told Alice that we might as well be prepared for the worst. So they're out. But we did get Stubby and Jean."

"That's good."

"Stubby and Jean. Bob Rothermel and Cynthia. That's two, four, six, eight. And Henry and Ad. There won't be much drinking with that group. Stubby's been on the wagon five or six years. Henry is AA, very active in it. Bob still likes to put it away, but Cynthia only drinks a little wine at dinner. Alice never did drink, as you know, and I limit myself to two before dinner, usually a bourbon on the rocks."

"What about Ad, and what about Jean?"

"Ad is AA, too. Jean is unpredictable. She's on and off the wagon from one month to the next. She may arrive tonight with the blind staggers. On the other hand, she may not take a drink. It all depends. You knew their daughter had to be put away?"

"No, I didn't. Was that Barbara?"

"Barbara, yes. Bobbie. Oh, yeah. It was a tragic thing. She cut her wrists, and another time an overdose of sleeping pills. Some guy in Wilkes-Barre she was crazy about, so they said. Stubby went on the wagon, but Jean still ties one on. They sold their house, and then Stub was out of a job for over a year. He's got something now, Henry gave him a job at the brewery as a sort of a coordinator with the advertising agency."

"Stubby? He's a civil engineer."

"He's not the only guy with a Lehigh degree that's doing something altogether different. Do you remember Chuck Rainsford?"

"Sure. General superintendent of the Dilworth Collieries. I used to play golf with Chuck."

"Not any more. I'm afraid he's come down in the world. He gives a course in geology at the adult education setup we have here. Two nights a week. They pay him something like a hundred and fifty dollars a term, and he tells me he's glad to get the money."

"I've seen him bet that much on a single putt," said George Denison. "Haven't you any *good* news, Andy?"

"Well, you know how it is. The good news is always less spectacular. Let me think. Of those coming tonight? Henry and Ad's oldest grandson ran for the state legislature and nosed out the Democrat."

"That's always good to hear," said George Denison.

"Well, it's a start," said Stokes. "Let me think, now. Cynthia's taken up painting, but I don't know whether you'd classify that as good news, exactly. It's what she calls non-representational. In other words, not supposed to represent anything—and believe me, as far as I'm concerned, it doesn't. Both their kids have moved away. Young Bobby is a test pilot for one of the big aviation companies in California. The daughter married a fellow from Chicago and they're living out there. The husband is with Continental, the bank. There's no money here, George. Not the way we knew it. We're losing population, a thousand a year. The town is back to where it was in the 1910 census, and no new industries coming in. These people that are buying your land, they'll put up a supermarket and a big parking lot, but sure as hell that's going to be the end of some more of the smaller stores. And if they lease the rest of the land to a drive-in movie, which is what I understand, that'll close down one of our movie theaters. Banking isn't much fun any more, the hard luck stories I have to listen to. When I first started working here I used to hear a lot of crazy schemes that we had to turn down, but at least there was some imagination at work. Not any more. It's the fast buck, the quick turnover, build as cheaply as possible, take your profits and get out. Some of our people drive as much as fifty miles to work and fifty back. Car pools. Our biggest cash depositor, week to week, used to be the old Stewart department store. Now do you know what it is? The numbers racket. A few of our old friends have made some money in the stock market, but that's not here. That's New York and Philadelphia, and representing industries as far away as California."

"That's enough good news for one day," said George Denison.

"I know, and I have to live with it three hundred and sixty-five days a year. If there was only some way we could reduce the population and become a small town, with enough work for everybody. I wouldn't mind being a small town again. But I'm a banker, and I have to keep up this pretense, like a booster. Well, in three more years I retire. A banquet at the hotel, a silver cigarette box, and the responsibility passes on to one of those young fellows you see out there. He's welcome to it."

"I've been away too long, you've stayed here too long," said George Denison.

"That's about the size of it, I guess," said Stokes. "Yes, I guess that's just about the size of it."

"I must be going, Andy. I'll see you a little later."

"Mike will let you out. You remember Mike Kelly? If you don't, he'll remember you. Used to pitch in the Twilight League, and was on the police force. About our age. He'll appreciate it if you remember him—and so will I."

Mike Kelly was waiting to unlock the heavy plate-glass door. His eagerness to be recognized was almost a supplication.

"Hello, Mike," said George Denison.

Mike Kelly put the door key in his left hand and shook hands with George Denison. "George, it's mighty good to see you. You're looking great, George. Great."

"Well, you might be able to go nine innings yourself," said George Denison.

"You remember those days? You used to play under the name of —what was the name?"

"George Denny."

"George Denny," said Mike Kelly. "So you wouldn't lose your amateur standing. You could hit. You were a good hitter, George. There was a couple times there where you threw to the wrong base—"

"Never. I never threw to the wrong base in my life."

"Now you know you did, George. But when it come to hitting that apple, you had the power. There was only one pitcher could get you out. Marty Boxmyer, pitched for the Knights of Pythias. Marty was such a little guy and he had so much steam that you never knew where the ball was coming from. But outside of Marty, you could hit any pitcher in our league."

"Yes, I could even hit you, Mike."

"I'll admit it. I wasn't the greatest pitcher in the league. But there was very few could get a long ball off of me, when my sinker was going right. How long you gonna be in town, George?"

"Just overnight."

"Living in Connecticut, I hear. How's your missus?"

"Fine thank you. And yours?"

"Passed away, George. I buried her two years ago the sixth day of May. But I have eight grandchildren. Five boys to carry on the name. One of them at Villanova was scouted by a couple of major league clubs. He has three one-hitters to his credit, one of them against your old college alma mater. A two-to-one win against a good Princeton team. Pardon my ignorance, George, but you didn't have a son if I recollect."

"Two daughters, but one of the grandsons is on the Harvard crew."

"Well, that's good, George. You could of been a great athlete if it wasn't for that one thing. You know what I mean. I don't have to say it."

"I guess you must be referring to the suds," said George Denison.

"Not the suds. It was the hard stuff."

"I don't think it made much difference, Mike. I wouldn't have been much better, and I wouldn't have had as much fun."

"I used to try to lecture you," said Mike Kelly.

"Yes you did. Mike, it's nice to see you, and maybe I'll see you again before I leave. If not—keep the faith."

"You remember that, huh? Keep the faith. So long, George. Glad we run into one another."

Back at the hotel George Denison found his wife standing at the window, looking down at the traffic on Main Street. "I was watching you," she said. "You came all the way from the bank without being recognized. I was trying to remember the stores between here and Scandinavian Street. Do you realize there's not a one that used to be here that's still here? Not a one, in the same place. There may be some that moved."

"They didn't move. They closed. At least that's what I gather from Andy. Did you get an appointment with the hairdresser?"

"No. They wouldn't take me before tomorrow."

"Then let's go for a ride," said George Denison.

"Where to?"

"Oh—wherever old Dobbin takes us. I'll just wrap the reins around the buggy-whip."

"What's this quaintness, all of a sudden? Old Dobbin? Did you ever know anyone that had a horse called Dobbin?"

"I knew a girl that had a dog called Dobbin," said George Denison.

"She must have been terribly affected. I suppose she had a horse called Rover."

"Towser," said George Denison.

"Frankly, I don't believe it," said Pammie Denison.

"Come on, put your coat on while there's still daylight," he said.

She put on her coat and hat. "Did you really know a girl that had a dog called Dobbin?" she said in the elevator.

"I really did," he said.

"When?"

"During what we sometimes refer to as the Tommy Williams Period."

"Oh," she said, and in the presence of the elevator boy said no more.

The green car was at the door. They got in and he drove south on Main Street. "Who *was* the girl that had—"

"With a dog called Dobbin? What difference does that make now? She was never as important to me as Tommy Williams was to you."

"All right. I was just wondering whether she was one that I knew about or one that you never mentioned. Where are we headed for?"

"You'll soon see," he said.

"Oh, then I guess I know," she said.

"Right," he said.

After a while he drove off the main highway and up into the hills, and presently he stopped the car on a township road, midway between two farmhouses. "Are you going to kiss me?" she said.

"Don't you think I ought to?"

"Yes I do," she said.

He kissed her on the lips, and when he drew away she was looking down at the floor, vaguely smiling. "That was very nice of you," she said.

"I feel rather self-conscious about it," he said. "But it's just about the only chance we'll get."

"Do you know something, George?"

"What?"

"After twenty-five years, twenty-seven, whatever it is, this is the first time I've really felt that you've forgiven me for Tommy Williams."

"Really? Well, maybe it is the first time. I don't know."

"I forgave myself a long time ago," she said.

He laughed. "I'm sure you did."

"Oh, it wasn't as easy as all that. A girl that's made a damn fool of herself—first she has to justify herself. Then she has to forget all about that and start being honest with herself—if she can. And I did. And that was when I was harder on myself than you ever were. It was at least a year before I could forgive myself for what I did to you and to myself."

"I didn't realize it'd taken you that long," he said.

"I know you didn't. That's why today, just now, is the first time I feel that you've really forgiven me. All those years in between, you took me back and we've been nice to each other, but there's always been something missing. Why is that?"

"I don't know," he said. "I've had it in my mind that I wanted to come here, to this very spot where I first kissed you over forty years ago. And I planned to kiss you. Then on the way to Gibbsville I more or less gave up the idea. Oversentimental. Forced. Awkward. But then I saw old Karl Isaminger. Then I had a long talk with Andy and heard what's happened to people we used to love. To this town. Life has been awful to them, Pam, the town and the people, and it hasn't been nearly as bad to you and me. Not yet, anyway. But our luck will start running out. We're getting there. And I wanted to bring you here and tell you that I've always loved you. Here, where I told you the first time."

"Then what I felt was right," she said.

"Yes," he said.

"From now on I guess we have to be ready for anything," she said.

"Yes," he said. With the tips of his fingers he caressed the back of her neck. "And don't be depressed by what we see tonight, at Alice and Andy's."

"Thank you," she said. "I won't. Now."

"Here comes a man on a tractor," he said. "He thinks we're lost."

The Locomobile

Shortly after getting out of the army in 1919, George Denison gave—*gave*—his mother's Locomobile limousine to Arthur Gow, who had been the lady's chauffeur. The car was a beauty, purer in line than the Pierce-Arrows and Packards that were generally chosen by women like Mrs. Denison. It was painted Brewster green, and it was the only one of its kind in the county. It had less than 15,000 miles on the odometer, six new Pennsylvania Vacuum Cups to replace the original tires, and it would have fetched five thousand dollars in a trade-in if George Denison had wanted to bargain. But his mother had neglected to mention Arthur Gow in her will—she had never got around to it in the years since the will had been drawn up—and George Denison wanted to do something for Arthur. Mrs. Denison's personal maid, Agnes, was left five thousand dollars, the cook, Margaret, a more recent addition to the Denison establishment than Arthur Gow, got two thousand dollars. Something had to be done for Arthur, whose nose was a little out of joint at not being included among the beneficiaries, but who had stayed on, taking care of the limousine and George's phaeton and doing odd jobs about the house and grounds, until George's return to civilian life. Arthur did not exactly say so in so many words, but he *as much as* told Agnes and Margaret that he would not quit the job until George had had a chance to do what was right and fair. George would surely do the right thing. He was a young fellow, George, but very fair, and when he had had time to study the whole situation would realize that the missus—well, it wasn't only the money. All those nights sitting outside somebody's house while the missus was at a dinner. Up at six o'clock every morning and sometimes not getting to bed again till after midnight. Supposed to have one day off a week, but how many times did she ask him to change to another day, so that he never knew for sure whether he could go fishing or plan a picnic with his wife and kids. And if it came to money, how much

New Yorker (20 July 1963); *The Hat on the Bed*

money he had saved the family by cleaning the spark plugs and vulcanizing inner tubes and things like that that other drivers, *some* other drivers, would take to a garage. The Winton salesman, the Cadillac salesman, the Peerless salesman had all approached him to use his influence with Mrs. Denison and he had turned them down flat, although some other women's drivers had used *their* influence and collected a nice cut. Could anyone say that there was a car anywhere in the whole county that was better taken care of than the Denisons' two Locomobiles? In all kinds of weather Arthur put on his gum boots and washed and polished those cars and caught many a cold doing it. Was *her* car, the limousine, ever once pulled up at the portecochere without fresh flowers in the cutglass vases? Didn't he always warm the laprobe in front of the carriage-house stove so she wouldn't have a cold cover over her knees? And who was it saw to it that the car never left the carriage-house without her little flask of brandy where she knew it would be?

George Denison knew most of these things about Arthur Gow and his diligence, his pride in his work. True, George took a lot for granted, as you do take a lot for granted in a good servant such as Arthur and Agnes and Margaret; but having so recently got out of the army, with its blundering and inefficiency in spite of the disciplined atmosphere, George was more inclined to observe and appreciate the quiet smoothness of a well-run household and of the persons responsible for it. "I want to do something for Arthur Gow," he told the family lawyer, Arthur McHenry, himself just returned from overseas.

"I had another look at that will," said McHenry. "I helped your mother with it, and I remember at the time thinking it was strange she didn't mention Arthur. But I didn't say anything. You know how your mother was. She came in here one day and had a batch of notes on how she wanted everything disposed of, right down to who was to get your father's cuff links. The diamond ones." He smiled.

"Who did get them? I forget," said George Denison.

"Nobody," said the lawyer. "Originally she was going to leave them to me, but I persuaded her not to. As her lawyer I didn't want to figure as a beneficiary. Somewhere you'll come across a letter suggesting that you give them to me, but it's not in the will itself."

"Well, I haven't taken a good look at her jewelry. It's all in one box," said George Denison. "I'll have another look and if they're there, I'll bring them down to you."

"No hurry," said the lawyer. "And I never saw the letter. But she told me she was going to write it, and when she said she'd do a thing she usually did it. So it's somewhere around."

"Yes. Mother had two desks, one in the library and the other upstairs in her sewingroom. I haven't even attempted to go through the stuff in the sewingroom."

"Well, it's around somewhere, you may be sure. And incidentally, when you come across it you may find some suggestion as to what to do about Arthur Gow. Although I'm inclined to doubt that. She was so explicit about the bequests to the cook and the maid, I think she had very positive feelings about leaving him out. I thought at the time, well, she might have lent him money, for instance, and had some understanding with him that she would forgive the debt."

"Oh, no, Arthur," said George Denison. "I doubt that very much. Unless it was a small sum, fifty dollars or something like that. But not anything like a thousand or two thousand. Mother liked to live well and she spent money with a fairly free hand, but she always considered that money as mine. That is to say, eventually mine, and from the time Father died, when I was eighteen, she always made quite a point of telling me how the money was going out. She didn't ask my permission, of course, but things like—oh, taking the cobblestones out of the carriage-house and putting down a concrete floor. When we got rid of the horses and turned the carriage-house into a garage, she showed me all the bills. And if she gave money to Farmington or the Children's Home, she was always careful to let me know how much and where and so forth. She wouldn't have lent Arthur Gow any considerable amount without telling me. And she wouldn't have forgiven the debt without asking me. Of that I'm sure. Also, Arthur never needed money. He was very stingy with his money. If I wanted a nickel or a dime outside my allowance, I could get it from Margaret or Agnes—although it was much easier to get it from Margaret than Agnes. But Arthur was hopeless. 'You're not supposed to ask me for money,' he used to say."

"I'm surprised that you have such charitable feelings for him now, considering," said the lawyer.

"Not charitable, Arthur," said George Denison. "I just don't want him thinking my mother was as stingy as he was."

"Oh, I understand," said the lawyer. "Discriminated against. Just what I thought when we were working on the will. But knowing your mother, I don't think it was an oversight."

"No, it couldn't have been an oversight. After all, Arthur drove her down here to this office, and he was sitting in the car downstairs while she was talking to you. It wasn't an oversight. But it was and is a good excuse for someone to have unkind thoughts about Mother, and she was too good for that . . . There's another thing."

"What's that?" said the lawyer.

"I'm going to let him go."

"Fire him?"

"Terminate his employment. I don't intend to stay in Gibbsville. You know that."

"Well, I guess you've thought that all out. You and Pammie. It's probably not very stimulating here."

"I want to be near the water, somewhere where I can go sailing every good day. And these past ten years, prep school, college, and the army, I've made different friends than those I grew up with."

"You've got the Gibbsville doldrums, and you want to get out. Well, why not? And if you don't do it pretty soon, you never will."

"That's exactly what Pammie says. I'm fond of my old friends, but I like my new ones, too. And since I can't afford to move Long Island Sound to Lantenengo County, we'll move to Long Island Sound."

"And you're not going to need Arthur Gow."

"What I thought I'd do—I don't want to give him any actual cash. Mother saw fit not to, so I won't. But there's that Locomobile limousine. It's probably worth at least as much as Mother gave Agnes, and if he wants to sell it, fine. That way everybody should be satisfied. I haven't gone against Mother's wishes, but he has no cause to complain."

"Certainly no cause to complain," said the lawyer. "I think it's the handsomest car in the county. He shouldn't have any trouble selling it in Philadelphia."

"Then you approve?"

"I have one slight reservation—that your mother knew exactly what she was doing, and *she* might not approve. But as you said a minute ago, she always considered that the money was yours. And I never knew her to really go against your wishes."

"No, not after I began to make some sense," said George Denison. "Whenever that was."

"Seems to me you've always made pretty good sense, George," said the lawyer.

George Denison found Arthur Gow in the carriage-house (which, from habit, they had not learned to call the garage). Appropriately, Arthur was giving the limousine windows a polish. "You like that car, don't you?"

"I do," said Arthur Gow. "That I do. You can have all your Pierce-Arrows and Packards—"

"And Rolls-Royces?"

"Well, I don't know as I'd go that far. The Rolls-Royce is in a class by itself. But it ain't only the make of car I was thinking of. It's this here car, this particular one, I have a fondness for. I guess if I put in the same hours on a Scripps-Booth I'd feel the same way. Only I never would—put in the same hours on a Scripps-Booth, I mean. I took a liking to this car the minute I saw it. Now for instance Mrs. Hofman has that Pierce, and you know what we call it? The drivers? We call it her china-closet. This ain't no china-closet."

"How would you like to own this car?" said George Denison.

"Yes, well if a man owned a car like this he could consider himself —he could consider himself very fortunate. I guess there ain't but two or three hundred like it in the whole country, if that. A car like this don't wear out, and you never get tired of looking at it. The Pierce-Arrow people are improving the looks of their new models, but they have a long way to go before they catch up to this one. You'll have this car another five years, at least."

"No, I've decided to give it away."

"Give it away? If you give this car away, I'll quit."

"Well, that's all right, Arthur. Because I'm going to give it to you. As a sort of a farewell present."

Arthur Gow went to the car and rubbed the door-window with his chamois. He was thinking. "I heard talk you were leaving town," he said. Even his incredulity was slow, as slow as belief might have been in a less cautious man. "Somebody said you were putting the house up for sale."

"Putting everything up for sale, except the closed car. I'm going to give you that."

Arthur Gow stopped polishing the glass. "You're in earnest?"

"Positively in earnest. Go down to Mr. McHenry's office, tomorrow morning if you like. He's making out the bill of sale."

"Sale?"

"To make it legal, I'm selling it to you for one dollar. But you can owe me the dollar."

"What do you want me to do with the car when I own it?"

"When you own it you can do whatever you please. You can keep it, you can sell it, you can fill it full of Singer's Midgets and go all over the country in it. What would you *like* to do with it?"

"What would I like to do with it? I'd like to ride in the back seat, from here to Reading and back. Just to see how it feels. Then when I got that out of my system—are you giving me my walking papers?"

"Yes, if you put it that way. I'd like you to stay on till Mrs. Denison and I leave for good. That'll be the first of June, we've rented a house in Connecticut. Mrs. Denison is giving the women notice to-day."

"Margaret not going with you? Or Agnes?"

"No. We have a couple, a man and wife, that go with the house in Connecticut. You don't seem very surprised at any of this."

"Well, there was talk around that you and your missus were moving away. Everything gets around in Gibbsville."

"Yes. What will you do? Take a vacation? I'm sure you've been thinking about this."

"I've been thinking. I'll get offers. There's always a couple ladies wants me to drive for them. When you were away in the army I had a couple offers. But I didn't know you were thinking of giving me this car."

"Does that change your plans?"

"To some extent. To *some* extent, it changes them. To some extent it don't change them at all."

"I see—although I don't see," said George Denison.

"What I mean is, George, I don't want to drive for nobody else. I want me own hours. And I got a little money put away. I was thinking of going in business for myself, driving for hire. There's a lot of ladies in town, widows and old maids, that your mother used to lend them the car with me driving. Most of them I got tips from. But now I can charge them all, like so much a head to drive two-three-four of them to the golf club. Reading. Philadelphia. Card parties. Evening parties, but double for parties after ten o'clock."

"You *have* given it some thought."

"There's a lot of these ladies, they got the money but they don't want to go to the expense of a car and a garage and a driver. They all know me, and they all rode in this car, most of them. It'll be the same as living retired but making money at the same time."

"You wouldn't like to work for whoever buys the house?"

"No more driving private, George," said Arthur Gow. He faintly, almost indiscernibly smiled. "When you come back for a visit you can ride in this car, and I won't charge you."

"Well, thank you," said George Denison. (Later he was able to recall that his was the only word of thanks offered during the conversation.) "You go see Mr. McHenry tomorrow."

"What would be a good time to go?" said Arthur.

"Oh, any time after ten o'clock, I should think."

"Yes, I guess there won't be much to it, just a bill of sale," said Arthur.

"Well, go on with your work, Arthur. I don't want to interrupt you."

"That's all right," said Arthur Gow, and resumed his task.

George Denison found his wife in his mother's sewingroom.

"Well, I just got rid of one Locomobile and one Arthur Gow," he said.

"That's good. I was never very fond of either," she said. "I don't look well in green, and as for that pickle-face Arthur, dignity is all right but he carries it too far. Before we were married I used to see him, chauffeuring your mother around, and from his expression he seemed to say, 'Look what I've got in the back seat.' Not in a complimentary way, either."

"Well, after the first of June," said George Denison.

"Yes," she said. "What do you want me to do with all these letters and little scraps of paper? Can I throw them away? Your mother was very efficient, but she kept everything. Every letter you ever wrote, from the time you were visiting your Uncle Joe and Aunt Something, I can't decipher her name."

"Not a real uncle and aunt. He was my godfather. Joe Riddle, friend of my father's. Aunt Sophie. They're both dead."

"Ah, you poor little orphan, let me give you a nice pat on the head. Go away. Now what *about* these things? I'm in favor of holding on to your letters and things like that, but here is a whole stack of miscellaneous. Reminders that your mother wrote to herself."

"Did you by any chance come across anything about Arthur Gow?"

"Arthur Gow? I'll say I did. A whole stack."

"Are they all together in one stack?"

"No, they're all mixed up in the miscellaneous. Do you want me to separate them? Some are from him to her, and some are memorandums she wrote herself."

"Memoranda."

"Memoranda sounds like a pancake flour," said Pammie Denison. "If you want me to go through this whole accumulation, I will, but having gone through it once I can assure you there's nothing worth saving. Unless you suspect your mother of carrying on a romance with Arthur Gow."

"Somehow, *somehow,* I have my doubts about that. Mother liked men, all right, but if she was ever going to have a romantic attachment it wouldn't be Arthur Gow. If she'd had some dashing French chauffeur—but not Arthur. Mother was more like you in that respect. Very impatient with dull men. Luckily you have me."

"Uh-huh. And if I should happen to forget how lucky I am, I have you to remind me."

"Yes, isn't that splendid? Very few wives—"

"Never mind. Just tell me what you want me to do with this junk. Your letters and other family letters are all tied together, but the rest of this hodge-podge, you'll have to decide. I mean I'm certainly not going to go through it all over again. So shall I leave it all here and you go through it? I warn you, you're in for a very dull three or four hours."

"I'll get to it after dinner," he said.

The miscellany turned out to be full of items that were easily discarded. They went back to his father's death six years earlier, at which time Mrs. Denison apparently instituted the practice of jotting down notes that covered repairs and changes in the house and grounds, wedding presents to be purchased, social engagements, books to be read, letters to be written, telephone calls to be made. All these notes were written on paper of uniform size and texture which bore the initials A.S.D. in the upper left-hand corner. Here and there would be an item of simple arithmetic—addition, subtraction, multiplication, short and long division—that indicated her attempts to estimate her income and expenses. Here George Denison was going in for guesswork, since the items were not identified by words or names; but he recognized figures that represented his recollection of her income for various years, which she seemed to have divided by twelve. Conversely, he found notes in which certain repeated figures were multiplied by twelve, indicating her attempts to arrive at a year's outlay on wages and other fixed expenses.

"This is rather fun," he said to his wife.

"Why?" said Pammie Denison.

"Well, for several reasons. First of all, I didn't realize that Mother didn't trust her memory. I wish I knew whether she kept notes before Father died. I doubt it. I think he did all this while he was alive, and she only started after he was dead. She wasn't very good at long division."

"Another thing she and I had in common," said Pammie.

"But I'll say this for her. When she did a problem in long division, she'd prove it."

"You multiply the thing on the right and the thing on the left, and it's supposed to come out the thing in the middle."

"Oh, you do know how," he said. "My compliments."

"Of course I know how. It's just those damn subtrahends that confused me. Those names for things. I have a very good mind for figures."

"Yes, as a matter of fact, you have," he said. "Ah, here's something I'm glad I came across. 'A. McH., C. Links.' "

"Oh, boy!"

"Well, it's important. It means that she really wanted Arthur Mc-Henry to have my father's diamond cuff links."

"Good."

"I'm sorry. Am I distracting you? What are you reading?"

"It's called *The Magnificent Ambersons,* by Booth Tarkington," she said. "He's the one that wrote those Penrod stories, but you wouldn't guess it from this book."

"Princeton man," said George Denison.

"Oh, *well.*"

"Class of—I'm not sure. I think he went to Exeter, too. Ivy Club."

"Naturally," she said.

"When you get finished with his book I'd like to read it."

"If you ever get finished with that stuff," she said. "At the rate you're going, checking your mother's long division."

"I'm almost finished that part, and practically all of it goes in the trash basket."

For an hour or so she went on reading, while he continued with his chore, and there was no conversation. But she chanced to look across the room at him twice in a five-minute period, and she saw that both times he was sitting back in his chair, his legs stretched out, a piece of paper in his hand, and he had hardly changed his position. He was no longer reading the notes, but he was deep in thought.

"Have you discovered something?" she said.

"I don't know," he said. "See what you make of it." He handed her not one but two sheets of the notepaper.

On one sheet she read: "Send A.G. away."

On the second sheet: "See A. McH—advice about A.G.!!! Afraid!!!"

"Well?" said George Denison. "Does it make any sense to you?"

"Does it to you?" she said. "You've been brooding over it for the last ten minutes."

"I've been letting my imagination run riot. She obviously never did see Arthur McHenry about Arthur Gow, or he would have told me so when I spoke to him about giving Gow the car. But she must have been afraid of Gow. Can you read any other interpretation into it?"

"No. I never realized it till now, but he does give me the creeps."

"I'm a little sorry now that I promised to give him the car."

"You can get out of that easily enough."

"Not so damn easily. What excuse can I give? What have I got to go on?"

"Go see Arthur McHenry first thing in the morning, and take these notes with you. What about the notes from Arthur Gow to her? Is there anything in them?"

"Not a thing. I've got them all here, but they don't tell anything. Here he wants a new hose. Here he wants a new nozzle for the hose.

Here's one that asks for a new storage battery for the car. This one is a request for three days off, 'next week,' whenever that was. This one —a long one with a list of things he's ordering at the hardware store. Chamois. Bon-Ami. Brass polish. Whisk broom. You saw all this, and there isn't a thing in it that gives any clue."

She was silent.

"Are you still with me?" he said.

"I'm thinking," she said. "Let me see his notes to her."

He handed her the sheaf of notes, and she quickly went through them, one by one. "I wonder," she said. "But I think I'm on to something."

"Like what?"

"In all the years he worked for us, Jim McGroarty, our chauffeur, never wrote a note to Mother or Daddy. They may have written notes to him, or left messages in the kitchen. 'Please have car to take me to eight-thirty-five train.' Things like that. But I don't even re- member that. The point is, all these things that Arthur Gow asked for in his notes, he could have much more easily asked her in person. Do you see what I'm getting at? Why write these things out, when all he had to do was say, 'Mrs. Denison, can I buy a chamois and charge it?' Do you see what I mean? They didn't speak to each other, he and your mother. At least any more than was absolutely necessary. For five or six years, ever since your father died, she's avoided con- versation by having him put everything on paper."

"So that she wouldn't forget anything."

"No! Because she was afraid of him," said Pammie Denison.

"You're basing that on that one note, the one about seeing Arthur McHenry. Afraid."

"No I'm not. I'm basing it on instinct. Intuition. And common sense. Here you have dozens of notes from Gow to your mother, dozens of them, and it must have been a nuisance for him, writing notes every time he wanted to buy a feather duster. But she made him do it, and why? Because she couldn't bear to talk to him, or more likely have him talk to her."

"Why didn't she fire him, if she felt that way?"

"Because she had no good reason to, that's why. I'm sure he never said anything, or did anything, that would give her grounds to fire him. But she had an instinctive feeling—yes, like me. And she was *fair,* your mother. She wasn't going to discharge a servant because he gave her the creeps, not as long as his work was all right. I couldn't have discharged him, either, not without reason, but I'm awfully glad he isn't going with us to Connecticut."

"And she left him out of her will," he said. "He was honest, sober, reliable, a very thorough worker. What do you suppose happened?"

"Nothing, I tell you," said Pammie. "But I swear to you, she was afraid something would happen, or could happen, or might happen. I know exactly how she felt, and you never will, because you're not a woman."

"I may be making a big mistake, giving him the car," he said.

"Possibly, but now you can't go back on your word, any more than your mother could discharge him without grounds. Let him have the car, and let's forget about him."

"If we can," he said. "From now on I'll always think of my mother, the last six years of her life, intimidated by a perfect servant."

"I agree with you, because that's the way I think it was."

"There's one thing that does worry me, a little," he said. "Maybe it shouldn't, but it does."

"What's that?"

"Oh—thinking of those old ladies, those friends of Mother's, that he's going to have for customers. Are they my responsibility?"

"No, George," said his wife. "You can stop being a captain."

"I suppose so," he said. "I suppose I should."

Zero

I t was so cold that no one was out. At the top of the hill, sitting in his car with the motor running, Dick Pfeister could see all of Main Street to the south, and in more than an hour not a soul had ventured forth on foot. Once in a while an automobile would come along, usually an out-of-town car on its way through. Once in a while it would be a truck, likewise on its way through and carrying five to ten tons of coal. Town people were staying in. The Orpheum had not even bothered to turn on its lights, and Richard Arlen and Carole Lombard, who were probably sitting in the sun in Southern California, or anyway had been doing so a few hours earlier, could not complain if their fans chose to stay home on such a night. The trolley from Gibbsville, due at eight-twenty, was reported two hours ago as stuck halfway up the mountain. The track was clear of snow, but something had gone wrong with the lubricating system and the trolley was just sitting there and the passengers had to wait until they could be transferred to a relief.

According to the information Dick Pfeister got from the traction company office, the trolley came to a halt and then the wheels would not turn. The motorman then had to walk down the track a couple of miles to the nearest emergency telephone. He was a brave and strong man, the motorman, to risk freezing to death. The thermometer outside the traction company office registered eight degrees below zero, and what it must have been like on the mountain was anybody's guess. The motorman was going to try to walk back to his car, which was at least better than sitting down and falling asleep. Meanwhile the passengers in the trolley had light and some heat, and help was on the way. They could have been a lot worse off.

The repair car, followed by the relief, had passed by about an hour ago on their way southward. The relief, with the passengers from the stalled trolley, should be along any minute now. Ordinarily the entire trip from Gibbsville took only fifty minutes, but this was not a night on which schedules were being observed. Tomorrow's papers would carry items giving the temperature in other Pennsylvania towns, like Snowshoe and Clarks Summit, and no doubt it *was* colder in those towns than in Mountain City, but it was cold enough to kill you here, and you died just as dead at Mountain City as at Snowshoe.

Down at the end of town a beam of light appeared, and Dick Pfeister watched it until the source of the beam, the relief car, came into view. He checked his fuel gauge; the tank was a little less than half full. He switched off his motor and got out of the car and went to the street corner where the trolley would stop. He stood in the doorway of Hutchinson's furniture store for protection from the cold wind. It was strange that no one else seemed to be meeting the trolley—and just then two automobiles came from different directions and stopped at the corner, apparently having heard at the last minute that the relief trolley was on its way.

The relief stopped at the corner, and three passengers got out. The first was a middle-aged woman with her arms full of bundles; the second was a man whom Dick Pfeister recognized: John J. Flaherty, the lawyer, who rode to and from the county seat five days a week. Flaherty was being met by his son; the woman by a man whom Dick Pfeister took to be her husband. The third passenger was Eva Novak. She was carrying a black imitation-leather hatbox and a heavy suitcase. She looked around, but Dick Pfeister did not come out of the doorway until the middle-aged woman and Flaherty had been taken away in their automobiles.

"Hey," he called to her.

She saw him, but she did not speak.

He went to her and picked up her luggage. "That's *my* car, across the street," he said.

"Okay," she said. "Where we going?"

"I'll take you to your sister's."

"I didn't have anything to eat. Is it all right if we get a sandwich or something? I didn't eat anything since I left Philly, only a milk shake in Gibbsville."

"Can't you get something at your sister's?" He opened the door of the car and she got in, and he put the luggage in the back.

"I'd sooner get something at the diner. I'll pay for it. I don't want to go to my sister's and the first thing I ask her for a meal. It's eleven o'clock at night, and she won't even be up at this hour."

"I'm not sure the diner's open," said Dick Pfeister.

"He's *always* open. You can see from here. Listen, if you don't want to come in with me, that's all right, but I gotta have a plate of soup or something. The last two hours all I could think of was a Yankee pot roast at Joe's diner."

"All right," said Dick Pfeister.

"You don't have to eat with me, if that's what you object to. You don't even have to let on you know me."

"It isn't that," he said.

"Yes it is. You don't want anybody to see me with you. Well, maybe I feel the same way, but first of all I'm hungry."

"Maybe there won't be anybody there."

"Don't be too sure of that. They're liable to come in. The best thing is you take me there and I go in alone, then you come in a couple minutes later. We don't have to leave together."

"It'll look fishy, you going in there alone on a night like this."

"Listen, Dick, I didn't ask you to meet me at the trolley. That was all your idea."

"What if I got a couple of hamburgers and a container of coffee? Would that satisfy you? I can't go in the diner with you, and that's all there is to it. And you can't go in there by yourself, not on this kind of a night."

"For Christ's sake then, get me a couple hamburgers and some coffee. Just so I get something or I'll faint dead away. Then you'd have to take me to the doctor's. I'm still weak. I only been walking on my two feet since Monday. You have no idea."

They drove to the diner and Dick Pfeister got the hamburgers and coffee. He put them in her lap. "We'll drive out toward your sister's."

"Did he put sugar and cream in the coffee?" she said.

"Both."

"The container's hot. That's good," she said. She took the wax paper off one of the hamburgers and commenced to eat as they headed for the edge of town. She finished the first hamburger before they reached her sister's neighborhood of company houses. "Now I can have some coffee," she said. "It is hot. Do you want some?"

"I'll take a sip," he said.

"There's a quart of it, I don't want it all. You want a bite of hamburger?"

"No thanks," he said.

"So much the better," she said. "I shouldn't eat so fast. It isn't polite, but what do I give a darn about politeness? Do you have a cigarette? We smoked all ours on the trolley. Everybody ran out of cigarettes. I only had enough to last me to Mountain City, then I was gonna get another pack, but I shared mine with a fellow sitting next to me. First we smoked all his, then we smoked all mine. He just come from burying his uncle in Gibbsville."

"What was it like on the trolley? Were you scared?"

"I wasn't. What was there to be scared of? I was worried for the motorman. He walked a couple miles to phone the trolley company, to say we were stuck. If it wasn't for him we'd be there yet. He bundled up warm. Two pairs of gloves, two mufflers around his head. But they had to give him first aid. He passed out as soon as he got back in the trolley. He was in terrible shape, the poor fellow. He was on the trolley I came in on. They were taking him to the doctor's. They said he had frostbite and might lose a couple toes. I don't know. That's what some person said. I know you *can* lose a foot if you get a bad frostbite. It happened to a buddy of my uncle's, worked at the Madeline Colliery. He got drunk and couldn't find his way home, a night like tonight. Stanley Bolitis. You probly noticed him, with the crutch."

"Yes, I know him," said Dick Pfeister. "What about you, Eva?"

"Oh, they told us we shouldn't worry. The electricity was connected up, so the lights were on and we got some heat."

"I didn't mean that."

"Oh." She took a long drag of her cigarette. "They said I wasn't supposed to take a job that I had to stand up all the time. I'll have to look for work that I can be sitting down. I thought of a telephone operator. They train you, and you don't have to have a high school diploma. They don't pay much to start, but they're all right to work for. I don't have any money left. I only had enough to get home."

"How much more do you need?"

"Well, that's up to you. Look in my purse, there's only a little over four dollars. I'll have to pay my sister board and room."

"How much did you tell her?"

"Oh, she guessed. She didn't tell her husband, or he wouldn't let me stay there. He'd put me out. He'd say be a girl in a house, but I can't even be that for a while. Not that I want to, but I couldn't if I wanted to."

"I don't have much money either. I brought fifty dollars with me you can have, but that's the last I can lay my hands on for I don't know how long."

"Well, I never said it was all your fault. It takes two. But this way is better than if I had the baby and I had to tell who the father was. That would sure be the end of you, Dick."

"I know that, for God's sake. You don't have to keep reminding me."

"No, but you don't have to act as if you were the one that was doing all the favors. *I* went to that crummy hospital, and I was the one that took a chance on dying. You pleaded and begged me, but since then you act as if you didn't have any responsibility. As soon as I can get work I don't care if I never see you again, the same as you feel about me. I'm going to save up till I have enough to go some place else, and then believe me, Dick, I'll get out of here so fast. I'm suppose to take it easy for two months, but I start looking for work tomorrow. Or anyway as soon as this cold spell lets up. I can't walk that far in this weather."

"Where do you expect me to get more money?"

"You work in a bank, you're suppose to know."

"Are you suggesting that I steal it?"

"That wouldn't do me any good, if you got caught stealing. I have enough to tell in confession without that on my conscience. No, don't start stealing on my account. But you have to get the money somewhere, till I find work."

"What if I can't get any more? Just can't?"

"Don't say you can't when you can. You can sell your car, borrow money on your house. Ask your father and mother."

"You might as well tell me to get it from my wife."

"Well, if she'd give it to you. You're doing everything to protect her, but what's she entitled to more than I am?"

He slapped her. It was not a hard slap, from his somewhat cramped position in the car, and it barely glanced off her face, but her left cheek received some of the blow. She put her hand to her cheek. "Wud you do that for? That was a lousy thing to do."

"I'm sorry I did it," he said.

"Yeah," she said.

"But you don't have to bring my wife into it."

"Bring her into it? She's in it whether she knows it or not. You can't keep her out of it. She's in it. Maybe she doesn't know it, but she is, and sooner or later she will know it. *Because you'll tell her.* I can keep quiet, I showed you that. But you'll tell her, if she don't find out for herself."

"Not me. I won't tell her."

"Yes, you. I got to thinking a lot about you, Dick, in that crummy hospital. I went in there and I signed my name Evelyn New. Evelyn New. As soon as I did that I was alone in the world, because if I died they didn't know my name. I couldn't have any visitors, I couldn't talk to anybody. They even said I couldn't have the priest if I was gonna die. All alone, see? So what I did was think, and I sure did think about you, Dick. All right, you were paying for it, but on account of yourself, not on account of me. I'm not surprised you slapped me."

"I apologize for that," he said.

"Apologize. That's just a word. If you thought you could get away with it, you'd murder me. Maybe you don't know that yet, but you would. That's why I wasn't surprised by you slapping me. You didn't only want to slap me. You wanted to murder me."

"That's what you figured out in the hospital?"

"Yes. When I thought you were in love with me I couldn't of figured that out, but down there I knew you weren't in love with me. That's all right. I wasn't in love with you any more, either."

"That sounds as if you wanted to murder me, too," he said.

"No, not murder you. I was doing enough killing for one person. Maybe the baby would have been another Paderewski, somebody famous like that."

"Paderewski? You mean the piano player? What made you think that?"

"Well, he'd of been only half Polish, so I guess not Paderewski. I don't know. Was there anybody famous in your family?"

"No."

"Well, maybe only a basketball player. That's when I got stuck on you, when you used to play basketball. You wouldn't even look at me then. I didn't know when I was better off."

"Oh, I looked at you, but you were too young."

"You only thought I was," she said. "Thank God for that, or we'd of been in worse trouble. Then my father was still alive, and speaking of murder he would of murdered you. If I had any brothers they would of murdered you. But instead of that you want to murder me."

"Ah, the hell with all this talk about murder. Nobody's going to murder anybody. That's all your imagination, because I gave you a slap in the face. I'm sorry for that, but I'm not going to keep on apologizing all night. I have to take you home or my alcohol will evaporate and the car'll boil over."

"All right. You said you had fifty dollars," she said.

"Here it is."

"Thanks. But don't forget, Dick, I'm gonna need some more."

"I'll try to get you another fifty next month, but I don't promise."

"How will you get it to me?"

"I'll mail it to you in cash."

"All right. Four weeks from tomorrow I'll be expecting it. Fifty cash. But don't put me off. Some of it has to go for medicine."

"I'll do the best I can, and whatever you do, don't you come in the bank. I don't want anybody to see me talking to you."

"It's no pleasure talking to you, either, Dick."

He moved the car closer to her sister's house. "Can you carry those bags all right?"

"Oh, sure. Those delicious hamburgers gave me my strength back."

He kept the motor idling until he saw the door open at her sister's house, then he drove home and put his car in the garage.

One lamp was burning in the kitchen in the otherwise darkened house, but he knew that Emily was still awake. As soon as he opened the kitchen door he knew she was awake. The house was still; she was not moving around upstairs; but from her to him came a hostile greeting. He put his overcoat and hat and arctics in the hall closet, making no sound. He went to the cellar and made sure that the furnace was all right for the night. When he returned to the kitchen she was sitting at the table in her blue flannel bathrobe and smoking a cigarette.

"I tried not to make any noise," he said.

"I was awake. I heard you come in."

"It's bitter out. Must be over ten below," he said.

"It's fourteen below outside the bathroom window," she said. "You want to tell me where you went to?"

"You mean after the meeting?"

"There was no meeting. Phil Irwin phoned to say it was called off."

"Yes, I found that out when I got there. There was a notice on the door of the gym. Alumni Association meeting postponed, account of severe weather. Phil didn't show up, but some of the others did, so we went over to the Elks and had a few beers. Jack Showers, Ed McGraney."

"Always Jack Showers and Ed McGraney," she said.

"They're on the athletic committee."

"And you never see them any other time. *I* never see them at all."

"Well, why should you? Got any pie or anything?"

"Pie on top of beer? You'll be yelling in your sleep all night. Why don't you have some pretzels?"

"Don't tell me what I'm hungry for, will you?"

"No, I won't tell you anything. You don't tell me anything but lies. You never went near the Elks tonight."

"I can prove it."

"Who by? Jack Showers and Ed McGraney all over again?"

"They were with me. Where do you think I was?"

"That's what I'm trying to find out. Listen to me, Dick. I know there's something funny going on, and I'm going to find out what it is. I'm not going to let you make a fool out of me. Whoever it is, it isn't one of my friends because I keep tabs on them. Norma. Elaine. Especially Norma. But it couldn't be her, because when I was checking up on you and her I found out she has another boy friend. But whoever it is, you might as well prepare yourself. I'm going to make trouble."

"Make trouble for yourself. That's what you're doing right now. And keep your voice down or you'll wake the kids."

"Oh, isn't that rich? You showing consideration for the kids. I like that, all right. It's all right to make a fool out of me and go whoring around, but we mustn't wake the kids. That's rich, that is. Go on up and wake them. Tell them where you were tonight, with some whore."

He slapped her. "Shut up," he said.

She drew away from him. "Don't you do *that* again, don't you *ever* do that again. I'll *kill* you first, Dick. I swear I will."

"Go ahead, you'd be doing me a favor," he said.

The strange, simple words shocked her. Whatever else he had said to her, these words she recognized as the truth; at this moment he wished to be dead and free, but not only free of her. More than to be free of her he wished to be free of the other woman. She could think of nothing to say, but she knew that no words of hers could threaten this man with trouble. She was looking at destruction, and she had had no part in it.

Eminent Domain

The Langendorfs and the MacMahons exercised a private version of the right of eminent domain over the Whitney property. The Langendorfs lived on Second Street, the MacMahons on Main, which paralleled Second. Between Second and Main there was an unnamed alley. Instead of going to one of the nearby corners, a MacMahon would go out his back gate, cross the alley, cut through the Whitney property lengthwise, and cross Second to the Langendorfs' front yard. It helped, of course, that the three families were friends and it helped even more that Mrs. Langendorf was Albert Whitney's sister. Actually she was a half sister, but that was close enough.

As a boy Gerald Higgins spent all or part of every summer with the MacMahons, who were his grandparents. He had no contemporaries in the Langendorf family, but he was often sent on errands to the Langendorfs', and in fact the Langendorfs would telephone the MacMahons to ask if Gerald would run an errand for them. Consequently he used the trespass privilege over the Whitney property many times in his boyhood, and he was well along in years, fourteen or so, before realizing that he had never been inside the Whitney house—except the kitchen. Mrs. Whitney and Beulah Bader, the Whitneys' hired woman, had occasionally interrupted him on one of his errands to invite him to have a glass of lemonade or a piece of huckleberry pie; but even on such occasions he had usually stayed on the Whitneys' back porch, where they kept the icebox. At fourteen he had begun to notice more and more of the subtleties of social relations, and to the discovery that he had never been in the front part of the Whitney house he added the observation that he could not recall that his mother, his father, or his grandparents had ever gone calling on the Whitneys.

It was not of itself much of a discovery; in Lyons, Pennsylvania, you could be friends with a family and still not have them to your

The Hat on the Bed (1963)

house or go to theirs. There was that kind of relationship: friendly, but not close. And in some houses they never used the front room, the parlor, except at the time of a death, a wedding, or the annual visit by the pastor. The Whitneys, however, did use their parlor every day, every evening. They most certainly did. Gerald Higgins, passing their house in the early evening, would often see Albert Whitney reading the Fort Penn paper that came in the mail, and smoking a cigar. The cigar was forbidden in those front parlors that were opened only for special occasions. The Whitneys, when they had friends in for a game of cards, would use their front parlor instead of the diningroom. Sometimes on a summer evening Gerald Higgins would be passing the Whitneys' house and he would hear their Vic playing Harry Lauder's record of "She's My Daisy," the same recording that his grandfather enjoyed so. It was hard to understand some of Harry Lauder, who did nothing to smooth out his Scottish burr. Was he singing, "I'd rather lose m' *straps* than lose m' Daisy" or "I'd rather lose m' *stripes* than lose m' Daisy"? Stripes, most likely, meaning chevrons. To Gerald Higgins, growing up with ragtime and jazz, Harry Lauder was a bore, and he replied to a Lauder record with a popular, very risqué parody that began, "I love a lassie/ a bony, bony lassie/ she's as thin as the paper on the wall." He could never finish it in front of his grandparents. It was very risqué, and very popular, and he had a feeling that it would not have shocked Albert Whitney, who smoked cigars in his front parlor and played cards without lowering the parlor shades . . .

Bert Whitney, as the older people called him, had a job as manager of the Valley Lumber Company, which was owned by the Langendorf family. Any business enterprise that went by the name Valley was likely to be owned by the Langendorfs. The Langendorf general store was called Langendorfs' but the lumber company, the brick yard, the water company, and a real-estate firm, all named Valley, were nominally separate from the store, which was almost a hundred years old. If anything happened to one of the Valley enterprises, the Langendorf name would still go on as it always had, symbolized by the store. Old Mr. Fred Langendorf was not sentimental about many things, but he was sentimental about that. He had sold his shares in the Valley Power & Light Company at a profit, and suspended the Valley Wagon Works at a loss, but the general store was not for sale at any price, and everyone knew it.

Everyone knew, too, that Bert Whitney owed his job to two people: to his grandfather, who had come to Lyons and stayed there in the early part of the previous century; and to his half sister, who had married Mr. Langendorf when the old man was a middle-aged widower. Bert Whitney was third-generation Lyons, representative of a family that had escaped mean poverty and never quite got rich. They had always had enough to eat; on the other hand Albert Whitney's father, Lawrence Whitney, had mortgaged his house to get his son through Franklin & Marshall; in eighteen years Lawrence Whitney had failed to stash away enough money to pay for Bert's college expenses. The mortgage was still outstanding four years later when Bert's half sister married the widower Langendorf. As a wedding present to his wife Fred Langendorf retired the mortgage, and Lawrence Whitney, free of debt, soon gave up the struggle that had ceased to be a struggle.

The next in an unending series of presents that Fred Langendorf gave his wife was to place her younger half brother in charge of the lumber yard. It had been Lawrence Whitney's hope that Albert would study law, but Bert had no taste for the law—or for study. Nor was he particularly good at selling; but all the lumber yard needed to survive was an order-taker. The carpenters and builders, the railways and the mines would buy what they needed, and they did so in sufficient quantity to make the lumber yard a profitable business. All that Bert Whitney had to know was what stock he had on hand and keep it from getting too low; his customers usually came to the yard and helped themselves to what they wanted.

Bert ate a good breakfast every morning and was at the office at eight, went home for dinner at half past eleven, returned to the yard an hour later to do business with the independent carpenters who used the noon hour for their small purchases, and at five o'clock he was through for the day. The tennis court, for which as a subscriber he had a key, was on the property adjoining the lumber sheds, and Bert could get in a set or two nearly every spring and summer day. He was one of two men in the town who could chop a ball so that it would go over the net and come back over the net on the rebound. He was also a keen trout fisherman and a better than fair shot. He had a very pleasant life, and his one regret, for which he could not blame himself, was that he had not had a son to whom he could teach the chop stroke, the tying of a trout fly, the timing of the second shot when going after quail. He had one daughter, Amy, to whom he taught the rules of lawn tennis, but she was so lacking in the competitive spirit that she was no fun to play with. When she finished high school she went off to Fort Penn to become a trained nurse, and her father was thereby relieved of the responsibility of her education and of the problem of what to say to her when they were alone together.

Amy Whitney was more like her mother, the former Jobyna Ortlieb, whose father was a blacksmith at the old Valley Wagon Works until his death. Jobyna's education ended with the eighth grade, not because the Ortliebs were poor, but because Jacob Ortlieb would not have a female in his house who knew too much. Jobyna went to work with the thirty-five other girls in the shirt factory and at the end of a year she knew too much about certain things that she had no business knowing about at all. Her father was not aware of the kind of conversation that went on among the factory girls, or of the privileges that the girls' foreman exercised. Jobyna Ortlieb was an apple dumpling of a girl, and after a year of her share of the foreman's attentions she quit her job. Her mother backed her up in her refusal to go back to the factory. "If she comes home some day knocked up it'll be your fault," the mother told the father. This argument carried weight, and Jobyna then got a job as cash girl in Langendorfs' store. By the time Bert Whitney finished college Jobyna was a full-fledged clerk, bringing home forty dollars a month and entitled to the employees' twenty-five percent discount on nearly everything sold at Langendorfs'. She sang in the Lutheran church choir—a mezzo-soprano—and was president of the Busy Bees, her sewing club. She was happy in her job, with its daily contacts with the customers and the promise of a secure lifetime if she did not find a husband.

She could almost forget the ugliness of her year at the shirt factory, but it came back to her when Bert Whitney asked her for a date. She had not had many dates, and although she had known Bert all her life, he was now a college graduate and requests for dates with her did not come from boys who had been to F. & M. or Lebanon Valley, Dickinson, Bucknell or State. A Lyons boy asking her for a date was more likely to be one who had had no more education than she, and if he came to her house with a fifty-cent box of chocolates he seemed to think he had made a down payment on her for life. She wanted something better than that. On the other hand, there was the question: what exactly did Bert Whitney want? She knew from the factory experience what men could want, and she did not want that, either. But if she was ever going to get anyone better than the box-of-chocolate swains, she had to start somewhere with the Bert Whitneys. She therefore agreed to let Bert walk home with her after choir practice, then to come to her house on a Wednesday evening, then to escort her to the band concert in the Grove, and then to kiss her as they sat on the front porch. Something told her that in the world they then entered, she was more knowledgeable than Bert. That, or Bert was behaving with such gentlemanly restraint that this would not be like the ugly ordeals with the factory foreman. In the succeeding months she watched Bert fall in love with her, and somewhere along the way she fell in love with him. The Busy Bees gave her a shower, her mother gave her a cameo brooch, her father gave her—or, just as good, returned to her—five hundred dollars. After the wedding trip the bride and groom took up residence in the Whitney house on Second Street, just across the street from Jobyna's former boss, Mr. Langendorf.

It was a full year before Jobyna realized that she might as well have moved to Pike's Peak. No one came to see her, and she did not feel right about taking up again with the girls of the Busy Bees. She had a feeling that Bert would not like them to return her calls. Not that he ever said anything derogatory about them. But the husbands of the married Busy Bees were not among Bert's friends. They pitched horseshoes; he played tennis. He was a Mason; they belonged to the P. O. S. of A. They slept in their underwear; he wore pajamas. They said ain't; he never said ain't. They spoke Pennsylvania Dutch; he knew only a few words in it. They saw each other; he never saw any of them. Jobyna would have liked the company of the married Busy Bees during her pregnancy, but to seek them out then would have seemed like asking for help, and when her daughter was born she was grateful for the help of Dr. Samuel G. Merritt. She needed all the help the doctor could give her, and he later admitted that he had needed a lot of help from God.

She was never again able to hold on to a baby long enough to have it brought forth whole and alive, and the older Amy got, the more precious she became to her mother. Bert never complained, but from the pleasure he took in showing his friends' sons what to do with their wrists in casting, where to hold their thumbs on a shotgun, how to grip a tennis racquet, it was obvious that he missed having a boy of his own. It was less obvious but apparent to Jobyna that he *tried* to love Amy, and she pitied him for having to make an effort to feel what he did not feel. For Jobyna it was so easy to love Amy, therefore sadder that the girl's father was missing that joy.

Jobyna Whitney could not teach Amy to play tennis, but from her Amy learned to cook, to sew, to market. It went without notice by the girl's father, but at fifteen Amy Whitney six or seven times a year would take over the cooking and other such household duties when Jobyna had to take to her bed with periodic pains. Amy would have to be excused early from the morning session at school to give her time to prepare her father's dinner. She was a good student, she made up whatever she missed, and the only thing she minded was when her duties at home took her out of biology class. She got 100 in every biology exam and her teacher apologized for giving her a mark of 99 for the year. "If I gave you a hundred that would mean you were perfect," he said. "Nobody's perfect. I tell you what I'll do, Amy. I'll give you 99-plus, then the only person that ever gets a higher mark will have to be perfect, so?" In junior and senior years Amy did moderately well in chemistry and not so well in physics, but since the same man taught biology, chemistry, and physics, she always had one subject that she enjoyed more than others. In senior year Prof Hunsberger told her she must study medicine. "You wish me to, I will speak to the father," he said.

"Well, I'd like to be a doctor, but I'm a girl."

"I speak," said Hunsberger. He called on Bert Whitney at the lumber yard. Hunsberger was a fellow alumnus of Franklin & Marshall, of the same time but not a classmate.

"What can I do for you, Hunsie?" said Bert Whitney.

"Whereabouts do you send Amy to college, Bert?"

"I didn't know she wanted to go. College. You mean four years, or Normal?"

"Not Normal, Bert. Don't send her to Normal. She wants to be a doctor, an M.D."

"A doctor, no less. No, Hunsie. If she wants to go to Normal, I can manage that. But pre-med, and then medical school. I'm not a rich man."

"Neither was your father, Bert. And Amy could maybe get a scholarship. Maybe you send her up to State."

"My father had to mortgage his house to—"

"*You* mortgage *your* house," said Hunsberger.

"And you mind your own business, Hunsie. I remember now, she got good marks in biology, but cutting up frogs is a long way from studying medicine. Is this your idea?"

"Cutting up frogs is a long way from studying medicine. But you make it longer than it is. This young girl has ability and wants to learn. Wants to learn, Bert."

"Do tell? It'd cost at least five thousand dollars before she got through, ready to start earning some money."

"I go to Mr. Langendorf, or *Mrs.* Langendorf then."

"You keep your nose out of my family affairs, Hunsie. If you say one damn word to my sister or my brother-in-law, I won't even let her go to Normal."

"This is a sin, Bert. A sin."

"Then the Lord will punish me. I'm very pleased with Amy. She's done well all through High, she's not a bit flighty. But she doesn't want to be a doctor. I know her too well for that. She just said that to please you. She's a very polite girl. We always saw to that."

Hunsberger shook his head. "And yet they call us the thick-headed Pennsylvania Dutch."

"Didn't you ever hear of the stubborn Yankee? That's what we are, a few generations back. I don't mind being called stubborn when I know I'm right. You just don't understand women, Hunsie. They try to please everybody, and you can't do that in this world."

"I'm in this world, too, Bert."

"No, you're always looking through a microscope, too busy to see what's going on around you. You better concentrate on your amoebas. By the way, are you going down to Lancaster next week? You fellows are having your twenty-fifth reunion."

"I was never to a commencement since I graduated."

"But your twenty-fifth reunion. You don't want to miss that."

"My fiftieth, I miss that too, if I am living yet. I was not one of you Chi Phi boys, Bert. Four years I only saw one football game. Saturdays I was clerking in a store. One dollar and fifty cents."

"I didn't have it so easy myself. That's the trouble, Hunsie. You have some idea that I'm a rich man."

"No, not now any more. I think you're a poor man, Bert."

"I'm not sure just how you mean that, Hunsie, but I don't want to get sore at you. So if you're not going to buy any lumber, I'm going to close up for the day."

It was a particularly inopportune moment for Hunsberger's appeal. Apart from an automatic resistance to such a radical notion as sending his daughter to medical school, Bert Whitney had certain notions of his own which would require financial assistance, inevitably by Fred Langendorf. Hunsberger encountered opposition that was confused with alarm, and Bert Whitney was proud of his self-control in his conversation with his old college acquaintance. For a year or more Bert Whitney had been turning over a scheme that if successful could make him independent of Fred Langendorf, although the first money would have to come from Langendorf himself; the bank would not be likely to make a loan for such a scheme. And the sum needed was five thousand dollars—minimum. The project was one for which Bert Whitney felt he was uniquely qualified, with his interest in athletics and games. He even had a name for it: the Olympia (if the movie theater could call itself the Bijou, pronounced By-Joe, an ancient Greek name would catch on in time).

The scheme, which Bert preferred to call a plan, was to get hold of some land back of the lumber yard, clear it, grade it, and construct four or six tennis courts, a trapshooting range, a swimming pool, a refreshment stand, men's and women's toilets, and eventually a pavilion that could be used for meetings and—not to be mentioned at first—mixed dancing. The land was only three blocks from the very center of town, whereas the Grove, where picnics and band concerts were held, was at the far edge of town and offered nothing but a stand of trees and a bandstand. In wintertime Bert would flood his tennis courts to provide skating rinks that would be safer than any of the nearby dams, and, again, closer to the center of town. People would pay small sums to use the various facilities, but the profit would come from the refreshment stand and the sale of sporting equipment, tennis balls, blue rocks, guns, skates. It would be a wholesome, family place where absolutely no alcoholic beverages would be served—certainly not in the beginning—and rowdyism would be strictly forbidden. Bert Whitney could envision a respectable, well-policed amusement park that on some future day would rival Willow Grove of Philadelphia, and Lyons might become famous as the site of Olympia. He would be the George C. Tilyou of Nesquehela County, without having gipsy fortune tellers or questionable side shows. Both railroads would have to do their share when he began to expand, but he would never let the common stock pass from his hands. It was, after all, his original idea. Hunsberger was up against a man's dream.

Fred Langendorf was usually described as being all business, a description that he earned in business dealings but that was not completely fair to his private generosity or his personal amiability. He was physically a rather frail man, ill equipped by Nature for the wrestling and the running and jumping, the camping out in the woods, the swimming in the coal-stained creeks that his boyhood companions enjoyed. Nor was he by temperament a player of games, a hobbyist. He was able to keep a lot of figures in his head, and his whole face would brighten up when he was called upon to perform his trick of adding three columns simultaneously. As an arithmetical gymnast he had no rival in the town; quail shooting and euchre he left to men like his wife's half brother.

"It's easy to see you gave this a lot of thought, Bert," he said.

"Been thinking about it and thinking about it," said Bert Whitney. "As I said a minute ago, it's too bad the bank can't go into it."

"Oh, they could, you know. Up to the value of the land."

"The assessed value," said Bert Whitney.

"Well, maybe a little more than that."

"But nowhere near five thousand dollars."

"No, nowhere near that," said Fred Langendorf. He put a finger in his ear and wormed some wax out of it. "How would you want this money, Bert? Would you want it all at once, or say half this year and half next, after you see how you're progressing? You'd be better off taking half now, you know. Then you'd only owe me twenty-five hundred and say two percent. Twenty-five fifty if it was a total loss."

"I'd have to have the whole amount now, Fred. I couldn't do it on less."

"And your job at the yard."

"Won't suffer, I promise you that," said Bert Whitney.

Fred Langendorf tried the other ear. He produced a wad of wax that stuck to the tip of his little finger. He studied it carefully for a long moment and then flicked it into the wastebasket. He was frowning, but he said, "All right. You have to give a man a fair chance, otherwise where would any business be? I'll make out a cheque and a promissory note. From then on it's up to you, Bert. But don't come to me for any more. Five thousand dollars cash is a very large sum of money. And keep me out of it. They'll guess you got the money from me, and you can't keep them from guessing. But if anybody asks me am I behind you in this scheme, I'm going to tell them no. I'm lending you five thousand dollars at two percent, and what you do with the money is your own business. That's what I'm going to tell them."

"Is it all right if I mention your name at the railroad companies?"

"No, Bert. You can't use my credit in this scheme. In fact, Bert, you be at the bank at ten o'clock tomorrow morning and I'll give you the cheque and you can deposit it right away."

"That sounds as if you didn't trust me."

"If a half a dozen people saw that cheque they might get the wrong impression. You have your money, Bert. Be satisfied with that, now, and don't ask for any extra. By the way, I understand Amy took second in general average. That's fine."

"Yes. What made you think of Amy all of a sudden?"

"Oh, I happened to. Maybe a little more than just happened to, but I don't believe in interfering in family matters. So I guess that's all today, Bert."

Amy Whitney, with the twenty dollars she got from her Uncle Fred and Aunt Lorena Langendorf and letters from Prof Hunsberger and Dr. Samuel G. Merritt, went to Fort Penn and enrolled as a student nurse at the big hospital.

One day in the summer of 1918 Gerald Higgins was taking a basket of grapes to the Langendorfs'. He had picked the grapes from his grandparents' arbor and now he was delivering them to Mr. Langendorf, who was convalescing from some illness. Gerald Higgins was fifteen, getting, he thought, a little old to run errands of that sort, but Mr. Langendorf was a nice man and Gerald's resentment vanished

when he saw the old boy. Mr. Langendorf was sitting in a rock-
ingchair, fully dressed in a white linen suit, his starched collar too
loose around his scrawny neck, his spotted hands fluttering as though
beating time to an inaudible tune.

"You ought to be out in the Glen on a day like this," said Mr.
Langendorf.

"I guess I will go, later," said Gerald Higgins.

"I never learned to swim," said the old man. "That water was so
cold, I couldn't stay in long enough."

"It's pretty cold, all right," said the boy.

"Watch out for snakes, too."

"We do. Billy Reifsnyder killed a copperhead the day before yesterday. That was the second one he killed this summer."

"It's been so dry. We need rain. Did you see Amy?"

"Amy Whitney? No. I didn't know she was home."

"Yes, she's home. On your way back, if you see her tell her I'm
expecting her."

"Yes sir, I will," said the boy.

The old man reached in his pocket. "A little something for you,
Gerald. Just between you and I." He held a silver dollar between
thumb and forefinger; his other fingers were curled up on the palm
of his hand and the hand shook so that as Gerald Higgins reached
for the coin it fell to the floor. "Excuse me. You'll think I don't want
to part with my money."

"Thank you very much, Mr. Langendorf," said the boy. "I'll tell
Amy you want her to come over."

"Come again, Gerald. I always like to see you."

On the way home the boy knocked on the screen door of the
Whitneys' kitchen. A voice from inside said, "Just put it on the porch
. . . Oh, it's Gerald. I thought it was the groceries." Beulah Bader,
her arms covered with flour, came to the door.

"Is Amy in?" said the boy.

"Amy! You got a visitor!" Beulah had a loud voice.

The boy could hear someone running down the back stairs, then
Amy appeared. "Oh, hello," she said. "You wanted to see me about
something?"

"Mr. Langendorf said to tell you he was expecting you."

"It's Gerald! Little Gerald. Why I never would have recognized
you in your long pants. When did you get them?"

"I had them for over a year, pretty nearly. Mr. Langendorf said—"

"I know, I'm getting ready. Come in and sit down, have a glass of
lemonade. Or would you rather have some grape juice?"

"I have to go, but thanks."

"Haven't you got time for one glass of lemonade?"

"Well, all right I guess so."

"Come on in out of the heat. Beulah, will you bring us a pitcher of lemonade in the front room?"

"I got my hands all sticky with dough," said Beulah Bader.

"Beulah's baking, but you go on in the front room, Gerald, and I'll be in in two shakes of a ram's tail," said Amy Whitney.

The Whitneys' front room was unlike any the boy had seen in Lyons. The chairs and sofa were covered for the summer, but the room gave the immediate impression of being in active use. There was mail on the secretary and spots of ink on the blotter. There were photographs of baseball and football teams on the walls; group photographs, and action photographs; not the sort of pictures that hung in Lyons front parlors, although there were the customary severe-looking men and women in oval frames as well. There was a large lithograph of the Franklin & Marshall campus. The boy counted four silver loving-cups of various sizes, and an elaborately designed beer stein stood alone on the top shelf of the secretary. A massive walnut cigar humidor rested on a mother-of-pearl inlaid taboret. The rugs had been taken up and the room was comfortably cool. The room was more like the boy's father's den than like any front parlor in Lyons.

"I brought a little sugar in case this is too tart," said Amy Whitney, setting down the tray. "Sit wherever you'll be comfortable."

"Thank you."

"I'm glad I saw you before I leave. Don't you wish you were going along? I'll bet you do."

"Where to? I didn't know you were going anywhere."

"You didn't? I was sure the whole town knew. I'm going overseas. I joined the army. I'm a nurse. A lieutenant. Don't you read the paper? It was in last week."

"I just got here Saturday," said the boy.

"Yes, my father just got out of the army and now I'm going in. So we can still hang the service flag in the window. I'm the only woman from Lyons in the army."

"I didn't know Mr. Whitney was in the army."

"Don't you ever hear *anything* in Gibbsville? My father was a first lieutenant. You should have seen him in his uniform. He had boots and spurs, and a swagger stick. He went in last September and he just got out in June. He was so disappointed, poor Father. Just about to go overseas, and they discovered he had kidney trouble. Didn't you know any of this?"

"I wasn't here in September. I had to go back to school," said the boy.

"Well, I don't think it'll last long enough for you to get in, but it might. I'll send you a German helmet when I get over there. That's because when you were a little boy, maybe you don't remember this, Gerald, but when you were a little fellow you and I used to play catch. Do you remember that? In the alley?"

"Sure, I remember."

"You must be what, now? Fifteen?"

"Yes."

"I thought so. You were about seven, then, and I was seventeen. That's just about when it was, the year before I went in training."

"For what?"

"To be a nurse. Didn't you know I was a trained nurse? I haven't seen much of you these last six or seven years. I guess I wasn't home much when you were here. Do you like the girls, Gerald?"

"Oh—well, some I do, and some I don't."

"Have you got a sweetheart in Lyons?"

"No!"

"Lyons girls too countrified for you?"

"They sure are. Dumb hicks."

"Well, don't be too sure about that."

"Oh, some of them are all right, I guess. One or two."

"Who, for instance?"

"Oh, I don't know."

"Ask me no questions, I'll tell you no lies, huh?"

"Uh-huh," said the boy. He had become conscious of her femininity during the latter part of the conversation, an awareness of resources of experience that he had not expected her to have. In the great division between girls who did and girls who did not, he now placed Amy Whitney among the girls who did.

"What are you thinking?" she said.

"Nothing. I wasn't thinking about anything."

"Oh, yes you were, but I'm not going to pursue the subject," she said. "You have eyes that give you away, Gerald. Did any girl ever tell you that?"

"No."

"Well, you have."

"So have you."

"Why Gerald Higgins. I have? Can you read my thoughts?"

"You were trying to read mine."

"And I did," she said. "Well, Mr. Mind-Reader, unless you want some more lemonade I guess I ought to go over and see my uncle."

"I had enough, thanks."

"If I send you a German helmet will you write to me?"

"Sure, if you want me to."

At this moment Bert Whitney appeared in the doorway. "Ah, I see you have a caller. Hello, Gerald."

"Hello, Mr. Whitney."

"How's everybody up at the MacMahons'? Is your mother here?"

"No sir, she's coming later. August."

"It is August," said Bert Whitney.

"Oh, that's right. Well, later in August," said the boy.

"How is your father? Keeping well?"

"Yes sir, as far as I know."

"Didn't I hear he was in the army?"

"The Navy. He's a senior lieutenant, the same as a captain in the army."

"And where is he now?"

"In Chicago. Great Lakes Training Station."

"Have a glass of lemonade, Father?"

"No thanks. If it lasts much longer they may get you into it. I suppose you wouldn't mind that."

"No, I wouldn't mind. I wish I was."

"Don't be in any hurry. It isn't all bands playing and pretty girls throwing kisses at you. Your mother asleep, Amy?"

"Yes, I gave her a pill a little while ago."

"Think I'll take a little tonic myself," said Bert Whitney. He opened a door in the taboret and got out a bottle of whiskey and a tumbler. He filled half of the tumbler and drank the whiskey in two gulps while his daughter and the boy sat silent. "Tonic," said Bert Whitney, to no one. "Amy, you have a lot of things to do this afternoon, so I guess you better start doing them."

"Yes. I was just getting ready to go over to Uncle Fred's."

"Oh, you're going over there? What do you want to go over there for?"

"I'll tell you later," said Amy Whitney.

"You mean not in front of Gerald? Good Lord, he's a MacMahon, and they all know I have no use for Fred Langendorf. They know why, too. Don't you, Gerald?"

"No sir. I guess I better be going."

"All right, Gerald. And I'll send you the helmet the first one I see. Goodbye."

"Goodbye, Amy. Goodbye, Mr. Whitney."

* * *

"The last time I saw you," said Amy Whitney. "Do you remember when that was?"

"Yes I do," said Gerald Higgins. "It was at your house in Lyons, the day before you were going away to be a nurse in the army."

"August 1918. And what are you doing now?"

"Right now I'm at Princeton, getting my M.A. And what are you doing, Amy? Are you still a nurse?"

"No. I'm in New Jersey, too. East Orange. Married to a doctor I met in the army. I have two children. Are you married?"

"No."

"I didn't think you would be. Either that, or you'd be married at nineteen. You were a rooty kind of a kid. I can remember thinking that even then. I wouldn't have been one bit surprised if you'd made a pass at me. I fully expected you to. Maybe I was a little bit disappointed that you didn't."

"Well, I'll make up for it now."

"No, you don't have to be gallant with me, Gerald. I'm fat and unattractive, but at least I know it."

They had a moment of silent, candid looking-into-each-other's-faces, the boldness relieved by a smile for nostalgia. Their chance encounter took place in a Childs restaurant on Fifth Avenue. "A long way from little old Lyons, P A," she said. "Wonder how many people here ever heard of Lyons."

"Not many, I guess," he said. "But we wouldn't know the places they came from either."

"I guess not. Do you ever get back there?"

"Oh, once in a while, to visit my grandmother. And I've been having correspondence with Robert Millhouser. Remember him?"

"Sure. The big scandal when he killed his wife. That's what he gets for marrying a girl not even half his age. But I guess he's paying for it, the poor old thing."

"That you can be sure of," said Gerald Higgins.

"I never go back. There's nothing to bring me back any more. I'm the last of the Whitneys, and I never had much to do with my Ortlieb cousins. They looked down on us."

"Looked *down* on you?"

"*You* know. The reverse of what it should have been. The Ortliebs worked with their hands, the Whitneys were all desk workers."

"Where is your father now? I know your mother died, but I lost touch with your father. Did he stay around Lyons?"

"Long enough to die, that's all," said Amy Whitney Robbins. "He would have lasted a few years longer if he hadn't hit the booze, but he never gave much consideration to anyone else and he ended up not caring what happened to himself. A man that never gave a thought to anyone else. The one thing I wanted to be in life, a doctor, he kept me from being. And why? Because it interfered with his plans. Do you remember Olympia Park?"

Gerald Higgins laughed. "Olympia Park, sure. Two tennis courts and an ice cream stand. Olympia Park. The courts are all overgrown with weeds, but the uprights are still there, to hold the nets."

"A memento of my M.D. My biology teacher in high school tried to persuade my Uncle Fred Langendorf to pay for my education. Pre-med and medical school. But my father wanted the money to build Olympia Park. So I became a trained nurse instead of a doctor. But at least I met my husband through that, so I guess I shouldn't complain. But I do complain, whenever I stop to think of it. That father of mine with his grandiose ideas, he never did anything he could be put in jail for, but he took five thousand dollars from Uncle Fred and bought that land and built those tennis courts, but there weren't enough people in Lyons that cared about tennis, so he took what was left and put up that dance pavilion. Four miles away was Midway."

"I remember Midway very well."

"My father thought Lyons people would rather walk to his place than ride to Midway. He never stopped to think that the young people wanted to get away from Lyons, even if it was only four miles away. Midway got the Lyons people and the Johnsville people, and Olympia got nobody."

"That was the summer I didn't go to Lyons. My family went to Ventnor that summer, near Atlantic City."

"He had two dances at his park. The first one, people came out of curiosity. The second, nobody came. He lost money on both dances, and finally gave up. Flat broke. Five thousand dollars down the drain, and I was emptying bedpans at the hospital. I could have filled those bedpans with my own tears, whenever I thought of that money. I never would have gone home again if it hadn't been for my mother. You knew Uncle Fred Langendorf."

"Sure. I liked him."

"People misjudged Uncle Fred," said Amy. "They used to go on about how he was money-mad, but I could tell you a few things. He tried to help my father get on his own feet, lent him that five thousand dollars knowing he didn't have much chance of getting it back. Believe me, no one else in Lyons would have lent Bert Whitney that kind of money, but Uncle Fred did. And a lot of men would have been good and sore at my father for losing it all, but Uncle Fred let him keep his job at the lumber yard." She paused, marshalling thoughts that she probably had never tried to organize before. "I wrote Uncle Fred a letter from the hospital and told him I had this chance to be an army nurse but I needed his advice in the matter. He supported my mother while my father was in the army, and he gave Father his job back when he got out, although my father was saying awful things about him. So he wrote back and said he thought I ought to do whatever my conscience told me to do, and I knew by that that he was telling me to go ahead and join the army. He never believed in interfering in other people's lives, but he as good as told me that I owed it to myself, it was a wonderful opportunity to see something of the world and at the same time do something for my country. He didn't come out and say these things, but it was what he meant. Well, he was right. I met my husband overseas, and we got married after the war was over."

"And now you live in East Orange," said Gerald Higgins.

"Not very far from Princeton. You ought to come and visit us sometime. Remember how you used to walk through our yard?"

"It was a good short cut, till your father stopped us."

"My father stopped you? Stopped who?"

"Everybody, I guess. Me. My grandmother. My aunts. He wrote my grandfather a letter. I never saw the letter, but Grandpa said we all had to stop going through the Whitneys' yard."

"I never knew that, Gerald. This is the first I ever heard of that."

"I think he put a padlock on the back gate, the alley gate. Yes, I'm positive of that."

"I wonder why he'd do a thing like that," said Amy. "My mother could have got away by the front gate."

The young man was silent.

"You knew my mother was a little out of her head, didn't you? Didn't the MacMahons ever tell you that?"

"No."

"Oh, that's why you looked surprised. Yes, my mother began acting strangely, oh, back when I was in High. She'd stay in bed for days at a time and later on she'd hardly ever come downstairs. I had to get out of that house or I would have gone a little coocoo myself. My father wouldn't send me to medical school or any place else, so I went into nurse's training. I guess if the truth be told, I was a little afraid of my mother. It wasn't natural for a person to sit in her room, rocking away. She was always good to me, mind you. She never slapped me the way mothers did their children. But she began acting rather peculiar when I was around sixteen or seventeen. I remember one day she said I ought to quit my job. But I didn't have a job. I was going to school. I asked her what she meant by that, and she didn't even remember saying it. But she said it again one time, and she said certain things that I don't want to repeat, poor thing, but if anybody would have heard them—well, she had some idea there was something going on between Prof Hunsberger and I. Poor old Hunsberger, my goodness. Did you ever remember Professor Hunsberger at Lyons High? He was science teacher, and taught me more than any other teacher I ever had."

"Did he keep you after school, Amy?"

"Oh, come on. What kind of a thing is that to kid about? He was the last person you'd ever think that of. You're almost as bad as my mother."

"I was only kidding," said Gerald Higgins.

"Well it could have had serious consequences, if it ever got out what my mother was thinking."

"Yes, especially then."

"She told me I ought to go to work for Uncle Fred, only she called him Mr. Langendorf, and I took her seriously. I asked my father if we were that hard up, and he said to pay no attention to my mother. She was living in the past, he said. Well that was putting it mildly. As far as I was concerned, she was living in the past and he was living in the future, with his big scheme to build an amusement park. With money that I should have had for my education. You never had to worry about that, going to Princeton, and the MacMahons were very well-to-do. I guess your own family, too. I'm going to see to it that my children never have to worry about that. By the time my daughter is eighteen we'll have enough saved up for her to go to Vassar or some place like that, and the boy, it depends on whether he wants to be a doctor or what. My husband got his M.D. at Northwestern, but we thought of sending the boy to P. and S. So far he hasn't shown much interest, but he's only nine. He looks so much like my father you'd almost take him for a son instead of a grandson, and he has that same athletic ability. Albert Whitney Robbins. He's never been to Lyons. Vacations we go to Toms River, so it may be years before Whitney ever sees my old home town, if he ever does."

"You call him Whitney?"

"Yes, because I never liked the nickname Bert or Al," said Amy. "Look at that poor woman over there, near the window. She's had what they call Szymanowski's Operation. Didn't do her much good, though, did it?"

"I don't know. I didn't see her before they operated," said Gerald Higgins.

"You're such a smart aleck," she said. "But I'll bet you never heard of Szymanowski's Operations. I should have been a doctor. I'll always regret it that I wasn't. But that father of mine, believe me. One thing they can never accuse me of and that's selfishness. There I'm more like my mother. That is, up to a certain point. I'd never let conditions affect me till the only thing left to do was go up in the attic and hang myself. Were you in Lyons when they found her?"

"Yes," said Gerald Higgins.

"Somebody could have stopped her. If not my father, Beulah Bader should have. But there was another selfish one, that Beulah Bader. She never went out of her way to be helpful. When one of us'd call her she'd pretend not to hear us. Just go right on doing whatever she was doing."

"Yes, I know what you mean," said the young man.

"Uncle Fred was paying here twenty—dollars—a week. Can you imagine?"

The Mayor

Yock Schindle usually opened up around nine-thirty, to be
ready for the first customers of the day. The first hour's customers were always the same men, each one had the same
thing every morning, each stayed about the same length of
time every morning. Most of the men would have a Coca-Cola with a
squirt of lemon or lime, a few would have a glass of milk flavored
with chocolate syrup, there were three or four who would take nothing to drink but would buy a cigar or two. At about ten-fifteen every
morning Yock's place would contain as many as fifteen customers, all
in the front room. Yock had no actual rule against their playing pool
at that time of day, but the back room, with its four pool tables,
would be empty of customers, the overhead lights were dark, the
tables covered with black oilcloth. Once in a great while a man
would say to a friend, "We have time for twenty-five points," and
they would play, but it was not customary, and it was not encouraged
by Yock, who was kept busy behind the tiny soda fountain (no ice
cream, no sundaes). The cigar smokers would help themselves out of
the case on the opposite side of the front room, and would put the
money for their purchases on the soda fountain. Six days a week
Yock's ten o'clock trade did not vary as much as fifty cents from day
to day, and nearly every man who belonged to the ten o'clock trade
would also drop in again later in the day, in the middle of the afternoon or after work.

Yock got the most enjoyment out of the ten o'clock trade because
it was as good as reading a newspaper. Better, really, because he
heard things that the newspapers could not print. The mayor was a
ten o'clock customer, and he usually had just come from sitting as a
magistrate in police court. Two doctors and three lawyers were
among the ten-o'clockers, as were a reporter from each of the two
newspapers, a couple of insurance men, a jeweler, the proprietor of
a ladies' specialty shop, a private detective, and a couple of profes-

The Hat on the Bed (1963)

sional politicians who were perennial office-holders. The men who owned the town seldom or never patronized Yock's place, but there was no other group who knew more than Yock's crowd about what was going on. Up to a point they trusted each other, and the morning conversations at Yock's were considered confidential at least to the extent that if you repeated something you heard at Yock's you were discreet about attributing the source of your information. The politicians were the only ones who used Yock's as a place to start rumors, and they were the only ones whom the others did not always believe.

The mayor was not a professional politician—dependent, that is, on public office or graft for his living. He was mayor because he wanted to be mayor and considered the office good publicity for his business, which was an already prosperous, second-generation shoe store. He was a Shriner and an Elk, a Lutheran, a former president of the Merchants' Association, a founding member of Rotary, a one-time captain of the Gibbsville High basketball team and currently a captain of one of the senior league teams at the Y.M.C.A. There were also *non*-memberships in certain organizations and institutions that were in his favor: he did *not* belong to the country club or the Gibbsville Club, the Catholic Church or the Ku Klux Klan. He lived on Market Street, in a house that was three stories high and had a marble stoop in front and a well-kept yard that went back to the next street, but it was on Market Street, and as long as a man continued to live on Market he remained a man of the people. The people, who voted for him in large numbers, were quite proud of the fact that he could buy and sell some of the upper-class aristocrats of Lantenengo Street. His money did not count against him. Saturday night you could still go to Lester Flickinger's store and be waited on by the mayor of the town. If you were buying a pair of shoes for your kid and Lester did not happen to be waiting on you, it was still Lester who came and handed you a scout knife (unofficial) or a school companion for your kid, depending on whether it was a boy or a girl.

Les Flickinger was such a natural for the office of mayor that the talk around town was that he got the nomination for five thousand dollars, then told the professional politicians that he saw no reason why he should spend any more of his own money to get elected. This did not sit too well with the politicians, but he had the Republican nomination ("Tantamount," the newspapers always said, "to election") and they could blame only themselves for not having put a bigger bite on Les in the beginning. As a consequence of their short-sightedness they were compelled to get money elsewhere, and to do so they had to make commitments that resulted in one of the most graft-ridden administrations in the town's history. The town council approved contracts for the paving of roads in outlying areas that were not yet cleared for the construction of houses; and the street railway company was once again threatened with a municipally owned bus system. But no one could say that Les Flickinger took a dirty dollar. He put through an appropriation for a car for the police chief, which he may have used more frequently than the chief. He took trips to Philadelphia and the state capital and other cities in the Commonwealth, extolling the virtues of his town and thereby justifying the expense accounts he submitted for these trips. No one seemed to care, or to notice, that those trips also coincided with lodge conventions and sporting events. He was the town's biggest booster, and whatever the cynical may have thought and said about those paving contracts for undeveloped areas, they doubted that Les Flickinger was getting anything out of it.

When Les turned up at Yock Schindle's for morning prayers, as someone called the ten o'clock gatherings, he often had some amusing or scandalous or pathetic story direct from police court. His magisterial powers were limited, and most of the prisoners brought before him were d. and d.'s—drunk and disorderly. The usual sentence was ten dollars or ten days. Not more than half the culprits had ten dollars cash on them, and Mayor Flickinger would suspend sentence and let the man off with a warning. Habitual offenders could be sentenced to thirty days in the county jail, and with the coming of cold weather there were some regulars who would request a sixty- or even a ninety-day sentence to the stony lonesome. The mayor never denied such requests: any man who would willingly prefer the county jail to freedom was on his last legs, and if he froze to death or got run over by a switching engine, the cost of burying him had to be borne by the municipal government. If he died in jail, the county had to take care of it. For the mayor it was a strange experience to be thanked for sending a man to prison, and especially to a prison that offered almost nothing but shelter from the elements. At Thanksgiving and Christmas the newspapers reported that the "guests of the county" would be served a turkey dinner, but the oldest con had never seen a scrap of white meat, for the reason that the prison cook carved the breast and sold it to the local restaurants. "When I think of those poor souls up there," said Les Flickinger one day.

"Makes you want to stay honest, eh, Les?" said Arnold Goble, one of the professional politicians.

"Sure makes you want to stay honest, all right," said Les. "But then on the other hand you have the ones that are the scum of the earth. I mean that. The scum of the earth. You wouldn't believe it possible in this day and age, how low some men can get. And women. They brought in Jenny Faust again last night. She kept everybody awake all night, yelling and screaming."

"What did Jenny do this time?" someone asked.

"Well, I guess Jenny always does the same thing, if you get the drift. But this time she set up business down in the lower yards, down near the Pennsy freight station. I mean the Reading freight station. I ought to know the difference between those two. Anyway, there she was and half a dozen men waiting in line when they arrested her. A woman like that, there ought to be some way to put her away for good."

"Well, I see the A's won," said Charley Dewey, another politician. "Al Simmons got a hold of one with the bases loaded. It must of been some poke, over four hundred foot. It's 468 foot from home plate to the center-field fence. If that fellow was with a better team you'd never hear of Ruth."

"Ah, nuts. They're both hitting the same pitching, practically," said someone. "You guys that root for the A's, what did Mack ever do for you? Connie Mack is in it for the money, and as long as you got him running the A's—"

"Aah, shut up. Connie Mack knows more baseball in his little finger than your Hugginses and the rest of them ever *will* know," said someone else.

"I agree with you on that," said Charley Dewey. He had a hard, loud voice, and when he wanted to take over a conversation he could do so. It was not until a little while later that he revealed to Les Flickinger that that had been his purpose.

He followed Les out into the street. "You know why I interrupted you in there?"

"Oh, you did it on purpose?" said Les Flickinger.

"Sure I did," said Charley. "What's the use of you making an enemy when you don't have to? Don't you know about Jenny Faust and Yock?"

"Jenny Faust and *Yock?* Yock Schindle? I never heard him so much as mention her name."

"You never will, either. You know, Les, there's a lot of things in this town you don't know. Being from well-to-do parents and a graduate of Lebanon Valley and all that, there's some things you're not familiar with, and you oughta ask me. Not that you could of asked me in this particular case, but hereafter, be a little more careful."

"Never mind about that, Charley. Don't start issuing orders to me, you know. But what about Yock and Jenny Faust?"

"What I ought to do is leave you flat, right here in the middle of the sidewalk, and let you go on making mistakes, but I got the party to consider. So this time I'll tell you for your own good, *and* the good of the party organization. I'm not just some guy that a year from now's getting out of politics."

"Maybe I'm not either, but what is it you want to tell me?"

"I want to tell you this, Les. You don't make enemies out of a fellow like Yock Schindle, and if I didn't interrupt you back there, that's what you were doing. Yock Schindle, Jacob W. Schindle, is responsible for Jenny Faust being a fifty-cent hooker. Now how do you like *them* for apples?"

"Well, how do I like them? I think you're crazy with the heat. I remember Yock's father and mother, lived over on South Canal Street. I waited on them in the store many a time, and Martin Schindle was a brakeman on the Reading. Martin L. Schindle. His wife came from near Swedish Haven, on a farm. There was I think one other brother and two sisters in addition to Yock. I waited on all of them. They had good credit and they were a very strict family. The father didn't say much, but you could tell."

"Uh-huh. Now tell me all you know about Jenny Faust."

"Jenny Faust? Well, I don't know which Faust she was. I don't remember her coming in the store when I was a young fellow, and I wouldn't *let* her in now. There was one Faust family up on North Second, and another 'way out Market. Then there were Fausts lived out there near the packing-houses."

"Well, you missed one family. Jenny's family. They lived down at the end of South Canal. There was the mother and two daughters. The old man was dead, and the mother took in washing. The two daughters used to carry the baskets with the wash, Jenny and her sister Lizzie. They used to go call for the wash and then lug it back when it was done. That was all they had to live on till the girls got big enough to get work. Lizzie got a job in the silk mill, and Jenny got a lot of jobs. I remember she had a paper route, and then she got work in the hospital for a while, and I guess when she was around fifteen or sixteen years of age she got a job in the silk mill with Lizzie."

"Where does Yock come in?"

"Then. Right about then. Yock was a call-boy for the Reading, through his old man being a brakeman. Yock was waiting to be notified that he could take the examination for brakeman, but they passed him over for bad eyesight and he got transferred to the weighmaster's office. He could never be a railroader, with bad eyesight, not on a train crew anyhow. But they fixed him up with a job in the weighmaster's office just about the time his old man took the examination for fireman."

"How do you know all this?"

"I lived on South Canal then. I'm only about four or five years younger than Yock. He just looks older. Them thick glasses he wears."

"And then what?" said Les Flickinger.

"Well, Yock took a liking to Jenny, only his parents put a stop to it. No son of theirs was getting mixed up with anybody as poor as that. They were poor, all right. The girls used to when they were kids walk the tracks to pick coal. We all did, but not our sisters. Only the boys did, except the Faust girls. They had to have a lot of hot water for the old lady to do her washing."

"Uh-huh, uh-huh."

"So one day Mrs. Faust knocked on their door and Yock's mother wasn't going to let her in, but she pushed right past her and back to the kitchen to the old man having his supper. Either Yock was going to marry Jenny right away, or she was going to the squire's office and swear out a warrant. Old Man Schindle got up and threw her out by the kitchen door, and then he went to work and beat Yock insensible. He didn't ask nobody no questions. Yes, no, or amen. He just threw her out, and then went to work beating up his son."

"How old was Yock?"

"Eighteen. Maybe nineteen by then."

"And what happened to Jenny? Did she have the baby?"

"Some say she did and some say she didn't. Some say she had it and got rid of it, and others said it was stillborn."

"You mean she may have had a live baby and killed it?"

"Who knows? Jenny knows, but her old lady kicked her out, just like Old Man Schindle done to the old lady."

"But that's, uh, homicide. It comes under the head of homicide. Manslaughter, maybe."

"Yeah, but who was going to take the trouble to find out? Jenny's old lady? And not Yock's parents."

"Where did she have the baby?"

"You ask these questions that all these things happened thirty years ago, and nobody knew the answer then. Now I doubt if Jenny herself could give you the answer. It was damn near thirty years ago. All she had to do was wrap it in a burlap bag and weight it with some ballast off the tracks, and drop it in the canal. One kid more or less on South Canal Street—especially down there at the lower end."

"Even so, human life—"

Charley's voice was harder than ever. "Come on, Les. Come on," he said.

"Don't talk to me in that tone of voice," said Les.

"Yeah? Well, I'll bet old Yock was glad to hear my tone of voice this morning."

"Yock Schindle," said Les. "And Jenny Faust. Yock Schindle and Jenny Faust. She's being held in the county jail for the next term of court. I could have made it harder for her, but I guess I'm just as glad I didn't."

"Yeah. Uh-huh."

At the Window

The first thing to go was the gilded-horse weathervane on top of the barn. From an upstairs window Moore had been watching it as it spun crazily, clockwise and counter-clockwise, resisting the wind and going with it. The ornament was a rather ugly thing, resembling—unintentionally, Moore was sure—one of those quarter horses that are raced in the Southwest, with a body that was too long and legs that were too short. Nevertheless Moore was sorry to see it go. In the last fifteen minutes he had come to forgive it its ugliness and admire its spirit, as though it were a real animal and putting up a struggle against the gale. Then the rod snapped, and the whole weathervane was carried away.

"There goes our horse," said Moore.

"What horse?" said Helen Moore.

"The weathervane," he said.

"Is *that* what you've been watching?" she said. "I thought you were sitting here brooding about the trees."

"I am. But I got fascinated by the weathervane," he said. "I wonder how old it was."

"It was here when we came," she said.

"I know it was. And that'll give you an idea of how it's blowing out there."

"I don't need that to tell me," she said. "All I have to do is listen."

"All the storms we've had since we moved here, but this is the one that finally blew away the weathervane. I hope we'll be able to find it."

"*I* hope we'll still *be* here," she said. "There's no electricity. The stuff in the refrigerator's going bad, and everything in the deep freeze. The water pump. I've been filling pots and pans with water, while you've been up here watching a weathervane. I just hope the wind doesn't come along and blow away our bottled gas."

New Yorker (22 February 1964); *The Horse Knows the Way*

"The wind isn't coming from that direction," he said. "I'm afraid we can expect to lose some trees, though."

"Yes, and the radio said to expect possibly four inches of snow."

"Are you worried?"

"Well, not yet," she said. "I mean, we have plenty of food in the house, and we can cook it. And there's lots of firewood down in the cellar."

"If it snows we'll have plenty of drinking water."

"Don't worry, it's going to snow. The phone is on the blink, and our only communication with the outside world is the radio."

"One-way communication, at that," said Moore. "There! The first snowflakes. God, they're big. Look, you can hardly see the Williamses'."

"I notice they've lit a fire."

"Oh, an hour ago," said Moore. "They must have lit theirs as soon as the electricity went off."

"Well, they have to have a warm room for old Mr. Williams. Now you can hardly see their house. I don't think I've ever seen so much snow come all at once."

"Every year I talk about getting a Delco and one of those little tractors."

"What's a Delco?"

"An electric power plant."

"Oh, that's a Delco?"

"There are different makes. The first one I ever knew of was a Delco and I call them all that. Isaac Hostetter. He was a farmer in our valley when I was a boy. He was the first one to have a tractor, too. The other farmers thought he was out of his mind. He was, a little, I guess. He went into deep debt to buy all sorts of modern equipment. The most modern thing most of them had was a De Laval. A cream separator, operated by hand. We had one. I used to crank it, sort of like winding the dasher when my mother made ice cream. Didn't I ever tell you about old Isaac Hostetter?"

"Maybe you did, I don't know. I guess there won't be any mail today."

"Oh, I doubt it now," said Moore. "I doubt if they'd start out in this weather. Last year we didn't get any mail for two days, remember?"

"Twice. Once for two days and another for three. No, I guess that was the year before when we didn't have mail for three days."

"Well, there's no use of their starting out and then getting stuck somewhere. How would you like to have Mr. Andrews as our house guest for two or three days?"

"The postman Mr. Andrews? Not very much," she said. "Why?"

"Well, if he got stuck in the road anywhere near our house, what else could we do but invite him to stay?"

"Oh, in that case of course we'd have to have him. We couldn't turn him away," she said.

"Actually, of course, he's not a bad fellow. Just a bit of a bore to talk to. And he's a talker."

"Now you can just about make out our barn."

"Imagine if we had cows?" said Moore.

"And you had to feed them?"

"Not only feed them. *Milk* them. If you were a real farmer's wife you'd have to do the milking twice a day."

"No thank you," she said.

"That's the way it used to be, when I was a boy."

"Your mother didn't have to milk cows."

"No, but the farmer's wife did. Mrs. Stroub. Pretty soon we won't be able to see our fence," he said.

"I hope it'll be there to see when this is over," she said.

"Isn't it strange what the wind does? It'll blow down a tree that's stood fifty years, a deeply rooted tree. But a tin mailbox stays right there. And a big thing that you'd think would make a good target, the tool shed, it hardly seems to shake. But my little weathervane with the horse on it, away it goes."

"Oh, I guess it's a lot like life. When your time comes, you go too."

"Uh-huh," he muttered. "I never get tired watching the snow-flakes. Do you ever try to pick out one snowflake and watch it all the way to the ground?"

"Yes, I have," she said.

"Really? We've been married thirty-three years and that's something we never knew about each other."

"You can't expect to know everything about a person, no matter how long you live with them. I wouldn't want to know everything about a person. And anyway, how could I? Every day you live you add something new to yourself."

"And lose something, too, I suppose," he said. "Think of the things we forget about ourselves. Mentioning old Isaac Hostetter, I remember something that happened fifty years ago, at least, and I haven't thought about it in all that time, till just now."

"I don't think you ever mentioned him to me before," she said.

"Oh, I must have mentioned him, years ago, but not lately."

"It's an unusual name. I'd have remembered it," she said.

"Yes, but there were a lot of unusual names, unusual to you when we were first married. Hostetter. Hochgertel. Fenstermacher. Womelsdorf. Wynkoop. Zinsendorf. Just thinking of names in our valley."

"How did a Moore get in there?"

"I must have told you that story," he said. "A farmer by the name of Billy Poffenberger. He ran up a big bill at my grandfather's store and for two years he didn't pay anything on account. He finally told my grandfather that he could have the farm for a receipted bill and a thousand dollars cash. It was a good farm, only Poffenberger'd let it go to hell, so my grandfather made the deal. He left it to my father in his will."

"I knew your father inherited it," said Helen Moore.

"To show you what neglect will do, it took my grandfather most of five years to get the property back in shape. I guess he must have spent quite a little money on it, but it was worth it. When my father died my mother sold the farm for forty thousand dollars, that's with everything on it. The livestock, the implements, and so forth. She had the house all fixed up nicely. Our house, that is. Jake Stroub, our farmer, he'd never spend any of his own money on their house. They had another house on the other side of the barn, he and his family. They kept it clean, but they didn't even have a picture on the wall. All the walls were bare. They used to have a calendar in the kitchen, and that was all. A farmer has a hard time getting along without a calendar. I don't remember their ever having a clock, but they always had a calendar. The Swedish Haven Bank gave out calendars every year, and every farm in the valley had one. The one thing you'd see in every kitchen. We had one in our kitchen, too, but that was natural because my father was a director of the Swedish Haven Bank. A funny thing was, we were never there much in the wintertime. We didn't usually open up our house till around Easter. My mother said it was too gloomy during the real dead of winter, and of course we kids had to be in school in town. But as soon as we opened up the house around the first of April, one of the first things my father always did was to hang the bank calendar in the kitchen. I can remember him tearing off January, February, and March, and every year he always said the same thing. 'Well, that winter passed quickly,' he'd say."

"Yes, he had a good sense of humor," said Helen Moore.

"I guess he had to have, to put up with me," said Moore.

"And I guess your mother wasn't too easy to get along with," said Helen Moore.

"No, I guess she was pretty neurotic. That's what they'd say about her today. Neurotic. I suppose they would have called me a juvenile delinquent."

"Well, that's what you were, weren't you?" said Helen Moore.

"Oh, I don't deny it," he said.

"No, don't deny it to me," she said.

"I never have, have I? You can't say I ever pretended to be any better than I was, Helen. That's one thing I never did."

"No, I guess if you'd have tried to be a hypocrite I never would have married you," she said.

"I never had any use for a hypocrite," he said. "I had one or two friends of mine, and I don't have to tell you who they were. But they were getting away with murder, only because they never got caught. But no matter what I did, I always got caught at it sooner or later. You take now for instance, Johnny Grattan. The night I had my accident, Johnny'd been driving the car and he almost went off the road a couple of times, so I made him change places with me. The result? When the truck hit us, he was sound asleep, dead drunk, in the back seat, and *I* was the one that was pinned behind the steering. But it could have been Johnny that lost his arm instead of me."

"I don't see how that makes him a hypocrite," said Helen Moore.

"Well, it doesn't make him a hypocrite exactly. But in a way it does. I mean, he pretended he was sober enough to drive, but he wasn't. That's the way he was, you know. He was always putting up a big bluff. Always bluffing. Oh, sure. He could drive the car. A whole bunch of people on the porch of the Sigma Nu house, and I started to get in behind the steering, but no. Johnny had to show everybody how he could drink twice as much as everybody else and still drive. He lasted to the other side of Allentown, and then I had to take the wheel."

"Well, which is worse? For forty years he's blamed himself for what happened to you," she said.

"Now that's what I call being a hypocrite. He blames himself, but he has both arms. And I wonder how much sleep he lost over me."

"He never took another drink," said Helen Moore.

"So he says," said Moore.

"Well, you *know* he didn't, Frank."

"Sure. Sure. Good for him," said Moore. "Let's move back to Swedish Haven so we can see more of John L. Grattan, the non-drinker."

She suppressed her reply. "Well, this isn't getting my work done," she said. "Do you want anything?"

"Do I want anything? What for instance?"

"Well, I thought I'd spend the rest of the morning in the attic, sorting out things for the rummage sale."

"The attic? Do you know what it'll be like up there? You'll freeze to death."

"Oh, I have my big thick sweater. I won't be cold. And if it does get too cold, I'll stop. But I promised the committee I'd be ready when they sent the truck."

"This snowstorm will put everything back at least three days," he said.

"Well, I'm more than three days late. I should have done this a week ago. There's coffee in the glass pot. You may want to heat it. I put the milk and cream out on the windowsill. It'll keep just as well there as in the refrigerator."

"We used to have a box to keep things in during the winter. It was just outside the kitchen window, and you could keep meat and vegetables there. It opened from inside the kitchen. We ought to have one of those."

"Yes, that'd be a good idea. I suppose we could get a carpenter to make one."

"You know damn well I couldn't," he said. "You need two hands for that."

"All right, we'll ask Mr. Rosetti. But first let's find out how much he's going to charge us. Not like the last time, when he charged us eighty-five dollars just to fix a few feet of fence."

"Well, he knows I can't do it."

"Oh, Frank, will you stop?" she said. She left the room, got her sweater and retired to the attic.

She did not remain there long. It was a hard cold in the attic, with the sound of the wind beating against the roofing, and the power failure keeping the room in just enough darkness to make her chore difficult. She gave up and descended through trapdoor to ladder to the second-story guest room where her husband was still sitting at the window.

"I couldn't get anything done," she said. "No light, and my hands got cold. Would you want an early lunch?"

"I don't know what came over me," he said. "How long is it since I bellyached about my arm? I don't do that often, do I?"

"No," she said.

"One thing leads to another," he said. "I got on the subject of Johnny Grattan and before I knew it I was back there forty years ago. Forty years, that's a good solid block of years."

"Well, let's hope it's out of your system," she said.

"It'll never be out of my system altogether. It gave me a good excuse for being a bum."

"Oh, you're not a bum, Frank. That's silly," she said. "They should have made you get an artificial arm, then you could have done certain things and you'd have gotten used to it, so that when those new ones came along, the World War Two arms, you'd have been ready. I don't know, maybe you could still learn to use one of the new ones. They say they're marvelous."

"No, I couldn't learn to use one now. I'd only get discouraged, and I'm bad enough as it is."

"Only when you're feeling sorry for yourself. Then you can work yourself into such a state that you can be a disagreeable son of a bitch."

"Well, I don't enjoy it when I'm that way."

"I should hope not," she said. "How would you like some soup and a sliced chicken sandwich for lunch? I have the last of that chicken. Or I could fix you some cold cuts with a hot soup? I have some ham and liverwurst."

"The cold cuts," he said.

"I'm going to give you a steak tonight. We had three left in the deep freeze. If they get the electricity back on soon—but I'm not counting on that."

"No," he said. "I guess they'll try to have it on for tonight, but I wouldn't count on it much before dark."

"Old Mr. Williams must be miserable."

"Do you know what the Eskimos do with their old people? They put them out in a storm and they just fall asleep and never wake up. It seems to me a very sensible way."

"Are you suggesting that that's what they ought to do with Mr. Williams?"

"Not seriously, no," he said. "But this would be their chance, wouldn't it? And the Lord knows, Mr. Williams isn't getting much enjoyment out of life. He's over ninety."

"His mind is all right, though," she said.

"For a man over ninety. But he hasn't got much control over himself. He's practically helpless, and he's nothing much to look at. One of the funny sights is to see that old man, born right after the Civil War, shaving himself with an electric razor."

"Well, he won't be able to use it today."

"Oh, he probably doesn't have to shave more than once or twice a week. I'm thirty years younger than he is, but I notice a shave lasts me longer than it used to."

"He must be a problem in weather like this," said Helen Moore.

"Yes. Well, he's clinging to that last spark of life," he said. "And I guess they have enough firewood to keep him warm. I imagine they have him in their livingroom."

"Yes, I would think so. He doesn't sleep upstairs any more. They more or less turned their diningroom into a bedroom for him."

"I didn't know that," said Moore.

"Oh, last year," she said. "They had that lavatory in the hall, so all they had to do was bring down a bed from upstairs. Once a week they take him upstairs and give him a bath. That's the part I wouldn't like, giving an old man his bath. But Rachel doesn't complain. She's very fond of the old man."

"Well, that was the understanding, you know. He put up the money for the farm, on condition they'd give him a home. I guess they never expected him to last *this* long, though. That was twenty years ago."

"Yes, he got his money's worth. But Rachel doesn't look at it that way."

"It's still coming down," he said. "I think the wind has let up a little. Slanting. I noticed one little spot behind the tool shed, no snow on the ground at all. Just that one little spot. But I'll bet you there'll be two feet of snow there tomorrow, if not before."

"Well, let's hope it fills up all the reservoirs. We don't want any more water shortages next summer."

"No. Just think if we farmed this place," he said. "I mean if we had to depend on it for a living. Tom Williams told me last fall, I forget how much he said he lost last year. He about broke even on the dairy end, but he lost on the sweet corn and his potatoes. And Tom's a pretty good farmer. He uses all modern methods and reads up on all the latest information. But if you don't get rain at the right time and in the right amount, you can be the smartest farmer in the country and for all the good it does you you might as well stay drunk."

"Tom doesn't drink," she said.

"I didn't mean *he* might as well stay drunk. Anybody. Although you're wrong about Tom not drinking. Once or twice a year Tom ties one on that lasts four or five days."

"Oh, he used to, but not any more," said Helen Moore.

"Have it your way, but I happen to know better. The difference is, now he goes away, and I know where he goes. He and his brother, from Wilkes-Barre, and one or two friends of theirs go up to a shack they have in the Poconos. To go deer-hunting, they say. But last year Tom took a case of bourbon with him and it was all gone when he came back. Figure it out for yourself. Twelve bottles of whiskey. Four men. Four days. That's pretty good drinking for a man that doesn't drink. I could have gone with them. He invited me. Just bring some money, he told me. They play poker. I almost went."

"What stopped you?" she said.

"Well, if you think back, that was when you just got back from the clinic that time. You were waiting to hear from the doctor."

"Oh," she said. "Well, I'm glad you didn't go. Thank you."

"What the hell? I knew you were worried."

"You didn't say anything," she said.

"Neither did you. But it was a natural thing to be worried. And I probably wouldn't have had any fun. I don't like to be around a bunch of men when they're drinking and they have a lot of guns around."

"Why do you have to spoil it? You do something nice, and then it's as if you were ashamed of it," she said.

"Well, I don't know," he said. "Maybe I would have gone, and maybe I wouldn't. I don't know."

"You *would* have," she said.

"Well, I usually win at five-card stud," he said. "But then somebody gets a little drunk and they start all those fancy variations. Seven-card high-low, wild cards. Takes all the pleasure out of it for me."

She kissed him.

The Hardware Man

Lou Mauser had not always had money, and yet it would be hard to imagine him without it. He had owned the store—with, of course, some help from the bank—since he was in his middle twenties, and that was twenty years ago as of 1928. Twenty years is a pretty long time for a man to go without a notable financial failure, but Lou Mauser had done it, and when it has been that long, a man's worst enemies cannot say that it was all luck. They said it about Lou, but they said it in such a way as to make it sound disparaging to him while not making themselves appear foolish. It would have been very foolish to deny that Lou had worked hard or that he had been a clever business man. "You can't say it was all luck," said Tom Esterly, who was a competitor of Lou's. "You might just as well say he sold his soul to the devil. Not that he wouldn't have, mind you. But he didn't have to. Lou always seemed to be there with the cash at the right moment, and that's one of the great secrets of success. Be there with the cash when the right proposition comes along."

Lou had the cash, or got hold of it—which is the same thing—when Ada Bowler wanted to sell her late husband's hardware store. Lou was in his middle twenties then, and he had already been working in the store at least ten years, starting as a stock boy at five dollars a week. By the time he was eighteen he was a walking inventory of Bowler's stock; he knew where everything was, everything, and he knew how much everything was worth; wholesale, retail, special prices to certain contractors, the different mark-ups for different customers. A farmer came in to buy a harness snap, charge him a dime; but if another farmer, one who bought his barn paint at Bowler's, wanted a harness snap, you let him have it for a nickel. You didn't have to tell Sam Bowler what you were doing. Sam Bowler relied on your good sense to do things like that. If a boy was buying a catcher's mitt, you threw in a nickel Rocket, and sure as hell when

Saturday Evening Post (29 February 1964); *The Horse Knows the Way*

that boy was ready to buy an Iver Johnson bicycle he would come to Bowler's instead of sending away to a mail-order house. And Lou Mauser at eighteen had discovered something that had never occurred to Sam Bowler: the rich people who lived on Lantenengo Street were even more appreciative when you gave them a little something for nothing—an oil can for a kid's bike, an ice pick for the kitchen—than people who had to think twice about spending a quarter. Well, maybe they weren't *more* appreciative, but they had the money to show their appreciation. Give a Lantenengo Street boy a nickel Rocket, and his father or his uncle would buy him a dollar-and-a-quarter ball. Give a rich woman an ice pick and you'd sell her fifty foot of garden hose and a sprinkler and a lawn mower. It was all a question of knowing which ones to give things to, and Lou knew so well that when he needed the cash to buy out Sam Bowler's widow, he actually had two banks to choose from instead of just having to accept one bank's terms.

Practically overnight he became the employer of men twice his age, and he knew which ones to keep and which to fire. As soon as the papers were signed that made him the owner, he went to the store and summoned Dora Minzer, the bookkeeper, and Arthur Davis, the warehouse man. He closed his office door so that no one outside could hear what he had to say, although the other employees could see through the glass partitions.

"Give me your keys, Arthur," said Lou.

"My keys? Sure," said Arthur.

"Dora, you give me your keys, too," said Lou.

"They're in my desk drawer," said Dora Minzer.

"Get them."

Dora left the office.

"I don't understand this, Lou," said Arthur.

"If you don't, you will, as soon as Dora's back."

Dora returned and laid her keys on Lou's desk. "There," she said.

"Arthur says he doesn't understand why I want your keys. You do, don't you, Dora?"

"Well—maybe I do, maybe I don't." She shrugged.

"You two are the only ones that I'm asking for their keys," said Lou.

Arthur took a quick look at Dora Minzer, who did not look at him. "Yeah, what's the meaning of it, Lou?"

"The meaning of it is, you both put on your coat and hat and get out."

"Fired?" said Arthur.

"Fired is right," said Lou.

"No notice? I been here twenty-two years. Dora was here pretty near that long."

"Uh-huh. And I been here ten. Five of those ten the two of you been robbing Sam Bowler that I know of. That I know of. I'm pretty sure you didn't only start robbing him five years ago."

"I'll sue you for slander," said Arthur.

"Go ahead," said Lou.

"Oh, shut up, Arthur," said Dora. "He knows. I told you he was too smart."

"He'd have a hard time proving anything," said Arthur.

"Yeah, but when I did you know where you'd be. You and Dora, and two purchasing agents, and two building contractors. All in it together. Maybe there's more than them, but those I could prove. The contractors, I'm licked. The purchasing agents, I want their companies' business, so all I'm doing there is get them fired. What are you gonna tell them in Sunday School next Sunday, Arthur?"

"*She* thought of it," said Arthur Davis, looking at Dora Minzer.

"That I don't doubt. It took brains to fool Sam Bowler all those years. What'd you do with your share, Dora?"

"My nephew. I educated him and started him up in business. He owns a drug store in Elmira, New York."

"Then he ought to take care of you. Where did yours go, Arthur?"

"Huh. With five kids on my salary, putting them through High, clothes and doctor bills, the wife and her doctor bills. Music lessons. A piano. Jesus Christ, I wonder Sam didn't catch on. How did *you* catch on?"

"You just answered that yourself. I used to see all those kids of yours, going to Sunday School, all dolled up."

"Well, they're all married or got jobs," said Arthur Davis. "I guess I'll find something. Who are you gonna tell about this? If I say I quit."

"What the hell do you expect me to do? You're a couple of thieves, both of you. Sam Bowler treated everybody right. There's eight other people working here that raised families and didn't steal. I don't feel any pity for you. As soon as you get caught you try to blame it all on Dora. And don't forget this, Arthur." He leaned forward. *"You were gonna steal from me.* The two of you. This morning a shipment came in. Two hundred rolls of tarpaper. An hour later, fifty rolls went out on the wagon, but show me where we got any record of that sale of fifty rolls. That was this morning, Arthur. You didn't even wait one day, you or Dora."

"That was him, did that," said Dora. "I told him to wait. Stupid."

"They're all looking at us, out on the floor," said Arthur.

"Yes, and probably guessing," said Lou. "I got no more to say to either one of you. Just get out."

They rose, and Dora went to the outer office and put on her coat and hat and walked to the street door without speaking to anyone. Arthur went to the back stairs that led to the warehouse. There he unpacked a crate of brand-new Smith & Wesson revolvers and broke open a case of ammunition. He then put a bullet through his skull, and Lou Mauser entered a new phase of his business career.

He had a rather slow first year. People thought of him as a cold-blooded young man who had driven a Sunday School superintendent to suicide. But as the scandal was absorbed into local history, the unfavorable judgment was gradually amended until it more closely conformed with the early opinion of the business men, which was sympathetic to Lou. Dora Minzer, after all, had gone away, presumably to Elmira, New York; and though there were rumors about the purchasing agents of two independent mining companies, Lou did not publicly implicate them. The adjusted public opinion of Lou Mauser had it that he had behaved very well indeed, and that he had proven himself to be a better business man than Sam Bowler. Only a few people chose to keep alive the story of the Arthur Davis suicide, and those few probably would have found some other reason to be critical of Lou if Arthur had lived.

Lou, of course, did not blame himself, and during the first year of his ownership of the store, while he was under attack, he allowed his resentment to harden him until he became in fact the ruthless creature they said he was. He engaged in price-cutting against the other hardware stores, and one of the newer stores was driven out of business because of its inability to compete with Lou Mauser and Tom Esterly.

"All right, Mr. Esterly," said Lou. "There's one less of us. Do you want to call it quits?"

"You started it, young fellow," said Tom Esterly. "And I can last as long as you can and maybe a *little* bit longer. If you want to start making a profit again, that's up to you. But I don't intend to enter into any agreement with you, now or any other time."

"You cut your prices when I did," said Lou.

"You bet I did."

"Then you're just as much to blame as I am, for what happened to McDonald. You helped put him out of business, and you'll get your share of what's left."

"Yes, and maybe I'll get your share, too," said Tom Esterly. "The Esterlys were in business before the Civil War."

"I know that. I would have bought your store if I could have. Maybe I will yet."

"Don't bank on it, young fellow. Don't bank on it. Let's see how good your credit is when you need it. Let's see how long the jobbers and the manufacturers will carry you. I *know* how far they'll carry Esterly Brothers. We gave some of those manufacturers their first orders, thirty, forty years ago. My father was dealing with some of them when Sam Bowler was in diapers. Mauser, you have a lot to learn."

"Esterly and Mauser. That's the sign I'd like to put up some day."

"It'll be over my dead body. I'd go out of business first. Put up the shutters."

"Oh, I didn't want you as a partner. I'd just continue the name."

"Will you please get out of my store?"

Tom Esterly was a gentleman, a graduate of Gibbsville High and Gettysburg College, prominent in Masonic circles, and on the boards of the older charities. The word upstart was not in his working vocabulary and he had no epithet for Lou Mauser, but he disliked the fellow so thoroughly that he issued one of his rare executive orders to his clerks: hereafter, when Esterly Brothers were out of an article, whether it was a five-cent article or a fifty-dollar one, the clerks were not to suggest that the customer try Bowler's. For Tom Esterly this was a serious change of policy, and represented an attitude that refused to admit the existence of Mauser's competition. On the street he inclined his head when Mauser spoke to him, but he did not actually speak to Mauser.

Lou Mauser's next offense was to advertise. Sam Bowler had never advertised, and Esterly Brothers' advertising consisted solely of complimentary cards in the high school annual and the program of the yearly concert of the Lutheran church choir. These cards read, "Esterly Bros., Est. 1859, 211 N. Main St.," and that was all. No mention of the hardware business. Tom Esterly was shocked and repelled to see a full-page ad in each of the town newspapers, announcing a giant spring sale at Bowler's Hardware Store, Lou Mauser, Owner & Proprietor. It was the first hardware store ad in Gibbsville history and, worse, it was the first time Mauser had put his name on Sam Bowler's store. Tom Esterly went and had a look, and, yes, Mauser not only had put his name in the ad; he had his name painted on the store windows in lettering almost as large as Bowler's. The sale was, of course, a revival of Mauser's price-cutting tactic, even though it was advertised to last only three days. And Mauser offered legitimate bargains; some items, Tom knew, were going at cost. While the sale was on there were almost no customers in Esterly Brothers. "They're all down at Mauser's," said Jake Potts, Tom's head clerk.

"You mean Bowler's," said Tom.

"Well, yes, but I bet you he takes Sam's name off inside of another year," said Jake.

"Where is he getting the money, Jake?"

"Volume. What they call volume. He got two fellows with horse and buggy calling on the farmers."

"Salesmen?"

"Two of them. They talk Pennsylvania Dutch and they go around to the farms. Give the woman a little present the first time, and they drive their buggies right up in the field and talk to the farmers. Give the farmers a pack of chewing tobacco and maybe a tie-strap for the team. My brother-in-law down the Valley told me. They don't try to sell nothing the first visit, but the farmer remembers that chewing tobacco. Next time the farmer comes to market, if he needs anything he goes to Bowler's."

"Well, farmers are slow pay. We never catered much to farmers."

"All the same, Tom, it takes a lot of paint to cover a barn, and they're buying their paint off of Mauser. My brother-in-law told me Mauser's allowing credit all over the place. Any farmer with a cow and a mule can get credit."

"There'll be a day of reckoning, with that kind of foolishness. And it's wrong, *wrong,* to get those farmers in debt. You know how they are, some of them. They come in here to buy one thing, and before they know it they run up a bill for things they don't need."

"Yes, I know it. So does Mauser. But he's getting the volume, Tom. Small profit, big volume."

"Wait till he has to send a bill collector around to the farmers. His chewing tobacco won't do him any good then," said Tom Esterly.

"No, I guess not," said Jake Potts.

"The cash. I still don't see where he gets his cash. You say volume, but volume on credit sales won't supply him with cash."

"Well, I guess if you show the bank a lot of accounts receivable. And he has a lot of them, Tom. A lot. You get everybody owing you money, most of them are going to pay you some day. Most people around here pay their bills."

"You criticizing our policy, Jake?"

"Well, times change, Tom, and you gotta fight fire with fire."

"Would you want to work for a man like Mauser?"

"No, and I told him so," said Jake Potts.

"He wanted to hire you away from me?"

"A couple months ago, but I said no. I been here too long, and I might as well stay till I retire. But look down there, Tom. Down there between the counters. One lady customer. All the others are at Mauser's sale."

"He tried to steal you away from me. That's going too far," said Tom Esterly. "Would you mind telling me what he offered you?"

"Thirty a week and a percentage on new business."

"Thinking you'd get our customers to follow you there. Well, I guess I have to raise you to thirty. But the way it looks now, I can't offer you a percentage on new business. It's all going in the opposite direction."

"I didn't ask for no raise, Tom."

"You get it anyway, starting this week. If you quit, I'd just about have to go out of business. I don't have anybody to take your place. And I keep putting off the decision, who'll be head clerk when you retire. Paul Schlitzer's next in line, but he's getting forgetful. I guess it'll be Norman Johnson. Younger."

"Don't count on Norm, Tom."

"Mauser been making him offers?"

"I don't know for sure, but that's my guess. When a fellow starts acting independent, he has some good reason behind it. Norm's been getting in late in the morning and when ha' past five comes he don't wait for me to tell him to pull down the shades."

"Have you said anything to him?"

"Not so far. But we better start looking for somebody else. It don't have to be a hardware man. Any bright young fellow with experience working behind a counter. I can show him the ropes, before I retire."

"All right, I'll leave that up to you," said Tom Esterly. On his next encounter with Lou Mauser he stopped him.

"Like to talk to you a minute," said Tom Esterly.

"Fine and dandy," said Mauser. "Let's move over to the curb, out of people's way."

"I don't have much to say," said Tom Esterly. "I just want to tell you you're going too far, trying to hire my people away from me."

"It's a free country, Mr. Esterly. If a man wants to better himself. And I guess Jake Potts bettered himself. Did you meet my offer?"

"Jake Potts wouldn't have worked for you, offer or no offer."

"But he's better off now than he was before. He ought to be thankful to me. Mister, I'll make an offer to anybody I want to hire, in your store or anybodys else's. I don't have to ask your permission. Any more than I asked your permission to run a big sale. I had new customers in my store that I never saw before, even when Sam Bowler was the owner. I made *you* an offer, so why shouldn't I make an offer to fellows that work for you?"

"Good day, sir," said Tom Esterly.

"Good day to you," said Lou Mauser.

Tom Esterly was prepared for the loss of Norman Johnson, but when Johnson revealed a hidden talent for window decorating, he felt cheated. The window that attracted so much attention that it was written up in both newspapers was an autumnal camping scene that occupied all the space in Mauser's window. Two dummies, dressed in gunning costume, were seated at a campfire outside a tent. An incandescent lamp simulated the glow of the fire, and real pine and spruce branches and fake grass were used to provide a woodland effect. Every kind of weapon, from shotgun to automatic pistol, was on display, leaning against logs or lying on the fake grass. There were hunting knives and compasses, Marble match cases and canteens, cots and blankets, shell boxes of canvas and leather, fireless cookers, fishing tackle, carbide and kerosene lamps, an Old Towne canoe, gun cases and revolver holsters, duck calls and decoys and flasks and first-aid kits. Wherever there was space between the merchandise items, Norman Johnson had put stuffed chipmunk and quail, and peering out from the pine and spruce were the mounted heads of a cinnamon bear, a moose, an elk, a deer, and high above it all was a stuffed wildcat, permanently snarling.

All day long men would stop and stare, and after school small boys would shout and point and argue and wish. There had never been anything like it in Bowler's or Esterly Brothers' windows, and when the display was removed at Thanksgiving time there were expressions of regret. The small boys had to find some place else to go. But Norman Johnson's hunting-camp window became an annual event, a highly profitable one for Lou Mauser.

"Maybe we should never of let Norm go," said Jake Potts.

"He's right where he belongs," said Tom Esterly. "Right exactly where he belongs. That's the way those medicine shows do business. Honest value, good merchandise, that's what we were founded on and no tricks."

"We only sold two shotguns and not any rifles this season, Tom. The next thing we know we'll lose the rifle franchise."

"Well, we never did sell many rifles. This is mostly shotgun country."

"I don't know," said Jake. "We used to do a nice business in .22's. We must of sold pretty close to three hundred of the .22 pump gun, and there's a nice steady profit in the cartridges."

"I'll grant you we used to sell the .22 rifle, other years. But they're talking about a law prohibiting them in the borough limits. Ever since the Leeds boy put the Kerry boy's eye out."

"Tom, you won't face facts," said Jake. "We're losing business to this fellow, and it ain't only in the sporting goods line or any one line. It's every which way. Kitchen utensils. Household tools. Paints and varnishes. There's never the people in the store there used to be. When you's first in charge, after your Pa passed on, just about the only thing we didn't sell was something to eat. If you can eat it, we don't sell it, was our motto."

"That was never our motto. That was just a funny saying," said Tom Esterly.

"Well, yes. But we used to have funny sayings like that. My clerks used to all have their regular customers. Man'd come in and buy everything from the same clerk. Had to be waited on by the same clerk no matter what they come in to buy. Why, I can remember old Mrs. Stokes one day she come in to borrow my umbrella, and I was off that day and she wouldn't take anybody else's umbrella. That's the kind of customers we used to have. But where are those people today? They're down at Lou Mauser's. Why? Because for instance when school opened in September every boy and girl in the public and the Catholic school got a foot-rule from Lou Mauser. They maybe cost him a half a cent apiece, and say there's a thousand children in school. Five dollars."

"Jake, you're always telling me those kind of things. You make me wonder if you wouldn't rather be working for Mauser."

"I'll tell you anything if it's for your own good. You don't have your Pa or your Uncle Ed to tell you no more. It's for my own good too, I'll admit. I retire next year, and I won't get my fifty a month if you have to close down."

"Close down? You mean run out of business by Mauser?"

"Unless you do something to meet the competition. Once before you said Mauser would have trouble with the jobbers and the manufacturers. Instead of which the shoe is on the other foot now. Don't fool yourself, Tom. Those manufacturers go by the orders we send in, and some articles we're overstocked from last year."

"I'll tell you this. I'd sooner go out of business than do things his way. Don't worry. You'll get your pension. I have other sources of income besides the store."

"If you have to close the store I'll go without my pension. I won't take charity. I'll get other work."

"With Mauser."

"No, I won't work for Mauser. That's one thing I never will do. He as good as put the gun to Arthur Davis's head, and Arthur was a friend of mine, crook or no crook. I don't know what Mauser said to Arthur that day, but whatever it was, Arthur didn't see no other way out. That kind of a man I wouldn't work for. He has blood on his hands, to my way of thinking. When I meet Arthur Davis in the after life I don't want him looking at me and saying I wasn't a true friend."

"Arthur would never say that about you, Jake."

"He might. You didn't know Arthur Davis as good as I did. There was a man that was all worries. I used to walk home from work with him sometimes. First it was worr'ing because Minnie wasn't sure she was gonna marry him. Then all them children, and Minnie sick half the time, but the children had to look just so. Music lessons. A little money to get them started when they got married. They say it was Dora Minzer showed him how they could knock down off of Sam Bowler, and I believe that. But I didn't believe what they said about something going on between him and Dora. No. Them two, they both had a weakness for money and that was all there was between them. How much they stole off of Sam Bowler we'll never know, but Arthur's share was put to good use, and Sam never missed it. Neither did Ada Bowler. Arthur wouldn't of stole that money if Sam and Ada had children."

"Now you're going too far. You don't know that, and I don't believe it. Arthur did what Dora told him to. And what about the disgrace? Wouldn't Arthur's children rather be brought up poor than have their father die a thief?"

"I don't know," said Jake. "Some of it was honest money. Nobody knows how much was stolen money. The children didn't know any of it was stolen money till the end. By that time they all had a good bringing-up. All a credit to their parents and their church and the town. A nicer family you couldn't hope to see. And they were brought up honest. Decent respectable youngsters, all of them. You can't blame them if they didn't ask their father where the money was coming from. Sam Bowler didn't get suspicious, did he? The only one got suspicious was Lou Mauser. And they say he kept his mouth shut for six or seven years, so he was kind of in on it. If I ever saw one of our fellows look like he was knocking down off of you, I'd report it. But Lou Mauser never let a peep out of him till he was the owner. I sometimes wonder maybe he was hoping they'd steal so much they'd bankrupt Sam, and then he could buy the store cheaper."

"Well, now that's interesting," said Tom Esterly. "I wouldn't put it past him for a minute."

"I don't say it's true, but it'd be like him," said Jake. "No, I'd never go to work for that fellow. Even at my age I'd rather dig ditches."

"You'll never have to dig ditches as long as I'm alive, and don't say you won't take charity. You'll take your pension from Esterly Brothers regardless of whether we're still in business or not. So don't let me hear any more of that kind of talk. In fact, go on back to work. There's a customer down there."

"Wants the loan of my umbrella, most likely," said Jake. "Raining, out."

Esterly Brothers lasted longer than Jake Potts expected, and longer than Jake Potts himself. There were some bad years, easy to explain, but there were years in which the store showed a profit, and it was difficult to explain that. Lou Mauser expanded; he bought the store property adjoining his. He opened branch stores in two other towns in the county. He dropped the Bowler name completely. Esterly Brothers stayed put and as is, the middle of the store as dark as usual, so that the electric lights had to burn all day. The heavy hardware store fragrance—something between the pungency of a blacksmith's shop and the sweetness of the apothecary's—was missing from Lou Mauser's well-ventilated buildings, and he staffed his business with young go-getters. But some of the old Esterly Brothers customers returned after temporarily defecting to Mauser's, and at Esterly's they found two or three of the aging clerks whom they had last seen at Mauser's, veterans of the Bowler days. Although he kept it to himself, Tom Esterly had obviously decided to meet the go-getter's competition with an atmosphere that was twenty years behind the times. Cash customers had to wait while their money was sent to the back of the store on an overhead trolley, change made, and the change returned in the wooden cup that was screwed to the trolley wire. Tom never did put in an electric cash register, and the only special sale he held was when he offered a fifty percent reduction on his entire stock on the occasion of his going out of business. Three successive bad years, the only time it had happened since the founding of the store, were unarguable, and he put an ad in both papers to announce his decision. His announcement was simple:

50% Off
Entire Stock
Going Out of Business
Sale Commences Aug. 1, 1922
ESTERLY BROTHERS
Est. 1859
Open 8 A.M.—9 P.M. During Sale
All Sales Cash Only—All Sales Final

On the morning after the advertisements appeared, Tom Esterly went to his office and found, not to his surprise, Lou Mauser awaiting his appearance.

"Well, what can I do for *you?*" said Tom.

"I saw your ad. I didn't know it was that bad," said Lou. "I'm honestly sorry."

"I don't see why," said Tom. "It's what you've been aiming at. Why did you come here? If you want to buy anything, my clerks will wait on you."

"I'll buy your entire stock, twenty cents on the dollar."

"I think I'll do better this way, selling to the public."

"There'll be a lot left over."

"I'll give that away," said Tom Esterly.

"Twenty cents on the dollar, Mr. Esterly, and you won't have to give none of it away."

"You'd want me to throw in the good will and fixtures," said Esterly.

"Well, yes."

"I might be tempted to sell to you. The stock and the fixtures. But the good will would have to be separate."

"How much for the good will?" said Lou Mauser.

"A million dollars cash. Oh, I know it isn't worth it, Mauser, but I wouldn't sell it to you for any less. In other words, it isn't for sale to you. A week from Saturday night at nine o'clock, this store goes out of business forever. But no part of it belongs to you."

"The last couple years you been running this store like a hobby. You lost money hand over fist."

"I had it to lose, and those three years gave me more pleasure than all the rest put together. When this store closes a lot of people are going to miss it. Not because it was a store. *You* have a *store.* But we had something better. We never had to give away foot-rules to schoolchildren, or undercut our competitors. We never did any of those things, and before we *would* do them we decided to close up shop. But first we gave some of the people something to remember. Our kind of store, not yours, Mauser."

"Are you one of those that held it against me because of Arthur Davis?"

"No."

"Then what did you hold against me?"

"Sam Bowler gave you your first job, promoted you regularly, gave you raises, encouraged you. How did you repay him? By looking the other way all the time that you knew Arthur Davis and Dora Minzer were robbing him. Some say you did it because you hoped Sam would go bankrupt and you could buy the business cheap. Maybe yes, maybe no. That part isn't what I hold against you. It was you looking the other way, never telling Sam what they were doing to him. *That* was when you killed Arthur Davis, Mauser. Sam Bowler was the kind of man that if you'd told him about Arthur and Dora, he would have kept it quiet and given them both another chance. You never gave them another chance. You didn't even give them the chance to make restitution. I don't know about Dora Minzer, but Arthur Davis had a conscience, and a man that has a conscience is entitled to put it to work. Arthur Davis would have spent the rest of his life trying to pay Sam back, and he'd be alive today, still paying Ada Bowler, no doubt. Having a hard time, no doubt. But alive and with his conscience satisfied. You didn't kill Arthur by firing him that day. You killed him a long time before that by looking the other way. And I'm sure you don't understand a word I'm saying."

"No wonder you're going out of business. You should of been a preacher."

"I thought about it," said Tom Esterly. "But I didn't have the call."

The Victim

One night Leonard J. Kanzler was on his way home from work—he was a pharmacist at Smith's drug store and it was his turn to close up on Tuesdays, Thursdays, and Saturdays—and a man stepped out from behind a chestnut tree and blocked his path. "Put up your hands," the man said.

"Put up my hands? What for? You robbing me?" said Kanzler.

"You're damn right I am. Back up against the tree, and don't try anything. This is loaded."

"You won't get much from me. A couple dollars at the most. My watch and chain."

"Come on, Kanzler. The money from the cash register."

"Oh," said Kanzler.

"Yes, oh. Your inside coat pocket. Put it all on the ground and then start walking as soon as I tell you."

"I think I know who you are," said Kanzler.

"You don't, though. So just put the money on the ground, and your diamond ring. You can forget about your watch."

"Yes, I think I know who you are. Are you J.M.?"

"No, I ain't J.M., and quit stalling. You don't know me, but I know you."

"Yes, I guess you do. All right. There's the wallet, and on top of it my ring. That's a Masonic ring, you know. Won't do *you* any good to wear it, because *you're* not a Mason."

"Who said I was gonna wear it?" The man, who had a handkerchief over the lower half of his face, reached down and picked up the wallet and ring.

"Now what do I do?" said Kanzler.

"Wait till I have a look inside of the wallet."

"The money's there. Two hundred and eighty-six dollars. Is that enough to go to jail for? If you're who I think you are, you wouldn't shoot me."

Saturday Evening Post (14 March 1964); *The Horse Knows the Way*

"You better not count on that, mister."

"Mister? I guess you're *not* who I thought you were."

"You wouldn't know me from Adam, bud. So don't take any chances. Now you can start going, but walk slow. If you start running I'll give you a bullet in the back. Just take it easy."

"Now?"

"Now."

"How did you know I—"

"Saturday night, you always take the money out of the cash register, and Smith comes and gets it from you Sunday morning. See, I know."

"As soon as I get home I intend to call the police."

"Sure. And tell them to go looking for J.M."

"No, I don't think you're J.M. any more. I'm glad you're not. He's in enough trouble as it is."

"Get going, Kanzler."

"No, you're not J.M. You're not from around here. You don't pronounce my name right."

"Do I have to root you in the tail to get you started?"

"I'm going," said Kanzler. "It's Con-slur, not Canz-lur."

He walked slowly to his house, which was up the hill in back of the Court House. His wife was in nightgown and bathrobe, her hair in curlers, and she was sitting at the kitchen table with a *Delineator* spread out before her. "Len? Will I put the coffee on?"

"Be with you in a minute."

"You going to the toilet?"

"Making a phone call."

"Who to at this hour of the night?"

"Come and listen," he said. He picked up the receiver. "Get me two-two-oh-jay, please."

"Who's that?" said Leora Kanzler.

"Hello, Police Headquarters? This is Leonard Kanzler speaking. Oh, hello, Jack. You sound like you had a cold. Well, there's a lot of it around. Come in tomorrow and I'll give you something for it. Or no, I won't. I'm off tomorrow. No, every other Sunday. Well, to tell you the truth, I got held up and robbed. Five minutes ago. On the way home. I'm all right, but the store is minus two hundred and eighty-six dollars and I'm minus my diamond ring. Young fellow with a pistol. A revolver. Came out from behind a tree on North Second, the 400-block. You know where that row of trees are. I had the night's receipts in my wallet. We never leave them there over Saturday night. I bring them home for safekeeping and—no, I thought I recognized him at first, but it was somebody else. This fellow was a stranger, an out-of-town fellow. Say about thirty maybe, medium height and build, wore a handkerchief for a mask. No, I'm all right. I wasn't even scared at the time, but now since I'm home I think he would have used the gun."

"Good heavens," said Leora Kanzler.

"I'm home. No, the wife and I usually have a little lunch on Saturdays that I'm not opening up the next morning. If you send anybody tell them not to make any noise, will you, Jack? We don't want to wake up the whole neighborhood. No, they're both away visiting their grandmother in Shamokin. They won't be back till Tuesday."

"Wednesday," said Leora Kanzler.

"Wednesday, my wife says. Okay, Jack. I'll be waiting for them. No, I don't keep a gun in the house. We have one in the store, but I don't even think it's loaded. It's not mine. Right." He replaced the receiver.

"Good heavens. Right here on Second Street? Are you all right? Are you sure?"

"That was Jack Riegler. Sounds asthmatic to me. No, I'm all right. But I wouldn't like to repeat the experience. As long as I was talking to him I wasn't worried, but all the rest of the way home I began thinking if he put a bullet in my back, I could lie there and bleed to death by the time somebody found me."

"Two squares from home."

"Or even less."

"I'll get you a drink of whiskey."

"No, some coffee'll be all right. I don't want any whiskey on my breath when the police come."

"They're coming here? The police coming here?"

"I'd rather they came here than I go there," said Kanzler.

"Yes," she said. "You sure you're all right, Len? I'd die if anything happened to you."

"We're safe and sound. The last place the holdup man wants to be is this neighborhood. I told him I was sending for the police."

"What kind of a man was he? A thug?"

"Well, I guess he is a thug. He had a gun, and he would have used it. A professional criminal, I'd say. Studied our habits at the store. Knew I brought the receipts home Saturday night. Got close enough to me to see my ring. Very little he didn't take in. Probably in and out of the store a half a dozen times, studying every move. One thing, it should teach Harry Smith a lesson. I told Harry three years ago, I said leave the money in the cash register and hang a light over it, an ordinary six-watt bulb, that you can see it from the street. He said that'd be a temptation, an invitation, but what he was thinking was the waste of electricity."

"Instead of the waste of maybe a man's life."

"Well, I did that for the last time."

"I'll say. Don't you ever risk your life for Harry Smith. I'd die if—"

"Gives me a good chance to get some other things off my chest."

"A raise," she said.

"No, I never had to ask him for a raise. That much I'll say for Harry. In another year and a half I'll be getting sixty, and that's as much as any other man in town gets, unless he graduated from P.C.P. But they start higher, the P.C.P. graduates."

"But you have your license, Philadelphia College of Pharmacy or no Philadelphia College of Pharmacy. More doctors depend on you than the college men."

"That's because I'm used to their writing. I have to admit, the college men got training I never got. When it comes to the U.S.P., I don't have to take a back seat to anybody, but—uh oh. That'll only be the police." He went to the front door. "Oh, it's Tom Kyler."

"Evening, Len. Understand you had a little trouble."

"Come on in, Tom. You all by yourself?"

"Norm is down waiting in the car. Norm Ziegler."

"You got here quick."

"Well, you know we have the blinker on the pole down at Main and Scandinavia. Soon as we see a certain signal we call headquarters. Jack said you had an armed robbery. You all right?"

"Fine and dandy. Not saying he wouldn't have used his gun on me. At first I didn't think so, but he was a cool customer. Have a cup of coffee with the missus and I. Tell Ziegler."

"Thanks, we just finished a little lunch at the Greek's. But all right, I'll have a cup of coffee while you describe the suspect. Evening, Mizz Kanzler."

"Oh, they have you a detective now, Tom," she said.

"On night duty I don't wear the uniform. It gives you away. Well, Len, tell us all about it. You's on your way home with the night's receipts. That was two-eight-six, Jack said. Then somewheres in the 400-block on North Second, about how far from the corner of Pine would you say?"

"I'll tell you the whole story from beginning to end," said Kanzler.

"First can I use your phone? Have to tell Jack we're here, then you can tell me your story," said Kyler.

"Under the hall light," said Kanzler.

"Tommy Kyler," said his wife. "I had him in seventh grade. More than once I whacked his little behind, I'll tell you."

"Shush," said Kanzler.

Kyler returned from his telephone call and sat stiffly in the kitchen of his seventh-grade teacher. As Kanzler told his story, Kyler would interrupt with pertinent questions, and whenever he did he could not keep from glancing at Leora Kanzler. She would nod and smile approvingly at her old pupil, but Kanzler was irritated. "Tom, you better let me tell it my own way or I'll lose the thread," he said. "Let me tell it through, then you come back with your questions later."

"Tom's an expert at this, Len. Don't tell him how to run his business," said Leora.

"Listen, the two of you act as if I couldn't tell it without your help. I'm the one this happened to, not you or Tom. Let me tell it my own way, while it's fresh in my mind."

"I just want to get a few details before you forget them," said Kyler. "You say the fellow sounded like he didn't come from around here. What do you mean by that? Did he talk southern, or something on that order?"

"Didn't talk southern, didn't talk northern, eastern or western. He didn't talk like a New York salesman, and he didn't talk like an Irishman from up the mountain."

"Was he disguising the way he talked?"

"Now, Tom, what kind of a question is that? Was he disguising. If I knew that I'd have to know what he was disguising, wouldn't I? There was the one thing gave him away, and that was how he pronounced my name. My *last* name, before you go asking me questions about it. He said Canz-lur. Now how does everybody pronounce our name around here? How do you pronounce it?"

"Like everybody else, I guess," said Kyler.

"Say it," said Kanzler. "What's my last name?"

"Con-slur," said Kyler. "Oh, *I* see. Canz-lur. Con-slur. Therefore you figured out he was from out of town." He wrote in his notebook and accompanied the writing with the spoken words: "Out, of, town."

"See how careful he is? Puts everything down. That's why he has to ask you those questions," said Leora Kanzler.

"He puts it down, but it's a lucky thing I noticed it or what would he have to *put* down? I've been doing a little detective work of my own, don't forget."

"How's that, Len?" said Kyler.

"Well, now, you take here's a fellow knows my name and my habits. But doesn't know how to pronounce my name. So he doesn't know me. Personally. All the same, he's been in town long enough to study my habits and find out that Saturday nights I always bring home the receipts."

"You told him all that before," said Leora.

"Will you please, Leora? Please? So therefore this fellow must of been in town a couple or three weeks at least."

"More than likely," said Kyler. "More than likely."

"Well, if I was in your place," said Kanzler. "What I'd do, I'd go around to all the hotels and rooming houses and find out if they had a fellow answered that description. Medium heightth, medium build, and somewhere around thirty years of age. If such a man took a room in the last two or three weeks you could get a complete description from the landlady or the hotel manager. His name. Fingerprints. Everything. He most likely told them he was some kind of a salesman."

"There's a lot of men answers that description," said Kyler.

"Yeah, but there's a lot more that don't. All tall men, all short men, all fat men, all skinny men. All Italians. All colored. All men that were raised here in Gibbsville. All one-legged men. All every kind of man except medium-heightth, medium-built men around thirty years of age. You'll soon narrow it down, just as soon as you find out what hotel or boarding-house he stayed at."

"Uh-huh. That's what they call routine police work," said Kyler.

"Routine common sense, that's what it is," said Kanzler. "But the thing about common sense is that it's so uncommon. If you'd listen to me instead of both of you interrupting, maybe we'd get somewhere."

"Now, now. Now-now-now," said Leora.

"*I* could probably catch this fellow, if he's still in town," said Kanzler.

"Maybe I ought to ask the mayor to have you sworn in, Len. Put you on the force."

"You don't have to get sarcastic, Tom. I meet a lot of people in my business, maybe just as many as you do, and I have to be a student of human nature. You know, people come in the store and they hand me a prescription, all folded up. I look at it and see what it's for and I just say to come back in a half an hour. But that person has just told me things about himself, if his friends knew, or his boss, or sometimes his *wife*—if I ever said a word about that prescription, entire families would be ruined. *Ruined.* And some of the most prominent people in this town, believe you me. Tonight I was thinking when this fellow held me up, first I thought I recognized him, and I said to him, I asked him if he was So-and-So and mentioned two initials. The initials of a certain young fellow that comes in to get prescriptions filled. They cost a lot of money every refill, and he'll be coming back for a long time. That's who I thought was holding me up. But the more I talked to the robber, the more I knew it wasn't the certain party, and I was glad it wasn't, because this party has trouble enough as it is, without robbing people at the point of a gun."

"Who did you have in mind?" said Kyler.

"It wasn't him, so I don't intend to tell you."

"How can you be sure it wasn't him? He was wearing a handkerchief over his face," said Kyler.

"You can ask me till you're blue in the face and I won't tell you. It wasn't him. What you ought to do, Tom Kyler, you better concentrate on the hotels and boarding-houses. This fellow that held me up, he won't be satisfied with any two hundred and eighty-six dollars and my diamond ring. I wouldn't be a bit surprised if he was robbing somebody else right this minute. He has to. He got two hundred and eighty-six dollars and a diamond ring from me, but now you police are looking for him. The question is, where does he strike next?"

Kyler looked at Leora Kanzler. "He's right," he said.

"Do you think he is?" said Leora.

"I know he is. He has it all doped out, and he has the right dope," said Kyler. "Earlier tonight we had a report of an armed robbery at Schlitz's. You know Schlitz's, the grocery store all the way out West Market? They stay open late Saturday night."

"Paul Schlitz's, sure I know them. Didn't I used to live at 1844 West Market?" said Leora. "They were held up too?"

"Not a whole hour before Len was held up. Paul and his wife, they closed up a little after nine. Shades down. A knock on the side door. They wouldn't of opened the front door, but the steady customers know about the side door. Paul went and opened the door and there was a fellow with a handkerchief over his face. A .32 or a .38 revolver in his hand. Pushed Paul out of the way, went right to the counter where him and his wife had the money in little piles. Close to four hundred dollars. Saturday's when a lot of their customers settle up so it may be more. They have to go through their ledgers to make sure."

"Were they injured?" said Leora.

"She fainted, but nobody was hurt. The robber put all the cash in a paper bag and then he took a meat cleaver and hacked the telephone wire. That was when she fainted, when she seen him pick up the cleaver."

"I would too," said Leora.

"Yeah. We didn't get the call on that till around a quarter to ten.

Schlitz had to go next door to phone the doctor. I guess she had some kind of a heart attack, so we were late getting the call."

"Was it the same fellow that held me up?"

"Well, it sure sounds like it."

"Funny Jack Riegler didn't mention anything to me."

"Well, I guess he wasn't sure it was the same fellow, and it don't pay to get people excited. But I guess you're right, Len. First the fellow robs Schlitz, out in the West End, then he can be on North Second in five or ten minutes. He has around seven hundred dollars on him, in small bills and silver. He won't be satisfied with under a thousand."

"Exactly the way I doped it out. Small bills. Now where else would you go for small bills on a Saturday night?" said Kanzler.

"The speakeasies. Only there he'd be liable to run up against some opposition. Drunks, full of Dutch courage. Too many people. This fellow is too smart for that."

"Well, all the stores are closed by now," said Kanzler.

"Yeah. Nothing open after eleven o'clock, except the speaks. Where there's any money, that is."

The telephone rang. "I'll bet that's for you," said Kanzler "Jack Riegler."

"All right, I'll answer it," said Kyler. He went to the telephone, and the Kanzlers stood in the hall to listen. "Kanzler's," said Kyler. "Yeah, Jack, it's me. Uh-huh. Yeah? Yeah? For Christ's sake. I'll be a son of a bitch. I didn't know he had it in him. Wuddia want us to do, Norm and I? No, they're all right. Well, maybe shook up a little, but we been talking. Yeah. I think he wants to be a cop. Ha ha ha ha ha. Okay, Jack. We'll get over there right away." He hung up the receiver and turned to the Kanzlers. "Got him. Got your man."

"Arrested him?" said Kanzler.

"No *sir.* Charley Paxton, old Charley, shot him dead as a mackerel. Four shots. I didn't think old Charley could shoot that good, but I was wrong."

"What *happened? Where?*" said Leora.

"Well, remember we were trying to figure out where there'd be cash at this hour of the night?"

"Uh-huh," said Kanzler.

"We forgot the Armory. They have them dances there Saturday night."

"What dances?" said Leora.

"Big dances, every Saturday. Gents seventy-five, ladies a half a dollar. They get good crowds."

"Oh, *public* dances," said Leora. "Yes, I've seen the ads."

"Your stick-up man seen the ads too. I guess. Anyway, he went out there to the Armory, and Ted Haggerty, he runs the dances, he was in the booth where they sell the tickets from. The ticket window was down, and he was getting the money ready to pay the orchestra. Knock on the door, and I guess he thought it was the fellow from the orchestra. He let him in, but it was the fellow with the gun. But this time he wasn't so smart. They always figure it out wrong. He told Haggerty to put the money in the satchel, and that was the last thing he ever said. One, two, three, four. Old Charley Paxton was sitting there in the booth, half asleep most likely. And he just took out his gun and he fired four straight shots and hit the guy with every one of them. Old Charley Paxton, getting ready to be retired. You sure have to hand it to him. Just quietly pulled out his .38 and one, two, three, four. Guy was dead before he hit the floor. Three in the body and one in the head."

"You would have thought the fellow'd know Paxton was there," said Kanzler. "I would have made sure of that."

"Surprises me, too. Only I guess maybe he didn't think old Charley was a cop. Well, he's a cop all right. I'm proud of him."

"For killing somebody? Tom Kyler?" said Leora Kanzler. "I'm ashamed of you."

"That was his duty. You wouldn't like it so much if the same fellow killed Len. I gotta be going."

"As I look at it," said Kanzler. "This young desperado was clever, very smart. He studied me and my habits, and did the same thing with the Schlitzes. Also the Armory. Had it all figured out to the last detail, including Charley Paxton. I don't agree with you that he didn't know Charley was a cop. I'm sure he knew he was a cop. But he probably saw Charley out there, half asleep or half intoxicated. Everybody knows Charley gets intoxicated, Tom. You don't have to cover up for him. Charley only had so much longer to go before they retired him, and he's been celebrating all winter. Was Charley wearing his uniform?"

"No," said Kyler.

"No. Because about two months ago he wasn't exactly suspended from the force, but they furloughed him. Isn't that correct, Tom?"

"Well, what they did, they didn't suspend him because he only has a little while before he's retired. They took him off regular duty and had him on standby. Like tonight, being a Saturday, he was on special duty. Saturday's our busy night, and those dances at the Armory draw a rough crowd, sometimes. All the same we can't spare a man unless it's somebody like Charley, but he was as good a cop as anybody else tonight."

"Because he killed a man?" said Leora. "Is that what he was there for?"

Tom Kyler patted his hip pocket. "I carry this in case I have to use it, Mrs. Kanzler. I'm supposed to protect life and property."

"I never thought I'd hear one of my pupils say they think it's all right to kill a man."

"Be fair, Leora. Be fair," said Kanzler.

"I don't understand you, either. The things you've been saying tonight," she said.

"I'll go now," said Kyler.

"Yes, I guess you have to, if you don't want to listen to a family argument, Tom. Goodnight. You know your way out."

"Goodnight, Len. Mrs. Kanzler," said Kyler, leaving.

"A while ago you would have died if anything happened to me, so you said," said Kanzler. "Well, just stop to think that if we didn't have the Tom Kylers and the Charley Paxtons—"

"Oh, I'm familiar with all that. But you, all of a sudden I don't understand you at all. First you put yourself in the same position as a robber and it was uncanny, your mind worked the same as his. Then you turn around and defend a drunken policeman for killing a man."

"Well, maybe I don't understand myself, either. But I was never robbed before. Never had a man point a gun at me and take my wallet and my ring. That's an experience that doesn't happen to me every day."

"I hope it never happens again, if it has this effect on you."

"What did you used to whack his behind for—Tom Kyler?"

"What do you want to know that for?"

"I guess you never thought about it this way, but you used to be a kind of a policeman."

"Go to bed. You and your customers and prescriptions and human nature."

"No, I'm going to stay up awhile. This makes my third cup of coffee. But you don't have to stay up, Leora."

"I don't intend to. Will you be sure and turn all the lights out?"

"Uh-huh. I wonder what his name was."

"Whose name?"

"Oh, the fellow tonight that didn't know how to pronounce my name."

"The sooner you start forgetting about that," she said.

"Shouldn't be hard. I don't have much to remember," said Leonard J. Kanzler, pronounced Con-slur, in Gibbsville, Pa.

The House on the Corner

It went all the way back to a day when George Wentz came home from shoveling the snow off the neighbors' sidewalks. "How much did you make?" said his father.

"Ninety cents," said George.

"For how many sidewalks?"

"Oh, gee, I don't know."

"Well—was it two? Four? Six? Eight?" said his father.

"It sure wasn't two, and it sure wasn't four. At least six. Do you want me to count up?"

"Wouldn't that be a good idea? You made ninety cents, and that could be a lot of money if you got it for one sidewalk. But if you did six, that's fifteen cents a sidewalk. And if you did nine, that's a dime apiece. Count up and see."

"Well-ll, starting with our house, Mama gave me a dime. That's one."

"One sidewalk, one dime," said his father. "Then who?"

"Mrs. Williams, fifteen. Mrs. Chester, ten. She didn't want the whole thing shoveled, just a path. It sure looked funny, just a path, and all the others swept clean. Let me see now. After Mrs. Chester, Mrs. O'Brien, fifteen. Next to them is the Reveres."

"And they have Jake Loomis to shovel theirs," said his father.

"No, I did it," said George.

"Where was old Jake? That's supposed to be part of his work."

"I don't know, but when Mrs. Revere saw me cleaning Mrs. O'Brien's she called to me and said would I clean hers."

"A man-sized job, all the way around the corner," said his father.

"And the driveway."

"And the driveway? How much did you get for that?" said his father.

"Twenty-five cents."

Saturday Evening Post (22 August 1964); *The Horse Knows the Way*

"A quarter? For the whole thing? The front sidewalk, and around the corner, and the driveway? A quarter for that? Is that all?"

"That was the most I got from anybody, a quarter."

"But the work. How long were you at it?"

"That took me the longest."

"Who paid you? Mrs. Revere herself?"

"No. Mr. Revere."

"Oh, *Mister* Revere. He came out and graciously bestowed upon you the enormous sum of twenty-five cents. What did you say to him?"

"What did I say? Oh, you mean did I say thanks? Yes."

"Tugging at your forelock," said his father.

"What?"

"Just an expression," said his father.

Amy Wentz called from the diningroom. "Supper's ready, you two."

"Be there in a minute," said the elder Wentz.

"No, now," said his wife. "It's on the table."

When they were seated George Wentz's father said to his wife, "Well, did you hear what Franklin Revere paid George for clearing his sidewalk and his driveway?"

"Twenty-five cents," said Amy Wentz.

"I have a good notion to go up there and tell him what I think. The boy should have got at least a dollar for that work. Twenty-five cents. Old Jake Loomis is no fool. He's not going to break his back on a day like this. I'll bet you Jake had a look out the window and went right back to bed—with a bottle of hooch, most likely."

"I wouldn't put it past him," said Amy. "But you're not going to say anything to Franklin Revere, do you hear? We're in no position to go around making enemies of people like the Reveres."

"Why not? They don't own us," said Wentz.

"I didn't say they did," said Amy. "But they come closer to owning us than we are to owning them."

"Nobody owns anybody in this country," said Wentz.

"No, but some people own their own houses and some people are paying rent."

"And others are mortgaged," said Wentz. "To the hilt. But the Reveres don't happen to hold our mortgages, and they don't have any financial control over us whatsoever."

"Ethel Revere was a Stokes, and who do you have to go to when you need money? Her brother, at the bank. So let's not start something because they underpaid George seventy-five cents."

"All right, all right," said Wentz. "But the boy's never going to do any more work for them, shoveling snow or anything else."

"I doubt if the opportunity will come up again," said Amy.

But it did. A few days later there was another heavy fall of snow, and the last thing Ben Wentz said to his wife before leaving for work was that under no circumstances was George to clear the Reveres' sidewalk. Shortly after ten o'clock the Wentz telephone rang, and it was Ethel Revere. "Amy, this is Ethel Revere. I was wondering, when George gets home from school this afternoon, could he come and clear our sidewalk? He did such a good job the other day, and Jake Loomis is staying home."

"I'm sorry, Ethel, but George won't be able to," said Amy.

"Oh, dear. I was really counting on him. He more or less promised. Franklin was so pleased the other day, and he told George he could have the job any time Jake didn't show up."

"You mean the job of shoveling snow?"

"Yes. Of course I didn't mean Jake's other work. Jake *is* a good gardener, and of course George has to stay in school."

"And George isn't going to be a gardener," said Amy. "He's going to study architecture."

"Oh, good for him," said Ethel Revere. "Well, you don't know any other boys in the neighborhood that I could ask?"

"I don't think you'll get anybody to do it for twenty-five cents," said Amy.

"Oh, *that's* why we can't have George," said Ethel. "Well, we could make it fifty."

"That's not enough, either."

"Then what do you think would be a fair price?"

"A dollar seventy-five," said Amy.

"A dollar seventy-five?"

"A dollar for today, and seventy-five additional payment for Tuesday," said Amy.

"*I* see. Holding us up, eh?"

"No, not holding you up at all, Ethel. Only getting a fair price. You won't get a man to clean your sidewalks and driveway for under a dollar. If you think you can, you're free to try. But we didn't call up and ask you to hire George. You called us."

"Very well, Amy. I'm sorry to've troubled you. Goodbye."

All day the Reveres' sidewalk and driveway was covered with snow, until late in the afternoon when Amy saw two colored men with shovels and ice-choppers on the job. She recognized one of the men, Peter Lejohn, who was a porter at the bank, and the other man might easily have been Peter's brother. Whoever they were, they were grown men and Amy guessed that each of them was getting at least two dollars for his work . . .

That was the start of it. Thereafter, whenever Ethel and Franklin Revere had to pass the Wentz residence on foot, they would nod and utter the greeting appropriate to the time of day, but without adding any names. This would occur three or four times a year, but the years multiplied the number of times and the combination of times and years hardened, solidified, the relationship between the Wentz family and the Reveres. There was nothing as dramatic as a feud between them, and nothing approaching cordiality. George Wentz came home from his last year at Princeton, having lived twenty-three years on the same block as the Reveres, and had never been inside their house. He brought with him a friend.

"Who lives in the big house on the corner?" said Adam Sturgis.

"People named Revere. Mr. and Mrs. Franklin Revere."

"Mr. and Mrs. Gotrocks?" said Adam.

"Not *the* Mr. and Mrs. Gotrocks, but they're well fixed. She has the money. He comes from Maryland somewhere."

"It's a nice house," said Adam.

"Yes it is," said George. "At one time it and one other house were the only houses on the block. The houses in between—our house, for instance—were built on ground that used to be a grove of trees. That was before I was born, but my father remembers it. He used to play there. They used to come and have picnics under the trees. It was almost like a public park, but then I guess the land got too valuable and the trees were cut down and they put up sixteen or eighteen small houses. Income producers. Although we never paid rent. My father bought our house when he and my mother got married. Subject to mortgages, of course, but he finally paid them off. I guess that's why we never had a car. My father and mother gave up a lot to own their own home. There were two things they were determined on. To own their own home, and send me to college."

"Well, you helped there. It didn't cost them much to send you to college."

"No, but they were ready, in case I didn't get any scholarships. In a way, I suppose the help I got at Princeton paid off the last mortgage, indirectly. And my father had the satisfaction of owning his own house the last year of his life."

"And knowing you were all set. Phi Bete junior year, he didn't have to worry about you," said Adam.

"He worried enough. I'm sure he never made more than three hundred a month, and he had to keep up appearances."

"Is that all? He owned a jewelry store," said Adam.

"It's Wentz's jewelry store, but my father didn't own it. It was owned by his older brother and my grandmother. My father was never anything more than a clerk. A combination clerk and bookkeeper. He had to wait on customers and keep the books. If they had a good year, the extra profit was cut up between my uncle and my grandmother, and maybe a small Christmas present for my father, but it was never much. My uncle liked the dames and the booze. Oh, the store made good money. Uncle Lou had a wife that knew how to spend it, too. But my father saw very little of it. He handled it, and that was about all. Handled it, is right. A clerk in a jewelry store has to have his hands clean and his fingernails just right. I remember every Sunday evening, my mother used to give my father a manicure. Every Sunday evening. My uncle had his manicured at the ladies' beauty parlor. The barbershops in town didn't have manicurists then. But my mother was my father's manicurist. As a matter of fact, she got good enough to give manicures to some of her friends. She never said so, but I'm sure she picked up a few dollars that way. Just from friends. They did a lot of things like that. My father kept the books for a couple of little stores. He'd bring their books home, or rather they'd bring them to our house. My uncle never knew my father did that. Little stores like Miss Jenny Albright's. She had a store in the front room of her house. Sold yarn and things like that. Linen and handkerchiefs. My father kept her books for her. A hundred and twenty dollars a year. And Joe Orsino, had a shoe repair shop on Second Street. My father charged him more, twenty-five a month. Three hundred a year. And he got something for being financial secretary of his lodge. He never told me how much that was, because everything about the lodge was secret. But it was probably two or three hundred a year."

"But you were never actually poor," said Adam.

"Compared to some, no. Compared to others, we were worse than poor. There was never a time when we didn't have enough to eat in the house, that's true. The cheaper cuts, but unskimmed milk. My mother used to want to deal at the Bell Store. It was a cash-and-carry chain store. But we had customers among the grocers and butchers, and believe me they put the pressure on people that bought at the Bell. And they were right. Why should they buy an engagement ring from us if we were spending our money at a store that was slowly putting them out of business? An early lesson in economics for me, when my father told my mother we had to stop buying at the Bell. One of the few times I ever heard them fight. 'Let Lou Wentz make up the difference,' she said. Money was the enemy in this house."

"It must have been," said Adam.

"But there's nothing like a common enemy for keeping people together. We missed a lot. Do you know that in four years at Princeton I've yet to see New Haven? My father used to say, 'All your friends are going up to Yale. It won't break me to treat you to one game there.' But I'd think of the train fare, and the tickets to the game, and meals for a girl and me, and it would just about amount up to a suit of clothes. My suits, Adam. Not yours. And I'd refuse. Then in junior year he sent me a check and said this was the last time I'd be able to see Princeton beat Yale on their own home ground, the Yale Bowl, and he insisted I go."

"But you didn't go. I remember. They beat the hell out of us, too," said Adam.

"No, I didn't go, but I didn't tell him. I wrote him a letter of thanks, faking it as if I'd gone. And I kept the money, fifty bucks, and that year I gave them both pretty decent Christmas presents. As it happened, that turned out to be my father's last Christmas alive. My mother asked me how I could afford such nice presents, and I told her I'd saved up my winnings at bridge. She gave me a look and she didn't say anything, but *she* knew I'd never gone near New Haven. That little gold bar pin. I got it wholesale through the store. She wears it all the time."

"What did you buy your father?"

"A cashmere sweater. He was wearing it when he died. He was down-cellar, tinkering with the oil burner, and he started up the stairs and got about halfway. Heart attack."

"You know, George, I have a confession to make," said Adam.

"Go ahead," said George.

"Ever since we've been friends, a little over three years, the one thing I had reservations about was your being a student of the dollar. I knew you weren't Rockefeller, but you used to get these letters from Wentz's jewelry store. Wentz's. Jewelers and Silversmiths, Established 18-something. And I used to think, well he doesn't have to play it *that* close to the vest. It was very hard to pull you loose from a buck. And then I thought, well, the Pennsylvania Dutch. Not notoriously spendthrift. So when you invited me here, frankly I came out of curiosity as much as anything else, and I fully expected to be met with a 1915 Pierce-Arrow. And when I saw that house on the corner, I thought it was going to be yours."

"Well, I guess I was stingy," said George. He laughed.

"You were never stingy in your life, you dumb bastard."

"Pretty stingy. There were times when I could have spent more than I did. But I'm not going to change right away, Adam. I'm pretty sure of getting the Prix de Rome, and I've had offers of jobs. By the time I'm thirty I should be making pretty good money, and then maybe I'll be able to do what I want to do. What I really want to do."

"Which is?"

"Give my mother the keys to that house on the corner."

"Why?"

"Because those bastards, they used to go by this house and they'd just barely speak to my father and mother. Just barely speak to them. And for no reason at all."

Aunt Fran

Mary Duncan heard her husband stomping his feet on the front porch, heard him kicking his shoes against the porch rail, and then there was the complaining squeal of the front door being pushed inward. She did not look up from her letter-writing. "Is the game over?" she said.

"No, there's about ten minutes left in the last quarter, but I began sneezing, so I came home. G.H.S. is ahead, eighteen to six." He took off his trench coat and hung it on the clothestree in the hall, then came in the front room. "Look, I just wanted to show you. Wringing wet." He held out a knitted Balaklava helmet.

"Well, don't wring it out here," she said.

"I just wanted to show you," he said.

"And you ought to get those shoes off," she said.

"My feet are dry. These shoes held up. A very good buy, although I didn't think so at the time. I paid fifteen dollars for them in 1917. That was when we wore shoes with leather puttees. Then we all had to get boots, before we were shipped overseas. Thirty-five, the boots were. They lasted me most of the time in France, then after the armistice I got a new pair to come home in. Sitting in the attic. If I knew somebody that rode horseback I'd give them away."

"Give them to Jimmy Malloy," she said.

"He has a pair, and anyway I don't think my boots would fit him."

"Well, then keep them. You wear them on Decoration Day."

"I didn't wear them last Decoration Day. I didn't go in the parade. Who are you writing to?"

"Aunt Fran. I'm trying to tell her we won't have room for her this Christmas. Take that wet cap out in the kitchen and wring it out. And maybe throw it away."

"You knitted it for me."

"I know I did."

"I get a lot of use out of it. Skating. Gunning."

Saturday Evening Post (19 September 1964); *The Horse Knows the Way*

"All right, don't throw it away. But please don't have it dripping all over my rugs. And go on upstairs and dry your hair, or you'll catch more cold."

"I'll dry my hair on the roller towel."

"All right, do as you please," she said.

"And I'm going to have a shot. Do you want one?"

"No thanks. I have to finish this letter," she said.

"A good slug of whiskey might inspire you."

"It might inspire me to tell Aunt Fran to go some place else for a change. Why does she always have to come here?"

"She doesn't have to. Why do I go to a high school football game, in rain and snow and mud?"

"Search me. Look at your trousers. They're soaking wet. I think you'd better go on upstairs and take off everything."

"I will if you will," he said.

"Oh, stop that kind of talk on a Saturday afternoon. It isn't becoming."

"I wasn't in earnest, for cripes' sake," he said.

"Get some dry clothes on and then maybe I'll have a highball. I got some ginger ale yesterday. It's in the pantry next to the preserves. The shelf on your right. You know what you ought to do is take a hot bath."

"Hell, I used to sleep in places that were worse than that field."

"Yes, but you haven't lately and you're seven years older. Go on, act sensibly and let me finish this darn letter."

She could hear him running a tub and moving about, and she went on with her letter to her aunt. She forgot about him until he reappeared, wearing white flannels, a crimson sweater with a white letter G, and a pair of sneakers. He handed her a highball. "You look like a cheerleader," she said.

"I couldn't button the top button of my white flannels, but everything else fits me."

"The sweater fits you quick," she said.

"A little quick, but I can still get it on."

"It's not the same sweater you had in high school, is it?"

"No. They used to give us coat-style sweaters."

"That's what I thought."

"I bought this one myself. Six bucks."

"When you were coaching. I remember."

"Coaching the backfield." He sat down and stretched his legs. "You finish your letter?"

"Finally," she said. "Do you want me to read it to you?"

"To correct your grammar?"

"Oh, when *you* can correct *my* grammar. No, to get our stories straight. 'Dear Aunt Fran. I am writing you this far ahead in order to make it possible for you to alter your plans in case you were planning to visit us this coming Christmas. As you know, we would always love to have you over the holidays but this year both children have invited school friends to visit them. Junior is bringing a boy from Seattle, Washington, who will not be able to go to his own home for the holidays and Barbara is inviting a girl whose father and mother are missionaries in China and she does not expect to see her parents for two more years.' "

"That sounds as if Barbara didn't expect to see *her* parents for two more years."

"Shut up. It does not. 'Barbara is also having two other friends for the Christmas festivities, namely the club dance and the Assembly and another dance being given by Judge Choate's daughter Emily. Therefore we will have a houseful with two girls sleeping in the guest room.' "

"Is that true?"

"Well, Barbara asked me if we'd mind having this girl from Scranton that has a crush on Bobby Choate. He asked her to go to the Assembly and she has no place else to stay. And Emily Choate's dance is only two nights before. To continue. 'Bill and I hope you will be able to visit us later in the winter when things have quieted down and there is more room.' Then some stuff about the people she knows in town, and love from you and I, Mary. All right?"

"Well, I hope so. We don't want her to cut you out of her will."

"She can't. Grandpa established a trust fund, and when she dies the principal goes to me."

"I know that. But she never spends any more than she has to and she must have saved some out of the income."

"I'm not worried about that," said Mary. "It's just that I don't want to hurt her feelings."

"Yes, and I guess it can get pretty lonely around Christmas, an old maid living in a hotel. But she has your other sisters to invite herself to."

"She never has, though. She's always come here. And I will say I was glad to have her when you were away in the army. A grown person. Those two Christmases you were away, the children were just the wrong age. I couldn't let them see I was miserable. They were so proud to have their father a captain, and at that age they got used to having you away. But if I would have shown any signs of how I felt, they would have started feeling sorry for themselves, too. So I was glad to have Aunt Fran to talk to. And cry a little."

"Then for cripes' sake let's have her," he said. "We can put cots in the attic, or something."

"No. We can't. I've made up my mind. I'm very fond of Aunt Fran and all that. But now it's the children's turn. You can't go on all your life doing things for the older people. The time has to come when you must start giving preference to the younger ones. Aunt Fran's had her life, but Barbara and Junior are just starting out. I may sound heartless and cruel, but if Aunt Fran has to spend Christmas in a hotel, that's not our fault. It isn't, Bill. She could have made more of her life. She always had enough money to live nicely and do what she wanted, and I'm not going to let sentiment spoil our children's Christmas."

"No, I can see you're not," he said.

"Well, whose side are you on, anyway?"

"I don't know. She may not be around much longer. In her late sixties. And the kids have all the time in the world ahead of them."

"No, this is the time when they store up memories, and the parties this Christmas are going to be the best this town ever had."

"You and I didn't have a country club to go to."

"No, and more's the pity. My parents wouldn't allow me to go to the Assembly till I was twenty. Chicken-and-waffle suppers. Sleigh rides. Picnics. Heavily chaperoned."

"But we got married, Mary. And I like those memories, even if you don't seem to."

"Don't twist what I say. I like those memories, too, but our children will have different ones. And I'm not going to let Aunt Fran deprive them of them."

"All right. No use getting all het up about it. Let's forget Aunt Fran." He sipped his highball and lit a cigarette. The telephone rang. "I'll get it," he said, and went out to the desk in the hall.

She heard him say, "Oh, hello, Joe," and thereafter she paid no attention. He was on the telephone about five minutes.

"That was Joe McGonigle. He promised to call me. Guess what happened. You won't believe it. You know when I left, the score was eighteen to six, favor of G.H.S. Well, then they fumbled and Reading recovered for their second touchdown, making it eighteen to twelve. Reading kicked the extra point. Gibbsville then received and I'll be damned if they didn't fumble again. You know, wet ball, a day like this. And Reading recovered and went for a touchdown in two plays. Maybe he said three plays. Joe's still so excited he can hardly talk. That made it Reading nineteen, Gibbsville eighteen. Then Reading made that extra point and it was Reading twenty, Gibbsville eighteen. Well then do you know what happened? Gibbsville returned the kickoff to Reading's thirty-yard line, a hell of a run by young Dvorshak on that sloppy field. Then with about two and a half minutes left to play, Dvorshak kicked a field goal from the forty-yard line, and it was Gibbsville twenty-one, Reading twenty. Why didn't I stay? You know Dvorshak's that kid that when I was coaching the backfield, I taught his older brother how to dropkick, and his brother taught him. But forty yards on that sloppy field, and the ball must have weighed ten pounds. *I'm* going to have another drink. How about you?"

"Yes, I'll have another," she said.

"He's a fine kid, too, this Dvorshak. I wouldn't be surprised if he went to Notre Dame. There's a whole family of them. Five brothers. One went to Fordham. One to Villanova. One to the University of Maryland, and one to Pitt. The one I coached went to Fordham. But I think this one is headed for Notre Dame."

"Have you got any stamps in your wallet?" she said.

"Yes," he said. "You want me to get you one?"

"Please," she said. "No hurry."

All Tied Up

One day Miles Updegrove, who did not ordinarily notice such things, noticed that Earl Appel came to work in a pair of loafers. They were not twenty-five-dollar loafers, they did not have tassels, they were not even polished. They were exactly the same kind of loafers that Miles Updegrove wore around the house on Saturdays, when he did the chores that piled up during the week. They were Miles Updegrove's version of the canvas sneakers his father had worn when he did his chores around the same house. Seth Updegrove would never have worn his sneakers to the bank; Miles would never wear his loafers to the bank; and he did not like to see Earl Appel come to work in loafers any more than he would have liked Earl to appear at the bank without a necktie. True, Earl's shoes did not show from his post behind the counter. Also it was possible that Earl was having his regular shoes repaired, and the loafers were a substitute. Miles, moreover, was a man who believed in keeping his distance from the members of the bank staff, and to speak to Earl Appel about shoes would be a violation of his own rule. Nevertheless when Miles Updegrove attended the next Monday meeting of the directors he made a point of checking on Earl Appel's footwear, and, as he feared, Earl was again wearing the loafers. A week later, again after the directors' meeting, Miles Updegrove was disturbed to see that loafers apparently were Earl Appel's regular shoes. They may have been polished once since Miles first noticed them, but they still looked out of place in a bank.

Miles thought of preparing a memorandum to the bank staff. In 1955 a memorandum to the male members of the staff had taken care of a problem of a somewhat similar nature. "It has been called to our attention," Miles then wrote, "that certain of our staff have recently been afflicted with attacks of 'five o'clock shadow,' a malady that in these days of a growing percentage of women customers does not add to the tidiness or prestige of The Bank. Upon inquiry we have learned that in order to achieve punctuality in the morning, several of our staff have formed the habit of shaving the night before, no doubt a continuation of a custom originating during army or navy service. It is our earnest hope that the habit will now be discontinued as several complaints have been received." The memo was signed "M.B.U., President, For the Board of Directors," and Miles took some pride in it because it combined firmness with a light touch, and it was completely successful. The offending night-before shavers—two others besides Earl Appel—obeyed the directive, and there never again was a complaint against five o'clock shadow.

This, however, was a different situation. (Actually, of course, there had been no complaints by women customers on the score of unshaven tellers. That had been an inspired detail that happened to coincide with a then current campaign to attract women's savings accounts. It was Miles Updegrove who noticed that the younger men's beards were heavier than the middle-aged men's in the late afternoon.) Earl Appel had almost no occasion in the course of his work to come from behind his counter and let the customers see that he wore loafers. It was not a problem that could be handled as the beard problem had been. Earl Appel was the only man who wore loafers to work, and a memorandum to the staff would be too pointedly directed at him. And yet something had to be done, or said, for although it was true that Earl Appel did not often have business on the public side of the counter, he did walk to work every morning, he did have lunch every noonday at the Y.M.C.A. cafeteria, and he did walk home every afternoon. In other words, he was seen, and everyone knew he was an employee of the bank.

"It gives such a bad impression," said Miles Updegrove, one evening at home. "A man too lazy to lace his shoes in the morning."

"Speak to him about it," said Edna Updegrove.

"When? I only go there twice a week, regularly."

"But you're president of the bank," said Edna. "What's to stop you going in any time you feel like it?"

"You don't understand, Edna. My father always told me, he said the cashier is the one to handle the personnel relations. Pop didn't say personnel relations, and now we call the cashier the manager, but that was the general idea."

"Then have a talk with Fred Schartle. Tell *him.*"

"I thought of that already, but if I say something to Fred he's going to get touchy. He'll take it like it was a criticism of his personnel relations. You know. Him not noticing it that Earl Appel comes to work every day wearing sport shoes. A person has to be very careful with Fred. You won't find a better manager of our size bank in the State of Pennsylvania. Absolutely as reliable, sound, as they come. But don't criticize."

"You don't have to be afraid of Fred Schartle. The other way around, would be my guess," said Edna Updegrove.

"Oh, I guess I'm not afraid of Fred Schartle. I guess nobody would think that. However, though, he's apt to be very sensitive if somebody trespasses on his territory. That time when we talked about voting a bonus for Clara Slaymaker. Remember Clara suggesting some little gift for new women customers?"

"Well, I don't remember, but go ahead."

"Yes, Clara suggested some feminine trinket or other. To go with every new savings account of ten dollars or over?"

"No, I guess I forgot about that," said Edna.

"Well, anyhow we put the ad in the *County News* and we got about forty-five new women customers, all told."

"What was the prize, I wonder," said Edna.

"Some kind of a plastic something or other. They ran us under two dollars each wholesale. I gave you one."

"Oh! Those picnic sets. I remember. They weren't much good if you left them out in the hot sun. Not that I blame Clara for that. I think they were made in Japan. I'm almost positive."

"What difference does it make where they came from, or what they were?" said Miles Updegrove.

"Excuse me, but you don't have to ask the whole neighborhood," said his wife.

"Well, you get me sidetracked on things that don't matter," he said. "I was trying to tell you about Clara Slaymaker and Fred Schartle, how touchy he is."

"Go right ahead."

"I will," said Miles Updegrove. "So at this meeting somebody had the idea that we vote a special bonus for Clara. Not anything big. In the neighborhood of fifty dollars, or maybe a week's pay. Fifty dollars, as I remember it, because it wasn't even a week's pay. Clara gets seventy-five, now, but I think she was only getting seventy then."

"Goodness, I didn't know she got that much. That's what my father got when he was superintendent of schools. Three hundred a month."

"Yes, but how long ago was that? Earl Appel gets a hundred and a quarter, plus the Christmas bonus. You ought to see our salary list. It would hand you a few more surprises. Very few years Fred Schartle doesn't make over ten thousand, *with* the yearly bonus, that is. But he was dead set against a special bonus for Clara. Nothing personal against Clara. But he didn't want us to be the ones that recommended a bonus for individual members of the staff. That kind of recognition should come from him, was his argument. They were his people, and he was supposed to know more about them than the directors did. Well, he was right, Fred. Maybe Clara did suggest the picnic sets for new women customers, but if that entitled her to a fifty-dollar bonus, then others were entitled to as much or more. Like it was Earl Appel that probably saved us a heck of a lot of money when he heard we were considering a branch bank out on Northampton Turnpike, the old Northampton Turnpike near the Zellerbach farm. We thought it'd be a good place for a branch, there at the intersection of the Northampton Turnpike and the Lehighton Road. But according to Fred, he was told by Earl Appel that some big outfit from Philadelphia were thinking of putting up a huge supermarket about a mile or so down the Turnpike. How Earl found that out, I don't know, but he was right. In other words, if we'd of gone ahead and put a branch bank at the Lehighton intersection, we'd of been a mile away from where the business was. Out in the cold, so to speak."

"Yes, I can see how that would be," she said.

"So if we were handing out special bonuses, Earl Appel was more entitled than Clara Slaymaker."

"I should think so," she said.

"With that information most people would have bought some land in the neighborhood, but Earl was either not smart enough or more likely carrying a debt load that was as much as he could carry. We don't like our people to go beyond a certain limit. It varies with different individuals, but our policy is a bank employee shouldn't obligate himself to more than one third of his weekly pay. And Earl Appel is always pretty close to that figure."

"How do you know?" she said.

"How do we *know?* Listen, if somebody like Earl Appel runs up a bill or buys anything on time, it's Fred Schartle's *business* to know. He watches them like a hawk. We never fire anybody if we can help it. It isn't good for the bank to have it get around that we fired somebody."

"You mean good for the person," she said.

"For him either, but it isn't good for the bank. People always want to know why So-and-so was fired, and nine times out of ten they don't believe the explanation. That's why we have to keep people on when we'd just as soon let them go. We give them a strong hint to quit, go look for another job. But firing them is another matter entirely."

"Well, now," she said. "Are you thinking of firing Earl?"

"Did I say that? No, I certainly did not."

"No, but that's what you inferred," she said.

"That's what *you* inferred. You can never get that straight about inferred and implied, as long as I've been married to you."

"All right. Hinted at. I think you want to fire Earl," she said.

"Well, to tell you the God's honest truth, I wish he'd resign. I don't like a man that's too darn lazy to lace his shoes in the morning."

"Well, in fairness, if it's gone that far you're duty bound to say something to Fred," she said. "Did Fred make any money on the supermarket thing?"

"Good heavens, no. That would have been a real estate speculation, one of the things we're most against."

"Then Earl's entitled to some credit for not speculating," she said. "What have you got against Earl, in addition to coming to work in sport shoes?"

"To be honest with you, I don't know. I wouldn't like to think it was anything personal. He's been with us now nine years in September, ever since he got out of the army. The Appels are all fine people."

"Except for Dewey, the one that married my cousin Ruth Biltzer. I couldn't say much for him. But he was only distantly related to Earl."

"About a third or fourth cousin," said Miles Updegrove. "Dewey was supposed to be shell-shocked from World War One. That's what they said. But I can remember from when I was little, before World War One, Dewey Appel drove the ice wagon for Noah Klinger, and they used to say you could get a cheap drunk on just from his breath. But Dewey was only a third or fourth cousin of Charley Appel, Earl's father."

"Hung himself, finally," said Edna Updegrove.

"No, you're thinking of Sam Klinger. Dewey Appel shot himself. Sam Klinger was Noah's brother, the hunchback, and *he* hung himself. But Dewey Appel shot himself with a .22 rifle."

"You're right. I was thinking of Sam Klinger. Goodness, do you remember that?" She put down her mending and looked back in her memories. "When I was going to First Street school, little Sam Klinger used to scare the life out of us. He was always there in the afternoon when school let out, and all our parents told us to never go anywhere with him. The boys used to throw stones at him. Yes, he hung himself, and Dewey shot himself. That was it. I guess I was going to High then."

"No, you were away at Normal, and I was still going to Muhlenberg, a junior or a senior, but I heard about it."

"That's right. I had a letter from Mom."

"Soozenserp," said Miles Updegrove.

"What?"

"That was the saying. He committed soozenserp. Anybody that hung himself, they used to say he committed soozenserp. I guess it was slang."

"Good grief! I haven't heard anybody use that expression since I was ten years old. How did you happen to think of it?"

"I don't know."

"Soozenserp," she said. "High German?"

"I doubt it. *Süssen* means sweeten in High German, but that wouldn't have anything to do with suicide. Sweet syrup? I don't know. Maybe it had something to do with taking poison. But I can remember we kids saying somebody committed soozenserp, whether it was poison or like Sam Klinger or Dewey Appel."

"If Pop was still alive, he'd know. He collected all those odd sayings."

"Yes, some of them pretty odd for a school superintendent to collect, I'll say that much."

"That was because when he retired he wanted to work on his Pennsylvania Dutch dictionary."

"It would have got him locked up if he put in some of those expressions."

"Oh, it was just an ambition of his," she said. "Mom threw all those notes in the stove, a couple of desk drawers-full. Pop's penmanship was terrible, for a schoolteacher. You could hardly decipher it. You never would have thought he had so much education. My, my. When you think of all that education. Even my cousin Ruth Biltzer graduated from Normal, and a lot of good it did her, married to Dewey Appel. A few dollars once in a while, substituting at First Street school, but he took it away from her to buy drink. Look at me. I had the equivalent of two years in college, but I don't know anything."

"What are you supposed to know?"

"What am I supposed to know?" she said.

"Yes. I'm a college graduate, with a bachelor of arts degree, but I make my money digging cement. I don't need a college degree for that. Pop didn't have a college degree, not even a high school diploma, but look how much he made."

"That's just what I'm saying," she said. "I got my certificate from Normal, but I never made any use of it."

"That's because you married young."

"And a man that was well off. But if you wouldn't have been well off I would of got a job teaching, and there would of been an altogether different story."

"I don't understand what you're arguing about," he said.

"I don't either. *Yes* I do. I was thinking my education went to waste, and how my father scrimped and saved to put us through school. My mother would think it was sinful, the money we spend. That trip to California. Twenty-five dollars a day for a room in a hotel. Just the room, no board."

"It'd be twice that now. But it's our money, and we didn't go in debt to pay for it. Now they don't think twice about going in debt for things. That's why we have the personal loan department at the bank. The big money-maker out at the Turnpike branch is the personal loan department, all those young couples."

"Thanks to Earl Appel," she said.

"How, thanks to Earl Appel? Oh, because he steered us away from the Zellerbach farm. Well, yes."

"Did you ever thank him for that?"

"Me personally? No, I just got through telling you, those are the things that Fred considers his territory."

"Did Fred thank him?" she said.

"Sure he did. I wasn't there, but I'm sure Fred Schartle wouldn't just take the information without saying thank-you for it."

"But no bonus," said Edna Updegrove.

"Why should he get a bonus for a thing like that? Earl works for the bank, doesn't he? Don't we pay him his salary every week? If the bank lost a lot of money on a bad location, Earl wouldn't get his bonus at the end of the year."

"Oh, he got a bonus at the end of the year?" she said.

"All employees of the bank get a bonus at the end of the year, if we vote one. But we couldn't vote one if we had a bad year. The bonuses come out of profits, don't forget."

"Oh, out of profits, eh? I see," she said.

"You don't see, but I'd be surprised if you did. Women never take the trouble to understand about banking."

"Clara Slaymaker does," said Edna Updegrove.

"No. She's pretty dumb. When she retires we won't replace her. All she ever knew was bookkeeping, and we got machines for that now. We could run the bank on half the number of employees we have now."

"Then why do you keep her?" she said.

"Because she and Walter Fertig are the last ones left that my father hired. If it wasn't for that they'd have been let go when we put in the new equipment. Sentiment. If it was me, I would of let them go, but Pop said take care of Clara and Walter, and I said I would. But I don't have any sentiment where certain others are concerned."

"Meaning Earl Appel," she said.

"Meaning anybody that don't have enough respect for their job to come to work in moccasins. I never had to tell Walter Fertig to put on shoes, or shave in the morning. It makes my blood boil."

"Yes," she said. "Well, then you better find some way to get rid of him."

In the succeeding two or three months, on his twice weekly visits to the bank, Miles Updegrove was aware of his mounting antagonism toward Earl Appel, but considerably less aware of the fact that it showed. Although he left personnel problems to Fred Schartle, it had always been his custom upon visiting the bank to stop and say hello to Walter Fertig and Clara Slaymaker, and while so doing to greet by their first names the other members of the staff. "All they want is for you to say hyuh to them," his father had once remarked. "But that much they do want." Miles did not realize that his growing dislike of Earl Appel was compelling him to abandon a habit that was almost a tradition, and when the fact was called to his attention he was disturbed. It was Fred Schartle who mentioned it.

"There's one other thing I've been meaning to ask you, Miles," Fred said one Friday afternoon.

"Why sure, what's that?" said Miles.

"It's kind of hard to bring it up."

Miles Updegrove smiled. "Only one thing could be that hard," he said. "You want to borrow some money. How much, and what for?"

"It isn't money, though," said Fred. "Money-wise, I'm contented. But one of our fellows, Earl Appel, came to me a week or two ago and said something that I thought he must be getting what they call a persecution complex."

"Who's persecuting Earl?"

"Well, now don't get me wrong, Miles. But what it comes down to is he thinks you are. Not persecuting him, but that you don't like him. He said you stopped speaking to him, but you speak to everybody else."

"As far as I know, I speak to everybody every time I come in the bank. If I see them. I can't speak to those I don't happen to see, but as far as I know . . ."

Fred Schartle hesitated.

"What is it, Fred? Come on, say it."

Fred Schartle shook his head. "Then I guess it's unconscious," he said.

"What is?"

"Well, since Earl mentioned it to me, I noticed every time you came in you always talk to everybody but him. A couple times you walked right past him. Once he even held the gate open for you and you didn't say anything to him. The gate that—"

"I know where the gate is. I could find my way around this place blindfolded," said Miles Updegrove. "I didn't know I was supposed to do a curtsey when somebody held the gate open for me. I often hold the gate open for this one and that one, depending on if I get there first. But I don't remember anybody telling me I was a nice fellow for that. That's a thing you do, whether you're president of the bank or a junior like young Bob Holtz, just starting out in the business."

"Well, it isn't only holding the gate open," said Fred Schartle. "It's when there's three or four staff people gathered together and you say hello to all but one. And if it's the same one several times, I feel it my duty to all concerned to inquire if there's any particular reason."

"Fred," said Miles Updegrove. "I hired you, and then I promoted you over some that had seniority on you. I was saying to Edna a little while ago, there isn't a better manager of our size bank in the entire State of Pennsylvania. I honestly believe that, and I'm as proud of your fine record as anything I ever did for the bank. But when you come to me with some story about a bank employee having a persecution complex, then I have to remind you, Fred, you're not perfect. Nobody's perfect. Not even you, Fred."

"I never—"

"Just let me finish what I have to say, *please.* That expression you used, persecution complex, I know where it comes from. It comes from nowadays I understand certain big banks in Philadelphia and I'm sure New York—New York, I'm *sure.* They employ full-time psychiatrists, and every time John Smith makes some mistake they send him to the doctor for a mental checkup. Maybe he's sneaking a couple drinks in the lunch hour, or has designs on some young woman in the filing department. I was out to Denver a few years ago and heard all about how some of those big banks have these so-called head-shrinkers. Oh, I know what they call them, and head-shrinkers is a good name for them. The bankers' convention in Denver. I was sitting next to another country banker like myself, and he said to me, 'Mr. Updegrove, I'm beginning to think we're in the wrong business.' He said we ought to turn our banks over to the head-shrinkers, if we can't fire a man that's undependable. Stop this wet-nursing of undependable young fellows before the whole banking structure falls into a state of collapse. And I'll tell you quite frankly, Fred, I don't take to it when a good reliable manager like yourself talks to me about persecution complexes. I've always backed you to the hilt, even when I didn't entirely agree with you. Personnel problems are your territory, and I won't touch them. But when you graduated from Temple University they didn't give you an M.D. degree. You were trained in commerce and finance, and if Earl Appel needs help along those lines, mental, then maybe I can speak to the board, or *you* can, and we'll see what we can do. Maybe a leave of absence. Maybe we'll just have to let him go. I don't know, Fred. I honestly don't know. And that's all I have to say for the present."

"For God's sake," said Fred Schartle.

"Hmm?"

"For Christ's sweet sake," said Fred.

"Now, Fred. Remember who you're talking to."

"Remember? I don't have to remember."

"Oh, yes you do," said Miles Updegrove. "You're on the verge of saying some things you may regret a long, long time—"

"But I'm quitting. I resign," said Fred.

"That's one of them. But be careful what else you say. Because regardless of what you want to get off your chest, I'm the one that will have the last say, Fred. Remember that. And you damn sure better remember it. You're not going to walk out of here and into as good a job as this, just like that. You may be out of work for quite a long while. I know I wouldn't hire a manager that wanted to turn my bank into a mental institution. You go home and talk to your wife, and I'll be here Monday as usual."

"You think you have me all tied up."

"Well, haven't I? The bank holds your paper. The question is, Fred, when I think it over am I going to *want* to have you all tied up? I don't fly off the handle as quick as some, but don't go too far with me. Goodnight."

Miles Updegrove drove home and had his usual two ounces of whiskey and listened to Edna through dinner. The Philomatheans, her old literary society at Normal, were having a get-together dinner in the spring. "What do they want to have a dinner for? The Philos went out of existence back there in the Thirties somewhere. You never go to your A.T.O. dinners, so I don't see why I should go to this. Still, it's kind of nice to have them go to all this trouble. And I have my pin yet. We were all Philos. My father, two sisters, and me. All Philos. Oh, how we hated those Keystones. They were full of

Catholics, the Keystones. A Catholic couldn't get into Philo when I was there. I wouldn't let a fellow carry my books if he was a Keystone. Paul O'Brien. No, *Phil* O'Brien. That doesn't sound right, either. He was from the coal regions. It *was* Paul. I understand he was a judge later. Me refusing to let a judge carry my books because he was a dirty Keystone. But a Catholic, too. Now I don't hardly mind them at all. I just found out those Bradleys are Catholic, and they've been here almost a year."

"What Bradleys?" he said.

"Out past the country club, on Heiser's Creek Road. He's some electrical engineer."

"Oh, that Bradley. No, he's with the light company but he's not an engineer. Assistant district manager. They won't be here long. Five years and they get transferred. A friend of Fred Schartle's, and *he* won't be around here much longer either."

"Oh, for goodness' sake, Miles. I knew there was something worr'ing you. Some other bank stealing Fred away from you. More money, eh?"

"Nothing of the kind," said Miles Updegrove. "My mind isn't made up for sure, but I don't know why I should keep him."

"You mean you're firing him, Fred Schartle? When was it—last summer you said you never fired anybody. It must be serious, a man you had such confidence in. It isn't—you didn't catch him in some kind of a shortage, I hope."

"Not a shortage of money. Although I'll have a look at his figures before I let him go. No, as far as I know now, he's clean. But I just found out that Fred Schartle considers himself an amateur headshrinker. That's slang for psychiatrist."

"Fred Schartle?"

"All this time I gave him a free hand with the employees, his idea of how to handle them was to see if they had a persecution complex. Well, are we running a bank or a mental institution? If Fred wants to run a mental institution, that's his privilege, but—"

"Somebody at the front door? Who would that be at this hour?" said Edna Updegrove. "Sit still, I'll go." She went to answer the doorbell. He remained at the dinner table, straining to recognize the voice of the visitor but unwilling to make an appearance. The first intelligible words he heard were Edna's. "You don't want to talk to me, Dorothy. You better save it for Mister. We're just finishing our dessert." Dorothy was the first name of Fred Schartle's wife. Miles got up and went to the front room.

"Good evening, Dorothy," he said.

"Oh, Mr. Updegrove? What did he *say* to you? He came home

around seven with some wild story. All I can get out of him was that he—"

"I'll leave you two be," said Edna Updegrove, and left them.

"Sit down, Dorothy. Have a cigarette if you wish to. Would you care for a cup of coffee? We were just having some."

"Nothing, thank you, Mr. Updegrove. He was like a wild man. I never saw him act like that before."

"Did he have anything to drink?" said Miles Updegrove.

"Yes, I'm sure he did. He wasn't staggering or anything, but he was an hour late, and I guess he had one or two. Yes, he did. Not when he came home, but before. But, oh, please tell me what he said. All I could get out of him was you and he had some kind of an argument."

"I'm sorry you had to be subjected to this, Dorothy," said Miles. "Yes, Fred and I were having a discussion about bank matters, and then all of a sudden out of a clear sky he started abusing me. Using strong language and making personal remarks that I couldn't tolerate."

"*Did* he quit? *Did* he resign?"

"Yes, he did," said Miles Updegrove.

"Oh, God," she said. Her hands dropped from the arm of her chair and the weight of them seemed to cause her torso to crumple. For the moment she had nothing to say.

"Can I get you a drink of something?"

"Water? Could I have a glass of water?"

He called to his wife. "Edna, would you bring us a glass of water for Dorothy?"

The woman opened her handbag and took out a pack of cigarettes. "I think I *will* have a cigarette," she said.

"Yes, have one," he said.

"Would you care for one?" she said.

"No thanks," he said. "I never use them. A pipe is all I ever smoke. Sometimes a cigar."

"Here we are," said Edna Updegrove, with a glass of water. "Is there something else I can get you? A cup of coffee?"

"No thank you. I just—my throat felt dry."

"Of course. Now if you want anything else, just call. I'll be in the kitchen, so call loud in case the dishwasher's going." Edna Updegrove departed.

"She's such a wonderful person, Mrs. Updegrove. So well liked all over town," said Dorothy Schartle. She sipped the water. "I'm all right now. My throat got suddenly dry."

"Yes," said Miles. "Well, I don't know what else I can tell you, Dorothy."

"What did he say when he resigned? Why? What reason did he give you?"

"Reason? Oh, he didn't give any reason. He took exception to certain things I said about personnel matters. I guess that was it. But there was no call for him to fly off the handle that way. Frankly, I left the bank before he could say a lot worse."

"It's so unlike him," said Dorothy Schartle.

"Yes, I guess it is. In fact, I just finished paying him a compliment a few seconds before he started in on me. That's why it's so hard to understand. But maybe you can explain it."

"How?"

"Well, I don't want to pry into anybody's personal affairs, but being's you came here, and you're naturally worried about him— have you noticed anything unusual about Fred lately?"

"No, I haven't," said Dorothy Schartle.

"Nothing worrying him? How is he sleeping?"

"Well, I guess he could use more sleep. He wakes up pretty early. Daylight, most of the time. They say you don't need as much sleep as you get older, but Fred's only forty-three."

"I always got my seven or eight hours when I was that age, but we're all different, I guess."

"He wakes up around six o'clock and goes down and has a cup of coffee. He drinks a lot of coffee, that I will say."

"Too much coffee isn't good for you. He has a cup of coffee at six A.M. And then I guess you give him his breakfast."

"Yes, with the children. He likes to have breakfast with the children before they're off to school. He usually walks to the corner with Phyllis, our youngest. She takes a different bus than the other children. The older two take the high school bus. Then he comes back to the house and gets the car."

"So I guess he has one or two cups of coffee at breakfast—"

"Two, as a rule," she said.

"And I know he always takes another cup at coffee break, at the bank."

"Yes, and at lunch," she said. "Do you think it's the coffee?"

"Oh, I wouldn't say. It may be something else entirely."

"Not that I know of," she said.

"What does he do for recreation?"

"Well, he has his carpentry. He has all these drills and lathes and all. Woodwork, you know. He just got finished making a birthday present for Earl Appel. A cigarette box."

"Earl Appel? I didn't know they were such friends."

"Well, not very close, but Earl has the same hobby. Woodwork. It's a sort of a rivalry, you might say. Last year Earl made Fred a stand for an ash tray. We have it in the family room. Earl does more complicated things than Fred."

"Is that so?"

"Oh, yes. Earl built all the cabinetwork for the Appels' hi-fi."

"Uh-huh."

"Earl got Fred innarested, in the first place."

"What else does he do, for pastime?"

"Fred? He takes walks."

"He and Earl Appel?"

"No, no. Sometimes with the children, sometimes by himself. On Sundays he usually gets up around ha' past seven and goes for a walk."

"Do the children get up that early on Sunday morning?"

"No, Sunday mornings he goes by himself. He goes up over Schiller's Mountain and down the other side and home by way of the county road."

"That's a good ten-mile walk," said Miles Updegrove. "Nobody with him, huh?"

"No, all by himself. He likes to be by himself," she said. "He says he sees plenty of people during the week."

"And doing this woodwork he's by himself, too, I guess."

"Oh, yes. I used to sit there with him, but the saws and the lathes make such a noise. I can feel it in my teeth. Not that he doesn't like to be with the children and I."

"But he has these times when he likes to be alone," said Miles.

"Yes," she said.

"How is his temper when he's home?"

"Well—he's very strict with the children."

"How is he with you, Dorothy? If you don't mind that question."

"Well, we've been married now almost twenty-one years. I guess we're just like any other married couple. You take the good with the bad."

"But you're satisfied the way things turned out," he said.

"Why, yes, of course. Except like tonight, my goodness. When a thing like that happens, I don't know what comes over him."

"A thing like that? What else was there like that?"

"Oh, when he loses his temper over something. But that's personal."

"And then he likes to be by himself," he said.

"He's not the only one. I want to be by myself, too," she said. "Mr.

Updegrove, what's going to happen? We have our home isn't paid for yet, and our eldest daughter wants to take a course in textile design. The boy wants to go to the Air Force Academy. That's free, I guess, but nothing will be coming in. We have some saved up, but we don't want to touch that."

"I don't know, Dorothy. Fred was very positive."

"Where does he get any right to be positive?" Now she began to cry, and only words, not sentences, were intelligible among her mutterings. Such words as ". . . positive . . . right . . . children . . . me . . . nice home . . . selfish . . . whole life . . ."

"Maybe I ought to get Mrs. Updegrove to come in," said Miles.

"No, no! Please don't. I don't want her to see me like this," said Dorothy Schartle. "I'll be all right." She stopped crying.

"I don't know what to suggest, Dorothy," said Miles Updegrove. "I told him I'd see him Monday, but naturally you can't expect me to have much to say. He just as good as threw his job in my face, and nobody's indispensable these days."

"But I know him, Mr. Updegrove," said Dorothy. "I know what he'll do. He'll go for one of his walks tomorrow afternoon—"

"Did he say anything about coming in tomorrow?"

She hesitated. "I'll be truthful with you. He's drunk. He won't be in tomorrow. He can't take more than two drinks and never could. He'll be sick all night and tomorrow he'll be no good for work. No, he won't be in."

"Saturday morning. One of our busiest days. But I guess it's better if he doesn't come in, for his sake as well as the bank's."

"Let me talk to him. He wouldn't listen to me tonight, but I know how he'll be tomorrow and Sunday. If I talk to him will you let him come and see you, Mr. Updegrove? Please?"

"I told him I'd see—"

"Not Monday. Sunday. Here. I know how to handle him, Mr. Updegrove. I really do."

"Maybe you do, but I don't."

"You won't have to when I get through talking to him. Just let him come here and apologize, and tell him you're willing to forget about the resignation. You're a *good* man, Mr. Updegrove. You'll do that, please? It takes a big man, and you're that."

"An apology won't mean much without good intentions behind it," said Miles Updegrove.

"I promise you, Fred Schartle will never give you the slightest trouble, ever again. I'll say the same thing to you that I'll say to him. If he ever causes any more trouble, I'll leave him. I'll go back to my parents in Quakertown, and the children with me."

Miles Updegrove tapped his fingers on his knee. "Well, if you're so sure that it will do any good—all right. He can come in Sunday after church. And if I'm convinced—"

"You will be! You will be! I promise you. And I'll never forget this as long as I live. I'll never stop thanking you."

"Well, let's wait and see what happens Sunday," said Miles. He put on a smile. "But I have a feeling that Mrs. Fred Schartle has a great deal of influence over Mr. Fred Schartle. The hand that rocks the cradle rules the world, they say."

Dorothy Schartle rose. "Thank you very much. Will you tell Mrs. goodnight for me? I don't want her to see my eyes all red."

"You run right along, young lady. I'll say goodnight for you, and see you to the door," said Miles Updegrove.

He stood in the vestibule until Dorothy's car moved out of the driveway. He turned off the porch light and went back to the kitchen. "Well, how much could you hear?"

"Hardly anything, from back here," said Edna Updegrove. "But she was in a state, I could see that."

"Yes. Well, the upshot is he's coming here Sunday noon, to apologize."

"Oh, Miles, we won't *be* here Sunday noon. We're going over to Amy's for the christening."

"I can't help that, Edna. This is bank business, and Amy isn't any relation."

"No, but it's her first granddaughter," said Edna. "Oh, well, you're just like your father. You and that bank."

"I want to see what this young fellow has to say for himself," said Miles Updegrove. "A great deal depends on that. Is there any more coffee?"

"I threw it out, but I could make some fresh."

"Never mind," he said.

Christmas Poem

Billy Warden had dinner with his father and mother and sister. "I suppose this is the last we'll see of you this vacation," said his father.

"Oh, I'll be in and out to change my shirt," said Billy.

"My, we're quick on the repartee," said Barbara Warden. "The gay young sophomore."

"What are *you*, Bobby dear? A drunken junior?" said Billy.

"Now, I don't think that was called for," said their mother.

"Decidedly *un*-called for," said their father. "What *are* your plans?"

"Well, I was hoping I could borrow the chariot," said Billy.

"Yes, we anticipated that," said his father. "What I meant was, are you planning to go away anywhere? Out of town?"

"Well, that depends. There's a dance in Reading on the twenty-seventh I'd like to go to, and I've been invited to go skiing in Montrose."

"Skiing? Can you ski?" said his mother.

"All Dartmouth boys ski, or pretend they can," said his sister.

"Isn't that dangerous? I suppose if you were a Canadian, but I've never known anyone to go skiing around here. I thought they had to have those big—I don't know—scaffolds, I guess you'd call them."

"You do, for jumping, Mother. But skiing isn't all jumping," said Billy.

"Oh, it isn't? I've only seen it done in the newsreels. I never really saw the point of it, although I suppose if you did it well it would be the same sensation as flying. I often dream about flying."

"I haven't done much jumping," said Billy.

"Then I take it you'll want to borrow the car on the twenty-seventh, and what about this trip to Montrose?" said his father.

"I don't exactly know where Montrose is," said Mrs. Warden.

"It's up beyond Scranton," said her husband. "That would mean taking the car overnight. I'm just trying to arrange some kind of a schedule. Your mother and I've been invited to one or two things, but I imagine we can ask our friends to take us there and bring us back. However, we only have the one car, and Bobby's entitled to her share."

"Of course she is. Of course I more or less counted on her to, uh, to spend most of her time in Mr. Roger Taylor's Dort."

"It isn't a Dort. It's a brand new Marmon, something I doubt you'll ever be able to afford."

"Something I doubt Roger'd ever be able to afford if it took any brains to afford one. So he got rid of the old Dort, did he?"

"He never had a Dort, and you know it," said Bobby.

"Must we be so disagreeable, the first night home?" said Mrs. Warden. "I know there's no meanness in it, but it doesn't *sound* nice."

"When would you be going to Montrose?" said Mr. Warden. "What date?"

"Well, if I go it would be a sort of a house party," said Billy.

"In other words, not just overnight?" said his father. "Very well, suppose you tell us how many nights?"

"I'm invited for the twenty-eighth, twenty-ninth, and thirtieth," said Billy. "That would get me back in time to go to the Assembly on New Year's Eve."

"What that amounts to, you realize, is having possession of the car from the twenty-seventh to the thirtieth or thirty-first," said his father.

"Yes, I realize that," said Billy.

"Do you still want it, to keep the car that long, all for yourself?" said his father.

"Well, I didn't have it much last summer, when I was working. And I save you a lot of money on repairs. I ground the valves, cleaned the spark plugs. A lot of things I did. I oiled and greased it myself."

"Yes, I have to admit you do your share of that," said his father. "But if you keep the car that long, out of town, it just means we are without a car for four days, at the least."

There was a silence.

"I really won't need the car very much after Christmas," said Bobby. "After I've done my shopping and delivered my presents."

"Thank you," said Billy.

"Well, of course not driving myself, I never use it," said Mrs. Warden.

"That puts it up to me," said Mr. Warden. "If I were Roger Taylor's father I'd give you two nice big Marmons for Christmas, but I'm not Mr. Taylor. Not by about seven hundred thousand dollars, from what I hear. Is there anyone else from around here that's going to Montrose?"

"No."

"Then it isn't one of your Dartmouth friends?" said Mr. Warden. "Who will you be visiting?"

"It's a girl named Henrietta Cooper. She goes to Russell Sage. I met her at Dartmouth, but that's all. I mean, she has no other connection with it."

"Russell Sage," said his mother. "We know somebody that has a daughter there. I know who it was. That couple we met at the Blakes'. Remember, the Blakes entertained for them last winter? The husband was with one of the big electrical companies."

"General Electric, in Schenectady," said Mr. Warden. "Montrose ought to be on the Lehigh Valley, or the Lackawanna, if I'm not mistaken."

"The train connections are very poor," said Billy. "If I don't go by car, Henrietta's going to meet me in Scranton, but heck, I don't want to ask her to do that. I'd rather not go if I have to take the train."

"Well, I guess we can get along without the car for that long. But your mother and I are positively going to have to have it New Year's Eve. We're going to the Assembly, too."

"Thank you very much," said Billy.

"It does seem strange. Reading one night, and then the next day you're off in the opposite direction. You'd better make sure the chains are in good condition. Going over those mountains this time of year."

"A house party. Now what will you do on a house party in Montrose? Besides ski, that is?" said Mrs. Warden. "It sounds like a big house, to accommodate a lot of young people."

"I guess it probably is," said Billy. "I know they have quite a few horses. Henny rides in the Horse Show at Madison Square Garden."

"Oh, my. Then they must be very well-to-do," said his mother. "I always wanted to ride when I was a girl. To me there's nothing prettier than a young woman in a black riding habit, riding side-saddle. Something so elegant about it."

"I wouldn't think she rode side-saddle, but maybe she does," said Billy.

"Did you say you wanted to use the car tonight, too?" said his father.

"If nobody else is going to," said Billy.

"Barbara?" said Mr. Warden.

"No. Roger is calling for me at nine o'clock," said Barbara. "But I would like it tomorrow, all day if possible. I have a ton of shopping to do."

"I *still* haven't finished wrapping all *my* presents," said Mrs. Warden.

"I haven't even *bought* half of mine," said Barbara.

"You shouldn't leave everything to the last minute," said her mother. "I bought most of mine at sales, as far back as last January. Things are much cheaper after Christmas."

"Well, I guess I'm off to the races," said Billy. "Dad, could you spare a little cash?"

"How much?" said Mr. Warden.

"Well—ten bucks?"

"I'll take it off your Christmas present," said Mr. Warden.

"Oh, no, don't do that. I have ten dollars if you'll reach me my purse. It's on the sideboard," said Mrs. Warden.

"You must be flush," said Mr. Warden.

"Well, no, but I don't like to see you take it off Billy's Christmas present. That's as bad as opening presents ahead of time," said Mrs. Warden.

"Which certain people in this house do every year," said Barbara.

"Who could she possibly mean?" said Billy. "I opened one present, because it came from Brooks Brothers and I thought it might be something I could wear right away."

"And was it?" said his mother.

"Yes. Some socks. These I have on, as a matter of fact," said Billy. "They're a little big, but they'll shrink."

"Very snappy," said Barbara.

"Yes, and I don't know who they came from. There was no card."

"I'll tell you who they were from. They were from me," said Barbara.

"They were? Well, thanks. Just what I wanted," said Billy.

"Just what you asked me for, last summer," said Barbara.

"Did I? I guess I did. Thank you for remembering. Well, goodnight, all. Don't wait up. I'll be home before breakfast."

They muttered their goodnights and he left. He wanted to—almost wanted to—stay; to tell his father that he did not want a Marmon for Christmas, which would have been a falsehood; to tell his mother he loved her in spite of her being a nitwit; to talk to Bobby about Roger Taylor, who was not good enough for her. But this was his first night home and he had his friends to see. Bobby had Roger, his father and mother had each other; thus far he had no one. But it did not detract from his feeling for his family that he now preferred the livelier company of his friends. *They* all had families, too, and *they* would be at the drug store tonight. You didn't come home just to see the members of your family. As far as that goes, you got a Christmas vacation to celebrate the birth of the Christ child, but except for a few Catholics, who would go anywhere near a church? And besides, he could not talk to his family en masse. He would like to have a talk with his father, a talk with his sister, and he would enjoy a half hour of his mother's prattling. Those conversations would be personal if there were only two present, but with more than two present everyone had to get his say in and nobody said anything much. Oh, what was the use of making a lot of excuses? What was wrong with wanting to see your friends?

The starter in the Dodge seemed to be whining. "No . . . no . . . no . . ." before the engine caught. It reminded him of a girl, a girl who protested every bit of the way, and she was not just an imaginary girl. She was the girl he would telephone as soon as he got to the drugstore, and he probably would be too late, thanks to the conversation with his family. Irma Hipple, her name was, and she was known as Miss Nipple. She lived up the hill in back of the Court House. The boys from the best families in town made a beeline for Irma as soon as they got home from school. Hopefully the boys who got a date with her would make a small but important purchase at the drug store, because you never knew when Irma might change her mind. A great many lies had been told about Irma, and the worst liars were the boys who claimed nothing but looked wise. Someone must have gotten all the way with Irma sometime, but Billy did not know who. It simply stood to reason that a girl who allowed so many boys to neck the hell out of her had delivered the goods sometime. She was twenty-one or -two and already she was beginning to lose her prettiness, probably because she could hold her liquor as well as any boy, and better than some. In her way she was a terrible snob. "That Roger Taylor got soaked to the gills," she would say. "That Teddy Choate thinks he's a cave man," or "I'm never going out with that Doctor Boyd again. Imagine a doctor snapping his cookies in the Stagecoach bar." Irma probably delivered the goods to the older men. Someone who went to Penn had seen her at the L'Aiglon supper club in Philadelphia with George W. Josling, who was manager of one of the new stock brokerage branches in town. There was a story around town that she had bitten Jerome Kuhn, the optometrist, who was old enough to be her father. It was hard to say what was true about Irma and what wasn't. She was a saleswoman in one of the department stores; she lived with her older sister and their father, who had one leg and was a crossing watchman for the Pennsy;

she was always well dressed; she was pretty and full of pep. That much was true about her, and it was certainly true that she attracted men of all ages.

The telephone booth in the drugstore was occupied, and two or three boys were queued up beside it. Billy Warden shook hands with his friends and with Russell Covington, the head soda jerk. He ordered a lemon phosphate and lit a cigarette and kept an eye on the telephone booth. The door of the booth buckled open and out came Teddy Choate, nodding. "All set," he said to someone. "Everything is copacetic. I'm fixed up with the Nipple. She thinks she can get Patsy Lurio for you."

Billy Warden wanted to hit him.

"Hello, there, Billy. When'd you get in?" said Teddy.

"Hello, Teddy. I got in on the two-eighteen," said Billy.

"I hear you're going to be at Henny Cooper's house party," said Teddy.

"Jesus, you're a busybody. How did you hear that?"

"From Henny, naturally. Christ, I've known her since we were five years old. She invited me, but I have to go to these parties in New York."

"Funny, she told me she didn't know anybody in Gibbsville," said Billy.

"She's a congenital liar. Everybody knows that. I saw her Friday in New York. She was at a tea dance I went to. You ever been to that place in Montrose?"

"No."

"They've got everything there. A six-car garage. Swimming pool. Four-hole golf course, but they have the tees arranged so you can play nine holes. God knows how many horses. The old boy made his money in railroad stocks, and he sure did spend it up there. Very hard to get to know, Mr. Cooper. But he was in Dad's class at New Haven and we've known the Coopers since the Year One. I guess it was really Henny's grandfather that made the first big pile. Yes, Darius L. Cooper. You come across his name in American History courses. I suppose he was an old crook. But Henny's father is altogether different. Very conservative. You won't see much of him at the house party, if he's there at all. They have an apartment at the Plaza, just the right size, their own furniture. I've been there many times, too."

"Then you do know them?" said Billy.

"Goodness, haven't I been telling you? We've known the Cooper family since the Year *One,*" said Teddy. "Well, you have to excuse me. I have to whisper something to Russ Covington. Delicate matter. Got a date with the Nipple."

"You're excused," said Billy. He finished his phosphate and joined a group at the curbstone.

"What say, boy? I'll give you fifty to forty," said Andy Phillips.

"For how much?" said Billy.

"A dollar?"

"You're on," said Billy. They went down the block and upstairs to the poolroom. All the tables were busy save one, which was covered with black oilcloth. "What about the end table?" said Billy.

"Saving it," said Phil, the house man. "Getting up a crap game."

"How soon?"

"Right away. You want to get in?"

"I don't know. I guess so. What do you think, Andy?"

"I'd rather shoot pool," said Andy.

"You're gonna have a hell of a wait for a table," said Phil. "There's one, two, three, four—four Harrigan games going. And the first table just started shooting a hundred points for a fifty-dollar bet. You're not gonna hurry *them*."

"Let's go someplace else," said Andy.

"They'll all be crowded tonight. I think I'll get in the crap game," said Billy.

Phil removed the cover from the idle pool table and turned on the overhead lights, and immediately half a dozen young men gathered around it. "Who has the dice?" someone asked.

"I have," said Phil, shaking them in his half-open hand.

"Oh, great," said someone.

"You want to have a look at them?" said Phil. "You wouldn't know the difference anyway, but you can have a look. No? All right, I'm shooting a dollar. A dollar open."

"You're faded," said someone.

"Anybody else want a dollar?" said Phil.

"I'll take a dollar," said Billy Warden.

"A dollar to you, and a dollar to you. Anyone else? No? Okay. Here we go, and it's a nine. A niner, a niner, what could be finer. No drinks to a minor. And it's a five. Come on, dice, let's see that six-three for Phil. And it's a four? Come on, dice. Be nice. And it's a—a nine it is. Four dollars open. Billy, you want to bet the deuce?"

"You're covered," said Billy.

"You're covered," said the other bettor.

"Anybody else wish to participate? No? All right, eight dollars on the table, and—oh, what do I see there? A natural. The big six and the little one. Bet the four, Billy?"

"I'm with you," said Billy.

"I'm out," said the other bettor.

"I'm in," said a newcomer.

"Four dollars to you, four dollars to Mr. Warden. And here we go, and for little old Phil a—oh, my. The eyes of a snake. Back where you started from, Billy. House bets five dollars. Nobody wants the five? All right, any part of it."

"Two dollars," said Billy.

When it came his turn to take the dice he passed it up and chose instead to make bets on the side. Thus he nursed his stake until at one time he had thirty-eight or -nine dollars in his hands. The number of players was increasing, and all pretty much for the same reason: most of the boys had not yet got their Christmas money, and a crap game offered the best chance to add to the pre-Christmas bankroll.

"Why don't you drag?" said Andy Phillips. "Get out while you're ahead?"

"As soon as I have fifty dollars," said Billy.

The next time the shooter with the dice announced five dollars open, Billy covered it himself, won, and got the dice. In less than ten minutes he was cleaned, no paper money, nothing but the small change in his pants pocket. He looked around among the players, but there was no one whom he cared to borrow from. "Don't look at me," said Andy. "I have six bucks to last me till Christmas."

"Well, I have eighty-seven cents," said Billy. "Do you still want to spot me fifty to forty?"

"Sure. But not for a buck. You haven't got a buck," said Andy. "And I'm going to beat you."

They waited until a table was free, and played their fifty points, which Andy won, fifty to thirty-two. "I'll be big-hearted," said Andy. "I'll pay for the table."

"No, no. Thirty cents won't break me," said Billy. "Or do you want to play another? Give me fifty to thirty-five."

"No, I don't like this table. It's too high," said Andy.

"Well, what shall we do?" said Billy.

"The movies ought to be letting out pretty soon. Shall we go down and see if we can pick anything up?"

"Me with fifty-seven cents? And you with six bucks?"

"Well, you have the Dodge, and we could get a couple of pints on credit," said Andy.

"All right, we can try," said Billy. They left the poolroom and went down to the street and re-parked the Warden Dodge where they could observe the movie crowd on its way out. Attendance that night was slim, and passable girls in pairs nowhere to be seen. The movie theater lights went out. "Well, so much for that," said Billy. "Five after eleven."

"Let's get a pint," said Andy.

"I honestly don't feel like it, Andy," said Billy.

"I didn't mean you were to buy it. I'll split it with you."

"I understood that part," said Billy. "Just don't feel like drinking."

"Do you have to *feel* like drinking at Dartmouth? Up at State we just drink."

"Oh, sure. Big hell-raisers," said Billy. "Kappa Betes and T.N.E.'s. 'Let's go over to Lock Haven and get slopped.' I heard all about State while I was at Mercersburg. That's why I didn't go there—one of the reasons."

"Is that so?" said Andy. "Well, if all you're gonna do is sit here and razz State, I think I'll go down to Mulhearn's and have a couple beers. You should have had sense enough to quit when you were thirty-some bucks ahead."

"Darius L. Cooper didn't quit when he was thirty bucks ahead."

"Who? You mean the fellow with the cake-eater suit? His name wasn't Cooper. His name is Minzer or something like that. Well, the beers are a quarter at Mulhearn's. We could have six fours are twenty-four. We could have twelve beers apiece. I'll lend you three bucks."

"No thanks," said Billy. "I'll take you down to Mulhearn's and then I think I'll go home and get some shuteye. I didn't get any sleep on the train last night."

"That's what's the matter with you? All right, disagreeable. Safe at last in your trundle bed."

"How do you know that? That's a Dartmouth song," said Billy.

"I don't know, I guess I heard *you* sing it," said Andy. "Not to-night, though. I'll walk to Mulhearn's. I'll see you tomorrow."

"All right, Andy. See you tomorrow," said Billy. He watched his friend, with his felt hat turned up too much in front and back, his thick-soled Whitehouse & Hardy's clicking on the sidewalk, his joe-college swagger, his older brother's leather coat. Life was simple for Andy and always would be. In two more years he would finish at State, a college graduate, and he would come home and take a job in Phillips Brothers Lumber Yard, marry a local girl, join the Lions or Rotary, and play volleyball at the Y.M.C.A. His older brother had already done all those things, and Andy was Fred Phillips all over again.

The Dodge, still warm, did not repeat the whining protest of a few hours earlier in the evening. He put it in gear and headed for home.

He hoped his father and mother would have gone to bed. "What the hell's the matter with me?" he said. "Nothing's right tonight."

He put the car in the garage and entered the house by the kitchen door. He opened the refrigerator door, and heard his father's voice. "Is that you, son?"

"Yes, it's me. I'm getting a glass of milk."

His father was in the sitting-room and made no answer. Billy drank a glass of milk and turned out the kitchen lights. He went to the sitting-room. His father, in shirtsleeves and smoking a pipe, was at the desk. "You doing your bookkeeping?" said Billy.

"No."

"What *are* you doing?"

"Well, if you must know, I was writing a poem. I was trying to express my appreciation to your mother."

"Can I see it?"

"Not in a hundred years," said Mr. Warden. "Nobody will ever see this but her—if she ever does."

"I never knew you wrote poetry."

"Once a year, for the past twenty-six years, starting with the first Christmas we were engaged. So far I haven't missed a year, but it doesn't get any easier. But by God, the first thing Christmas morning she'll say to me, 'Where's my poem?' Never speaks about it the rest of the year, but it's always the first thing she asks me the twenty-fifth of December."

"Has she kept them all?" said Billy.

"That I never asked her, but I suppose she has."

"Does she write you one?" said Billy.

"Nope. Well, what did you do tonight? You're home early, for you."

"Kind of tired. I didn't get much sleep last night. We got on the train at White River Junction and nobody could sleep."

"Well, get to bed and sleep till noon. That ought to restore your energy."

"Okay. Goodnight, Dad."

"Goodnight, son," said his father. "Oh, say. You had a long distance call. You're to call the Scranton operator, no matter what time you get in."

"Thanks," said Billy. "Goodnight."

"Well, aren't you going to put the call in? I'll wait in the kitchen."

"No, I know who it is. I'll phone them tomorrow."

"That's up to you," said Mr. Warden. "Well, goodnight again."

"Goodnight," said Billy. He went to his room and took off his clothes, to the bathroom and brushed his teeth. He put out the light beside his bed and lay there. He wondered if Henrietta Cooper's father had ever written a poem to her mother. But he knew the answer to that.

Mrs. Allanson

Mrs. Frank B. Allanson's great gift is her ability to impart importance to people and things because they are her people and things. Back in the days when the motor car provided a precise and subtle index of taste and financial circumstances, the Allansons owned a series of Franklins. The late Frank Allanson had chosen the Franklin because it was an air-cooled car, and the cult of the Franklin included three or four men with whom Allanson was congenial in many matters. But Sara Allanson, although she did not drive, very soon was proclaiming the Franklin to be the superior of the Pierces and Packards, the Stearns-Knights and Peerlesses, the Hayneses and Paiges and Chandlers that belonged to the families she knew best. She was particularly hard on the Pierce-Arrow, since the Pierce spoke for itself as an indication of money spent, while the Franklin in its way spoke for itself as an example of money saved. It would have entailed no financial hardship for the Allansons to have bought a Pierce; Frank Allanson's firm was the local legal representative for the Lehigh Valley Rail Road, the Prudential Insurance Company, and the Ingersoll-Rand people, as well as one of the larger independent coal companies, a lumber company, a department store, and the Keystone Bank & Trust. But as it happened, Robert B. Stokes, whose firm represented the Pennsylvania Railroad and the M. A. Hanna Company locally, owned a Pierce-Arrow, and so did George W. Ingersoll, lawyer for the Light, Heat & Power Company. Sara Allanson never missed an opportunity to say something disparaging about Althea Stokes's and Pansy Ingersoll's Pierces, always with the implication that anyone who went higher than the Franklin price range was doing it for show. (It was a major-minor triumph for Sara when the Allansons' William learned that the Ingersolls' Pierce was technically a second-hand car, almost brand-new but purchased from the estate of a Chestnut Hill widow. "Frank and I would never own a second-hand car," Sara said.

The Horse Knows the Way (1964)

She did not specifically identify the Ingersolls' Pierce, but her friends could infer what they pleased about all Pierce-Arrows and Packard Twin Sixes.)

Frank Allanson died of pneumonia in 1927. He was given a nice, dignified send-off at the Second Presbyterian Church, and in a very short time Sara had so successfully adjusted herself to widowhood that most of her friends had a hard time believing that Frank's death had been so recent. George Ingersoll, who had a forked tongue, described her as a born widow. She was only in her late thirties, with a daughter in boarding-school, but it never occurred to anyone to suppose that Sara Allanson would ever marry again. She wore black for the full year's period of mourning, but as she went on wearing her Persian lamb after the year was up, there was an illusion that publicly the mourning period was being continued. This is not to say that she flaunted her grief. Not even her closest friends had been subjected to any teary outbursts, and when she spoke of her late husband it was with admiration and respect, but no one was permitted to be witness to a display of emotion. During his years on earth Frank Allanson had been so completely protected against invasions of his private life with Sara that she was not going to let down the bars now that he was dead. There had not been much curiosity about their intimate life, but there had been some. There is always some. But as George Ingersoll said, when a man like Frank marries a woman like Sara it's the wife that's in charge of such matters and the husband does exactly what he's told. If there was some truth to George Ingersoll's comment, it explains why it was so easy for Sara to achieve the transition from matrimony to widowhood. She had always wanted to be a widow, a single woman whose husband had been taken away from her in orderly circumstances.

At that time, early in her widowhood, Sara was somewhat inclined to be stout, with a tubular torso that was restrained by a foundation garment. Her breasts were small and created no problem in corsetry. But she had never had a slim waist, and the most she could hope for was a figure that would not be called fat. She wore very high heels to give her legs a better line, and she watched her weight. The overall effect was favorable. She dressed well, she was tidy and clean, a member of the female sex, a widow. She was not unpretty. Her nose was too large, long and hooked, and her lips were so thin that without lipstick her mouth would have been only a horizontal slit in her face. Nevertheless she had gone through girlhood and young womanhood with her fair share of compliments to her looks, and if the specific compliments invariably concerned her blue-green-gray eyes, they were uniquely hers. She had often—fairly often—sat amused at the bridge table while the other three at the table discussed the true color of her eyes. "What are they, really, Sara? What do *you* think they are?" someone would always ask.

"Father always used to say they were blue, like Mama's, and Mama said they were gray, like most of the Doerflingers'. Frank thinks they're grayish green. I honestly don't know."

"Fascinating, really fascinating," someone would say. "Now where do we go? Isn't that table finished *yet?* How many rubbers are you *playing* over there?"

Sara's daughter Marjorie had not inherited the polychromatic eyes of her mother, and in the field of feminine beauty she was generally considered—as early as sixteen—a hopeless case. Her misfortune began, ironically, with her eyes. She had had to wear glasses since the age of five, and as frequently happens, the only thing she liked to do was to read. She was not good at games; a ball would come at her and she would not see it until too late for her to raise her hands in self-protection. She would come home from school, do her homework immediately, and resume her reading of the multi-volume *Our Wonder World, Stoddards Lectures, The Girls of Bradford Hall,* and the latest *St. Nicholas* magazine. Her father worried that she was not getting enough fresh air, and her mother would send her out to play, but Marjorie would go only as far as a friend's house, where she would read whatever books were available there. She was not a particularly unhappy child, nor an especially brilliant one. She was, let it be noted again, her mother's daughter, and Sara Allanson saw to it that the other mothers ordered their sons to be at least polite to Marjorie at parties and dancing school. Marjorie was known as a duty-dance, but so were most of her contemporaries at that age. As for her intense reading, it supplied her with a large store of information without stimulating her to any creative effort of her own, but because she had always been a reader of books, she was not repelled by textbooks. Consequently she was regarded as a good student and was rewarded by her teachers with marks just below the top. It was nice for Sara Allanson to be able to say that Marjorie had never failed a subject during her entire school career, and it was quietly comforting to look back upon Marjorie's sixteen years and find nothing to be ashamed of. Being a plain child had some advantages, at least for the parents, and Marjorie had not been mentioned among the girls whose behavior was being criticized. Virginia Stokes, for example, was carried home from a picnic in a state of intoxication; Annabell Ingersoll was asked to leave Westover for the *announced* reason that she habitually violated the rule against smoking; and lower down the social scale was the scandal in the public high school

involving four girls of Marjorie's age and several members of a visiting football team.

The high school mess was kept out of the papers, but it became a
topic of discussion among Sara Allanson's friends. Sara, recently
bereaved, was rather less concerned for her fatherless child than
some of the mothers whose daughters were beginning to show signs
of prettiness. "Thank heaven my Marjorie has always had a level
head on her shoulders," said Sara. "Not that any of our girls would
do that sort of thing. I actually heard that there were more than four
boys involved, you know. Yes, there were four of the high school
girls, but I've heard as many as ten boys. That sounds exactly like the
Germans in Belgium, except that these girls were willing. Much too
willing, from what I hear. It's going to be very difficult to know who
to punish if any of those girls turn out to be pregnant. They wouldn't
even know themselves who to blame, and you can't just put a whole
football team in jail. Well, the whole unfortunate affair ought to
make some of our friends stop and think, not mentioning any
names."

With so many other things on her mind—what to do with Frank's
law books and his clothing and personal effects; papers to sign; letters to write; accounts to be settled; furniture to be rearranged—
Sara did not stop long to think about the high school scandal. If she
had been able to look into the future and see what it held for
Marjorie (and for her) she might have lingered over the high school
situation to fortify herself with the knowledge to handle a somewhat
similar situation. For in Marjorie's next to last year at boarding-
school, with her marks holding up well and her deportment practically faultless, the girl became a problem. It was a rather nasty problem, and yet the absence of any dramatic episode to point it up was
almost worse than the problem itself. The simple facts of the problem were that Marjorie had practically overnight developed a figure
that was voluptuous enough to compensate for the beauty that Nature had withheld from her face, and that boys were hanging around
the Allanson house.

Sara Allanson, being Sara, could quickly attribute this sudden
popularity to a remarkable discovery of Marjorie's worthwhile qualities by boys who had been too immature to make the discovery
earlier. "It's so nice to have the boys dropping in that way," said
Sara. "Marjorie isn't what you'd call—well, you know how some girls
are *forward* with boys. And boys do need a little urging at that age,
fifteen or so. It wasn't till just recently that she showed the slightest
interest. Gave them the least encouragement. But this summer, just
since she got home from school, she seems to've suddenly realized

that boys are just as interesting to talk to as girls. And the boys have been finding out that my Marjorie, the little girl that they used to tease about always having her nose in a book, she can talk on almost any subject. And I daresay hold her own in conversation with most of the boys."

The summer was well along before Sara noticed that the boys would come to call on Marjorie only in the afternoon; Marjorie and her caller would go off in the direction of the tennis club and be gone until suppertime. For the rest of the evening Marjorie was alone, unless one of the girls in her crowd dropped in. Sara knew that Marjorie was not one of the best dancers, but it seemed odd, to say the least, that none of the boys had taken her to *any* of the weekly club dances. Apparently the new popularity had its limits, and Sara was not sure she liked that. Then along about the second or third week in August the very disturbing incident of Herbie Ingersoll and Roger Bell occurred.

Roger was a new boy in town, the son of a construction engineer on the new dam, and he had lived in many places and undoubtedly was more sophisticated than the other boys his age. It was common talk that all the young girls were crazy about him and that the boys could not stand him. He played the ukulele-guitar and sang songs in Hawaiian and Spanish, and he had just finished his freshman year at Leland Stanford. He did not hesitate to ask any girl for a date, even though he had been in town long enough to have seen for himself that certain girls had understandings with certain boys. They were all too young to be formally engaged, and some mothers forbade their daughters to go so far as to accept the boys' fraternity pins; but some of the understandings were well rooted in time, and one of those was between Herbie Ingersoll and Sue Lauderbach, the daughter of Jefferson Lauderbach, head chemist at the steel mill. Herbie and Sue had been sweethearts for five or six years, but that made no difference to Roger, nor did the fact that Sue repeatedly refused to have a date with him. He kept trying. He also appeared at the Allansons' at least one afternoon a week and would go for a walk with Marjorie.

Marjorie was out walking with Roger on the August day that Herbie turned up. "Is Marjorie home, Mrs. Allanson?" he said.

"Why, no, Herbie. She and Roger are up at the tennis club. Roger Bell. Why don't you go up there? I imagine they'll be on the porch."

"She was supposed to go for a walk with me," said Herbie.

"Oh, was she? Are you sure? Because I know Roger called up shortly after lunch."

"Will you tell her I'll be back around six, please?"

"Yes, I'll tell her that. But Herbie, does Sue like it when you spend so much time with Marjorie? I know you're not engaged or anything serious, but I understand that you object if Sue goes out with another boy, and I just wonder."

"Who told you that? Roger Bell?"

"No. Long before he ever came to town."

"Well, I have to go now, Mrs. Allanson. Will you give Marjorie my message, please?"

Herbie left quickly and thus put an end to further discussion, but he was back at six o'clock, waiting unannounced on the Allansons' porch, when Marjorie and Roger Bell returned from their walk. Sara Allanson, upstairs and getting ready for her bath, could not hear the conversation that was taking place on the porch, but presently Roger Bell left, and a few minutes later Marjorie and Herbie crossed the street and headed in the direction of the tennis club. It was seven o'clock before Marjorie came home, and she was alone.

"Marjorie, you *know* we have dinner at six-thirty this time of year. I think it was very inconsiderate of you to go off like that, and I don't want it to happen again. If you wanted to talk to Herbie you could have just as easily stayed on the porch."

"I'm very sorry, Mother."

"You look a sight, too," said Sara. "The least you can do when you come to the table is—go comb your hair, and honestly, Marjorie. Look at your dress. You look as though you'd been playing with mudpies, at your age. I'll wait dinner for ten minutes more while you make yourself presentable. I declare."

"You go ahead. Don't wait dinner for me."

"I'll do nothing of the kind, and then I want to talk to you about Herbie."

"No. I'm not going to talk about Herbie. Or anyone else."

"How *dare* you speak to me that way?"

"Mother, I'm not going to talk about Herbie Ingersoll and that's all there is to it, no matter what you say."

"Well, I'll say this. You're not going to *get* any dinner. If you want to behave like a naughty child, that's the way you'll be treated. Stay in your room without any supper, till you remember your manners."

"I don't want any supper."

"You can suit yourself about that, Miss Impudent. But we're going to have a talk about certain things, whether *that* suits you or not."

"No! I will not!" said Marjorie. She went upstairs and slammed her bedroom door.

All evening Sara waited, but the girl did not appear, and in the morning her room was empty, her bed not slept in. Sara was made dizzy in the rush of all the possibilities of disaster and disgrace, and

by the realization that in this crisis she had no one to turn to. The
fact lay bare that in the whole world, among all the women she
counted as her friends and the men who had been friends of her
husband, there was not one whom she loved enough to share her
terror. Out in that bleak world, and now a member of it, was her
child. *Her* child. But as a member of that world Marjorie could not
love her, and she could not love Marjorie. She sat, for physical rest,
in a Windsor chair at Marjorie's desk, and listened to this report
from herself to herself, that testified to her loveless condition and
her supreme remoteness from other flesh and blood. The ecstatic
shudders of a kindly man, the water break, the cries in the night and
the soiled diapers and the second teeth and the simulated pride and
the secret appraisals were all lies, all equally spurious and unexperi-
enced. There were some things to do, because out in that world was
that world that must not be surrendered to, that billion of flesh and
blood or chalk. Say nothing today, tomorrow call the police. No, next
day call the police. No, never call the police. No, never say anything
to anyone. Yes, call a detective agency. No, do it through Judge
Eaton. Regret Althea Stokes's luncheon. Confide in Dr. English. At
least have some coffee. A good strong cup of coffee. And think up a
good story for the help.

"Mother?"

Sara Allanson did not turn. "Yes?"

"I'm sorry I was rude."

"Well, I should think you would be. Where did you sleep?"

"In the attic."

"In the *attic?*"

"In the old playroom."

"Why? What did you sleep *on?* There's no bed made up."

"I know. I'm stiff. I slept on the floor."

"Why? What made you do that?"

"I don't know. I just did."

"Well, you'd better get yourself a hot bath or you'll be stiff the rest
of the day. I see you haven't changed your dress."

"I know."

"I was just going down to breakfast. What do you want? And
rumple your bed. I don't want Agnes to think you stayed out all
night."

"Mother, I don't *care* what Agnes thinks."

"I'm sure you don't, but I do."

"But I wish you didn't."

"You have to care what people think in this world."

"I don't."

"Well, you'd better start."

"It's too late for me to start."

"Oh, ridiculous. What shall I tell Bertha you want for breakfast?"

"Two soft-boiled eggs."

"And how soon will you be down?"

"Three quarters of an hour."

"Very well. One thing more. If Herbie wants to come calling this afternoon, I want you to tell him no. I think you're getting in too deep there, and I'd rather you didn't see him unless Sue comes along."

"Well, she won't come along."

"No, and I don't trust Herbie Ingersoll. Not that I trust Roger Bell, either, but *they're* only going to be here another year. Two soft-boiled eggs, you said. Three quarters of an hour."

"Mother?"

"Yes?"

"Nothing."

"Well, whatever is on your mind, Marjorie, I'll be home all day except for luncheon and bridge club at Mrs. Stokes's. I have a few things to say, too."

The things that were to be said were not said. The summer vacation dragged and spurted along, and Marjorie went back to school, the fall meetings of Sara's Tuesday bridge club were inaugurated, and Sue Lauderbach had a tiny diamond—embedded in Herbie's fraternity pin. At Christmas, having made her reservation in October, Sara took over the country club for a dinner dance for Marjorie, which turned out to be as good a party as all the other parties that it duplicated: same people, same orchestra, same food, same place. But the occasion was ruined for Sara by an overheard scrap of conversation between two young men. She did not know either boy; they could have been out-of-town house guests, and they could have been town boys who were not invited to parties until they went away to college, whose parents were not members of the club. Sara, on her way from a visit to the ladies' room, halted in the vestibule behind the stag line, and over the heads of the boys she saw Marjorie dance by.

"Marjorie Allanson," said the first boy.

"Yeah. Lots of lovin'," said the second boy.

"You said it," said the first boy.

"The hottest necking in town."

"I'll say."

Sara drew away unseen; there was more, but it was in slang terms that she did not understand, and she had heard enough. She was angered but not particularly shocked, not genuinely surprised. It was her understanding that the word necking clearly implied incomplete consummation; the word was not used in such cases as the high school girls and the football players. From this Sara drew some small but at least temporarily reassuring comfort. If the boys had been able to say more, they would have said it.

The music stopped at four o'clock, and Sara went home with Jim and Esther Truesdale, Frank Allanson's law partner and his wife. She undressed and took a bath and got into bed. She could not let herself go to sleep until Marjorie got home, but she was not fully awake when she heard a car and voices and the storm door and front door closing, then Marjorie's footsteps.

"I'm awake, Marjorie," she called.

Marjorie opened her door. "Thank you for a very nice party. It was really swell, Mother. Everybody had a good time."

"Yes, I thought it went very well. Who did you come home with?"

"Just now? That was Ralph Munson. I didn't come home with Bud Ogilvie because he got tight. We all went to the hamburger place."

"But you had scrambled eggs at three o'clock."

"Oh, we didn't go to the hamburger place just to eat, Mother. We go there to finish up the evening."

" 'We.' You make it sound as though you went to parties every night of your life. Well, it's over, and next year it'll be someone else's turn. Is Ralph Munson Dr. Munson's son from Mountain City?"

"No, he's no relation. As a matter of fact, Ralph Munson wasn't at our party. You don't know him."

"Well, explain that. How did you happen to come home with someone that wasn't even at the party?"

"Well, he works. He's the night manager at the Gibbsville Bakery, and he works every night from eight to four."

"How did you ever meet him? Have you ever seen him before tonight? No wonder I never heard of him. Is he married?"

"Separated. He came here from Allentown last year. Mother, can we talk about this tomorrow?"

"We'll talk about it now, whatever it is. Are you aware that your father helped to get the Gibbsville Bakery started? I have stock in it. Not enough to interest a fortune-hunter, I can assure you, but your father was one of those that put up the money for the bakery. How did you *meet* this Ralph Munson?"

"I don't know, I don't remember. But he isn't a fortune-hunter. He's nothing like that."

"He's a married man, and my guess is this isn't the first time you've seen him. A married man—"

Marjorie did not wait to hear any more, and the next day Sara did the only thing she could think of in the circumstances: she summoned Jim Truesdale.

"Yes, I know Ralph Munson," said Jim.

"Are you holding anything back from me, Jim? I have a feeling you are, and it's not fair to Frank."

"I guess I was Frank's best friend, but he never discussed family affairs with me. Or with anyone else, for that matter. I'll answer any questions you ask, Sara, but don't expect me to stand *in loco parentis*. In other words, I'm not going to take on the problem of Marjorie's love affairs. That's one thing I have no intention of doing."

"I only wanted to know about this Munson man."

"Well, they're pleased with him at the bakery. He makes about seventy-five dollars a week, somewhere in there. He isn't what you'd call a handsome fellow. Ordinarily you wouldn't give him a second look, and when I heard about him and Marjorie I was inclined to dismiss the whole thing as gossip. Exaggerated. I figured you must have known all about it and were letting it run its course, so to speak. I didn't like him being a married man, but it wasn't up to me to say anything. These girls, they seem to grow up overnight nowadays, and suddenly you hear all these stories. If you believed half the stories you hear, you'd wonder what's becoming of the young girls today."

"Now look here, Jim, don't start inferring that there were stories about Marjorie. That's just the kind of a remark that gets stories started, and coming from you I don't like it a bit. I could remind you that it was Frank Allanson that was responsible for getting all the best clients in the firm, not you. You never would have got very far without Frank, and it seems to me you're forgetting your obligations."

"Now, Sara, don't let's indulge in personalities. Frank and I were equal partners in every way, and I'm very sure that Frank never said anything to imply otherwise. If you wish to believe that Frank Allanson *carried* me, you're quite mistaken, but I won't go into that."

"Well, *I* will," she said. "You wouldn't have the Lehigh Valley for a client but for Frank, and as far as that goes Frank had all those big clients before you were made a partner."

"Sara, Sara, come on now. This is getting out of hand. You put me on the defensive, and I don't like it. Let me say this much, to correct any wrong impressions you're harboring. The firm has all the clients it always had, plus certain ones that came to us *after* Frank passed on. *After.* Do I make myself clear?"

"You make it clear that you've taken clients that Frank probably didn't want to have anything to do with."

"Would you say Wadsworth & Valentine was one of those clients? One of the biggest construction companies in the United States? We handle all their legal business in this region now, but only in the past year, Sara. *Only* in the past year. You get some of that fee, but under the terms of the partnership, I didn't have to give you a nickel of it. So don't make such rash statements about our clients. I can understand your being upset about Marjorie, and all the talk. I don't think Marjorie is a *bad* girl. Small town, everything exaggerated out of proportion, and I don't know who's worse. The boys, or the mothers of the girls. If Frank were alive—"

"If Frank were alive he'd throw you out of this house, bodily," said Sara.

"Well, I doubt that, but that's my cue to leave."

"It certainly is. It most certainly is," she said.

Marjorie was still asleep after her party, and Sara sent Agnes to wake her. "Take her breakfast up to her, and tell her I wish to see her as soon as she's finished," said Sara. "I'll be in my room."

"Are you going to have it out with her?" said Agnes.

"Why? What do you mean?"

"Just so she don't think we tattled on her," said Agnes. "The lawyer here and all, I know you're getting ready, ma'am. But I wouldn't want her to think it was us, because it *wasn't* us. Not me or Bertha. We think we have a pretty good idea who you might say spilt the beans, but make sure the poor girl don't blame Bertha and I. It *was* William, wasn't it? *He* informed on her."

"I won't say," said Sara.

"It was him, all right. He was in the kitchen getting warm when the front doorbell rang and I went to answer it. He just come back from driving you to Mrs. Stokes's and was in the kitchen getting warm. I answered the door, and then I went back in the kitchen and William asked me who it was. I should of told him it was none of his business, but I didn't. That's how he found out. Worse than a woman for gossip. He hung around and hung around till it was time to go fetch you, and that's how he seen Munson. Munson went out the front door the very same minute William was driving away. But before you believe everything William told you, you gotta take this into account, that Munson fired William's elder boy from the bakery. I don't say Munson wasn't here. That he was, and I'm not denying that. But Munson did give William's boy the sack, and he has a grudge against Munson."

"Agnes, there were a lot of things you could have told me that you didn't, and you should have."

"Well, you were bound to find out sooner or later, and I don't think much of people that carry tales. I'd a cousin was murdered in the old country through a man carrying tales. Ambushed and shot down in cold blood. Left a wife and four small children. No, regardless of the provocation I'd still not inform on a person. I send a portion of my wages to help those children, the innocent victims of circumstances. It's only five dollars a month, but that's sixty dollars a year. Twelve pounds, in Ireland, you know."

"Well, I'm very glad you don't believe in carrying tales," said Sara. "There's altogether too much of it."

"Meaning would we say anything to outsiders? The answer is no. What goes on in this house is nobody's business outside, no matter how much they try to pump us. And they did, employers and servants alike, but got very little information for their trouble. As long as *I'm* living in this house, and the same for Bertha, they can pry around and snoop as much as they want to, but we're loyal. Loyal to the bone. A pity some women don't have something better to occupy their time. Naturally it's m'self they try to wheedle the information, Bertha being mostly in the kitchen and refusing to answer the telephone. But they don't get much out of me, you can be sure of that. There was one of them I'm ashamed to say give me a ride home from Sodality last Tuesday, and I was no sooner in her auto than she begun her cross-examination. And the two of us just come from Benediction, with the smell of the incense still in our nostrils."

"I can guess who that was. What did she want to know?"

"Well, what they're all asking these days. Last summer they'd be asking did young Ingersoll and that newcomer, Bell, did they come to blows? There was talk they'd a fist fight on the front porch. But now it's all Munson. Do you let him come to call, et cetera. I said to Miss R, I appreciated the ride home on a cold night, but if I had to pay me fare with bits of confidential information, then I'd sooner pay me dime and take the trolley. There the conductor'll take your ten-cent piece and worry about his own troubles."

"So true," said Sara Allanson.

"I'll be getting her breakfast, poor thing," said Agnes.

Sara Allanson, who had found no joy in the sexual act, was nevertheless a former participant in it, with a simple and straightforward definition of what constituted the act and what did not. She could no longer solace herself with that earlier use of the word necking and its implication of incompleteness: Marjorie had smuggled a married man into this house, and a married man did not go to all that trouble for anything less than completeness. Therefore Marjorie must be dealt with not as a girl but as a woman.

Sara did not have to wait long. She could read the household sounds, and obviously Marjorie was taking a cup of coffee and turning down the rest of her breakfast. Now, in her nightgown and bathrobe, wearing her glasses and with no sign of makeup, she was at her mother's bedroom door.

"Well, come in," said Sara.

Without a doubt the girl had been given some warning by Agnes. A defensive apprehension was in her manner. "What is it?" she said.

"Do you know what happens to girls like you if they're poor? They get sent away to the Protectory, and all the rest of their lives they're never able to live that down. And do you know what happens to men like Mr. Munson? If he was some kind of a day laborer he'd be put in prison."

"Oh, that's what it is," said Marjorie. *"That's* why you had Mr. Truesdale here. Well, if you do anything to Ralph, I'm in it too."

"Indeed you are."

"I know you're not going to have me sent to the Protectory, but you could do something to Ralph like have him lose his job. If you do that, Mother, I'll leave this house."

"You wouldn't get very far—not that I'm so anxious to keep you here. You've shown how much respect you have for a good home. I suppose you're thinking of going away with Mr. Munson. But I wonder how enthusiastic he'd be about that? Can you picture him going to some strange town and getting a job in a bakery, with an eighteen-year-old girl, not his wife, tagging along?"

"He knows all that."

"Oh, then you've discussed your predicament?"

"Yes."

"And what did you decide, may I ask?"

"You'll soon find out."

"I want to find out now. You're not a child any more, young lady. Let's not have any childish bad temper. What did you and your Mr. Munson decide?"

"He's leaving town."

"I should—say—he—is. And planning to take you with him, I suppose?"

"No."

"Oh, leaving you here."

"Yes."

Sara considered this for a moment. "Where is he going?"

"I don't know. Out West somewhere. He's told them at the bakery that he's resigning his job and leaving at the end of the week."

"Do you propose to join him?"

"No. He's going away and not telling me where. But if you do anything to get him fired, keep him from getting a reference, I'll go away. Even if I don't know where he is. I won't live here another minute."

"When did you, or he, decide all this?"

"Last night."

"At the hamburger place?"

"We didn't go to the hamburger place."

"Where did you have your rendezvous?"

"At the bakery."

"At the bakery! The bakery? How did you get there, for heaven's sake?"

"Roger took me. Roger Bell. What does it matter who took me there? I couldn't invite Ralph to my party—"

"No, you can have him in your room, but not to your party. That's the kind of a love affair this was. Even you can see that."

"Yes, I saw that, and so did he, and that's why he's going away. And I never expect to see him again, so does that satisfy you?"

"I must say you don't seem very upset about it."

"What's the use of getting upset about it?"

"Well—you couldn't have loved him very much after all."

"I didn't, and he didn't love me. Who would love me?"

"What?"

"That's what I said. Who would love me?"

"Marjorie, what a terrible thing to say."

"Yes, isn't it? How could my daughter Marjorie say such a thing, and everybody talking about her? That's supposed to be the excuse. Love. Why should I have to love anybody? Nobody ever loved me. No I don't love Ralph Munson, but he was nicer to me than anybody else ever was. Except Roger. But people like you, and Herbie Ingersoll—you were ashamed of me."

"Thank you not to put me in the same class with Herbie Ingersoll."

"Why not? You wanted me to be one thing and Herbie wanted something else, but you never cared what I wanted."

"As far as I know, as far as *I* know—as far as I know you were never deprived of anything. And as to your relations with the opposite sex, I just don't understand how you could cheapen yourself. I couldn't believe it possible, even when I could practically see it with my own eyes. On my own doorstep. In my own *house*. Well, the first thing is to see Dr. English."

"What for?"

"Don't *tell* me you aren't aware of the consequences of your behavior."

"Oh, you mean pregnant. You don't have to worry about that. I'm not pregnant."

"You're sure?"

"Of course I'm sure. Nobody gets pregnant if they're careful. We're not living in the Dark Ages, Mother."

"Well, that's a relief. I'm sure I don't welcome the prospect of taking you in to see Dr. English. And I won't have to take you out of school. But when you go back I'm going to write a letter to Miss Crowder and make sure you stay on the school grounds. In other words, you're going to have to change your ways—here at home, and at school, and everywhere else. You think you know so much, with your talk about the Dark Ages, but you haven't even learned self-control."

"And having Miss Crowder lock me up is your way to teach me."

"Yes, and seeing to it that you associate with the right sort of boys."

"Like Herbie Ingersoll? All the mothers considered him the right sort of boy."

"You don't intend to change your ways, I can see that, but you're going to find that it'll do you no good to defy your mother. You won't have a cent till you're twenty-five, and if I went to court I could prevent you from getting anything even then."

"Yes, but you wouldn't do that. The noto*riety.*"

"You're wrong. It can be done very quietly. In fact, Marjorie, those sort of things usually are done very quietly, especially when all the judges are personal friends of mine. It wouldn't be in a courtroom, you know. That kind of thing takes place in the judge's chambers."

"You'd have to say I was insane."

"No, I wouldn't. Just enough to convince the judge that you weren't ready to administer your own affairs. Financially. You wouldn't have to be certified as insane. We won't even *talk* about *that*. I'm only telling you now what can be done without any notoriety, and hope it will serve as a warning to you. There are lots of other things I can do. I can take you out of Miss Crowder's and put you in a much stricter school. I could send you abroad, to Switzerland, a school that handles difficult girls. And if you refused to go, or ran away, then I could do something more drastic, because a girl that runs away has proved that she's difficult. If you ran away now, for instance, seven years from now I could tell the judge that that was what you'd done when you were eighteen, and that would be a black mark on your record. I hold all the trump cards, and any false move on your part is going to count against you in the future as well as the present. So don't attempt anything foolish."

"That's what Ralph said, and he didn't even know you," said the girl.

Marjorie was coming out of this inquisition unscarred, and Sara knew it. She could not compel herself to be more severe than she had been thus far, with her threats of restrictions at school and vague hints of financial pressures and court actions. But neither could she force herself and Marjorie into an open, candid discussion of the girl's intimacies with men, the heart of the matter. So long as they skirted the topic, the conversation remained just that, a conversation, and Sara could already see that she was getting nowhere, that Marjorie's ways would not be changed. But if the only way to effect a change was by probing more deeply, the result was not worth the discomfort and unpleasantness it would cost Sara. In a sudden burst of futility and renunciation she said, "Well, it's your life. Make a worse mess of it if that's what you want."

The abruptness of the statement took Marjorie by surprise. "May I go now?"

"I don't know what else I can say. Yes, go," said Sara. She spoke with weary solemnity, but as soon as the girl closed the door behind her Sara experienced a sense of relief that started in her abdomen and leapt strangely to the back of her neck. She recognized the cause of this relaxation of tension: she had done everything, absolutely everything, that she could do, and now it was up to the girl herself.

And so it was, just as Sara had foreseen, and rather much as she and Marjorie had wanted it to be. The atmosphere had been cleared of particles of love, and nascent hatred was gone too. What remained, or was substituted, was a formal arrangement, a modus vivendi that functioned extremely well. Having no love to give, Sara was no longer obliged to simulate love or the giving of it; having had no love, Marjorie, under the new arrangement, was not obliged to accept her mother's counterfeit of it. She obeyed her mother's household rules that governed her hours, and she brought no one to the house, surreptitiously or otherwise, who did not meet with Sara's approval. Away from the house she behaved wholly on her instincts, and she became a convenience for thwarted men. Their number did not increase, but their age level was raised. They were husbands. At the country club, in the shopping district of the town, Marjorie's progress was frequently and momentarily halted by men who urgently wanted to see her but were reluctant to hold lengthy conversations with her in public. A man would stop her on the street or follow her from one room to another, and while making a pretense of casual conversation he would mutter, in some degree of desperation, "When can I see you? Same place, five o'clock tomorrow? Quick, Marjorie. Here comes Mrs. Hofman." She had forbidden them to call her on the telephone, and they were dependent on such chance encounters.

Their need of her gave her a special strength that enabled her to ignore the cold hatred that she saw in the faces of their wives. It was a cold and special hatred. The women knew she was not out to break up their establishments, and they would not permit themselves to recognize this faceless body as a declared enemy. Marjorie was not even a rival whom a woman could discuss with a friend, and she became in consequence the object of unexpressed and individual hatreds. "You're a menace to society," said Jap Wilson, one of her few bachelors. "One of these days you're going to wake up with your throat cut, and they won't know who did it. Too many suspects."

"Just so they get the right one," said Marjorie.

"Aren't you ever afraid of them?"

"No. If they really loved their husbands I would be. But all they care about is having a house on Lantenengo Street and their charge accounts and being Mrs. So-and-so."

"Not all of them, Marjorie. Betty Langdon isn't one of those."

"If I were as pretty as Betty Langdon I wouldn't worry about Marjorie Allanson. But that isn't all there is to it. How would you like to be told that you were a pansy?"

"Is that what Betty told Ben?"

"Told him, and almost had him convinced of it. Something she read sounded like a description of Ben, and pretty soon he couldn't get interested, if you know what I mean. For over a year she had him in such a state that every time he went near her it got worse. That's one marriage I could have broken up. Ben would have married me. Anyway, now you know why Betty hates me. I showed her up. She *wanted* Ben to be a pansy so she wouldn't have to sleep with him any more, and now I guess he sleeps with anybody."

"You guess?"

"Not with me. He went and told Betty about me, so I told him that he and Betty were just right for each other. And they are. I think some married couples get as much of a thrill out of quarreling as anything else."

"Some do, I guess."

"Those I know about seem to. I wouldn't get married for anything. I'm *never* going to get married. When I'm twenty-five I'm going to move away from Gibbsville and live in New York. I'll get some kind of a job, maybe work in a settlement house or something like that. And when I get to be forty or around there I'll move to Italy and settle down with those elderly Englishwomen you read about. Widows and old maids. Have a garden, and tea every afternoon. I'm always reading about them in books, and it sounds like a nice life. They all have something in their past, but they mind their own business, and they're polite to each other. Some of them turn Catholic and the priest is practically the only man they ever see. I don't know about that part of it for me. I've never met a priest, but Agnes, our maid, talks about her priest as if he were a saint, and I just don't believe it. It's going against nature, and I just don't believe it, especially Italians. My goodness, I knew a girl at Miss Crowder's that spent a year in Florence, and American men are bad enough, but those Italian men must be a hundred times worse. But I guess when I'm forty I'll be safe. I'd just like to think that in my old age I could have a nice little villa and a few friends to talk to if I felt like it, and if I wanted to stay home and read and not see anybody, I could do that. Some of them take up painting. I wouldn't be any good at that. I probably wouldn't be very good at gardening, either, but they say anything grows over there, the land is so fertile. Genteel old maid. Can you see me as a genteel old maid, you genteel old bachelor? Kiss me while I'm young, Jap. I won't talk any more, I promise."

She was twenty, and a year out of school. She had not tried very hard for the colleges that were acceptable to her, and tried not at all for the others. In anticipation of her twenty-first birthday she was given a Chrysler convertible coupe, which she drove badly and continually. She took golf lessons and played dutifully in the lowest sixteen; she went to the movies with her friend Blandina Tuckerman. She had her hair done. She enrolled in a business college for a course in shorthand and typing, and dropped it halfway through. She continued to read a lot, novels and magazines, not for stimulation or for entertainment but purely for the consumption of time. She never, for instance, would mention a book to Blandina for the purpose of a discussion of it. Blandina was her companion rather more than she was her friend; a small, thick-ankled girl whose father owned a shoe store, whose mother was a Christian Scientist, whose brother was studying to be an ornithologist. The Tuckerman family were lost in mediocrity and bound by such respectability that they were unaware of Marjorie's special notoriety among the country club set. There was no way in which the gossip would have reached the Tuckermans, and Marjorie confided nothing in Blandina. Marjorie was the bright spot in Blandina's life, and if love can exist in a vacuum, Blandina's feeling for Marjorie was love. Marjorie, of course, was not unaware of the drabness of Blandina's life—the brick house in a row of brick houses, the father's devotion to his business, the mother's hypochondria, the brother's preference for birds over all human beings, and Blandina's own unimaginative spirit—and she was not ashamed to use Blandina in a quid pro quo relationship. Blandina did not question the fairness of the arrangement: she rode around in a pretty car, she was waited on by the Allanson servants, she never had to pay to see a movie, and twice a year she was taken to the country club, where her father and mother never had been. Sara Allanson made no effort to understand the relationship, but she approved of it. As dull a girl as Blandina could do no harm, and she even, by her dullness, suggested a certain conventionality. Sara reasoned that no one would look upon Blandina as an evil influence or a partner in misconduct—and no one did.

In a few years Marjorie Allanson became a fixed figure in the town. She was a young woman who was known to be immoral, and yet there was no dramatic evidence of her immorality, and as time passed there was a more moderate judgment of her misconduct. She was not invited to the small parties of the younger set, where misconduct was not exceptional. Consequently her name was left out of the minor scandals of her contemporaries, and her reputation, though bad, was static. The old label was there, but it was old. One indeterminable day it became a fact that several years had passed since Marjorie Allanson had been involved in an episode worth talking about. It was no secret that Jap Wilson took her to hotels down country, but there was not much interest in Jap Wilson's amours. He was well in his thirties, a bachelor, and was said to have been turned down by every marriageable girl in town since his graduation from State. The prevailing opinion was that Marjorie Allanson had quieted down or was being extremely discreet, and in the absence of a spectacular incident it did not matter which. She was also putting on a little weight, and the voluptuousness of her figure had ceased to be alarming or startling. It would not be long before she was actually stout, and she was getting close to twenty-five.

Then one morning the town learned that Marjorie Allanson had eloped with Chester Tuckerman, and the sensation could not have been greater if the man had been one of the husbands who had been her lovers. "How did it *happen?*" was the common question, and first to ask it was Sara Allanson. Along with the rest of the citizenry she had not known that Marjorie had ever had five minutes alone with

Blandina's brother. The young man's name had never come up even during the times when Sara was present at lunch with Blandina and Marjorie, and Sara would not have recognized Chester if she saw him on the street. She did not, indeed, recognize him when Marjorie brought him home with her from Elkton, Maryland. "Mother, I want you to meet Chester Tuckerman, my new husband. We were married this morning."

"Yes, the paper called. How did this happen?"

"Well, aren't you going to welcome us home? We're married, Mother."

"Yes, of course. How do you do, Chester. I take for granted that you're Blandina's sister. I mean brother, of course."

"Yes, ma'am. My father owns the shoe store."

"Yes, and what do you do? How old are you? Tell me something about yourself."

"I'm twenty-six years old and I'm working for my master's degree at Bucknell."

"Bucknell. Then are you a Baptist?"

"No. My father is a Reformed, and my mother's a Christian Scientist."

"Oh, yes, I believe I did know that. There aren't many Christian Scientists in Gibbsville, are there?"

"Two hundred and fifteen, but my mother says the Scientists are getting their own church next year. Now they meet in Odd Fellows Hall."

"And you're at Bucknell. That's up near Sunbury, isn't it?"

"Lewisburg. I guess we're about fifteen miles from Sunbury. I go through Sunbury on the way home."

"Marjorie has cousins in Sunbury. Judge Doerflinger is my first cousin. That ran for State Attorney General several years ago? At least he ran for the nomination."

"I don't know many Sunbury people, unless they went to Bucknell."

"Well, Cousin Will is a graduate of Dickinson," said Sara. "Then you plan to finish your education? How long have you got before you get your degree?"

"Till June."

"And then what do you plan to do?"

"I have a job next fall, teaching science at Swedish Haven High."

"Oh, science? That must be interesting. Does that include chemistry and physics?"

"Yes, I'll have to teach chemistry, but biology is my field."

"Biology. Oh, yes. I took physiology in school, but I guess biology is much more advanced. Do you expect to support yourself and Marjorie on your teacher's pay?"

"No, but I'll work in the store during the summer. That's three hundred extra, and my mother's going to give me a thousand dollars for a wedding present."

"Marjorie of course will have her own income fairly soon. I suppose she told you that."

"Yes, I guess that'll come in mighty handy."

"But what are you going to do in the meantime?"

"Marjorie, I guess you better tell her that," said Chester.

"Yes, I haven't heard much from you, Marjorie," said Sara.

"You will," said Marjorie. "First of all, I'm having a baby."

"That doesn't surprise me. I was surprised when you eloped, but not by this piece of news. Looking at your figure, I almost asked you."

"You'd have been wrong. I just found out, and the baby isn't due for seven more months."

"Approximately," said Chester. "We're not quite sure about that. Marjorie is very irregular, and the—"

"Oh, be still," said Sara. "I want to hear what my daughter has to say."

"Your *daughter* is his *wife*, Mother. And I was the one that proposed, because I want to have a baby."

"You didn't do this deliberately, I trust," said Sara.

"No, but when I found out, I decided I wanted it. I could have put a stop to it. I know doctors that do it for other girls in town. But Chester was willing to marry me, so we eloped."

"I wasn't just *willing* to marry her, Mrs. Allanson. I'm very fond of Marjorie. She's always been very nice to Blandina, and she isn't stuck-up, like some of the girls in this part of town. In fact, I always admired Marjorie, although I never knew her very well."

"Till recently, let's put it," said Sara.

"Well, yes," said Chester.

"As they say nowadays, you made up for lost time. Well, I still don't know what your plans are. For instance, when do you begin to support your new wife?"

"He can't support me now. He only has enough money to finish at Bucknell."

"And I live in a fraternity house. I guess I could take my mother's thousand dollars and we could board in Lewisburg, but Marjorie put her foot down on that."

"Why should we live in a boarding-house and there's this house with all the empty rooms, and servants and conveniences?"

"Don't you want to be together, like most newly married couples?" said Sara.

"He can come down on weekends. It isn't far."

"I can get a ride nearly every weekend. There's over two hundred boys and girls from Lantenengo County, and four Lambda Chis live around here. Lamba Chi Alpha, that's my fraternity."

"Marjorie's father was a Phi Kappa Sigma."

"They're good. Older than we are."

"So he can come down weekends," said Marjorie. "It isn't a question of money, Mother. Mr. Truesdale said if I ever needed money I could always borrow on my inheritance."

"It isn't exactly an inheritance, you know. I hope you made that clear to Chester. You'll have the income, but you can't touch the principal. This new child of yours will get that, and share it with his brothers and sisters."

"What does it amount to, the income?" said Chester.

"Well, I suppose it's all right to tell you, since you *are* Marjorie's husband. This year it comes to a little over eight thousand dollars."

"A year?"

"Yes. If the stock market comes back it'll be more. It used to be more," said Sara.

"I don't see why Chester can't take my car to Lewisburg and then he won't have to depend on other people to come home weekends. I don't want to drive till after I've had the baby. If I want to go anywhere, William can take me."

Sara was silent.

"Do you object to that, Mother?"

"No. I was just thinking it'd be nice if you'd *ask* me to do all these things. Instead of which you're just informing me that this is going to be so, and that is going to be so. I have no voice in any of these matters."

"Would you rather I lived with Mr. and Mrs. Tuckerman?"

"Where do they live?"

"Oh, Blandina would love that," said Chester.

"No. Mrs. Tuckerman is a Christian Scientist, and they don't approve of doctors," said Sara.

"I wanted to be a doctor originally, but my father said it would kill my mother. They had fights enough over Blandina and I."

"No, you stay here, Marjorie, and tomorrow first thing we'll have Dr. English come and see you."

"Don't have him. Have Malloy," said Tuckerman.

"Dr. Malloy has never been in this house and if I have anything to say about it, he never will be. Some things, Chester, that you're going to have to leave up to me. Don't be so hasty your first time in the house."

"Pardon me," said Chester.

"Marjorie, will you tell Agnes where you and Chester want to sleep? She can get William to help her move the furniture," said Sara. "And I was wondering whether your mother and father would like to come here for dinner this evening. What would you think about that, Chester?"

"Well, I don't know. I guess that'd be all right. I mean *sure*. I guess the two families might as well get acquainted."

"What is your telephone number?" said Sara.

"Three-nine-eight-four Jay. It sounds like a party line but it isn't. I don't know why they have the Jay there."

The announcements went out, the presents began pouring in, and the social amenities were observed to the extent that Marjorie was guest of honor at an older ladies' luncheon and another luncheon for younger women. The temporary absence of the groom in Lewisburg provided Marjorie's lifelong acquaintances with a good excuse to postpone mixed parties until the fall, and it was firmly understood by them and by Marjorie that the postponements would be permanent. No one had the slightest intention of giving a dinner dance for Marjorie Allanson Tuckerman and her bird-loving husband. The nut dishes and bread plates were duly acknowledged and, when not engraved, exchanged for credit; and Marjorie stayed out of sight as her pregnancy grew more noticeable. Her baby was born on the dot, according to Dr. English's prediction, or two months prematurely, according to the explanation by Sara which no one paid any attention to. And Chester was awarded his master's degree.

Now, with a husband and a baby daughter, Marjorie vanished as completely as though she had moved to Florence, Italy. She and Chester rented a house in Swedish Haven, four miles away, but a thousand leagues removed from the people she had always known. All reports on her life had to come from Sara. "Marjorie's all wrapped up in that little girl, and I can't say I blame her. Chester's brown eyes and curly hair. They both try to keep each other from spoiling that child, but I'm not sure how well they're succeeding. I'm so pleased with Chester. He's brilliant, you know. They won't be able to hold him very long at Swedish Haven High. He's already turned down several offers from *colleges*, but he's going to stay at Swedish Haven to get experience, and besides he'd given them his word. I hope he does stay, because I couldn't bear to have them take little Robin away. I go there every Monday afternoon, but if I had my way I'd be there *every* afternoon. By the way, did you know that Chester's family are descendants of William Penn? They were an old Pennsylvania family before Gibbsville was ever thought of. I just happened to find that out when they were deciding what to name the baby. Some of these upstarts at the country club are in for a rude shock when they hear that. Chester got in, of course, but I had to laugh when I heard of some of the people that were trying to keep him out. Not that he cares. They never go to the club. But as I said to Marjorie, her father was one of the founders of it and one of these days she might have a son and I'm going to turn over Frank's bonds to Marjorie's son. Can you imagine somebody like that Harry Reilly questioning Chester's right to be in the club? If he knew how close he came to being kept out, and it was Frank Allanson that spoke up for him. I wish we had a college in Gibbsville, that would keep Chester here. He's a brilliant young man. Brilliant. I gave him a microscope for his birthday. It was the only thing he wanted."

Marjorie's second child was a son, and he was named Frank Allanson Tuckerman. "Such a chubby little fellow, and his initials are f, a, t. Just like his mother," said Marjorie.

"You're not fat. What they call pleasingly plump," said Chester.

"Well, I'm not as fat as I was. God, I was big this time. A hundred and seventy. Dr. English said that was too much, and I think we ought to wait a while before we have another."

"Suits me," said Chester. "If we have any more we're going to have to look for a bigger house, and I like this one."

"I love it. Why don't we buy it? It's so silly to go on paying rent, money down the drain."

"I'm against mortgages. I can pay the rent here, but I couldn't scrape up the cash to buy it."

"But I can, and you're so popular with Mother, she'd lend you the money in a minute."

"Yes, but I could get unpopular with her, too."

"Not any more."

"Besides, I may want to get out of Swedish Haven. That would make me unpopular with your mother, and we'd be saddled with a house. You don't know how long it'd be before we could sell it, and we'd be paying taxes and the mortgage on this house and paying rent on some place else."

"Yes. Well, I love this house, and if we move away I hope we can find one exactly like it."

"With certain improvements. If we bought this house we'd want to spend some money on it. The wiring should be done all over again, it really isn't safe. And I'll never buy a house that doesn't have oil heating. This furnace is a darn nuisance. Just because we live in the coal region. My father's always saying we sell shoes to the coal miners, therefore we have to use coal."

"My father said the same thing," said Marjorie.

"Well, maybe I'll get a job in Oklahoma and we'll *have* to get an oil burner. Or maybe out in the western part of the State. I filled in another application today. Spring Valley. It's a good little college. Better than a lot of them. The money's about the same, but I'd be willing to take less at a college as good as Spring Valley. I don't want to give up my job here for less money unless it's a good opportunity."

"When will you know?"

"Oh, not for a month or two. These things take time, and I'm not the only applicant, you can be sure of that. There'll be Ph.D.'s applying for this particular job. I'm not very hopeful."

"Chet, why don't you get your Ph.D.? When I have the money it's so ridiculous for you to go on teaching in a high school. Is it Mother?"

"Well, only partly. It's my mother, too. She says I'll be principal here and make as much as a college professor, and she's right. The principal of Swedish Haven High makes as much as some full professors. She looked it up. But I don't put all the blame on them. I have to take some of it. I like it here."

"Well, if you like it that much, we'll stay. We can buy this house and spend some money on it."

"You're so impulsive. It'll take me about two more years to finish my book, and then if that gets accepted I'll get better offers. I won't need my Ph.D. And this fat little fellow won't have to move till he's almost three years old."

"All right, but then let's buy this house. Let's *own* it for three years. I really want that, Chet. Our own house. We can get it for twelve thousand."

"Well, let's see what I hear from Spring Valley."

"You just don't want to be pinned down."

"Probably," he said. "How would you like me to pin you down?"

"It's too soon. Another two weeks or so."

"All right, two more weeks. But then I start looking."

"You'd never do that to me, would you?"

He rubbed his nose with the back of his forefinger. "No, I don't guess I ever would."

"I couldn't endure that, Chet. I mean it. The only person I ever really loved."

"Well, that goes for me too. My father, and our kids. But nobody else. No girl, no woman."

"I don't even like to have you joke about it," said Marjorie.

She was far more afraid of what her own reprisals would do to her than of the seriousness of Chester's threat, and this fear was some measure of the insecurity of her new life. She had forsaken all others, and—with the exception of a single half-hearted overture by Jap Wilson—they had abandoned her to her high school teacher. She was as happy as anyone she knew, proud of her children, content with her husband. But the three years of marriage had not yet made her ready for any such test as a casual infidelity on the part of Chester. She no longer entertained herself with a contemplation of a far-off Italian villa in a far-off future. She did not need to be strengthened by other wives' cold hatred of her or by the uncritical devotion of Blandina Tuckerman. And her present relations with her mother were reasonably satisfactory. She knew that Sara could not resist the impulse to take possession of Chester through flattery and offers of financial help, but after a certain point of skepticism Chester was a naïve man in his relations with Sara, and he simply did not believe that Sara's patronage was obsessive. Since he did not recognize Sara's motives, Marjorie did not see fit to educate him. Instead she rationed Sara's visits and made sure that her mother was given no opportunity to take advantage of Chester's naïveté.

The Spring Valley application was turned down; the college took a man who had already had five years' teaching experience in a large university, and Chester did not even get as far as a personal interview. "Let's face it," he told Marjorie. "I made my mistake when I didn't stay at Bucknell. By now I'd have put in four years as a college teacher. I'd be an assistant professor, and I'd most likely have my Ph.D. All of a sudden I'm a middle-aged man as far as teaching is concerned. I mean it's too late for me to change. I'm a high school teacher, and that's that. So from here on I'm going to *be* a high school teacher, not a frustrated college professor."

"All right," said Marjorie.

"George Beck is going to resign, and when he does they'll offer me his job. He's had a good offer from Tech High, in Fort Penn, and his wife's from around there. He's going to recommend me. He told me so, and the only thing they'd be afraid of is if I took the job and then up and left two or three years from now. Is that all right with you?"

"Yes."

"I'd have to promise the board to stay five years."

"You don't hear any objection from me. But there's one thing I do want."

"I know. You want to own this house," he said.

"Yes. No more putting it off. We'll buy it tomorrow."

"Tomorrow? All right. Tomorrow."

"Good! We can give them a cheque tomorrow, and the next day we can have the electricians out to look over the wiring. Next week I'm going down to a place near Philadelphia and talk to a man about putting up a hedge. I have his name in my desk."

"A hedge? A fence'd be a lot cheaper."

"But not as pretty, and the hedge will keep the kids from straying off, even better than a fence. Also keep stray dogs out."

"Then you're pleased? I mean, you're not disappointed in me?"

"Chet, you know how I've wanted to own this house, and tomorrow night we'll be able to say it's ours."

"Well, if you want to know how I feel about it, I'm glad we didn't have to move to Spring Valley. I must be getting set in my ways."

They bought the house during the noon recess on the next day, and when Chester got home after school Marjorie had filled every vase with flowers and she handed him an unopened bottle of Canadian Club whiskey. "Where did you get *this?*" he said.

"I stole it. It was in my father's private stock, and I just went and took it."

"You went to see your mother?"

"I went there, not to see her. She was out. But I wanted to get this bottle and to ask Agnes if she'd mind the children when I go to Philadelphia. I didn't see Mother, and I didn't say anything about buying the house. I'll tell her some other time. This is just us. Our own private celebration in our own house. Would you rather I'd stolen some champagne?"

"To tell you the truth, I've never had champagne. I've never had this, either, but I've heard about it. And it's pre-Prohibition?"

"Open it, and we'll drink a toast."

"Now, or after supper? You know my capacity, and on an empty stomach."

"Let's have one drink now, and we can save the rest for when company comes. I didn't mean we should get tight, but I suddenly remembered all that liquor Father stored away, and how it would be nice if we used his whiskey to toast our new house. Not Mother's. His. And I'm certainly entitled to one bottle."

"All right. Here's to our new house. Do we have to drink this bottoms-up?"

"Here's to our new house, and the happiness you've given me in it."

"That goes without saying, as far as I'm concerned. To you, Marjorie. My wife."

"And to you, the father of my lovely children."

"I guess we'll have to drink it bottoms-up for all those toasts. Bottoms-up!"

"Bottoms-up!" she said.

"Oh-ho-ho-ho," he said. "That's the real thing all right. You can feel that going down all the way. I've got tears in my eyes, and it isn't sentimental."

"I'd almost forgotten how much I like the taste."

"The taste, or the kick?"

"Both, I guess. But I always liked it. The taste as well as the effect."

"When did you acquire a taste for it?"

"Oh, on dates, you know. Some boys always had a flask or one of those flat bottles."

"You're probably more of a booze hound than I am. I used to chip in and buy a bottle after a football game, but that was just showing off. You never went around much with those girls like Virginia Stokes. I used to hear about how she got slopped, and Annabella Ingersoll."

"I have to get supper. No, I never went around much with them. Are you going to have another?"

"Not unless you do," he said.

"No, I have to put the potatoes on," she said.

"Where's Robin?"

"They're in the kitchen. She's having her supper and he's in the crib."

"Marjorie! I smell smoke."

"So do I. *No! No!*" She ran through the diningroom and pushed open the swinging door, and as she did so a blast of flame leapt into the diningroom before the door swung shut again. "Chester! Chester!" she screamed. He ran to the swinging door, pushed it open and was blasted with flames. Marjorie was picking the baby out of the burning crib, and he did not immediately see Robin. Then he saw her roasted body on the floor. He wrapped her in his coat and carried her to the front room, and Marjorie came in with the body of the baby. Marjorie's dress was burning and her hair was on fire. He pressed his hands on her head and extinguished the flame, and lifted a small rug from the floor and smothered the flames on her burning dress, now nearly gone.

"Put the baby down," he said.

"No, no. Go away," she said. "Oh, Robin. Robin, is that you, Robin? Chester, your shirt's on fire."

He beat out the fire on his sleeve. "Put the baby down, Marjorie. It's no use."

"Call Dr. Straub. Get somebody," she said. "Is that Robin? Is that Robin, Chester?"

"Yes."

"Aren't you going to call the doctor?"

"Yes, but it won't be any use. Marjorie, let me take them out on the lawn. The whole house is going up in a minute, and you need a doctor."

"Are they dead?"

"Goodness, yes. Thank God."

"Thank God?"

"Look at them. You'd pray they were dead."

"Look at your hands. Chester, you're burned."

"Please take the baby out on the lawn, and I'll take Robin. You must get out of here. Do you hear me. Look at the diningroom. Marjorie, get out of the house for God's sake."

"Do you want me to take the baby out on the lawn?" she said.

"Yes, please. Hurry."

"All right. Will you take Robin?"

"Yes, I'll take Robin. Come on, Marjorie. Come with me."

"I'll take the baby out on the lawn, Chester."

"That's a good girl. You take the baby, and I'll take Robin."

"Is your baby dead, Chester? My baby is."

"Yes, they're both dead. And the house is ready to go."

"You be sure and take your baby, Chester."

"Yes, I will, dear."

"This whole house is going to go. Unngg, that smell. Isn't that an awful smell?"

"Yes. You go first, Marjorie."

"And you follow me," she said. The front door opened. "Oh, hello, Mr. Hartman. Did you come to help us?"

"Good God," said the neighbor, Hartman. He turned his face away.

It always takes a little while to get to know Mrs. Frank B. Allanson, a somewhat unusual trait in an American lady. To some degree her seclusion may be attributed to Miss Tuckerman, her paid companion, a bouncy little woman who speaks very little Italian—nouns, mostly—and takes it upon herself to suggest that Mrs. Allanson's callers restrict themselves to two or three innocuous topics and to visits lasting less than an hour. Miss Tuckerman is hardly ever successful, but not for lack of trying. A lady whom Mrs. Allanson herself has invited to tea will get a surprise visit from Miss Tuckerman in advance of the appointed day. "I hope you'll pardon this intrusion," Miss Tuckerman has been known to say, "but Mrs. Allanson has been a bit under the weather, you know. She gets these chest colds and they hang on and hang on. So she tires easily. And at seventy-six. She doesn't look it, but she is. So when you come for tea on Tuesday, don't be surprised if I walk in and tell her it's time for her to rest. Otherwise she'd go on for hours."

"I think you can count on me not to outstay my welcome," the lady—sometimes a noble lady—has been known to say.

"Of course. But then there's this other thing is even more important. I'm referring to subjects to talk about. Not to talk about, is more like it."

"Very well, what are they?"

"First of all, you don't want to say anything about fire. A house on fire. That kind of a fire. Or grandchildren. You don't want to bring up the subject of grandchildren. Avoid that like the plague, because most of the ladies here do have grandchildren and naturally they're liable to say something about them."

"Yes, I have six of them."

"You see what I mean? And do you have anybody in your family or some friend of yours named Marjorie? Because if you do, I'd appreciate it if you didn't bring the name up."

"Isn't it a fairly common name? I should think it'd pop up quite frequently. But go on, please. Any more?"

"Well, the name Chester."

"As a place name, or as a wuddiacallum Christian name? We have a Chester, you know. Rather picturesque town."

"I meant as a man's first name."

"No. No, I don't believe I know a Chester. Chester and Marjorie. Fire and grandchildren. Extraordinary. I know a woman can't bear the very mention of snakes. I'm not too keen on the filthy things myself. But have I got it right now? One, two, three, four. Chester and Marjorie. Grandchildren and fire. Yes, four. Any of these things is apt to set her off, I take it. Oh, well. Thank you for coming, Miss Tucker, and you'll show yourself out?"

From an inner compulsion or a less excusable motive many of the forewarned women lose no time in bringing up the topics on Miss Tuckerman's proscribed list. To some it is a relief, to some a disappointment, to discover that Mrs. Allanson is apparently undisturbed by the introduction of the forbidden names or references to fires and grandchildren. If she is upset at all, it does not show. Her outward composure is wholly ladylike, and the contrast between Mrs. Allanson's dignity and Miss Tuckerman's effervescence has led some of the ladies to suspect that of the two it is Miss Tuckerman who needs watching.

Mrs. Allanson never goes beyond the garden walls. Her villa is four stories high, of which the bottom two stories are backed up against the side of the hill, and the third story is on the level of the road. Miss Tuckerman's small Fiat is usually parked outside the third-story main entrance to the house, and Mrs. Allanson's older acquaintances have learned to wait until Miss Tuckerman has driven down to Florence before entering the house. Nothing comes of a visit to Mrs. Allanson if Miss Tuckerman is hovering about, in and out, interrupting the conversation. Miss Tuckerman has no friends of her own, and to some of the ladies it seems as though she tried her best to prevent Mrs. Allanson from having any. But there are a few ladies who call on her, one at a time, perhaps two or three times a year, and keep her from being lonely. And there is no doubt, from the stories she tells in Miss Tuckerman's absence, that she is lonely. She has had a very sad life.

"She finally confided in me," Mrs. Jessop, her nearest neighbor said one day. "I had a *devil* of a time getting that Tuckerman woman out of the way, but I was determined to find out all about Mrs. Allanson. She interested me from the start. Lovely hair and eyes. Imagine she must have been quite striking-looking in her younger days. They were here, I guess about two months, before I ever met her. I could *see* them from my garden, and at first I thought they must be English. But when Dr. Rossi told me they were Americans I decided to go call on them. So I fixed up a little bunch of my hyacinths and took them down to her place, and left them with a note. One American welcoming another. That sort of thing, and I was on my way back up the hill when I heard this voice calling 'Yoo-hoo, Mrs. Jessop,' and it was the Tuckerman person. She came stumbling along after me on her fat legs and when she got her breath she introduced herself and thanked me. Asked me to come for tea, and then proceeded to instruct me on how I was to behave. I didn't get that much preparation when I was presented at court. But they were new, and I know how it is for an American here, especially if you don't speak the language, and they didn't.

"So I had tea with them, and I was quite surprised to see how quickly Mrs. Allanson had made herself at home. You'd have almost believed that she'd been here all her life. She talked about *her* view, and I didn't bother to point out to her that my view was just a little better. And *her* servants. I kept quiet about that, because she'd hired that Anna Valenti, who's a terrible thief but threatened a friend of mine with a carving knife when she caught her stealing. Her villa. Her view. Her companion, Miss Tuckerman, who turned out to be a friend of her daughter. 'And where is your daughter?' I said. 'Passed on,' she said, and I thought I was going to be in for it, but Miss Tuckerman firmly announced that it was time for Mrs. Allanson's rest, and I took the hint.

"Miss Tuckerman came to see me a couple of times to ask my advice on one thing or another, and once again I was invited to take tea with Mrs. Allanson, but at the last minute I couldn't go, and the next day I got a crazy angry note from Mrs. Allanson. I wish I'd saved it. But the gist of it was that I had snubbed her and who did I think I was? She had some strange thing in it about her connection with William Penn, that I couldn't make any sense out of. Something about her grandchildren and William Penn. But since I'd been practically ordered not to mention grandchildren in front of her, I was completely at a loss, and nobody'd said a word about William Penn. Then I realized that Mrs. Allanson was like quite a few of the ladies that come here to live. We come here because it's first of all cheap, and the climate is good, and mostly because we don't want to spend our last years at home. In my case, Chicago, in her case a little town in Pennsylvania. And usually there's something sad or unpleasant behind it. Nothing particularly tragic about my coming here. My husband simply told me that he wanted to marry a snip that was younger than our youngest child, and I agreed so quickly that I took his breath away. That fixed him. He had to marry her, then. But there was nothing like that in Mrs. Allanson's history. She'd been a widow for many, many years.

"Naturally I was curious about her grandchildren, because of what the Tuckerman person had told me and the thing in Mrs. Allanson's note. It centered around her grandchildren.

"Well, Blandina, Miss Tuckerman, again asked me to call on Mrs. Allanson, apparently unaware that she'd written me that angry letter. And I went. And I was fascinated by Mrs. Allanson's behavior, because she never gave the slightest indication of having written me at all. There was only one thing, and that was just before I was getting ready to leave. We were both standing up, and Blandina was out of the room, and Sara Allanson said she'd had a letter from Marjorie but please not to tell Blandina. I knew that Marjorie was the name of her daughter, but what was this business about Marjorie's having passed on? She couldn't say any more because Blandina came back in the room with my coat.

"The next thing was to see what I could extract from Blandina. But all I could get out of her, in answer to a direct question, was that

Marjorie was dead, and her eyes filled with tears. I had a nasty suspicion that Blandina turned on the tears to keep me from asking any more. But I did notice that from then on she saw to it that I was never alone with Sara. I had a devil of a time learning the whole story, until I did some detective work and discovered that Blandina drove down to Florence three mornings a week. And then it was so easy that it was like taking candy from a baby. Not only because she left Sara all by herself, but Sara herself wanted to talk. It poured out of her, and she made me promise not to tell Blandina that I went to the house.

"The grandchildren were burned to death in a fire, sometime back in the early Thirties. It was a terrible thing, because the daughter, Marjorie, and her husband, were drunk. They'd left the children in the kitchen, all by themselves, and Marjorie and her husband were so drunk that they didn't even know the house was on fire until a neighbor came to help. He could see the whiskey bottle on the table, and he had to testify that Marjorie and her husband were obviously drunk. A schoolteacher, the husband was, and very pleased with himself, but the kind of a hypocrite that would never be seen in a speakeasy but made Marjorie steal the liquor from her mother's cellar. But Marjorie had a terrible punishment. Not only the horrible death of her children, but she'd apparently been a beautiful girl. Strikingly beautiful. And *she* was badly burned in the fire and disfigured for life. Not that she lived much longer. She underwent some skin-grafting that wasn't at all successful, and she wouldn't let anyone see her. Only her mother. Not even her husband. Yes, one other person. Blandina, the Tuckerman woman. She visited her in the hospital as often as she could, and that's why Sara gave her the job as companion after Marjorie jumped out of the hospital window. Sara didn't want to talk about the husband, and she gave me some rather conflicting stories about him. One time she told me that he was teaching at some little college in Pennsylvania. Another time she said he moved to Canada after Marjorie killed herself, and spent all his time studying the habits of birds. Of course I don't accept everything Sara told me as gospel, but I remembered having gone to school with a girl from Gibbstown or Gibbsville, Pennsylvania, and I wrote and asked her about the story. And most of it appears to be true. She sent me a clipping from an old newspaper, and it was all there about the children and the fire, and Marjorie being badly burned. I hadn't really known the girl very well, and she only sent me the one clipping, but it confirmed the story Sara told me.

"Interesting, you know. I mean Sara's reaction to it all. It all happened a long time ago, and you can't go on living if time doesn't help you some. But Sara's reaction is quite unusual. It seems to me that only a very remarkable woman would have her courage. Almost as if she took as much pride in her tragedy as some women do in—oh, I don't know. In other things. It was a *terrible* tragedy, but it was *hers,* if you know what I mean. And Blandina must be a trial to live with."

What's the Good of Knowing?

The social evening was at an end and Mr. and Mrs. Young got in their car and went home. Beatrice Young stayed in the car all the way into the garage; she and her husband got out together. He lowered the garage door, and in the driveway he looked up at the sky and said, "If it wasn't the wrong time of year, I'd say we could expect snow."

"Well, we don't get snow in September. Have you got your key?"

"In Wyoming they get snow in September," said Albert Young. "Yes, I've the key. You mean the kitchen door key?"

"What else would I mean?"

"Well, you could mean the garage key, or the front door key."

"Since when did we start locking the garage door? I don't remember it ever being locked."

"I used to lock it during the war, when we had gas rationing," said Albert Young.

He unlocked the kitchen door and they went inside. "Want a bottle of beer?"

"Good heavens, no," she said.

"Good heavens no? Don't make it sound like a crime, Beatrice. You *asked* for beer at the party."

"That doesn't mean I'm going to sit up drinking beer all night, does it? I'm going to bed. Goodnight."

"Sit down, Beatrice. Just sit down and tell me what the hell's the matter with you?"

"All right. I won't sit down, but I don't mind telling you how disgusted I was with you tonight. You, and George and Archie and all the rest of you."

"I knew that was it."

"Did you? Do you have any idea how you sounded, a bunch of older men suddenly talking like prep school boys."

"I guess we did," said Albert Young.

The Horse Knows the Way (1964)

"And believe me, I wasn't the only one that was disgusted. There wasn't a woman there that didn't wish her husband would shut up."

"No, I guess there wasn't."

"Even the ones that haven't always lived here. Edith Morgan, I could see her mentally thanking God her husband never knew Sadie Carr. He probably would have been just as bad as the rest of you. How on earth you ever got started on the subject of Sadie Carr, I'll never know."

"Well, I'll be glad to tell you if you'll listen."

"I don't want to listen," she said.

"Sit down and listen, for Pete's sake. It'll do you good."

"Do me good? Well, I like that."

"It'd do you all good if you'd listen," he said.

"Thanks just the same."

"Sit down, Beatrice. We talked like prep school boys, but you're pouting like an eighth-grader. I'm going to get myself a beer, and you can sit or stand, but I'm going to have this out with you." She sat at the kitchen table, her chin up, her gaze fixed on the wall straight ahead. He opened and poured a bottle of beer, taking his good time about it.

"We were sitting out on the porch," he said. "You women were all upstairs so you didn't hear the beginning of it. I'm not sure whether it was George or Archie or who it was that first brought up Sadie's name, and I don't even know why. But I know the first time I heard her name I laughed, and that's the same reaction the other men had. We all laughed except the men that didn't grow up here. Then hey wanted to know what we were laughing for."

"I can imagine what came next," she said.

"And there you're absolutely wrong, because you *can't* imag e. Sam Morgan said who was Sadie Carr, who *was* she? And th e wasn't a man there that volunteered the answer. Not a one of .. Finally I spoke up and said she was a girl we all used to know."

"It would have to be you, of course."

"It had to be me because I just happened to be sitting next to Morgan. Morgan pursued the subject. He would. He wanted to know why we all laughed when her name was mentioned and then suddenly shut up about her. What was she? Some kind of a town tart?"

"A very good guess on Sam's part, I must say."

"You can say what you like, but I'll tell you this. There wasn't a man there that wanted to say anything derogatory to Sadie. We all did laugh, that's true, when her name came up. But after the original reaction we all wanted to—we didn't want to say any more about her. I think we were all thinking the same thing. That Sadie never did anybody any harm, that she didn't have a mean bone in her body. I doubt if any of us had even thought about her for years. That's why we laughed at first, because when we were younger we used to make jokes about her. But she's been dead for over thirty years, and maybe we realized as we got older that Sadie was really quite a sweet girl."

"Oh, for God's sake."

"All right. What did *you* know about Sadie? Actually *know?*"

"Well I'm sure I was glad to take your word for it, all of your words, you gay Lotharios. None of us girls knew her to see hardly, but you Don Juans hinted at plenty."

"Mm-hmm. Hinted is right," he said. "Always hinted that more went on than actually did."

"All right. Point-blank. Did you go all the way with her?"

"Yes."

"Did George?"

"I don't know."

"Did Archie?"

"He certainly did. He wanted to marry her. He gave her his fraternity pin and had her up to State for one of the proms."

"Well, he's a sap anyway. But at least two of you in the same crowd had intercourse with her. And what about Mr. Codway that she worked for?"

"All right, maybe he did."

"You realize of course that it's just coming out, about *you* and this quite-sweet little girl, and we've been married thirty-six years. Why were you so protective about *her?*"

"I don't know. I just didn't tell you. I don't know why. Any more than I know why the other fellows there tonight were protective, as you call it. I guess George slept with her, too. I'm not sure he was one of those that laughed tonight. He was at the other end of the porch away from me."

"He probably did. You and he were the ones that disgusted me the most, trying to pretend that she was a kind of a harmless innocent that you all had fun with. Good clean fun. Ha ha ha. Well, now it comes out, and if that's all, I'm going to bed. I'll leave you to your tender memories of Sadie Carr."

He remained in the kitchen but did not finish his beer. He rinsed out the glass and the bottle, and he was in his bed before Beatrice was in hers. He was asleep before she was, and in the morning he was gone before she got out of bed. There was a new engineer at the factory, a young fellow named Robert Stannard who looked promising but in this, his first week, was suffering from shyness. The simplest way to overcome that was to spend a lot of time with him, show

him the equipment and let the personal relations take care of themselves. "Now about this boiler," said Albert Young. "This isn't going
to be one of your problems. We're getting a new one. Of course the
job of installing the new one *is* going to be one of your problems, but
at least you know now that you're not going to be saddled with this
one."

"It has seen better days, all right," said Stannard.

"Yes it has," said Albert Young. "But it was a good one. I'm going
to introduce you to Eddie Thomas, foreman of our steamfitters. Eddie helped to install the boiler and he's kept it in good shape ever
since. I suggest you spend an hour or so with Eddie. It won't be a
waste of time. Get Eddie talking about this boiler and that way you'll
find out more about Eddie and he about you than any other way I
can think of. He's a good man, but he's a Welshman and they can be
hard to know. I'll make myself scarce while you two get acquainted."

He took Stannard to lunch at the hotel. "Next week I'd like to
make a suggestion, after you and Mrs. Stannard are more or less
settled in. It's just a suggestion, but it's worth thinking about.
Namely, get into the habit of once in a while—not every day, but
once in a while—bring your lunch to the factory. Most of the time
you'll eat it alone, because one of the worst things you could do
would be to try to be pals with the men. Their lunch hour belongs to
them, just as yours and mine belong to us. But an engineer is something like a doctor. He has no hours. And if the men get used to
seeing you around like that, they'll separate you from the sales department. Do you see what I mean?"

"I think so, sir."

"You don't have to do the things the men are paid to do, such as
crawling inside the boiler, or climbing up on top of the water tower.
Actually the men resent that. Our men know their jobs, for the most
part, and what they say you can rely on. For instance, you'll find that
some of them have a lot of theoretical knowledge—metallurgy, electricity, things like that—that may surprise you. When I came here I
had an engineering degree, and even though I'm the third generation to own the factory, and had worked here part of every summer,
I made the great mistake of underestimating the practical men's
technical knowledge. Luckily my father'd made the same mistake, so
he saw to it that I didn't repeat it. He put me in the hands of a man
named Jacob Carr, one of our foremen, a man who only got as far as
eighth grade in school but came here to learn his trade when he was
about fourteen or fifteen. He was apprenticed to old Matthew Logan, a master mechanic that had started out with my grandfather,
and Jacob Carr was just as tough on me as I imagine Matthew Logan

was on him. It was quite an experience, you know, getting slapped down every once in a while by a man that hadn't finished eighth grade. He'd say things like, 'What is two-eighteen point eight?' "

"That's the boiling point of oxygen," said Stannard.

"Of course, but Jacob Carr—Mr. Carr, I always called him—he was testing me to see how much I learned at State."

"And showing off a little," said Stannard.

"Yes, he was showing off, but doing it for a reason. My father had told him to put me in my place, and he did. Every day for a year I reported to Mr. Carr at seven A.M. And by the way, I had to be shaved. 'I shave before *I* come to work, so you come shaved too,' he said. My, was he strict, and my father backed him up in everything. At the end of that year I was cut down to size, but I knew more about the factory than I would have learned in five years, or ten, if I'd gone right into the office. My second year I was transferred to the accounting office under Henry J. Ingalls, and I had more of a knack for that work than for the manufacturing end, but I missed Mr. Carr. I asked my father to put me back on the floor, but he wouldn't. He finally told me why—oh, five or six years later. He said that Mr. Carr had told him I'd never make a real floor man. I didn't have the real mechanical turn of mind, he said, and he was right. I could follow everything, but I didn't look at a problem and lose myself in it. I was, in other words, an office man. That was before we heard so much about the word executive. I've often thought that Mr. Carr was just as disappointed as I was—or would have been, if my father had told me I didn't measure up. He didn't tell me that until after Mr. Carr died. Was killed, actually."

"In an accident at the factory?"

"Yes," said Albert Young. "Yes, he was."

"How?"

"How? Well, this was before you were born, so I guess it's all right to tell you. From a teetotaler, not even a glass of beer, Mr. Carr suddenly became a heavy drinker. So much so that he began to bring a pint of rotgut to work with him in his lunch-can. My father found out about it and fired him, hoping that would knock some sense into him. And it did for a while. He went on the wagon for a month and came and saw my father, and my father was only too willing to give him his job back. But the reform didn't last. He didn't bring the booze in his lunch-can any more, but he still brought it with him and had it hidden somewhere. One day he'd been hitting it a little more than usual, because some of the men said later that he was obviously drunk. One man told him to go home, before my father caught him in that condition, but Mr. Carr told the man to mind his own business. Then a little while later he went into the generator room, where he had no business to be, and went behind the switchboard and fell against a bus bar. Twenty-two hundred volts. A.C."

"Yes, D.C. might have knocked him away."

"He knew that, Bob. I didn't want to say anything to my father. He was upset enough. But Mr. Carr grabbed hold of that bus bar. It was no accident."

"Sounds to me as though he'd found out he had cancer," said Stannard. "Something like that."

"He'd found out something," said Albert Young.

"Did they call it accidental death?" said Stannard.

"Oh, yes. The insurance company wasn't very happy about that, but the coroner's jury wasn't made up of insurance people, and the insurance company couldn't go against their verdict."

"So naturally the family was taken care of," said Stannard.

"The widow and two daughters. One of them named Sadie. The other one—I think her name was Peggy. Or maybe it was Betty. Doesn't matter."

"Dessert for you gentlemen?" said the waitress. "Mr. Young, we have the first punkin pie you asked for last week."

"Just coffee for me, Mildred, but Mr. Stannard might like some. Bob?"

"Yeah, I'll try the punkin pie."

"You want the whipped cream on it? It comes with or without. In other words, you don't have to have it with," said Mildred.

"Without, then," said Stannard.

Albert Young lit a cigarette. For some unaccountable reason he was disliking this young man—and then he knew it was not this young man he disliked. It was the remembered image of himself that he had succeeded in obliterating for nearly forty years. He wondered if enough time remained to hide himself again. What the damn hell had brought the Carrs back into his life?

He took young Stannard to the factory and left him in the draughtsmen's room; he had no wish to be with anyone so young. In his private office the afternoon dragged on because he knew that at five o'clock he was going to the club in the hope of encountering George Watson, and yet he could not count on seeing George or make an appointment with him. It was going to be enough of a surprise to George to see him at the club at that hour of the day.

He was lucky. George was there, sitting in the bar with Sam Morgan. "Sit down, Bert. Take the load off your feet," said George.

"I had a slight hangover today. Did you fellows?" said Albert Young.

"I told you years ago," said George. "Moderation is no good for anybody. You didn't drink enough last night to bother anybody, except one of your moderation addicts. Have a good stiff snort. Have a boilermaker, for God's sake."

"No. I'll have a bourbon on the rocks."

"All right, but don't say I didn't warn you. Moderation. Moderation."

"It's not that I drank any more than usual last night. But it seemed to hit me."

"I didn't notice anything—except I did notice that you got sort of reminiscent there about Sadie Carr. My God, if you have to go back that far."

"I was talking about Sadie Carr?" said Albert Young.

"You wouldn't stop. Right out of nowhere you started talking about her."

"No," said Sam Morgan. "Bert wasn't the one that brought her name up. It was Archie. Archie said that the young girls nowadays all take some kind of a medicine that keeps them from getting pregnant, and then he said what a godsend it would have been for Sadie Carr. Naturally I didn't know who that was, and I asked Bert. It wasn't Bert that brought her into the conversation."

"Well, maybe not, but he kept talking about her," said George.

"So did you, George," said Sam Morgan.

"Well, I didn't say anything derogatory," said George.

"Far from it," said Sam. "The only derogatory thing was Archie's remark about the godsend if they'd had that medicine then."

"Oh, well I didn't hear that," said George. "If I had, I sure as hell would have lit into Archie. He had no cause to make disparaging remarks about Sadie. Him least of all. Bert, were you ever favored with Sadie's tender ministrations? I don't seem to remember you being on her list."

"If you think a minute, you'll remember, so there's no use my lying about it. Yes."

"By God, you did. I remember now. It was some picnic or something out at the old Park. Didn't you have some fight with some Irish boy? Fellow, his father used to own the marble yard on the East Side. Mc-Something. McCahill. McCahill. The Irish were having a picnic. The Knights of Columbus. And there was a dance. Some big orchestra. Was it Paul Whiteman? I think it was Paul Whiteman, or maybe it was Vincent Lopez. Anyway, she went out with you at intermission, and then when you came back McCahill—no, I'm wrong. That was Archie. I remember now it was Archie, because he had a shiner. But there was something about you and Sadie. I'll think of it."

"Don't wrack your brains. I admitted it," said Albert Young.

"Poon-tang," said George. "A little piece of poon-tang, that was Sadie. All the same, she was a hell of a good kid. I never knew what she wanted out of life. Not money. You wouldn't think of offering her money. Never occurred to me to offer her money. Her father was a—hell, he worked for *your* father, Bert. In fact he was killed in an accident out at your factory."

"Yes he was," said Albert Young. "Electrocuted."

"And Sadie always worked. She had a job there with R. D. Codway when I knew her. Codway was an optician, had a place on South Main. He was a widower or maybe a bachelor. Single, anyway, when he came to town. And what went on between him and Sadie I never knew for sure. But she had to look presentable, and she did. She had style about her. Always very *neat,* wasn't she, Bert? So was her father. They were very clean-looking people. I never knew her mother. But their house was very neat and tidy. I was inside the house several times. Do you remember their house, Bert?"

"I never got inside."

"I never understood about the Carr family. I used to call for Sadie to take her out. Eight o'clock. Ring the doorbell. Sadie'd let me in, and there wouldn't be a sign of anybody else. And you wouldn't hear anybody moving around. Not a sound. She'd tell me to wait in the front parlor and I'd sit there and all I'd hear was the clock ticking. I don't know whether her father and mother went to bed right after supper or what. But she'd come downstairs with her coat and hat on and out we'd go. Maybe the father and mother were in the kitchen, I don't know. But they stayed out of sight. Strange. Those kind of people, I guess they were anxious to get their daughters married off. Some of them of course were very strict, but some of the mothers gave the girls plenty of leeway, and that must have been the case with Sadie. Didn't seem to make any difference what time I got her home, just as long as it was before daylight. I was the one that caught hell from my family for staying out late. Two, three, four o'clock in the morning."

"Did she finally snag a husband?" said Sam.

"Sadie? No. She died. What was it she died of, Bert?"

"Appendicitis. Peritonitis."

"An abortion, maybe?" said Sam.

"No," said Albert Young. "Malloy was their doctor. He was a big Catholic surgeon around here in those days, and he wouldn't touch that kind of a case. He could always send a woman to another doctor, but he was the one that operated on Sadie. She never came out of the ether."

"And even before that she'd begun to go downhill," said George. "I think her father's death was a great shock to her. She began to lose her looks, and I think it was her father."

"Had a lot to do with it, all right," said Albert Young.

"Well, even today you can't fool around with a ruptured appendix," said Sam.

"No, I guess you can't," said George. "I had mine out when I was sixteen."

"I've never had any trouble with mine," said Sam.

"Now they have them up and walking around the next day," said George.

"Yes, I remember when Beatrice had hers out, she was home from the hospital in just over a week," said Albert Young. "And that was a good ten years ago."

"They still don't know what the hell it's there for," said George. "What good it does."

"Well, unless you want to take into consideration a lot of Cadillacs and mink coats," said Sam.

"You mean doctors' wives got the mink coats," said George.

"And the doctors got the Cadillacs," said Sam. "Gentlemen, I have to head for home. George. Bert." He rose and departed.

The two friends said nothing for a little while. "I don't know, Bert. We're getting on."

"Yes, we are," said Albert Young. He waited, without knowing what he wanted from George, for he had never known.

"When I get a little stitch in my belly, I know it can't be appendicitis, because I've had that out. But I'd just as soon not know, wouldn't you?"

"I suppose so, George."

"It's going to make damn little difference whether I know or I don't," said George.

"So in other words, what's the good of knowing? I think you're absolutely right, George."

"And if you'll just tap that bell, I'll let you in on the secret of eternal life and connubial bliss and good fellowship and all the rest of it. The magic formula, my friend."

"Right you are," said Albert Young, and tapped the bell.

Clayton Bunter

There was neither excitement nor rejoicing over the death of Clayton Bunter, and certainly no one carried out the threat, heard so many times over the years, to commit certain acts of desecration on his grave. It is possible that Clayton Bunter, by taking a long time dying, extended the potential drama of his passing until nothing was left of it, so that he was allowed to leave this world almost unobserved, just like any other sick old man. The quiet departure of a man who had been so roundly hated was curiously disrespectful to him, and he would not have liked it one bit. Several months after Clayton was laid to rest the newspapers published the information from the Orphans Court that appraisals had been concluded and that the total value of the estate was just under $800,000. "The son of a bitch wasn't even a millionaire," was the rather weak comment in the barber shops and cigar stores, and so real was the citizens' disappointment in the size of the Bunter fortune that the comment became his epitaph. They hurried to forget him, and no one talks about him today.

And yet Clayton Bunter during the first quarter of the century was regarded, not unjustly, as something of a financial wizard, a shrewd guesser in real estate transactions and a clever trader in the stock market. Although he was not even the twentieth richest man in Gibbsville—he probably did not belong among the top thirty—he was more conspicuous than most of the rich men because of his eccentricities. To begin with, there was his mode of dress. Other rich men wore cheap suits and wore them threadbare, but Clayton, having paid twenty dollars for a suit, would never again subject it to the presser's iron. He understood as well as any man with an extensive wardrobe that sponging and pressing shortens the life of a garment. It was not true that Clayton refused to sit down because he did not want to wear out the seat of his pants. He had another reason for wanting to remain standing, a painful one, and he did not like to be

The Horse Knows the Way (1964)

kidded about it. In general, though, he was not disturbed by disrespectful or insulting remarks, whatever they might pertain to, or whoever made them. Only on Sunday and on Monday morning when he attended his bank directors' meeting, would he wear a collar; the rest of the week he went without collar and tie, and his flesh rolled over the neckband and all but hid his brass collar-button. During the warm weather he went without coat and vest, but he continued to wear long underwear. He would roll up his shirt sleeves and tuck in the neckband, and all day long he would stand under shopkeepers' awnings, fanning himself with his straw hat and soaking his underwear with his sweat. It did not pass unobserved that he always started the week with clean underwear that got progressively soiled by Saturday.

With the coming of cold weather Clayton would put away his straw hat and get out his fedora and his rubber overshoes. He wore rubbers not so much as a protection against the damp as an economical protection for the soles of his shoes. Except in severe cold he wore a fireman's rubber coat, one of several gifts from the man who handled his fire insurance.

Clayton was a fat man, whose dimensions were no larger than those of some men who were called stout; but no one ever called him stout. He was fat. He would have been fat if he had weighed twenty pounds less than his two hundred ten. He was on his feet most of the time; owing to the already mentioned ailment he was seldom at his desk for long periods. But it was also a part of his disposition to be moving about, to be where he could see people, watch them, talk and listen to them even though the things they sometimes said were insulting. "I don't consider it an insult when I can buy and sell a fellow, when all I have to do is get a dispossess and he'd be out in the street. Water off a duck's back," he would say. He was often insulted by men, particularly young men, who were ignorant of the fact that he was their landlord. He operated behind numerous business names, all representing holdings of Bunter & Company, some of them better known than others, and some not identified with him at all. These latter were the nominal owners of Clayton's slum tenements, among the worst in town. Clayton's refusal to proclaim his possession of his filthy firetraps was not out of a sense of shame, but merely precautionary. He did not wish to be bothered with his tenants' complaints of leaky roofs and falling plaster; even more he dreaded the wrath of tenants whom he had had dispossessed. He did not like to part with the fees he paid his collectors, but he knew, from having tried vainly, that you can't get something for nothing in this life, and the collectors contributed to his peace of mind.

But it would be a mistake to think of Clayton as an unhappy man. Miserable, perhaps; but not unhappy. He lived with his wife and his older sister in a red brick marble-stoop house in a neighborhood of red brick marble-stooped houses that he owned and that his wife and sister dominated. Laurie, his sister, and Florence, his wife, were life-long best friends, and as a team they kept 752 West Market Street spotless, from attic to cellar, from windowpane to stove lid. Their cleaning work was never done because women's work is never done. On Sundays, when dust gathers just as much as it does on other days, they put aside their mops and dustrags, but they noticed things that they would have to get started on Wednesday, after the Monday washing and the Tuesday ironing. They took turns with the cooking of supper, the big meal of the household day, and they shared the preparation of Sunday dinner. Clayton did not come home for the noon meal on weekdays, but supper and Sunday dinner were planned to please him, and he in turn pleased them by being a good eater. He would compliment Laurie by eating two platefuls of her sauerkraut, pork, and knepp, and still have room for two wedges of Florence's shoofly pie. (All three Bunters were of English and Welsh extraction, but their church was the German Lutheran and their kitchen was Pennsylvania Dutch.) Sauerkraut was the Saturday night fixture on the Bunters' menu, as firm as Clayton's full hour in the bathtub, when, contrary to legend, Clayton would soak and scrub away the week's grime and be ready to start the new week bright and early on Sunday morning with a fresh union suit, put on his collar and tie, and accompany his wife and sister to divine service.

The women would walk arm in arm, in step, and Clayton would go along as a kind of outrider on foot. After church the Bunters would walk home together at a somewhat more leisurely pace, the women stopping now and then to exchange greetings with parishioners of other denominations while Clayton stood aside like other husbands and brothers and let the women do the talking. If, as infrequently happened, the women's conversation threatened to be overlong, Clayton would take out his watch and say, "The roast," and in simu-lated alarm the women would end the conversation and the Bunters would proceed homeward. The Bunter women did not need any reminder from Clayton; they knew precisely how long a cut of beef or lamb ought to remain in the oven; but they liked to linger (with *some* acquaintances) to give Clayton the opportunity to be the domi-nant male, which in turn gave them the opportunity to be the domi-nated females. It was a harmless fiction that deceived absolutely no one. The Bunters never had any guests in their house, but everyone knew that the sisters-in-law, although proud of Clayton's business head and pleased to make him comfortable, ran the household at 752 without the slightest interference by Clayton.

It was, in fact, an ideally happy ménage, with no member of it having cause for envy. Laurie had her consanguineous relationship as her claim on Clayton, and Florence performed her wifely duties according to Clayton's dwindling demands. Clayton was correspondingly pleased that he was able to provide a home for his sister while at the same time providing company for his wife. The basic marital relationship gave Laurie no cause for jealousy since she regarded Clayton's needs as a male weakness that was better administered to by Florence than by some woman who would fill the house with children. Florence, submitting to Clayton's spasmodic urges, never gave Laurie reason to suspect her of taking advantage of her position. The topic was not discussed in detail, but Laurie had been given to understand that Clayton himself regarded his urges as a weakness, and Laurie was almost positive that she could tell better from her brother's diffident manner than from any indication by Florence when he had yielded to his desires. Laurie admired Florence's dignified fortitude at such times, and was if anything a little embarrassed that it was her brother who had imposed on her friend. But these were no more than minor crises, having neither great nor lasting effect on the happiness of the ménage. Florence hardly seemed to notice them, and for Laurie it became less and less a problem to hide her gratitude from Florence. Her gratitude was a practical thing; she knew, as Florence did not, that Clayton was the owner of several houses that were of ill repute, and without Florence he might have been compelled to patronize the dreadful places. Laurie remembered only too well that their father taunted their mother with his boasts of visits to such houses. He had come very close to being found dead in one, and all her life, but especially in Clayton's young manhood, Laurie had been apprehensive for the first sign that Clayton would follow in their father's footsteps toward Railroad Avenue. But when she was seventeen or eighteen Laurie realized that she had an almost ready-made solution to that problem: Florence. Florence was in and out of the Bunter house every day, and Clayton, then about thirteen years of age, liked to be with his sister and her friend. He liked to be with them when they made fudge, he held up willing hands when they were winding balls of yarn, he would sit on the back porch and help them shell peas, he ran errands for them in rain and snow. He asked to sleep with them when Florence spent the night at their house, and Laurie remembered her father's boisterous consent, "Sure, let him! Do him good," and their mother's weary refusal. Boys her own age began to take an interest in Florence

Cutshall, but they were discouraged by Florence's insistence on their finding a boy for Laurie, an impossible condition. Consequently Florence emerged from the bloom of her teens into the plainness of her early twenties without having formed any attachment that threatened Laurie's plan. When Clayton reached twenty-one, already stout and looking older than his years, and making money in real estate since his graduation from Gibbsville High, he asked Laurie if she thought Florence would marry him, and Laurie said yes, but to postpone his actual proposal until their father died. Laurie did not want Mr. Bunter to say some dreadful thing that Florence and the Cutshall family would not be able to forgive. Bunter died, obscenely delirious to the end, and his wife died a few days later from—Laurie believed—the effects of listening to the terrible things Bunter had said to her on his deathbed. The doctor said she died of a stroke.

Laurie had the house ready for Clayton and Florence on their return from Niagara Falls. In the busy first days of showing Florence where everything was and helping with the housework she put off making her speech about finding a room elsewhere, and the speech was never made. She became indispensable as unpaid houseworker and companion to her sister-in-law, and steadily and soon the friends, now relatives, had a pattern for their lives that was to endure for a quarter of a century—until the death of Clayton Bunter, who was only the third party to their arrangement. The sisters-in-law did not need any outside friends; they did not need Clayton except as the payer of bills; but he did not get in their way, and he was useful as the excuse for their devotion to their house and the pleasure they got out of their teamwork.

Except on Sunday morning they did not care how he looked or how he smelled. They wanted him nice for church, but he was a man, and on weekdays, taking care of his business affairs, he had a right to look as he pleased. As his fortune grew—they were aware that it was growing, without being told how much—they became more resistant to any change in themselves and in him.

"You two want to buy an automobile?" he said one evening.

"An auto? What for?" said Laurie.

"You can't drive," said Florence.

"No, I can't, but if George Wizmer can learn, I sure can. I went for a ride with him today. He just bought a new Haynes. Electric lights. Doors in the front. Self-starter."

"How much was it?" said Laurie.

"Well, I guess it was around three thousand, but I don't know."

"We don't want an auto, do we, Florence?" said Laurie.

"What would we ever use it for?"

"To go on trips," said Clayton. "A lot of people buy cars and go visiting."

"Who would you ever want to visit, Florence?" said Laurie.

"Nobody that I know of," said Florence. "I have my aunt and uncle in Buffalo, New York, if it'd get that far."

"Supposed to be a very good car, one of the best. Rudy Schmidt says it compares with the Peerless. I don't know how the roads are between here and Buffalo, but it'll go that distance."

"Sounds to me like an awful lot of money," said Laurie.

"Don't worry about the money if you want one. If you two say we ought to buy a car, I'll put up the money. Otherwise, we can forget about the whole matter."

"Don't buy one on my account," said Florence.

"Do we have that much, that we can put that much money in an auto?"

"Was I ever the kind of a fellow that bought a Haynes car to drive to the poorhouse?" He laughed. "Yes, we could buy two and it wouldn't break us."

"Two cars, huh. Lantenengo Street," said Laurie.

"I was sorry when my father sold the horses, but I never wanted an auto," said Florence.

"Want me to buy you a team?" said Clayton. "Doc English is getting rid of his team of sorrels. He's in the market for an auto. Took a demonstration in the Haynes, George said."

"No thanks," said Florence.

"I'm afraid to death of horses," said Laurie. "But worse of autos."

"All right, then we won't say no more about it. Subject is closed. Meeting adjourned. Pass me the paper, Florence. See what's going on in the world." He took the paper, folded it several times down to one-column width and handed it back to Florence. "I take notice you didn't read the paper."

"Laurie, lend me your glasses," said Florence. She then read: "Clayton Bunter to bank board. Clayton Bunter, well known real estate man, of town, was elected to membership on the board of the Citizens Bank & Trust Co., South Main St., at the recent meeting. Mr. Bunter, who resides at 752 W. Market St., is a native of town. He was graduated from Gibbsville H. S., then entering the real estate business. He is married to the former Miss Florence Cutshall—*my name in the paper!*—daughter of Mr. and Mrs. Percy D. Cutshall, also of town. Poppa will kill them for saying Percy. Mr. Bunter is a member of Trinity Lutheran Church. He is the son of the late Mr. and Mrs. Daniel C. Bunter, the former a well known carpenter and builder of town. I didn't know your father was a builder."

"Every carpenter is a builder, according to the *Standard*. They always have to fancy it up," said Clayton.

"Well. Bank director," said Florence.

"Do you get paid for that?" said Laurie.

"Get a two-and-a-half gold piece every meeting I go to."

"How often is that?" said Florence.

"Once a week. Monday."

"Ten dollars a month, a hundred and twenty a year," said Laurie. "I don't see why that's worth bragging about."

"All right, then I won't give you any of the gold pieces. I was going to give them half to Florence and half to you."

"Oh, come on, Clay-ton. I didn't mean anything by it," said Laurie.

"Then hereafter you'll know better."

"It's a big honor, Laurie," said Florence. "But I'll make him give you half of the gold pieces."

"I wouldn't take them if he didn't give them to me of his own free will," said Laurie.

But she did, and saved them, two dozen of them a year until she had an accumulation of more than two hundred gold pieces. Once a year she would take them out of their woollen sack and wash them with soap and water, dry them, and arrange them in stacks of ten. They were pretty little coins, and though she knew that sometimes there was a nickel premium on them at the banks, she never regarded them as money to spend. They were playthings. After she had the stacks lined up on her bedroom table, as a boy would do with lead soldiers, she would mow them down with a sweep of her hand and push them into a glittering pile, and lift handfuls of them and pour them back onto the pile. Although this was a game she played only about once a year, it always happened on nights when Clayton had said to Florence, "Let's turn in." It was well understood by all three that when Clayton said that to Florence, Laurie was not to attempt to prolong the conversation. She was, in fact, being told to go to her room on the third floor and to stay off the second floor until morning.

There were, of course, many nights when she was given the signal to retire to her room, and she had other quiet pastimes to occupy her until she was ready to turn out the Welsbach and go to bed. She was not much for reading, and in any case she kept the Welsbach burning low so as not to waste gas. Crocheting was too fine to be done in that light, but knitting was all right; she could practically do that with her eyes closed. She could have darned Clayton's socks or patched his shirts, but Florence had assigned that chore to herself, and Laurie would not have liked to work on her brother's clothes at such times, when she was trying not to think of Clayton or of Florence. It was bad enough to be made to feel out of it without having a basketful of her brother's socks to remind her of him and Florence in that terribly still house. And so she would knit something for the church bazaars, or work on her rag rugs for the house, and some nights she would turn off the gas and sit at the window.

That was one of the best ways to get your mind off things. The Market Street trolley, going west or coming east, went by every fifteen minutes; the Collieryville trolley, to or from town, passed the house at half-hour intervals until the last one from Collieryville, which passed 752 West Market Street at a quarter to midnight, headed for the carbarn. After nine o'clock the trolleys bound for the western end of town or for Collieryville would be half filled with young couples and a few married ones on their way home from the moving pictures. Later on Laurie would see the single young men, riding in the trolleys or walking to save a dime after their dates were over. From her window it was impossible to get a very good look at the passengers, except those who were seated next to the window on the Collieryville trolleys. The Collieryville trolleys were twice as big as the Market Street trolleys, which were known as dinkies and were operated by one-man crews. The conductors and motormen were trying to organize a union to fight the one-man trolleys, but the Irish were afraid that the Pennsylvania Dutchmen would run the union, and the Pennsylvania Dutchmen were afraid that the Irish would get everybody fired from their jobs. Clayton said that the Company couldn't put an Irish motorman on the same car with a Dutch conductor or vicey versa. The conductor would get out to throw a switch, and the motorman would leave him a hundred yards behind and make him walk in the rain and snow. Such foolishness made the trolleys go off their schedules, but Clayton said that as long as the crews were fighting among themselves the Company didn't have to worry about any union. The Irish were the real troublemakers, but they were that way about everything, Clayton said. The only tenant who had ever actually hit Clayton was an Irishman he had dispossessed. Walked right up to him on Main Street and gave him a bloody nose. Clayton must have bled a lot, too, from the condition of his shirt and underwear and his handkerchief. A terrible thing to have happen to your own brother, in broad daylight and right on the main street of town. Ripper Hennessey, the man's name was. He got thirty days in jail for it. People were always picking on Clayton, because he was that much smarter than they were. His own father had picked on him, but which one was the director of a bank, and

which one could talk about buying two Haynes automobiles? Sometimes even Florence didn't seem to fully appreciate Clayton, but
Laurie would never say anything in criticism of Florence. Never.
Florence was the best thing that ever happened to Clayton, and even
if she didn't seem to fully appreciate Clayton, she never complained.
Some women complained about their husbands when it came to
certain things, but not Florence. When Clayton said, "Let's turn in,"
Florence would get up and have a last look at the kitchen range and
see if the back door was locked and say goodnight to Laurie and
then go upstairs and wait for Clayton, and you would not know from
anything she said or did, not even from the expression on her face,
that there was anything different about that particular night from
any other night. If you knew what kind of a woman Florence really
was, you'd know that she was keeping up her end of the bargain
without so much as one word of complaint. And in the morning she
would have the coffee on at seven o'clock and everything just the
same as every other morning. It was Laurie who was inclined to be a
little grouchy on those mornings, and the last thing in the world she
would blame it on was not having slept very well.

The Gambler

What had been four months was now four days, the time left before he would be leaving town for good. "We'll give you till the first of March to clear out," the chief of police had said. "You'll do your thirty days in the sneezer. That shouldn't be too tough. You've done that before."

"Oh, sure. Like the fellow says, I can do thirty days standing on one foot," said Marvin. He tried to keep the sarcasm out of his voice; there was no use irritating the chief. At the same time, he could not resist saying something. Thirty days in the county jail was thirty days and nights of the jail smell, the jail food, the howls of the prisoners having nightmares.

"Well, it could of been a lot worse," said the chief. "It could just as easily been ninety days."

"I know," said Marvin.

"Where do you figure on going next?" said the chief.

"I don't know. You got any suggestions?"

"One. But you won't pay any attention to that," said the chief.

"You mean get a nice, decent, respectable job."

"Tzright," said the chief.

"Doing what?" Marvin looked at his right shoulder, at his left shoulder, at his frail torso. "What am I built for?"

"It don't have to be, uh, carrying bags of cement. You don't have to swing a pick and shovel."

"You know the only thing I'm good for, Chief."

"Yeah, and where does it get you? Another thirty days up the hill, and I gotta run you out of town. Where do you *think* you'll go?"

"South."

"You ever *been* South?" said the chief.

"You mean those small towns? Hell, I wouldn't spend the night in one of them. I was figuring maybe I'd take a train and go to Miami. I'd send the wife and kid on ahead of me in the car."

New Yorker (1 May 1965); *Waiting for Winter*

"This is after you got out of the cooler?" said the chief.

"Yeah, or before," said Marvin.

The chief thought for a few seconds. "We're going up the hill in about fifteen minutes. I'll sign you in with the warden before twelve noon, and that way you'll get credit for a full day, instead of a half a day."

"Yeah?" said Marvin.

"You do your thirty days," said the chief.

"Yeah?"

"That leaves you three months till the first of March," said the warden. "You gotta be out of town the first of March."

"Yeah."

"Why do you want to hang around here for, those three months? The Miami season is just about over then."

"Well, it was my lawyer. Dunphy. The mayor said he'd give me ninety days on the hill, or if I agreed to leave town when I got out, he'd reduce it to thirty days. Then Dunphy said I needed more time to find someplace to live, for the wife and kid."

"I didn't understand that, either," said the chief. "I don't know why you need three months. If you so much as pick up a pair of dice, I'll throw you in the can again. Does Dunphy want you to do something for him?"

"I don't know. I honestly don't know," said Marvin.

"Why would Dunphy want you around?"

"For that matter, why did the mayor give in to Dunphy?" said Marvin.

"Yeah," said the chief.

"I just as soon leave town when I get out, but them two got something cooked up between them."

"The mayor and Dunphy?"

"Uh-huh," said Marvin.

"How about your wife? Dunphy has a reputation for a ladies' man."

"Four months gone. You can't go near her."

"You're having another kid, huh? You getting to be a family man, Marvin?"

"Well, it looks that way. It wasn't my idea. Hers, either, I guess. But there you are, you know."

"Telling me. I got five," said the chief. "Anyway, they want you to leave town, but they got it cooked up that you stay three months after you do your thirty days. And Dunphy isn't after your wife. I wonder what's the mayor's angle?"

"They both want me to do something, but I don't know what," said Marvin.

"Yeah, all the signs point to that. Does your wife have enough money while you're up the hill?"

"We got enough. We got enough if I can go someplace else and start operating. But we don't have enough to hang around here doing nothing for three months, nothing coming in, all going out."

"Well, we'll see what happens," said the chief. "If you're all ready, I'll drive you up the hill and turn you over to the warden."

"I'm ready any time you are," said Marvin.

"You know, you oughtn't to be going up there, a young fellow like you with brains. The tough guys, I don't mind locking them up. As far as I'm concerned, they could throw the key away, when I take some of them up there. But I hate to see a young guy with brains, wasting them. This makes three times they put you away. Twice here, and once in Massachusetts. One of these days it won't be a gambling rap, Marvin. They'll get you on some felony and instead of a month or two, you'll be in for a year or more. So far you only got misdemeanors against you, but once you get in the felony class, we gotta treat you different."

"I know," said Marvin. "I got no complaints against you, Chief."

"I'll say you haven't," said the chief. "Well, take a good breath of fresh air. Fill your lungs with it."

They got in the chief's Dodge sedan and Marvin denied himself a cigarette on the brief ride to the county prison. He was checked in by the warden and the turnkey put him in a cell by himself, a luxury that cost him ten dollars. He lay down on the leather straps that would be his mattress for the next twenty-nine days and stared at the ceiling.

He caught a cold the second day, and it stayed with him a week. The bedbugs and crabs attacked him the first night and were with him the full time of his imprisonment. His wife came to see him on the four Sunday visiting days, but she did not like the visits and neither did he. He could not tell her to stay away and she could not neglect him. There were no long-term prisoners; they were sent to state penitentiaries. Consequently the turnover was steady and neither the prisoners nor the turnkeys were inclined to establish a fixed relationship toward each other. The queers among both discovered each other quickly, and had the only unity that existed in the entire prison. Marvin got through his sentence without a single long conversation with anyone, but he was unable to use his solitude for a successful analysis of the motives of Dunphy and the mayor. In every way the thirty days was a waste of time.

"How much money we got left?" he asked his wife on his first day out.

"It's around eight hundred and forty dollars," she said. "I kept pretty good track."

"Okay. Tomorrow we go to Miami."

"That suits me," she said. "This town got nothing for me."

"How do you feel?"

"Oh, all right, I guess. I don't throw up as much. This'd be a good time to leave town. Then I'd have three-four months in Miami before the baby, and maybe we could stay there permanent."

"There's nothing doing there in the summer. I'd have to come back North."

"Unless you got something steady."

"Not that again, Arleen," he said.

"Well, you ought to start thinking about it. Three times you been arrested—"

"Ten times I been arrested, but only three times I got locked up. What do I know except gambling?"

"Maybe the next time you get put in jail they'll keep you there long enough to learn a trade."

"What kind of a remark is that? I ought to give you a smack in the mouth."

"Just you try it," she said. "You don't have the least sense of humor."

"Did I get any mail?"

"Not since Sunday. Oh, Dunphy wants you to phone him."

"I been expecting a letter from Harry Brisbane. Coral Gables. I should of had a letter by this time."

"All you got was a phone call from Dunphy, unless you want to read a letter from my sister. They're moving to Providence. Everybody's moving. My mother's people lived in the same house for over a hundred years."

"Did you talk to Dunphy?"

"His stenographer. He'll be in all afternoon."

He went to see Dunphy.

"You put on a little weight, if I'm not mistaken," said Dunphy.

"What they feed you. Potatoes and bread is all you can eat."

"Didn't they give you turkey at Christmas?"

"Yeah, it was the only good meal I had the whole thirty days. Christmas dinner in stir. I'm getting out of town."

"Yes, I know."

"I mean right away. Not the first of March," said Marvin.

"Will you close that door behind you? Thanks. Why do you want to get away so fast?"

"I'm going down to Florida."

"Yes, this is the season. I suppose you have something lined up there?"

"I'm waiting to hear from a fellow."

"Well, suppose you don't hear from him?" said Dunphy.

"I'm going anyhow. There's nothing here for me. I can't operate. You know that. Bradley says if he sees me with a pair of dice in my hand, I go up the hill again."

"That's just it. He has to see you, first. He has to see you, and he has to be chief of police. And if he isn't chief of police, it doesn't make any difference if he sees you."

"Oh. You mean Bradley is on the skids?"

"He may be," said Dunphy.

"Well, say he is. Where does that put me?"

"It could put you at Number 112 East Scandinavia Street."

"The old joint? You get rid of Bradley and open up again?"

"That seems to be the general idea," said Dunphy.

"How do you get rid of Bradley? I never heard of him being on the take or anything."

"Not lately, but there's no cop in town that hasn't been on the take at some time or other. They have to be, to live."

"I never shelled out to him, and he pinched me twice."

"Yes, but we have a new mayor, now," said Dunphy.

"And the son of a bitch sent me up for thirty days."

"What's thirty days in your young life?"

"Try it, and see," said Marvin.

Dunphy laughed. "Not if I can help it," he said. "Here is the picture, Marvin. Certain people in town expected the new mayor to adopt a more liberal attitude toward gambling and so forth. But George Daimler is no fool. One of the very first things he did was to send you up the hill, much to the surprise of a lot of people. Probably one of the most surprised people was Tom Bradley. I'm sure he fully expected that I could persuade the mayor to get you off with a fine, or a suspended sentence. But lo and behold, you go up the hill for thirty days."

"I was a kind of a fall guy."

"Yes."

"Well, Daimler's a lot smarter than I gave him credit for," said Marvin. "Or is it you?"

"Daimler is no fool, but he isn't all that smart."

"It *was* you, huh?"

"It was I," said Dunphy. "And that's who it will be from now on. Weren't you fortunate that you asked me to handle your legal mat- ters?"

"Yes, I guess I was," said Marvin. "How do you tie a can to Bradley?"

"You'll see," said Dunphy. "Oh, hell, I might as well tell you. We don't go back to when he was pounding a beat and taking a few bananas off the fruit stand. We had to have something more recent than that."

"Yeah, you sure would."

"He has a car. A Dodge sedan. It's registered in his name, and he's the legal owner. But in the two years he's had it, I doubt if he ever bought a single gallon of gas for it. The dealer put two new sets of tires on it and billed the city. Twice it was overhauled at city expense, and he brings it in for a washing once a week. If we wanted to, we could easily prove that he had the tank filled several times before taking out-of-town trips. It adds up to quite a sum. Sheer carelessness on his part. We're going to let him resign, and be eligible for his pension. If he makes a stink, we'll make a stink. He *could* go to jail."

"Boy!"

"Well, do you still want to go to Miami?" said Dunphy.

"You're kidding," said Marvin. "When do we open up?"

"Shortly. Very shortly," said Dunphy.

The Neighborhood

Some of the houses on Tuscarora Street were numbered and some were not, but it was not necessary to look for the number of the Rellinger house. Across the street from it were standing perhaps a dozen men and women, the women clutching their shawls across their chests, the men standing with their hands in their pockets or their arms folded; and whether they were in conversation or silent, they all kept their eyes on the Rellinger house. Directly in front of the Rellinger house, on the skimpy front lawn, was a policeman in uniform, chatting with two young men in civilian clothes. Every once in a while the policeman would leave his post on the lawn and tell some slow-moving pedestrian to keep moving. Or there would be a man or oftener two men who turned in at the Rellinger footpath and the policeman would stop them and take a look at their credentials, and if they satisfied him, he would let them proceed to enter the house.

It was a semi-bungalow, with a gabled roof that cut the upper-story bedrooms to half size. A narrow slag driveway passed the house and went back to a one-car garage. The double doors were open, and parked in the garage was a small Nash touring car, pointed inward, with a trunk at the rear. The black imitation-leather cover on the spare tire had lettering in white which read: "Walter J. Klug—Nash—128 S. Oak St., Swedish Haven, Pa."

In the backyard a clothesline was strung from the kitchen door to a corner of the garage, and on it hung stiffly the articles of a family wash: a man's overalls, shirts, and underwear, and a couple of gingham housedresses, lingerie, bath towels and tea towels. They had all been hanging there since the day before, and they had collected some soot and cinders.

The Rellinger house stood between two others like it, and Allan Rogers went to one of them and rang the doorbell. He waited and was about to ring again when a woman came to the door. "Good morning, is the lady of the house in?"

"What is it you want? I don't want to buy anything," said the woman.

"I don't want to sell you anything. I wanted to inquire if you had a room for rent."

"No rooms for rent," said the woman. She began to close the door and he put out his hand. In it were two ten-dollar bills.

"They're yours if you let me sit at your diningroom window."

"What are you, some kind of a newspaper fellow?"

"You guessed it," said Rogers. "All I want to do is sit at your diningroom window and see who goes in and out of the Rellingers'. I promise not to bother you."

"I don't know what my husband would say."

"He'd say take the money. It's like picking it up off the ground."

"Well, I don't know. You look all right," she said. "What paper'd you say you're from?"

"The Associated Press."

"Where is that? Is that Philly?"

"Oh, it's all over the world. Everywhere."

"How long would this be for?"

"Oh, it might be a week. Might even be longer than that."

"You'd have to pay me the twenty dollars every day," she said.

"Of course. Naturally. And if you'd like to make a little extra, maybe you could fix me up with something to eat. Right now, I only had a cup of coffee for breakfast."

"All right, come on in. What's the name again?"

"My name is Allan Rogers. I'll be glad to show you my identification." He took out a hip wallet and opened it wide to show a large quantity of bills. "For two dollars would you fry me a couple of eggs and make me some coffee?"

"All right. You want toast?"

"Yes, buttered, if it's not too much trouble."

"You can have it buttered, and if you'd care for some strawberry preserves."

"Home-made? You put them up yourself?"

"Well, my sister put them up. She has the time. There's the two diningroom windows, take your pick."

"Thank you. And you never told me your name, Mrs.?"

"Mrs. Kenneth R. Schumacher—but don't you go putting that in the paper. You mind, now."

"I won't do anything to displease you, I promise you, Mrs. Schumacher. Say, this is a nice house you have here. Look at that sideboard. That didn't come from Sears, Roebuck."

"I guess not. My grandfather made it."

"I was going to say, that kind of workmanship. If some of those antique dealers ever got a look at that."

"Oh, I wouldn't sell."

"No, it's nicer to keep a thing like that from generation to generation. And of course they get more valuable the longer you hold on to them."

"What would a sideboard like that be worth, do you think?"

"Well—I'm no expert, but you'd be foolish to take a penny under eight or nine hundred dollars. Possibly a great deal more. They pay all kinds of fancy prices for the genuine article."

"Do you know the name of any of those dealers?"

"I don't, but I could easily find out for you. I have a friend in New York that knows all about these things."

"You come all the way from New York to report next door?"

"Yes, I drove down this morning. I left my car back on the street where the church is."

"They won't let no cars on Tuscarora unless you live here. Well, this ain't getting you your breakfast," said Mrs. Schumacher.

"Mind if I smoke a cigarette?"

"No. The mister smokes cigarettes, pipe, cigars. I'm used to it. There's an ash tray on the sideboard you can use." She went to the kitchen and Rogers took up his vigil.

As he expected, there was nothing to be seen; the shades in the Rellinger house were lowered, and it was not hard to guess the business of the men who went in and out of the Rellinger house. Police. District attorney's office people. Local newspaper men. Family connections and close friends. So far he had not recognized any of the newspaper men, which seemed to indicate that he was the first man from an out-of-town newspaper on the scene. He was sure of it. The others who would soon be arriving would be dismayed to find that he was already established in the house next door to the Rellingers'.

The smell of coffee and bacon came in from the kitchen, and he began to think of ways to persuade Mrs. Schumacher and her husband to let him rent a room in this warm, comfortable, spotless monument to banality. Eight years as a reporter had not made him cease to be astonished when bizarre events occurred in banal surroundings. Very probably, the interior of the Rellinger house was as commonplace as the Schumachers'. He moved about and studied the Schumacher family history from the framed photographs. The wedding picture. The posed photograph of Kenneth R. Schumacher in olive-drab uniform and campaign hat, with a collar device that indicated he had been in the Corps of Engineers. Numerous photographs of, obviously, the Schumacher daughter and son, including two recent pictures of their own husband and wife. Daughter and son had married young. Son and daughter's bridegroom were wearing Tuxedos and white bow ties. Presumably the Schumacher young had homes of their own, and if Rogers passed inspection by Kenneth R. Schumacher, it ought to be easy to persuade Mrs. Schumacher to accept payment for room and board at an exorbitant rate. It was too bad the daughter lived elsewhere; she was a rather pretty little thing. The mother may have been, too, but not any more, not any more.

She brought in an asbestos place-mat and set it on the table. "It's near ready," she said. Then she went back to the kitchen and returned with a lacquered tin tray, with his breakfast on it.

"Boy, I feel like a privileged character," he said.

"Oh—it's nothing," she said.

She stood and watched him as he ate. She grinned at his compliments to her coffee, her just-right eggs, the home-baked bread, the strawberry jam. "Don't you feel like a cup of coffee?"

"Well—" she said, and got a cup and saucer. He wanted her to sit down. He had work to do, and she had to be sitting down and relaxed for the kind of work he had in mind. He waited until she had had her first mouthful of coffee.

"You'd never think a thing like that could happen in such a nice neighborhood," he said.

"Nor anywheres else," she said. "I can't get used to it happened."

"No," he said. "They sound like the last people you'd expect to have a thing like that happen to them."

"Oh, I don't know. Not the way it happened, nobody'd expect that. But I guess everybody thinks back now."

"You thought maybe something would happen?"

"Something," she said. She pronounced it like *sumpsing*.

"Well, you were in a position to know. Seeing them every day, naturally you'd get to know them better than most people."

"Not him. Her I knew. Always borrowing. I took notice her wash is still on the line, with my clothespins she borrowed off me. They can stay there. I don't want to touch them."

"I don't like it when people don't return things, either," said Rogers. "I don't mind helping out, but people get in the habit of borrowing things and they impose on you."

"Oh, I'll say. He made good money, but he was tight-fisted. She had to ask him for every penny. If she wanted a cake of soap. Sooner than ask him, she'd borrow off of me. He wouldn't trust her with money."

"Well, he probably had his reasons. She was young and probably extravagant."

"Young? Forty-two, she was."

"Well, forty-two isn't old," he said.

"Well, not old, but it ain't young."

"What was he? Fifty or so?"

"Over that. He was the same years older than her that my mister is older than me. She was forty-two and he was fifty-two. Ten years difference in age, exactly."

"Had he been married before?"

"Who? My husband?"

"No, Rellinger."

"No, I never heard of him being married before. They weren't married long, you know."

"No? How long?"

"I gotta think. They come here next door. Our two were in high school, our son and daughter. I guess they come here about six or seven years ago. They were just married, a bride and groom, but not a young couple if you know what I mean. She was in her thirties and he was in his forties. Then."

"Had you known them before?"

"Well, the town ain't so big. She used to work in Bachman's ice cream parlor, over on West Main. It's where people go when they want a plate of cream or a soda. There's some like Luger's drug store, but Bachman makes his own cream. He charges the same as Luger, but Bachman's burnt almond is famous. That, and his peach. You can't get peach this time of the year. He'll only use fresh peaches."

"I see. And that's where she worked before they were married. I guess he must have seen a lot of her before that."

"I don't know. A man that feels like a soft drink or a plate of cream, he'll very seldom go to Bachman's. They go to Luger's. Some men go to Luger's in the morning and the afternoon, every day. But Dory Rellinger, I don't know. Every time you went past his store you'd see him in the window. He was a watchmaker, by trade. He didn't have anybody working for him. Just this little store, if it was half the size of this room. You could put three of his store in this room, easily. It's over there on West Main. Next door to the Eyetalian fellow that has the shoeshine and cleans hats. Two little bits of stores, you could put them both in this room. But Dory Rellinger knew how to charge you. There's only the two watchmakers in

town, and the one's in Slazinger's jewelry store. If you didn't buy
your watch at Henry Slazinger's, you could wait a month before he'd
fix it. But Dory Rellinger would promise you your watch in a couple
days, and he'd have it ready when you came in. But charge! He made
good money. Paid cash for the house. Paid cash for everything, my
husband said. Used to send away for everything to save money that
way. Them gingham dresses of hers out on the clothesline. Sears,
Roebuck. They got near all their furniture by mail order. That she
told me herself."

"He was stingy, eh?"

"Well, he had the cash. If you didn't have the cash, he wouldn't let
you have your watch. Here was I, his next-door neighbor, but one
time he made me go home and get a dollar and a half, or else he
wouldn't let me have my husband's watch. Being a railroader my
mister has to have two watches so he don't have to go without one."

"Your husband is a railroader," said Rogers.

"He has a regular run. Freight conductor on the Pennsy. The
mixed freight from Philly to Gibbsville."

"Oh, is that so?"

"Twenty-two years on the Pennsy, starting from call-boy."

"What did he think of Rellinger?"

"He didn't think much of him after he wouldn't trust me for a
dollar and a half, and living next door."

"No, I shouldn't think he would, not after that," said Rogers.
"Was he surprised when this thing happened?"

"Next door? He couldn't sleep last night. I couldn't either, but he
had to be up at ha' past four. Maybe he'll get a little sleep in the
crummy. The caboose. I hope so. My God, when you think of it."

"Try not to think of it, Mrs. Schumacher," said Rogers.

"But I can't help it. How could a man do such a thing? Not only
the one time but two times. Twicet."

"I understand he chloroformed them," said Rogers. "Is that what
you heard?"

"Chloroformed them, yes. That's what Billy Hughes said. The policeman. Billy and Ed Reid, the chief, and another fellow from the
county asked me didn't I hear anything yesterday afternoon, and I
said no. I seen Dory come home early, about ha' past two."

"Put his car in the garage?"

"No, he was walking. He never took the car to work with him. She
put the car in the garage. I seen her with her mother, and they got
out of the car and went in by the kitchen door. That was shortly
before noontime. Then I happened to notice them in the kitchen,
and I almost went over and told her to get her wash off the line. It

was there since morning, and dry by that time, and it looked like we were gonna have snow. I thought for sure we were gonna have snow yesterday. It still feels like it."

"Yes, it does. But you didn't go over. Probably a good thing you didn't."

"Or a bad thing. Maybe if I went over she would of come back to borrow something, and then she wouldn't be there when he got home."

"Don't blame yourself. This man was going to kill them sometime. If not yesterday afternoon, last night. Then he came home and went in the house. Did you see him again?"

"Yes. When they came to take him away," she said. "Ed Reid and Billy Hughes, they come in a car. They got out of the car and they both had a pistol in their hand. Billy went back to the kitchen door and Ed went in the front door. I thought, my goodness, why did they have their pistol in their hand. I thought maybe there was a robber, and I got scared. But I guess it was about an hour later some more men came and then Ed and Billy came out the front with Dory, and he had handcuffs on him."

"Did you happen to notice the condition of his clothes? Was there blood on his clothes?"

"No, sir! He was wearing his Sunday suit as if he was on his way to church. And you know what he did?"

"What?"

"He saw me at the window. And he laughed and stuck his tongue out at me. I thought to myself, you'll pay for that, Mister, when I tell my husband. See, I didn't know what they were arresting him for. Then I saw the dead-wagon pull up, from Koenig the undertaker. Koenig and young Hennessey that works for him, and there was two other men with them."

"I don't understand that, the dead-wagon. Is that the hearse?"

"No, it's what they use instead of the hearse. The hearse has windows on the side, but the dead-wagon is when they take the body to the funeral parlor. You know, to embalm them? We call it the dead-wagon. I guess you have another name for it."

"Now I understand it," said Rogers. "They went inside, Mr. Koenig and the men with him?"

"Carrying two rough-boxes. Do you know what that is? It's instead of a casket. Just a wooden box, the size of a casket."

"I see."

"When I saw that, I knew there was something bad. Two dead people, that meant. And who else could it be? His wife, and his mother-in-law."

"Uh-huh."

"Then they went inside, but a minute later, not even a whole minute, one of the men came out of the house and got sick. One of the men with Koenig. He was as sick as a dog, and he sat down on the porch step. My God, I thought. What's going on in there? Then Koenig came out and said something to the man, but the man just shook his head and waved at him to go away. And Koenig went back in the house and I guess about fifteen or twenty minutes later, I don't know, Koenig and Hennessey came out carrying the one rough-box. They put it in the dead-wagon. Then they went back in and come out with the other rough-box. But they didn't look good, either. Koenig or Hennessey, or the other fellow. They drove away in the dead-wagon and then come another car with some other men and two police. The police stood on guard in the front and back, and the other men went in and stayed there."

"How soon was it before the news got around?"

"Inside of ten minutes after Koenig went away the people started coming. That was when my daughter phoned. She knew more about it than I did. She asked me if it was true about Dory Rellinger, and I said I knew somebody was dead. Probably two people dead. Then she told me."

"Did she have it right?" said Rogers.

She nodded. "Said Dory Rellinger murdered his wife and his mother-in-law. And I said how, and she didn't want to tell me, but I made her. She said he cut their heads off. And I fainted dead away. Left the receiver hanging off the hook and all. The last time I fainted was the morning the mister and I got married."

"Well, you mustn't talk about it any more, Mrs. Schumacher," said Rogers.

"Oh, I'm all right now. It's like it never happened. Only I know it did. But I don't know. Who'll they ever get to live in that house? This was such a nice neighborhood," said Mrs. Schumacher.

A Good Location

R ed Walters watched the Hofman Pierce-Arrow pull away from the gas tank. He continued to wave his hand, although Mrs. Hofman was as always staring straight ahead. "There's no doubt about it," said Red Walters. "The bigger they are, the nicer they are."

"You're right," said his partner, Charlie Connors. "The bigger they are, the nicer."

"You know how much she's worth?" said Red Walters.

"Well, I heard reports she had over a million," said Charlie.

"A million? She come into over a million when the old man passed away. She must be worth over two million, if not three," said Red.

"Three million dollars," said Charlie. "Most people would be satisfied if they had *one.*"

"Did you ever stop to think how much the income is on a million dollars?"

"The income? No, I don't guess I ever did," said Charlie.

"Well, if them stocks and bonds give her a five-percent return, that comes to fifty thousand dollars a year on one million. You take and multiply that by three—"

"A hundred and fifty thousand dollars a *year?*" said Charlie.

"A hundred and fifty thousand a year just in income," said Red Walters. "That's what she got coming in."

"Holy Jesus Christ, that's pretty near three thousand dollars a week," said Charlie.

"Well, it ain't all clear. Some of it goes into taxes," said Red. "But supposing she paid out a thousand a week in taxes, that still leaves her two thousand dollars."

"That old lady got two thousand dollars coming in every week," said Charlie.

"Somewhere around that figure," said Red.

New Yorker (4 September 1965); *Waiting for Winter*

"Seven into two thousand," said Charlie.

Red nodded. "Pretty close to three hundred a day."

"Three hundred dollars a day. When you look at it that way—what would we do if we took in three hundred dollars a day, Red?"

"We'll never take in no three hundred dollars a day in this location. We're lucky if we take in that much in a week."

"Yeah, and how many weeks do we come near that much?" said Charlie.

"Not so many, and with us it ain't profit. That's everything."

"That's a fact," said Charlie.

"If we can split up a hundred between us, week in and week out, we had a good year."

"Well, we been doing that, Red. Sometimes more."

"I know, but we don't put anything back in. You take your fifty, I take my fifty, and all we are is standing still."

"Yeah, but if I come home at the end of the week with forty dollars instead of fifty, Mary would let out a yell you could hear in the next county."

"Bess, too. She wouldn't let out a yell, but she'd start crying, and that's just as bad if not worse. They're so used to the fifty, they never stop and think if the two of us put back five a week, inside of a year that'd come to five hundred and twenty dollars."

"That's right," said Charlie.

"And with that money maybe we could go to the bank and borrow the money for a better location. We gotta get a better location and that's all there is to it, Charlie. Old Lady Hofman was running out of gas or we never would of had her for a customer. You heard what she said to me."

"No, I was pumping," said Charlie.

"Well, she said to me she didn't know I was in this business. She remembered from before the war when I used to deliver her papers. Always five dollars every Christmas. The only one I ever got five dollars from, and I was the only one got five dollars from anybody. There wasn't another kid in town delivering papers that got five dollars. Not that she give it to me herself, but the butler did. Most kids were lucky to get a quarter."

"I never had a paper route," said Charlie.

"What we used to do, during Christmas the paper gave us calendars to deliver to the people on our route. It was an extra delivery, but the customers were supposed to give you a little something. Some gave a dime, some a quarter. But Old Lady Hofman's butler gave me a fi'-dollar bill. Four of it I kept. My mom didn't know how much I got from any of the customers, but she knew I got something. So I said I got a dollar from Old Lady Hofman and kept the other four for myself."

"What'd you do with the other four?" said Charlie.

"I hid it to run away with. The old man used to beat me, and my mom did, too, so I used to save up till I got enough money so I could run away."

"You never run away, did you?" said Charlie.

Red shook his head. "No. She found it. Sixteen dollars and forty-five cents in one of them Bull Durham sacks the Bull Durham tobacco used to come in."

"Sure, I remember them. A little string on them," said Charlie. "Where did you hide it, that she found it?"

"Under the mattress on my bed. Then one day she decided to turn it over when I was at school, and there it was. They both beat me. They asked me where I stole it. And when I finally told them the truth, they beat me like I stole it from *them*. Sixteen dollars and forty-five cents. I was saving up till I got twenty, and then I was gonna run away."

"Huh."

"You know, thinking about that, Old Lady Hofman coming here got me thinking about it. If I didn't put it off, if I ran away when I had the sixteen forty-five, I'd of been out of this town and God knows where the hell I'd be, but I wouldn't be here."

"Where were you going?" said Charlie.

"Philly. You remember, I was a pretty husky kid for fourteen. I was gonna get a job on a ship, and if I didn't get a job I was gonna join the navy. Once I was gone they wouldn't of worried about me. All they gave a God damn about was my paper route. Every week if *she* didn't take the money off me first, *he* would. We got paid on Friday. My route was all the way out Lantenengo Street starting at Second. I got a flat rate of a dollar a week. I was supposed to get more, but the son of a bitch in charge of delivery would take your route away from you if you didn't split with him. Pay him, or lose your route, and that was all there was to it. Johnny Minzer."

"Oh, that son of a bitch," said Charlie. "Crazy Artie's brother."

"I made three hundred and eighty-four deliveries a week, and I was supposed to get a cent for each. Three dollars and eighty-four cents a week. Instead of that I got a dollar. Only I didn't get it. My parents did. 'Who pays for your shoe leather?' my old man used to say. Yeah, and who paid for my left shoulder being lower than the right, from carrying those papers six days a week? They say Johnny

Minzer made over a hundred dollars a week, stealing from us, and it all went for booze and whores. You remember when he got killed on that motorcycle? We didn't shed no tears."

"I'll bet you didn't," said Charlie.

"We sure didn't," said Red. "The only thing I was sorry for, it happened too late to do me any good."

"Oh, yeah, that was after we got out of the army," said Charlie.

"The summer of '19," said Red.

"Right around there sometime," said Charlie. "I'm surprised he didn't try to take your calendar money."

"Try to? He did. You didn't get your calendars unless you forked over a half a buck. If he ever knew Old Lady Hofman used to give me five bucks, he would of delivered the calendar himself. But he figured the most anybody gave was a quarter, and some of the cheap-skates didn't give us a nickel. Some of the maids give us a dime that I bet they were supposed to give us more."

"I guess they couldn't see giving a kid more than a dime," said Charlie.

"No, but they should of given us what we were entitled to," said Red. "I'm positive some of them maids held out on me. Bess had an aunt cooking for one of the Stokeses. I always meant to ask her if she knew anything about it, because those particular Stokeses'd be the kind that'd shell out better than a dime. The Stokeses and Old Lady Hofman were related."

"You can't always tell by that," said Charlie.

"No. Some were stingy and some were big-hearted," said Red. "What was I thinking? I was thinking about something I wanted to tell you."

"Uh—about Johnny Minzer?"

"No, no, no, no, no. About Old Lady Hofman," said Red.

"Search me. We were saying how rich she was."

"Yeah. That had something to do with it," said Red.

"Something she said when you were talking to her," said Charlie.

"I wish to hell I could remember. Wait a minute! She said she didn't know I was in this business, and that got me thinking, if we got a better location, there's people like Old Lady Hofman would just as soon give us their business. They used to like me when I was carrying papers, a lot of those people."

"Well, there's plenty of good locations, if we had the money."

"*I* know! That got me started on if we kept out five dollars a week, five hundred and twenty a year. You know what that's around? That's around five-percent interest on ten thousand dollars."

"Those things I leave to you, Red. You know me and arithmetic."

"Well, just supposing the bank would lend us ten thousand dollars at five percent. They'd want more, but around that figure. Just say ten thousand we borrowed and five hundred we paid interest. We'd take in more than we take in here, Charlie. A good location, say out around Eighteenth and Market, out that way. If we had a good location we'd stand a much better chance of getting an agency. Christ knows we'll never get an agency if we stay here. Here we can't even get a good tire agency, let alone a car. I don't say we'd get an agency right off the bat, but if we had a halfway decent garage in a good location, *they'd* come to *us.*"

"You mean the manufacturers?"

"I mean the manufacturers," said Red.

"Well, it sounds all right to me, Red. I wouldn't be afraid to work on any kind of a car on the road today. I could run the shop, all right, providing you ran the business end. And the selling. You'd have to do the selling. Like the fellow says, I couldn't sell a life preserver to a guy that was going down the third time. But the mechanical end I wouldn't be afraid to tackle."

"What I was thinking a while back," said Red. "There I saved up that sixteen dollars and forty-five cents. Three fifty-five to go and I was ready to run away. What happened? My mom discovered where I hid it, and all I got out of it was a couple of beatings off of her and my old man. I waited too long. I should of lit out when I had fifteen dollars."

"Yes, but if you ran away when you were fourteen and got a job on a boat, or joined the navy, maybe you'd of ended up with the syph, or got a knife in your back. How do you know you're not better off here?"

"Here? What do I have here? The both of us put in ten to twelve hours every day, and if we don't bring home that fifty bucks every week, we got one of our wives yelling bloody murder and the other one bawling her head off like it was the end of the world. Your kids and my kids are too young to show any appreciation, but they never will, Charlie. Their mothers got them thinking the same way. Bess wouldn't even let one of my kids pull weeds out of the neighbor's garden. 'I won't have my children pulling no weeds for the neighbors,' she says. It don't do no good to try and tell her how some of the rich kids on Lantenengo pull weeds and sell the *Saturday Evening Post*. Bess *Walters'* children are too good for that. It's all right if I vulcanize tires all day, just as long as I bring home that fifty a week. Charlie, we gotta get out of here. That's all there is to it."

"Well, how soon did you figure on getting out?"

"The sooner the better," said Red. "If I was wearing my good clothes you know what I'd do?"

"No, what?"

"I'd get in my car and drive downtown to the bank. Right now," said Red. "No, I guess they close at three o'clock."

"You mean without talking it over with the women?" said Charlie.

"Without talking it over with the women. I'd go down there to that bank, and if they gave me any encouragement, this week we'd start. You keep out five dollars, I'd keep out five dollars."

"Well, I don't know, Red," said Charlie. "We ought to talk to the women first."

"Charlie, if we talk to the women we'll never do it. It'll be my sixteen forty-five all over again. That's the truth and you know it. Whatter you shaking your head for?"

"I was thinking, five dollars a week. Mary bought a couple things on installment. A new Maytag. A davenport. I got them to pay for."

"I got them kind of things, too," said Red. "Bess makes me carry a lot of insurance, as if she was afraid I was gonna croak. But you gotta back me up the same as I gotta back you up. That's the first thing they'll want to know. Is Charlie taking five dollars less? Is Red taking five dollars less?"

"Red, if we do this, I don't know when we'll hear the end of it. She won't give me a minute's peace, Mary."

"Oh, I know how they'll be," said Red. "If Mary so much as buys a new apron for herself, Bess'll want to know where she gets the dough. They'll be watching each other like a hawk. But I swear to Christ, I got a feeling that if we don't do it now, we never will."

"You didn't have this feeling yesterday," said Charlie.

"Maybe I did and maybe I didn't. I don't think it come over me all of a sudden. I think I had the feeling a long time."

"You know what I think?" said Charlie.

"No, what?"

"I think if Old Lady Hofman didn't stop and fill up her tank, you wouldn't of had this feeling," said Charlie.

"Well, I guess that had something to do with it," said Red. "God Almighty, three hundred dollars a day. If she wasn't so old I'd marry her."

"Marry her anyway, she don't have long to last," said Charlie. "Call her up and tell her you decided to marry her. Here's a nickel, I'll pay for the call."

"You son of a bitch," said Red.

"And let me know how you make out. But now *I* got a lot of work to do."

"All right, you son of a bitch. I'm gonna keep this nickel," said Red.

"Buy a pack of gum," said Charlie.

Afternoon Waltz

In many American towns it often happened that on the main residential street there would be one or two blocks that for one reason or another gave an impression of retiring. Sometimes it was because the leafage of the trees in those blocks darkened the sidewalks. Sometimes the character of the dwellings was uniformly conservative, as if an early house or two had set a style that succeeding builders felt compelled to follow. Whatever the reasons, it was certainly true that when such a block had remained intact for a full generation, it attracted (or held) the kind of people who belonged in that particular neighborhood. The block, the houses, seemed to be occupied by grandparents and the unmarried sisters and brothers of grandparents.

Between Tenth and Eleventh on Lantenengo Street all the houses on the north side were porchless and none was set back from the building line. Most of them had vestibules. A few were constructed to have the front parlor half a story above the street level, so that not even a very tall passer-by could see in the parlor windows. Where the front parlor was on street level, the passer-by's curiosity was frustrated by curtains of heavy lace and lowered window-shades. But the residents of the ten-hundred block were their own best protection against casual peering-in on the part of men on their way to work and women on their way to market. What was there to see in the front parlor or anywhere else in the John Wesley Evans house at 1008?

In point of fact, if an accurate count had been kept of the persons who had set foot in the Evans house since its construction in the 1890's, the total number would not have exceeded a thousand, and that would have included invited visitors, physicians, clergymen, tradesmen and craftsmen. Wesley John Evans, the father of John Wesley Evans, had built to stay, and as there never had been any small children or careless servants in the house, the wear and tear

Saturday Evening Post (23 April 1966); *Waiting for Winter*

had been kept at a minimum. Wesley Evans and his wife got sick and died, but only in their terminal illnesses had they required doctors and nurses. Their social life was so severely restricted that they had never served a meal to a non-relative on a purely social occasion. When John Wesley Evans entered the house for the first time, he was a college senior on Christmas vacation, and it would never have occurred to him to invite a friend to be his house guest.

As the only child of his parents to reach maturity, John Wesley Evans was brought up in an atmosphere that was compounded of desperate affection and conscientious discipline. He rebelled against neither. He was, in fact, a good boy; obedient, honest, and clean. When in senior year he told his father and mother that he was not yet ready to study for the ministry, they deferred to his wish. It was just as well, since his father died the next summer and his mother would have passed the remaining two years of her life alone in the house at 1008. In the thirty years of her marriage to Wesley John Evans she had never been separated from him for more than three days at a time, and the continual presence of her son was her only comfort against pain and terror. She could not have stood her last ordeal without him. Then too, if he had gone to a seminary and become more imbued with religious doctrine, he might have refused to place within her reach the medicine that enabled her to put an end to her agony. "An accidental overdose," said Dr. Phillips. "But she didn't have long anyway, so if you don't say anything about it, I won't say anything about it."

"I won't say anything about it, Dr. Phillips," said John Wesley Evans.

"No, I was sure you wouldn't," said Dr. Phillips. "If you're ever asked what your mother died of, tell them it was a complication of diseases."

"Is that what my father died of, too? A complication of diseases?"

"Oh, no. He died of quinsy. I was *here* when *he* died," said the doctor. "Nobody was here when your mother died."

"I was in the next room," said John Wesley Evans.

"Yes, I know," said the doctor. "Best we don't carry on any more conversation now, John. We'll just let her rest in peace, as they say." The doctor smiled. "I hope my son'll be as considerate when my time comes. Maybe I might have to send for you."

"If you send for me, I'll come," said John Wesley Evans.

"Well, it'd be only fair. I brought you into the world," said the doctor. "But now let's stop talking. I'll most likely see you at the service."

Thus at age twenty-five John Wesley Evans found himself virtually alone in the world, with capital amounting to $160,000 and a rather large, comfortable house to live in. It surprised him to discover that the freedom he now enjoyed could so quickly become so much of his life that it was all of it. He had not been conscious of being contained by his mother and father, but now that they were no longer there to say or do anything, anything at all, he began to understand that what he wanted most was the release that had come to him through their deaths.

Every morning almost his first thought, which carried through breakfast and beyond, was of a new day in which he could do as he pleased. The small things of major importance gave him opportunities to indulge himself. He never, for instance, had been permitted to lie abed past the hour of eight; now he sometimes appeared in the diningroom at nine. Like all children of his day, he ate what was put before him, a habit which he continued during his four years in college. Now, at twenty-five, he broke the habit, broke it and abandoned it. Sarah Lundy, who did the cooking and general housework, never knew what he was going to want for breakfast. She would bring him his first cup of tea and stand in the doorway while he considered the meal that was to follow. "Today I'll have liver and bacon. Corn bread. Apple butter," he would say. Whatever he ordered, it was never quite like the breakfast that other people ate, and there had to be a lot of it. Breakfast was his big meal. Everybody else ate a big dinner at noon and a light supper, but John Wesley Evans would often eat nothing but fruit, cheese, and bread for the noon meal; then in the evening, at six o'clock, he liked a thick soup and hot apple pie with heavy cream. Throughout the day he might eat a bunch of grapes, some Seckel pears, or whatever else Sarah Lundy had put on the sideboard. Where all the food went she did not know; he remained, as he had always been, all skin and bones; the kind of child and young man that parents feared would die of consumption. Also, he was unusually tall, six foot one, and tall, thin people were often said to have a tapeworm. But if John Wesley Evans had a tapeworm it did not affect his disposition, and people with a tapeworm were generally cranky. John Wesley Evans was generally cheerful, so that Sarah Lundy did not mind much if he put her to a lot of extra work with his unpredictable menus. Until her final illness his mother had done the cooking in the Evans household, and Sarah Lundy was agreeably shocked when John Wesley Evans told her that she was a much better cook than his mother had been. It was the kind of thing he often said to her, the unexpected kind of thing that he had never said while his parents were alive. Sarah Lundy was the first person to realize that John Wesley Evans was an altogether different person from the shy young scarecrow who had always come straight home from school every afternoon and done his sums on the diningroom table. In those days you would hardly know he was in the house. Many times she had entered a room to do her dusting and would be startled to discover him, lying on the floor and reading a book. Thick books, they were, from the glassed-in bookcase in the front parlor, which had a key in the lock. The boy's father and mother did not read the books, and Sarah Lundy was not at all sure that the boy had permission to remove the books from the case. The books, which did not fill all the shelves, were for show, and had been there throughout Sarah Lundy's employment in the Evans house-hold—at the old house on Second Street and the house at 1008 Lantenengo. Sixteen years she had put in with the Evans family; watched two Evans children pass on before either of them reached the age of seven; helped carry W. J. Evans to his bedroom when he had his second stroke; been kept awake at night by Mrs. Evans's moaning and groaning; and now she was being witness to changes in the household that she would have liked better if she understood them better.

There was no doubt about it; her own lot had improved. She did not have to be washed and dressed and downstairs by six-thirty in the morning. As long as the house looked neat and clean she could do her chores on her own schedule. She was practically her own boss, and once John had had his breakfast and his bedroom tended to, she could leave the house to do the marketing three or four days a week, which gave her an opportunity to chat with outsiders and gossip with friends along the way. The walk back up the Tenth Street hill was a little tiring, but the exercise of authority at the grocer's and butcher's and the pleasant conversations made it worth it. Before Mrs. took sick Sarah Lundy had never done the marketing; now she made decisions. "How is your lamb chops today? . . . Do you have any turnips fresh? . . . Let me have a basket of them peaches . . . What are your sweet potatoes selling at?" She had not yet been designated housekeeper by John, but she so considered herself. She could not quite get up the nerve to enter the house by the front door, but that would come. John had voluntarily raised her pay to $35 a month, which was a good sign, especially as he had not raised the pay of the woman who came in on Monday and Tuesday to do the washing and ironing. The week's wash was not as big as it had been, and there were plenty of women only too glad to work for a dollar a day and dinner. (You had to keep an eye on them or they'd walk home with a pound of sugar under their cloaks.) No doubt about it; for both occupants of 1008 Lantenengo Street an era of ease and comfort had begun with the passing of John Wesley Evans's mother.

On the other hand Sarah Lundy, who was Irish and a Roman Catholic, had never been *un*comfortable in a household that was Welsh and Methodist. There were no blacker Protestants than the Welsh Methodists, and they were actively and deeply hated by Sarah Lundy's Irish Catholic friends, particularly those whose menfolk worked in the coal mines. Of very recent memory was the execution of the Mollie Maguires, and the feeling persisted that the Mollies had been hanged because they were less powerful than the Welsh bosses. In theory the Mollie Maguire organization had been broken up by the hangings, by the threats of excommunication by the higher clergy, and by the public indignation over the Mollies' crimes. In fact the organization continued to meet in greater secrecy, necessarily in smaller numbers, keeping their hatred alive and making absurd plans for the future. For the time being murder was ruled out, and violence took the form of beatings administered to non-Mollies by Mollies. No one had to distinguish between one and the other; all the Irish knew which was which. In spite of the division, the non-Mollies were loosely united with the Mollies by the common enemy, the Welsh Protestants, and when Sarah Lundy first went to work for the Evans family neither party could guess how the arrangement would turn out. Sarah, with her distrust of Welsh Protestants, correspondingly was distrusted by Wesley and Gladys Evans. Sarah had come highly recommended by her previous employers, but as it happened she was the first servant ever employed by the Evanses, who had just begun to make money. Gladys Evans was not a lady, and her treatment of Sarah Lundy was unsure, varying from unreasonable demands to spurts of kindness, until Sarah Lundy subtly and patiently established a reasonable relationship. Thereafter she fitted into the household. The Evanses were not a family to inspire affection, but their Methodist morality matched in many ways the aversion to sin that had been drummed into Sarah Lundy by her own people. Liquor, beer, tobacco, snuff, card-playing, dancing, breaking the Sabbath, and free intermingling of the sexes were forbidden in the Evans household. So had they been at the Lundys'. When Patrick Lundy came home drunk, he had the choice of sleeping in the woodshed or the privy, but not in the house, and Rose Lundy was a strong enough woman to enforce her rule. Life as the Evanses' hired girl was thus not much different from Sarah's life at home, except that she got paid and the food was better and there was more of it. Gladys Evans did not like Sarah's having a crucifix over her bed and holy pictures on her bureau, but as it was unlikely that Wesley Evans would ever enter Sarah's bedroom, the tokens of Sarah's papist affiliation were allowed to remain. It was well known, of course, that churchgoing Catholics never stole, and Gladys Evans never refused Sarah permission to go to church.

Sarah Lundy was not critical of John Wesley Evans and his ways. Compared to other women in her position in the ten-hundred block she had it soft, and she knew it. Nevertheless she was bothered by a superstitious feeling that things were going too well. Life was not that easy. For a little while a person might go along unplagued by trouble and sorrow and pain, but Sarah had been taught that God had not intended that the life here below was to be anything but preparation for the life hereafter. The godless, the sinful, who took their pleasures on earth, would all too soon learn that they had paid for them at the price of eternal bliss. God had given man a free will, and he could make his choice between earthly satisfactions and heavenly salvation. Sarah Lundy believed that Wesley and Gladys Evans, who presumably had been baptized Christians, were quite possibly. in purgatory, expiating their venial sins. That was what could happen to Protestants if they lived good lives. The worst that could happen to them would be to spend eternity in limbo because they had not been baptized. The important thing about Wesley and Gladys Evans was that they had served God as well as they knew how, avoiding sin and the occasions of sin, and God would take into consideration the circumstances that kept them from becoming Catholics. Sarah Lundy did not for one minute forget that bad Catholics could be condemned to eternal damnation. God would be more severe in His judgment of Catholics, because they were supposed to know better. It was a very complicated subject if you got into it too deeply, and it was not a subject to discuss with non-Catholics, who asked ignorant questions. But it was a subject that Sarah Lundy occupied her mind with much of the time, and most of the time she was thinking not of just anyone but of John Wesley Evans.

There was no harm in him, no evil. True, he did not have a job, he did not work. Indeed, he seldom went out of the house. But she could not judge him guilty of sloth, one of the seven deadly sins. Some men were meant to work with their hands, some were meant to work with their brains. John Wesley Evans escaped the charge of sloth because he was doing something with his brains. Bit by bit he was converting the sitting-room back of the parlor into a workroom. "It sounds a little fancy, Sarah, but from now on we'll call this the library," he announced one day.

"The liberry," she said. "All right. I'll get used to it."

"I'm going to build some bookshelves, and some day both these walls will be lined with books from top to bottom."

"Covering the wallpaper?"

"Covering the wallpaper. You'll be able to say you remember this room when it didn't have a single book in it."

"What would I want to say that for?"

"Well, if you don't want to say it there's no reason why you should. But the time will come when you'll be *able* to say it. And the time may not be too far off. This was always the room I liked best. Not the way Papa and Mama had it, but my way. The nicest thing about it is the bay window."

"Where the Mrs. would sit and do her sewing."

"It has the north light. I may take up painting as my hobby."

"Picture-painting?" said Sarah Lundy.

"Oh, I have no such intention, but if I had, this would be a very suitable room for a studio," he said. He paused. "I wonder if I have any talent in that direction. You never know till you try."

"You was always drawing pictures when you was little," said Sarah Lundy.

"When I was little," he said. "The trouble is, I wouldn't know how to start. I never knew anyone that painted pictures. No, it won't be painting I'll do here."

"What will it be?"

"Reading. Thinking."

"Just reading and thinking? What's that for a young man to be doing? You ought to be out on these nice days, making friends with people. Enjoying the sunshine. Here you're only twenty-five years of age and a body'd think you were up in your fifties. Reading and thinking. You'll be an old man soon enough, John Evans. The years go by before you know it, I can say that knows."

"Then you should be told that I intend to spend the rest of my life in this house and the greater part of it in this room," he said. "Reading, and thinking."

"Then you'll never live to your father's age, cooped up like that. Your father never would of seen sixty-two if he didn't move around and get the fresh air in his lungs."

"They went to a great deal of trouble to protect me from the fresh air."

"Only because they were terrified you'd get the consumption."

"Well, I didn't, so they must have been right. And since they seem to've been right, I'll continue their methods. Take a miner out of the mines and he dies in a year."

"Little do you know. And that's not saying how many die of the miner's asthma before they're forty."

"Sarah, I'm properly grateful for your concern, but I've made up my mind. I've already sent away for over a hundred books. At least a hundred."

"A—hundred—books?"

"Before I'm through there'll be at least a thousand in this room, and I'll be able to tell you what's in them."

"I wouldn't listen," said Sarah Lundy. "Nor neither would anyone else in their right senses."

"That I'm sure is true," said John Wesley Evans.

"There! Then what do you want to read a thousand books for? You say yourself nobody's going to listen to you tell what's in them. So what's the good of stuffing your brain with what's in them? I ask you that. Your brain won't hold all that. A thousand books. My Lord and Savior, that's a terrible, terrible thing, John. A terrible thing. I could read and write when I was seven years of age, not saying how long ago that was, and I read me prayerbook and the newspaper, and the leaflets we get after Mass. I could read more if I had to. But a thousand books!"

"I may go to two thousand."

"Your eyesight'll give out before that. There's another thing to worry about. Your eyesight."

"Yes," he said.

She had frightened him and she was sorry. "Not that your eyesight won't last forever if you don't strain it too hard. You understand that. It's the same as anything else. Too much of a good thing's as bad as none at all, and that goes for reading and thinking and fresh air and all."

Sarah Lundy's discovery that John was fearful of damage to his eyesight came as a surprise to her, with a surprising effect. For not only was it news that he worried about his eyes; it was news that he ever worried about anything. Until now she had thought of him as a skinny, bloodless individual; a vegetable of a boy, who lay on the floor and read books when he ought to be out climbing trees. She could not remember his ever crying at night, or coming home with a bloody nose, or threatening to run away, or being punished for sins with his own or the opposite sex. If he had been a pretty or a handsome child, or a remarkably ugly one, a troublesome or happy one, she would have been better prepared for the unmistakable admission contained in the single word "yes" and the way he uttered it. After saying it he left the room, and her female instinct, flabby from disuse, returned to life in a surge of compassion. This aging virgin now knew that he could use her pity. He was afraid of something.

II

Two doors to the west of 1008 lived Mr. and Mrs. Percy B. Shields, and theirs was the first house in the block to have striped awnings over the front windows, upstairs and down. There was not much practical use for awnings in that block. The trees that stood on the edge of the brick sidewalk kept the sun from being too bothersome, and the other residents of the block found curtains and roller-shades and inside shutters very satisfactory. But Mrs. Percy Shields wanted striped awnings, upstairs and down, and it did not bother her that some of her neighbors said the awnings made her house look like a circus. In the first place, they did not make the house look like a circus or like anything else but a house with striped awnings. In the second place, they made the house cooler. She could open her windows, which her neighbors could not do if they insisted on keeping their shades lowered. In the third place, it was her house and as long as she was not breaking any law she could have striped awnings or blue awnings or yellow awnings or any other kind she wished. What her neighbors objected to, if they would only come out and say it, was any bright touch, anything unusual. They might object to her striped awnings, but it might interest them to learn that the most disgraceful houses on Railroad Avenue had exactly the same kind of lace curtains that her neighbors had in their windows. And no awnings. How did Mrs. Percy Shields know about houses on Railroad Avenue? Never mind, she knew. She had it on good authority.

Never for a moment was it suspected that the authority might be Percy Shields. For one thing, he was much too old. Age had kept him from going to the defense of the national capital in 1861, and he was now forty years older. It took him a good twenty minutes to go from his house to the Gibbsville Club, a seven-block downhill walk all the way, and in recent years he had had to depend on his carriage to bring him home. It was true, as they said, that on the way home he had to carry in his belly a quantity of Old Overholt, but he never could have got home if he relied on his legs. Even the downhill walk to the club took some courage; at his time of life a tumble could result in a broken hip, and he had never known any of his contemporaries to recover from that. He therefore walked with care; slowly, and never raising his feet higher than was necessary to keep them from scraping the ground. During the winter months, when there was ice and snow, he was compelled to suspend his walks. Arthur

Hawkins, who was hostler, gardener and man-of-all-work for the Shieldses, would help Percy into the swan-type cutter, cover him up with a buffalo robe, and take him to the club. Percy would spend the same amount of time at the club as he did in kinder weather, but he would miss the exercise. Percy's need of Arthur and the horse also interfered with his wife's morning schedule, as it postponed her marketing. Consequently the wintry weather inconvenienced both Harriet and Percy Shields, and on the afternoons of extremely inclement days they could hardly bear to be in the same room with each other.

Harriet Shields observed the custom of afternoon tea, which was made possible by the fact that they had no children and could have their evening meal at a later hour than most households. Harriet served tea six days a week to a different woman friend every day. The amount of information she thus acquired was considerable and of a large variety. Her guests had been chosen for that purpose, and they represented the well-to-do, the genteel poor, the witty, the vicious, and ages from forty to sixty-five. Women past sixty-five, Harriet had found, did not hear much gossip, possibly for the reason that they had difficulty hearing anything at all, and worthwhile gossip could not be shouted to a deaf person. For one maiden lady and one widow Harriet's teas were an ample substitute for the evening meal; the four other regulars came because Harriet Shields had invited them to come, and no one wished to incur her displeasure. They all were, in a word, afraid of her. They had all heard her comments on other women and some men, and the faithful six preferred to remain on her good side. In the course of their weekly conversations with Harriet Shields they had entrusted her with personal confidences, which were safe only so long as her visitors were in good standing with her.

But if they were afraid of her, they also were addicted to the opportunity she provided for a free expression of their own observations and opinions. From week to week they saved up items of confidential and unprintable news for Harriet. Since there were never more than two women present, Harriet and her guest, it was possible to repeat intimate and slanderous details without reckoning with a third person. And while Harriet was duly appreciative of interesting items, she was never shocked and seldom surprised by anything. Another good thing about Harriet was that she did not interrupt; a friend who was emboldened to tell a lurid story did not lose her courage halfway through. If Harriet had heard the story before—as often she had—she would hear the new version all the way out, and then, but not until then, supply corrections and additions. It could be said of Harriet that she practiced scandalmongering as an art.

She, of course, was invulnerable. Such displays of eccentricity as her striped awnings and her taste in millinery were irritating, but not such stuff as gossip is made on. Harriet Shields was still pretty, healthy, and vigorous, but she was not in the least flirtatious or concupiscent. A glass of wine was all she ever drank. She had never taken laudanum. She paid her bills promptly. She did not lose her temper in public or have hysterics. She had a personal fortune, inherited from her father, which gave her a social and financial background that was very nearly the equal of any in the town, and made her immune to the charge that she married Percy Shields for his money. Indeed, it was the other way around: if anyone was vulnerable in that respect it was Percy, who had married a woman with much more money than he and who was a great deal younger. But Percy Shields had always been an affable mediocrity; everyone wished him well, and when Harriet consented to marry him there was universal sanction of the union. No one would have to worry about Percy any longer, and Harriet Stokes's share of the Stokes wealth would remain in Gibbsville. It was also said at the time that it was a real love match. Later this was amended to "ideal marriage." At sixty Percy Shields retired from the practice of the law, a formality which consisted only of his giving up his office in the second-floor rear of the Keystone Trust Company building and moving his law books to a hallway bookcase at 1012 Lantenengo Street. He never looked at them again. Not even once. Not even to notice that a couple of them had been put in upside down.

Harriet Shields's house had somewhat more grandeur inside than the other houses in the ten-hundred block. At the foot of the front stairway was a bronze statuette, mounted on the newel post, of a knight in dull armor holding a spear which supported a gas lamp. The gas line went through the hollow spear. One day Harriet detected a strong odor of gas leaking from the burner. Someone somehow had turned the valve half on. She immediately sent for the plumbers and had the pipeline sealed permanently. The statuette remained on the newel post for decorative purposes, but as a lighting fixture it was useless. "Why don't we get that lamp fixed?" Percy would say once or twice a year.

"Yes, I must remember to do that," Harriet would say. But she had developed a theory that Percy, after one of his long days at the club, had reached out for support on his way upstairs and inadvertently turned the key of the gas valve. Right or wrong, the theory covered a possibility, and the bronze knight provided no more light until he was electrified.

In her front parlor Harriet Shields had a crystal chandelier that was the largest in a private house in all Lantenengo County. Twice a year her maids unhooked each of the thousand and more bits of glass, washed and dried each one and replaced them. The task always took two days, and the entire operation was supervised by Harriet. It was not as simple as Percy Shields made it out to be, for not only was there the job of unhooking the bits of crystal and washing away the six months' collection of grime, but there was also the polishing with ammonia. Harriet and the maids would have to interrupt their work to get away from the smell of the ammonia. On the second day Harriet was at her efficient best, directing the rehanging of the bits of crystal, like stringing pearls. This she accomplished with the help of a detailed sketch of the chandelier, and when the task was completed and the gas turned on, even Percy admitted that there was beauty in the sparkling, subtle changes of color. "Louis Quatorze," he would say. "We must give a ball."

"You always say that, Percy," Harriet would say. "And you'd sooner die than have a ball."

"I'd rather die than arrange for one, is what you mean. But if you did all the work I'd enjoy it."

"We could never have a ball without inviting our neighbors, and who'd want to have *them?*"

"Not me, I'm sure. Consider the subject closed." It would be closed until it was reopened after the next cleaning of the chandelier.

Elegance, luxury, modern conveniences were not put in for the pleasure of Harriet's neighbors. When she added something to the interior of her house she did not even feel compelled to display it to her daily visitors. "Harriet, is it true that you've put in a laundry chute?" said Ellen Walker one day.

"Now where did you hear that?" said Harriet.

"I forget who told me, but I understand you have a new laundry chute that's lined with tin, all the way from the third floor to the basement."

"We have one, but it's been there for over a year. Think of attaching so much importance to a laundry chute."

"There aren't very many in town, you know," said Ellen.

"I'm sure I have no idea how many there are, Ellen. By the way, it's lined with copper, not tin. If I'd thought you'd be interested in a *laundry* chute, I'd have shown it to you a year ago. But good heavens, I'd never think of boring my friends with things like that."

"It would surprise you to know how curious people are, especially about your house."

"It wouldn't surprise me in the least. Not in the least."

"So many people have asked me if I've ever seen your wall safe. A wall safe with a combination lock?"

"Are you asking me if I have one? At least that's more interesting than a laundry chute. Yes, we've had one for a long time."

"Is it because you don't trust banks? That's the rumor I heard."

"Well, all I can say is it wasn't a rumor that started at the Keystone Trust Company. That's where I keep my money and Percy keeps his, and my father kept his and my brother Harry keeps his. That kind of a rumor could do a lot of harm. It *could* have been started by one of the other banks."

Ellen Walker's husband Louis was cashier of the Coal City Trust Company. Momentarily Ellen was on dangerous ground and having difficulty composing a suitable comment.

"I'm sure Louis'd scotch that rumor," said Harriet, who was positive that Ellen was repeating Louis Walker's very words. "Yes, we have a wall safe to keep our things in. My jewelry. Percy's good studs. Things I got from Mother. We're not worried about things being stolen, but the safe is fireproof. Fireproof, Ellen."

"Of course. I never thought of that."

"Well, I had to, you know," said Harriet Shields. "Some day all my things will go to my nieces and my nephews' wives. I can't expect to last forever."

"Looking at it that way, it's a responsibility," said Ellen.

"There's no other way to look at it. Those things increase in value every year. Mother's solitaire—well, it isn't polite to talk about such things, but it's worth three times what Papa paid for it. Tripled in twenty years, mind you."

"It's the largest diamond in town, I know that," said Ellen.

"No, there's one larger. But mine is better cut. It isn't only the size of a diamond, Ellen. For instance, yours I imagine is worth more than some I've seen, because it's newer, and the cutting methods are constantly improving."

That was another thing about Harriet Shields. She *knew* so many things. She never went away; a spring trip to Philadelphia to see the new styles, and another in November to do her Christmas shopping. But she did not like to leave Percy, and he could not travel in comfort. Nevertheless Harriet kept up to date on everything in the outside world as well as on matters pertaining to her own circle of acquaintances. She was the only woman on Lantenengo Street who had taken the trouble to find out all the reasons for the war with Spain, which she had done by writing to the district member of the House of Representatives. The name Harriet *Stokes* Shields and the Lantenengo Street, Gibbsville, address carried weight. She knew about Spain, and diamond-cutting, and the superiority of copper over tin, and how to rehang strands of crystal on a chandelier. She spoke French and had once taken lessons on the flute. There seemed to be no end to the variety of subjects that could claim her interest. Imagine writing to a Congressman for information on a war that only lasted a few months!

One day she came out of her house and saw her neighbor, young John Evans, standing in front of his own house but staring at her striped awnings. "Well, Mr. John Wesley Evans. Are you trying to stare a hole through them?"

He removed his hat. "Good morning, Mrs. Shields. I didn't hear what you said."

"I *asked* you if you were trying to stare a hole through my awnings. They've been there, this is the third year. No, next year will be the third. But haven't you ever noticed them before?"

"I noticed them, but I never took a good look at them."

"I'd heard you didn't leave your house much, but even so."

"Well, I was thinking of getting some. I didn't know so much for the front of my house, but my bay window in the back. If it wouldn't be prying, would you mind telling me about how much they ask for an awning?"

"I couldn't say exactly, but if you want to come in I'll look it up. Come on," she said, and turned about, fully expecting that he would obey. He did.

It was his first visit to the Shields house, and he was the first Evans to visit the house. "I've never been in here before," he said.

"Is that so? Well, just sit down a minute and I know right where to find the receipt. Hillyard and Son. Hall. Hill. Hillyard. Here it is. Goodness, I'd forgotten about that."

"What?" said John.

"How much they overcharged me. Eight windows. Two, three, and three. I thought it was going to be forty dollars for the whole thing, but he charged me three dollars extra for the windows on the top floor. He said he had to rent ladders from somebody. His ladders wouldn't go that high. Here, you can see on one receipt, 'Received $40 and no cents, part payment.' Then here's the second receipt, balance due on awnings, paid in full. That was Bert Hillyard. His father was a man of his word. If he said forty dollars, he meant forty dollars. No charging extra because his ladders wouldn't reach. Unfortunately, there's no one else in town that does that kind of work, so you'll have to go to Hillyards'. But if you deal with young Bert, get it all down in black and white first. Now that you're here, would you care for a glass of root beer? We have it on ice, so it should be nice and cool on such a warm day."

"Well, if it wouldn't be going to too much trouble," he said.

"Amy! Two glasses of root beer, and a plate of salty pretzels. Now, John, tell me what you do with yourself all day. I heard that you were writing a book. Is that *true?*"

"No, I'm not writing anything."

"That's what I said. I know you graduated from college, but I was sure they didn't teach you to write. What was the name of your college?"

"Wesleyan. Middletown, Connecticut."

"How far is that from New Haven?"

"Uh, let me think."

"Never mind. I only asked because you knew my brother went to Yale. Harry."

"Yes, I guess everybody in town knows that Mr. Stokes went to Yale."

"What was that again?"

He smiled, and said nothing.

She glared at him, but her glare changed to a smile. "Well, it *is* true that my brother's very proud of having gone to Yale."

"He spoke to my father about sending me there, but Yale was too stylish for us. That was when I was thinking of becoming a preacher."

"I take it you've given that up," said Harriet Shields.

"Yes, I've given it up."

"What do you plan to do instead?"

"Nothing. At least, not take a job, or learn a profession."

"Why, everybody does something in Gibbsville. At least till they're old enough to retire. But you're not old enough to retire."

"I don't have to retire. I never did anything to retire from."

"Then it's not going to be easy for you to find a wife. A man that sits around the house all day isn't what the modern girl is looking for."

"Probably not, but there are two sides to that question, too."

"Meaning, I suppose, that you're going to remain a bachelor."

"I guess that's what I am. A bachelor. I never thought of myself as a bachelor. Just a fellow that wasn't planning to get married. But after you reach a certain age I guess they call you a bachelor."

"You're not a woman-hater, are you?"

"No, I like some. I never got to know many girls."

"What kind of girls do you like?"

"What kind do I like? My goodness, that's another thing I never thought of. I'd have to think."

"I should imagine that a girl would have to show how much she appreciated you before you'd take a fancy to her."

"Then I have a long while to wait."

"Not necessarily. If you gave them a chance. Girls are intelligent, too, you know. But you'll never meet the intelligent ones just sitting at home all the time. You have to get out once in a while. Otherwise you'll be an old bachelor before you know it. There are so many different ways to meet girls. Do you play cards?"

"In *our* house?"

"That's true. You're Methodist. They don't allow dancing, either, do they? Well, here's our root beer. I thought you were going to take all day, Amy."

"No ma'am," said the maid. "I had to move a big cake of ice. The iceman pushed everything in back of the box so there was fifty pounds of ice in front of the soft drinks. I told him a hundred times—"

"Thank you. We'll talk about it later," said Harriet. She sipped her root beer. "Yum! Go ahead, drink it while it's nice and cool."

"I was enjoying the smell of your cologne. Is that what you call it? Cologne?"

"Roger and Gallet's Eau de Cologne. Thank you, I'm glad you like it. You see, you're not a woman-hater at all, if you appreciate scent."

"I never said I was a woman-hater. I just don't know any, or hardly any."

"And those you've known haven't been the right kind. Would you like to join the Assembly, now that your parents are gone?"

"What for? You know I don't dance."

"The Assembly isn't only a ball, John. Mr. Shields doesn't dance any more, but we'd never miss an Assembly. Why, for some people in town it's the only opportunity they get all year to put on their best bib-and-tucker, display their party manners. It's a very nice occasion."

"I guess the women would enjoy it, but do the men?"

"Ah, indeed they do. As much as the ladies. I think there's a meeting in a week or two. Suppose I ask Mr. Shields to put your name up? If *he* puts you up, you'll get in, then you'll be a member for life. As long as you pay your ten dollars a year."

"Ten dollars?"

"Oh, now ten dollars won't send you to the almshouse, and some day you may be very glad you joined."

"I can't dance, I don't have a full-dress, and I hardly know any of those people."

"It's time you rectified all those things. A young bachelor who lives on Lantenengo Street has certain obligations. If you don't agree, then you ought to move to the other side of town, where such things don't matter."

"My father was never in the Assembly."

"No, and if he had wanted to be, he couldn't have been."

"Then why should I want to join it? What was the matter with my father?"

"Morally, or financially, nothing, I suppose. But socially, everything."

"I'm no better, socially."

"Oh, yes you are. You have more finish."

"Not so's you could notice it."

"You're wrong. I *have* noticed it. You haven't got *la politesse,* as the French say, but you have a manner. I don't quite know how to describe it, but it's there. Now I suggest that you arrange to take dancing lessons—privately, of course. Then by the time New Year's Eve is here, you'll be able to trip the light fantastic as well as any of them. And you have a great advantage over most of the men—you're tall."

"Dancing lessons?"

"Professor Long and his wife. They give private instruction in Union Hall, you know."

"I couldn't do that, Mrs. Shields. I'd feel foolish."

"Very well, then *I'll* teach you. Tomorrow afternoon you come here at two o'clock, and we'll start our lessons."

"Here?"

"Of course, here. Look at this floor: It was meant for dancing. Take up a few rugs, move a few chairs, and this is really a ballroom. From two o'clock to three. If you haven't got the proper shoes, go down to Schoffstal's and buy a pair. That's where Mr. Shields buys his and most of the other gentlemen. And don't let Bert Hillyard overcharge you the way he did me." She rose. "I'm sorry there isn't room for you in my buggy, or you could ride down to Schoffstal's with me. But the walk'll do you good."

He walked with her to her carriage, and even in the open air her perfume was inescapable.

III

During the rest of that summer and into the months of autumn John Wesley Evans was seen going in and out of the Shields house twice or three times a week, always early in the afternoon. At that time of day Percy Shields was invariably at the club, and his absence from home during John Evans's visits was duly noted, as was the fact that young Evans had departed before the tea-time arrival of Harriet Shields's daily callers. When the visits had occurred frequently enough and regularly enough, the curious advanced beyond mere speculation: they questioned Sarah Lundy when they encountered her at the meatmarket, the grocery store, and on the slow climb up Tenth Street. Even a less subtle woman than Sarah Lundy could not have failed to notice the new friendliness of housewives who in the past had ignored her entirely or had thought nothing of preempting her place in the customers' lines. "Good morning, Sarah. No, you go right ahead, you were here first," they would say. Then they would manage to engage her in conversation which unfailingly included a reference to her young employer. "Busy as ever, with his French lessons," said one woman.

"What French lessons?" said Sarah Lundy.

"I understood he was taking French lessons from Mrs. Shields," said the woman.

"First I heard of it," said Sarah Lundy.

"Oh, yes. Three or four days a week he has a lesson. At least that's what I understood. Well, it's nice for him that he has someone so near."

"First I knew about any French lessons. He goes over there, but I didn't know that's what it was for."

"In connection with a book he's writing," said the woman.

"Ah, that I knew about. He's forever talking about books," said Sarah Lundy.

It was as exasperating to Sarah Lundy as to the curious that she had so little information to give. John Wesley Evans had never so much as told her that he was going to call on Mrs. Shields. At five minutes to two in the afternoon, three afternoons a week, he would leave the house, destination unannounced, and be gone till five or ten after three. Sarah Lundy soon knew that he went to call on Mrs. Percy Shields, but did not know why. When he got home he would close the door of his library, but she could hear him muttering, *"One* two-three, *one* two-three, *one* two-three," over and over again, and once when she made some excuse to enter the library he was doing some kind of exercise.

"You know I don't like to be disturbed when I'm working," he said. "What *is* it?"

"I thought I heard you call me," she said.

"You didn't think any such thing. Go on about your business."

"Either you called me or you're getting the habit of talking to yourself. Is that from one of your French lessons?"

"What French lessons?"

"The ones you're taking off of Mrs. Shields."

"*French* lessons? I see. Is that something you figured out for yourself, or someone else figured out for you? I hazard a guess that it was someone else. Well, you're both wrong. And I'm going to keep you in the dark as long as possible. Forever, if I can."

"I'm sure I care little enough what goes on with you and the old lady. Although she isn't that old that a young man's company—"

"Go on about your business, I said."

He weighed the matter, and after eating a banana and a whole bunch of grapes he came to the conclusion that he must report the conversation to Mrs. Shields.

"Well, I do declare," she said, when he had finished.

"You're not angry?" he said.

"Of course I'm angry," she said.

"Not at me, I hope," he said.

"Good gracious, no. Nor at your clumsy Sarah. But I am angry with whoever tried to pump her. I'll find out who that was, and make her pay for it. I love gossip, but I believe in certain rules."

"Certain rules about gossip?"

"Well, yes, in a way," she said. "A lady doesn't descend to gossip with a servant. It's mean and disloyal. They gossip about us, every chance they get, and that's to be expected. But when a woman of our station in life tries to extract juicy morsels from a servant, that's treacherous. Servants find out enough without any help from one of us. I'm going to punish that woman, whoever she was."

"How will you find out who she was?"

"I don't know, but I'll set a trap for her. It could be one of my own little toadies. I rather suspect it is."

"Your own little toadies? One of your servants?"

"Don't you pay attention to what I say? *Not* one of my servants. One of the ladies I have in for tea every day. Those are my toadies."

"Oh, I thought they were your friends," he said.

"I have no friends. If I had any, I lost them when I married Percy Shields. It was perfectly all right for him to marry me, but it was all wrong for me to marry him. You probably won't see the difference, but there was one."

"Why *did* you marry him?"

"Because he was ardent. You're too young to know about such things, but when you're thirty years older you'll know that a man in his fifties *can* be ardent. And he can seem especially so to an ignorant, inexperienced young woman. I adored him."

"But you don't any more?" he said.

"That doesn't last very long, even with two people of the same age. They have children, and that's what makes the marriage last."

"But you had no children, and your marriage has lasted."

"I had a child. A man in his sixties. A toothless baby that had to learn how to walk. Yes, and even had to have his bottle every day. Haven't you ever noticed that my husband walks as if he were afraid he was going to fall, like a little child?"

"I never thought of it that way," he said.

"That's why I love to dance with you, John. When I was a young girl I loved to dance. Not just round-dancing, but any kind. My mother used to tell me that I was getting too big to skip on my way home from school. But I wasn't skipping. I was dancing. Well, let's get to our lesson."

"I don't think you feel like it today," he said.

She looked at him and frowned. "No, I don't," she said. "But how did you know?"

"Oh—mental telepathy. Something like that," he said.

"Call it that, I suppose. It's not a term that has any sweetness, tenderness. But you're afraid of tenderness, aren't you?"

"I don't know," he said.

"You are. And so am I," she said. "I could show you what it can be, but then you'd never come back. Don't look at my neck, my chin, John. The rest of me is very nice."

"I want to see the rest of you," he said.

"Sometime I'll let you, but now you must go."

"Why not now? The door is closed," he said.

"Please go. But if you want to, you can come back tonight."

"How can I? Your husband will be here."

"Come at eleven o'clock. The front door will be unlocked, and I'll be here."

"Where will your husband be?"

"My baby will be sound asleep, snoring, and dead drunk. And nothing will wake him before five o'clock tomorrow morning. At eleven o'clock there won't be anyone on the street, and most of the leaves are still on the trees. I'll be waiting for you, I promise. And if you decide not to come, don't ever come again."

IV

The great doctor in Philadelphia said there was nothing to be done. "This is a thing that started in your left eye, most likely when you were no more than ten or twelve years old," said the doctor. "That was when you started wearing glasses."

"Yes sir," said John Wesley Evans. "Fifth grade. I'm going by the teacher I had the first time I put them on."

"Your parents took you to a man in a jewelry store, and he gave you your first pair of glasses. But Dr. Phillips tells me there was a good eye-ear-nose-and-throat man in your town. I don't understand it. Your family weren't poor."

"My mother bought my glasses at the same place where she bought hers," said John. "I guess she didn't know any better."

"That was it, I suppose," said the doctor. He studied his patient. "I can't say now how much difference it would have made, Mr. Evans. But a good eye-doctor would have looked at your left eye and noticed things that needed attention. By that time your right eye had started to go."

"Yes, I had to get new glasses every two years."

"Always from the man in the jewelry store?" said the doctor.

"Yes sir. He let me try on different glasses till I found the ones that were the most comfortable."

"And you'd wear them for two years?"

"Just about. Maybe a little longer. When I went away to college I got thicker ones. Stronger lenses."

"You used your eyes a lot, studying."

"I always did, not only studying but reading. I like to read."

"You haven't spent much time outdoors, have you?"

"No, I liked to read," said John.

"The sunlight bothered you?"

"Yes, I guess it did, thinking back."

"Dr. Phillips tells me you thought of studying for the ministry."

"I gave that up a long time ago. Why?" said John.

"I was thinking of your future," said the doctor. "You ought to plan for it, have something to do."

"It won't be the ministry. I don't believe in God, and I believe in Him less now than I ever did."

"That's understandable, but in the times I've seen you you impressed me as having quite a lot of courage."

"That's bluff," said John.

"Bluffing takes courage under the circumstances, Mr. Evans," said the doctor. "Now I'll be frank with you, because I've found out that I can be. There are probably some doctors who would perform an operation on your eyes. I won't put you through that, because in my opinion the operation would not be successful. However, if you feel that you owe it to yourself to have the operation, Dr. Phillips knows the names of other doctors in my field."

"That isn't giving me much choice, is it?"

"No, and that's why I put it that way. I'm usually the doctor that they come to as a last resort."

"Dr. Phillips said you were the best," said John.

"Well, I don't believe in false modesty, especially in a surgeon. If I knew of a better man, I'd send you to him myself. In about six years I'm going to have to stop doing surgery, and by that time we'll know more and there'll be new men coming along. But not in time to do you any good."

"How long is it going to be before I go completely blind?"

"You'll be able to see, to get around, for another eighteen months, I should say. But you're not going to be able to read more than four or five months. Reading is going to be more and more difficult for you. It is already. Have you done much traveling?"

"None at all," said John.

"Would you like to see the Parthenon? The Eiffel Tower? In other words, I'm suggesting that since you can afford it, now is the time to travel, to see things. And people. If *I* were in your position I'd spend part of that time looking at beautiful women, preferably in bed, and all sizes and colors. But my morals have never been my strong point, as anyone in Philadelphia will tell you."

"I have no morals, either," said John Wesley Evans, more to himself than to the doctor.

"I find that hard to believe," said the doctor.

"Oh, I've never disgraced my parents or anything like that, but *inside* I have no morals. I've never wanted to be a good man. I just wanted to be left alone. You go your way, and I'll go mine. That was my philosophy of life. You find it hard to believe that I have no morals, but I once killed a person."

"You did? How?"

"I didn't shoot them or anything like that. But I helped this person to commit suicide. The person could not have committed suicide without my help."

"Well, legally I suppose you could be held responsible for manslaughter. Not knowing the circumstances, I can't say. But right here on Walnut Street there are dozens of men of the medical profession who face that problem every day. Religious men, too. As an eye doctor I don't have to face the problem as much as a man who does abdominal surgery, for instance. But here on Walnut Street, and all over the country, all over the civilized world, surgeons operate on men and women, make the incision, and discover an absolutely hopeless condition. The patient is asleep, under chloroform. Why not let the poor man, or woman, stay asleep?"

"Why not?"

"Ah, but it's not that easy. There may be another doctor there, and there are always surgical nurses. Some of them know as much about surgical techniques as some doctors. That's the practical side, the chance of being reported and ruined professionally. On the ethical side, it's as bad or worse. Doctors discuss ethics while they're medical students, but after medical school you don't hear as much of that talk. We doctors tend to keep those thoughts to ourselves, the older we get and the more set in our ways. We confine our ethical discussions to something we call ethics, but is really no more than professional courtesy."

"What if I see a woman naked and fall in love with her? Isn't it going to be worse when I can't look at her any more?"

"I was wondering what you were thinking during my speech about ethics," said the doctor.

"Why did you think you had to make a speech?"

"That leaves two questions unanswered," said the doctor. "Well, I mentioned the Parthenon. I was in Athens a great many years ago, and I've never gone back. But I remember the beauty of the Parthenon, and always will. I'm very glad I saw it when I could. That should answer your first question, especially since you're not going to lose your sense of touch. I have often touched women in the dark, and so will you. As for your second question, I make these speeches to get you to talk. I want you to be stimulated to ask me questions. Remember, Mr. Evans, this has been my lifework, and I've had to tell other patients the same thing I've told you. If I can't help you in one way, I may be able to help you in others."

"Now I understand," said John Wesley Evans. "Will I ever stop being afraid?"

"You've already begun to stop," said the doctor. "But that's not saying you aren't going to have a difficult time later on. The fear will pass, but getting reconciled to your blindness may take time. Have you got a friend, a very close friend?"

"One, yes," said John.

"You're lucky," said the doctor. "Man, or woman?"

"A woman."

"She's older, and she's married. Am I right?"

"Yes."

"Does she know you've been to see me?"

"Yes."

"Could you ask her to come and see me?"

"What for?"

"To answer the questions she wants to ask me," said the doctor.

"You certainly do know a lot, Doctor," said John. "She's here in Philadelphia. She's staying at the Bellevue-Stratford Hotel."

"You might as well tell me her name. I'm very close-mouthed. I've had to be."

"Her name is Mrs. Percy B. Shields."

"I could ring up the hotel on the telephone."

"You don't have to. She's waiting outside in a hansom cab."

"Will you go out and ask her to come in?" said the doctor.

John Wesley Evans smiled. "She wanted to come in with me, but I wouldn't let her. She's always right."

V

There is nothing more that need be added to this small story. The reader can fill in for himself the assumption that the news of John Wesley Evans's blindness created genuine dismay. The devotion of Harriet Shields to her young neighbor was soon of a piece with her devotion to her aged husband. When Percy Shields died, the towns-folk were prepared to be tolerant of a marriage between Harriet and John Wesley Evans, but it did not take place. In a little while John Wesley Evans became truly if prematurely a typical resident of the ten-hundred block, one of the sequestered men and women who gave a character to the neighborhood that was as solemn as brown-stone and brick. But sometimes on a summer afternoon, on a favorable day in May, a warm day in September, there would be the sound of a waltz coming from Harriet Shields's talking-machine. It was not loud enough to disturb anyone.

Fatimas and Kisses

Around the corner from where I used to live there was a little store run by a family named Lintz. If you wanted ice cream, by the quart or by the cone, you could get it at Lintzie's; you could buy cigarettes and the less expensive cigars, a loaf of bread, canned goods, meats that did not require the services of a butcher, penny candy and boxed bon-bons, writing tablets and pencils, and literally hundreds of articles on display-cards that novelty salesmen had persuaded Lintzie to put on his shelves, and which he never seemed to reorder. I doubt if there are many stores like Lintzie's around any more, but his place was a great convenience for the people in the neighborhood. When a housewife ran short of something she would tell her child to go down to Lintzie's for the bottle of milk or the half pound of butter or the twenty cents' worth of sliced ham. And Lintzie would charge it. He well knew that the housewives in the neighborhood preferred to deal with the downtown meat markets and grocery stores, and that his trade was at least partly on a semi-emergency basis. That, and the fact that he allowed people to charge things, gave him the excuse to maintain a mark-up on most of his stock, and the housewives called him a highway robber. They called him that to his face. But they were careful how they said it. O'Donnell's meat market was the best, and Gottlieb had the best grocery store, but they were downtown and they would not open up for you if you needed a can of soup or a quart of milk at half past eight in the evening. Lintzie and his wife and two children lived upstairs over the store, and someone would always come down and open up for a customer.

Lintzie was a thin man with a Charlie Chaplin moustache and hollow cheeks that were made hollower still by his habit of leaving out his upper plate. He was young to have false teeth; in his late twenties. He had been in the Marine Corps, although he had not gone overseas, and all his worldliness, all his travels, were by benefit

New Yorker (21 May 1966); *Waiting for Winter*

of his having been a Gott damn chyrene. He was a Pennsylvania Dutch farm boy, from somewhere east of Reading, and it wondered me, as the Dutch say, how he had ever heard of the marines. So, being in my teens and curious, I asked him. "How I heart abaht the Marine Corps? I didn't never hear about them till once I seen one of them there posters in the post office. I seen a picture of a marine, all dressed up in his plues, his rifle at right shoulder arms, his bayonet in a white scabbard. He looked handsome to me, so I went home and said to my old man I was going to enlist. I won't tell you what the old man said. He said to go ahead, only he said other things besides. Glad to get rid of me. Him and my brother could run the farm without me. My brother was glad to get rid of me too. That way the old man would leave him the farm and me nothing. So I went to where it said on the poster and signed the papers. By Jesus if I knew what it was like them first three months I would of never enlisted. Son of a bitch sergeant with a swagger stick. Drill. Bivouac. Snakes. By Jesus nights I was too tired to cut my throat. That's no joke. But I guess it all done me good. I come out stronger than I went in, but minus the most of my teeth."

"How did that happen?"

"Oh, I got in a fight with a sailor, me and another Gott damn chyrene we were on duty in the Lackawanna Railroad Station in Hoboken, New Chersey. We took him in custody, he was drunk. But then all of a sudden from all over come them sailors. I had a .45 in my holster but it done me no good. They must of been ten of them chumped us all at once, and one of them hit me across the mouth with my own billy club. That was all the fighting I ever done in the Gott damn chyrenes. The Lackawanna Railroad Station in Hoboken, New Chersey. I got a discharge in October 1918, two weeks before the armistice. But I used to raise a lot of hell in Philly and New York City and Boston, Mass. I could tell *you* some stories if you was older. I was a pretty good-looking fellow till them sailors chumped me. But the son of a bitch that started it, he got something like thirty years' hard labor."

"You identified him?"

"I sure did. I picked him out of twenty of the bastards. I hope he rots. I would of got corporal if it wasn't for him. Maybe I would of stayed in and got gunnery sergeant. But they let me go and now I can't even chew a steak, not with the teeth I got now."

Lintzie's wife was a placid, rather slovenly woman whose hair was never in place. She had an extraordinarily lovely complexion and white little teeth and large breasts that swayed unencumbered by a brassiere. When he addressed her by name, which was seldom, he called her Lonnie. She called him Donald or Lintzie; Lintzie, if she was shouting to him from the back of the store or upstairs, and Donald if she was standing near him. He hardly ever looked at her unless her back was turned. In front of people my age and younger he would say to her, "Go fix yourself up decent, for Christ's sake."

"Aah, shut up," she would say.

But when older people were present they hid their animosity by paying no attention to each other. One day when I went to buy cigarettes, which he was not supposed to sell to me, I waited for Lintzie or Lonnie to appear and wait on me, but neither came. I went back and reopened and closed the door so that the bell would ring again, and she came running downstairs. "Oh, it's you," she said.

"Will you give me a pack of Camels and a pack of Fatimas," I said.

"Charge or pay?"

"*Pay,*" I said.

"Who are the Fatimas for? Some girl?"

"For my uncle," I said.

"Yeah, your uncle standing out there with the bicycle. You better watch out, Malloy. Her old lady catches her smoking cigarettes, they'll tell your old man and you'll get hail-Columbia. Give me thirty-five cents."

"Where's Lintzie?" I said.

"To Reading. Why?"

"Just wondered," I said.

"Why?"

"Just wondered," I said. I looked out toward the sidewalk and at the half-ton panel truck parked at the curb, driverless. She put two packs of Camels and two packs of Fatimas on the counter.

"I'll treat you to the butts," she said. "Okay?"

"Thanks," I said.

"The next time her old lady comes in, I won't say anything about you buying her kid Fatimas. Okay?"

"All right," I said.

They never knew—older people—at just what age you started to notice things like a driverless truck and a husband's absence and a delayed appearance, and put them all together. But now Lonnie knew that I had put them all together, and I knew that I had put them together accurately. My discovery was too momentous and mature to confide in the girl who was waiting with her bike. It was too much the kind of thing that I wanted to protect her from, and was indeed eager to protect her from all her life. Those were things I already knew too much about, along with the sight of death and the ugliness of things I had seen in my father's office and in ambulances, hospitals, the homes of the poor, when my father was still trying to make a doctor of me. I could barely endure to see those things myself, but I was a boy. She was a girl, and in ten years or maybe less she was going to be my wife. *Then* I might tell her some of those things, but now Fatimas and kisses were as much as she was ready for.

The bell tinkled as I opened Lintzie's door and tinkled again as I closed it. I guess it was the sound of the bell as much as the Fatimas I flashed that made her giggle. "You got them?" she said. It was a throaty whisper.

"Sure," I said. "Fat-Emmas for you, humps for me. Where do you want to go?"

"Have you got matches?"

"We don't need them. I have my magnifying glass." Matches in a boy's pockets were prima facie evidence of the cigarette habit, like nicotine stains on the fingers. A magnifying glass only created the suspicion that he had been seeing too much of Craig Kennedy, the scientific detective, in his struggles to outwit The Clutching Hand.

I went away to school around that time, and during vacations my hangout was a downtown drug store. Lintzie's was not that kind of place; the neighborhood kids congregated on the sidewalk, drawn to the store by the candy and ice cream, but Lintzie and Lonnie discouraged them from remaining inside. "Get your fingers off them Easter eggs," Lonnie would say. "Stop fooling around with them searchlights. Do you want to wear out the battery?" Lintzie and Lonnie would threaten to put items on the kids' family bills, and sometimes they made good on the threats. Sometimes they billed the wrong family; a fair amount of pilfering went on in spite of the Lintzies' vigilance, and you would see a kid who had just been driven out of the store furtively but proudly displaying a mechanical pencil or a put-and-take top or a carton of fig newtons that he had stolen. One of my younger brothers never came out of Lintzie's empty-handed, even if all he got was a cucumber. I did once see him steal a cucumber. The custom was known locally as the five-finger-grab, and it contributed to the Lintzies' pedophobia, which did not exclude their own messy children. "Go on up and wipe your nose," Lintzie would say. "Tell your mother to sew them buttons on." As a young buck who had danced with Constance Bennett and visited the Pre Cat, I stayed away from Lintzie's as much as possible during that period.

But then my father died and I had to get a job as cub reporter on one of the town papers. Temporarily—and I never considered it anything but temporary—my sphere of activity was limited to my own county. We had almost no income, and my mother kept us going by converting her bonds to cash, a desperation measure that obviously could not last forever. It did not make economic sense—nothing did —but very soon we were steady customers at Lintzie's instead of at the cash-and-carry a block away, where everything was much cheaper. My mother ceased to be a customer at O'Donnell's and Gottlieb's; lamb chops and asparagus seldom appeared on our dinner table. We bought a loaf of bread at a time, a jar of peanut butter, a half dozen eggs, a quarter pound of butter, a half-pint of cream, because at Lintzie's prices nothing must go to waste, to turn stale or sour. "On your way home, stop in at Lintzes' and get a can of tomato soup," my mother would say. She had never referred to it as Lintzie's and she was not going to start now. I had always been able to tell that she did not like Lintzie or his wife, and she liked them less when she owed them money twenty-nine days out of every month. They were not overly fond of her, either; she was a better bookkeeper than they, and never hesitated to prove it.

I had become, among other things, quite a drinker, although I was not yet twenty years old. How I managed to drink so much on no money is still somewhat of a mystery to me, but cheap booze was cheap, and politicians and "members of the sporting fraternity" were expected to buy drinks for newspaper men. "Why not?" an old-timer said to me. "It's small recompense for the dubious pleasure of their company." Lintzie was neither politician nor prizefight promoter, but one afternoon, when I stopped in for a last-minute purchase, he invited me to have a drink with him at Schmelinger's, a neighborhood saloon that had never bothered to pretend to be a speakeasy. "I'm broke," I said.

"I'll buy," said Lintzie.

"That's a different story," I said.

Schmelinger had been a patient of my father's, and I therefore had never been a patron of Schmelinger's, but Lintzie was greeted with the gruff politeness of the barkeep toward the good customer. We sat at a table and had three or four whiskeys—straight, with water chasers—and spent a most enjoyable hour together. In that neighborhood nearly all the men were at work all day, and Lintzie had no men friends. I gathered that he would run over to Schmelinger's for a shot in the middle of the morning and along about three or four in the afternoon, before the housewives' and schoolkids' rush. That was on a Lincoln's birthday, a school holiday. I was rather sorry that I could not count on being fitted into Lintzie's schedule, but I need not have worried. He changed his schedule to fit mine.

At that stage of my life I took my charm for granted; I did not inquire into the possible reasons why a man who was ten years older than I would want to buy me four dollars' worth of expertly cut rye whiskey once or twice a week. But slowly I began to understand first that he had somehow become indifferent to the difference in our ages. From our conversation it appeared that during my time away at school I had somehow added ten, not four, years to my age. Secondly, like everyone else, he needed someone to talk to. And he talked. He had certain recollections of his Marine Corps days that he liked to dwell on repetitiously: practical jokes on comrades-in-arms, small revenges on young officers, standing two feet away from Woodrow Wilson, visits to a whorehouse on Race Street, Philadelphia. From his whorehouse reminiscences he would often proceed, with unconscious logic, to some revelations concerning Lonnie. Her people had intended her to be the wife of his brother, but when Lintzie came home on his first furlough he threw her on the ground and gave her what she'd been asking for. On his next furlough he married her despite the fact that his brother had meanwhile thrown her on the ground and given her what she'd been asking for. But Lintzie had been first, and the baby was almost surely his. Now that the kid was old enough to look like somebody, he did look more like Lintzie than like his brother, so Lintzie guessed he had not made any mistake in that respect. He was not so sure about the second kid, the daughter. She didn't look like anybody, like a Lintz *or* a Moyer (Lonnie having been a Moyer). But by the law of averages it was probably Lintzie's kid, and he had never been able to prove anything. Lonnie hardly ever went out of the house. Most of the time she waited on customers in her carpet slippers. When she had to go back home for her brother's funeral her shoes did not fit her, so she had to stop on the way to the station and buy a new pair. Two months later, when she was taking the kids to their first day at Sunday School, the new shoes were too small for her. It was hard to believe that she had ever been pretty, but when she was seventeen or eighteen she was as pretty as any girl in the Valley. Some girls didn't care what they looked like after they got married, and Lonnie was one of them. Well, which was worse: the ones who didn't care, or the ones who cared about nothing else and flirted with every son of a bitch with pants on? In another year or two you'd be able to leave her at a hose company picnic and she'd be as safe as if she stayed home. Lintzie had told her as much, and all she said was, "Aah, shut up." That was her answer for everything. Shut up. To Lintzie, to the kids, to her mother, but most of all to Lintzie, and she had said it so often that it sunk in, finally sunk in, and he *did* shut up.

After a while it sunk in on *her* that he had practically stopped talking to her, and she complained about it. He told her he was only doing what she had been telling him to do: she had been telling him for years to shut up, and that's what he did. If she didn't want to listen to anything he had to say, he would talk to her only when it was positively necessary. And her automatic reply to that statement was to tell him to shut up. He realized that she used the expression the way some people say "Go to hell" or "Aw, nuts" but "Aah, shut up" was actually what she said, and he took her at her word. To some extent it made life livable, not to have to talk to her. She was not very much of a talker, not what you'd call a chatterbox, a windbag, but half of what she said was complaints, bellyaching. If it wasn't about money, it was about her feet getting bigger, and if it wasn't about her feet it was why didn't he do more about raising the kids instead of sneaking off to Schmelinger's morning, noon, and night? The funny thing about her complaining was that it was never twice about the same thing. It was probably better than if she harped on the same thing all the time, which would soon drive a man crazy, but on the other hand, she would complain about something and if you paid enough attention to go and do something about the complaint, you damn soon found out that she didn't even remember complaining about it. Like the time he went out and paid $185 for a new Stromberg-Carlson and she asked what the hell did he want to have two radios for, entirely forgetting that she had complained about the old radio and had specifically mentioned the Stromberg-Carlson as the one she wanted next. One day, out of a blue sky, she said to him, "Why didn't you stay in the marines? If you stayed in the marines we'd be living in Hawaii instead of a dump like this." It was such an infuriatingly unreasonable complaint that he hauled off and gave her a kick in the behind. "What'd you kick me for?" she said. Sometimes he thought she didn't have any brains in her head, but she was no dumbbell. In some things she was pretty smart. He let her do the ordering when some of the salesmen came around. She didn't know that seven eights was fifty-six, but she never took the first price on anything, and every time she ordered something, say a gross of pencils, she made the salesman fork over something for nothing. Before she would even begin talking about a sale she would demand free samples—candy, chewing gum, novelties—and use them later to reward kids who went on errands for her.

In the strictest confidence and after more than the usual ration of rye and water, Lintzie told me one day that Lonnie had discovered that most housewives did not bother to keep tabs on what they bought. My mother did not let her get away with it, he said, but other women in the neighborhood did not seem to notice when Lonnie added items to the monthly bills. She was pretty good at it, too. It was hardly ever more than a dollar's worth of stuff per account, but if you added a dollar to every bill it came to around a hundred a month clear profit. At Christmas it was even more. Anyway, it was well over a thousand dollars a year, which was Gott damn good for a woman that couldn't multiply seven eights. Like picking it up off the floor. Thereafter I did not mind taking Lintzie's free drinks. I was, so to speak, the guest of the neighborhood housewives, among whom were a few who had failed to settle accounts with my father's estate.

It also occurred to me that I was receiving a bribe from Lonnie that supplemented the original four packs of cigarettes. It probably would have done her no good to complain, but she could have protested when Lintzie rang up a No Sale on the cash register and helped himself to the money to pay for his hospitality to me. No doubt she was glad to get him out of her sight. Nevertheless I became convinced that Lonnie was appreciative of my early silence, if possibly a little apprehensive that I might break it now that Lintzie and I were drinking companions. Ethically I was not standing on firm ground, but my ethics and my morals and my conscience were taking a continual beating in other areas as well. I was giving myself trouble over girls and women and love and theology and national politics and my uncontrollable temper. Not the easiest of my problems was my willingness to spend as much time with a man whom I regarded as a moron. It was true that I was the victim of circumstances back beyond my control, but I was unable thereby to justify my association with this loquacious lout. Since I could not justify it, I gave up trying to.

Downtown, in back of a second-rate commercial hotel, was another saloon that was as wide open as Schmelinger's and served the same grade of whiskey. Unlike Schmelinger's it catered to a considerable transient trade, principally the traveling salesmen who stopped at the hotel. It was a busy joint, and often half filled with strangers. I went there one night, alone, and sat at a table to drink beer, eat pretzels, and read the out-of-town papers. At the next table were two strangers drinking rye and ginger ale. Salesmen, most likely, and getting drunk. They did not bother me, but I began to pick up some of their conversation. One was telling the other about a customer of his, nothing much for looks, but a positive, guaranteed lay. Nothing novel about that conversation between salesmen, but the speaker gave his companion directions on how to find the accommodating customer, and the address was Lintzie's store. "I got put on to her a couple years ago," he said. "Don't look for any great

beauty. This is for a quick jazz when you don't have a date. No
money. You give her a dozen samples or shave your prices a little.
And you gotta watch out for the husband. He's in and out of the
place all day. A boozer. My last time in this town, I was upstairs with
the broad and the husband came back from the saloon. I had to hide
in a closet till he went out again. All he had to do was open that
closet door and I'm cooked, but I been taking off her for a couple
years and that's the first time we ever had a close one. Don't tell her
I sent you. The first time, you gotta make it on your own, but I want
to tell you something, that—ain't—hard. And buddy, she likes it."

I could easily have struck up a conversation with the traveling man
and learned more about Lonnie's behavior, but a friend of mine
joined me and we were town people against strangers. The salesman
had confirmed my suspicions about Lonnie, dormant suspicions because I had not realized that Lonnie was quite so adventurous or
quite so careless. Oddly enough, my immediate impulse was to warn
Lonnie to use some caution, and my second, contradictory to the
first, was no more than a feeling of pity for Lintzie. The practical
effect of what I had overheard was to give up my pleasant enough
drinking sessions with Lintzie. There was going to be trouble there, I
knew it, and I had a very positive wish to stay away from it. I did not
want to be drinking with Lintzie while Lonnie was using his absence
to entertain a gabby salesman.

In later years I came to believe that Lintzie's first suspicions of
Lonnie dated from my withdrawal from our sessions at Schmelinger's. My excuse to him was flimsy, although based partly on fact:
that the paper had promoted me to columnist, an extra job that had
to be done on my own time. It was flimsy because Lintzie did not
believe me. Whenever I saw him he gave me the special look of small
dignity offended, the look of small people who do not feel entitled to
anger. My subsequent theory about Lintzie's suspicions of Lonnie
was that without me (or anyone else) to talk to, he was left entirely
with his thoughts, and his world was very small. He had a wife, two
kids who gave him no pleasure, and the clientele of his store for
whom he had no respect. And of course he had the memories of his
ten months as a private in the Marine Corps, patrolling railway stations and piers and being sneered at by sailors and petty officers;
occasional visits to whorehouses along the Eastern Seaboard; the
time he stood frozen at attention when the President of the whole
Gott damn United States passed within two feet of him at the Union
Depot in Washington. His brother had never been as far as New
York, his father had never been as far as Philadelphia, his mother
had never even been to Reading before she was thirty. For a Berks

County farm boy Lintzie had seen a lot of the world, but he had not been seeing much of it lately. Schmelinger ran a very sober saloon; the only decoration in the place was a pre-Prohibition framed brewery advertisement, depicting a goat in Bavarian costume raising a beer stein. Schmelinger himself was a strict Roman Catholic who had a daughter a nun and a son studying for priesthood. It was in these surroundings that Lintzie was spending a great deal of his time, probably as much of it as in his own store.

A full year and a little more passed during which I did not have a drink with Lintzie and actually did not set foot in his store. (My mother could send one of my brothers for those last-minute quarts of milk.) I was getting twenty dollars a week on the paper, and the owner, in his benevolence, allowed me to fill the tank of my four-cylinder Buick at the paper's expense. So I was coming up in the world, and I loved my column, which was one of the numerous imitations of F.P.A.'s Conning Tower. One afternoon, after the paper had gone to press and the other reporters had gone home, the phone rang on the city editor's desk and I went to answer it. "Malloy speaking," I said.

"Oh, it's you, Malloy. This is Christine Fultz."

"Hello, Chris, what have you got?" I said. She was a "correspondent" who picked up a few dollars a week for news tips and unreadable (and usually outdated) accounts of church suppers.

"Well, I'll tell you, there's something very funny going on out here."

"Is it funny enough to go in my column?"

"What column is that?" said Chris.

"Never mind. What have you got? Spill it."

"I want the credit for the tip, mind you."

"I'll see that you get the credit for the tip, but first you have to tell me what tip on what," I said.

"It's at Lintzie's. There's a whole crowd of people standing outside there."

"Maybe they're having a bargain sale."

"Be *serious.* Somebody said he shot her."

"Lintzie shot Lonnie?"

"That's what I said, didn't I? But I don't know if it's true or not. I couldn't get very near, there's such a crowd. There was another story circulating that he shot her and the two children, but I don't know that either."

"Are the police there?" I said.

"If they are, they're inside. I didn't see no police."

"When did this happen, do you know?"

"Well, it couldn't of happened very long ago, because I went past Lintzie's an hour ago and there was nobody there. But when I came back you should of seen the crowd. So it must of happened between the time I went past there an hour ago and when I was on my way home."

"Now you're using the old noodle, Chris. What else?"

"*Somebody* said he shot a *man.*"

"Lintzie shot a man?"

"Don't go blaming me if that's just a rumor, but that's what one person told me. There's supposed to be a dead man in there, and Lonnie and the two kids."

"But Lintzie? Where is Lintzie?"

"I don't know. He's either inside or he got away. Or maybe he's dead too."

"That's the old noodle again, Chris. Well, thanks very much. You'll get credit for the tip."

"Are you coming out?"

"Try and stop me," I said.

In less than ten minutes I parked my car across the street from Lintzie's. It was my neighborhood, and everyone knew that I was working on the paper, so they made way for me. A cop, the newest on the force, got between me and the door. "No newspaper reporters," he said.

"Who said so? *You,* for Christ's sake? Get out of my way. If you'll turn your thick head around you'll see your boss waving to me to come in." Inside the store Joe Dorelli, a sergeant and detective—all detectives were sergeants—was signaling to me. "You see?" I said to the rookie cop. "I was covering murders when you were playing high school football." It was a lie, but rookie cops were our natural enemies. I went inside.

"What the hell is this, Joe?"

"Lintzie, the Dutch bastard. He come home and caught her in bed with a guy and he shot them. Then the kids come running in from the yard and he shot them too. You want to see the gun? Here's the gun." On the counter was a holster stamped USMC and in it was a Colt .45 automatic pistol.

"Where is Lintzie?" I said.

"Back in the kitchen, talking to the chief. You'd think he just got elected mayor, honest. He phoned in. Me and the chief come right out and the first thing he done was offer us a cigar. Then he took us upstairs and showed us the wife and the boy friend. Wait'll you see *them.* We're waiting for the fellow to come and take their pictures. Then Lintzie took us down in the cellar and showed us the two kids."

"He shot them down in the cellar?"

"No, on the stairway, between this floor and the bedroom. Then he carried them down in the cellar. I don't know why, and he doesn't either. I said to him why didn't he shoot himself while he was at it? That's what they often do. But he was surprised at such a question. Why should he shoot himself? He looked at me like I wasn't all there."

"Is he drunk?"

"You can smell it on him, but he don't act it. He asked were you here."

"He did?"

"By name," said Dorelli. "That's what I wanted to talk to you. Did you know this was gonna happen? Nobody knows who the guy is. Well, we know his name and he was some kind of a salesman. His wallet was in his pants pocket, hanging on the back of a chair. From Wilkes-Barre, he is, but working for a company over in Allentown. Sidney M. Pollock, thirty-two years of age. But did you know about him and the Lintz woman?"

"No, but I might recognize him."

"We'll get him identified all right."

"I'd like to take a look at him."

"From the front you would. You know what a .45 slug'll do. The right-hand cheekbone it went in. She got it in the heart. Two. He gave her one for good measure. The kids he gave one apiece. Five shots, four dead. But he was a marine, and they teach them to shoot in the marines. I took notice there was a picture of him in the bedroom. Marksman and expert rifleman. Well, do you want to take a look at them?"

I only wanted to see the dead man, and I did recognize him. He was the companion of the traveling salesman who had talked so seductively of Lonnie Lintz. Even after a year there was no mistaking that nose and that hairless skull. I could not have recognized the bigmouth salesman; he had been sitting on my right; but Pollock had been facing him, and me. It was perhaps too much to say that if I had struck up a conversation with them that night, Pollock would not now be lying dead in his underwear on a messy bed in a strange town, in disgrace. I thought of Pollock's wife, if any, and his probably orthodox mother and father in Wilkes-Barre.

"Now you got another treat in store for you," said Dorelli. "Down in the cellar."

"No thanks," I said.

"Me either," said Dorelli. "I had to, but if I didn't have to I wouldn't have. Two kids, for Christ's sake, around the same age as two of mine. This guy is crazy, but don't you write that. That's what he'll claim—and maybe he had a right to kill her and the Jew, but not the kids. He can't pull that unwritten law on the kids. For that he deserves to fry."

"I didn't know you were such a family man, Joe."

"Listen, what you don't know about me would fill a book," he said. "You had enough, we'll go down and see if the chief'll let you talk to Lintz."

I waited in the store while Joe conferred with the chief. A cop named Lundy came in while I was there. "That's something you don't often hear in this town," he said.

"What's that?" I said.

"Them women out there, they want to lynch him."

"We've never had a lynching in this town," I said.

"We never will. It's just talk, but you don't often hear that kind of talk in Lantenengo County. Just talk, but all the same I'm gonna tell the chief to get him outa here."

"You mean you're thinking of *suggesting* to the chief," I said.

"Aah, smart guy," said Lundy. "I hear Lintz and you was great buddies."

"Doing some detective work at Schmelinger's, eh, Lundy? Do you think you'll solve this case?"

"I'll solve you one right in the puss, Malloy," said Lundy.

"Then you'll be right back on the garbage truck. We supported *this* mayor," I said.

Dorelli, at the rear of the store, beckoned to me.

"Any message you wish me to convey to the chief, Lundy?" I said.

"No, you wouldn't get it right, just like that rag you work for," said Lundy. He laughed and I laughed. Lundy was a good cop and he knew I thought so.

"I'll put in a good word for you, then," I said.

"Jesus, don't do that. That'd be the ruination of me, a good word from you."

I joined Dorelli. "You can talk to him, but one of us has to be there."

"Oh, come on, Joe. There's no mystery about this case. Let me talk to him alone."

"We'll do it our way or not at all," said Dorelli.

"Then we'll do it your way," I said.

Dorelli led me to the kitchen. A uniformed cop was standing outside the kitchen door; the chief was sitting across the table from Lintzie, his chin on his chest, staring at him in silence. Obviously the chief had momentarily run out of questions to ask Lintzie. Lintzie turned when I entered. "Oh, there's my buddy. Hyuh, Malloy."

"Hello, Lintzie," I said.

"Say, Chief, let me send over to Schmelinger's for a pint," said Lintzie. "I'll pay for it."

"Pay for it? You got a lot to pay for, you son of a bitch," said the chief.

"I'll be down in the cellar," said Dorelli, and left.

"Well, I guess I went and done it," said Lintzie.

"How did you happen to pick today?" I said.

"I don't know," said Lintzie. "I was over at Schmelinger's and I guess I started to thinking to myself. There was a whole truckload of stuff piled up on the kitchen porch, waiting to be unpacked. I knowed Gott damn well Lonnie wouldn't start unpacking it. It had to be unpacked and put down in the cellar out of the way. So I said to myself if I got it all unpacked I could make the kids take it down in the cellar when they got home. It was a truckload of stuff from the wholesaler. Canned goods. Heavy. In wooden boxes. All I needed was my claw-hammer and I could unpack the stuff and the kids could take it down the cellar a couple cans at a time. Ten or fifteen minutes' work for me and I could be back at Schmelinger's. So I said to Gus I'd see him later and I come home."

"What time was that, Lintzie?" I said.

"Search me. I lost track of time," said Lintzie.

"About quarter of three," said the chief. "Between half past two and three, according to Schmelinger."

"I come in the store door, and I took notice to the salesman's car outside. But I went inside and no Lonnie, and no salesman. The chief don't believe me, but I caught her once before with a salesman, only it wasn't the same one."

"Why don't you believe him, Chief?"

"Because this was a deliberate murder. All this stuff about the packages on the back porch, that's the bunk."

"Look outside, the boxes are there right now in plain sight," said Lintzie.

"He pretended he was going to spend a couple hours at Schmelinger's, the way he usually did. But he only went there long enough to give his wife and the salesman time to go upstairs," said the chief. "He admitted himself he usually kept the .45 upstairs but today he had it hanging on a peg in the cellar stairway. This was a planned first-degree murder."

"How about that, Lintzie?" I said.

"The chief don't have to be right all the time."

"But why was the gun hanging in the stairway?"

"To get it out of the way of the kids. Lonnie said she caught the boy playing with it and I was to get it out of the way. So I took and hung it on a peg in the cellar stairway, where he couldn't reach it. That was two-three days ago. Lonnie could—I was just gonna say Lonnie could back me up on that, but I guess not now."

"No," I said. "So then what?"

"Yes, listen to this part, Malloy," said the chief.

"Then what? Then I went upstairs and caught them in bed."

"Wait a minute, Lintzie. You're skipping a lot. Did you get the gun and then go upstairs?" I said.

"Me? No. I went upstairs and caught them and then I got the gun."

"Did you, before you went upstairs, did you call Lonnie to see where she was? Upstairs or down-cellar?"

"Well, she could hear the bell when I come in the store."

"But you could have been a customer. You didn't call her, or did you?"

"He didn't call her, and he *didn't* come in the front door," said the chief. "He told Dorelli one story and me another, and now he's an altogether different one. He told Dorelli he went around the back way and got his claw-hammer and started opening the boxes. There's no mark of a claw-hammer on any of the boxes, and anyway you make a certain amount of noise opening a wooden box with a claw-hammer. You know, you put the claws under the slats and you start using leverage and it makes a peculiar kind of a noise. But that would have warned the people upstairs. No, he came in the back door, where there is no bell, and he got the .45 and sneaked upstairs and took careful aim and killed the salesman. One shot. Then he let her have two slugs right in the heart. I had a look at the .45 and I'll tell you this much, Malloy. If all my men kept their guns in as good a condition I'd be satisfied. I know something about guns. If you leave a gun in a holster for any length of time, the oil gets gummy, but not this gun. This gun was cleaned and oiled I'd say in the last twenty-four, forty-eight hours."

"I always kept my gun in good condition," said Lintzie.

"Yes. For just such an occasion," said the chief.

"Tell me what you did, Lintzie," I said.

"I shot them, for Christ's sake. And then the Gott damn kids come yelling and screaming and I shot them, too. I ain't denying it. Go ahead and arrest me."

"Oh, we'll arrest you, Mr. Lintz," said the chief. "You *were* arrested, nearly an hour ago. Sergeant Dorelli placed you under arrest, but you don't have a very good memory."

"You shot the kids on the stairway, and then you told Dorelli that you carried them down to the cellar."

"That's what I done. Yeah."

"But I understand that a bullet from a .45 has a terrific impact, that it'll knock a grown man back several feet. So I was wondering, maybe when you shot the kids the impact knocked them down the stairs, and then you picked them up and carried them to the cellar. Is that about right, Lintzie?"

"No," he said.

"What did happen?"

"I held the kids, one at a time, and shot them," said Lintzie.

"Jesus," I said, and looked at the chief.

"They wouldn't hold still," he said.

"Jesus Christ," I said.

"Oh, this is quite a fellow," said the chief. "It takes a real man to grab hold of a kid with one hand and shoot him with the other. And do the same thing all over again with another kid."

"Which did you shoot first, Lintzie? The girl or the boy?"

"Her. Then he come at me. I don't remember holding him."

"The boy tried to defend his sister," said the chief.

"He didn't try to defend nobody, that kid. He was getting ready to shoot me. Him and Lonnie."

"But I thought Lonnie told you to hide the gun," I said.

"Till he got older, that's all. She was gonna wait a couple years till we had more money saved up."

"Oh, and then she was going to let him shoot you?" I said.

"You got the idea," said Lintzie. He grinned at me and sneered at the chief. "She thought I was dumb, but I wasn't so dumb."

"You said something about catching her with another man once before," I said. "You never told me about that."

"Yes, I did. Didn't I?"

"No, you never told me that. When did you catch her? Was it like today, you came home and found her with another man?"

"Night," he said.

"Oh, you came home one night and found her?"

"No! I was home. Upstairs. The night bell rang and she went down to see who it was."

"You thought it was a late customer," I said.

"I thought it was, but it was a foreigner. He had whiskers and he wore those funny clothes. You know. He had whiskers on his chin, all the girls were stuck on him."

"Oh, yes. Once I had a billygoat, he was old enough to vote. He had whiskers on his chin. I remember the song."

"This was *him*, though. Not a song."

"Oh, really? And he came in the store and made passes at Lonnie?"

"*She* made passes at *him*. She made passes at everybody except you. She didn't like you, or your mother, or any of you. Boy, oh, boy, the things she used to say about your old man."

"She never knew my old man, but what did she say about him?"

"How he used to operate on people when they didn't have nothing wrong with them. Any time your old lady wanted a new dress, your old man would operate on somebody."

"Oh, well that was true, of course," I said.

"Stop humoring him," said the chief.

"And that's why Lonnie never made passes at me, because she didn't like us. But what about this foreigner with the beard, Lintzie? Did you ever see him any place else? Did you ever see him at Schmelinger's?"

"He used to come in there but I never talked to him."

"He did come in there, though?"

"I seen him there," said Lintzie.

"He had whiskers. Did he wear a kind of a coat with little straps across the front?"

"Such a coat, yes," said Lintzie. "But I never seen him when you were there."

"No, but I think I knew the fellow you mean."

The chief looked at his gold hunting-case watch. "You had long enough, Malloy. I'm taking this fellow down to the squire's office."

"Charging him with first-degree murder?" I said.

"We sure are. An open-and-shut case, like this watch."

"I'll make you a small bet he never goes to Bellefonte," I said.

"I wouldn't take your money," said the chief.

"Bellefonte? Where the electric chair is?" said Lintzie. "Huh. Not me."

"See? He doesn't think so either," I said.

"Who did I used to guard during the war? Tell him, Malloy," said Lintzie.

"Woodrow Wilson, the President of the whole Gott damn United States," I said.

"Can I go upstairs a minute, Chief?" said Lintzie.

"No. You mean you want to go to the toilet?"

"No, I want to get something for Malloy."

"Call Lundy, tell him what it is and he'll get it," said the chief.

"My picture of me, upstairs on the bureau," said Lintzie.

"Oh, for Christ's sake. All right," said the chief.

Lundy went upstairs and brought down the photograph, which I had never seen before, of Private Donald Lintz, U.S.M.C., in his greens and the old-style cap that sat squarely on the top of his head, two badges for shooting pinned to the blouse.

"Put that in the paper, Malloy," said Lintzie.

"That I promise you," I said. "And how about pictures of Lonnie and the kids?"

"You want them too?" said Lintzie. "What do you want them for? I don't want them in the paper."

"Are there any more up there, Lundy?" I said.

"Sure," said Lundy. "Plenty. Her before she got fat, and the two kids."

"No, you can't have them," said Lintzie.

"Get them, Lundy," said the chief.

"You son of a bitch, Malloy," said Lintzie. "You want to make people feel sorry for them."

"Maybe he doesn't, but I do," said the chief. "Malloy, why do you think this fellow has a Chinaman's chance? You can tell me. The D.A. prosecutes, I don't."

"Can you spare five minutes?" I said.

"What for?"

"Will you come with me? It'll only take five minutes at the most," I said.

The chief called Dorelli, told him to keep an eye on Lintzie, and accompanied me to Schmelinger's. I pointed to the old-time beer ad on the wall. "There's Lonnie's other boy friend," I said. "Any fifty-dollar alienist will keep Lintzie out of the chair."

"Maybe you're right," said the chief.

"Something on the house, gentlemen?" said Schmelinger.

"Maybe you're right," said the chief.

"You, Malloy?"

"Not on the house," I said. "You've just lost your best cash customer."

"I won't miss him," said Schmelinger.

"He was good for fifty bucks a week and he never gave you any trouble," I said.

"I won't miss him," said Schmelinger. He ignored me and addressed the chief. "After this fellow stopped coming in with him he just sat there and stared at the Bock beer picture. And I bet you he don't even know it was there."

"Is that so? Well, thanks, Gus. Next time I'm out this way I'll have one with you," said the chief.

We walked in silence halfway to Lintzie's, then the chief spoke. "I thought a great deal of your father. What's a young fellow with your education throwing it all away when you could be doing some good in the world?"

"What education? I had four years of high school," I said.

"You were away to college," he said.

"Away, but not to college."

"Oh, then you're not much better than the rest of us," he said.

"I never said I was, Chief."

"You never said it, but you act it. Your father *was* better than most of us, but he didn't act it."

"No, he didn't have to," I said.

Yostie

It was going to be a busy day. It was sure to be, no matter how unpromising it looked now. All twenty boats were tied up neat and orderly at the pier, all forty oars were stacked in the office. There was not a soul in either the men's or the women's bathhouses, but the clean, dry bathing suits were on the office shelves, arranged according to sizes; and a hundred and fifty towels, still wrapped in bundles as they had come from the laundry, were resting on the floor behind the counter. The bathhouse keys were hanging on hooks that were numbered from 1 to 50.

Irwin Yost looked at the wall clock, which bore the name and an advertising slogan of an ice cream company. He checked the time against his pocket watch, a silver potato attached by a leather thong to one of his suspender buttons. The hour was 7:26. The people would not start coming much before 8:25, when the trolley that left Gibbsville at seven-thirty arrived. Nevertheless he decided that he might as well open the safe now and be ready for them when they arrived. At 8:25 things would begin to happen all at once, people renting bathhouses and suits and towels and rowboats. He did not like to do it so soon, but he opened the safe and got out stacks of silver—halves, quarters, nickels and dimes. He broke open each stack by slapping it hard on the edge of the counter, and he poured the coins into the separate craters in the cash drawer. Now he was ready to make change in case some customers came by automobile, although he knew from experience that the automobile people always came later than the trolley people, and anyway there never were very many automobile people. Today, because it was Decoration Day, there would be some farm people in small trucks, but even so they would not be here much before the trolley people, if at all. Decoration Day or no Decoration Day, farm people had their chores to do. Yostie closed the safe and locked the cash drawer and went out and had a look around.

Saturday Evening Post (4 June 1966); *Waiting for Winter*

He could tell that the day was going to be a scorcher. The sun had not yet burned off the haze on the water, and at this hour that meant a hot day. He hoped he had put in enough ice to last through the afternoon. If the word got around that the soft drinks were not cold, sales would fall off. Most of his customers brought their own picnic lunches, but they bought their Coca-Cola and Whistle at the refreshment stand. The kids drank Whistle by the gallon, practically, all day long, but they wanted it cold, which was no more than right. The ice cream for the cones—combs, the kids called them—was no problem. It came packed in ice from the factory. But the only way to keep the soft drinks cold was to put the bottles in galvanized iron tubs and see that there was plenty of ice.

"What say, Mildred? Do we have enough ice?" said Yostie.

"I guess maybe, if it don't get too warm," said Mildred Kunkel. "If she's too warm a day, I don't know for sure."

"She'll be a warm one all right," said Yostie. "I wisht we wasn't shorthanded. Paul Miller got his arm broke playing baseball."

"I heard," said Mildred. "Such a nuisance."

"Do you have any suggestions who I could get in his place? One of your brothers, maybe?"

"All them is at Reading down, taking in the baseball," said Mildred.

"Can you manage by yourself?"

"The soft drinks I can manage but maybe the wieners I'm slow with."

"Do as good as you can," said Yostie. "I go now and ask one of the Seiberling boys to help out."

"Them? They don't need the money."

"Their daddy don't need the money, you mean. But he's so stingy."

He left the pier and walked to one of the cluster of cottages a hundred yards away.

"Hello, Yostie. You ready for a big day?" said Samuel Seiberling.

"Shorthanded. I come to ask if maybe one of your young fellows wanted work."

"How much would you pay?" said Seiberling.

"Three dollars is the most. It's near eight o'clock already. Not a full day, but I'll pay three."

"Not enough, Yostie. Henry Ford pays five, so I wouldn't let them work for less. Anyhow, they all went to town for the parade and I don't expect them back before noon."

"You know anybody wants work?"

"Maybe one of my kids would work half a day, for three dollars," said Seiberling.

"No. I guess me and Mildred Kunkel have to do it all by ourselves."

"Do you do it to Mildred, Yostie?"

"You got a dirty mouth, Sam, and dirty thoughts also. Mildred is decent."

"They're all decent till you get the red part in," said Seiberling.

"Shut your dirty mouth, Sam."

"Tell her to come over after work and I'll give her three dollars."

"I could say something, but I won't," said Yostie. He turned and walked back to the pier.

"Did you get somebody?" said Mildred.

"No, nobody," said Yostie. He looked at his watch. "Only a little while now before the eight-twenty-five trolley. Sit down, Mildred. You'll be on your feet all day. Rest while you can."

"Oh, I'm used to it. You sit down and take the load off your feet. Will I give you a drink of something?"

"Too early in the day. I don't have a thirst yet, thanks."

"Soon is the trolley," she said. "I come over and help in the office. They don't come off the trolley thirsty. Right away they want their keys to the bathhouses. Some want boats."

"You know this business as good as I do, Mildred."

"Well, I work for you two summers now," she said.

"Today I pay you double. Yes I do, now don't you argue. It's only right you get double. You'll do the work of two, with Paul away."

"But Paul can swim and I don't know how to swim. I ain't a lifeguard."

"I forgot that," said Yostie. "Now you got me worried, if somebody falls in."

"There was nobody ever drowned here yet," she said.

"No, but Paul always has to fish some person out, and I can't and you can't."

"If some person falls in maybe some hero will pull him out," she said. "I tell you what, Mr. Yost. You watch when the trolley comes, and the first one you see that's a good swimmer, you offer him the job, lifeguard. No charge for the bathhouse, no charge for a boat all day, and we give him lunch free. There's always some good swimmers from Gibbsville, young fellows."

"A good idea, Mildred. I'd be willing to pay him money, too. It worries me, without Paul. I don't want nothing to happen. We never had no drowning yet, but it only needs one to give the place a bad name."

"I didn't mean to worry you."

"I know, but I should have thought of that myself."

"Well, what could you do?" she said.

"I could have made Paul send somebody. He knows the good swimmers."

"It was his place to offer to send somebody," she said.

"Yes, he should of," said Yostie. "Well, ten more minutes before the trolley."

"Here comes the first customer, before the trolley," she said. She pointed to a lone man, walking up the road from the main highway. He was carrying a small, imitation leather Gladstone, and Yostie and Mildred silently watched his approach.

He was hatless, and the jacket of his suit was slung over his shoulder. He was holding the jacket with a finger hooked into the tab in the collar. "I don't like his looks," said Yostie. "I seen that kind before. They want to start a dice game and rook the farm boys out of their money."

"Maybe so," said Mildred.

The man came onto the pier. "Hyuh, you open for business?" he said.

"Just about," said Yostie.

"Where can I get a cup of coffee and maybe a couple sinkers?"

"Sinkers we don't have. Wieners, cake and pie is all. But I got coffee," said Mildred.

"Well, a piece of pie'd go good. You got cigarettes for sale?"

"Yes sir. We got Camels, Luckies, Piedmonts, and Philadelphia Hand-Mades. They're cigars, of course," said Mildred. "You follow me."

"All right. I'll follow you," said the man. Unseen by Mildred he looked at her behind and winked at Yostie. "Can I leave my suitcase here, temporarily?"

"Do you want to rent a bathhouse?" said Yostie. "I can give you your key now. Fifty cents, that's for the whole day."

"Well, can't I just leave my suitcase while I get some grub in me?"

"There's a lot of people'll be here in a few minutes. The trolley's due. If I was you I'd hold on to the suitcase if you don't want to rent a bathhouse."

"Oh, you got a lot of people coming," said the man. "Well, here's a half a buck. I'll take a bathhouse. You can give me the key later."

"You care to rent a bathing suit, or do you have your own?"

"How much'll a suit set me back?"

"With the towel, that'll be seventy-five."

"That comes to a buck and a quarter," said the man. "Well, all right. I guess I might as well. What are all the people coming for?"

"It's Decoration Day. We always get a big crowd Decoration Day," said Yostie.

"You sure as hell don't have many now."

"No, but when the trolley empties there'll be thirty or forty. Maybe more."

"What's the name of this place?"

"Yostie's. It's my place. My name is Yost. That's how it got the name."

"Uh-huh. You got a pretty good proposition here. They rent those boats and all? What do you charge for a boat?"

"Fifty the first hour and twenty-five cents an hour after that."

"Uh-huh. So a fellow rents a boat eight hours it runs him two and a quarter a day. But on the other hand, you most likely hope you rent a boat four or five times a day, huh? Eight times a day, at a half a check every time, you make four bucks instead of the two and a quarter. What's to keep a guy from renting a boat for the day, and then rowing down the lake and making a few dollars on his own?"

"The lake ain't that big. I can keep my eye on all my boats, just from here."

"Uh-huh. You got about twenty boats out there."

"Exactly twenty," said Yostie.

"Say, you probably make ten dollars an hour minimum. How long do you stay open?"

"We're open till eight, but most of the people go home by seven."

"Eighty dollars a day, just from renting the boats," said the stranger. "You could make five hundred a week that way. And I see you got fifty keys for bathhouses. That's twenty-five a day, times seven is a hundred and seventy-five. Soft drinks. Wieners. Pie and cake. Say, you got a nice little business here, Mister. You don't sell any liquor on the side, I guess."

"I don't allow no drinking on the place. This is a family place."

"Yeah, I can see that," said the stranger. "It's not a regular amusement park, or you'd have like shooting galleries and wheels and rides. But you could make a lot more dough without changing the place much."

"You're a stranger around here, or you'd know about the big park. There they got all those things. Ferris wheel and all. This ain't that kind of a place. Here you don't have to spend as much money. Are you connected with the amusement business?"

"Well, not exactly. I worked in parks here and there."

"What as, if you don't mind me asking," said Yostie.

"Christ, I was everything from a short-order cook to a shill."

"A what?"

"A shill. A shillaber. That's a kind of an assistant, I guess you'd call it. Hey, she brought me my coffee? I call that service."

Mildred placed a tray on the counter. "Coffee. I didn't know whether you wanted it with milk and sugar, so there they are. And a piece of apple pie."

"That's real service. Thanks, young lady. What do I owe you?"

"Fifteen. A nickel for the coffee, ten for the pie," said Mildred.

"Does everybody get this service?" said the stranger.

"No," said Mildred, and picked up his nickel and dime and left.

The man drank some coffee and had a bite of the pie, which he held in his hand without using the fork. "She makes good coffee. The pie is bakery pie, not home-made, but she knows how to make coffee," said the man. Yostie nodded and waited until the man finished the pie.

"You don't have a butt on you," said the man.

"I don't use them," said Yostie. "I can give you a cigar."

"No, no thanks. I stick to Piedmonts."

"Would you be looking for a day's work?" said Yostie.

"What made you think of that? Don't I look as if I had any money on me?"

"Some, but not much."

"What kind of a day's work, and what do you pay?"

"Helping out here in the office. Renting the bathhouses and handing out the towels."

"Sounds like a whorehouse, handing out the towels. What do you pay?"

"Three dollars. That's what I pay the regular fellow, but he broke his arm playing baseball."

"He sure as hell didn't break it carrying home his pay. No, you gotta talk more money than that, Yostie," said the man. "When did your guy break his arm?"

"Yesterday."

"Yesterday, huh? I tell you what I'll do, Yostie. You give me thirty-five a week and a place to sleep. The bathhouse. I don't care where. An army cot. I don't care, I'm not particular. And I'll help you out till your guy's arm knits."

"Can you swim?"

"Can I swim? I could swim across your little lake under water. Where I come from originally everybody's a good swimmer."

"Where was that?"

"Well, now, let's say it was Atlantic City, New Jersey. You don't have to know all that, do you? All you want is some guy to help you out till your regular man is ready to go to work again. Now my name is Ed Smith. You just call me Ed. If you call me Smith, I'm not used to that name, but I am used to Ed. Is that your trolley up there? You better make up your mind quick, before the big rush."

"All right. Thirty-five a week, or five dollars a day."

"It takes an arm five or six weeks to knit properly. I broke mine when I was a kid and it took about that long. So you can figure on me being around long enough to collect a month's pay at least. You pay at the end of the week?"

"Sunday night."

"Sure, when the Saturday and Sunday money is in. And where do I sleep?"

"I'll bring you a cot," said Yostie. "You might as well hang up your coat and vest and roll up your sleeves."

"I'm ready for business. I'll watch how you do it the first two or three customers, but I catch on quick."

"Say, that's some tattoo you got there," said Yostie. "What is that? Some kind of a dragon?"

"A genuine Chinese dragon. Cost me thirty-five dollars. But how do you like this one, on this arm?" He held out his left arm and showed the inner side. "Now watch." He opened and closed his fist, and the tattooed figure of a nude woman moved its hips. "The twitching twat, I call that," he said. "That only cost me twenty-five, but I get more laughs from that than the dragon. The dragon is real art work. Tessie the twitching twat is for laughs, and you know who likes it best? Women. They laugh their guts out."

"Uh-huh. Well, here they come," said Yostie.

"My God, they are family people. They look like a Sunday school picnic," said Ed Smith. "I'll give you even money there isn't two hundred bucks in that whole crowd."

"I don't bet," said Yostie.

Thus against his instincts and his better judgment Yostie hired a man who refused to tell anything about himself, and what could be guessed was all unfavorable. Yostie excused his action on grounds of necessity, although he knew that there was more to it than that. Ed Smith was such an unlikable man that you wanted to get rid of him two minutes after you met him, but instead of that you were hypnotized by his all-around badness. Even Mildred, who usually had such good sense, had fetched his coffee and pie for him. But the decision had to be made so quickly; the people were leaving the trolley, the stampede was on, led by two small boys who wanted to be the first to line up for bathing suits, although they would have to wait until their parents got to the pier with the money for the suits.

It was a good-sized crowd. Those that Yostie recognized were mostly from Gibbsville, with a few from Swedish Haven and the other stops on the trolley line. They were mostly family groups, parents and young children, although there were several couples who were going steady and would spend the day off by themselves. Yostie recognized Walt McLoughlin, who worked in a printing plant in Gibbsville, with his wife and three children; Jerome Stumpf, formerly driver of a three-horse beer wagon and now helper on an ice cream delivery truck, with his wife and two children; Bucky Stahlmyer, from Swedish Haven, who clerked in a hardware store, with his wife and seventeen-year-old daughter; John Adams, weighmaster at one of the Gibbsville coal yards, with his wife who had to walk with a cane because she had the dropsy; Adam Klein, boiler fireman and general handyman at one of the Gibbsville bank buildings, with his wife and two sons; Fred Alexander, the widower who operated the projection machine in the Swedish Haven moving picture theater, who was accompanied by his own two small children and by Irma Dreibelbis with her two; Sam Gottschall, head hostler at the Murray Brothers mule yards, with his wife and five children; Artie Minzer, alone, about forty-five, who was said to be not all there and had to be watched; Danny O'Brien, who had lost an eye at Soissons and probably had a couple of half-pints of whiskey in his hip pockets, with his thin little wife and two children; and many others whose names did not immediately come to Yostie. They brought their lunches in shoeboxes and market baskets, and they were all dressed in their best clothes, most of the men in stiff straw skimmers, new and last year's; the women in summer hats or carrying sunbonnets for later on. Some of the younger men wore freshly laundered khaki pants or white ducks, and a few of them wore white or brown sneakers. As an indication of how business was to be on this, the season's opening day, the first trolley-load was very promising, and Yostie hoped he would not run out of ice; but what was most reassuring to him was that they were there, that they had come at all with their saved-up dollars and halves and quarters, and that he and they together greatly outnumbered Ed Smith. Yostie despised himself for his weakness in hiring Ed, but there was nothing to do about it now, and he tried not to think about it. If only he had thought in time he would have remembered that he did not even need Ed. Nearly all the grownups were completely trustworthy and could be counted on to keep their young ones from doing anything dishonest; and as for needing a lifeguard, Jerry Stumpf was the son

of the Swedish Haven locktender and had once belonged to the
bunch of canal kids who were known as the Water Rats. There
wasn't a better swimmer in the county than Jerry Stumpf.

But Ed was at work, and he was catching on quickly. He had a
personal remark for every customer who wanted a bathing suit and
towel. "These suits are guaranteed to keep you afloat," he said to
one hesitant woman.

"Guaranteed?" she said.

"Well, in two foot of water. And if you start sinking, just yell for
me."

It was the kind of joking that early in the day and in the holiday
mood the people were ready for. "Lady, you're not gonna take this
young fellow back in the women's bathhouse," he said.

"I am so," said a woman. "He's only four years of age."

"He looks like five to me, and when *I* was five years old, believe
me."

"Oh, you," said the woman. "I thought you was serious."

"Don't anybody get serious today," said Ed. "Everybody have a
good time on their day off. Yostie wants everybody to have a good
time and get good and thirsty, buy a lot of soft drinks. Especially you
folks that brung your own lunches. Me and Yostie gotta live, too,
hey, Yostie?" Yostie pretended not to hear him.

They disposed of the first rush of bathhouse and bathing suit customers, and the men and boys and young couples who wanted to
rent boats gathered near the stacked oars. On the pier was a large
sign that read: "Children Under 12 Not ALLOWED in BOATS unless Accompanied by ADULT By Order of the Management." Yostie
had never strictly enforced his own rule, but he was startled to see
that Ed Smith was renting boats to boys who obviously were not yet
ten years old. "Listen, I don't want them little bits of kids out on the
lake. Be more careful who you rent the boats to," said Yostie.

"I'll keep an eye on them. Nobody's gonna drownd as long as I'm
here."

"Never mind about that. That's my rule, and I want you to do what
I say around here," said Yostie.

"All the time?" said Ed Smith.

"All the time," said Yostie. "You better get that straight or else
you won't be here long."

"Is that any way to talk to the man that's going to be your partner?"

"No, that'll never be," said Yostie. "I don't go partners with anybody."

"Man *or* woman?"

"Man *or* woman," said Yostie.

"Uh-huh. Well, I'm kind of that way myself. He who travels fastest travels alone, is my motto."

"I'm not traveling anywhere," said Yostie. "You're the one that's traveling, not me."

"I only meant that as a kind of a saying."

"I know," said Yostie. "Now we gotta start getting ready for the nine-twenty-five trolley. That'll be the big one of the day, the nine-twenty-five. The ten-twenty-five there'll be hardly anybody on it, or the eleven-twenty-five. The twelve-twenty-five there'll be a few, those that stayed in Gibbsville to watch the parade. Then there won't be many till the two-twenty-five, and by that time some of the early ones will start going back. There's some men has to work tonight, men on the four-to-midnight shift."

"Where is that?"

"Oh, there's the Pennsy roundhouse, they got a four-to-midnight shift. There's the maintenance crew at the steel mill, they go on at five. And the fellows that work the night trick on the trolley lines. Pretty near half of the men here this morning will be working somewhere tonight. All good solid, reliable working men, with families."

"And very slow spenders."

"That's because they don't have it to spend, and they don't spend what they don't have, these people."

"I had the understanding that there was a lot of coal miners around here."

"To the north," said Yostie. "But they don't come here. They got their own places to go, closer to home. Maybe that's where you were headed for."

"Why do you say that, Yostie?"

"Because that's what I think. You seem more like a fellow that wanted to be where there was a lot of spending."

"Well, that's no lie," said Ed Smith.

Yostie smiled. "Maybe you would of been disappointed, though."

"Why?"

"The miners are on strike. There isn't a ton of coal coming out of the coll'ries. I hear they got soup kitchens in some of the mining patches. That's because your spenders don't save up for the rainy day. My people, maybe they don't make as much as a miner, but they know how to save. You don't see my people coming here in a Hudson Super-Six. They take the trolley, or else the farm boys, they ride bicycles. Pretty soon now you'll see the farm boys, eight or ten at a time, riding their bicycles. Some of them'll ride a good ten miles to get here, and ten miles back. How would you like to ride a bicycle twenty miles?"

"I'd sooner the Hudson Super-Six. So the miners are on strike, eh?"

"Yep. You ought to read the papers more," said Yostie.

"I didn't see nothing in the papers about any strike."

"Well, maybe where you come from the strike isn't big news."

"To tell you the truth I don't read the papers much. To me it's a waste of time. In the big cities the papers are all full of stuff about Europe and Washington, D. C. And in the small towns it's all about the local people that I never heard of. About the only time I ever read a paper is when I take a dump, if there happens to be a paper there. I'd sooner spend two cents for a couple sticks of gum. I don't have a rotten tooth in my mouth. That's because I chew gum all the time. It keeps them healthy, exercising the gums."

"Well, I had all mine out some years ago, and I should of done it sooner and saved myself a lot of misery," said Yostie. "Now I tell you what we do now. I'm gonna put you in charge of the boats. You took notice every boat has a number painted on it, and we wrote down the time every boat was rented."

"Yeah."

"What you do, you keep track of how long a boat was out, and when their hour is up, you see that megaphone I got hanging on the pole. You take that megaphone and you call out the number of the boat and tell them their hour is up, and if they don't bring the boat in, we charge them the twenty-five cents for the second hour. Most of them keep their boats over an hour, but you have to let them know, because some of them only want to spend fifty cents, and they don't want to pay the extra quarter. If they're a few minutes over I don't make them pay the extra, but if they're ten minutes over they can't say they weren't warned. I got twenty boats, but it's very seldom they're all out at the same time. And make sure the oars get taken out of the boat and put back where they belong. If you do things orderly it makes it a lot easier. Paul Miller has it all down to a science, but he knows most of the people and he can usually tell without looking at the check-list when they took a boat out."

"Do you turn the boats upside down at night?"

"If it looks like rain. But all my boats are in A-one condition now. I painted them and caulked them myself this spring, before Paul and I put them in the water."

"You stayed here all winter?"

"Sure. I got plenty to do, fixing up, making my repairs. You don't think this place looks so nice by accident. Takes a lot of work to run a place like this."

"How old are you, Yostie?"

"How old am I? What do you want to know for? I'll be sixty-two my next birthday, if that's any your business. Why?"

"You ought to be getting ready to retire, instead of working all winter."

"Not me. If I didn't earn my daily bread I wouldn't know what to do with myself. Man lives by the sweat of his brow. I got a rupture I had to have operated three years ago, or I'd do it all myself. But since I was operated I need some help. Lifting, I have to be careful. All right, we done enough talking already."

"Where is your house? Where do you live?"

"Where do I live? This is my house, here. I got a room upstairs over the office. It suits me."

"How do you keep warm in the winter?"

"Coal oil heater. That's all I need. I got two of them for the real cold weather. I keep one here in the office, and one upstairs. That way I only have to keep one going at a time."

"And you live here by yourself all winter?"

"Yes."

"And don't see anybody?"

"Sure I see somebody. I got salesmen and people coming here near every day. Paul comes down Sundays. And my goodness, I go in town when I have to, once or twice a week."

"Oh, you have a car?"

"I have a car. A half-ton truck, a Ford."

"And you cook your own meals and all that?"

"Sure I cook my own meals. You didn't think I had a servant-girl or something?"

"You do your own washing?"

"No, that I don't do. I give my shirts and underwear and the bedsheets to a farmer woman down the road. Costs me a dollar a week, but I'm no good at ironing. And she darns my socks. That's fifty-two dollars a year for her, and that's a lot of cash for a farmer woman. That and her egg money. In ten years she can save up five hundred dollars, and with the egg money she'll probably have over a thousand. A farmer woman with a thousand dollars drawing three percent interest, she can hold her head up with any millionaire."

"They put it in the bank now, do they?"

"They sure do. Thirty dollars a year for nothing, and the money locked up in a vault? They sure do. That's one of the ways these country banks make their money. The farmer women that used to keep their money in a crock. Now the husband can't steal it off them any more. We got forty-five, fifty farmer women with savings accounts in our bank."

"You got a bank, Yostie?"

"I'm a director of one."

"I'll be a son of a bitch. A banker, and you don't even put a collar on your shirt."

"When I go to the bank I put a collar on. When I'm painting my boats I wear my overhalls. When I go to bed at night I put on my nightshirt. All right, that's enough talking for one day."

It was enough talking, and yet whenever he was alone with Ed Smith he talked some more. He would begin by explaining something that had to do with the work on the place, but before he finished he was telling the stranger things about himself that he did not usually talk about. There was an intensity in the way the stranger looked at you that forced things out of you. He seemed to be calling every man a liar, and Yostie found himself not only revealing but attempting to justify his actions and his beliefs. And even when he had spoken he was not satisfied that he had convinced Ed Smith of his honesty and sincerity. Ed Smith was so lacking in honesty and sincerity that Yostie knew it was useless to try to make him believe in worthy motives, but he was compelled to go on trying. It gave Yostie a dirty feeling of doubt as to his own honesty and sincerity. "That's all right," said Ed Smith. "You can worry about them kids all you like, Yostie. But you're not worrying about the kids as much as you're afraid one'll drownd and they won't come here no more."

"That's the way you look at it," said Yostie. "But I'd sooner close the place right now than have one little kid lose his life."

"Sure, sure. But how deep is your lake at the deepest?"

"In places, it goes down eighteen feet. It ain't a natural lake. It's a dam."

"I could see that," said Ed Smith. "Well, you built your dam so's to have a place for people to pay money to swim and go boating. But what do you have them life preservers for? Because where the water's that deep, people can get drownded. That's the chance you took, that somebody will fall in that can't swim, or they'll get cramps. You knew that when you built your dam. But you're hoping luck'll be on your side, and nobody'll get cramps or fall in that can't swim. If you're real lucky, nobody's gonna drownd before you get back the money you put in this place."

"What the devil did you come here for, anyway, just to pester me?"

"No. I bring you luck. If it wasn't for me coming here today, you would of worried all day because you didn't have no lifeguard. Now you got a lifeguard, me. So you can stop worr'ing. I don't only swim good. I can do artificial respiration. I'm the luckiest thing that happened to you today."

"A person would think you were the only man that could swim," said Yostie.

"There's nobody in that dam now that can swim half as good as me. You only got one real swimmer there now. The fellow named Jerry. But he don't have any wind. He's too fat to stay under. If you got a kid lying down there in eighteen foot of water, you need a man that can get down there and stay long enough to pull the kid out. Your friend Jerry couldn't do it. Maybe your friend Paul could, but he ain't here."

"Paul could do it all right. And some of the farmer boys."

"Maybe. But would they know what to do with a kid after they brung him up? How to get the water out of his lungs and start him breathing again?"

"Paul knows. Paul got a badge from the Boy Scouts."

"Well, I never got no badge from the Boy Scouts. But I saved a couple people. Not saying where, but I saved them. I could of put in for a medal. The old guy that owns the steel mill, that gives away medals."

"You mean Andrew Carnegie?"

"That sounds like the name. What was it again?"

"Carnegie. Andrew Carnegie."

"I'm pretty sure that's the name. Who's another guy that owns a steel mill?"

"Charles M. Schwab."

"No, it was the other one. Carnegie. He gives away these medals for lifesaving. But I would of had to tell my right name."

"And you didn't want to do that," said Yostie.

"You're damn right I didn't. You wouldn't either, if you was me."

"Why would a fellow like you want to risk your life to save somebody else?" said Yostie.

"Well, you don't think. I seen this guy fall in the water, and I took off my shoes and my coat and went in after him. He fought me, the dumb son of a bitch."

"He was trying to commit suicide?"

"No, Christ no. Just the opposite. What they call panic. Frightened. But I let him have one right over his left ear and I pulled him out. You know what? Some bastard run off with my shoes. Then they stard taking up a collection to give me, and they got about eight or nine bucks and just then I seen a cop coming towards us and I beat it the hell out of there. Soaking wet and no shoes, but I didn't want to talk to no cop."

"Where did you go?"

"No, if I told you where I went you could maybe figure out where it happened, then you'd know too much about me. Anyway, that was one guy I saved. The other was a woman. She didn't have any looks, but she ga' me a hundred bucks out of her purse, and I humped her a couple times. I went to the hotel where she was staying. This was after I kept her from drowning and she give me the C-note. I was broke again, and I figured she ought to be good for a few bucks more. She said, 'But I gave you a hundred dollars.' And I said if that was all it was worth, she didn't have to give me any more. So she went and got her purse and gave me another fifty, but that was gonna be all, she said. And I said all right, and let's have a drink on it. I took notice she had a brand-new quart on the bureau. She said she was saving that for a friend, for when she got home, and I said well what the hell did her friend ever do for her? So we went to work on the quart and I gave her a hump. The upshot of it was she stayed a couple days longer before she went home, and about a week later I come down with one of the worst doses of clap I ever got anywhere. She was a hooker, and there I thought she was just some married dame out for a good time."

"Are you over this thing?" said Yostie. "Don't you use my toilets if you got something."

"Hell, that was three-four years ago. I'm all right now."

"You sure you never had the other thing?"

"Big Casino?"

"No, the syphilis."

"That's what Big Casino is. No, I don't know why I didn't, but I didn't. So far. I'll probably get it sometime. You talking about all these farmers. I know a friend of mine that got it off a farmer's wife in Nebraska. You know, out West? You'd think a farmer's wife'd be pretty safe, but I guess the old man took a wagonload of cattle into town and went to a whorehouse, and come back home and give it to the frau. If you had to have a doctor's certificate from every broad, you'd never get laid. So what do you do? You take your chances. Clap I had three times. The syph, not so far. You never had a clap, did you, Yostie?"

"No, I did not," said Yostie.

"No, I didn't think you did. Where's your wife? Dead?"

"Passed on eight years ago."

"Do you have any kids?"

"I have two daughters, both married and living some distance away. I have five grandchildren."

"Yeah, I almost called you Grandpa. When I get your age I guess I won't miss it either, if I'm not dead before then. I never had any money in the bank, and ever since I was sixteen years old I been more or less traveling. I got no desire to stay put, and I never did from my own free will, but that ain't saying I didn't have to."

"You mean like prison?"

"I don't mean anything else but. I never wear a hat, because that's the only way to fool the cops. If you done time it takes a hell of a long while before you get rid of the jailbird look. Any cop can spot it, around the eyes. The mouth. The far-head. Even the hair. Most cons I know lose their hair. I think it's because they all get some scalp trouble from the dirty clippers that the prison barber uses. I don't know. That's just my idea. But if you get plenty of sunshine and fresh air, like at the shore or caddying at a golf course, it fools the cops. The first thing I always do when I get out of the can—well, first I want to get a good hump. But I go get a job caddying or at the shore, and inside of a week's time I got a good sunburn. Caddying. Do they have a golf club around here?"

"About five miles up the state road, past the next town."

"Is it public?"

"No, private. Only the rich people, near all from Gibbsville. That's the county seat."

"You don't belong, do you?"

"Goodness, no. I never was inside the place, only once. A banquet when they had a conwention. The county bankers' association. And that was at night, so I didn't get much of a look. The diningroom and the men's toilet was all I got a look at. They had a nice fireplace. I guess I never saw such a *big* fireplace. They had the wheels and axles off a mine car for the wood to set on. That I remember. And such a lot of silver cups on the mantelpiece. It was a good meal. Steak. But I only had my new teeth in a few weeks, I guess, so I couldn't chew so good. They had a good speaker, though. Very educated, and a good sense of humor for telling jokes."

"So you never played pasture pool?"

"What's that?"

"That's slang for golf. No, you wouldn't look right in them knickerbockers. The short pants they wear playing golf."

"I never played any games," said Yostie. "When I was a young fellow we used to rassle."

"Did you ever get in any fights?"

"Not real ones. I was raised on the farm. There was only me and my two sisters home. They used to fight one another, but not me. And I went to the township school, October to the end of April. I got as far as the sixth grade. But there wasn't so many boys to fight with my age."

"How did you make all your money?"

"All my money?"

"You made a bundle. You're the director of a bank."

"I have some. I guess I did pretty well for had to give up school in the sixth grade. Oh, when I was ten years of age I started in working in a store. My parents both passed on and I was supposed to be put in the orphan asylum, but Lucius P. Mueller offered to raise me and my uncle didn't have no objections, so I went there to live. Lucius P. Mueller and his wife. They were supposed to send me to school, but they didn't, and there was nobody checking up on whether they did or not. They had a little kind of a grocery store in the poor section of town. They sold vegetables and the regular staples like rice, dried fruit, tea and coffee, spices of one kind another. Sugar. Salt. Some hardware. Dry goods. My goodness, you went in that little store and there was barrels of molasses and pickles down cellar. Flour by the sack, or loose. Hardly room to turn around. Pails and buckets, market baskets, hanging from the ceiling. Stacks of brooms. It was a poor neighborhood and most of the business was done on tick. I had a cot in the attic where I slept. They used the attic to store things they didn't have room for downstairs. Cold in winter and hot in summer, but no worse than the farm. They didn't have no children of their own, the Muellers, and they were getting old and crippled with the rheumatism, so I got up every morning at five o'clock and went down in the kitchen and put the kettle on. Take the dust covers off of everything in the store. Open up. Then she'd come down and cook breakfast. A good breakfast. Oatmeal that stood overnight. Sometimes fried scrapple or mush, with molasses. She always gave me enough to eat, I'll say that for her. The smell of the coffee'd wake him up and he'd come down and have a big cup of coffee and smoke his pipe. Always a cup of coffee and sit there *inhaling* his pipe till he got ready to go out and sit in the privy, sometimes for a half an hour. Then he'd come back and eat something. You asked me if I do my own cooking? That's how long ago I learned to cook, when I was ten years old working for the Muellers. She liked to eat, but everything he ate disagreed with him. I guess I was around fourteen years of age before I realized what was wrong with him. He was taking a tonic, and *he* wasn't sick. He was *drunk* half the time."

"And doped up, most likely."

"Yes," said Yostie. "Alcohol and morphine. That and milk toast he lived on. I ate good because she ate good. Nothing wrong with her appetite. She waited on the trade, her and I. He took care of the money. Every night he put all the cash in a leather tobacco pouch with a drawstring on it and kept it under his pillow."

"How long did you stay with them?"

"Five years, till one night he died. I come down one morning and she was there ahead of me, drinking a cup of coffee. 'Go fetch the undertaker, Irwin,' she said. 'Mister passed away.' They had the funeral the next day and that night she wanted me to sleep in the bed with her. She said she never slept alone for thirty-five years and she was afraid. But I was more afraid than she was. I was fifteen and I guess she must of been somewheres in her late fifties, but she was still a woman. I didn't take to that."

"What did you do?"

"Well—I gave in."

"You humped her?"

Yostie nodded. "Mm-hmm."

"Was she your first? How did you like it?"

"She was my first. I wanted to run away, but I didn't have nowhere to run away to, or no money."

"Oh, then you stayed. Humping her every night?"

"I stayed a week, till I got a job. Callboy for the Pennsy."

"How did you get that job?"

"Heard about it in the store, and went and asked for it," said Yostie.

"As easy as that, eh?"

"Well, no. They usually give those jobs to railroad families, so when I went and applied they said I had to have references. The only person I could think of was my pastor. Reverend Jacoby, pastor of the Lutheran Church I attended. So I went to him and asked him would he give me a reference, and he wanted to know why I was quitting the store. I couldn't tell him outright, but he guessed. He didn't come out with it, either. But he said maybe it was time I got some other work. So he put on his hat and took me over to the roundhouse and asked to see the Road Foreman of Engines, C. L. Butz. Him and Butz had a few minutes' conversation and then Butz said all right I could start the next night."

"So you went to work for the railroad. But you didn't have no place to stay. Did the reverend find you a place to stay?"

"Yes, he did. I had to work at night, and he got me a room in a boarding house that the man worked in the daytime. Doubled up. That was a common practice among railroaders."

"Uh-huh. What were you getting paid?"

"Eight dollars a week, as I remember it."

"You never got rich that way."

"No," said Yostie. "But it had a lot to do with it. The reverend made me go back to school. By going to classes in the daytime I was able to finish the eighth grade. Then I took the two-year commercial course. Bookkeeping, shorthand, and typewriting."

"Who paid for all this?"

"The school district. The public school. The Pennsy didn't raise any objections. They encouraged me. And Reverend Butz was backing me up."

"Why? Was he sweet on you?"

Yostie froze. "Reverend was a good, kind man. I guess you wouldn't know a good man if you saw one," he said. "You don't have the right kind of eyesight, that's your trouble."

Yostie turned away from Ed Smith and unnecessarily rearranged the piles of towels—something to do with his hands, something to keep him busy. Then and there he made up his mind to fire the stranger at the end of the day, and, if necessary, to drive to Gibbsville that night and persuade someone to act as lifeguard the next day. He would pay any amount of money, ten dollars a day if he had to, but someone else was going to be working for him tomorrow. Anything to be shed of this evil man.

He did not speak to the stranger again until past the noon hour, and then it was Ed Smith who spoke to him. "Where do you eat your dinner?" said Ed Smith.

"At the lunch counter," said Yostie.

"Is that where I eat mine?"

"Suit yourself," said Yostie.

"Do I get it free, or do I have to pay for it?"

"You can tell Mildred it's free," said Yostie.

"Do I have to fill up on weenies?"

"Don't ask me what you eat. Maybe you like a ham sandwich, I don't know."

"What about supper?"

"She stays open till seven," said Yostie.

"The same bill of fare?"

"It's always the same bill of fare. You can have ham sandwiches, cheese sandwiches, wieners, if she don't run out. Pie, cake, and coffee. And the soft drinks."

"Is that how you live all summer?"

"No, I cook my own," said Yostie.

"Well, how about if I eat with you? I'm gonna get pretty tired of ham sandwiches."

"You want me to do your cooking for you?"

"Well, you were bragging about what a good cook you are. You know what I'd like is a couple pork chops."

"In the warm weather I never eat pork chops," said Yostie.

"Well, what will you cook yourself tonight?"

"I don't know for sure."

"I wouldn't mind if it was just some ham and eggs."

"Well, I ain't gonna cook it for you," said Yostie.

"Oh. That means never?"

"Never."

"But what do I do for supper? When I have a job I gotta have one square meal a day. I'd rather it was two, but at least one. Some kind of meat, and potatoes. Cooked warm. I been a short-order cook. I can hustle up a good meal myself, but I gotta have the raw materials. Do you have an icebox where you keep your meats and all?"

"Yes."

"And what have you got? A coal stove, and where is it? I didn't see any around. I only seen a little kerosene stove. Is that what you cook on? You can't cook much of a meal on that. As soon as you light the second burner the flame on the other goes down. I never knew it to fail. So you can't cook two things separate at the same time."

"I don't have any trouble," said Yostie.

The mind of Ed Smith was working, and Yostie waited for the results. He guessed that the stranger was considering the advantages and negative aspects of throwing up his job.

"I don't know," said Ed Smith.

"You don't know what?" said Yostie.

"I was thinking something."

"Giving your brain a little exercise?" said Yostie.

"Oh, don't you worry about that, Yostie. Maybe I don't look it, but my brain works overtime. Always look at all the angles. You pay me Sunday, right?"

"That's when I pay the regular help. Sunday."

"Let's see now. What'll I have coming then, this Sunday?"

"If you got a mind that works overtime, you ought to be able to calculate five dollars a day. This evening, at the end of the day's work, I'll owe you five dollars."

"Then that would be Wednesday, Thursday, Friday, Saturday, Sunday. Twenty-five bucks, I'd have coming."

"That's what it comes to," said Yostie.

"That's what it comes to. But you don't have the sound of a man that wants to keep me till Sunday. You didn't tell me where I was gonna sleep. And you practically told me I had to do my own cooking." He pulled out a pack of Piedmonts, lit one, and sent streams of smoke out of his mouth and nostrils without removing the cigarette from his lips. He put the pack back in his shirt pocket and shook the little box of safety matches in his right hand. "What did this Paul Miller do for his scoff?"

"His what?"

"His scoff. His meals."

"Noon hour he ate at the lunch counter. Supper, sometimes he went back to town, sometimes he took supper with me."

"That's what I figured," said Ed Smith. "A privileged character."

"No. A regular employee. He works for me all year round," said Yostie.

"And when his arm gets better, I get the air."

"Paul gets his job back, if that's what you mean," said Yostie.

"Yostie, you don't wanta come out and say it, but I bet you fire me at the end of the day. You use me to get you through today, but night comes and you hand me a five-spot and I'm through."

"That's about the size of it, yes," said Yostie.

"You don't deny it."

"No, I don't deny it," said Yostie. "I'll pay you for your day's work, but then I want you to go. This ain't the place for you."

The stranger catapulted his cigarette with thumb and middle finger in the direction of the water, which it did not reach.

"That could start a fire, your cigarette," said Yostie. He walked to the edge of the pier and crushed out the cigarette with the toe of his shoe. "I notice you got a pack of cigarettes. You didn't have any before."

"What of it?"

"You been to the lunch counter," said Yostie.

"Is that against the law, to buy a pack of butts?"

"No. But I guess you snuck down there when I wasn't looking," said Yostie. "That's what I mean, this ain't the place for you."

"I didn't know I was supposed to get permission to take a leak."

"You didn't go that far to take a leak," said Yostie. "And I told you what your job was. To keep an eye on the boats. You can't do that from down at the lunch counter."

"Yostie, you're just looking for some excuse to fire me. You don't need no excuse. You own the joint. But I know what's eating you. You didn't want me hanging around Mildred."

"I don't want you anywheres near Mildred," said Yostie.

"That's too damn bad." The stranger clenched and unclenched his fist and looked at his tattooed arm. "She got a laugh out of it. I told you they always do."

Yostie reached in his pocket and took out a roll of bills. He removed a rubber band, which he slipped over his fingers, wetted his thumb with his lower lip, and peeled off a five-dollar bill. "Here's for the whole day. Now you can go, and I don't want you hanging around no more. You can get the next trolley to Gibbsville." He put the rubber band around the money and restored the roll to his pants pocket.

Ed Smith took the money, folded and refolded it into a small square, and put it in the watch pocket of his pants. "You don't care if somebody gets drownded."

"There's plenty of good swimmers there now," said Yostie.

"I just happened to think. I gave you a buck and a quarter for a suit and a locker. Don't I get that back?"

Yostie unlocked the cash drawer and gave the stranger $1.25 in silver. "Now're you satisfied?"

"Let me think a minute. No, I guess I can't get any more out of you."

"I gave you more than you're entitled to already," said Yostie. "You only worked a half a day. So now go."

"All right. So long," said the stranger.

"Don't forget your valise," said Yostie.

"I damn near did. That would of been terrible, if I had to come back for it." The stranger was grinning. "You don't want me coming back here for something."

"If you know what's good for you, you won't come back," said Yostie.

For the first time, the stranger allowed himself to show some ugliness. He picked up his Gladstone and slung his jacket over his shoulder and glared at Yostie. "Yeah, and if *you* know what's good for *you,* you won't make threats," said Ed Smith. He cleared his throat of phlegm and spat it on the office floor. Then he left, and Yostie watched him until he reached the state road.

For the next hour or so Yostie's relief at getting rid of the stranger was mixed with his worries over the problems of handling the bathhouse customers and providing some protection for the boaters and swimmers. He could have postponed firing the stranger, he told himself. He had acted selfishly and left his people in some danger. But there were other dangers that a man like Ed Smith symbolized. Ed Smith could be just as dangerous to their welfare as eighteen foot of water, and not only to the customers; Mildred Kunkel was not very bright. She was twenty-six or seven, not a child. But in the two seasons she had been working for Yostie, during which he saw her every day between Decoration Day and Labor Day, none of the male customers had taken any interest in her and she had treated them all alike. Now, today, a total stranger had leered at her (without her being aware of it), and she had gone out of her way to go to the trouble of bringing him that pie and coffee. And the stranger had had at least one conversation with her that she as a decent young woman should not have tolerated. But she did not appear to have been insulted by it. The motions made by the nude tattoo were unmistakable, even to a virgin or to a man who had never watched a belly-dancer at a carnival, and if Ed Smith had accompanied the demonstration with suggestive words, Mildred must have been disturbed. Yostie was still disturbed when he thought of the tattoo, and his thoughts went from the tattoo to Mildred and back to the tattoo, and then to the stranger's leering wink. Indeed, the stranger's leering wink had been disturbing enough in itself, without the extra provocation of the nude figure so explicitly outlined on human flesh. The face meant nothing, but the figure could have been posed for by a woman of Mildred Kunkel's build. Yostie wondered if the stranger had said anything to Mildred about the resemblance. He had to know, he *had* to know what the stranger had said to Mildred.

Yostie's troublesome thoughts were interrupted by the appearance of young Kenneth Seiberling, sixteen or seventeen. "Hyuh, Mr. Yost," said Kenneth. "My pop said you had a job for me."

"Oh, did he? Well, I guess maybe I do," said Yostie. "You know how we keep track of the boats. Put down what time a boat was rented and all."

"Sure, I ought to know. Is that the job? Do I get three dollars for it? That's what Pop said."

"You have to stay here till all the boats are put away, and the oars and all. And you heard about Paul breaking his arm? So you have to watch out in case some person falls in."

"Lifeguard? I can swim as fast as Paul," said the boy.

"All right. You're hired. And maybe if you do good work I got a steady job for you till Paul comes back."

"Twenty-one dollars a week?" said the boy.

"That's what I'll pay, but that's from seven to seven, don't forget."

"Is it all right if Lamarr helps me?"

"If you want to pay him," said Yostie.

"He's only a kid. I'll give him fifty cents a day. That's all he gets a week from Pop."

"All right," said Yostie. "Start now by seeing how long the boats were out. I'm going down and get a little lunch."

One problem solved as another was created, Yostie thought on his way to the lunch counter.

Mildred had a thin streak of perspiration on her upper lip and the hair at her temples was matted down. She took off her steel-rimmed glasses and wiped them with her apron. "You come near forgetting your lunch," she said.

"I was kept busy," said Yostie. "How is the ice? Do you have enough?"

"We may need another fifty pounds," said Mildred.

"Well, I'll take the truck and get some," said Yostie.

"Send the new fellow, Ed."

"I fired him. I don't want him around," said Yostie.

"What did he do? Something bad?"

"I didn't trust him. What did you think of him?"

"Oh, I don't know," she said. "You wish I should make you a cheese sandwich? Put down mustard for the marketing. They all used up a lot of mustard on the wieners. That's good, though, because mustard makes a person thirsty. My goodness, they drank such a lot of Whistle. You have to order from the bottler already."

"Sit down now, Mildred. I fix my own lunch. You sit down a while."

"First I gotta go out back," said Mildred. "My back teeth is floating."

"Didn't you go all this time?" said Yostie. "That ain't good for the kidneys."

"I was too busy," said Mildred. She hung up her apron and went to the women's bathhouse. Yostie prepared a Swiss cheese sandwich, with plenty of mustard, and while he was filling his coffee cup he heard the flushing of the bathhouse toilet. He was rather proud of having flush toilets in the bathhouse. Other resorts of this size did not have them. He was pretty sure that Mildred Kunkel did not have a flush toilet at home in a poor section of Swedish Haven, and he was especially pleased that the one she used now was his.

"I couldn't of waited much longer," said Mildred. She smiled. "Here, let me cut the crust off." She took his sandwich away from him and sliced the crust with a bread knife. "That's better, ain't it?"

"Thanks," said Yostie.

"It's nice to have a minute's peace," said Mildred.

"Yep, there's nothing like it," said Yostie. He took a bite of the cheese sandwich and a gulp of the coffee.

"You didn't trust that fellow. I didn't either," said Mildred. "Well, I trusted him for a pack of Piedmonts."

"Didn't he pay you for them? He had money on him."

"Some, but not much," she said. "He said would I trust him till Sunday, and I thought being's he was working here."

"What else did he have to say?" said Yostie.

"Oh, I don't know. The kind of a fellow that talks a lot but they don't say anything. I didn't believe half of what he said. He said he was in Europe six or seven times, and China. Did you take notice he had such a dragon tattooed on his right arm? He got that over in China, so he said. But you don't have to go to China for that. My cousin got it done in Philly once. They take and pick it out with such an electric needle. A needle run by the electricity. A scap forms on the skin so you don't want to look at it, but the scap falls off and my cousin said they can never remove it, the tattoo. An eagle. He was in the United States Navy. Herman Ziegenfoos that his parents used to have the farm next to Peter Schlicter's out past the old flour mill."

"I know the Ziegenfooses," said Yostie. "Herman was tattooed yet? I wouldn't want that. A person could have the wrong thing tattooed on them and then they could never get rid of it."

"Herman had such an eagle, but I guess an eagle is better than a dragon."

"Yes. Better than a lot of things," said Yostie.

"Much better," said Mildred. "An eagle you don't have to be ashamed of it."

"No. The American eagle is very patriotic," said Yostie.

"Some sailors, they put a girl's name on their arm, in tattooing, and then they went out and married some other girl. That I wouldn't like, if I was married to some man and he had a tattooing with some other woman's name. How would my husband like it if I had some other man's name tattooed on me? Women get tattooed."

"I know. I seen one in the carnival once. Ugh. It hurt me to think about it. She was wearing such a costume, but every place you could see she was tattooed."

"You in a carnival, Mr. Yost," said Mildred. "That I can't picture."

"Oh, I don't know," said Yostie.

"Honest. If some person told me you went to a carnival I would call them a story-teller. A real carnival?"

"It had a tattooed lady. A snake charmer. A strong man. It was a regular carnival," said Yostie.

"I don't trust them kind of people," said Mildred.

"Well, I don't either."

"They're like them gypsies. You know them gypsies that used to come around in wagons? When I was little they used to come in their wagons like the wagons in the circus. They used to have a lot of horses with them, on halters, and my Poppa said the horses was all stole. Now they come in autos. They don't work. They just steal. My uncle, Herman Ziegenfoos's daddy, he used to stand down by the road with his shotgun. Them gypsies never camped on his farm you bet."

"No, you couldn't trust them. They used to run them out of town."

"No wonder," said Mildred. "They used to kidnap the children."

"So I heard," said Yostie.

"That's what I heard, too," said Mildred. "Was you ever to Europe, Mr. Yost?"

"Me? What would I want to go there for? The farthest I ever was was to Wilmington, Delaware. That's past Philadelphia."

"I seen it on the map, in geography."

"We took one of the men from our lodge there. That was where he was getting buried. Four from our lodge accompanied the remains. We got our carfare both ways, also dinner from the Wilmington lodge. We left Swedish Haven on the morning train and changed at Philadelphia. Stayed right with the coffin to make sure it got on the Wilmington train. Then at Wilmington there was a delegation from the lodge to meet us. They took us to the hotel and I guess there was about eighteen or twenty of us sat at the same table there. No beer or whiskey or anything like that, but plenty to eat. Then from there we went to the church and we had the regular lodge ritual, and burial was in the churchyard right outside. After that we drove back in time to catch the train to Philadelphia. We had to change trains again there, but we caught the flyer home. That was George Hoffman. Knew him twenty-five or thirty years, but I never knew he was born in Wilmington, Delaware. Came here with his parents when he was two years of age, but I always thought they were local people too. George Hoffman. Before your time, Mildred."

"Yes, I didn't hear of any George," she said.

"It's an interesting city, Wilmington. Much hillier than I pictured it."

"Oh, I wouldn't picture it hilly, either."

"Very hilly. Not as hilly as Gibbsville, but hilly."

"Gibbsville is too hilly for me," she said. "I wouldn't care to live in a place that hilly."

"Well, then you wouldn't care for Wilmington, either."

"I don't care for any place except around here. Reading is hilly, too. I was to Reading twice already. No, I don't care for hilly towns or big towns. I couldn't get used to so many strangers."

"No, me either," said Yostie.

Two boys came to the lunch counter and each put a nickel on the oilcloth cover and each covered his nickel with his hand. Yostie watched and listened to Mildred's behavior toward them. "What can I do you for?" she said.

"Can I have a Whistle?" said one boy.

"Sure," said Mildred. "You want a straw with it?"

"Can I have two straws?" said the boy.

"It won't last as long," said Mildred.

"I don't care," said the boy.

She removed the cap from a bottle of Whistle and stuck in two straws. "There you are, Billy. You, Normie. You want a Whistle too?"

"No, I want a Coke," said the boy called Normie.

"You want two straws?" said Mildred.

"No, I'll drink it out of the bottle," said Normie.

"Oh, my. Such a big drinker," said Mildred. She decapped the bottle and the boy took a couple of swigs.

"Now will you fill it up with water?" said Normie.

"You want water in your Coke yet?" said Mildred. "You make it weak."

"Yeah, but not as weak as Whistle," said Normie.

"Well, my goodness. You learn something every day," said Mildred. She dried their damp nickels on her apron and dropped them in the cash drawer. She made more conversation with them as they drank, and Yostie was pleased with her. He was more than pleased with her. He valued her, her willingness to work, her friendliness, her contentment. She was only twenty-seven, and he was past sixty, but it came over him now that before summer was out he would ask her to marry him and he was sure she would accept. She had too much sense to say no to an offer like that; she would never have a thing to worry about the rest of her life—long after he was gone.

A young couple wanting soft drinks interrupted her conversation with the boys, and she greeted the newcomers by name. Yostie looked down at his left hand and found that he was opening and closing his fist. The moment he realized what he was doing he stopped and looked at Mildred, but she was too busy to have noticed.

"I go get the ice, Mildred," he said.

"All right," she said. "They're getting thirsty again."

The General

Their house, be it noted, was in the old part of town, in a section that had ceased to be fashionable but that at one time had been not just one but the *only* neighborhood for the very rich to live in. It was two blocks long, this section, on both sides of the street. There was no uniformity to the design of the houses, and yet they all looked the same because they were all built of brick or brownstone and presented a solid, substantial front of planned severity. The houses of plaster-covered brick were even more forbidding than the houses built of cut stone. Stone, being stone, retained the marks of its ancient porosity and therefore had that much more life than the bland, grey-brown artificiality of the plaster. Not until the rich began to desert the neighborhood and the plaster cracks were neglected did any of the houses begin to look human. Thereafter the houses and the people in them commenced to look very human indeed. The residential character of the neighborhood changed completely between 1915 and 1920. Nearly every house was drastically altered to accommodate commerce. There was a beauty parlor, a tire shop, a bakery, a grocery store, a motorcycle-bicycle agency, two automobile showrooms, an army and navy surplus outfit, a paperhanger-painter's establishment, a shoe repair and hat cleaning establishment, an electrical supply store with a crazy assortment of lighting fixtures hanging like stalactites from the ceiling. The upstairs rooms were used for storage, for the offices of painless dentists, and for apartments. By the time Mr. Coolidge was inaugurated President, the only house in the neighborhood that was strictly a private residence was Number 444, the home of General Dixon L. Hightower and his wife. It surprised no one that they went on living there. It would have amazed their friends if the Hightowers had moved.

The feeling that the Hightowers *belonged* in 444 was not so much due to the fact that Sophronia Hightower had been born in that house as to the widely held belief, among the young and uninformed, that it was General Hightower's lifetime residence. Actually the Stokes family had built 444 and Dick Hightower did not occupy it until his marriage to Sophie Stokes. Thereafter, however, he never left it for any considerable length of time except for his army service during the Spanish-American War, and the annual encampments of the National Guard at Mount Gretna. The coal millionaires of the neighborhood guarded their privacy and the comparative anonymity of their houses, but 444 was the home of the town's only general and in many ways he gave it its character. A workingman who lived to the south of Number 444 would often explain that he came from "down past General Hightower's," and people would know what section of town he lived in. There was not much town left beyond General Hightower's house. Tourists passing through the town without leaving Main Street would get the impression that there was only one really nice house in the community. Unquestionably, in the post-war years Number 444 and the Hightowers belonged together to a degree that house and owner too rarely achieve. Dick Hightower, the general, had added a few touches of his own to the original boxlike structure: two bay windows that could be mistaken for turrets, a crenelated cornice, a stone heraldic eagle clutching arrows over the front door. It was a corner property and the Hightowers had a side yard as well as a back yard, which were protected from trespassers by an iron fence consisting of simulated spears. In the geometric center of the side yard was, of course, a flagstaff topped by a screaming gilt eagle. Every five years or so someone would reinvent the name Fort Hightower for the place, but it never caught on. The joke was always short-lived because in the milder seasons Sophie Hightower was to be seen in the yard, tending her rose bushes and peonies and entertaining her friends in the summer house in the back yard.

Dixon Hightower was a military man, fully qualified by Regular Army experience until he resigned his commission to marry Sophronia Stokes, and entitled to his brigadier's star by virtue of his subsequent promotions in the National Guard of Pennsylvania. At West Point he had remained in the bottom half of his class and therefore upon graduation was assigned to the infantry instead of to the cavalry. Nevertheless he had been under fire in the Indian Territory and had spent ten years at army posts. He knew the difference between a button-stick and a Gatling gun, although the young and uninformed were inclined to be skeptical of their elders' somewhat vague assurances that the general had once been a warrior. He had five or six medals that he wore to military funerals of former officers of the Guard. The younger crowd, those who were reaching maturity after the 1918 Armistice, had stopped calling him a toy soldier, but they did not seriously believe that he could ever have been in battle. In his blues, wearing his medals and his sword, he would go to funerals and review the local militia, but when the troops went off to the Mexican border in 1916, he marched with them only as far as the railroad station, remounted his horse and rode back to Fort Hightower. It was the same in 1917, when the Guard and the conscripts went away to war, with the difference that now he no longer wore a uniform or rode a horse. He marched with the leaders of the community who were members of the Patriotic League, and instead of a sword he carried a malacca stick. He was past the age when he could be useful except as a member of the draft board, and he was not even in command of that.

"If I'd stayed in the army," he said to Sophie, "I'd have my own division."

"Well, are you sorry you didn't stay in?" she said.

"Oh, please don't misunderstand me," he said, *"You* know I've never regretted that decision. You *must* know, Sophie. Don't you?"

"Well, that's what I've always thought," she said.

"What I meant, all I meant was that there are men my age, or just a few classes behind me, that are divisional commanders today. Joe Westman has a division. Ted Maguire is a major general on Pershing's staff. And other fellows I used to know have two stars and two of them have three stars. Lieutenant generals, they are. Peyton March, and Jack Pershing, not much younger than I, with four stars. My goodness, but the time flies. But I suppose I'm well out of it. I was never very good at army politics, and now I hear that there's no love lost between March and Pershing, and Leonard Wood and Pershing have had a tussle."

"You told me before we were married that you weren't very tactful."

"Well, you've found that out for yourself," he said.

"Yes, I have. But I was thinking of army politics. I wonder how I'd have been as an army wife."

"You'd have managed, for a while," he said. "But if I know you, my girl, some captain's wife would go just a little too far and you'd give her a piece of your mind. As my old friend Sam Bannister used to say, an army officer wears the insignia of his rank but an army wife doesn't have to."

"No, I don't think I'd have made a very good army wife," said Sophie.

"Mind you, you'd have gotten through it if you'd *had* to. I am not saying *that,* Sophie. But I never could have asked you to put up with the discomforts and inconveniences. Not to mention the snubs and the discipline. That kind of a life would have broken your spirit."

"Oh, do you think so?"

"Might have. It very nearly did mine, and I was used to it. It's a very contradictory thing, army life. I remember having a long talk with a British officer I got to know in Washington. He was a career man, then about forty, and a major. I was a good deal younger, but we hit it off well together, and used to see a lot of each other. Charles Willing-Lloyd, hyphenated. Haven't thought of him in years. Welsh, I suppose he was, with the name Lloyd."

"You had a long talk with him?"

"Many. But one I remember particularly. I'd just come up from Brownsville and he and I were comparing notes. The rigors of army life and so on. He'd been in Africa and India and all over, and he was a very interesting conversationalist. There was a small group of us that used to meet for dinner once a month. Army and navy officers, attachés, and we'd play cards for not very high stakes, or some of us would just sit and chat. One evening Charles and I were comparing notes, and he made to me what was a very profound observation. He'd been in action, mentioned in dispatches and so on, but he insisted that it takes a different sort of man to be a good career officer. A war, he said, doesn't demand as much of a man as the day-to-day army routine. When the bugles sound, and the shooting begins, the amateurs rush in. Ready to die, ready to shed their blood, it's true. But they're amateurs. And they will die and they will shed their blood needlessly if we haven't done our jobs between wars. That fact is never understood by the civilian mind. All they see of us in peacetime is parades, gold braid, unloaded weaponry. Military funerals, military balls, the governor's inauguration. And a few weeks of camp in the summer in neat rows of tents with canvas flies over them and flooring underneath. But we've been living under discipline and our men have been too. So that when the amateurs get into it, the professionals can show them that orders are there to be obeyed."

"You wrote me all this in a letter one time," said Sophie.

"Did I? Well, that doesn't surprise me," he said. "I was very full of it at the time, when I was hesitating about whether to resign my commission."

"Your friend nearly persuaded you to jilt me," said Sophie.

"Oh, Sophie, he did no such thing!"

"I know he didn't, Dickie. I'm only joking."

"But you mustn't joke about such things," he said. "There've only been two things in my life I've ever cared deeply for. Our marriage, and the army. And I'd never joke about our marriage. I wish I could feel as deeply about religion, especially now that we're both getting on in years."

"You've always been a good Christian, dear. I don't think the good Lord above will punish you for your doubts. We all have them."

"Not you," he said. "Every year in June, when you take such pride in your roses, all your doubts disappear. You always say the same thing. There has to be a God to create such beauty."

"I haven't said that in years," she said.

"Maybe not in so many words, but it's what you feel."

"There are many times when you haven't the slightest notion what I feel."

"So you say. But that's what you'd like me to think. You're a woman and you like to be mysterious. Perfectly all right, of course. No harm done, as long as it doesn't get out of hand. It's like my saying that I could have my own division. Yes, I'd have my own division, *if.* And you'd be very mysterious, *if.*"

"If what?"

"If I'd stayed in the army," he said.

"No, I meant, I'd be very mysterious if what?" said Sophie.

"Well, if you'd been an altogether different kind of a person. And if you'd been an altogether different kind of person I assure you I'd never have resigned my commission to marry you. What's more, if I'd been the kind of man who refused to resign his commission, you never would have married *me.* If, if, if. My goodness, but we waste our time with our ifs. Haven't we got something better to do than that?"

"Well, I have, thank heavens," she said. She rose, put on her wide-brimmed Panama, and picked up her gardening pouch. The Panama had once been his, the pouch was an old musette bag.

"Mysterious? You and I mysterious?" he said.

"I didn't say *you* were," she said.

He smiled and went to his desk, where there were always a great many letters to be answered. She had her flowers, he had his correspondence.

Four times during the winter months they asked friends in for dinner. Once there had been little jokes about the neighborhood to tease the dinner guests who had moved to the west end of town. "Welcome back to The Bowery," Dixon Hightower would say, but the jokes wore a bit thin. Their elderly friend Mrs. McMasters, who had never liked jokes of any kind, put a stop to them. "Since you bring up the subject, Dick Hightower," said Mrs. McMasters. "I don't see why you stay down here. It may be all right for you, but it's no place for Sophie."

"Why not? She's in her old homestead."

"I was in my old homestead, too, but I had sense enough to get out. The smoke from the locomotives—*you* don't know what it is to keep things clean, let alone breathe decent air."

"Get rid of your Reading Company stock," said Hightower.

"I will not get rid of my Reading Company stock. I didn't say the smoke wasn't necessary, but I had sense enough to get out of the thick of it. I own stock in the steel mill, too, but I don't have to listen to the noise. This is no place for Sophie to live. It isn't safe to walk the streets at night."

"Then I'll see that she doesn't. She never has, but I promise not to let her start any bad habits."

"Bad habits?" said Mrs. McMasters.

"Such as walking the streets at night," said Hightower.

"Dixon Hightower, sometimes you go too far with your attempts to be humorous. I prefer to talk about something else, if you don't mind."

The mortality rate among their friends reduced the Hightowers' social obligations. The death of Elsie McMasters not only struck her from their list but made it inconvenient for George and Laura Cromer, who had been dependent on Elsie and her gigantic Locomobile limousine, to get to Number 444. The Cromers had to watch every penny, and taxicabs were out of the question. The Hood McGowens could afford taxis, but when Minnie McGowen discovered a naughty word scratched in the varnish of their Pierce-Arrow outside the Hightowers' house, she resolved that they had paid their final visit to the neighborhood. She did not blame Tom Duffy, the McGowen chauffeur, who was keeping warm in the Hightower kitchen. She was somewhat inclined to blame Dick Hightower for his stubbornness in remaining in that section of town. Daniel Wynkoop, their bachelor friend, showed up on the wrong night, twenty-four hours early, and took pot-luck with Dick and Sophie. Unfortunately he finished off most of a bottle of pre-Prohibition rye before going home, and was beaten and robbed of $25 and a gold watch less than a block away from the Hightowers'. He was unable to give the police an accurate description of his assailants. The Hightowers' surviving friends went on inviting them to their houses, but the balance of social exchange was too one-sided. More and more people were finding excuses not to accept invitations to 444, and even in the dinner season there would be periods two months long in which Dick and Sophie dined alone. Those evenings were not unpleasant for him; he had more time for his correspondence, and the World War had produced a whole new library of military histories, battle reports, and even a crop of novels that viewed war with a jaundiced eye. Dick Hightower disliked the novels and some of the histories, but it amused him to find so many authors who were discovering for the first time an obvious truth that Sherman had stated profanely nearly seventy years before them. His correspondence—at least his part of it— expanded as a result of his reading of the new books. He was in fact quite busy.

Sophie, however, was not much of a reader. She read the local paper in the evening and the Philadelphia *Public Ledger* in the morning; the *Delineator, The Ladies' Home Journal* and *Life*. If a friend strongly recommended a novel by Booth Tarkington, Edna Ferber, or John Galsworthy she would read it, and get all through it no matter how long it took. She had a Philadelphia friend who was related to Joseph Hergesheimer, and that was Sophie's nearest connection with a living author. In their evenings at home after dinner she sometimes envied Dick and his absorption in his books and letters. He would laugh aloud at something he had written and triumphantly read it to her. He would exclaim, "Bully!" when he came upon a telling passage in a book, but he would often have to read back over ten or twenty pages of a military campaign to explain why a single line had met with his enthusiastic approval. It was seldom worth it; Ludendorff's right flank was too hard to follow. "I know it doesn't mean the way it sounds to me," she said. "But when any general exposes his right flank, you can imagine what I think."

"Not Ludendorff, though. *He* was never caught with *his* pants down."

"Then why don't they find some other way of saying it?" she said.

After dinner they would have coffee and a thimbleful of a liqueur from their dwindling stock. He was perfectly willing to let her have his share of such things as Benedictine, but the tiny drink was more ceremonial than gustatorial and they agreed that it was the ritual and not the drink that they would miss when their supply was gone. Already they had begun to substitute applejack for their good gin and whiskey in cocktails when guests were not present. Applejack, they had discovered, made an acceptable "whiskey sour," if you limited yourself to two. They had not yet found it necessary to patronize a town bootlegger. When that time came, Dick was going to have to wrestle with his conscience. "Everybody breaks the law, and it's a law that I'm opposed to," he said. "However, I'm not going to feel right about it. I don't like the thought of having some bootlegger say he has General Hightower for a customer. Then there'd be the question of delivering it here. I wouldn't like that at all, and I'm most certainly not going to their place and bring it home with me. I don't keep any at the club, so when someone offers me a cocktail, I just say no, because I can't return the favor. If I knew everybody at the club it might be a different matter, but they have a lot of lawyers from out of town come there for lunch. As long as people call me General I don't think I ought to flout the law of the land. Do you, Sophie? Am I being inconsistent, or hypocritical?"

"Not you, Dick. The law is hypocritical."

"No, I wouldn't say that. It was a constitutional amendment, had to be approved by two thirds of the states, and the law itself isn't hypocritical. Very well meaning. But it doesn't work. The people have tried it, and they don't want it, and those that do want it should step out of the way. Take defeat gracefully. I'll vote in favor of repeal of the law and I know I will. Therefore I think I'm being consistent. But I'd hate to think I was being hypocritical about it, drinking at home and not at the club."

"Where do we get our applejack?" she said.

"You think I'm being inconsistent because I won't deal with the bootleggers?"

"Well, I just thought of it."

"Schertzinger, the farmer, delivers it. He leaves it in the stable, in one of the old box stalls. I leave the cash in an envelope, behind that picture of Dan Patch. A gallon every two weeks."

"Do we drink that much?"

"Just about. Four ounces apiece, every day. That's twenty-eight ounces a week. In four weeks we dispose of 112 ounces, or seven quarts. There are four quarts in a gallon. We never run out of it, because we keep that much ahead of our supply. But I don't consider Adam Schertzinger in the same category with those bootleggers. We've always bought our sweet cider from him and his father, since time immemorial. Nearly all our vegetables. Your mother dealt with the Schertzinger family when you were a little girl."

"Yes, they came to market every Friday."

"I know. Didn't I help them get one of their sons into West Point? Or at least I tried. If he could have overcome that Pennsylvania Dutch accent they'd have taken him."

"He turned out all right," said Sophie.

"Actually much better than if he'd tried to be an army officer. The accent is no handicap to a country doctor, but it would have been at The Point. They're used to southern accents, but they'd have laughed at young Schertzinger. Just imagine how they'd ridicule him.

It rains a lot at West Point, and they wouldn't know what he was talking about when he said, 'It makes down uckly.' "

"And 'The pie is all.' "

"Hmm. He wouldn't have much occasion to say that. We saw damn little pie when I was there. Mince pie at Christmas, my plebe year."

Their conversations had a way of drifting toward army life no matter how they started, but it could hardly have been otherwise with Dick Hightower. Other husbands, Sophie had found, did the same thing in conversation with their wives. Doctors digressed to medicine, lawyers to law, bankers to finance. Unlike other husbands, Dick Hightower was a chatterbox, and though his topics might be sandwiched between one army reminiscence and another, he did hold forth on other things. In fact—and she said this about once a year—if other people could know Dick Hightower as she knew him, they would realize that he was one of the most fascinating men you could ever hope to meet. In his youth he had traveled a great deal throughout the United States and territories, he had acquired a knowledge of history and could read French and German without much difficulty, he read the New York and Philadelphia papers at the club every day, he subscribed to magazines like *The Literary Digest,* the *Review of Reviews,* the *Army & Navy Journal,* the *National Geographic,* and *Foreign Affairs.* She did not see where he got the time to read them all, but he could quote from them and did so. Once a year, on Memorial Day, he would give the principal address at the ceremonies at the Soldiers & Sailors Monument, and he would begin the preparation of this speech right after the Christmas holidays. It was such a thorough, painstaking piece of work that both newspapers printed the speech *in toto,* from the copies given them in advance. This was in the nature of a precaution against being misquoted and for the purpose of providing the full text to history students in the public and Catholic high schools. The General Dixon L. Hightower Prize of ten dollars cash and a certificate suitable for framing was awarded annually to the student in each high school who had the best marks in American history. Dick's attendance at the commencement exercises was only one source of the kind of pleasurable experience that animated his conversations with Sophie. ("A little Italian girl won the prize at the Catholic school. Her father and mother can barely speak English.")

But his interests were not all on the intellectual side. He would return from a walk to the post office with ever so many things to tell her, little things that he had noticed that would escape the attention of a less observant man. Every morning, Monday through Friday, he would leave the house at ten o'clock, beautifully dressed in fine weather, with one of his walking sticks and bowler, Homburg, or Panama; grey spats and never the same suit two days running. On cold days he had his fur-lined black broadcloth or his long tweed ulster, and on rainy days inevitably his trench coat. He was so punctual that the motormen on the trolley lines had their own little custom of saluting him with taps on the floor bell, which he would acknowledge with a semi-military wave of the hand. As there were ten-o'clock trolleys for several out-of-town points the general's progress northward to the center of town was, as he said, tintinnabulated. ("You knew that Edgar Allan Poe went to West Point, briefly.")

His first stop was Joseph Ostertag's cigar store. Joseph Ostertag dealt only in cigars, pipes, pipe tobacco, and snuff. He had never sold a cigarette or a box of candy, and he stocked only Piper Heidsieck chewing tobacco for a few special customers (two county judges and a few Catholic priests). Back of his store, invisible from it, was his small cigar factory, in which three men and an apprentice were kept busy hand-rolling the two grades of Ostertag cigars: the twenty-five-cent straight Perfecto, and the two-for-a-quarter Special. Joseph was a dour man who owned the building in which he sold and made his cigars, the adjoining building, which contained a shoe store and three stories of offices, and a large storage warehouse in the North End of town. There were men in a position to know who said they would like to have what Joe Ostertag had *over* a million dollars. Nevertheless he was his own store clerk and did his own sweeping and cleaning. In his store he had a single bentwood chair, not for sociability but because one of his steady customers had once had a heart attack and was compelled to lie on the floor. No one—wife, friend, or customer—was permitted to call him Joe.

Dick Hightower had been a regular customer of Joseph Ostertag's for twenty years, but their opening exchange had not changed.

"Good morning, Joseph."

"Good morning to you, sir."

"Two Perfectos, please."

Ostertag would raise the lid of the box and allow Dick Hightower to choose, although the cigars were individually foil-wrapped.

"Will you put that on my account, please?"

Ostertag would write in a ledger. "Two . . . Per . . . fec . . . toes . . . D . . . L . . . High . . . tower . . . 4 . . . 4 . . . 4 . . . South . . . Main." It was not necessary to record the price; it had not changed either. As for the quality of the leaf, it had if anything got better, but that was a matter not to be discussed wih

Ostertag. That was *his* business. In recent years, however, Ostertag and Hightower, having completed their transaction, permitted themselves some additional conversation. It usually concerned the stock market, which, since it was not the cigar business, was not a closed topic. Ostertag, surprisingly enough, traded on margins. But he made up for this uncharacteristically risky practice by getting out of a stock the moment it showed a three-point rise. Weeks would go by in which he did not trade at all, then one of the five stocks in which he specialized would be offered at an attractive price and he would again buy for the three-point profit.

Hightower, using Ostertag's information, would stay in for a five-point rise, but he never bought on margin, and his profits were smaller. He was content with small profits. His speculation was satisfactory if it made him pocket money, two to three thousand dollars a year. Sophie's fortune was administered by a Philadelphia trust company and he never interfered. She gave him $6,000 a year, paid all the household bills and reinvested the surplus income of her trust funds. The surplus had accumulated to more than $100,000, which would be his in the event of her death. The trust funds were not hers to dispose of, but he would never require more than the income from $100,000. And as she pointed out, the $100,000 rightfully belonged to him, inasmuch as she would have given him $7500 a year or $10,000 a year if he had wanted it. But he did not want it. He wanted no more than he had, no difference in the scale of their living, no change in his way of life that would take the fun out of careful spending. He did not wish to wear ready-made clothes, but he made his tailor-made suits and handmade shoes last, so that the arrival of a new suit or a pair of Oxfords was an event, not merely a purchase. "The small pleasures," he would say. The motormen's salute. The conversations with Joseph Ostertag. The reasonable profits in the stock market. The twenty-five-cent-straight cigars.

From Ostertag's he would go to the railroad station newsstand and pay a nickel for his New York paper, if the New York papers had made the train connections. If not, he would buy a Philadelphia *North American* because there was nothing else he cared to buy, and he had to buy something. He would exchange greetings with the station agent, the baggagemaster, and the telegraph operator, and return to Main Street. The traffic policeman operating the semaphore would salute him, and he would raise his hand in a return salute that was a trifle more military than the gesture he accorded the trolley motormen. The policeman, after all, bore arms, and Dick Hightower happened to know he was a former member of the National Guard.

For the next hour or so he would occupy a chair in the board room of the local branch of Westmore & Company, stock brokers. He would leave his overcoat on a hanger but keep his hat on or in his lap. All the customers kept their hats on unless they were seated next to one of the women customers. (Their patronage was invited, but they did detract from the once all-male atmosphere.) Dick Hightower's hour in the Westmore board room was a high point of his day. He would trim the first of his two Ostertag Perfectoes with his gold cutter, and take his place in the front row of chairs. All the customers knew each other, and they felt free to make running comments as the board boys chalked up the quotations coming in on the stock ticker. The regular customers, the daily visitors, were not only acquainted with each other but they also knew which men were trading in which securities. It was a motley crowd of retired business men, merchants, bootleggers, insurance salesmen, lawyers, two old maids and a madam. It was not considered good form for a bank employee to be seen in the board room, a restriction that did not apply to bank directors. Notwithstanding the presence of the women, the board room atmosphere was that of a sporting event, an uninterrupted race meeting five hours long. The chairs were comfortable, the temperature was kept under control, there were plenty of ash trays, and there was a customers' toilet with two urinals. Dick Hightower was a light trader, whose commissions covered only his share of the firm's overhead, but he added tone to the place and Westmore & Company knew it and he knew it. No other firm in town could claim the simultaneous patronage of the general and the madam, and his manner of saying "Good morning," to her, without ever uttering her name, was precisely correct and an example which the other men followed. One word from him and the firm would have discouraged the madam's visits; but he did not speak that word, and the firm was tacitly grateful for his tolerance.

"You see that woman every day?" Sophie once said.

"Every single day," said Dick Hightower.

"What do you say to her?" said Sophie.

"I say good morning."

"You speak to her? How did you ever get to know her?"

"We were never formally introduced."

"Who does she sit with?"

"Oh, she knows some of the men."

"Do the other women speak to her?"

"Do the other women speak to her? No, I don't believe they do. They never sit with her, I know that."

"She just talks to the men?"

"Well, she's rather used to that," he said.

"What if you had to sit next to her? What would you say to her?"

"It's very doubtful that I'd ever find myself in that predicament. After all, I know how to maneuver myself."

"What if she maneuvered herself next to you?"

"That will never happen. If you didn't know who she was, you'd never take her for a prostitute. She's quite ugly. She wears a sealskin coat, but no jewelry except a wedding ring."

"A wedding ring?"

"Most of them do," he said.

"*Most* of them?"

"When I was a young officer we were often entertained by them. Every good-sized town has at least one madam that young officers know about."

"You never told me that. Did you patronize them?"

"I did."

"Oh, Dick, you didn't."

"Sorry to disillusion you, but I did."

"I suppose I knew that, really."

"You could have found out any time you asked me. Remember, I was past thirty when I met you."

"So was I."

He smiled. "I'd never have known if you hadn't told me."

"That was about all I had to tell," she said. "Think of the difference between that woman and me. I mean in what she knows about life."

"Life? Whatever she knows about life, it hasn't done her much good. If you could see her you'd understand that. It's all written in her face. Women of your sort tend to think of them as tarnished beauties. They're tarnished, all right, but very few of them were ever beauties. You know the expression, as ugly as sin."

"Then why would a nice young man want to have anything to do with them?"

"Because nice young women have to stay nice or they aren't nice any more, if I make myself clear."

"Perfectly," she said.

Unless there were unusually active trading in the market, Dick left Westmore & Company before noon, to be a little ahead of the midday rush at the post office. He had a large mailbox to receive his books and periodicals. He would open it with his key and take out what he wanted and leave the rest for a dull day. He did not wish to be overburdened on his walk to the club, in the course of which he often had to stop and chat with ladies; and while he could manage his cane and a book or two and the removal of his hat, as an officer he had been trained not to carry small parcels while in uniform. Early habits were hard to break. Later habits were easily formed. At the club he would go to the cloakroom and put away his things, wash his hands as in a ceremonial ablution that symbolized his withdrawal from the contacts of commerce and common folk, and his return to the world of the gentleman. Not all the members of the club met his standards, but every gentleman in town was a member of the club. He would rub his soap-softened hands and enter the billiard room, where even at half past eleven in the morning at least one game would be in progress. "I'm up," he would say, and write his initials on a blackboard to signify his intention of challenging the first winner. A wooden plaque, listing the club billiards champions of other years, had D. L. Hightower as champion for 1911 and 1912 and runner-up in 1913, 1914, and 1917. He would never reign again; the younger men were too good for him; but no member could beat him every time they played. He could still run out a string of twenty-one points. He was a slow player, which gave him a psychological advantage over the younger men, and he would play more slowly than usual against those who showed impatience. This strategy delighted his contemporaries, the members of the Old Guard who occupied the same luncheon table every day. "Dick, you old fox, you had young Choate half out of his mind," they would say.

"Don't call me an old fox. Call me an old tortoise," he would say. "The race is not always to the swift." He managed to win enough money to cover his house charges. The seventy-five-cent table d'hôte came to six dollars a week, and he had usually won that amount by the Wednesday. In weeks that he had fallen behind he could count on making a comeback on the Saturday, when he could play all afternoon until he made six dollars. The players were more apt to imbibe on Saturdays.

As a rule there was a lull in the billiard room after lunch on weekdays, but there was likely to be some activity in the card room. Dick Hightower tried to stay out of the post-luncheon auction bridge. He had found that his contemporaries got sleepy after the meal, especially on Monday, Wednesday, and Friday when the club specialty, deep-dish apple pie, was on the menu. The stakes were never high, but it was no fun to see one's partner's eyelids begin to droop, to hear the heavy, regular breathing that portended a nap at the table. "Whitfield is in the land of Nod," someone would say. "Shall we leave him there?"

"What? What? Is it my lead?" the sleepy one would say.

"Not quite. Your partner just said two no trump, and I passed."

"Two no trump? Let's see now, can we review the bidding?"

"All right. I opened with a heart, you said a spade, my partner raised my hearts to two, and Dick said two no trump. I passed."

"And you were the original heart bidder, eh? Oh, yes, now it's coming back to me. I'll have to say three spades."

"And you do say three spades?"

"Yes. Three spades. I *said*, three *spades*. Oh, wait just a second. Two no trump would have given us game. However, I said three spades and three spades it is. Yes, three spades."

Yet even on days when the deep-dish apple pie was not having a toxic effect Dick Hightower would have preferred to be elsewhere. The club notepaper, of stiff stock and nicely embossed, was just right for certain items of his correspondence. At the writing desks, moreover, were sticks of sealing-wax and birthday-cake candles, and envelopes bearing the imprint of Dick's signet ring went out almost daily to sick friends, the lately bereaved, classmates who had achieved honors or grandparenthood, recent hostesses, and the beneficiaries of his spontaneous acts of charity, to whom he did not wish to give his home address. Foremost among these were non-commissioned officers and their families whom he would read about in the newspapers, men whom he had never known and who frequently were residents of distant communities, who had met with misfortune that a five-dollar bill, a ten-dollar bill, might help to alleviate. These gifts, and the acknowledgments of them, were a secret from Sophie and from everyone else. They never amounted to $100 a year, and on several occasions they had invited requests for larger donations, but he refused to be disillusioned by the greedy or the suspicious. Over the years the practice gave him much satisfaction.

"You know, General, a lot of people must think you live here," said Walter Beers, the paid secretary. "You get more mail than the club, outside of bills."

"Well, I do live here, about a quarter of my waking hours, Walter," said Dick Hightower.

"Yes, I guess that's right, when you stop to think of it. You eat one-third of your meals here, leaving out Sunday."

"That's correct, and I get most of my exercise here."

Beers laughed. "Exercise? Here?"

"At the billiard table. Someone, I believe, calculated that an hour at the billiard table is the equivalent of a three-mile walk. I have my doubts, but we must find out if one of the members has a pedometer. You don't happen to know of any?"

"To be truthful, General, I don't know what one is. A what did you call it?"

"A pedometer. Measures how far you walk."

"What do you do, attach it to your foot? I never heard of one."

"You attach them to your belt, but between us I don't consider them very reliable."

"I wouldn't, either. I don't trust the one I got on my car."

"Is that so? Walter, will you put stamps on these and see that they go out this afternoon?"

"I'll drop them by the post office on my way home."

An incredibly dull man, Walter Beers, but he had come home with a wound chevron from Château-Thierry, and Dick Hightower first had known him as company clerk and bugler in old Company B. A dull, unmilitary man, who nevertheless had battle stars on his Victory Medal and a *fourragère* on his now tight-fitting uniform. He would be club secretary as long as Dick Hightower had anything to say about it. "Walter, can you still sound pay-call?"

Walter laughed. "You mean on the bugle, General? Now what ever made you think of that? My goodness. Pay-call. I can't even remember how it went, let alone play it. I got my youngest boy, he's a second-class Scout, and they decided to make him a bugler on account of me. But they don't have pay-call in the Scouts. One less he has to learn than me. The neighbors ought to be glad of that. Pay-call. My goodness, General. I wasn't a bugler overseas. We just used the whistle over there, but I still got the same original old horn I had in B-Company."

"Hold on to it, Walter. It's government property, but I think you're entitled to it."

"They'd have a hard time getting it away from me," said Walter.

Four-thirty or five, time to return to 444, and timed carefully. The outpouring of the children from the schools was over, the departure of people who worked in shops and offices had not yet begun. At home there was tea (after a careful scrubbing of his hands). Because it was still daylight, Sophie would often have a visitor or two, and Dick was always the only male present. He would be at his courtly best; the head of the house, the host, the man in women's territory like a boy visiting his sister's boarding-school. All that, and The General, the highest-ranking military man in town. His hands were clean, his thin grey hair smoothed down, his necktie in place, the smudges on his shoes rubbed away. There would be a mechanical, innocuous flirtatiousness in his manner, put there as soon as he entered the sitting room, so that Sophie's guests would envy her her life with him. "Haven't you ladies got any gossip for me? There's nothing new at the club, I can assure you," he would say.

Although they might have been exchanging information on the

town's latest scandal, they offered none of it to him. He would not have welcomed it if they had. But the pretense of curiosity added a sparkle to the ritual of tea. Any real gossip Sophie had picked up would be duly passed on to him when they were alone, in language of the utmost purity but with illustrative gestures, and as completely descriptive as a police report. He had never asked her how her women friends were able to communicate details without using the language of the gutter or of the physician; they would not repeat naughty words, and they were ignorant of medical terminology. Nevertheless Sophie and her friends made their stories graphically real, and there was nothing in the calendar of sin that she had not at some time been able to convey to him in the telling of an episode. A day or two later—or a day or two earlier—the same story would be told at the club without the language restraints, but the women left nothing out.

Sophie was an accomplished gossip, a talent that compensated for her inability to concentrate on the printed word. As she was childless she was not compelled to protect her own son and daughter from reprisals. As she was beyond reproach in her conduct, she was invulnerable to gossip about herself. And as her husband led a blameless life, she had nothing to fear from misconduct on his part. Not even her chambermaid could find any evidence of the methods by which they took pleasure in each other, and it was assumed that if there had ever been erotic excitement in their marriage, that time had long since passed.

In the early days of their marriage, when Dick was a newcomer to the town, the obvious comment had been made that Sophie was a fortunate young woman to have captured such a handsome young man. She herself was plain, and though a good-sized fortune went with her, the eligible young men of the town had failed to be attracted by it. It was not unusual for a young army officer to marry for money, but when Sophie's husband resigned his commission and took up residence at 444, with no apparent inclination to enter the world of business, he came in for some harsh, if guarded, criticism as a fortune hunter. The criticism was not entirely fair. Investigation revealed that Dixon Hightower was not a nobody. The Hightower family were old Chester County stock who had scattered over the southeastern section of the Commonwealth, and who numbered among their living members a college president, several clergymen, some successful farmers, and a Philadelphia banker. Sophie's bridegroom was the only son of a weekly newspaper publisher and job printer in Montgomery County, a first cousin of the Philadelphia banker. William Hightower's business brought in little cash, but he accepted goods and services in lieu of it, and he always had a roof over his head and enough to eat. He was a graduate of a Friends Seminary, and had hoped to send his son to the new college at Swarthmore, but the opportunity to educate the boy at government expense was not to be denied. The rich cousin in Philadelphia offered no financial assistance, and as William Hightower had not been raised a Quaker, the cousin's scruples against a West Point education were considered to be all foam and no beer.

Dixon Hightower's army experience, beginning with West Point, taught him frugality and at the same time helped him acquire expensive tastes. The frugality was, of course, a refinement of the manner in which he had been brought up at home; the expensive tastes were new, but he took to them readily. Throughout his army career he needed financial assistance from his parents. As an army officer his credit was good, but sooner or later his boots had to be paid for, and he could not safely rely on his carefully hoarded winnings at cards for the expenses of the mess and visits to the cities. His father therefore practiced small economies; he smoked a cheap grade of Lancaster County tobacco, wore homemade carpet slippers in his shop and at home. His mother competed with her neighbors in fancywork and dressmaking. Together they were able to contribute as much as $500 a year to the maintenance of their son's standards, and it was worth it to them when he came home on leave, dressed in his blues and bringing them presents that they had paid for. He would be invited to hunt the fox with the nearby gentry and he was popular with its younger members. Their parents, however, knew to the penny what Dixon Hightower's financial expectations must be, and they were vigilant in keeping him at an unromantic distance from their daughters. It did not matter to them when Sophie Stokes, daughter of an upstate coal fortune, determinedly and unabashedly threw herself at the impecunious young lieutenant. Indeed, the mothers were all in favor of a union that would get Sophie a husband and young Hightower safely married. Dixon was well behaved, but not all the young wives were completely happy with their husbands.

Sophie Stokes was already courtesy aunt to the children of her friends, a readily available companion to the young wives during their confinements. She had acquired all the essential information about the young army officer, and knew from her friends that his mother earned pin-money by such work as letting out dresses for the expectant young matrons. She paid a visit to his father's newspaper-printing shop and saw him in his carpet slippers. As a Stokes she was a realist, a member of a family that demanded good value and had been remarkably successful in getting it. There was no doubt in her mind that Dixon Hightower represented good value for her, but he had never visited her part of the Commonwealth and could not be expected to know that she might also represent good value for him. He had been polite to her without displaying any of that extra politeness or cordiality that indicated an attraction. He still called her Miss Stokes.

Toward the end of his leave, before returning to his army duties at Fort Niagara, he was seated next to her at a dinner party, and this, she knew, might be her last chance. "Where is Fort Niagara?" she said. "I suppose it's somewhere near Niagara Falls."

"Quite near. It's on Lake Ontario. They call it the Niagara Frontier. It's a very pleasant place to be after the heat of Texas."

"And the city of Buffalo is somewhere near, is it not?" she said. "I have friends in Buffalo. The Watsons."

"I've been to their house. Colonel Watson, on Delaware Avenue? Is that the same one?"

"He made his money in railroads. It's the same one. I went to school with his daughter Jessica. Now Mrs. John Fisher."

"Yes, I know Jessica. The Watsons and the Fishers entertain on the grand scale."

"So I'm told," she said. "Is that the sort of life you care for? The entertaining on the grand scale?"

"Yes, I confess I do."

"But you can't do much of it on army pay."

"No, and if I were married I couldn't do it at all."

"Unless you had a rich wife," she said. "Why haven't you got a rich wife?"

He smiled. "Because no rich young lady has ever proposed to me."

"Very well. I do."

"Be careful, I might accept," he said.

"If you knew me better you'd know that I want you to accept."

"Here? Now?"

"Yes," she said.

"Assuming for the moment that you're not pulling my leg, I couldn't accept. Right now, I'm in debt, in no position to marry."

"How much in debt?"

"A little over eight hundred dollars."

"I have it in my purse, upstairs. You may consider it yours."

"It's very unwise to carry that much cash about with you," he said. "Why do you?"

"Because I like to. And if I'm robbed, I have more. Do you know who my father was? The name Stokes doesn't mean anything to you people down here, but I assure you, Lieutenant Hightower, eight hundred dollars wouldn't make a very large dent in my inheritance."

"Really? Are you a millionairess?"

"Yes."

"As well-to-do as our host," he said.

"Oh, I rather think so."

"In other words, you rather think you are richer than he is."

"I shouldn't be at all surprised. On the other hand, I'm not as rich as the Watsons."

"They're almost too rich, aren't they? I can imagine myself the owner of four horses, but not fourteen. And I don't think I'd care to live in that house on Delaware Avenue. I have a batman, an orderly, in the army. He has the duties of a servant, a valet. But Colonel Watson has a butler, valet, footman, coachman, groom, and I don't know what else. He must have many more at the farm in Batavia. Have you been there?"

"Yes."

"Then you know their scale of living. It's too grand for me. If I should leave the army, I'd share bachelor quarters with another officer, and one man would do for the two of us."

"But you're not going to share bachelor quarters. You're going to marry me. You would love my house. I have Patrick, who was my father's butler and coachman, and we have Rex and Ray, a pair of sorrels. I sold the farm to a cousin of mine, but I could buy it back if you were to insist. My cousin would extract his pound of flesh, but he's entitled to something. What are you thinking?"

"What am I thinking? I was thinking about this conversation. It sounds like a storybook conversation, in a novel, yet it's actually taking place. Nothing surprises me any more, except the commonplace. That's not quite what I'm trying to say. Let's put it this way. The first time I was ever under fire, it didn't seem possible that two hundred yards away, those men were actually firing shots at me. There they were, partly concealed by a rock formation, rocks that had been there since the beginning of time. Men that had been on earth—oh, twenty or thirty or forty years. They were members of an Indian tribe and not many of them live beyond forty. In between them and me was sand and sagebrush. All very commonplace, don't you know? And even the sound of their rifles was nothing new to me. But it all changed in the fraction of a second, when one of my men was picked off, in the middle of a sentence. He'd never been under fire, either, and he was in the midst of saying something to me. Before he could complete the sentence he was dead. I don't mean to shock you with this grisly story, Miss Stokes, but you asked me what I was thinking and that was it. The unpredictability of things."

"Such as having a proposal of marriage from your dinner partner."

"Yes."

"I could have predicted it, though. As soon as I heard you were leaving on Saturday afternoon. I asked to be put next to you at table."

"Did you? Then I believe you are quite serious."

"Oh, yes," she said.

"In that case, I accept. But I'm so accustomed to rules and regulations that I must insist on one thing."

"What is that?"

"That I propose to you. Miss Stokes, will you do me the honor of becoming my wife?"

"Yes, Lieutenant Hightower, I accept with great pleasure."

"Shall I rise and startle the guests with our announcement?"

"No, let's wait. But some of them wouldn't be as startled as you might think," she said.

Even the Philadelphia banking Hightower came to the wedding when he learned that his cousin was marrying a Stokes. Dixon Hightower, no longer in the army, wore a Prince Albert, but his six ushers were in uniform and provided the arch of swords. The bride was given in marriage by the cousin who had purchased her farm, and Jessica Watson Fisher was matron of honor. The groom's father, at the reception, could not resist saying to his banker cousin, "Well, Howard, the boy turned out a lot better than you expected."

"So it would seem, Cousin William," said Howard Hightower. "Are you planning to retire?"

"No. Just not going to worry quite as much," said William Hightower.

"You won't have to. We take care of her money, or some of it."

"Isn't that congenial?" said William Hightower.

The maladjustments between the bride and groom continued after their wedding night until well into the first year of their marriage, and were prevented from becoming disastrous only by their being treated as incidents of the night, not to be discussed in the daytime and never discussed at any great length when they occurred. "It hurts," she would say. "It always hurts."

"It won't always," he said.

"Do you think we'll ever have any children?"

"Do you want children that badly?"

"No. Do you?"

"I'm in no hurry," he said.

"That means you really don't," she said. "But if I'm ever going to, I ought to start now."

"Not everybody has them. And you're an only child and so am I. Do you honestly *want* to have a child, Sophie?"

"I don't think I do. And I'm getting afraid. They say you should have your first before you're thirty, and I'm past that."

"Well, there's only one way to have them, and we can't seem to do that. But we mustn't let it worry us. Our life is very pleasant as it is, don't you agree?"

"Oh, yes. I'm happy. I hope you are."

"Of course I am, Sophie. And I'm not at all sure if I'm cut out for fatherhood. Children don't like me."

"They don't like me, either," she said.

"Then we needn't lose any sleep over that," he said.

By concentrating their sensual ministrations in the first hour of retirement, by ignoring their failure to achieve conventional coitus, they reached a tacit agreement on the relative unimportance of that side of their married life. They were in no frenetic haste to produce offspring; Sophie had never experienced heterosexual or homosexual orgasm; and Dick, who had experienced both, showed her the ways by which she could produce orgasm in him, and for her there was enough excitement to give her pleasure. In the beginning she had been fearful that her failure might drive him away from her, and when it did not, when he turned out to be both patient and understanding, she accepted their modus vivendi as the solution to a problem that existed as a problem only because other women had told her of other experiences. She refused to see a doctor, and Dick supported her in her wish to preserve the secret of her failure. Thus their days contained neither frustration nor the torments of it. Other things mattered more and occupied their thoughts. For her there was the running of the household, her gardening, her friends, her gossip; for him there was the constant contrast between his new regimen (in which he was in full, supreme command) and the years of military restrictions. He was getting used to doing exactly what he wanted to do, without being required to supply explanation or excuse to anyone. For this he was learning to love Sophie, whose money had made his freedom possible, and he now loved the army for the preparation it had given him for this new life.

He was easily persuaded to accept a captain's commission on the governor's staff, was promoted to major at the outbreak of the war with Spain, and returned from Tampa, Florida, a full colonel. He had been out of the Commonwealth a total of three months, quite long enough to convince him that his decision to resign from the Regular Army had been the right one. Sophie had convinced herself that his decision to resign had been a sacrifice on his part, and he allowed her to continue to believe it, since it was something she wanted, but what he wanted now was to keep what he had.

A series of welcoming ceremonies, large and small, public, semi-public, and private, restored him to civilian life once more. Nearly half a century had passed since the town had been able to demonstrate its pride and gratitude to its military men, and the short duration of the hostilities with Spain and the absence of gunshot casualties was additional cause for rejoicing. Colonel Dixon L. Hightower was the man of the hour. There was even talk of running him for Congress. Not many outsiders had so quickly been adopted by the citizens of the town.

In the name of the borough a group of men of substance presented to Dixon Hightower a dress sword from Bailey, Banks & Biddle, at a subscription banquet in Odd Fellows Hall. But he had already, a week earlier, on the night of his return to 444, received a welcome from Sophie that surprised her as much as him: in the course of their first embrace, with neither of them expecting more than there had ever been for them, they were possessed by an intensity, a drive, that was wholly instinctive and that carried them forward into complete copulation. "How did it happen?" he said.

"I was going to ask you," she said.

"Was it because we missed each other?"

"I guess so. It must have been," she said.

"And it didn't hurt?"

"Not really. I didn't notice it. Did it hurt you?"

"Pinched a little, but only a little. Nothing would have stopped me."

"Or me either," she said.

"You haven't been going to see a doctor or anything like that?"

"Nothing. But I missed you. Oh, I wanted you so much. Just to have you in the house with me. Every night I took something of yours to bed with me, held it to my bosom."

"And elsewhere?"

She nodded. "Yes, and elsewhere."

"What sort of thing?"

"Different things. A cravat. A riding crop. A muffler. Whatever I happened to see in your wardrobe. I very nearly sent you something of mine, but how could I tell you that in a letter?"

"I wish you had sent me something of yours," he said.

"Oh, dear. What would you have liked?"

"Oh—some intimate something. Something feminine."

"Something I'd worn?" she said.

"Oh, yes. Lacy, satiny." He got out of bed and turned up the burner.

"What are you going to do?" she said.

"You mustn't look. Close your eyes, or turn away till I tell you to look."

She turned away. "What on earth are you doing?" she said.

"Just be patient, and don't look till I tell you," he said.

"You're getting something of mine, I know that."

"Just be patient," he said.

"How much longer?"

"Count to fifty, slowly," he said.

She commenced to count. When she reached the forties he said, "All right, now you can look."

He stood at the foot of their bed, and he was wearing an evening dress of hers and a pearl necklace, and on his head he had a silken scarf.

"Dixon!" she said.

"Are you surprised?"

"You could almost be a woman," she said.

"I thought you'd laugh," he said.

"I would have, but you even stand like a woman. A *pretty* woman, too. Not pretty, but handsome. You look a little like Madge Prestock."

"Well, that's a compliment. Madge is a handsome woman," he said. "Do you like me this way?"

"I don't know, I'm not sure. It's such a surprise. How can you suddenly transform yourself? Do you like to dress up like a woman?"

"I never have before," he said. He stood in front of her full-length mirror. "If my feet were smaller I could wear your shoes. The next time you go shopping, buy me a pair of high-heeled shoes."

"Do you mean it?"

"Yes. And a wig. You might have to go to Philadelphia for a wig. That place where you rent masquerade costumes. You know the place I mean, down on Chestnut Street. Van Something."

"What color wig?"

"Get two. Blond and brunette. Nobody else has to know," he said. "They could be all your things, and don't you think it would be fun?"

"I don't know. I suppose so," she said.

"I've always wanted to do this," he said.

"What about me? Would you want me to dress up as a man?"

"Haven't you ever wanted to?"

"Oh—when I was little."

"Only when you were little? Didn't you ever go to a fancy dress party in a man's costume?"

"We were never allowed to."

"What would you have gone as if you'd been allowed to?"

"A cowboy, with those white furry trousers."

"Chaparejos. Chaps. I have an old pair of leather ones in the attic. How would you like to put on my blues? Not the breeches, but the trousers and short coat."

"Now?"

"Unfortunately they're at the tailor's, but you could put on one of my civilian suits if you'd like."

"I'd feel very strange," she said.

"We'll do it some other time."

"You really want me to?"

"Yes, I do," he said.

"All right, I will. But I won't make as good a man as you do a woman."

"Oh, what difference does that make? It's just for the fun of it, you and I. Neither one of us would ever think of telling anyone else."

"All right, now please come back to bed."

"I will if you undress me," he said.

"You mean as if I were a man?"

"There's nothing wrong in it, Sophie. I don't see anything wrong. We're husband and wife."

"Yes," she said.

It became so that when she wanted him she would retire early and lay out lingerie, a dress, silk stockings and shoes on the chaiselongue in their bedroom. Without this preliminary, he could not be stimulated. He very soon tired of her awkward efforts to pose as a man. "I'm afraid you'll never learn to tie a four-in-hand," he said. But he never grew weary of his own part in the game, and for the sake of its consummation she played it with him. "I bought you a nice present today," she would say. "Don't ask me what it is. You'll see it sometime this evening." It would be an inexpensive necklace, a bracelet, an article of lingerie. In the mornings before breakfast she would put everything away, out of sight of her chambermaid, and he would shave and dress with no word, no look, no conspiratorial smile that referred to the rites of the night before. At breakfast he would read his newspaper and make his comments on the events of the outside world. He was the same man, because she knew him to be, and as she said about once a year, if other people knew him as she did they would realize that he was one of the most fascinating men you could ever hope to meet.

The Skeletons

George Roach went to the club every day, had his lunch, played his bridge, and returned home late in the afternoon. That was all right. He kept out of sight most of the day, and that, among other things, is what clubs are for. But his brother Norman, who was only two years younger than George, was not a member of the club, and the people of the town could see Norman going from place to place, doing nothing but go from one place to another, idling, trying to make conversation with busy people. "Uh-oh, here comes Norman Roach," they would say, and take action to avoid being buttonholed by him.

There was no sad reason why Norman Roach was not a member of the club. He had resigned from it in 1931, when many men were making such economies all over the country. "A hundred dollars a year isn't going to break you," said his brother George. "Two dollars a week."

"Will you give me two dollars a week for the pleasure of my company?" said Norman.

"I will not," said George.

"Then mind your own business," said Norman.

"All right, but I just want to remind you, if you stay out two years you won't be able to get back in without paying the initiation. That's two hundred and fifty."

"I may not want to get back in, and if I do, let me worry about how much it'll cost me," said Norman. "There's also the possibility that two years from now there won't be any club. And the further possibility that you won't be able to afford it either."

George laughed. "I'll always be able to afford it as long as my pigeons bid no-trump."

"You don't win that much playing bridge," said Norman.

"That's where you're wrong. I do win that much. As long as I've been in the club I'd never had a losing year, and one year I came out six hundred dollars ahead."

"I'd be ashamed to admit it if I were you," said Norman.

"Well, you're such a lousy bridge-player," said George.

"I have better things to do with my time," said Norman.

"Such as what? Such—as—what?"

"Well, for one thing, we have a very sick mother. If you'd pay a little more attention to her instead of every afternoon stopping at the club and playing cards with a bunch of nitwits. You don't show her the slightest consideration, and she'll be lucky to last out the year. If you want to know what I think, you're an ungrateful bastard."

"And you're a sanctimonious son of a bitch. You go see Mother every day because you think it's your duty—"

"It *is* my duty, and yours too."

"I haven't finished. You go there, and sit with her, and you never let her forget that you're being a dutiful son. But I'll tell you something, Norman. You bore the Christ out of her. You're going to bore her to death, and in less than a year at that."

"If you want to make excuses for yourself," said Norman.

"No. I got it straight from Mother."

"You're a liar, too. Mother would never make such a statement."

"As good as. And to me. 'Norman shouldn't feel that he *has* to come every day,' she said. So don't be so God damn high and mighty. Give the old girl a break, and stop boring her every afternoon. You're not exactly jolly company at best."

"She knows I care for her. That's more than she ever gets from you. And I'm not going to forget this conversation, George. You've said some things to me that aren't going to be easy to take back."

They were in their middle thirties. The Roach brothers. People who had not known them all their lives sometimes mistook the younger for the older. The looks, people said, had all gone to George, and it was not only the better nose and set of the eyes and chin. The older brother had more pep, as people said in those days, and Norman seemed to be continually watching him in mystification, baffled by his exuberance and his ease with the human race. It came so easy to George; to Norman it came not at all. Their mother dressed them alike throughout boyhood, in matching clothes that came from a rather special shop in Philadelphia; but the uniform attire was nearly the only thing they had in common. The boys were different from each other in so many respects that their clothes produced no fraternal effect. When they were old enough to select their own suits and haberdashery the brothers made their personal declarations of independence, and they extended their individuality in 1917 when George joined the navy and Norman the army. George was assigned to a gun tub in an army transport and never saw a submarine; Norman returned from France with two battle stars. But once again George in his officer's cape was a more dashing figure than Norman with his Croix de Guerre (avec paume).

In such cases the stodgy one is expected to be the more reliable, more substantial citizen, but Norman was neither a more nor a less successful man of business. They both had the same amount of money from the equal division of their parents' estates, and neither George nor Norman was conspicuously enterprising as a member of the business community. Their father, Patrick Roach, had made his fortune as a capitalist, by being there with the cash at the right time. He diversified. He went to work as office boy in a law firm at fifteen, with a parochial school education that had included bookkeeping and shorthand. He was accomplished in penmanship and made a few pennies by writing calling cards. He read law and in time was admitted to the bar, but he saw that the making of money in a law firm was a slow process for a young man who was not related to the partners. Through his experience as rent-collector for the firm's clients he became interested in real estate; as the firm's office boy he had paid almost daily visits to the local banks, where he had made a favorable impression for his neatness and politeness. He was, of course, scrupulously honest. Thus when he decided to open his own office as a lawyer specializing in real estate, he commenced with the blessing of some of the bankers. There were a few murmurs by his former employers as certain clients transferred their real estate affairs to the ambitious young Patrick Roach, but he had been careful not to influence the officials of the corporation clients, the coal company and the iron foundry, and publicly the old firm wished him well. Now, for the first time in his life, he was on his own.

By the time he was thirty he owned at least one building in each of the eight blocks of the principal business section, and he had married Sophie Richardson, daughter of one of the old families of the county. They were married in the First Presbyterian Church, and Patrick's mother, a County Limerick girl, refused to attend the nuptials. The Roaches, however, were represented by Patrick's brother and two sisters, who had been told that Sophie was taking instructions in Catholicism. She was doing no such thing, but she had told Patrick that some day she might, and Patrick was more in a hurry to get married than to make a convert of his bride. Thereafter Patrick Roach became by degrees a man without a church, and when he died room was found for him in the Richardson plot in the Presbyterian cemetery. His mother stayed away from that ceremony too, but her absence was not noticed by many of the leading citizens and their wives, come to pay their last respects.

The Roach brothers grew up without knowing their Roach cousins. It might even be said that they grew up without knowing their father, who went to his office every day of the week including Sunday. The citizens on their way home from church would see his Winton 6 standing at the curb and say, "Pat Roach—upstairs counting his money." It was a fair comment. He took no one into his confidence, and when it was said that Pat Roach was all business, there was very little left to say. His wife and his sons belonged in the large stone house on Lantenengo Street (that had once been owned by a corrupted judge), and he went home to see them. But he had no interest in Sophie's friends or in the details of his sons' upbringing. His games were played with other men, in offices. He joined the club because he was Sophie's husband and he remained a member because there were certain gatherings of certain men that more desirably were held at the club than in the good hotel. After such meetings Patrick Roach would return to his office or to the stone house out the street, without socializing, without the need to socialize.

Sophie chose the boys' schools. Lawrenceville because the Presbyterian minister thought well of it; Lehigh for George because her father had gone there, and Cornell for Norman because her brother had gone there. George joined Chi Phi because his grandfather had been a Chi Phi; at Cornell, where it was almost impossible to be overlooked by a fraternity, Norman joined Delta Upsilon in his junior year. None of this mattered to their father. "You could just as well send them to Harvard," he told Sophie. "I have the money."

"They have no roots in Harvard," said Sophie. "My mother's uncle went there, but he died a bachelor. We have nobody to write letters for them."

"All right, I leave that entirely up to you," said Patrick Roach. He had said the same thing so many times that she knew it was what he was going to say in this instance. Indeed, he would not have known how to oppose her; he was not sure of the dates of their birth, of their age at any given moment. It was the kind of thing he left entirely up to her. When she finally discovered that his bookkeeper had been his mistress, her only real curiosity was about where they had *gone,* where was the *bed?* And he refused to tell her. "I've admitted it," he said. "You don't have to know any more." He died without telling her that for fifteen years he had kept a room in the Roach Building to which only he and the bookkeeper had a key.

"Did you ever know that the old man had an apartment at 214?" said George to his brother.

"An apartment? What kind of an apartment?" said Norman.

"An apartment, to live in."

"Well, I guess if he wanted to have an apartment—although I don't know what he'd want it for. He had that big sofa in his office if he wanted to take a nap."

"I'll tell you what *I* think," said George. "It wasn't for taking a nap."

"*Him?* You mean there was a woman involved?"

"I'll take you down and show it to you. A bed. Chairs. A toilet."

"I don't wish to see it."

"Sheets all folded up in the closet. I'll bet it was he and Irma Michaelson."

"The bookkeeper? Quit your kidding."

"I'll bet anything."

"Well, you can't prove it by her. She croaked before he did. It doesn't surprise me, though."

"You acted surprised," said George.

"I am surprised in a way, but anything he did wouldn't surprise me. I just hope Mother never found out, that's all I care about. And don't you ever let on."

"I'll bet she did know," said George.

"You're crazy. She wouldn't have tolerated it for a minute."

"No? Who had the money?" said George.

"She has her own," said Norman.

"Nowhere near what he had. Nowhere near. I don't know what she has, but he had over six hundred thousand dollars. It may turn out to be a lot more. He owned stocks in companies I never heard of."

"I'll never touch a cent of it," said Norman.

"Oh, horsefeathers. You'll take all that's coming to you," said George.

George's prediction was accurate. Norman believed such things as he was saying them, but having said them, having registered his protest, he never again wished to be reminded of them. Not to accept his share of his father's estate would have made life uncomfortable for him, as it would have for his brother to have renounced his share. The Roach brothers, notwithstanding their differences in character, had a similar attitude toward work. They never quite got started in real jobs. Each of them had been left $100,000 by their father, and the income was just enough to keep them from having to earn a living. They had, moreover, expectations; half a million would be divided between them when their mother died. George improved his financial situation by marrying Elsie Stokes, who was really rich and had never considered marrying anyone else. Norman married Bertie Smith, whose family were not rich, but as a substitute for money she brought with her the habit of frugality and a lack of style that made for compatibility with Norman's. Of the brothers it was said that George was a gentleman of leisure and that Norman didn't do anything.

George and Elsie never invited Norman and Bertie to their parties, and Norman and Bertie never gave parties. Consequently the brothers might as well have been living in different towns. That was literally true for half the year, when George and Elsie were in Florida or Maine or traveling abroad. After two miscarriages Elsie had a hysterectomy and devoted herself to golf and the maintenance of her position as one of the town's outstanding hostesses. Having done no one any harm, having given people a few laughs, she suddenly died of cancer at the age of forty-two, and the gloom that afflicted the town was the greater because even George had not known the true nature of the operation on her gall bladder. Without being told to do so, the steward at the country club lowered the flag to half-staff, and George Roach was so benumbed that for months thereafter he failed to comprehend the universality of the sadness over Elsie's death. Now he was a rich man with nothing to do and no one to do it with.

He had been everywhere that he wanted to be, and in any case travel without Elsie was unthinkable. The war came, and he tried to get back in the navy, but they would not take him. The army took Norman, who had not had as many cocktails or eaten so much good food between wars, and Norman was shipped to North Africa as a staff officer in the belief that a man who had been decorated by the French in 1918 might be useful in liaison work. He came home in 1945 a lieutenant-colonel and wearing three ribbons that had not existed during the earlier war. "What are they?" said George.

"This is the Legion of Merit, this is the American theater, and this is the African campaign," said Norman.

"The Legion of Merit? Is that ours?"

"Certainly. Haven't you ever heard of it?" said Norman.

"I guess I've heard of it. Very impressive. Congratulations. I got one, for serving on the draft board."

"They gave medals for that?" said Norman.

"I was surprised, too. One day it came in the mail. However, I don't think I'll ever wear it. At least not when you're around."

"If they gave it to you you must have earned it," said Norman.

"Norman, why is it that you can be such a patronizing bastard even when you're trying to be nice?"

"Well, I must say you haven't changed much yourself."

"Probably not," said George.

"I hear you have a new lady friend. I was glad to hear that. You brooded too much over Elsie."

"I'd rather you didn't talk about Elsie. As for my having a new lady friend, undoubtedly Bertie was referring to Mrs. Green. But as usual Bertie is a little late with her gossip. Mrs. Green is back with her husband, running a poultry farm down near Reading. It never was a great romance, you know. Just a couple of middle-aged crows trying to hold on. What did you do while you were overseas, Norman? About women, I mean."

"If you knew me better you wouldn't even ask that question."

"I guess I shouldn't have. But you were gone three years. Weren't there any WACS, or nurses? Never mind, never mind. As far as I know, the breath of scandal never touched Bertie, either."

"If I'm not permitted to speak about Elsie, I'd rather you didn't speak about Bertie."

"That's a very good thrust. A point well taken. And to change the subject, what do you contemplate doing between now and the next war? If it comes soon enough you'll undoubtedly end up a general."

"I thought of entering politics. I got so disgusted with what I saw that I'm seriously thinking of it. I may run for Congress."

"Well, that seems like a good idea. It'll cost you a lot of money, but I'll be glad to help some. Have you sounded out the right people?"

"I haven't said a word to anybody, and don't you. I'm going to wait and have a look first."

"Yes, but they're not going to come to you, you know. And you'll want to take advantage of your war record. You might even want to run as a Democrat. The old man was a Democrat."

"You're not serious. They're the ones I want to get rid of."

"Just a suggestion. If you decide to run, you'll want to win, and they're winning everything these days."

"I would like to reverse that trend," said Norman.

"Well, good luck to you," said George.

Thereafter Norman thought of himself as a man engaged in politics, but the politicians did not sense his availability and he did nothing to alert them. The years passed, two at a time, one Congressional election after another, and no one thought to ask Norman to run for office. In a state where politics was every man's second, if not his first, occupation, Norman's comments and opinions did not draw attention to himself. But then Norman had the great misfortune to make any conversational topic seem dull. He had inherited some of his father's secretiveness, and his mother had told him once or twice that it was not good manners to talk about oneself. The result was a habit of reticence that restrained him from full expression of the idea in his busy mind. Not even two World Wars had produced a single good story for him to tell; not even his own wife knew the circumstances that led to his getting the Croix de Guerre and consideration for the Distinguished Service Cross. He had no conversational assets and he had one incurable liability—head tones that made his simplest remarks sound like utterances from a Presbyterian pulpit.

Norman and Bertie had two daughters, Sophronia and Alberta, who were never called anything else by their parents. They went from Gibbsville High to Wellesley and back to Gibbsville and jobs that did not take salaries away from young women who needed the money. Sophronia worked in the office at the Children's Home, and Alberta managed a gift shoppe that two friends of her Aunt Elsie's had opened as a hobby. It had never shown a profit, but it was a nice place to have a cup of tea, which Alberta served every afternoon, or to borrow an umbrella or go to the bathroom. Alberta loved the shoppe and its genteel clientele, who for the most part were women and girls with whom she rightly associated herself on quasi-social terms. With new customers who did not come from her acquaintanceship she was extremely polite. "Yes? Can I help you?" she would say. But even before the stranger had stated her needs Alberta would be smiling sadly, nodding pitiably, and she would interrupt. "I think I know what you have in mind, but we haven't carried it for ever so long," she would say. If the customer was persistent and asked if the item could not be ordered, Alberta would shake her head. "We're such a small shop," she would say. "You'd do much better to order it direct." The silent partners went on footing the bills, unaware that Alberta was maintaining the shoppe's prestige but fully aware that no one else would take the job for such small pay. And the toilet *was* spotless and the telephone was not a pay station.

Sophronia dropped in every afternoon on her way home from work, to hear about Alberta's interesting encounters with their mutual friends and strangers. Sophronia did not like her job at the Children's Home. The woman who superintended the Home was a former nurse, the only person the trustees could get at the salary, and Sophronia was frankly disgusted at the amount of food the woman put away. "She doesn't eat with the rest of the staff. Has hers cooked specially for her and served on a tray. But there's a darn good reason for that, let me tell you. We eat the same as the children, but Miss Mack has steak one day, roast chicken the next. But she pretends she's so busy she can't take time out for lunch. Busy, my foot. She has her nap after lunch till three o'clock every afternoon. Last month she had her sister staying with her for two weeks and this month it'll be her mother, fattening up at the Home's expense. She's trying to get the trustees to buy a station wagon, and here I am, a graduate of Wellesley, getting twenty dollars a week."

Alberta was sympathetic, but she did not respond to her sister's strong hints to be taken on as assistant in the shoppe. Sophronia, with her hair-sprouting moles on her chin and her not always clean fingernails, would not have added any daintiness to the shoppe, and might easily discourage the silent partners from dropping in. Alberta did not run the most successful shop in town, but it was the neatest. Also, in every respect but financial, the shop was her own. Notwithstanding a lifelong habit of obedience and respect to her parents' wishes, Alberta firmly resisted her mother's attempts to have Sophronia take part in the business. Fortunately Bertie understood Alberta's argument that the silent partners might be unwilling to support a losing proposition just to give employment to *two* Roach sisters. One, yes; two, no. "I wish we could go to your Uncle George," said Bertie. "He got all that money from your Aunt Elsie."

"No, Mother," said Alberta. "The only thing that keeps the shoppe in business at all is Aunt Elsie's friends. *Those* people. If they lost interest, we'd have to close."

"But you don't make a profit."

"No, but we don't show a very big loss either. The ladies come in and use the john, because they feel they have a right to. And they have. Then they buy something, and their friends do. But if they didn't own the business, they'd never come in. They'd wait till they got home to do wee-wee. The shoppe is just a comfort station, really."

"A strange way to put it," said Bertie. "Vulgar, to say the least."

"Not as vulgar as what I have to do there. But I'm perfectly willing to be a chambermaid, as long as they let me run the shoppe the way I like. It's a small luxury for them, the women that put up the money, and it's just wonderful for me. You have no idea how much I love it."

She did not often use the word love. It was not often used in the Norman Roach household. Such words as cabbage, and chair, and window, and rain, and dollars, and yesterday, and indigestion, and hairbrush, and rug got used, but not the word love. Soap was a word that they had used a thousand times more frequently. It was as far as they went in intimacy, and love as a word had taken on a bitter extra meaning as the girls grew into womanhood that promised nothing they had not already achieved.

"Then I'd go to Uncle George, if I were you. If it means that much to you. You want to be able to keep the shop when those ladies pass on."

"I want to do it *my* way, Mother, or not at all!"

"Oh, dear. You don't have to bite my head off."

"I'm sorry. I didn't mean to speak sharply. But—well, I'm sorry."

The conversation was too unusual not to be reported to Norman, and Bertie gave her account of it that evening. "Hmm. Last year I believe the loss was somewhere in the neighborhood of two thousand dollars," said Norman. "That's more than I'd care to underwrite."

"Of course it is," said Bertie. "And if you did, you'd have to give Sophronia the same amount. No, I wasn't suggesting that you put your money into the shop."

"Then what *did* you have in mind?"

"I don't exactly know. But if you spoke to George and got him to promise that he'd put up the money if the backers passed on, or decided to withdraw their support. In other words, just so we have some assurance that the shop isn't going to have to close."

"That seems like meddling, to me. Also, plus the fact that I'm not on very good terms with George."

"I didn't know you'd seen him lately."

"I haven't. About the only time I ever see him is if I happen to run into him on the street. I don't say we're on the outs or anything like that. But in a thing like this, going to him for a favor, I'd first want to be sure of where I stood with him."

"Oh, he's free with his money—and it's really Elsie's money, most of it."

"I know that, for heaven's sake. But what if he says it was Elsie and her friends that started the thing in the first place? Wasn't that enough for her to do? I don't know. If I happen to run into him, and he's in a good mood, maybe I'll mention it and maybe I won't."

"Not a word of this to Alberta, of course," said Bertie.

"Of course not. What do you think I am?" said Norman.

By a paradoxical misfortune George was in a jovial mood when Norman next encountered him; instead of a casual greeting and a quick leavetaking, with nothing much said in between, the brothers, at George's invitation, went to the hotel bar and had a beer together.

"What put you in such high spirits?" said Norman.

"If you thought a minute, you'd be able to figure it out for yourself. It's my birthday," said George. "Entering my sixtieth year."

"You're fifty-nine today? By gosh, that's right," said Norman. "Well, many happy returns and so forth. What are you doing to celebrate it? Anything special?"

"Well, tonight Dorothy Williams is having a few people in for dinner."

"Oh, is that on again? We heard something to the effect that you and Dorothy had broken off because you didn't want to get married."

"Always one little error in what you hear, Norman. *I* wanted to get married, and still do, but Dorothy doesn't."

"I should think you'd be quite a catch. Dorothy's no spring chicken. Let's see. She's about two years younger than I am, making her fifty-five."

"Yes. But she says we're both too set in our ways. We both like our independence, and she likes hers more than I like mine."

"I should think for companionship."

"My argument precisely. But she says what's the use of building up a companionship at this late date? One of us will outlive the other, and then be that much worse off later on. I see her point. It took me a hell of a long while to get used to not having Elsie. There's such a thing as getting too dependent on someone else. And at least I can be sure that Dorothy won't marry someone else and take away what we have. It would be nice to be living in the same house with her, but it would probably have its drawbacks."

"You'd save money, having the one household."

"That was one consideration."

"A pretty big one, I should think. The size of your house, and the size of Dorothy's. Cut down on servants. Taxes."

"Yes. Well, when Dorothy said no, she meant it. I'm going to get rid of my house and probably buy a smaller one. I've had a very good offer from Thomas Brothers."

"The undertakers?"

George nodded. "They like everything about it, particularly the cellar. Did you ever know that undertakers are partial to houses with a large cellar? And ours has a concrete floor and water fixtures and so on. Ideal, they said. I won't get what Elsie paid for it, but they named a good price and they'll go a little higher. I'm going to give the money to the hospital or to cancer research. Not sure which. I've wanted to do something like that for a long time."

"Leaving yourself enough to live on, I hope," said Norman.

"Oh, I'm not likely to become a public charge. Or to ask you for assistance. I know approximately what you have, and you have to think of your wife and daughters."

"I'm never sure when you're being sarcastic," said Norman.

"Most of the time," said George. "You bring out the sarcasm in me, and always have."

"Oh, I don't mind it any more. It's just your way. The older brother versus the younger brother."

"Very generous of you to take it that way. As we get older, and this being my fifty-ninth birthday, I can look back and think of times when I needn't have been quite so rough on you."

"It may have done me good," said Norman.

"Oh, now let's not get carried away, Norman."

"It's true, though. The three things that probably did the most for my character were *a*, being passed up by the fraternities my first two years in college. *b*, the army. And *c*, having you always take the wind out of my sails."

"I'd like you to elaborate. What did they do for your character?"

"Well, at Cornell I went there from a good prep school. Much better than most of the boys there. But Deke and Kappa Alpha and so on left me out in the cold, although they took in some fellows I'd gone to school with. Ithaca can be a pretty damn lonely place, I can tell you, and about the only friend I had there was a Chinaman. They had lots of Chinese there. They even had their own fraternity, and I'd have joined it if they'd given me a bid."

"Then came the army."

"That was altogether different. I wasn't a very popular officer. In fact, far from it. But I was a *good* officer. The same things that were against me at Cornell were in my favor during the first war. Namely, the fact that I had gotten used to being off by myself. If I had to send a couple of men out on patrol, I didn't have to think twice about whether a man was a particular favorite of mine. If it was his turn, and I could depend on him, I sent him. He would look at me and as much as say, 'You son of a bitch, you know I'm going to get killed.' But at least he couldn't accuse me of sending him and not somebody I liked better. I treated them all alike, and I ended up more respected than some officers that they liked better."

"This is the first time you ever talked to me about your army experience. How did you get your medal?"

"Oh, that's too long a story."

"I have all day," said George.

"No. It only makes me sore. I was up for the D. S. C., and all I got was the French medal. It was with palm instead of with star, but even so it griped me that the French would give me a medal and one of my own people—it must have been—fixed it so I didn't get the D. S. C. I think it was the major of my battalion. One of the popularity boys. A National Guard fellow from East Orange, New Jersey, and a graduate of Peddie. He always had it in for me after he found out I'd gone to Lawrenceville. But I'll tell you this much, Brother George. I knew of cases where they gave the Medal of Honor for less than I did to get the Croix de Guerre. *I* know it, and a few of my men knew it, and I guess that ought to be enough satisfaction. Only it isn't."

"Then you wouldn't exactly call it helping to improve your character."

"That part didn't. But I look back on the army as a good thing for me, generally speaking. Altogether I spent nearly seven years of my life as an army officer. A lot of fellows, retreads like myself. You were a retread, but I guess the navy is different than the army."

"Very. And I wasn't a retread. I didn't get back in."

"That's right, you didn't. But anyway you tried."

"I'm an honorary retread," said George. "I wonder why you didn't stay in the army in 1919?"

"If I'd known better, maybe I would have. But I was just as anxious to get home as anybody. Bertie was waiting for me, and I wanted to settle down and raise a family."

"Well, you did that," said George.

"Yes. Yes, I did that," said Norman, and then he was overwhelmed by the impulse that he had been denying. "George, I—you're feeling pretty good and there's something I want to take up with you."

"Go ahead."

"Well, you know the little gift shop that Alberta runs. That Elsie and those others got started. It's not much of a money-maker, you know."

"I always understood it wasn't a money-maker at all."

"It isn't. It falls behind every year, and one of these days Norma Blair and Frances Cookson are going to stop supporting it."

"Yes. Frances Cookson especially. She's not going to be around much longer. Why?"

"That's just it. One or both of them won't last forever, and if you had any idea how much that shop means to Alberta. It's her *life*. She's there at half past eight every morning and never gets home before six. She only takes thirty-five a week salary out of the shop, and the amount of work she puts in. What I was wondering is, would you be willing to—in case anything happened to Frances or Norma, or both—would you be agreeable to becoming the backer?"

"Me? Why not you?" said George.

"Because you wouldn't miss the money, and I would. Two thousand dollars a year is nothing to you, but it is to me. But it isn't only the money. If people knew you were behind it they'd be more apt to patronize it than if they knew it was me. Those people are your friends, not mine."

"Somehow I don't see myself as a magnet drawing customers to a gift shop. It isn't the way I picture myself. On the question of money, I suppose I could buy out Frances and Norma and later on take some kind of a tax loss. I imagine Frances and Norma have some such arrangement. In my case, of course, the tax boys might complicate things because Alberta is my niece. Those are things I don't know too much about. On the other hand, Norman, is it such a good idea to have your daughter go on year after year, taking charity just to give her something to do? Wouldn't she be much better off if she got a real job?"

"Both girls are against taking jobs that other girls really need."

"That's going on the assumption that you're a lot richer than you are. Who gave them that idea? You did. Except for the army, you've never had a job. Neither have I, of course. But Elsie had more than enough for both of us. She backed the gift shop so that Alberta could be independent some day, but I know she never had any idea of making Alberta *dependent* for the rest of her life. Elsie helped a lot of people to help themselves, to get them started. But if she had known the shop was going to turn out this way, she wouldn't have put up a nickel. That being the case, I'm afraid my answer is no."

"By God, I never thought you'd be tight-fisted."

"Oh, very," said George.

"You think nothing of giving away large sums of money to the hospital, but when it comes to your own flesh and blood . . ."

"Alberta? That'll be news to Bertie. Or maybe I don't understand the term, flesh and blood. I'll tell you what I'll do. If Norma and Frances have to stop supporting the shop, I'll *give* Alberta two thousand dollars if she'll promise to close the damn place, and go hunt for a job."

"Who are you going to leave your money to?" said Norman.

"A home for abandoned kittens."

"You're not serious," said Norman.

"No. There'll be small bequests to your daughters. But the major portions of it will be divided up among various institutions that Elsie was interested in. I'll enjoy the income while I'm alive, but when I depart it'll all be cut up."

"Some of that you inherited from Mother and the old man. It wasn't all Elsie's."

"You'd be surprised how little I had left when I married Elsie. I wasn't as careful as you, Norman. I almost had to go to work, and you know what a terrible thing that would be."

"You mean to say you squandered four hundred thousand dollars?"

"I took what you might call a post-graduate course in commerce and finance."

"Oh. The stock market."

"Foolish pride, it was," said George. "I thought I could run my little fortune up to somewhere near Elsie's. But when I was long, the market was short, and vice versa."

"You never told *me* you were losing in the stock market."

"It was hardly the kind of thing I wanted to brag about. I did everything wrong. Or everything right, except that I didn't do the right things at the right time. But I learned my lesson the hard way, and in all the time we were married I never gave a single word of advice to Elsie. Financial advice, that is. Well, one piece of advice. I told her never to pay attention to anything I told her about common stocks. And she didn't. In the long run that advice was worth over a million dollars to her. Not many husbands can make that claim. We knew any number of women who lost fortunes through taking their husbands' advice, but Elsie was always very proud of me as a non-advisor. Of course I helped her spend it. I was glad to cooperate there. We discovered a lot of places before the tourists spoiled them. Travel agent, that's what I should have been. A travel agent and a non-advisor to wealthy women. But I straightened out her slice."

"What was that?"

"Elsie. I was just trying to think of what I had done for her, and I remembered that when she took up golf I was the one that cured her slice."

"You had big things to worry you, you two," said Norman.

"*I* had, if I'd let them worry me. I'd taken a bad licking in the market. But I didn't let it worry me. With Elsie's money, the only thing to bother me was the fact that I was living off my wife. But she cured me of that, as effectively as I cured her slice. She pointed out to me a rather obvious fact, that the money I had had came from the old man and Mother. I didn't earn it. It was left to me, most of it by a man who happened to be my father but for whom I had no love."

"But he *was* your father," said Norman.

"Undoubtedly. But Elsie's point was that it was no worse to live off her, whom I loved and who loved me, than to live off my dear departed father, who had no love for me or you or Mother. Or even poor Irma Michaelson. It's no wonder you and I never developed the acquisitive instinct. He didn't make it seem very attractive, did he?"

"I'm still living off his money. I don't think I want to criticize him."

"Oh, God, you're pompous, Norman. Your whole life you've always talked as if you were afraid someone was taking down everything you say. Don't you know that no one cares?"

"I do. I have certain beliefs, certain standards. I don't consider that my life has been what I wanted it to be. But I can sleep nights—"

"I'll bet you do, too," said George.

"Well, I'm not sure how you mean that. Probably some reference to my home life, so I'll ignore it. I always remember the casual way you took it when we discovered about the old man and Irma Michaelson. Almost as if you were on his side."

"Not on his side. But I wonder how much Mother was to blame. She couldn't have been much fun."

"*Fun?* He didn't marry her for fun. He married her because she was Sophie Richardson and he was nobody."

"Yes, but why did *she* marry *him?* Sophie Richardson could have done a little better. Socially and financially, that is. Elsie used to say that Mother was itching to go out and have a good time, but didn't know how."

"That *sounds* like one of Elsie's ideas," said Norman.

"It was. I just told you. And like many of her ideas, or observations, very acute."

"I wouldn't have taken much stock in anything she had to say about Mother. I know she was very good at giving parties and that kind of life, but I wasn't aware that she had a serious side."

"Unfortunately, you didn't get to many of her parties, so you never really saw much of either side of her. But did you ever hear of Sven Svensen? The scientist? One of the men on the atom bomb project?"

"I may have read about him," said Norman. "Why?"

"We met him on the old *Kungsholm.* Saw quite a lot of him. He must have thought she had a serious side, because he turned up here one day for the sole purpose of getting Elsie to leave me and marry him."

"That was pretty fresh. What did you do?" said Norman.

"Well, first I had to make sure whether Elsie had given him any encouragement. And she conceded that a man like that might have got the impression that she was encouraging him. She had told him to come and see us when he came to America. And he took her literally, at her word."

"And you were satisfied with that explanation?"

"Not entirely. Not at all, really. But we'd been through something like it once before, only I was the one that had to make the explanations that time."

"So what did you do? With the Swede, I mean."

"Well, I took him to the club a few times. I showed him around the coal mines very politely. Then I insisted on having a dinner party for him. Elsie didn't want to, but I was adamant. I made up the list. The younger crowd. The prettiest girls in the county, and the big drinkers among the young men. It got a little out of control, I must say. But it gave Svensen a rather discouraging picture of the kind of life we led. You could almost see his mind working. If that was the way we lived, how long would it be before Elsie wanted to get back to that kind of carryings-on? There wasn't a soul there he could talk to. Elsie got a little tight, and tried to teach the guest of honor how to do the Lambeth Walk. Do you remember the Lambeth Walk? Nothing dirty about it, but nothing dignified, either. Like most Swedes, Svensen could put it away, but it only made him morose. As a matter of fact, he got rather disagreeable, and left the next day, with a terrible hangover and an extremely bad impression of Gibbsville society. It was the only time Elsie ever called me a son of a bitch. She knew what I was doing, all right. How could she not? But she forgave me. If I was willing to go to that much trouble to get rid of Svensen. She wasn't alive when they began writing about the men that built the atom bomb. I wonder if she would have been sorry she hadn't gone with Svensen. Her chance to go down in history."

"Yes, I remember the name now," said Norman. "He got the Nobel Prize."

"Oh, he'd already got it when we knew him. With someone else. But we didn't even know what he'd got it for, even after he told us. The Something Effect on Something of Heavy Water. Anyway, Elsie had her serious side. You've listened very patiently. Now would you care to tell me about Bertie's serious side?"

"That *is* sarcasm, and I think you're getting drunk. You'll be nice and drunk by dinnertime at the rate you're going."

"No, this is my usual time for my nap after lunch. What you think is intoxication is merely auto-intoxication. Fifteen minutes in a comfortable chair to let my food digest. Ten or eleven minutes of sound sleep, dead to the world, and I'm as good as new. You haven't got your car, have you?"

"No."

"It's only three blocks to the club, but I think I'll take a taxi."

"Why don't you go home?"

"In the middle of the afternoon? I'm never home in the afternoon."

"This would be a good day to go home. You're going to have to sooner or later, to change for dinner."

"Now that is a cogent argument. It makes so much sense that I wish I'd thought of it. But I'll give you the credit. Tonight at Dorothy's I'm going to make sure that you get proper credit for my well-rested appearance, my sparkle, my this, that, and the other. I'm sorry you won't be there to take a bow, but they aren't people you'd enjoy very much."

"No, they're all practically strangers to me, even though I don't know who's going to be there."

"As a matter of fact, Dorothy asked me if she should invite Bertie and you, but I said I couldn't imagine why. You've never had me to any birthday party of yours in the last fifty years."

"I haven't had one in that time, but if I had, I wouldn't have invited you. If I'd had any say in the matter you wouldn't have been invited to the ones when we were kids."

"Yes, we get along much better if we don't see each other. Every once in a while I think of asking you to have lunch with me, maybe even persuade you to come back to the club. But that would be a great mistake all around. A club is usually one of the places you try when you're looking for a man. 'Try him at the club,' they say. But in our case it works another way. You can be pretty sure that I'm at the club during certain hours of the day, therefore you don't have to worry about running into me someplace else."

"That's quite true. I *have* thought that."

"I'm not deliberately avoiding you. I have other reasons for going to the club. But if you were to rejoin, you'd feel that you had to go there to get your money's worth. And then we'd have to see each other. And then I *would* have to avoid you, deliberately. My friends, to be polite, and out of consideration for me, would feel they had to invite you to have a drink, or take a hand in a bridge game. Some of them might remember that you're a terrible bridge player, but they'd invite you anyway. And you might accept. Then you'd sit down and play a couple of rubbers, botching it. Leading from the wrong hand. Revoking. Misunderstanding the bidding. Arguing over the score. And before long you'd have a set of enemies that aren't your enemies now. Real enemies, too. In a club that's really a club a man likes to have everything just so. I'm sure you've heard about how a member can hate another member who sits in his favorite chair. That's been going on, I suppose, since the early days of White's Club."

"You mean Dick White?" said Norman.

"No, I don't mean Dick White. White's Club is a club in London, two hundred years old."

"Do you belong to it?"

"No, but I've been there."

"Does each member have his own special chair?" said Norman. "I wouldn't like to belong to a club where I couldn't sit where I pleased."

"If you're talking about White's, that's one thing you'll never have to worry about. You're as close now as you'll ever be to belonging to White's."

"I'm probably as close as I'll ever be to the Gibbsville Club. I never got anything out of it. I only joined the country club for my daughters, and they get very little use out of it. The swimming pool. That's about all. As far as I'm concerned, I go to the Y. M. C. A. three times a week, and that helps me keep in shape. That's why I was able to get back in the army without any trouble. I've always kept in shape. For someone my age, the doctors say I have the constitution of a man half my age. I walk at least a mile a day, rain or shine. Swim three times a week. I smoke, but I've never inhaled. Alcohol in moderation. Plain, wholesome food. Never any trouble with my bowels. First thing, right after breakfast, I'm on the can. That's the whole secret. Don't let yourself get constipated."

"What are you saving yourself for, Norman?"

"Saving myself? I don't know that I'm saving myself for anything."

"But you must be, to take such exceptionally good care of yourself."

"I wouldn't say that necessarily. I was given a good physique and I've always felt it was my duty to take care of it and not let it go to pot."

"That's not what you just said, but never mind."

"Whereas you should have taken warning when you couldn't pass the physical back in '42. Instead of which, you ought to consider yourself lucky to reach fifty-nine."

"I took warning when Elsie died. The warning was that a young person, comparatively young, who'd never had a serious illness, could get cancer and be dead in a few months. So what the hell was the use of going for walks in unpleasant weather, or playing volleyball at the Y. M. C. A., or giving up the good things to eat and drink? They told her she had cancer, and she kept it from me as long as she could. But *they* didn't. The doctors told me she had it, and so the two of us pretended she was going to have an operation and get well. Knowing better, both of us. It went to her brain, but at least she died thinking I'd been spared the truth. And at least I was able to be some comfort to her, up to the end. Now why should I change my ways? I couldn't possibly change my body. But what if I could? To restore my youthful vigor? And then what? Find myself at sixty, chasing after young women? Beating young men at tennis? What the hell for? Young women aren't very interesting in bed, and I'd done about as well at tennis as I ever cared to. I never had any trouble beating you, for instance. And I beat some fellows who were better than you. I didn't have to go out on the tennis court and show off my new vigor. Dorothy and I will go to bed tonight, if we haven't had too much to drink. If not tonight, maybe tomorrow night or the next. One of these days I won't have that any more, and when that time comes I hope I'll be ready for it. Although I suppose you never are."

"As a married man it's something I prefer not to talk about," said Norman.

"Why of course not, Norman. I wasn't hoping for an exchange of confidences on that subject. I've always thought of you and Bertie as fully clothed. In fact, with your hats on and maybe an umbrella."

"Don't go too far, George. Just don't go too far," said Norman. "I don't mind a little good-natured kidding, but leave my family out of it."

"But you can't object to what I just said. I always think of Bertie as fully clothed. If I'd said the opposite, then you would have every right to object. By the same token, I think of your daughters as virgins, which I'm sure they are. But if—"

Norman struck him. It was a clumsy and ineffectual blow of Norman's fist in the direction of George's face. But George was holding his drink halfway to his lips and Norman's fist struck his brother's arm. The glass was driven out of George's hand, the hand was driven against his chest, the contents of the glass spilled over his waistcoat.

"Now what did you do that for, you poor slob?" said George. The few other people in the tavern had not seen the actual punch, such as it was, but it was obvious that something unusual had occurred between the brothers. The onlookers waited in frozen attitudes for the next development. George addressed them: "It's perfectly all right, ladies and gentlemen," he said. "Slight altercation between brothers. This is my brother, Norman Roach, and I'm George Roach. It's my birthday. And we're half-Irish, you know. Now if you'll all just relax and mind your own God damn business, I'll be very much obliged." He had his handkerchief out and was sopping up the liquid on his waistcoat. The waitress handed him a napkin. "Thank you," he said.

"Would you care for a refill?" said the waitress.

"Ah, you understand about these things," said George. "But no thanks, Jennie. We know when we've had enough. You've had enough, haven't you, Norman?"

Norman had stood up during George's speech to the others. Now he reached in his pants pocket and took out some money. One by one he peeled off three dollar bills, then added a fourth, tossed the whole on the table and walked out.

"It came to a little more than that," George called to him, but Norman did not hear him. "Jennie, you take that."

"Jessie," said the waitress. "Thanks. Thanks very much. You want the check, Mr. Roach?"

"As soon as you call me a taxi," said George.

"You mind telling me what that was all about?" said Jessie. "You were sitting there peaceful and then all of a sudden."

"Just call me a taxi, Jessie," said George. "Chivalry, I am happy to say, is not dead."

"Who?"

"The taxi, Jessie, please. The taxi," said George.

The Roach brothers' quarrel over a woman who was supposed to have died but hadn't—a strangely unsatisfactory thing to quarrel about—did not long remain a topic of conversation in the town. The only accurate report of the altercation was given Dorothy Williams by George Roach, and her comment was, "You had it coming to you. You ought to know better than to tease a man like Norman. And especially over a thing like that. The virginity of two girls like Alberta and Sophronia is no joking matter. It's not a question of their morals, one way or the other. It's a reproach to their parents for not having produced someone more attractive. And it's a reminder to Norman that he's going to have to support them the rest of their lives. A man as stingy as Norman, not to mention a woman as stingy as Bertie—you should have known better. You must write him a letter of apology, this instant."

"You were going fine till you came to that," said George. "A letter of apology would be absolutely meaningless. And why wouldn't it be better all around if Norman and I disown each other? Now and forever. Thanks to Mother, I spent the first fourteen years of my life saying, 'I love my little brother.' When as a matter of fact I could hardly stand the son of a bitch. He had colds all the time. They took out his tonsils, but he still got colds. He always had something the matter with him, always suffering in silence, brave little man. But the brave little man always saw to it that everybody knew he was suffering. The only thing was, half the time there was nothing really the matter with him. The old man said to him one time, 'Norman, I believe you're a little faker,' and the little faker got sick to his stomach and threw up. He was of course a tattle-tale. We had a maid who used to let me watch her take a bath. Thanks to Norman, she got the sack, and eventually ended up in a house on Railroad Avenue. I've forgotten half the things he did that made me dislike him. 'I love my little brother,' I was forced to say. My father said one time, 'Sophie, maybe he doesn't love his little brother,' and my mother, in front of us, said, 'Kindly stop interfering.' Nothing ever convinced me that Mother was very fond of Norman, especially when we were older. But she had some notion that if I told that lie often enough, about loving my little brother, I'd begin to believe it was the truth. When he went to Cornell she made me write a letter to the Cornell chapter of my fraternity to try to get him a bid. She mailed the letter herself so that I wouldn't accidentally forget to. But I wrote a second letter, not exactly telling them to ignore the first letter, but quite frankly admitting that it had been written at the suggestion of a member of my family. They got the hint."

"I should think they would," said Dorothy.

"I've always been rather grateful to Bertie for marrying him. She didn't have much choice and it was a step upward for her in more ways than one. But they were so perfect for each other that they could have been living in another world. Think what it would have been like if she'd been some friend of Elsie's. Then we'd have had to see each other all the time and God knows what would have happened. I probably get along fairly well with most people because when I get through hating Norman, other people don't look so bad."

"Hate him? No, you don't hate him."

"Yes, I really do. I've come to that conclusion. And God knows, he hates me."

"I won't argue with you on that," said Dorothy. "But he hates everybody, without knowing it. Bores do. Bores are supposed to be pitiful, but I've never thought so. They can't help knowing that they're bores, but they go right on boring people because they hate them. It's their one weapon of revenge."

"Do people who hate people become bores? In other words, does it work both ways? I'd much rather do without the luxury of hating my brother than become a bore."

"Haters can be bores, but not because they're haters. On the other hand, people who don't hate anybody are the biggest bores. They're lacking in human emotion. Norman is more of a bore than a hater. He even bores me to talk about him," said Dorothy. Then, as an afterthought, she added, "But he doesn't hate you, George. Not you in particular. The one that would really hate you would be Bertie."

"Why do you say that?" said George.

"Speaking as a woman," said Dorothy. "If I were Bertie Roach, coming up from nowhere—"

"*To* nowhere," said George.

"Yes, to nowhere, but expecting more out of life than she ever got. Doing all the housework, raising those two hopeless specimens, and having to be Norman's wife. And all the time so near and yet so far from the fun you and Elsie had—I think Bertie must have had the dullest existence a woman ever had."

"It could have been worse," said George.

"Oh, it could have been. But she'd never think of that. She's had to spend her life thinking of how it could have been better. She's never really had anything. I almost feel sorry for her."

But now George began to tickle her in a way she liked to be tickled, and they quickly abandoned themselves to the special pleasures that the tickling usually produced. "You're *terrible,* George," she said.

"You think I'm terrible, Dorothy?" he said.

"Yes, I do. And I'm just as bad as you are, for liking it," said Dorothy. "Did you always know this was what I'd like?"

"Quiet," he said.

"Nobody else—"

"Quiet," he said.

The death of Frances Cookson was noted with suitable regret on the part of her limited circle of friends and acquaintances. It had been, as they said, a long time coming, which could have meant—but did not—that her friends were impatient to see her go. Her death put an end to her misery, but it was the beginning of active distress for Alberta Roach. Lawyers came to the shoppe and looked at her books; two sets of lawyers, one from the firm representing Frances Cookson's estate and the other representing Norma Blair. The settling of Frances Cookson's estate took more than a year, a year of harassment for Alberta, which told on her nerves, her appetite, her sleeping habits. The suspense was bad enough, but she got no relief when the problem was resolved by the agreement between Frances Cookson's and Norma Blair's lawyers. They decided that the shoppe must go out of business.

"It's cruel, it's cruel," said Alberta. "Mrs. Blair could have kept it going. I cut down the overhead to practically nothing. I was willing to have them reduce my salary. But Mrs. Blair said she didn't want to be bothered with it any more. Why did Father have to have that fight with Uncle George?"

"You must try to make the best of it," said Bertie. "It may turn out to be a blessing in disguise. With your experience, running your own shop, you shouldn't find it hard to get a job that will pay you much better, and you'll be able to do a lot of things you deprived yourself of."

The sisters were taking a more realistic view of jobs. Sophronia was no longer employed at the Children's Home, and the Roach girls no longer felt so strongly about competing with women who really needed money. Sophronia, with nothing else to do, had even offered her services as baby-sitter, with no takers. Alberta now discovered that her policy of running the shoppe for an exclusive clientele had made her an undesirable candidate for jobs in the larger stores. "Frankly, Miss Roach," said one manager, "you'd drive some customers away. You ran your own place for the country club crowd, and we don't get many of them in here." Alberta recalled now that the manager's own wife had been one of the women she had rebuffed.

"Something will come up," said Bertie Roach. "You have your degree from Wellesley."

"So has Sophronia," said Alberta.

"Well, you mustn't get discouraged."

"I *am* discouraged. What have I got to look forward to? Sitting home all day? Listening to Sophronia complain about her oily skin? And I wish you'd speak to her about rinsing out the tub. It doesn't do any good when I speak to her."

"Well, now you're not perfect either, you know. You could get into the habit of making your bed in the morning instead of leaving it till noon. It was different when you had to go to the shoppe every day. Your sister and I were more than glad to save you those few minutes. But each must do their share of the housework."

"Does that include Father? What does he ever do, I'd like to know. This house seems to be run for his convenience and comfort. Isn't he ever going to do anything?"

"What?" said Bertie.

"Yes, *what* is right. Lost his temper with Uncle George, and that ruined my chances of getting any help there."

Bertie Roach was not a subtle woman, but in matters that concerned her husband, her daughters, and her house she was perceptive. She liked watching pennies and bread crusts and fly specks and things that were in their proper place and things that were not in their proper place. She listened for the sounds that were the first signs of a cold in the head, for slightly prolonged gurgling in the water pipes that indicated trouble with the plumbing, for the variables in the pitch of greetings that revealed a mood or a change in mood. All her senses were continually at work, and little escaped her notice if it pertained to the objects and the beings in her house. She did not always or even often correct or improve what she observed; the effort would have been too great, and would have taken her away from her preoccupation with observation. Then too, her husband and her daughters treated her with a slight condescension that their formal respect for her did not altogether hide. But nothing got past her, and as the days and some months went by she had some new developments to watch.

These developments concerned Norman and Alberta, and affected Sophronia only indirectly. Norman, Bertie began to notice, would leave the house after breakfast, go for his walk in the shopping district, and return home before the morning was half gone. At first he would say he forgot something, and make a pretense of looking for a clean handkerchief or a pipe cleaner. But after a while he abandoned the making of excuses; he would turn up at home at ten o'clock, take his accustomed seat in the front parlor with his hat resting in his lap, and then abruptly announce that he was off again. He would be back in time for lunch, then leave once more. Bertie noticed that he seldom stayed away from the house for more than an hour. He offered no explanation for the changes in his former routine, and Bertie could not bring herself to the point where her curiosity would overcome her diffidence. If Norman wanted to be back and forth all through the day, there was no law against that. It was his house, and he was free to come and go as he pleased. In years past he had usually left the house after breakfast, come home for lunch, and then gone out for the afternoon. As men got older, they sometimes got bladder trouble, and Bertie made sure that that was not Norman's reason for the brevity of his absences from the house. She was not given much to finding the reasons for things, but Norman was her husband and whatever reason he had for a change in his habits was quite possibly important. She could not—though she tried—make herself believe there was no reason more important than caprice. Something was going on, something was happening.

When she learned the truth, she wished she had not. She wished she had remained ignorant and unashamed. The truth was, simply, that Norman had become a town character, an object of derision, a buffoon. In a most disrespectful way he had become known as *Norman,* with no need for further identification. One of the town drunks was known as Dory, one of the prostitutes was known as Mae. In like manner, Norman was Norman, a bore who had become an eccentric whom people laughed at behind his back and who would soon be laughed at to his face. It had taken time—a year or more—but she made the cruelly shameful discovery that her man, *her man,* was being called harmless! Not a harmless idiot, not a harmless nut, but "Norman, he's harmless." This strong man, well educated and brave, honest and decent, good husband and good father, with almost sixty years of blameless behavior to his credit, was being rewarded with the contempt of people who were not fit to lick his boots.

And he knew it.

He knew it before she did, and it was through his own small admissions that she pieced together the truth. First there were the occasional references to people who had got fresh; his being called Norman by people who had no right to call him Norman. Next came the incidents of impertinence in which he nearly lost his temper. Thinking back, Bertie realized that there must have been many such incidents and many times when he had come home to take temporary refuge from impertinent people. Her mind was unencumbered by the processes of psychoanalysis and her vocabulary was innocent of its jargon, but she recognized without being able to define his compulsion to return to the scenes of the abrasive attacks on his self-respect. He just couldn't keep away from those people.

Her method of dealing with Norman's problem was to observe silence, since she knew no other method. She could not tell him that he ought to stay away from people; to do so would have been the same as telling him that he was an outcast, and where was there to go that offered a race of people who were more understanding and tolerant? Here, at least, the enemies were not strangers. Here the bad people were not strangers who had never known that Norman was ever a brave and strong man. Another place would only be worse, cold and alien and seeing only the man he had become. There were just so many years a man could live (or a woman), and of the years that remained to Norman, some of them—the final ones—would be home years, when he would stay off the streets and away from the bad people. Some men got bladder trouble, some got the arthritis, and they sat in a chair and read books and took naps. Those were the home years, and as much as half the years remaining to Norman might turn out to be home years. Suddenly, and temporarily, Bertie had the material for a compromise that was not a solution, but was the next best thing to a solution of an unsolvable problem. When you know, and admit, that your husband bores people and inspires ridicule, you can plan for the day when you have him entirely to yourself. He did not, it must be remembered, bore Bertie. Long ago he had rescued her from a vegetable patch; for most of her life he had given her a house and the money to run it; and when she wanted him to, he made love to her. No one, it seemed, was going to do all these things for her daughters, and the bleakness of their future reminded her of what her life could have been.

For Sophronia there was no hope. She was a female, but men were repelled by her and thus had made her afraid of them. A certain few of the women of the town had friendships with other women that substituted for marriage. Bertie knew what they did; it had been described to her by Norman out of his limited supply of information. If Sophronia could have formed such an attachment, Bertie could have accepted the friendship part and deadened her imagination to ignore the secret kissings. In time Sophronia and her imaginary friend would be permanently designated as man-haters, and once so classified they would be forgotten. People were much more cruel to the fairies, as Norman called them—the men who corresponded to the women like Sophronia and her imaginary friend. It was sometimes argued that there was nothing but friendship between two such women, but the fairies were adjudged guilty, potentially if not actually. And, of course, they usually were. An odd sort of respectability attached to the female virgin perverts. In the history of the community none of them had ever been arrested, beaten up, or run out of town; whistled at, blackmailed, or driven to suicide by public scorn. Bertie did not know why this was so; she was not given much to finding the reasons for things. But she knew it was so, and if Sophronia could get someone, almost anyone, to be her companion and friend, Bertie would not stand in the way.

But women rejected Sophronia, and Sophronia was not constituted to make the effort of friendship. She was scornful of the people below her station in life, and jealous of those above it. The condescension she could not hide from her mother, a nobody, differed only in degree from her attitude toward her father, whose mother was a Richardson but whose father was undeniably Patrick Roach. And she had not tried to forgive Alberta for refusing to give her a job in the shoppe. Once, years ago, Sophronia had liked cats, but cat-hair made her father sneeze, and she was not allowed to keep one in the house. That had been years ago, a buried and forgotten oddment in the hideous history of Sophronia Roach, who had certain rights as a citizen of the United States of America that included her nullified right of the pursuit of happiness. God wasted no miracles on her.

Alberta at least had tried, and the shoppe was her hope. Had been her hope. A little store in an office building, full of trinkets and gadgets that were for sale more cheaply elsewhere; a place where nice women could borrow an umbrella and go to the bathroom and have a cup of tea. Almost a club for nice women, but nice women who had not appreciated it enough to support it. Bertie, thinking these things, progressed easily to intemperate thoughts of George Roach and his club and his failure to come through with the few dollars that would have kept the shoppe going, and his responsibility for what was happening to Alberta's hope and to Alberta. It was not hard to see what was happening to Alberta; before her time she was getting to be like her father. The details were not the same; Alberta had not yet become a laughingstock, a street bore. But when she telephoned the nice women they would not come to the phone or they would not return her call. Everybody—all the nice women—seemed to know that Alberta wanted to talk to them about starting a new shoppe. She had had to mention that project to only one or two of the nice women, and the others were told. The nice women were avoiding Alberta by telephone as the people on the street were looking the other way at the approach of her father. One day Bertie knew that that was so, no longer a truth to shrink from, but a hard, harsh fact to add to the other hard, harsh facts. As long as there was some hope for Alberta there could be some hope for Norman, for Sophronia, and for Bertie herself. It was a small family, and when there were only two children, if one of them turned out half well, the rest of the family could be sustained by that one's small hope. But Bertie had seen what those vigils beside the telephone had done to Alberta. ("Don't anybody use the phone this afternoon. I'm expecting a very important call.") The catalogs continued to come from the jobbers, and as though to add to the taunts the post office demanded its extra pennies for the insufficient postage on free samples of merchandise. ("I saw old Mrs. Reeves today. She told me how much she missed the shoppe—ha ha ha. I'll just bet she does. She used to bring things in to be rewrapped that she'd bought at the dime store.")

"What if we turned the front room into a shoppe?" said Bertie.

"It can't be done," said Alberta. "It's against the zoning laws, for one thing, and Father says it would put us in a different category with the insurance company."

"You spoke to your father? I didn't know that."

"Long ago. That was one of the first things I thought of, was having a shoppe here temporarily. Just to keep the business going."

"I wish you'd spoken to me first. I'd have known what to say to your father."

"It wouldn't have done any good. It would have cost around ten thousand dollars to get started again, and Father was against it. He won't touch his capital, because that's all we'll have to live on when he dies. He never took out life insurance, because he said you got better returns for your money in common stocks."

"Well, I never did know much about those things."

"After the holidays I'm going to start looking for a job. I was thinking of taking a course in shorthand and typing. Sophronia and I could take it together."

"Do you want to do that?"

"No, but for God's sake I have to do something or I'll go stark, staring mad!"

Her intensity frightened Bertie into silence.

"I mean it, Mother, and I'm not going to say I'm sorry, so don't expect me to. I'd rather wash dishes than sit around this house another year."

"You weren't given a college education to learn to wash dishes. But if that's what you want to do."

"It isn't what I want to do. But we'd have been better off if you hadn't given us a college education. It wasn't because we wanted it, but you and Father had a lot of ideas. That we were better than the girls in Gibbsville High and the rest of that baloney. Just because Father didn't have to work for a living. Well, if he hadn't deluded himself that he was a gentleman, he might have made enough money to do something for us. But he isn't a gentleman. He inherited money from his father, a cheap Irish skinflint who slept with his stenographer. Even so, if he'd been more like his father he could afford to live like a gentleman instead of what he is."

"What *is* he?"

"A tiresome old freak that people run away from. Oh, I know. I'm not blind."

"And what am I?"

"I wasn't talking about you," said Alberta.

"You were when you talk about your father that way, your own father. You might just as well call me a tiresome old freak too."

"Don't try my patience too much, Mother."

"Don't you try mine, either," said Bertie. But there was no force to her counter-threat. For thirty years she had ruled her children on the strength of her own belief in parental authority, with the result that in all that time they had not doubted or questioned her right to rule. But now neither she nor Norman could *do* anything for them; there was nothing now to take the place of feeding them, dressing them, binding their small wounds and performing all the other attentions that they needed as children. Bertie, when they were children, could find other children for them to play with, and did so by arrangement with other parents. No longer was that true. Bertie and Norman were of no use to their daughters. They were not even in the way.

Four lives were being lived in the Norman Roach house, four individual lives and not the collective family life that was Bertie's delusion. She did not wish to have any member separated from the family unit, and now that she was confronted with the accomplished fact of their individualities, the fact of her own individuality greatly disturbed her. She had not wanted to be alone, and through the years of her marriage to Norman she had not been alone. Now, however, the separate miseries of the others produced a separate misery for her, and she was unequal to the control of it. Upon discovering the collapse of her family as a unit, she rushed into the discovery that the collapse was also the destruction of the unit and of the individuals. *They* were deserting *her*. The spurious unity in which she had so long believed (and in which she had taken secret pride as the central factor) gave way to hysterical terror, in which every act of every individual was to be interpreted as protest, criticism of her, and, ultimately, persecution of her. The collapse of the unit was unreal because the unit as she understood it had never really existed; but there was nothing unreal about her belief in their persecution of her. It was real *because* she believed it, and could turn any word and any act into proof of it.

Soon—and very soon; it did not take long—the others noticed that Bertie was behaving strangely. She was snappish, she would argue over nothing, she would leave the table and lock herself in her room. Norman, with his massive ignorance of women, concluded that she was having a secondary menopause or had not graduated from an earlier one. As his knowledge of the climacteric consisted entirely of the information she had given him, and as she had refused to discuss it (reticence was her excuse, but her own ignorance was the reason), he had to be satisfied with his explanation of her conduct. One of the few things she had told him about the menopause was that it lasted an indefinite length of time and then it went away; she had not said anything about its coming back, but he convinced himself that she was having a recurrence. The *recurrence* would go away, and until it did he must be patient. The girls, too, must be patient, and he told them so. "Your mother is at a certain time of life," he told them. "I'm sure you know what I have reference to."

"I know what you have reference to," said Alberta. "But I thought that was over. And anyway—"

"I'd much rather we didn't discuss it," said Norman.

"I was going to say, whether it's change of life or not, it still doesn't give her the right to behave like this. She imagines things."

"Just you bear that in mind when you reach that age," said Norman. "Women, women."

"*Men! Men!*" said Sophronia.

"Now there, Sophronia, don't you be disrespectful," said her father. "*I'm* going for a *walk.*"

"Don't get lost, Father," said Sophronia. She grinned at him, half expecting to be slapped (as her mother would have slapped her), but unafraid.

Having more or less agreed that Bertie was a problem, the father and the daughters treated her as such, thereby confirming her suspicions of a union against her—the only unity in the household. She made up a bed in the attic and slept there. The protest she expected from Norman was not forthcoming, since he was doing everything to humor her. But the connotations of a bed in the attic did not escape the notice of Alberta and Sophronia; their mother had often sent them there to punish them when they were naughty, and only a woman who had something the matter with her would choose to sleep in a cold, dark room which had once been inhabited by bats. Every night at bedtime she would take her flashlight and retire, and Norman and the girls would exchange glances but say nothing. They would listen for the last sounds in the plumbing that indicated she was through in the bathroom and was on her way to the attic. The sounds had a relaxing effect on them. Norman could resume his reading of the *Congressional Record;* Alberta her study of the jobbers' catalogs, and Sophronia her endless knitting of scarves for the poor.

"Maybe you better go up and see how she is," said Norman one night at the beginning of Bertie's removal to the attic.

"And have her accuse me of spying on her? *You* go," said Alberta.

"Don't anybody go," said Sophronia. "That's what she wants—to get attention."

"I thought just the opposite, but maybe you're right," said Norman. "You may be right."

"Well, I'm glad I'm right for once, anyway," said Sophronia.

"Don't worry," said Alberta. "If there's anything wrong we'll hear from her."

"I suppose so," said Norman.

Interminable day followed interminable day for each and all of them, and yet they were sustained by a sense of waiting that was common to them all. At a quarter to seven one evening Bertie said, "I'm not going to wait dinner any longer. Sophronia's three quarters of an hour late as it is."

"Did she say anything to you about where she was going?" said Norman.

"She never tells me anything," said Alberta.

"It isn't like her," said Norman.

"It isn't like her to be late for a meal, if that's what you mean."

"And she was supposed to mash the potatoes," said Bertie.

"I'll mash them," said Alberta.

"No, I will. You stay where you are," said Bertie.

Sophronia did not appear all evening, and at eleven o'clock Norman announced that he was going to call the police station.

"I wouldn't if I were you," said Alberta.

"Why not? Is there something you're not telling us? You've been sitting pretty quiet all evening," said Bertie.

"Yes, out with it," said Norman.

"Out with nothing," said Alberta. "I just think it would be a mistake to call the police. She's not some sixteen-year-old juvenile delinquent. What would—"

At that moment Sophronia entered the house.

"Where on earth—" said Bertie.

"We were just about to call the police," said Norman.

"I was going to phone, but I didn't have any money," said Sophronia.

"I'm sure anybody in this town would lend you the price of a—" said Norman.

"Where *were* you?" said Bertie.

"Oh, leave me alone!" said Sophronia. "Can't a person go for a walk?"

"You could have walked to Reading by this time," said Norman. "You've been gone since two o'clock this afternoon."

"And what do you mean you didn't have any money? You had twenty dollars this morning," said Bertie.

"You're not going to get it out of her that way," said Alberta.

"Oh, you shut up, too," said Sophronia. "I'm going to bed."

"Have you had any dinner?" said Bertie.

"Are you still up? I thought you'd be in the attic," said Sophronia. She hurried upstairs and slammed the door of her room. Wherever she had been and whatever she had done, the only clue to her nine-hour absence was the delivery the next day of her purse. Mr. Grossman, the manager of the movie theater, delivered it in person. "It was turned in by the cleaning-woman," said Grossman. "There's seventeen dollars and forty-two cents in it. I guess she must of fell asleep."

"How did you know who it belonged to?" said Bertie.

"Oh, she always sits in the same place," said Grossman. "And I put two and two together. Miss Roach, I said, right away. We don't get that many customers for the matinee. Saturdays we do, but not on a weekday."

"Well, thank you very much. Here, give this to the cleaning-woman," said Bertie. She held out a dollar.

"Oh, that's all right," said Grossman. "Your daughter's a good customer."

"But the cleaning-woman ought to have something."

"Well—I'll make it a dollar if you make it a dollar."

"Isn't a dollar enough?"

"I guess a couple dollars is all right," said Grossman. "It comes to better than ten percent, if you want to look at it that way."

"Then let's give her five dollars."

"You mean you two and a half and me two and a half?" said Grossman.

"Yes," said Bertie. "Here's two-forty-two. I'll go get the other eight cents."

"Skip it, skip it."

"Or why don't we just give her two dollars apiece? Four dollars ought to be enough."

"Yes ma'am. Whatever you say," said Grossman. "Is she all right now, your daughter?"

"Yes. Why?"

"Well, you know she sat through four shows, pretty near."

"Oh, she did?"

"I guess she slept through part of them," said Grossman.

"Four shows. You didn't tell me that."

"Well, I seen her buy a ticket around ha' past two, and I noticed her going out when we broke about ten of eleven. Listen, she's no trouble, ma'am. That other time was water over the bridge, over and done with."

"What other time?"

"When her sister came and got her," said Grossman.

"Oh, then," said Bertie. "Well, thanks, Mr. Gross. I'll see that she gets the purse and I'll explain that I took the two dollars."

"She's all right. She's nothing to some of the characters we get," said Grossman.

Alberta at first refused to enlighten her mother on the occasion of having had to go and get Sophronia.

"Is it that wicked?" said Bertie.

"I don't know whether it was wicked or not. The woman wanted to have her arrested."

"What woman?"

"The mother of the little girl. Don't you know any of this? Sophronia followed a little girl into the ladies' room and the child became frightened."

"At something Sophronia did?" said Bertie.

"I—don't—know. *I* wasn't there. Maybe it was something Sophronia did, and maybe it was just the child's imagination."

"Good heavens," said Bertie. "When was all this?"

"Oh, several years ago. After she lost her job at the Children's Home. She used to come in and hang around the shoppe and I finally told her I'd give her the money to go to the movies, and that's what she did. I couldn't have her annoying my customers. They used to come in and see her there and turn right around and walk out. You don't *know*."

"And she followed the child into the ladies' room and then what?"

"Oh, dear. Well, as near as I could make out, the child must have screamed and the mother ran in, passing Sophronia on the way out. The woman went to the manager, Grossman his name is, and said her child had been molested. For all I know, Sophronia may have been only trying to be nice to the kid, but her looks were against her. On the other hand, that dreadful woman at the Children's Home, Miss Mack, she spread some story around about Sophronia."

"I never heard it," said Bertie.

"How *would* you? You never see any of the trustees. Whether it was true or not, Miss Mack fired her and nobody, least of all Sophronia, made any fuss about it."

"Then what happened, at the picture theater?"

"The manager calmed her down, the mother, and sent for me. He knew me because we were both members of the Merchants Association. He was very nice. I think he was inclined to believe the woman's story, but the woman had nothing to go on but the word of a frightened child, and Grossman is only the manager of the theater. He wants to have a good record so he'll be promoted to someplace else. So he told me as much as he knew, and said he realized we were a prominent family and so forth and so on. In other words, he wanted us on his side. So I told him I'd see to that, all right. The Roaches would stand behind him in case there was any kind of trouble."

"Your father knew about this all along?"

"Father? Can you imagine me telling any of this to Father? It's hard enough to tell you, a woman."

"Sophronia is one of those degenerates," said Bertie.

"Probably."

"My daughter, one of those degenerates," said Bertie.

"Well, now maybe you'll understand why I didn't want her in the shoppe."

"I do," said Bertie. "You didn't have any pity for her."

"Pity! *Pity?* Where were you when I was covering up for her at Wellesley? You never knew till just now what she was like. Tagging along after me all her life. The only good times I was ever allowed to have were my two years at Wellesley before she arrived there. But she made up for those two years, don't think she didn't. My friends had to be her friends, she couldn't make any friends of her own. I couldn't go anywhere or do anything without her horning in. My senior year I didn't have a friend left, thanks to her. They couldn't *stand* her, and neither could I. Even the Lesbians didn't want her around."

"I don't like that word," said Bertie.

"You don't even know what it means," said Alberta.

"There you're wrong," said Bertie. "And if she's one, maybe you are too."

"I have been," said Alberta. "And I think you are. And God knows what Father is. You don't know. I wouldn't expect you to."

"If you say another word, I'll slap you."

"Do, and I'll leave this house," said Alberta. She put her head forward, held up her chin defiantly and irresistibly close to Bertie, and Bertie slapped her. Alberta laughed. "Now I can leave," she said.

She stood up, looked around at the articles of furniture, then left the room. An hour passed, long enough for Bertie to stop wondering what she was doing. At the foot of the stairs Bertie called out, "Alberta, I'm going next door to borrow their vacuum."

"Yes, Mother," she heard Alberta say.

"I have to borrow their vacuum. Ours is being fixed."

"Yes, Mother, I heard you," said Alberta.

When Bertie returned Alberta was gone. Bertie had heard and seen the taxi come and go, but the conversation attendant upon the borrowing of the vacuum cleaner involved the ritual of apology, of explaining the absence of the Roaches' vacuum, of a few words of conversation unrelated to the vacuum, of Bertie's promise to bring the vacuum back that very same day, and the consumption of a piece of home-made fudge that her neighbor pressed upon her. A good twenty minutes was spent in the ritual. Bertie went upstairs to Alberta's room to determine the extent of her packing. It was extensive. The dressing table had been stripped of silver-backed hairbrush and comb and manicure set; the bureau drawers were open and empty; the clothes closet contained only a few old dresses and shoes.

Bertie looked everywhere for a note, but found none. There was nothing to do now but wait. She had neither bus nor train schedule, although she guessed that Alberta would be going southward toward Philadelphia. Northward were Scranton and Wilkes-Barre, of no interest to Alberta. Bertie wanted to be sick, but she did not want Norman to come home and find her being sick. Sophronia was probably at the movies.

Bertie plugged in the vacuum cleaner and started to do the front room. It was better than doing nothing while waiting for Norman to come home.

When he did come home she was doing the diningroom. "Don't stop, it's only me," he called to her. She switched off the vacuum and joined him in the front hall.

"Get ready for a shock," she said. "Alberta's run away."

"Run away? Where to? What do you mean *run* away?"

"Left. Packed her things and left. Where to, I don't know."

"You have some kind of a quarrel or something?"

"She was contemptible and I slapped her."

"Well, maybe she deserved it. She's been acting like an I-don't-know-what lately. Where's Sophronia?"

"Dear knows."

"Didn't go with her, though. Well, we'll hear from Alberta when she runs out of money. Do you happen to know how much she had on her?"

"No."

"Her bank balance doesn't amount to much. I doubt if she has over a hundred dollars there, if that. You given her any lately?"

"No, did you?"

"Not since the first of the month. Her hundred dollars monthly allowance. That wouldn't leave her much. The bank's closed, so she couldn't cash a cheque, although I guess one of the stores would cash one for her."

"It wouldn't be for much, though," said Bertie.

"I'm going on the theory that she'd write a bad cheque," said Norman. "If she was going to run away from home, writing a bad cheque wouldn't faze her. At least I don't think it would. It wouldn't be the first time she was overdrawn, not by a long shot. Going back to her Wellesley days she formed bad habits. More careless than dishonest, but one's just as bad as the other at the bank. We'll hear from her."

"You don't seem very worried," said Bertie.

"What good does it do to worry now? She's not a young girl, she's a full-grown woman, and maybe it was a mistake to slap her for that reason. But I'm not holding that against you. Many's the time I felt like it myself, but I never spanked them when they were little and I couldn't begin now. The other one is just as bad. She never apologized or offered me any explanation for staying out that night. I'm frankly more worried about her than Alberta. God almighty! We've given them every advantage, decent home and a fine education, and the thanks we get. Compare that with the letter I got every year from the man I saved the life of in 1918. In 1918! An ignorant Italian fellow but they're famous for their politeness. Right up to the time he died. 'Dear Lieutenant.' Always lieutenant, never mister."

"Where are you going? Are you getting ready to go out again?"

"I thought I'd go and inquire if they saw her at the bus station. Ivor Jones there would recognize her. You'll be all right, won't you? Or would you rather I stayed?"

"Stay. There's no use letting outsiders know we're worried."

"I guess so. Where do you think she'd head for?"

"She probably didn't know herself."

"What did you quarrel about?"

"Oh, any number of things. We've been getting on each other's nerves."

"In other words you don't care to tell me."

"Not now," said Bertie.

"I could phone Ivor Jones and make up some story and maybe that way find out which bus she took."

"No, let's wait till we hear from her. If anybody asks, we can just say she went away for a few days."

"Yes, if anybody asks. That may be the root of the trouble. Nobody's liable to ask. I guess there are probably some poor people in town that envy us because we have a nice home and plenty to eat. But you can be as rich as Andrew Mellon and still have your troubles. You don't even have to go as far as Andrew Mellon. We have some in town with ten times our money and they're no better off. We all had it too easy, that was our trouble. Except you. In this whole family, you were the only one that really did anything. It isn't natural for a man to spend their lives like George and I. It wasn't natural, not in this country. Over on the other side, Europe, maybe they can get away with it, but not here. Here I am, getting to the age where most men think about getting ready to retire. But I've always lived retired. So has George. The two of us, as different as we can be, but neither of us ever did a tap of work and now there's George'll fall over dead some day in the midst of a game of bridge. Me, I'll fall over talking to somebody like Ivor Jones. That's the way it'll be for me, and that's the way it'll be for George."

"Why are you bringing his name into the conversation? It's the first time I heard you mention him in I don't know how long," said Bertie.

"Why do I mention him? Because I guess there's that connection between him and Alberta. He wouldn't offer to help her out, and now she's in some kind of trouble again."

"Do you know what she is? She's as good as having a nervous breakdown. I know of people that had nervous breakdowns, and they remind me of Alberta, or she reminds me of them."

"Who, for instance?" said Norman.

"Who?"

"Yes. There aren't so many people that have nervous breakdowns. I've seen men go suddenly haywire, but that was fear. Strain. Just before an attack. I saw a man climb up over the parapet and stand up full height. The machine guns practically cut him in half. That was a real nervous breakdown. I don't consider Alberta having a real nervous breakdown. You shouldn't use that expression for a female tantrum. You go move your things up to the attic, but I never considered that a nervous breakdown. That was a tantrum. That was like me going for a walk when I want to get out of the house. If you called it a nervous breakdown every time someone wanted to avoid some unpleasantness, everybody in the world is crazy."

"Maybe everybody is," said Bertie.

Norman smiled. "Well, sure they are, to a certain extent. I am. You are. Alberta. Sophronia. I see plenty of examples of it, of people acting a little crazy. But that wouldn't justify me calling them all crazy. The real nuts are the ones that think they're sane and everybody else is out of their minds. They're the real nuts. I have to admit I sometimes feel that way myself, when I look at the way things are going. They're spending all that money paving the North Side but in five more years there won't be anybody living there. A bond issue for that, mind you. Everybody I talk to agrees with me, but they're all going to vote for the bonds. They say it'll provide employment. Typical Gibbsville thinking, and it's just as bad or worse nationally. The trouble is we have no real leadership. Nobody wants to take any responsibility. They all agree with me, but they go right on electing the same people year after year. If the right people would only get together."

"Yes," said Bertie.

"Instead of spending that money paving the North Side, what they ought to do is cut down on the population. Australia is looking for people, paying people to go there. They have to be British subjects, but they'd take Americans I'm sure. I wrote to the State Department but I never got any answer. I had a scheme to send our unemployed to Australia. Operation Gibbsville, I called it. Give our people the fare to Australia without losing their American citizenship. It'd cost four or five hundred dollars apiece, but that's cheaper than paying them unemployment insurance. I never got any answer, although several people I talked to in town said they'd be willing to go. The people I'd send aren't paying taxes, they're on relief, not doing anyone any good. But if we sent them to Australia they'd be welcome there, and they'd be doing some good for themselves, for Australia, for the United States, and the world in general. I met quite a few Australians in Africa. They're a lot like Americans, once you get to know them."

"Maybe Alberta ought to go to Australia," said Bertie.

"I don't know whether they need women," said Norman. "As I understand it they're looking for married couples. Homesteaders. I wasn't thinking of Alberta when I concocted my scheme, but you remember Jamestown. And the Far West. Once they got started they sent for women. Not that Alberta fits into that category, but she might like Australia. You never know. I'll take it up with her when she calms down."

"Are you going to finance a trip to Australia for her?"

"Well, I don't want to commit myself that far. We don't even know where she is."

"Or if we're ever going to see her again," said Bertie.

"I'm not worried about that. As soon as she runs out of money, that's when we'll hear from her and not before."

"Why are you so sure? I'm not," said Bertie.

"Well, it's what I think," said Norman. "And more than half the time I'm right. I'm right a good deal more than half the time."

As is often the case with a man whose mind is always busy, Norman Roach was more frequently right than wrong. He was right now. The circumstances were not as he had envisioned them—a financially distraught Alberta telephoning from a distant city for the funds to pay her way home. But as he said, when she ran out of money, they heard from her.

Less than forty-eight hours after she left home, she returned, accompanied by Edgar Fleischer, a lawyer and former classmate of Alberta's at Gibbsville High. The doorbell rang at five minutes past six and Norman went to answer it. "Well, come in," he said. "You didn't have to ring. Hello, Edgar." Norman chuckled. "You didn't have to bring your lawyer," he said. "But come on in."

He held the door open for them, and when they were inside he called out to Bertie. "We have visitors."

Bertie came forward from the kitchen. "Alberta!" she exclaimed. "We were so worried."

"Mother, you know Edgar Fleischer," said Alberta.

"Is that who it is? I didn't recognize him in this light," said Bertie.

"She brought her lawyer," said Norman.

"Don't anybody say anything till I get back," said Bertie. "We're having calves' liver and it'll be burned to a crisp. Are you staying for dinner, or what?"

"No, we're not staying," said Alberta.

"I don't see why you had to bring a lawyer," said Norman. "I don't understand that at all."

"He's not my lawyer, he's my husband," said Alberta.

"Your husband? Since when?" said Norman.

"I won't say any more till Mother gets back from the kitchen."

"This once it doesn't matter," said Bertie.

"Calves' liver will smoke up the whole house," said Alberta. "Go on, take it off."

"I won't be but a minute," said Bertie. She hesitated and looked at Edgar Fleischer. "This isn't some kind of joke, is it?"

"No, she's serious," said Norman. "Go tend to the meat and come back. We won't say anything."

Bertie hurried away and was back so soon that Norman and Alberta and Edgar Fleischer were still standing in the front hall.

"All right, I guess we can go in and talk," said Norman. He led the way, pointed to chairs for each of the others, and sat down. "I understood you to say you were married to Edgar. When did this happen? You weren't secretly married to him all the time, were you?"

"No. We were married yesterday, in Shoemakersville," said Alberta. "Edgar has cousins there."

"I thought your mother came from Phoenixville," said Norman.

"No sir. Shoemakersville," said Edgar.

"Why did you have to go down there? You could just as easily got married here in town," said Norman.

"Alberta wanted it that way," said Edgar.

"Let me tell them," said Alberta. "When I left here the day before yesterday I realized I only had a little over thirty-five dollars. That wouldn't get me very far. So I tried to think of who I could borrow from and I remembered Edgar."

"Why Edgar? I don't understand that either," said Norman. "He was never our lawyer."

"No, but he was a friend," said Alberta.

"I didn't know that, either," said Bertie. "Of course we know Edgar, but when did you ever see him since high school?"

"I didn't, except to say hello to on the street. And he always used to wave to me when he passed the shoppe. But we were always friendly."

"Tell her what I said," said Edgar.

"You mean in high school?" said Alberta.

"Yes."

"In high school he said he wanted to marry me and didn't care how long he had to wait."

"Really?" said Bertie. "And he waited all this time? Didn't he ever propose again?"

"I never got much chance to," said Edgar. "We never went out together or anything."

"But you didn't go to his office and say you were ready to marry him, did you?" said Norman.

"No, no, no, no, no. I kept the taxi waiting while I went and asked him if I could have the loan of a hundred dollars."

"Oh, I see. Then before you knew it you were telling him what you wanted it for," said Norman.

"That's just about the way it was, Mr. Roach. That's just about the way," said Edgar Fleischer.

"But it doesn't tell how they got married," said Bertie.

"If you'd use your imagination," said Norman. "One word led to another, and Edgar said he'd always wanted to marry her. I can see how that would happen. Yes, I can understand that."

"But I want to know—" said Bertie.

"I'll tell you," said Alberta. "He suggested that we get married, and I couldn't think of any reason why not. If I knew him well enough to ask him for money, and he still wanted to marry me after all these years. So I said I would, and he went down and paid the taxi and I waited in his office till he got his car out of the garage."

"I phoned Shoemakersville," said Edgar.

"He phoned one of his cousins in Phoenixville. I didn't hear that conversation," said Alberta.

"I have this cousin by marriage, a judge in Common Pleas. He's married to my mother's first cousin, and a very likable man, although I don't see him very often. He said he'd take care of all the necessary preliminaries."

"That was while Alberta was waiting in your office," said Norman. "You'd paid the taxi and brought her luggage upstairs."

"Didn't anybody see you carry the luggage upstairs?" said Bertie.

"They could have without knowing it was Alberta's luggage," said Norman. "Mrs. Roach is wondering how many people know you eloped."

"Nobody in town knows it, so you don't have to worry about that," said Alberta.

"Where did you go from the office?" said Bertie.

Alberta looked at Edgar Fleischer and he looked at her. "We spent the night at a motel, near Reading," said Alberta.

"Oh, well, you were getting married the next day. I suppose you signed the register Mr. and Mrs. Edgar Fleischer."

"No. Mr. and Mrs. Edgar Fisher," said Edgar Fleischer.

"If you drove there in your car they could check your license," said Norman.

"What difference does that make?" said Alberta. "Good heavens, Father."

"Then the next day you went to Shoemakersville and your cousin married you?" said Bertie.

"The Methodist preacher," said Edgar Fleischer. "We were married in his house."

"Did you have any attendants?" said Bertie.

"Edgar's cousin, and the preacher's wife," said Alberta.

"What time of day was it?" said Bertie.

"What time was it, Edgar? I guess about quarter to twelve," said Alberta.

"Yes, we got there about eleven-thirty and we were out by twelve noon. It didn't take long."

"Then where'd you go?" said Bertie.

"To a motel. A different one. We were both exhausted. We stayed there till this afternoon. Then Edgar had to come back to see about things in his office."

"I'm supposed to be in court tomorrow morning," said Edgar Fleischer. "But I think I can easily get a postponement. It isn't anything big."

"Do you want Mrs. Roach and I to make the announcement tomorrow? Where were you thinking of living?"

"You could stay here," said Bertie.

"Edgar has a room at Mrs. Buckley's, but we're going to have to start looking for an apartment."

"You won't have any trouble finding one. Vacancies everywhere. Meanwhile why don't you make this your headquarters?" said Norman.

"No thanks," said Alberta.

"You'll stay for dinner, of course," said Bertie.

"No, we just wanted to tell you. And I wanted to see Father for a minute. Alone."

"All right," said Norman. "We can go back in the diningroom."

They did so, closing the sliding doors. "You want to talk about finances, no doubt," said Norman.

"Yes."

"Well, I guess if you'd had a regular wedding, with a reception, I don't know what that would amount to. But what would *you* say?"

"I don't know."

"Two thousand? Three thousand?"

"I guess so. It'd depend," said Alberta.

"Say three thousand. And I'll continue your allowance."

"That would be very satisfactory, if you did that."

"How much does Edgar make?"

"I didn't ask him. I know he supports his mother. She lives with his sister in Akron, Ohio, but he supports her."

"Maybe I ought to include Edgar in this conversation," said Norman.

"No, don't. Whatever you want to give me is all right. We know we're not going to have much to start with. But his mother is over seventy and probably isn't going to last much longer."

"You'll have some from me, later on. Not much, but some. Your mother will have a trust fund, then you and your sister will divide the principal. Of course no one knows when that will be, but maybe by that time Edgar will be better fixed. I never heard anybody say whether he was good or bad, as a lawyer, that is. I've never known much about him."

"Neither have I. But when I needed somebody I turned to him," said Alberta.

"Are you going to be—all right? I don't mean financially."

"I hope so. I'll try. I'll do my best."

"It isn't easy to talk about such things," said Norman.

"It probably doesn't do any good to talk about them. The two people have to work it out themselves."

"Yes, that's what I meant. They always have to work it out. If you have children, you think about them a lot. That saves you from thinking about yourself and the other person."

"Was Mother horrid to you, Father?"

"Oh, no. No no. Nothing like that. No, we seemed well suited to each other most of the time. They say that opposites attract, but similars attract too. My mother and father were opposites, and my brother and his wife were similars. And your mother and I were similars. Just as long as you don't expect too much, that's the thing to remember. Look at your Uncle George. He expected too much, and when Elsie died he didn't know what to do with himself. But you see I never expected too much. Well, I don't keep that much cash in my checking account, but I'll arrange tomorrow to have the three thousand put in your account. They'll accommodate me at the bank, and you can draw on it any time after tomorrow. I'll write you a cheque now for five hundred, and you can cash that tomorrow. That ought to tide you over. I'd like to give Edgar a wedding present, but I will later. I don't like to give him a post-dated cheque. Creates the wrong impression. You can tell him I'm going to give him a thousand dollars."

"Thank you. I will."

"You know, now that I think of it, Edgar was a D.U. We had a D.U. dinner at the hotel a few years back, and I remember seeing him there. Swarthmore. He was a member of the Swarthmore chapter."

"Yes, he went to Swarthmore."

"Not important. I just happened to think of it. Well, young lady. Now you're a bride. A married woman. Customary to give the bride a kiss, I believe."

"All right," she said. She held up her cheek, and he brushed it with his thin, dry lips.

"Just don't expect too much, daughter. Nothing's the way we plan it," he said. "Where are you and Edgar staying, tonight?"

"We're taking a room at the hotel and then we're going to Atlantic City. Only for a week."

"A week. Well, I guess you'll be in and out of here. Or will you?"

"I'll be in and out to get my things, I guess."

"We ought to give some kind of a party for you," said Norman.

"I'd rather you didn't."

"I was thinking, that way Edgar could meet your friends, and that might be helpful to him professionally."

"They didn't help *me* much," said Alberta. "Edgar knows all those Roach cousins that we never had very much to do with. Those are the kind of people I'll be seeing more of."

"Well, they're good honest people, most of them. One or two bad eggs, but they average out pretty well. Are you going to wait for Sophronia?"

"Speaking of bad eggs?" said Alberta. "No. You can tell her all about it."

"Do you want me to do anything about your Uncle George? On the practical side, you know, he has a lot of money."

"He can read about it in the paper," said Alberta.

"That's what I was wondering. Will he like that?"

"If he wants to give us a wedding present, he will. But I'm not going to call him up and ask him for one. That's what it would amount to."

"I think he'll give you two thousand dollars. Why do I think that? Because that goes back to the time I had my quarrel with him. It would take too long to explain."

"Well, we've been in here long enough. I don't want to leave Edgar alone with Mother. There's no telling what she's liable to say. Or do. Anyway, thank you, Father."

"I wish there was more I could do, but it's too late for that. You're not even going to stay for dinner?"

"No."

"It isn't a bit the way I expected it to be," said Norman, shaking his head.

"Did you think you'd be wearing a cutaway? You said yourself, you're always saying, don't expect too much."

Bertie and Edgar were eagerly grateful for their return to the front room. "Everything all settled?" said Bertie.

"Everything," said Alberta.

"Well, anyway till after they get back from Atlantic," said Norman.

"Oh, you're going to Atlantic? Edgar wouldn't tell me," said Bertie.

"I didn't know whether Alberta wanted people to know," said Edgar.

"Ah, well that's nice," said Bertie. "It shows consideration."

The bride and groom soon departed. "How do you think they'll be?" said Bertie.

"I guess there's no telling this early in the game," said Norman.

"Did you notice he's a little cross-eyed?" said Bertie.

"I wasn't sure whether it was him or the lenses. He wears very thick glasses. They use their eyesight a lot in the legal profession. Fine print."

"No, he has a cast in one eye," said Bertie.

"I never knew what that meant, a cast in the eye," said Norman.

"I wasn't sure which eye to look at, and he gave me the impression of staring at me. What took you so long? Was she worried about money?"

"We took care of that," said Norman. "Did you ever have a long talk with Alberta about married life?"

"No, but girls nowadays get all that information from other sources."

"How did she seem to you?" said Norman.

"About that?"

"Yes," said Norman.

"Well, I guess he isn't very experienced, and they're new to each other. Why? Did she say anything about it to you?"

"Good Lord, no."

"Well, it's up to them," said Bertie.

"I couldn't tell anything. I guess they slept together both nights, but I'll just bet they didn't do anything."

"Well, we didn't either," said Bertie. "But at least you knew what we were supposed to do."

"So does Edgar, you can rely on that."

"But it isn't only knowing what you're supposed to do. Some women never get accustomed to it. He'll have to be very careful with Alberta."

"Good Lord, I thought we could stop worrying about her. You're holding something back from me. What is it?"

"It's only natural to worry about your own daughter. I won't be satisfied till she tells me she's having a child. She never took much interest in young men."

"I see. You're worried about her being frigid. But that's up to him now, and we have to stay out of it. If she has any trouble she can go see a doctor. So can he."

"If they tell him the truth. But there's no use in seeing a doctor if—"

"What the devil are you holding back from me? Out with it."

"Very well. If you insist. Alberta is a man-hater. She told me so herself."

"Rats! So were you till you found out you weren't."

"I thought I was a man-hater, but I was never a woman-lover. That's what Alberta is."

"You don't know what you're saying. She's too feminine to be that. Those kind of women wear a collar and tie, tailored suits. Over in France they even wear pants and men's hats. Why, they actually get all dressed up like men and pick up prostitutes."

"You told me all about that."

"It didn't sink in, or you'd know that Alberta isn't that kind."

"I'm going on what she told me herself."

"She said it to shock you, or else you misunderstood her."

"I misunderstood her, all right. I misunderstood both of them. I misunderstood everybody."

He paused. "I want to tell you about those women, something I didn't tell you before. Then maybe you'll realize what you're saying about Alberta. Those women, over in Paris and I guess other places too. They have a kind of a belt that they strap on, and it has a thing in front like a man's private parts, made of rubber. It's an exact

facsimile of a man's private parts, and they put it in a woman just as
if they were a man and having intercourse."

"How do you know? Did you ever see them?"

"Of course I never saw them, but I heard it described to me more
than once."

"Where would they buy a thing like that?"

"Listen, in Paris and when I was in Africa, they have things you
could never imagine."

"What about the woman-lovers here in town? Do they have them?
Not mentioning any names, but you know."

"How would I know that?"

"I don't think you know as much about such things as you let on
you do."

"Well, maybe I don't want to know," said Norman. "There are
plenty of other things to think about besides that. I want you to get
such ideas out of your head about Alberta, and twisting things she
said."

"She said she was a Lesbian."

"See? There you are. That's just what I mean. If she said she was
an Amazon you wouldn't expect her to go around with a bow and
arrow."

"She didn't *say* she was an Amazon. She said the other."

"Well, do you know what they were? They were a bunch of women
in Greece that wouldn't have anything to do with men, and do you
know why? Because they wanted to stop the men from going to war.
So they told the men that if they didn't stop fighting, they wouldn't
go to bed with them. That's *history.*"

"It may be history, but that's not what Lesbians are."

"Are you going against history?"

"No, I'm not going against history. I'm not against it, and I'm not
for it. But there are certain women in this town that like other
women the same as there are certain men that like men."

"I could tell you what the men do, but I won't. We had them in the
army. They had them in the navy, too. They say they were worse in
the navy. In fact, they had them in prep school."

"Oh, I know what the men do. The women do the same thing."

"How could they? They're built differently."

"Oh, all right. Have it your way. Only you're wrong. I can see that
I know some things that you don't know, especially where women
are concerned."

"I should hope so. Not being a woman, I bow to your superior
knowledge of the subject. Thank God I'm *not* a woman. Thank God
for that."

"Thank God I'm not a man."

"I'll second the motion," said Norman.

"I'll third it," said Bertie.

"Now where is that Sophronia again? Don't tell me she's gone off and eloped too."

"If she only would," said Bertie.

"Not this year, I hope," said Norman. "I'll manage, all right, but Alberta is going to put a dent in my capital. Did you say we were having calves' liver?"

"I may have to throw it away and open a can of something," said Bertie.

"Anything at all. A quiet dinner. We've had enough excitement for one day. When Sophronia gets home, *you* tell her about her sister. I'll prepare the notice for the paper and take it there myself. Walk'll do me good. We don't happen to have a recent photograph of her, do we?"

"No, she never liked to have her picture taken," said Bertie.

"Call me when dinner's ready. I'll be at the desk."

The telephone rang. "That'll probably be Sophronia," said Bertie. "I'll answer it."

Norman stood beside her as she spoke into the telephone. "Yes. Where are you now? . . . You should have called sooner . . . All right." She hung up.

"Short and to the point," said Norman.

"Sophronia. She's having dinner with some friend of hers, she didn't say who or where, and I didn't bother to ask. She'll be home later."

"Then it's just you and me. We can eat in the kitchen. What does she *do* all day?"

"You're a fine one to ask," said Bertie.

The Gunboat and Madge

It had to be a very small town indeed that had no place that stayed open all night, and in this town there were two competing Greek restaurants, two diners at opposite ends of the town, a second-floor-back speakeasy that seldom closed before five A.M., a gambling joint that did not usually get going before midnight, and Jay Fitzpatrick's place, which had been a saloon, a restaurant, a speakeasy, a poolroom, and which at the time of this story retained the character and equipment of all but the poolroom. Ever since Jay Fitzpatrick had been in business there had been, summer and winter, a large vat of bean soup on the kitchen range or on the gas stove. The soup was made of white, marrow-fat beans and a few potatoes and a tomato or two and an onion or two. It was said to be the oldest bean soup in the county. Fitzpatrick, who was a chronic liar anyway, claimed that it was the same soup he had started in 1910. He had never let the vat get empty, he said, and never let the soup get cold. He would add water and beans and potatoes and onions, but it was the same soup. In Spain, he said, they made sherry wine that way. They took a cask of wine and added to it whenever they took some out, but it was the same cask and the same wine. How did he know anything about sherry wine or any other kind of wine? Because he had once jumped ship in Barcelona and lived in Spain two years. He did speak a little Spanish, nobody could deny that. Customers had heard him speak it with vaudeville actors who played split weeks in the theater around the corner. He was a habitual liar, but he always had a little of the truth to back him up. For instance, his soup. His older customers knew that the original vat got a hole in the bottom and had to be replaced, but he said he had never claimed that it was the exact same vat; the soup *was* the same, because he had poured the old soup into the new vat. There had been no interruption in the soup. Any damn fool would know that a copper vat would not last forever, but no son of a bitch could call him a liar on the question of the soup. Ask any woman that baked her own bread. She always left a wad of dough from one batch to another; what they called a starter, to start the next batch with. It was the same with his soup. He always left a half a gallon or so at the bottom of the vat, and built up the soup from that. How did he know about the baking of bread? How did he know about anything? How did anyone know about anything? You found things out as you went along.

The arrival of Jay Fitzpatrick in the town was attended by some publicity, although the publicity was for Gunboat Dawson and not Jay Fitzpatrick. As Gunboat Dawson he had won a few fights against undistinguished Philadelphia middleweights, and he was signed to meet a county boy at a lodge picnic at an amusement park. The town had ordinances prohibiting prizefighting in the borough limits, but what went on at a lodge picnic outside the borough was a matter between the lodge and the township. Every saloon in the county had posters proclaiming the match between Gunboat Dawson, of Philadelphia, and Young Kid Flynn, the promising Collieryville boy, who was said to have killed a mine mule with a blow of his fist. Young Kid Flynn, whose true name was full of c's and z's, had a large following among the Poles and the Irish. The Germans and the Welsh devoutly hoped that Gunboat Dawson, who could have been a Protestant, would slaughter Flynn. Every seat in the dance pavilion was sold days before the fight. The lodge also stood to sell large quantities of beer. On the eve of the fight the whores from Reading and Allentown flocked to town and arranged for the pitching of tents on farm land adjoining the park.

Fitzpatrick-Dawson and his manager, Al Pincus, arrived two days before the picnic. Pincus hired a horse and buggy and took an expert look at the preparations that had been made for the contest. As a result of his findings he went to the lodge officials and informed them that his boy had had an attack of ptomaine poisoning and would be unable to go on. The lodge officials replied that Pincus and his boy would also have a couple of broken legs if Dawson did not go on. Pincus said he would get a lawyer, and the lodge men said that two of the county judges were members of the lodge, if he was thinking of going to court about it. The sparring between Pincus and the lodge men came to a satisfactory conclusion when it was agreed that two friends of Pincus's would not be molested if they set up games of chance. This compromise was reached after the lodge men refused to raise Dawson's guarantee by so much as a nickel. If Pincus and his friends wished to risk getting their throats cut, that was their own lookout, but $600 was what the lodge had guaranteed and $600 was what they were going to pay.

The betting on the fight was in small sums, none higher than ten dollars per bettor. But when Pincus learned that the Protestants had raised a pool of $500 to bet on Dawson, he had one of his Philadelphia friends take it all. His instructions to Dawson were simple. "Stay away from this ox the first three rounds. After that, the first time he lands a good punch, you go down and stay down. That's what they want to see, and that's what you give them."

"What if he lands a good one the first round?"

"Don't let him," said Pincus.

"Yeah, but what if he does?"

"Then it'll be on the square, and it'll look good. But you better keep away from him till after the third. These hicks don't know the first thing about boxing, but you do. At least enough to go three."

"What if I accidentally clobber him?" said Dawson.

"With what?"

"Well, you never know," said Dawson.

"If he hits you on the top of the head with his chin, maybe. Otherwise, we got nothing to worry about. You lose a fight that nobody knows you were ever in. It won't count against you."

"Maybe we could get a return match," said Dawson.

"No. When I get out of this town believe me I'm never coming back," said Pincus.

"You doing something funny? You better let me in on it, Al."

"You got two hundred bucks coming to you, win, lose, or draw. Don't try to be partners with me, please. I got enough troubles. I never welshed on a bet and I never held out on a fighter of mine. That's my reputation. But please don't try to be partners with me. Two hundred dollars is a lot of money for a young fellow used to getting sixteen dollars a month working on boats."

"All the same, if you're doing something funny I ought to know about it."

"Why? You don't have long to go in this business. Inside of two years you'll be weighing a hundred and ninety. A *slow* a hundred and ninety and a *fat* slow a hundred and ninety. You wouldn't last one round with any heavyweight in the business."

"You pick a fine time to tell me I'm through," said Dawson.

"I been meaning to tell you," said Pincus. "For your own good. I'll never get rich off of you, son. So you might as well know now."

"Why couldn't I be partners with you? I thought you took a liking to me. I just as soon give up boxing, as a fighter, but I could make a living managing."

"Not with me. I don't need a partner for that," said Pincus. "You go out there to that picnic and make yourself a quick two hundred simoleans, and don't let that mine-boy knock your block off."

Some groans went up at the beginning of the contest when Gunboat Dawson made the sign of the cross. The German Catholics were not unhappy, but the German Lutherans and the Welsh Methodists and Scotch Presbyterians were chagrined. Those who had not backed their prejudice with their money joined the Irish and the Poles in rooting against the Philadelphia boy. The Gunboat stayed away from the Polish boy during the first round. It was July, and everybody in or out of the ring had got up a sweat, and the spectators seemed to be of the opinion that they were watching a fight. Any activity more strenuous than mopping the brow was exaggerated. "They sure ain't many on my side," said Dawson to Pincus, who was acting as his second.

"Don't worry about that. Just stay in there two more rounds," said Pincus.

Right on schedule, the Polish boy, who was getting angry at being outboxed by the city fellow, threw a roundhouse punch that caught Dawson on the left side of the chin. Dawson remembered not to shake it off or to go into a clinch. It was a case of one idea at a time, and the idea was to go to sleep. Later he admitted that the punch was hard enough to excuse a brief nap; the Polish boy hurt him harder than he had expected. Dawson's knees bent, and he slowly collapsed. The spectators got to their feet and joined the referee in counting to ten. Pincus climbed in the ring and knelt beside his boy. For the moment he kept the smelling salts in his pocket, letting Dawson act out the knockout and give the customers their money's worth. But when The Gunboat rolled over on one side and appeared to be composing himself for slumber, Pincus decided he was overdoing it. He put the smelling salts to the boy's nostrils and in a loud voice said, "Come out of it, son! It's all over!" The Gunboat opened his eyes, and Pincus looked up at the referee and some other men and said, "He had me worried. Are any of you gentlemen a doctor?"

"I am," said a man in a pongee suit. "You won't have to send for the priest." The man left the group, and now Young Kid Flynn, still wearing his gloves, squatted down and lifted The Gunboat to his feet and assisted him to the stool in The Gunboat's corner.

"You don't know your own stren'th," said The Gunboat.

"Yeah, my old woman says I don't know me own stren'th," said Young Kid Flynn. "You feelin' any better?"

"Oh, I'll be all right," said Fitzpatrick-Dawson, rubbing his jaw.

"That ain't the side I hit you," said Young Kid Flynn.

"Maybe I'm hurt worse than I thought. It feels bad on both sides."

The two fighters were momentarily alone, while their managers were engaged in private conversation.

"Get your clothes on," said Young Kid Flynn. "Then we go have some fun, me and you."

"What do you call fun?" said Fitzpatrick-Dawson.

"The hoors. They got a bunch of hoors up the hill there. You see them tents? Me and you go up and have some fun."

"I gotta get a train back to Philly tonight," said Fitzpatrick-Dawson.

"We got plenty of time," said Young Kid Flynn.

"Wait'll I tell my manager. Hey, Al."

"What?"

"Him and I want to have some fun with the hoors," said Fitzpatrick-Dawson. "You want to come along?"

"We don't want him. Just me and you," said Flynn.

"I gotta talk to this fellow here," said Pincus. "You go have your fun."

"What time is our train back to Philly?"

"Nine-something, but you don't have to worry about it. Have some fun. You're entitled," said Pincus. "Go get your clothes on and I'll bring you your money."

"We don't need no money," said Flynn. He held up his gloved right hand, rotating the fist.

"I do," said Fitzpatrick. "I only got about nine dollars."

"We'll take some off of the pimps," said Flynn.

"Oh, now wait a minute, Paul," said Flynn's manager. "None of that again. I don't want no more trouble with the police." He turned to Pincus. "This boy can't stand a pimp. They run when they see him coming."

"You bet they do," said Flynn. "Come on, Dawson."

The fighters put on their street clothes and together they ascended to the tents. Early the next morning they awoke in separate tents, very sick from Mickey Finns and covered with mosquito bites. They put on their clothes and hitched a ride back to town with a farmer who was on his way to get a load of manure.

"They took every God damn cent I had," said Fitzpatrick. "I don't have a nickel for a cup of coffee."

"Wrong," said Flynn. "Pincus gave me this to keep for you." He handed Fitzpatrick an unsealed envelope containing twenty ten-dollar bills.

"Say, you're the first honest man I ever met," said Fitzpatrick. "Why did he give it to you, I wonder."

"He says to me I looked honest."

"But why didn't the hoors and the pimps take it off of you?"

"The lodge. The lodge is all over, everywhere. Philly. Allentown. Chicago. Don't get in trouble with the lodge. They're bigger than the cops."

"Do you belong to the lodge?"

"Not me, but I got friends in it. I can't join it because I'm a foreigner, but I got a lot of friends in it. It's all over. Allentown. Reading, Cleveland, Ohio, Buffalo, New York. All over."

"It looks like it's all over for me, too," said Fitzpatrick. "Pincus giving you the money to hold for me, that was the same as goodbye from Pincus."

"Because I knocked you out?" said Flynn.

Fitzpatrick looked at him and there were things he wanted to say, but he did not say them. It was more than likely that the Polish boy could beat him in a fight that was not fixed; in the present condition of his bowels, mangled as they were from the Mickey Finn, Fitzpatrick did not have enough fight in him to take on anybody. "He told me yesterday I ought to quit the ring," said Fitzpatrick. "He said to me why didn't I hang up the gloves and be a manager."

"I wouldn't want to manage. I don't see no fun in that," said Flynn.

"No," said Fitzpatrick. "Do we have far to go? How long before we get to town?"

"Through them trees you can see town. Through there you can see the Court House. That's the building with the clock. It says ten after seven. Why?"

"I'm a sick man, that's why. I want to go to the crapper and stay there all day."

"I'll stay there with you," said Flynn. "We'll go to John Bressler's. He'll be open now. Hey, mister, do you go near Bressler's saloon?"

"Near," said the farmer.

"We'll get off there," said Flynn.

"This wagon don't have any springs to it," said Fitzpatrick. "Shakes the hell out of you. But I guess it's better than walking. You know, I seen an old guy die from a Mickey."

"What's a Mickey?"

"A Mickey? A Mickey is what they put in our drinks. They invented it to give it to constipated cows, and that's what they gave you and me. You don't have to be old to die from it, either. You know what appendicitis is?"

"Sure. They have to operate on you for that," said Flynn. "My sister had it."

"Yeah, but if you got it and they gave you a Mickey before they operate on you, the appendicitis bursts open inside your gut and all the pus goes all over."

"I guess that's right," said Flynn.

"I know it's right. I seen a guy die of it. A young guy. You should of seen him, all doubled up with the pain. The cops thought he was faking. We were in the cooler, in Baltimore, Maryland. We were all pinched in a raid, and somebody give this young guy a Mickey and it hit him when we were in the wagon, on the way to the cooler."

"Stop talking about it. I don't feel so good," said Flynn.

"Your imagination's getting the better of you," said Fitzpatrick.

"Just stop talking about it."

"O.K."

The farmer stopped the wagon at a livery stable and the two fighters made their way to Bresslers' saloon. Young Kid Flynn got a boisterous greeting from the bartender, but he hurried to the toilet. The fighters spent most of the morning in Bressler's back room and Bressler kept his customers away from them. Late in the afternoon their internal organs got better; they could hold on to a little hot tea. Flynn's manager, who said he had been looking all over for him, dropped in at Bressler's for a beer.

"This ought to learn you to stay away from the hoors," said the manager, whose name was Charley O'Donnell.

"It wasn't the hoors, it was the pimps," said Flynn.

"Where there's hoors, there's always pimps," said Charley.

"Like where there's fighters, there's managers," said Fitzpatrick.

"I consider the source of that remark," said Charley.

"You'll consider the source of a good puck in the teeth," said Fitzpatrick.

"What are you picking on Charley for?" said Flynn. "He ain't done nothing to you."

"He's a manager. That's enough for me," said Fitzpatrick. "Him and Pincus should of stuck with us."

"I'm no nursemaid," said Charley. "Now listen, Paul, I got good news for you. I got the best news so far. I think I got you a fight in Philly."

"He means Pincus got you a fight in Philly."

"That's exactly right, smart guy," said Charley. "Me and Pincus partnered up, Paul. Pincus will put you on the card two weeks from Friday, in Philly. You fight a boy named Young Sam Langdon."

"I licked him in four rounds, two years ago," said Fitzpatrick. "He only got one eye."

"Then maybe we'll match you with a guy from Atlantic City that I forget his name."

"I'll tell you his name. It's Battling George Moran. I licked him in three. I can tell you all the names of who Pincus'll match you with. I tell you something else, Paul. You got two managers and maybe you'll get twice as many fights, but you won't be making twice as much money. The same money, Paul—for you. More money for them, but the same for you."

"Don't listen to this guy," said Charley. "He's through."

"I'm through, Paul. But two managers'll have you through quicker than I was."

"I gotta have fights," said Flynn. "I got a wife and two kids, and I ain't going back in the mines. I just as soon fight. I fight anyway, every payday, working in the mines. Only I don't get paid for it."

"That's the way to talk, Paul," said Charley.

"You'll take my advice and—"

"I don't want no advice. Get me a fight every two weeks, that I get paid for. Easy money. And fun. There's only one thing is more fun than fightin'. But I never got paid for that."

"No, and you gotta save your stren'th these next couple of weeks," said Charley.

"You hear that, Paul? Him and Pincus, they're all alike. He wants you to stay away from women so you'll get a nasty disposition and fight better."

"Huh. He don't know my wife," said Flynn.

"I know your wife," said Charley. "It's the hoors I want you to stay away from."

"She's as much of a hoor as any hoor, that woman. They all are, they're all the same."

"Your mother wasn't a hoor," said Charley.

"She wasn't? I could tell you some stories about her," said Flynn. "I don't care who they are, they're all hoors. That ain't saying I want to get rid of them. But I ain't fooled by them. Hoors, hoors, hoors."

"You're feeling better," said Fitzpatrick.

"Go home to your wife," said Charley.

"How much I got coming to me?" said Flynn.

"About a hundred dollars," said Charley.

"That's only half," said Flynn.

"You owed me for expenses," said Charley. "I got it all down in black and white."

"Gimme fifty and give her the other fifty. If I go home she'll take the hundred off of me. You take her fifty and tell her I'll be home tomorrow," said Flynn.

"What are you going to do?"

"Me and this fellow, we go to Jelly Bean's."

"You stay away from Jelly Bean's. You get in trouble there and they'll cut you up with a razor," said Charley.

"You coming with me, Gunboat?" said Flynn.

"Not now I ain't. I want to take a bath and get some sleep. I'm too shaky."

"Aah, the hell with you. The hell with all of you," said Flynn. "Gimme my money."

Charley counted out fifty dollars and gave it to him. The Polish boy took the money and went to the bar, had a couple of drinks of whiskey, and was driven in a carriage to the place known as Jelly Bean's on Mission Street. It was still daylight, and a lot of people in the streets saw the triumphant Young Kid Flynn in the railroad station hack on his way to Jelly Bean's. It was the last they saw of him alive. Sometime before midnight he died, not from a razor but from the bullets from a Colt .32 automatic, which was the stylish weapon among the Mission Street people who could afford it. The man who killed him was Jelly Bean, the fat and solemn Negro who was king of Mission Street. Accompanied by his white lawyer and five witnesses, he gave himself up at the local police station before the police knew anything had happened. The lawyer produced one witness, a woman in her late twenties, who had a broken jaw; and he called the attention of the chief of police to a cut over Jelly Bean's left eye. There were not many Poles in the town, but it was decided to put Jelly Bean in the county jail that night, just to be on the safe side.

Those were the circumstances of Jay Fitzpatrick's arrival in the town. His business career was less dramatic. He went to work for Bressler as bartender, short-order cook, and bouncer. He managed to steal enough money inconspicuously to become the nattiest dresser in that part of town. His personal profit out of a quart bottle of whiskey, sold by the drink, ranged between forty-five and sixty cents a bottle. It was a simple matter of watering the contents of the bottles from which he served the second—never the first—drinks. As there were no complaints from the customers, whose first drinks were full strength, Bressler was unable to verify his suspicions that Jay Fitzpatrick was doctoring the booze. He tried to trap Jay Fitzpatrick in the act of knocking down the till, but Jay was too wise to steal actual cash that Bressler counted twice a day. Bressler did not like Jay, had been afraid of him from the beginning. He had hired Jay out of fear. A couple of days after Jelly Bean shot Young Kid Flynn, with the town still buzzing about the story, Jay said he wanted to have a talk with Bressler. "It's this way," said Jay. "I'm kind of running short of coin, hanging around this town."

"What are you hanging around for?" said Bressler. "You're from the city. Why don't you go back?"

"It's cheaper here," said Jay. "I was thinking, what if you was to give me a job? I can tend bar, cook, and I know how to handle tough guys. I don't have to use a gun, like Jelly Bean. The trouble with a gun, any time a saloonkeeper has to use a gun he has to go out of business. If a tough guy started trouble in your place, maybe you have a gun and you could shoot him. But the cops would close you down. I hear there's talk of taking away a lot of saloon licenses. The law and order people are up in arms." There was truth in what he said; the Anti-Saloon Leaguers were using the Flynn shooting to their advantage.

"I don't need another man. I got a day man and a night man, and the cooking I can do myself," said Bressler.

"What if I was to get drunk here, tonight? Could your night man handle me? No. Maybe you could send for the cops, but it'd get in the papers, and you'd stand a good chance to lose your license."

"I get the drift," said Bressler. "If I don't hire you you *will* cause trouble."

"You get the drift," said Jay.

"I'll have to let one of the men go," said Bressler.

"Well, they're both probably stealing from you. Fire the one that steals the most."

"Cassidy," said Bressler. "He don't steal more than Green, but he drinks up some of the profits."

"When do I start? I'm ready to start tonight. And don't you worry about Cassidy. I'll give him the bum's rush if he argues."

Fear of Fitzpatrick continued to influence Bressler. On the other hand, Fitzpatrick livened things up among the customers. He was a good storyteller, a collector of dirty jokes, an entertainer who had been to Europe, Africa, and South America. He was a scrapper, and he made bean soup the like of which Bressler had never tasted. In fact, Bressler forgave him a lot for that bean soup. Bressler would sit in the back room, putting away platefuls of soup while out front Jay Fitzpatrick was making himself congenial with the customers, so completely taking charge that the customers assumed that Jay was Bressler's partner. Bressler did not mind. He was well up in his fifties, and if Jay had any idea of buying him out, all he had to do was make a good offer. Jay could go to one of the breweries and get help in financing the takeover, and with a little money from the saloon and a small political job, Bressler would be comfortable for life. It was such a logical, mutually profitable proposition that Bressler was incredulous when Jay turned it down.

"What's in it for me?" said Jay. "I never saved any money on what you paid me. I don't have over five hundred dollars in the bank to show for the time I worked for you. They say this Prohibition is coming in and they'll close down the breweries."

"The country'll never stand for it," said Bressler. "The working-man has a right to his glass of beer."

"Herman, you're just like all the rest of the Dutch. You are as thick-headed as any of them. One state after another is voting for Prohibition, and you dumb bastards keep on saying they'll never take away the workingman's glass of beer. A year or two ago you were saying this country'd never go to war against Germany. No, I don't want to buy your saloon. I wouldn't take it for a gift. Pretty soon I wouldn't take a brewery for a gift."

"Well, I ain't offering it to you for a gift," said Bressler. "When the boys get home from the army, you'll see about this Pro'bition."

"Yeah? Well, if I'm wrong maybe I'll open up a place of my own, but I ain't going partners with you."

The shock of Prohibition—and obesity, nephritis, cancer of the prostate, and heart disease—was too much for Bressler. He died in February 1920, and his widow was advised by her lawyer to sell the good will and fixtures for $1,000 cash. The buyer was Jay Fitzpatrick, and the only fly in the ointment was the fact that he had to pay rent to the Greek brothers who owned the hotel and restaurant on the corner and the adjoining buildings. In one of those buildings was Bressler's saloon, now Jay's. It was a hell of a note that he had to pay rent to a couple of foreigners, but they had the coin. Everybody talked about the Jews having all the money, but that was because there were more Jews than Greeks, and more people had to deal with the Jews in different lines of business. Like for instance there was any number of clothing stores and shoe stores and jewelry stores owned by the Jews, and ordinary people got to know about them. People saw them every day; they lived in town, had their own syna-gogue, had kids in school. What ordinary people did not know about the Greeks was that they all belonged to some kind of a Greek organization, exactly like a Chinese tong. Jay Fitzpatrick, who was born and grew up in Newark, New Jersey, was full of information about the Hip Sings and the On Leongs. Ignorant people did not know about the Chinese tongs, which were first of all *business* orga-nizations. The only time the tongs ever got in the papers was when they began hacking each other up and shooting each other; but the rest of the time they were just like the God damn chamber of com-merce. It was the same with the Greeks. The Speer brothers, Jay's landlords, got all the financial help they needed from their organization, and if anybody wanted to know where the headquarters of the organization was, it was in Boston, Massachusetts. Boston, Massachusetts. How many people in town knew that? Not many; but Jay knew it because you kept your eyes and ears open, you found things out as you went along. These foreigners came over here with no money but they saved every penny. (The Chinese, for instance, ate rice and rats.) But they helped one another, they had an organization. They paid dues, no matter how little, two bits a week. But two bits a week was a dollar a month, and if you had a thousand Greeks in Brooklyn, that was a thousand dollars a month in the treasury, twelve thousand in a year. An organization that had a sure income of $12,000 a year could go to any bank and buy a building, a theater, a peanut stand, and by keeping expenses down show a profit. All because the foreigners knew how to stick together and were willing to pay two bits a week dues.

Jay was now thirty-six years of age, not old by any means, and in pretty good shape. On the other hand he had to take into consideration the fact that in four years he would be forty, and if you did not start having some coin stashed away by the time you were forty, you were not going to get many more chances. He was doing all right day-to-day, month-to-month. Contrary to his predictions, the breweries did not go out of business. In order to make that slop they called near-beer they had to make good beer first and then reduce the alcoholic content; and when the right arrangements were made with the federal agents, the breweries delivered beer that was just as good as it had ever been, or almost. Sometimes the heat was on and the breweries had to deliver slop, in which case the individual saloonkeeper had to do his own doctoring of the slop by spiking it with ether. But there was still money in beer, and even better money in booze. Consequently Jay was able to maintain the standard of living to which he had accustomed himself. Five suits of clothes, silk shirts, twelve-dollar shoes, three-dollar neckties, ten-dollar fedoras. He bought himself a second-hand Kissel-Kar painted yellow, and he had a girl friend. Madge Shevlin was herself a business woman, half owner of the LaFrance Beauty Salon, and she and her partner were coining money with permanent waves at five dollars per curl. She did not need Jay to support her; but he took her to the professional football games and the amusement parks when the name bands played, and he was her escort when she attended the conventions of beauty experts. She and Jay were mutually complimentary on their taste in clothes, and they enjoyed the admiration of the people in hotel lobbies and ball parks who could not fail to notice such a striking couple. Jay's diamond ring was a present from Madge, and she gave him a manicure at least once a week. The question of marriage was avoided after one frank discussion in which Madge revealed herself to be deeply concerned with the future. "I wouldn't mind marrying you, dearie," she said. "But you're not putting anything away for a rainy day. This Prohibition, they got all these laws that they could put you in jail and padlock your place. Then when you got out I'd have to support you. It'd be different if I didn't have my mother near seventy and it looks like she'll be good for another ten years. The Muldoons are all long livers. And even if I didn't have Mom, I'm thinking of opening up branches in Swedish Haven and Taqua."

"Yeah, and I guess it would look kind of funny if I was kind of your manager," said Jay.

"If you *what?*"

"Well, if you started opening up branches all over the county—"

"Oh, you better get *that* idea out of your head," said Madge. "You mean *you* to *manage* the LaFrance? I'd be out of business inside of two years. You don't think past the week after next. I been planning on these branches since the second year I was in business. But first I have to buy out the partner I have now. If you had some capital I could buy her out and you and I could start up. I'd marry you then, if you put some capital in the business. But don't ask me to have you for a manager or a business partner, dearie. Except silent. If you could raise twenty thousand dollars cash, I guarantee you we'd have a business to support us in our old age."

"What if I sold my business and put the money in yours?"

"No good," she said. "You gotta have a business of your own, or at least a job. I wouldn't want you hanging around the business I built up."

"Why? Are you ashamed of me? I never knew that before," he said.

"Not ashamed of you. Don't I go everywhere with you? Including to bed. But a saloon and a salon are two different things. You stick to your saloon and I'll stick to my salon. Don't take it to heart, dearie."

It was not a rebuff that he took to heart; the proposal of marriage had been a courtesy that he extended to her because he thought it was time she was expecting it. Somewhere in Essex County, New Jersey, he had a son or daughter who would now be about eighteen, by the Italian girl he had married and deserted before the kid was born. He had never gone to the trouble of finding out whether he was divorced. He had shipped out as deckhand on a banana boat, and thereafter he followed two rules: never again work on a banana boat and never work on any boat that had for its destination one of the New Jersey ports. He did not want to arrive in Hoboken or Jersey City and find the law waiting for him. Almost as bad as the prospect of prison was the thought of having to live with Rosie. He was ashamed of himself for having had relations with such an ugly, fat little thing when all the other guys were having a good time with the pretty girls; and he never quite forgot Rosie's two brothers, one on each side of him, taking him to the priest's house for the marriage ceremony. The brothers did not even offer him a glass of wine after the wedding. They left him with Rosie and the priest, and as soon as Jay saw them turn the corner he gave Rosie a clout on the chin and left her with the priest. Two days later he was on his way to Guatemala, and at the time he did not even know where Guatemala was.

He became adroit at avoiding the topic of marriage, and in almost twenty years he was equally successful in avoiding the topic and the condition. But Madge had something about her that made the prospect of a full-time, permanent, legal union seem attractive. No matter how rowdy and dirty-talking she got when they were alone in a bedroom and she had had a few drinks in her, when she put her corset on and was dressed for the street she became an altogether different person. Lawyers and bankers tipped their hats to her, and not only because she knew a thing or two about some lawyers and bankers. She had taken bookkeeping, shorthand, and typewriting from the nuns, and for the first ten years out of school she had worked as stenographer in the office of a planing mill. Her boss, the owner, seduced her in her early twenties. Since there was not the remotest possibility that he would ever marry her, she gave herself a raise in pay and he gave the raise his approval. She remained his mistress until he had a stroke and had to let his son take charge of the mill. The son was a namby-pamby college graduate whose first official act was to call Madge into his office and inform her that she was through at the end of the week. "Don't I get two weeks' notice?" said Madge, and then she saw that on his desk were several bookkeeping ledgers. He smiled at her and pointedly looked down at the books and up again at her.

"The end of the week, Miss Shevlin," he said. "I took accounting in college. You were pretty crude."

"What about a reference?" she said.

"As what?" said Junior. "No, you'll never get a reference from me. Half the money you've been stealing here belonged to my mother."

"How do you expect me to get another job?"

"I don't expect you to, if it means handling money. If you're going to handle old men, maybe my father would give you a reference.

Only he can't hold a pen in his hand. You're getting off easy. You can tell your friends you're quitting, and if anybody asks me if you quit, I'll say you did. But that's as far as I'll go. You got away with over twelve thousand dollars, at least."

"Why don't you have me arrested?"

"If it was up to me, you'd have been on your way to jail a week ago. I'm not protecting you on account of my father. It's on account of my mother."

"A hell of a lot of use she was to your father these past five years."

"He always went home to her, Miss Shevlin. And he's with her now. Let me tell you something else. If any of this reaches my mother, I'll take these books to the district attorney. The statute of limitations won't save you. As recently as a month ago you put through a cheque for three hundred dollars payable to the J. J. Smith Lumber Company. But *you're* the J. J. Smith Lumber Company."

"Your father signed that cheque."

"Would a handwriting expert agree with you? How about all those cheques to the McDonald Machinery Company? Never very big, but a lot of them. A lot of specimens for a handwriting expert to examine. You endorsed the cheques, filed them, and then drew cheques made out to cash for the same amount, which you cashed yourself. That way we were never overdrawn at the bank, because the bank never saw the cheques to McDonald and J. J. Smith. But all the same it was pretty crude, Miss Shevlin. It was bound to catch up with you."

"Well, we're not all as clever as you are," said Madge. "Do I have to stay till the end of the week?"

"By no means," said Junior. "I've already hired a new girl, starting tomorrow. And I certainly don't want her to learn the office routine from you."

"Well, I'll bet she doesn't learn as much from you as I did from your old man," said Madge.

She had about four thousand dollars in a savings account, but she had a lazy mother and no job. It was an occasion for clear thinking. Obviously if she applied for the kind of job she had had at the mill, she not only would not get the job but the story of her dishonesty would be all over town. There were certain men in town who had given her little presents in the past, but the presents had never amounted to much and it was one thing to have a date with a man in Philadelphia and come home a few dollars richer, and quite another thing to try to make a living that way. Prostitution was abhorrent to her, and blackmail was liable to be both temporary and dangerous.

In the midst of these reflections she came upon an ad in one of the Philadelphia papers. It offered instruction in hairdressing, manicuring, and how to run a beauty salon. The course was intensive, lasted six weeks, and cost $500. She went to Philadelphia, enrolled, and took a room in a boarding-house. She had always been fastidious about her appearance, and she learned so quickly that the woman who operated the school offered her a job as instructress. Philadelphia was exciting, but she went home where the competition would be almost nonexistent. At home there was only one beauty salon, and it catered to the swells; there was no place that was not condescending to the women like Madge herself, who were willing to spend money to look nice but got good and sore when their appointments were changed or canceled because some Mrs. Gotrocks wanted a permanent at the same time. Madge Shevlin's LaFrance Beauty Salon was an instantaneous success, and Madge began coining money. She catered to the wives of the Rotary Club and Kiwanis, and before a Purim Ball or a Knights of Columbus Annual she would have to begin her appointments at seven-thirty in the morning to accommodate her patrons. She got great satisfaction out of turning down the swells who thought they could get last-minute appointments before a country club dance. "Why don't you try Mrs. Dunbar?" she would say, knowing that the swells had tried Mrs. Dunbar first.

Her first and only male customer was Jay Fitzpatrick, who came in one day for a manicure. "We don't take gentlemen customers," she said. "They have a manicurist down at the hotel barber shop."

"Yeah, but I don't go to the hotel barber shop," said Jay. "You have to be a judge to get a haircut there."

"May I see your nails?" said Madge.

He extended his hands, palms down.

"Did you ever have a manicure before?"

"No, can't you tell?"

"Why do you want one now?" said Madge.

"I don't know. I just got thinking. I spend money on clothes, I get a facial every day, but the dukes look like I just come out of the mines. And I never even been in the mines."

"Oh, I know who you are," said Madge. "I often saw you on the street."

"Well, wuddia say?"

"To tell you the truth, I never worked on a man's hands. But if you come in tomorrow morning around ten o'clock—no. Come in this afternoon, after ha' past five. That's when we close."

"You don't want the customers seeing me in your place," he said.

"Well, can you blame me?"

"Jesus Christ, you're no soft-soaper, are you? All right I'll be here a quarter of six."

When he arrived for his appointment and put his hands on the table she burst out laughing. "What's so God damn funny?" he said.

"I don't know where to start," she said. "I never saw such ugly hands in my whole life."

"I used to be in the ring. Some of them fingers I can't straighten out and some of them I can't bend. But I'll tell you this, Miss La-France Shevlin, I know what to do with them, in or out of the ring."

"Don't get fresh," she said.

"Who's getting fresh?"

"You're getting ready to."

"Give it a chance. Maybe you'll like it," he said. "Or aren't you that kind of a girl—and who do you think you're kidding? I'll buy you a steak. Wuddia say? You ever been to the Stage Coach?"

"Listen, I've been to Kugler's, the Arcadia, the Bellevue-Stratford, the L'Aiglon."

"Yeah, but were you ever to the Stage Coach? Them joints in Philly, that's a hundred miles away. I never saw anybody take you to the Stage Coach, closer to home."

"What are you inferring?"

"What am I inferring, you with the big words? I'm inferring that the guys you go out with don't take you any place around here."

"Did you come here to get a manicure or act insulting?"

"I come here to get a manicure and buy you a steak at the Stage Coach. I got my car outside and a bankroll in my pocket. You saw me on the street? *I* saw *you* on the street, and I said to myself, there's a handsome-looking woman going to waste."

"You don't see me worrying about that," she said.

"What's the matter? Is this your night for Sodality?"

"Sodality is Tuesday night," she said.

"She remembers!" he said.

"Listen, big boy, you're here to get a manicure, not a date."

"Sure. I'll pay you for the manicure, and the steak I'll throw in free. A nice big juicy two-inch steak? Don't that make your mouth water? With mushrooms, and a big baked potato with paprika on it? They don't serve a steak like that anywhere in town."

"I do, at home. Whenever I feel like it," she said.

"All right, then we'll go to your house," said Jay. "Who have you got living with you?"

"My five brothers and two sisters," she said.

"*That* I know *better*," said Jay.

"Then why did you ask?"

"I wanted to see what you'd say," said Jay.

She picked up his left hand and examined it professionally. "I saw prettier hands on a carpenter," she said.

"That's what I'm here for, to get my hands as pretty as a carpenter. Then I get them as pretty as a banker, then as pretty as a piano player."

"Not a chance," she said. "All I can do is improve the appearance of the nails."

"All right, go ahead and do that. And think about a nice juicy steak, smothered with onions."

"I thought you said mushrooms," she said. "If it's a real good steak you don't need anything on it."

"Now you're talking!" he said. "And blood-rare, is that how you like it?"

"The only way to eat a good steak," she said.

"A woman after my own heart," he said.

They went to the Stage Coach and the proprietor said he had just the steak for people who would appreciate it. He recommended a mixed-green salad to go with it. No potatoes. No nothing. Nothing but the steak for people who would appreciate it. Madge and Jay ate in silence except for occasional murmurs of appreciation of the meat. "What do you want for dessert?" said Jay.

"I couldn't eat any," said Madge. "I'm full up to here." She put her hands on her chest. He grinned and was about to say something. "No cracks," she said.

"I was only gonna say I like to see a woman that's not afraid to eat."

"Oh, sure," she said. "But I do have to hand it to you. I never ate a better steak in my whole life."

"This is where we'll go any time you feel like a steak. You want seafood, I know a place in Reading where they give you a shore dinner as good as Hackney's. You ever been to Hackney's, on the Boardwalk?"

"If you're trying to get it out of me did I ever go to Atlantic—yes. And I stayed at the Traymore. And if you want to know who with, that's for me to know and you to find out."

"Yeah, but from now on it'll be with me," he said.

"Pretty darn sure of yourself, aren't you?"

"I don't go for a person unless they go for me too," he said. "We don't have to kid around, me and you. Have a B-and-B."

"All right. I'm not much of a drinker, but a B-and-B would go good. I thought they had an orchestra here."

"Friday, Saturday and Sunday. You feel like dancing?"

"Oh, I don't miss it," she said. "But I notice they have a dance floor."

"Friday, Saturday and Sunday they have an orchestra, and entertainment. But not during the week. During the week it's pretty quiet, but Saturday they come from all over."

"I heard they have rooms," she said.

"If they know you they'll let you have a room," he said. "You want to have a look at the rooms?"

"Not this time," she said.

"No time like the present," he said.

"You know, you're the first fellow I went out with in over three months," she said.

"Then we ought to go and have a look at the rooms," he said.

"Wait till I have my B-and-B," she said.

"As far as that goes, you could have your B-and-B in the room."

"Don't rush me, big boy," she said.

The Stage Coach became their favorite place, and as it was the favorite place of other couples who could not meet at home, Jay and Madge became members of a set that consisted of free-spending, hearty-eating, heavy-drinking patrons of the Stage Coach and of sporting events and charity balls given by fraternal organizations. The women among them were all customers of the LaFrance Beauty Salon; the men patronized saloons and speakeasies that were frequented by men who shaved every day, and most of Jay's customers did not shave every day. The source of his spending money, however, was at least as legitimate as that of other members of the Stage Coach set. The only trouble about his money was that he had less of it than the bootleggers, the gamblers, and the contractors who shared income with the politicians. He tried to move in with the bootleggers and the gamblers, and they politely brushed him off; the contractors would have no part of him. The politicians liked his bean soup, and they would come to his joint at four o'clock in the morning after committee meetings, but they gave him no opportunity to present his case as a prospective committeeman.

He spent all he made, and he did not object when Madge would slip him a couple of twenty-dollar bills as her share of an evening's expenses. Although she would not marry him, they were getting to be more and more like a married couple in many ways. She gave up her little trips with other men, and he stopped fooling around with other broads. He rented a couple of rooms over a printer's shop in the alley back of his saloon, and by the time Madge got it all fixed up for him it was as nice as any apartment in town. She never went there in the daylight hours, but they gave parties there and their friends all knew about the apartment. "I ought to pay half the rent," said Madge.

"No."

"I want to," she said. "I want to make sure you don't take some other woman there."

"Aw, cut it out," he said.

"Seriously, I want to have a say in who you lend it to," she said. "Like if Charley and Edna want to go there, that'd be all right. But if Charley wanted to borrow it to take somebody else there, I'd be against it. If he ever cheated on Edna, that'd be the end of him for me. She gave up plenty for him and she's *true* to him."

"Isn't he true to her?"

"Well, you hear things at the salon," she said. "You're not always sure whether to believe them or not. But he's supposed to of gone off in the woods with that new buyer at Stewart's, at the store picnic. You know the one I mean. The buyer for children's wear at Stewart's. What's her name, now?"

"Borgman. Gloria Borgman," he said.

"You knew all right. You didn't have to think twice."

"No, I only had to think once-and-a-half. She's too skinny for me to go for, but some guys say the nearer the bone, the sweeter the meat."

"Oh, is that so? Well, I consider her nothing but an underfed tramp, and don't you go lending the apartment to her and Charley."

"My God, woman, who said anything about lending her the apartment? Talk to Charley, don't talk to me."

"Don't think I won't if I hear any more about him," she said. "Here, here's my half of the first month's rent."

"O.K., I'll take it," he said. "On the one condition."

"What's that?"

"That if I ever catch *you* there with Charley, I'll—"

She slapped him, playfully but hard.

"I forgot to duck," he said. "Famous last words."

They were, as they agreed, getting to be more and more like a married couple in many ways, in congeniality, in compatibility, in sharing the pleasures of the table and the bed, and in a fondness for dressing up and jointly accepting the compliments of their friends on their stylish appearance. Jay was one of the first men in town to wear the brim of his fedora turned up on one side and down on the other, and one of the last to give up spats. Madge, still a long ways from mink or sables, compensated by concentrating on her accessories— handbags, for instance, and hats and shoes and belts and earrings and bracelets. "When old lady Choate dies, I'm gonna make an offer for her sable coat," she told Jay.

"Who is old lady Choate?" said Jay.

"That's your trouble. Lived in this town as long as you have, and don't even know who old lady Choate is."

"She never comes in *my* place," he said.

"She never comes in mine, either. But if I had her money—boy, what I could do with it!"

"Does she have a husband?"

"She did have. He left her all the money," said Madge. "Her, and old lady Hofman. If I had their money!"

"This town is full of rich old ladies, to hear you talk."

"You bet it is," said Madge.

"You ought to let one of them borrow me for a year. Fix it up, will you? She'd die happy and me and you'd be rich."

"Listen, big boy, I could spare you for a year to get hold of that Choate money or the Hofman fortune."

"What would you be doing during that time?"

"I'd get me an old man," she said. "Or maybe a young one."

"Why not a rich one?"

"Find me one," she said.

"And what if I did? What would be my end? If I was your manager I'd want a third. That's what a fight manager takes."

"Find me one rich enough and I'd go halves with you. But unfortunately there don't happen to be any in town. They all have wives, or the widowers have children that would keep me away from them. There's one rich old guy, but he has a preference for young boys."

"Who's that?"

"*Young* boys. You're too old for him."

"Where do you hear all that stuff?"

"You know where I hear it. At the salon. That's where I hear everything. I got more dirt on the people in this town—and it's all true, or most of it."

"Yeah, but what about the other beauty parlor? Dunbar's. Does she have any dirt on you?"

"Well, I guess there was a time."

"Those guys you used to go on trips with."

"I guess so," said Madge. "That didn't worry me. The only time I was ever worried—I never told you this before." She then related the story of her embezzlements at the planing mill.

"Well, I'll be a son of a bitch," said Jay, when she finished. "The young guy comes in my place once in a while. Him and the golf players, they'll come in around three or four o'clock in the morning for a plate of soup. The others'll be plastered, but not him."

"No, not him," said Madge.

"You know, Madge, I often think up an idea to make a few bucks, but I never even mention it to you. I always thought you'd put the kibosh on it."

"What are you thinking now?"

"I don't have no ideas at present, but the next time I get a good one I'll talk it over with you. See, I didn't know you had that much larceny in you. I figured you saved your money and went into business for yourself. I didn't know you stole it."

"I didn't steal it all."

"No, but enough."

"Yeah. Enough."

"It's funny how you think you know a person, and then when you come right down to it you don't know them—well, as good as you think you did. I do have a kind of a scheme I been thinking about, but I don't have it all worked out in my mind."

"Tell me about it," she said.

"All right, I will," he said. "This has been brooding about in my mind for a couple years now. How the hell do I start making a bigger buck than running a saloon? You said one time I don't think two weeks ahead. That shows you didn't know me either. I always think ahead. You don't give me credit for much brains, but I could tell you a few things that—"

"When you get done patting yourself on the back, what's your scheme?"

"I just want to tell you, you stole the money to start your business. *I* stole the money to start *mine*. I didn't have practically a nickel when I went to work for Bressler, but I stole enough off of him to buy the place when he died. Right under his very eyes, I stole it. Him standing there half the time. No bookkeeping tricks. So credit where credit's due, Madge. I got *some* brains."

"All right. You're a financial genius," said Madge. "The scheme, let's hear the scheme."

"You know the Speer brothers, those couple of Greeks that—"

"I know the Speer brothers, yes," she said.

"Right. But did you ever hear of the Hip Sings and the On Leongs?"

"No. The Speer brothers, but not those others."

"Damn right you didn't. They're tongs. Chinese tongs. The Hip Sings and the On Leongs. You forget I was born-brought up in Newark, New Jersey."

"I think your mind is wandering," she said.

"In Newark they had as big a Chinatown as, well, second only to San Francisco. And shut up, will you?"

"Sure. I don't want to interrupt your train of thought," she said.

"All these Chinamen, all these Greeks, practically all the foreigners, they all belong to some organization. Some of them they only pay two bits a week. Some more. But they all pay dues. Then the organization puts the money in the treasury, and pretty soon you got a pretty nice bundle."

"Like the unions," said Madge.

"Exactly. Now you're beginning to catch on."

"I didn't have to be born in Newark, New Jersey, to catch on to that. We always had unions here. Are you going to start a union? A union of what?"

"Saloonkeepers. Guys that run speaks. Grocery stores that sell wine. Whorehouses. I was thinking I'd start with the whorehouses."

"Start what with the whorehouses?"

"Well, like I go to Daisy Minzer's, the joint on the way to the Stage Coach, and I go in there and I say, 'Daisy, you give me so much a week, and I'll make sure nobody makes trouble in your place.' Then I go to the Ace of Clubs, and the Pussy Café, and all over the county. Make the same proposition."

"I thought all those places paid graft to the police," said Madge.

"Sure they do. To keep from getting raided. But my proposition is to keep out trouble."

"Don't they all have bouncers?"

"Bouncers, yeah, but I'm Gunboat Dawson."

"You mean you used to be Gunboat Dawson," said Madge.

"I don't always tell you when I have to flatten some drunk. I do it on the average once or twice a month. I won't have no trouble with bouncers. I was thinking, the first time I go to Daisy Minzer's, she has a bouncer by the name of Jack Welch. I never did like the son of a bitch. So I was thinking I'd go in there and flatten him before I said anything to her. Then I make my proposition, with him lying there. She'd get the idea pretty quick."

"Oh, I see. In other words, where there wasn't any trouble, you'd start it."

"Right."

"Were you going to do this all by yourself?"

"When I was starting out, yes. Then when I got the thing going, I'd send for some guys I know in Philly."

"Do you want to know what I think of your scheme?"

"Sure."

"I think you're crazy in the head," she said. "Do you know who runs those whorehouses?"

"Yes, do you?"

"Yes. A fellow from up the mountain," said Madge. "Frank Something."

"Focci. How do you know that?"

"How do I know everything? And he's not the owner, he only runs them. They're all owned by a gang in New Jersey, your part of the country. They own houses all the way from New Jersey. They get the girls from the coal regions and they keep moving them from one house to another."

"Come on, *I* told you that," said Jay.

"You told me, but I knew it anyway," said Madge. "I think you're out of your mind. They'll kill you. And if they don't, the bootleggers will. The bootleggers won't stand for you making trouble in the saloons. They just won't stand for it, and why should they? They'll come and get you and shoot you, up in the mountains somewhere, and then they'll set fire to you. It wouldn't be the first time."

"You mean that whore they found? She was a squealer."

"And would you be any better in their estimation? If you go through with this scheme I'd be afraid to go out with you. I'd never come to this apartment again, I mean it. What if they came to get you and I was here? They'd have to take me too, if I was here. And I'd get the same thing they gave that whore. We wouldn't be safe anywhere, me *or* you."

"Now what are you doing? Who are you calling?" he said.

"I'm calling a cab to take me home."

"Put down that God damn phone," he said.

She replaced the receiver. She knew better than to go against him when he used that tone. Once or twice she had seen what his quick fists could do to a man, and at this moment he was not thinking of her as a woman but only as somebody that had got him into a boiling rage. He struck the palm of his left hand with the heel of the right. It was the heel of his hand, not his closed fist, that he used to uppercut men. She let the tears come. "I wished I never met you," she said. "I wished I never saw you."

"That goes double for me," he said. "That—goes—double, that does." He stood up, and she looked at him questioningly. "Put your dress on. I'm taking you home," he said.

They are old now, living retired the year round on the gulf coast of Florida. He uses a cane, but he goes in the water almost every day and floats on his back, swims a few strokes, and does not look his age. She stays out of the sun, and wears large sunglasses with rhine-stones studding the rims. Her hair is dyed blue. A little while ago they had some friends in to celebrate their fortieth wedding anniver-sary, pretty unusual these days when almost everybody has had at least one divorce. None of their present-day friends ever heard of Gunboat Dawson; Jay Fitzpatrick, retired restaurateur, and Madge Fitzpatrick, retired beautician, is how they are known to their Flor-ida friends. They have enough to live on nicely, and it is not surpris-ing that he, having been in the restaurant business, is quite a good cook. He makes a specialty of his bean soup, very popular among friends who have a hard time with steak and corn on the cob. Their men friends say she is smarter than he is about business conditions and investments, but she does not agree with them. "I could tell you one scheme Jay had, he'd of made a fortune on it, a fortune. But he was way ahead of his time," she says.

"What scheme was that?" a man will say.

"What scheme was that? Well, on the order of your protective associations. All the men in a business band together and form an association. Keep out unfair competition—"

"And government interference?"

"And government interference," says Madge. "He was way ahead of his time, Jay was. That was forty years ago."

"Well, if you have enough to live on . . ."

"That's what I say," says Madge. "If you have enough to live on. A few of the luxuries. Your friends in for a game of cards."

She is always trying to get up a game of cards, but it is not easy. Her friends say she is much too lucky. That, at least, is what they say to her.

How Old, How Young

You did not often see a woman crying on the street. You sometimes saw one in the neighborhood where the doctors had
their offices, coming out of an office with another woman or a
man and crying from pain. Sometimes they would be coming
from a dentist's office, but they would be holding bloodstained handkerchiefs to their mouths. Doctor's office or dentist's office, they
would usually get in a waiting car or a taxi and not be on the street
very long, and anyway their crying was easily explained. You just
about never were walking along the street and saw a young woman
crying out of emotional anguish, weeping tears that were tears of
sorrow and not caring that she might be making a spectacle of herself. But on this particular afternoon a long while ago James H.
Choate, who had a summer job as runner for the family bank, was on
an errand to a law office and coming toward him he saw this young
woman and if he had not known her he would have said she was
plastered. She was wearing white shoes with brown wing tips and
medium high heels, and yet she walked as if she had on ski boots.
She was wearing a simple dark blue linen one-piece dress with a thin
black belt and a white collar, and a straw hat that was varnished
black—pretty much of a uniform among certain types of girls in
those days. But she was walking like a drunken tart. Then when she
got closer he saw that it was Nancy Liggett and that she was weeping
without any self-restraint and leaving her misery naked for people to
stare at. Jamie Choate wanted to cover her, as though her nakedness
were the real thing. He stopped and stood in her uncertain path, but
she walked around him. "Nancy!" he said. She kept on going and he
watched her indecisively until she reached her car. She got in, and he
was glad that it was a coupe; it offered her some shelter from the
mystified stares of people, including himself. It was twenty minutes
of three, and he had to get to the lawyers' office and back to the
bank before closing time. He had not been told the nature of the

New Yorker (1 July 1967); *And Other Stories*

envelope he was to pick up, but he had been ordered to get it back before three, without fail. He was very unimportant at the bank; they did not think much of him there. He made a special effort on this errand. He got back in plenty of time—five minutes to spare—as much because he wanted to see if Nancy's car was still in the block as to make a good impression at the bank. The car was gone.

There was a swimming-party-picnic that night that Nancy Liggett should have been at but wasn't. Some people had a boathouse at a damn in the woods about fifteen miles out of town. The water was always very cold and so was the air, and even though the bank thermometer that day had registered above ninety degrees, people at the picnic were drinking straight rye to keep off the chill. Quite a few people got tight. It was a Friday, the beginning of the weekend for most of the people, but Saturday morning was a very busy time at the bank, and Jamie Choate stayed sober. His cousin, Walker Choate, was at the picnic to remind him, in case he forgot. Walker was an assistant paying teller and a regular member of the staff. Very patronizing toward Jamie. "Remember, you have all those blotters to change in the morning," said Walker. "Need a steady hand and a clear mind for that."

"Oh, go to hell," said Jamie. "I wonder why Nancy Liggett isn't here tonight."

"Why the sudden interest in Nancy?" said Walker.

"Because I've fallen in love with her," said Jamie.

"Then why didn't you bring her?"

"I don't know. I was hoping you would and then I'd take her away from you."

"If I ever brought Nancy to anything it wouldn't be hard to take her away from me. Even you could. Why don't you go take a look in the woods. Maybe she's here and forgot to check in with you."

"Walker, you *are* a wet smack," said Jamie.

"Yeah, and you're not dry behind the ears," said Walker.

It was a fairly large party and included people who were still in prep school and people who had children of their own, and a greater number of those in between. It would have been possible for Nancy to have arrived at the boathouse, stayed there a few minutes, and vanished in the woods without Jamie's having seen her. To make sure she hadn't, he went to the hostess-chaperone, Gwen Lloyd, and said, "I've been looking all over for Nancy Liggett."

"She isn't here," said Gwen. "She called up and said she wasn't coming. Offered no excuse, and she was supposed to help out with the food."

"Oh, you spoke to her? How did she seem?" said Jamie.

"How did she seem? She seemed rude and inconsiderate," said Gwen. "She was supposed to bring three dozen ears of corn for corn on the cob, and when I started to ask her about them, she just hung up."

"Not like her," said Jamie.

"Well, it'll be a long time before I count on *her* again. I don't know what's got into her lately. Don't tell me you have a sneaker for her, Jamie."

"What if I did?" said Jamie.

"Well, that's your business, but you'd do better with someone your own age."

"Nancy's the same age. Exactly the same age. We were both born in 1904."

"Girls mature earlier," said Gwen. "You're still in college, and she's been home two or three years."

"What are you not saying that you're kind of hinting at?"

"Just that she's older than you, even if you were born the same year."

"Well, at least she called up and said she wasn't coming," said Jamie.

"Yes, you do have a sneaker for her," said Gwen.

"I'm not as naïve as you'd make me out to be," he said.

"You're away most of the time. I just hope you don't fall for Nancy Liggett," said Gwen.

"I think maybe I have."

"Then forget everything I've said," said Gwen. "Heaven knows she needs someone she can depend on. And that's *all* I'm going to *say.*"

"You married people! You'd think you had some monopoly on how people react."

"In certain things we have more experience," said Gwen.

"I'll say you have," said Jamie. "Who's going to chaperone the chaperones, that's what we always say."

"Uncalled for, that remark," said Gwen. "If you're not having a good time, nobody's asking you to stay."

"Then I bid you a fond adieu," said Jamie. It was close to eleven o'clock and from his point of view the party had been a frost. Some of the people had paired off and vanished; the singers were going through their repertory; two tables of bridge had settled down in the boathouse; Walker Choate was trying to persuade an out-of-town girl to go canoeing with him. It was all very much like every other swimming-party-picnic the Lloyds had given, except that on this one Jamie had had no fun, no fun at all.

On his way home he slowed down as he passed the Liggetts' house. There was a light on in the room that he knew to be Nancy's bedroom, but Mr. and Mrs. Liggett were not the kind of people who sanctioned midnight visitors. At home Jamie went to the icebox and got a glass of milk, to the cakebox and got a couple of brownies. He sat on the kitchen table with his feet resting on a chair and pondered the newest mystery in his life: why had he never fallen in love with Nancy Liggett until he had seen her good looks washed away by tears, her face made plain by misery? Ah, well, it was not much of a mystery, really. Her good looks had always kept him away, and now she was just like anyone else—except that he was in love with her. And he would never be the same again. A new organ had come to life, somewhere in his chest, and it was pumping something warm and sweet through the rest of him. Nancy Liggett, who needed someone she could depend on.

He had a ladder match to play the next afternoon, and he thought of defaulting, but his best chance of seeing Nancy would be at the club pool. He played the match and won, had a ginger ale with the kid he had beaten, took a shower and put on his bathing suit and went to the pool. She was there, sitting by herself with her chin on her knees and her arms clasping her legs. She looked up at him as he dropped his towel and sat beside her. "Hello," she said.

"Do you mind?" he said.

"I'm not being very conversational," she said.

"Well, that makes two of us," he said. "You didn't go to the Lloyds'."

"No," she said.

"I left fairly early. It was still going strong, but the only person I wanted to talk to wasn't there."

"No?"

"No," he said.

"I warned you I wasn't being very conversational," she said. She picked up her bathing cap and pulled it on, tucking in wisps of her blonde hair, cocking her head as she did and unconsciously being extremely feminine and attractive. She stood up and went to the edge of the pool, hesitated, and dived in. He waited to see her when she got out, with her wet bathing suit sticking to her body, but he also wanted to see if she would return to their place. He had quite a while to wait. She swam very slowly up and down the length of the pool, floated a bit, and finally climbed out.

"You weren't going to get rid of me that way," he said.

"It was worth a try," she said. She took off her cap and dried the back of her neck and ran her fingers through her hair. She lit a cigarette and lowered herself to the concrete.

"How's the water?" he said.

"Very damp," she said. "You ought to investigate it."

"All right. Will you be here when I get back?"

"Why not? I was here first," she said.

He dived in and repeated her slow swim and float, and climbed out. "Can I have one of your butts?"

She pushed the pack and matches toward him. He lit one and took a couple of drags. "Don't be sore at me, Nancy. I didn't do anything. I just happened to *be* there, coming out of the bank."

"I'm not sore at you—just as long as you don't ask any questions," she said.

"I want to know, though. And it isn't just idle curiosity."

"What else is it?"

"Do you really want to know?" he said.

She turned and faced him. "Yes."

"It's love," he said.

"Oh, for Jesus' sake," she said.

"You said you wanted to know, and I told you," he said.

"I certainly didn't want to know that," she said.

"It doesn't put you under any obligation."

"I'll say it doesn't," she said.

"I just found out myself, last night."

"Because you saw me blubbering on the public street, you came to the conclusion that you're in love with me. You'd change your mind pretty quickly if you knew *why* I was crying," she said. "And you'll know soon enough. Everybody will. All of you. Everybody at this pool. Old Mr. Griffiths down there on the eighth tee. Johnny Wells, Mr. Charlton, Stanley Griffiths. The fussy foursome. You'd better get away before they all see you with me."

"What's the matter, Nancy?"

"Oh, for God's sake leave me alone," she said. She pulled up her knees again and rested her chin on them, and wept.

"What *is* it? I *love* you, Nancy."

"Oh, Christ almighty, Jamie. I want to die. I want to *die.*"

"Let's go someplace. Get dressed and we'll go for a ride," he said. She looked at him and she was not pretty, but there was the beginning of trust in her eyes.

"Where will you take me?" she said.

"Anywhere you say."

She put her towel to her face and sniffled. "Where's your car?"

"In the second row, halfway down the hill."

"I'll be there in ten minutes," she said. "Don't you come with me. I'll meet you in your car."

It took them longer than ten minutes, but she was there waiting when he got to his car. She was pretty again, in a flowery print sleeveless dress and a necklace of tiny Tecla pearls.

"Any place you want to go?"

She shook her head, and with her fingers only she waved to the clubhouse. "Goodbye, club," she said. "Nice to have known you."

They passed through two towns before either of them said anything. "Are you thirsty? I am," he said.

"Very," she said.

He stopped the car at a roadside stand and got a couple of mugs of root beer. "This is all they had," he said. "Out of everything else."

"I love root beer," she said. "Remember those picnics when we were very little? At the Griffiths farm? I got stung by yellow-jackets one year."

"I was there. You were certainly a mess. All puffed up."

"And Mrs. Griffiths put clay all over me, supposed to take the sting out but it didn't."

"The wrong kind of clay, I guess."

"I minded that worse than the sting, that mud all over my face and arms," she said. "Well, I should have gotten used to it. The mud's going to fly thick and fast."

"You don't have to talk about it, Nance," he said.

"Oh, I can now. We're not even in the same county, so I can talk, and I want to." She handed him her mug, and he returned it to the refreshment stand. They drove away.

"Do you think I'm pregnant, Jamie? Is that what you think it is?"

"The possibility occurred to me."

"Well, it might be a possibility but it doesn't happen to be what I was crying about," she said. "It's my father."

"Your father?"

"They came and arrested him this morning. It'll be in the paper this afternoon. Judge McDermott released him on bail, but he's going to have to go to prison."

"For what?"

"Misappropriation of funds. Daddy is a thief. He stole over sixty thousand dollars in three years."

"At the Trust Company?"

"Yes. When you saw me yesterday he had just signed a confession. I was there when he signed it. I went to his office to ask him for some money. Poor Daddy. He hated to refuse me anything, and didn't very often. But there I was, and some lawyers and a detective—although I didn't know that that's what they were. 'Gentlemen, my daughter is here to ask me for some money. Shall I tell her what my excuse is for turning her down?' One of the men said no, it would be cruel. But Daddy said I had to find out sometime. Sixty thousand dollars, and he doesn't know where it all went. He told me to go home and be with Mother when she got the bad news. Today I went to the club for the last time ever. Monday I start looking for a job."

"Your mother has some money, hasn't she?"

"Some. Enough for her to live on, I guess, but not in our house."

"I wondered why you said 'Goodbye, club.' I had a feeling it meant something."

"And you were right," she said. "About *that*. You weren't right in suspecting I was pregnant. I'm much too careful for that."

"I wouldn't know," he said.

"No, and the only person that would know—I don't expect to see *him* any more. Not after he hears about Daddy. So I guess I'm going to start being virtuous, for a change."

"Oh, stop trying to be so sophisticated. You make me sick. Whoever the guy is—and I'll bet I could guess—you don't know *what* he's going to do."

"Don't I? He's quaking in his boots right now, terrified that he'd somehow get mixed up in this."

"If that's your opinion of him, why did you have an affair with him?"

"Oh, Jamie, what a question. I knew what I was letting myself in for, but that didn't stop me."

"Well, at least his wife doesn't know. Although she is sore at you."

"How do you know?"

"Because you were supposed to bring three dozen ears of corn to her picnic last night," he said.

"Oh," she said.

"Who else could it be? As soon as I knew I was in love with you, I spent all last night figuring out all the possibilities. I finally narrowed it down to two."

"Who was the other?" said Nancy.

"That wet-smack cousin of mine, Walker," he said.

"No. Not Walker."

"I'm glad of that, anyway," he said.

"He is a wet smack, isn't he? And his wife is so unattractive. At least Gwen is pretty. A bitch, but pretty. At least I never felt that I was taking candy from a baby."

"Gwen thinks you ought to have someone you can depend on," he said.

"How touching."

"I think so, too," he said.

"And so do I. That makes three of us."

"Why don't you marry me?" he said.

"Let me find a job first," she said. "What do they pay you at the bank?"

"Fifteen dollars a week."

"Which is probably what I'll get, if I'm lucky. We could be gloriously happy on thirty a week, you and I."

"I'll have some money when I'm twenty-five."

"Yes, but what do we do in the meantime? Thanks for the offer, Jamie. But you have another year in college, and then I suppose they'll pack you off to the Harvard Business School, and then you ought to have a year or two in Wall Street. You and I are exactly the same age, but do you see how young you are? And how old I am?"

"I didn't like the sound of that when I heard it from Gwen," he said.

"Ask me again four years from now," she said.

"I don't want to have to wait that long," he said.

"We don't have to wait, for everything," she said.

Barred

I t was a fact that Jimmy Bresnahan got so mad at Nora Muldoon that he was ready to kill her. He went to her house that night and her mother answered the door. "Good evening, Jimmy," said Mrs. Muldoon, showing polite surprise. "Would you like to come in?"

"Why, yes, or I'll wait on the porch," said Jimmy. "That is, Nora's expecting me."

"Oh, I don't think so," said Mrs. Muldoon. "She went to the movies right after supper."

"That's funny," said Jimmy. "She was supposed to go to the Lake with me."

"You must have the wrong evening," said Mrs. Muldoon.

"Thursday. That's the night for the big orchestras. George Olsen is playing tonight. We made the date over a week ago."

"Then it must have slipped her mind. She and Isabel and Mary went uptown soon after supper," said Mrs. Muldoon.

"I was supposed to call for her at ha' past eight."

"Well, it's that now, but the movie won't be over till after nine. Then they go for a soda. I don't expect her much before ha' past nine. If then. Sometimes they go to Isabel's after the picture show, and Bud walks her home."

"Is it all right if I wait a little while?" said Jimmy. "I'll just sit out here on the porch."

"Well, I wouldn't count on her," said Mrs. Muldoon. "Knowing her, she wasn't dressed to go to the dance, and she's liable to stay at Isabel's till quite late. I think the whole thing must have slipped her mind."

"Are you sure she's not standing me up, Mrs. Muldoon?" said Jimmy.

"Well, I couldn't be sure of that either," said Mrs. Muldoon. "You wouldn't be the first one, and you've never had a date with her before. Nora's as changeable as the weather. I tell her time and again, if she wants to remain popular she has to start thinking of other people's feelings."

"She is standing me up, isn't she?" said Jimmy.

"Now I didn't say that, Jimmy. But it looks that way. I don't say she's standing you up, but I'm positive she isn't going to the Lake tonight."

"Why are you so positive?"

"Why am I so positive? Well, I just remembered, they *are* going back to Isabel's from the picture show. Yes, Isabel has a new Victrola, the table model to take to school with her. Yes, now I remember."

"Then there's no use my waiting," said Jimmy.

"No, I honestly don't think there is. I'll tell Nora you were here promptly at ha' past eight."

"Why is she standing me up? You know why, Mrs. Muldoon," said Jimmy.

"No, I can't exactly say I do, *if she is.*"

"You know she is, and you know why. Maybe you told her to break the date with me."

"Now, Jimmy, I don't intend to stand here letting the flies in while we discuss Nora. If you have anything to say to Nora it'd be better to say it to her."

"I'm right, though. You told her to break the date with me. You won't let her go out with me, is that it?"

"She made that decision without any help from me, Jimmy. Not many mothers—"

"That's it. It was you."

"No, it wasn't. Nora thought it over and then she thought better of it."

"With a little help from you."

"Don't get personal, Jimmy. Have more respect for your elders."

"It was you. Nora wanted to go out with me, but you wouldn't let her."

"I didn't have to say a word. Nora made up her own mind. And it's against the law to leave your car there with the motor running."

"You! You and those mothers!" said Jimmy. He heard her say something about a good thing some mothers—but he missed the rest in his angry haste to his car. He drove away noisily and recklessly, hating Mrs. Muldoon but even more so hating Nora for her treachery. For a week he had been saying that Nora Muldoon was the only one of the so-called nice girls who had the courage to make a date with him. She was the prettiest of them all, the only one worth taking to a dog fight. He had taken George McLoughlin's two-dollar bet that Nora would back out at the last minute. "That shows you how much you know about girls," he had said to George. "The real pretty ones are sure of themselves."

"Maybe I don't know so much about girls, but I'm related to those Muldoons and I know Nora better than you do."

"Two bucks, two bucks," Jimmy had said.

Now, driving through the streets of the town, he recognized cars and couples in them, off to an early start for the Lake. They would all know that he had a date with Nora Muldoon—and some of them would already know that Nora had stood him up. They would have seen Nora and Isabel Murphy and Mary McCorkindale—sometimes known as Faith, Hope, and Charity—marching together to the movies. It was bad enough that Nora had broken the date, bad enough if she had broken it and stayed home; but she had made it worse by going to the movies with Isabel and Mary, passing the homes of their friends who knew she had made the date with Jimmy. She did not even pretend she was sick or something. In a way it was worse than if she had gone to the Lake with someone else. At least then she could have pretended there was a mix-up on the dates. Or he could have pretended it.

He had almost twelve dollars in his pocket, the family Nash, his good white linen suit—the man in the saying: all dressed up and no place to go. It was too early for the Busy Bee. Nobody went there this early. George McLoughlin would be shooting pool at the Olympic, but one of the last people he wanted to see was George McLoughlin right now. Not that George would give him the razz, but he did not want any kind of sympathy from George. Or from anybody. He would like to get Nora Muldoon by the throat and throttle her, to tear the clothes off her and make her walk down Main Street half naked. He would like to disgrace her, the dirty little double-crosser. Why not? It was what they all expected of him.

One bad thing, one really bad thing that he had told in confession and got absolution for, that had brought shame and disgrace on his mother and father and cost his father a lot of money. The whole town knew it even if it never got in the papers. Jimmy Bresnahan caught in a raid on Sally Minzer's roadhouse by the state police. Taken to the county jail and held as a material witness because he offered resistance. The older men were let go, but he had taken a swing at a statie and they put him in the truck with the whores and locked him up overnight. Lawyers. Politics. Money. Disgrace. New Year's Day in the county jail. Hysterical mother. Angry father. Embarrassed sister. Pompous priest. Condescending neighbors. Hesitant friends. Leering acquaintances. The delayed return to college escorted by his father, and the interview with the prefect of discipline. "Yes, we heard all about James," said the prefect of discipline. "A truism that bad news travels fast, and there always seem to be volunteer informers in cases like this. Well, Mr. Bresnahan, you did the honorable thing coming here. Father Rector put it entirely in my hands when he heard you were coming with James. I will say parenthetically, Father Rector recommended clemency in recognition of your honorable behavior, and I was inclined that way myself, but I don't say the rector's attitude hurt any. Now then, Mr. Bresnahan, the university has no *official* knowledge of James's peccadillo, misconduct, whatever you wish to call it. It took place during the vacation, hundreds of miles from here. And according to our information, James's name doesn't even appear on the county records of your home county. How fortunate indeed. Because regardless of official record or no official record, I doubt very much whether James would have been admitted as a freshman if he had such a mark on his record. You wouldn't say such a mark testified to his good character. But when a boy is home on vacation he's supposed to be out of our jurisdiction, so to speak. Back in the jurisdiction of his parents, you might say, and in view of the fact that the university got no official report on the unfortunate episode, we decided to look the other way. Taking into consideration, of course, the fact that James has a record here that's about average—not as good as some, not as bad as others. Average."

So they let him back in the university, never officially having put him out. His father reduced his allowance. "None of my money goes for prostitutes," said Mr. Bresnahan. His mother sent him five dollars a week, or he would have had little money for cigarettes and movies. That second semester he did penance, but when he got home in June it was soon apparent that the mothers and fathers of the so-called nice girls deemed the penance inadequate. He was not fully ostracized; they nodded to him when they could not avoid it. But he was no longer welcome on their porches, he was not invited to picnics, he was left out of several birthday parties. His father had got him a job, not a soft job in a law office where he might learn something about the profession he expected to follow, but a three-dollar-a-day job cutting brush for a surveying party with the power company. He chopped away a lot of brush and killed a dozen rattlesnakes, got browned by the sun and learned just enough about civil engineering to confirm his preference for the law. In the evenings he played pool with George McLoughlin and spoke often of Nora Muldoon. "Why don't you ask her for a date?" said George. "All she can do is say no."

"If she says that," said Jimmy. "I haven't said two words to her all year."

"She didn't stop talking to you, did she?".

"No, but she never did say much to me," said Jimmy.

"Does she look at you with those big brown eyes?"

"Boy, those big brown eyes," said Jimmy.

"I'd like to dip my socks in her coffee, all right," said George. "Cousin or no cousin. Go ahead and ask her for a date, see what she says."

Jimmy discussed the problem with an older man, the chief of the surveying party, who had lived all over the world and had what he called his own personal League of Nations—his recollections of the women he had slept with. "Well, if she's as pretty as you say," said McDowell, "you can ask her anything, provided you ask her in the right way. The pretty ones you don't have to worry about. The homely mutts are the ones that sic the dogs on you. Now this kid knows you were pinched in a whorehouse, so she isn't expecting any saint. If it was me, I'd go right up to her and say, 'What about it?' But I don't live here, and you do. I can afford to put it all on one roll of the dice, because I'll be getting out of here after Labor Day. Don't be shy. One time in Mexico City I made a play for my boss's wife, expecting to get fired and sent home. It turned out quite the opposite. She said if I hadn't made my play when I did, she was going to make the first move herself. You never know what's in their minds."

Thus encouraged, Jimmy Bresnahan blocked Nora Muldoon's progress on the sidewalk one afternoon. "I'll treat you to a malted," he said.

"Thanks, but I'm on my way to the hairdresser," said Nora Muldoon.

"How long'll you be?"

"Two hours, maybe more," she said.

"What I wanted to say was, would you care to go hear George Olsen, at the Lake?"

"You mean on a date with you?"

"Or with another couple?"

"It's next Thursday, isn't it?"

"Yes."

"All right."

"I'll stop for you at eight-thirty," said Jimmy.

"I have to be home by one," she said.

"Whatever you say," he said.

"All right," she said.

"Thanks, Nora," he said. He was grateful to her for making the transaction so simple. As he said later to George McLoughlin, she did not make him get a letter from his pastor, or promise to behave like a gentleman.

"We'll see," said George, and his skepticism led to the two-dollar bet. McDowell, the civil engineer, provided a piece of advice. "Get her away from that dance," said McDowell. "Otherwise she'll be bored to death and you'll never get another chance at her. She's ripe for plucking. If you don't get anywhere maybe I'll have a go at her myself—or even if you do."

"She's not that kind of a girl," said Jimmy.

"My boy, they all are," said McDowell. "Take it from a man that's been everywhere, seen everything, and done everything, and ready to start all over again. If she's a she, she's a she."

Now, driving up and down the streets of the town while this particular she sat watching a movie, Jimmy Bresnahan fully agreed with McDowell's opinion of the female sex. He hated her, he hated them all. In the morning McDowell would want to know all about his date with Nora, and he would have nothing to tell. He hated McDowell for having raised his hopes, and hated him in advance for the glib explanation he would have for her having stood him up. But the only explanation worth a damn was that Nora Muldoon had wanted to humiliate him publicly, and he tried to think of a way to humiliate her that would not get him arrested.

Well, everybody expected him to show up at the Lake with Nora Muldoon. What if he showed up, not with her but with the worst tart in the county? They would all be looking for Nora Muldoon, but what if he showed up with Sally Minzer instead? And if not Sally herself—who was nothing to look at—one of Sally's girls.

He swung around in the middle of the block and headed for Sally Minzer's joint.

It was early for Sally Minzer's, but that meant that the girls would not be busy. They would have no objection to going to the Lake for a couple of hours. On the way to Sally's he imagined Nora's friends when he showed up with one of Sally's girls. Nora's girl friends would not recognize any of Sally's girls, but some of the boys would. He could imagine the whispers. "That's one of Sally Minzer's you-know-what. What happened to Nora Muldoon?"

That would be the cream of the jest, his bringing one of Sally Minzer's girls to the Lake instead of Nora. It would get back to Nora before the night was over. Some of Nora's friends were quite likely to telephone her from the Lake. As the prefect of discipline had said, there was always some volunteer informant.

It was early for Sally Minzer's place, but there were a few cars in front of the entrance and all the lights were on inside the house and in the driveway. Obviously the authorities had given Sally permission to open up. Jimmy parked his car and walked to the barroom, where two men were sitting at a table, having drinks. They were strangers to Jimmy and they paid little attention to him. The bartender was likewise a stranger. "What'll it be?"

"Rye and ginger ale," said Jimmy. "Is Sally in?"

"Sally? Do you know her?"

"Sure I know her."

"Does she know you?"

"Sure she knows me. You're new here," said Jimmy.

"Not so new. Who will I say wants to see Sally?"

"The name is Bresnahan."

"I'll go see if she's in," said the bartender. He left the barroom, but he was not gone long. Sally Minzer came in, stared at Jimmy and shouted, "Get him the hell out of here! Get him out! Who the hell let him in? This kid is poison. He hits cops. You, Bresnahan, get out of here and I never want to see your face again. You cost me plenty, you young punk."

"He owes for the rye," said the bartender.

"The hell with that, just get him out of here," said Sally Minzer. "And you, if you ever show your face in here again, I'll put them to work on you. *You're barred,* you understand that? *Barred.*"

The men at the table had got to their feet. "You heard what she said," said one of them. "You're barred."

The Gangster

Milo Brady was supposed to have become a doctor, but when his father died he stayed home to run the saloon and he never went back to college. It was only going to be one year that he would be staying home. He and his mother would find a buyer with no trouble at all, everybody said. Brady's had an ideal location, where the men on their way home from the mill would drop in to cut the dust with a beer and on payday go for the hard stuff. At night it became the neighborhood saloon, with a steady trade all evening long. Bartholomew Brady was a great big man who did not often have to come from behind his bar to keep order, but when an argument went beyond the talk stage and into the exchange of punches, Bart Brady knew exactly how to handle it. "Out!" he would say. "Do your fighting on the street, not in my place." And he was big enough and strong enough to enforce his orders. Consequently he had the tacit support of the police and of the mill officials, the parish priest and the neighborhood wives, and Prohibition did not close him down. His place remained so open, so unchanged, that he did not even remove the swinging doors. The beer was not always as good as it had been, but it was not as bad as in some other places. The whiskey was pretty bad as to taste, but no one ever went blind from it. His prices went up because his wet goods cost him more and various official palms had to be greased, but his customers always found the money to drink at Brady's. Bart Brady was a fine man who ran a decent, honest saloon, and when he died he was mourned by Catholic and Protestant alike. Every pew in St. Mary Star of the Sea Church was fully occupied for his funeral. No one had been given such a fine send-off since the death of the beloved Father John Mooney, St. Mary's pastor. Two touring cars full of floral offerings, not to mention the fact that Daley, the undertaker, had had to make a special trip to Boyertown for a casket large enough for the remains. Bart Brady was held in such high esteem that the Sons of Italy Band showed up uninvited, and no one could remember a non-military funeral that was attended by a band. It was not that the Italians had been Bart's customers. They liked him because he would not stand for their being bullied by his own people. "Stop pestering them Dagoes," he had said. "They're as good a Catholic as you are and maybe better." He was a strange man; he even had a good word for the Masons, and on that point he had had a falling-out with Father Mooney which was patched up before the priest died but not very long before.

He was indeed a strange man, Big Bart. Maybe once every two or three years he would leave the house and go to the bank and cash a good-sized cheque and he would be gone for as much as a week. When he came home he would pay a call on Father Mooney or a curate and sign the pledge, and for another year or two he would drink neither whiskey nor beer. If a customer invited him to have a drink he would take a cigar out of a box, hold it straight up, and put it in his vest pocket. Everybody in the neighborhood knew that Bart's periodic absences were for the purpose of going on a brannigan, and some knew that he had once said he went away—to Philadelphia, New York, Boston, Pittsburgh—because he was afraid of what he might do while drunk, and one of the things he might do was to kill a man with a punch.

The older customers could tell when Bart was just about due for a brannigan. He became, they said, short with people; absentminded, untalkative, very punctual about closing. Among themselves the customers would try to recall how long it had been since his last disappearance, and if two years had passed, he was due. After one particular absence he came home from Baltimore and the regulars observed that for a couple of months he rode the trolley car to and from the center of town several times a week, to be treated by a Protestant doctor for "strain." The regulars put two and two together and surmised what kind of strain it was that Bart would not let a Catholic doctor treat, but partly out of sympathy and partly out of fear they kept their guesses to themselves. No one wanted to be the man that Bart Brady killed with a punch, and no one had any wish to add to the discomfort of a man who had run into a bit of hard luck out of town. It could happen to anyone, and if you were a giant of a man and married to as cranky a little woman as Jenny Brady you ought to be entitled to go away once in a while.

For Jenny Brady the sun rose and set on their boy Milo, and it had always been that way. In a neighborhood where a couple with an only child was exceptional, Milo Brady attracted special notice because he was also bright and unusually well behaved. His good conduct could not all be explained away by the discipline of his parents. The nuns, for instance, and Father Mooney used him to run errands and do small chores; Slattery, the sexton of St. Mary's, had him shoveling snow before the six-thirty Mass. The boy was always somewhere in the vicinity of the church and convent, and all the way up to the eighth grade it was taken for granted that Milo Brady had a true vocation for the priesthood. Soon, they said, he would be off to St. Charles Borromeo in Overbrook, and St. Mary's parish would have another seminarian to its credit. But in eighth grade Milo got diphtheria and was taken to the hospital for a tracheotomy, and during the five long weeks he was a patient there he switched allegiance from Father Mooney to Dr. Malloy, from the nuns to the nurses, from the holy priesthood to the practice of medicine. "I want to be a doctor," he whispered to his father.

"What did he say? What did you say, Milo?" said Jenny Brady.

"He said he wanted to be a doctor," said Bart Brady.

"Ah, now, how can you be a doctor when you're as much as entered in the seminary?" said Jenny Brady.

"Don't make him talk," said Bart Brady. "It's a strain on his throat."

"Huh. Strain. Somebody here knows all about strains," said Jenny. "Milo-boy, what would you want to be a doctor for? You'll get over that idea when you're home again, safe and sound, and wait'll you see the new surplice Sister Mary Theodore crocheted for you. I tell you, it's a real work of art. A real work of art."

The boy shook his head. "I quit being an altar boy," he said.

His mother smiled. "Never mind, I'll speak to Father Mooney and you won't have to serve the six-thirty Mass any more." She looked about the room. "I think they must be spoiling you here, with all their attentions and the like of that. Be good to have you home again in your own bed and with your own things."

But when he was home again he put off going to see Sister Mary Theodore to thank her for the surplice, and Jenny caught him in a barefaced lie about going to call on Father Mooney. "Why didn't you go and see Father Mooney as I told you to?" she said.

"I went and he wasn't there," said Milo.

"Milo Brady! He waited for you till supper-time. You be sure and tell that lie in confession." She turned to her husband. "This young lad deserves a good spanking. Will I get the strap?"

"You'll do no such thing. When I want to give him the strap I'll give it to him, but he's only two weeks out of hospital."

"Oh, encouraging him to tell a lie to his own mother," said Jenny.

The next and the worst setback for Jenny Brady came from Dr.

Malloy, who came to see the convalescing boy every afternoon. "Did you give him the idea he wants to be a doctor?" said Jenny.

"No—and what if I did, Jenny?" said Dr. Malloy.

"We'd change doctors, that's what if you did. The child had a vocation for the priesthood till he went in that hospital."

"Well, I didn't take *that* out of him. Only about an inch of his windpipe. But I put a silver tube in to make up for it, and I explained that to him."

"Then it was you that gave him the idea," she said. "God will punish you, Doctor."

"Indeed He will, for a lot of things," said the doctor. "But who knows? The boy might have made a bad priest."

"How dare you?"

"I've known one or two," said Dr. Malloy. "They're subject to temptations, you know. Even Milo might be subject to them, and surely you'd rather see him a bad doctor than a bad priest. You know the old saying—*we* bury *our* mistakes."

"Doctor, you're only tormenting her," said Bart Brady.

"Not him, with his blasphemy," said Jenny.

"He saved the boy's life, remember that," said Bart Brady.

"And what's he done to his immortal soul?" said Jenny.

"I'm not here to talk about his immortal soul," said the doctor. "You take that up with Father Mooney. But if I were you, Bart, I'd send the boy away to school next year. Anyway, send him to Gibbsville High. Let him learn something about biology, and if he doesn't take to it, he can still go to the seminary. But I'd bet you five hundred dollars he'll end up studying medicine."

"What makes you think that?" said Bart Brady.

"Say it's a hunch," said the doctor. "The questions he asked, the interest he displayed. The last week he was there I took him through the surgical ward, and he remembered everything I told him. When he's a little older I'm going to let him watch me operate."

"Not as long as I have any say about it," said Jenny.

"All right, Jenny. Then he'll have to wait—unless Bart has *his* say."

"What if he fell over in a dead faint?" said Bart Brady.

"That's what I did, at my first dissection," said the doctor.

"Did you, now? You keeled over, did you?" said Bart Brady.

"I did indeed, and two others with me."

"And that's what you want for my son," said Jenny.

"No. That's not what I want for your son, Jenny. I'd be hoping that the day would come when he'd be able to take a little piece of windpipe out of a child's throat that was strangling. That's all. That I can do. The immortal soul—maybe that's your long suit, my dear woman." He rose.

"Well, don't go away mad, Doctor," said Bart Brady. "Will I get you a temperance?"

"Got any root beer?"

"I do, and birch, and sass. Come along with me and we'll see what's cold," said Bart Brady. "I'll be glad of the company."

Within the year Dr. Malloy was dead, and Milo Brady was in the public high school, studying, among other things, botany. From botany he progressed to biology, to physics and chemistry, and to other things as well, and among those other things were dancing and an interest in girls. They were years of torment for Jenny Brady, seeing her son abandon his vocation and, even worse, questioning the very articles of faith that it was sinful to question. He would not always tell her the names of the girls he danced with at the public dances in the Armory. In his senior year at high school he failed to make his Easter duty of going to confession and communion sometime between the first Sunday of Lent and Trinity Sunday, a failure which meant automatic excommunication. "Don't forget, tomorrow's Trinity Sunday," she warned him. "Go to confession today." But the next morning, when she wakened him for Mass, he said he had neglected to go to confession and was therefore unable to go to communion. "Milo! You know what that means! I want you to go and ask Father Gifford to hear your confession today, and you can receive communion tomorrow."

"Oh, I can go to confession next Saturday," he said.

"I said today, not next Saturday. You've had since the beginning of Lent, and you kept putting it off. You're not to put it off another day. What if you were hit by a trolley? You wouldn't be in the state of grace."

"Mom, I won't go to Father Gifford today and that's all there is to it," he said.

She wept and carried on and threatened to report him to his father, an empty threat since they both knew that Bart Brady had likewise neglected his Easter duty. She sulked for a few days, but when he came and asked her for money, she gave it to him. She always gave it to him, in amounts that had increased year by year. Bart Brady had at long last bought a car, a Velie touring car, but he had not learned to drive it and it had become practically Milo's personal property. He would drive his parents to wherever they wanted to go, but the car was really Milo's, and every time he took it out he asked his mother for money to buy gasoline. In the summer he was out in the car nearly every night, going to the dances at the amusement parks and getting home at two or three o'clock in the morning. The young people who went with him were from other parts of town, not the society kids, but certainly not the children of the mill section. He was rather stubborn when she asked him who they were, but sometimes on his own he would mention some names, and they were the sons and daughters of carpenters and paperhangers and proprietors of small stores—Protestants, most of them. She would not say to him, or admit to herself, that she suspected they cared more for his car than for his friendship. Somehow she knew that that was not true. Nearly all the telephone calls that came to the Brady house were for Milo, and as many of them were girls' voices as boys'. "Is Milo there? Can I speak to Milo? Is Milo there? Can I speak to Milo? Is this the Brady residence?" The voices told her that Milo was popular, genuinely so.

And in spite of the bad time he was giving her, Jenny was thankful that he was not a *bad boy*. He did not, for instance, drink. He had not started to smoke. And he did not have to be told to study. "Our James has the ability if we could only get him to apply himself," a mother would say. "All he cares about is baseball." Not so, Milo. He would bring his books home from school and after supper go to his bedroom and do all his homework, and along about nine o'clock the telephone would ring and it would be a classmate wanting to have Milo's help, in geometry, in French, and especially in the sciences. Milo's end of the telephone conversations was unintelligible to his mother, who had never reached hypotenuses and valences and periphrastics. That such words were present in the vocabulary of one member of her household was a matter of pride and anguish. She would turn down her radio, ostensibly to accommodate Milo, but only the better to eavesdrop. There were certain voices she came to recognize without identifying them. Girls. Certain girls. "Is Milo there?" And when these voices called and Milo went to the telephone Jenny would hear him say, "Where are you? Home?" And he would hang up and go downstairs to the barroom, where there was a phone booth. When he came back upstairs he would say, "Pop says I can have the car if it's O. K. with you. Will you let me have a couple dollars?" She could not refuse him. It was enough that for so many years she had refused his father until his father no longer came to her for anything but his meals.

For nearly twenty years she had been refusing his father, and she had never been able to accuse herself of that sin in the confessional. Twenty years of sacrilegious confessions, blackening her soul, with admissions of other sins but never a word about that one. Once, many years ago, Father Mooney had said through the grill, "And is that all, my child?", and she had almost confessed to the sin of rejecting her husband. But she could not, she could not. She could not say the words that would expose her soul to a priest who had heard the final confessions of condemned murderers. Priest or not, secret of the confessional or not, he was a man, only too unmistakably a man, with the heavy smell of his last cigar coming through the grill and the softened bass of his voice uttering the routine, "Is that all, my child?" A near saint he may have been, Father Mooney, but he was as male as Dr. Malloy and Bart Brady himself, and it was the male that had made her blacken all her confessions.

By keeping him out of her bed she gave him the excuse to go away on his awful trips, but he would have found another excuse, and she refused to blame herself for appetites he had acquired long before she married him. By his own admission he had been with many women, that kind of women, since he was sixteen years of age. He had fallen in love with her, *he said,* but he had not fallen in love with *her;* he had been attracted by her purity after those earlier adventures with the sluts. He had married her because there was no other way for him to possess her and her purity, and having married her he had made it sinful for her to deny him and thus he had been the cause of the sinful, soul-blackening lies she had told in confession. "And is that all, my child?" the priest would say, and she would lie and say that that was all.

She was ever conscious of what other women were thinking, of the giant of a man he was and the tiny woman she was by comparison. She had seen other women look at Bart, their faces dumb while their evil thoughts took possession of them. They would gaze up at him with eager smiles that were supposed to be innocent friendliness, but always, as if by accident, they would get to touch him with their fingertips, with their elbows brushing against him. They would look at him and then look at her, as though measuring them. They would linger after Mass, just to have a moment's chat with him. And they would look at her and wonder, wonder, wonder, terrified for her but wanting to experience the perils of making love to such a man. The men made jokes about the size of his feet and the amount of food he could put away, but the women made no jokes. The jokes they would make if they made them would not be funny; they would be too self-revealing. "Ach, and it's too bad little Milo don't have a little brother to play with, or a sister," they would say, tacking a question mark on to the end of their remark.

"Maybe some day he will," was Jenny's answer.

"The good Lord willing."

"The good Lord willing," Jenny would say. They never got anything out of Jenny Brady. No one did, except Milo, but he got everything out of her that was not a sin to give.

He came back from Villanova to go to his father's funeral. He went back to college to take his exams, but Lawyer McCaffrey suggested to him that he inquire about a scholarship for the next year. "There's not as much there as we thought there'd be," said Lawyer McCaffrey. "I'll talk to you again in June, after we've had a little more time, but meanwhile it won't do a bit of harm if you land yourself a scholarship. As it is, Milo, the automobile will have to go. I can tell you that right away. There may not be enough cash to pay the outstanding obligations. Luckily you're still a young fellow."

"I always thought Pop was pretty well fixed," said Milo.

"Hmm, well, we'll see," said Lawyer McCaffrey. "He may have stashed away some money we didn't know about, but I doubt it. If I were you, m'boy, I'd count on less rather than more."

"You're holding something back from me, Mr. McCaffrey."

"Yes."

"What?"

"Well—all right, I'll give it to you straight. It'll save trouble later on," said the lawyer. "During the course of some conversation with your mother, I happened to mention to her how I noticed a big difference between what your father took in and what he deposited in the bank. To tell you the truth, Milo, I harbored the suspicion that maybe you were knocking down, helping yourself at the till. That was how it came out that you weren't the one, but your mother was. She said she didn't know how much, but five dollars here, ten dollars there. Whenever you wanted a little extra, she'd help herself."

"Didn't Pop know that?" said Milo.

"I guess he knew, but he never said anything to her."

"Maybe he thought I was stealing from him," said Milo.

"Hard to say what he thought, and we'll never know. He could certainly see the difference between what he wrote down for the day's receipts and what he deposited in the bank."

"Then he knew one of us was a thief, only he didn't know which one," said Milo.

"He didn't want to know."

"No, he didn't want to know," said Milo. "I wish he didn't think it was me. My mother had a right to the money, she was his wife. But I wish he would have asked me."

"It's possible he didn't care that much, who took it," said the lawyer.

"He cared, all right. And so do I."

"Well, there you are, m' boy," said McCaffrey. "It all went in spending-money for you. New suits. Your car. You got in the habit of asking her for money instead of him, and she could never say no to you."

"No, she didn't spend it on herself, that's certain."

"Well, you were the only boy in this part of town that got his suits from Jacob Reed's. The old saying, it's a poor family that can't afford one gentleman."

"That's not why she did it," said Milo.

"No? Then why?"

"I'm not exactly sure why, but I know that wasn't it," said Milo. "I guess I better forget about going back to college."

"Well, you're going to need a lot more than you have now if you want to go on studying medicine. You've got your pre-med, then medical school, then interning someplace. Be seven or eight years before you start earning anything. You might be able to do it if the place went on making money, but don't forget, Milo, you'll have to pay a man to run it. You'll have to pay a good man fifty dollars a week. You can get a bartender for less, but you won't only need a bartender."

"What if we sold the place?" said Milo.

McCaffrey shrugged his shoulders. "If you want to do that I'll see if I can find a buyer for you. But bear in mind, boy, the interest off what you get from a sale won't support your mother."

"Then suppose I run it myself for a year and see what happens."

"Do you know anything about running a saloon?"

"What I don't know I can learn," said Milo.

"How would you handle Saturday night? Bart Brady could keep order with a flick of the eyebrow. They'll take advantage of you, boy. And it does seem a pity you losing a year of your education, but I guess you have to give it a try. If it doesn't turn out right you still have your mother to support."

"It doesn't look so good, does it?"

"If I didn't have my own three to educate, I'd like to offer to help, but there's the one at Georgetown and the other at State and next year the girl goes away to the Eastman Conservatory."

"She is? Noreen's going to study music?"

"Yes, a man from there listened to her play and she's been accepted for next year. Sixteen years of age, think of it. Our Noreen."

"Say, good for Noreen, good for her," said Milo.

"Thanks, boy. In case anything turns up, that I think'd make it possible for you to continue your studies—but don't count on it," said the lawyer. "I don't see anything on the horizon. They say look for the pot of gold behind the rainbow, but you had your rainbow—those fancy sweaters and gawlf stockings."

No good would come of talking to his mother, Milo knew. She would only lie to him, and when she finished lying she would weep and tell him she had stolen the money to please him. And when she finished with that she would very probably seek to justify herself by pointing out that if he had not abandoned his true vocation, he would not have learned to care so much for cars and dancing and expensive clothes. No good ever came of finding Jenny Brady in the wrong. Milo therefore firmly stated to her his intention of running the saloon, and stated it with such firmness that she gave him no opposition. "There's just not enough money for me to do anything else," he said, and stared at her. She got the import of the stare.

Having grown up in the same house with the saloon, Milo was not ignorant of the mechanics of running one, and within a year of his taking over, Brady's had a character of its own that was not so different from its old character that the customers minded much. The new proprietor was a slender man, a dancing man, an educated man, and not a giant of a man who could fracture your skull with a blow of his fist, whose schooling had ended in the fourth grade. But Milo kept a blackjack under the bar, and on a couple of occasions he showed he had the spunk to use it. What he lacked in bulk, he made up for in meanness; he waded right in and went for the nose, and a blackjack blow on the nose is an ugly and effective attack. It also commanded more respect for Milo than if he had sent for the police, and Brady's remained an orderly place. Inside of two years, or just about the time he should have been a junior in college, he was invited to listen to a proposition by the liquor mob.

They were Irish. There were some Irish in the beer mob, but only for show; control of beer was in the hands of the Italians who had come in from Jersey City in the early days of Prohibition, brought in some New York Jews, and in a short time had the manufacturing and distribution of beer on a highly efficient basis. It was no great secret that the real power belonged to the beer mob and that the bootlegging of liquor was conceded to the Irish to keep them quiet. Paradoxically, the liquor mob were somewhat more respectable, but public opinion was more sympathetic to the workingman's beer. The men in the mines and the mills never threatened to strike if they were denied their whiskey. Even the farmers who voted dry were grateful for the availability of beer while opposing every threat of the return of liquor.

One Monday morning the collector for the liquor mob, a man

named Rafferty, made his usual stop at Brady's and after handing a receipt to Milo said, "Jimmy O' wants to see you."

"What for? Isn't everything all right?" said Milo.

"As far as I know, everything's fine and dandy," said Rafferty.

"Then what does he want to see me for? I only ever met him three times in my life, and one of them was Dad's funeral."

"Go see him anyhow," said Rafferty.

"Did he say when?"

"Any time this afternoon. He'll be at the hotel," said Rafferty.

"Give me a hint, for Christ's sake," said Milo.

"I would if I could. You know that."

"You're a God damn liar."

"I'll give you one hint," said Rafferty. "Don't bring your truncheon. You won't need it."

"Who'll I get to mind the place?"

"Hang up a sign. 'Closed till five.' It'll be worth it. It isn't that often that Jimmy O' sends for a fellow. If it's going to be trouble, Jimmy O's the kind of a man that goes and sees the fellow in person. You know that."

"I don't know that or very much else about him," said Milo.

At half-past two in the afternoon he called at the hotel where Jimmy O'Dowd kept a suite of rooms. It was the second best hotel in town, owned by a renegade Catholic who was married to a cousin of Jimmy O' and herself a backslider. She acted as room clerk, and always stood behind the front desk.

"Well, now, if it isn't Milo Brady," she said.

"Hello, Mrs. Harris," said Milo. "I came to see Jimmy O'."

"You're expected," said Mary Harris. "It's the second floor front. You'll save time walking."

The parlor door of Jimmy O's suite was open, and Jimmy O' was sitting in a large plush chair in the far corner, where he could look out two windows and see everything that was going on in the neighborhood. At the moment he was reading the Philadelphia *North American*, an unlit cigar in his mouth and his spotless grey fedora on his head. At Milo's appearance he folded the newspaper and put it on his lap. "Young Brady, isn't it?" he said, taking off his glasses and putting them in a gunmetal case that sprang shut with a *plop*.

"That's me," said Milo.

"Sit down, boy. Will you have a cigar?" Jimmy O' held out a fistful of foil-wrapped cigars.

"No thanks, I don't smoke," said Milo.

"Don't start till you have to," said Jimmy O'. "And you don't drink, either, I'm told. But I hear you like the girls."

"I don't have any objection to them," said Milo.

"Well, they can get you into more trouble than cigars and booze put together, but every man to his taste," said Jimmy O'. "There's been a lot of favorable talk concerning how you took over your father's place. I hear those things, Milo. I get full reports."

"From Rafferty, I suppose," said Milo.

"Not only Rafferty. Others as well. You smashed some bohunk in the nose with your blackjack. I hear that took a lot of nerve, a man half again your size."

"It was that or he'd start wrecking my place. I paid the doctor bill, and we made up. He's still a customer, the man."

"Uh-huh. And one of those nights he'll have one too many and try to kill you."

"If he does, he'll get a bullet where he got the blackjack," said Milo.

"Oh, my. You went and got a gun. Well, it's always nice to be ready."

"The gun was always there. It belonged to my father, a .32 revolver."

"It's oiled and all, I trust," said Jimmy O'. "If it was only sitting there all that time it gets gummy. If you ever have to use it be sure and pull back the hammer before you pull the trigger."

"It's in workable condition," said Milo.

"And you'd use it if you had to?"

"If I had to."

"Yes, I believe you would," said Jimmy O'. "But that isn't why I sent for you. Firearms aren't the way I run my business. You can cause a man plenty of trouble without resort to firearms. You can get the same results with a pair of thick-soled shoes, and nobody has to go to the electric chair. I'm against *all* rough stuff, but that's not saying I'll let anybody walk all over me. Nobody walks all over Jimmy O'Dowd."

"Would anybody try?" said Milo.

"You're young, but you been in the business about two years, and you learn quick. Therefore you must of heard from time to time that I don't run my business, that I'm only fronting for certain other people, that they could run me out of business any time they felt like it. What's your candid opinion of that?"

"You mean do I believe it?"

"Yes," said Jimmy O'.

"Well, I only run a small saloon near the steel mill. I'm not up there with the big shots."

"Quit stalling and answer my question," said Jimmy O'.

"All right. Yes, I believe that."

"You think I'm just a second-rater?"

"No, now don't get me wrong, Mr. O'Dowd," said Milo.

"Well, what else do you think? You think them ginnies across the street are the boss of me?"

"Oh, listen, that's not what I think. The way I understand it, you're partners with them. You run the liquor end, and they run the beer."

"Well, there you're wrong. I wouldn't *be* partners with them. I wouldn't have anything to do with the whorehouses, or I could of been partners with them. As soon as they begun taking over the whorehouses, I got out. Whores are a necessity, they have them all over the world, whether it's Dublin or Cork or Allentown, Pa., or Gibbsville, Pa., or I don't care where it is. But that's money I don't take a cent of. So get it out of your head that I'm partners with those lads across the way. I got an aunt in the convent, a wonderful old lady up in her late seventies. I go see her three-four times a year and take my whole family with me. How could I face her with money in my pocket that came from the whores?" He reached in his pocket and took out a roll of bills bound in a wide elastic band. "Do you see that? You'll notice they're all clean fresh bills. Eight thousand dollars. Brand new from the bank. I like my money clean, in more ways than one. Here." He put his thumb to his tongue and peeled off two $100 bills and handed them to Milo. "That's for your time, coming up here to see me."

"Oh, I didn't—"

"Take it, for God's sake," said Jimmy O'. He replaced the rubber band and put the bankroll back in his pocket. "All right, let's get down to business. I want you to come and work for me."

"Doing what?"

"Well, if I was still in the army, you'd be my orderly. I'd make you a lance corporal. A dog-robber was what we used to call them, out of spite and envy, because they ate officers' food and could stay out of the rain. That was in sunny France, in '18. What I want you for, I want a clean-cut looking young fellow to go with me wherever I go—"

"A bodyguard?"

"I got Tiny Devlin for a bodyguard but he *looks* like a bodyguard. Every time I go any place the people all look at Tiny because of his size and that kisser, and that attracts attention. I want a clean-cut looking young fellow like yourself that has plenty of guts but don't attract attention."

"But what happens to my business?"

"I'll put Tiny in there to run it, and that'll support your mother.

You I'll pay a hundred-and-a-half a week and expenses. You'll drive my car and go with me every place I go. Dick Harris will give you a room here at the hotel."

"I don't live at home?" said Milo.

"I hear you won't mind that much. Listen, boy, I know all about you. I wouldn't be putting my life in your hands—you're a very good automobile driver."

"That isn't what you started to say, Mr. O'Dowd," said Milo. "Do I carry a gun on this job?"

"Well, I very often have large sums of money with me. Yes, you'd be better off carrying a gun, some of the time," said Jimmy O'.

Milo did not speak. He got up and looked out the window and saw, across the street, three members of the beer mob come out of the Greek restaurant, carefully setting their identical grey fedoras at a jaunty angle, lighting cigars, and getting into a large Paige touring car. Jimmy O', who could see them without rising, said, "They're not our kind, Milo."

"No, I guess they're not," said Milo.

Now a younger man in a powder blue suit with a long soft roll to the lapel and eighteen-inch bottoms on the trousers and a brown Homburg came out of the restaurant, and got in the Paige. "That's one I never saw before," said Milo.

"He's one of them's younger brother," said Jimmy O'. "Studying to be a doctor in Philly."

"I came near doing that," said Milo. "I wanted to be a doctor since I was thirteen."

"So I understand," said Jimmy O'. "Well, there was a time in my life I wanted to be another John McCormack, only my voice changed and that ended that. We all start out wanting one thing and end up something else. Lawyer McCaffrey had his heart set on being an actor. He used to give recitations. ' "We are saved by God's might," cried the guard with delight, "for the sign of the cross is the password tonight." ' Are you acquainted with that poem?"

"No," said Milo.

"It was one of Mac's recitations in school. He used to deliver it with gestures and all, act it out till you wanted to cheer at the end. It's a poem about this fellow that escaped from the redcoats in the Revolutionary War, only when he got to the Continental lines he didn't know the password and they were going to shoot him as a spy. But the guard gave him one minute to say his prayers, and he went down on his knees and blessed himself. 'You are saved by God's might, cried the guard with delight, for the sign of the cross is the password tonight.' That's how it went. Mac was a born actor. But between you and me and the bedpost, he's better off what he is. Two boys graduated from college and a daughter a promising pianist. 'Ye call me chief, and ye do well to call me chief—' "

"That one I do know," said Milo.

"One of Mac's recitations. Friday afternoon in the auditorium. And I'd sing 'Danny Boy' or 'The Dear Little Shamrock.' Oh, those were the days before we got a little sense in us, before we got rid of our foolish ambitions."

"You think wanting to be a doctor was a foolish ambition on my part?" said Milo.

"Bein's you didn't have the money for it, it was."

"I guess so," said Milo. "It'd take a lot."

"How much?" said Jimmy O'.

"Oh, I guess ten thousand at least," said Milo.

"Your Dad could of raised that, if he lived. But it's a good thing he didn't or now you'd be paying that off and you still wouldn't be a doctor. The good Lord moves in mysterious ways, his something to perform."

"You know, I never thought of it that way at all," said Milo.

"Oh, sure. I wanted sergeant so bad I could taste it, but Joe Mulcahy got sergeant and two nights later he was deader than a mackerel, trying to bring back a prisoner for interrogation. You come and work for me and you'll be living as good as any doctor in town."

"A hundred and fifty dollars a week is a lot of money," said Milo. "You'll want me to earn it."

"Only the once," said Jimmy O'.

"Only the once, eh?" said Milo.

"And maybe not that. There won't be any gang wars around here, Milo. We don't have gangs. It's only between me and them. But I put you down as the kind of a man that once you start taking my money, if I ever need you, you'll be there. Gang wars you read about in the paper. Chicago. New York. Detroit. St. Louis. Here we say the beer mob and the liquor mob, but the liquor mob is me, James Aloysius O'Dowd, five guys driving my trucks, four guys at my warehouse, an old man that used to work in the chemical laboratory at the coal company. Tiny Devlin. That's my whole operation. Across the street, they got a hundred men working for them, maybe more. During the summer, the latter part of August, around Labor Day, somewhere around there, a friend of mine I used to know in the army gave me the tip that there was something funny going on. He runs a little speakeasy way the hell down Canal Street, never good for more than a case of booze a week. Twenty-four dollars a week, and very slow pay at that. A guy come in his place one day and told him I was moving to Florida, retiring. He knew better, because I stop and say hello to him every Sunday at the eleven o'clock Mass. A couple days later I get the same identical story from a couple more customers, that I was retiring and moving to Florida. Who'd want to start a rumor like that? And why? Well, it didn't take much brains to figure that one out. It was the ginnies across the street. Six of my customers stopped ordering. The next move I figured would be rough stuff with my drivers. But that's where they crossed me. My drivers went around the same as usual, delivered two cases to two-case customers, five cases to five-case customers, and Monday when Rafferty showed up to make his collections, he got paid as usual. What the hell was going on? I said to myself. So I went over across the street and sat down and had a cup of coffee with Ed Charney. He said what was eating me, and I told him, I said I wanted to know what was the big idea starting those rumors and the rest of it. He said he didn't know a damn thing about it, and ordinarily I don't believe him, but this time I did. He said he'd try and find out and let me know in an hour. He did. He came over here himself, all alone, and gave me the story. He got a new guy working for him by the name of Williams, married to a cousin of his wife. Williams is from Jersey City. He has big ideas, too big. He decided to show Charney how easy it would be for anybody to take over my business. That was all there was to it, barring the fact that Williams wanted to be the one that took over. 'Well, I'm not going to let him,' I said to Charney. And Charney said, 'No, I'm not going to let him either. He's on his way back to Jersey City tonight.' But then Charney said it started him thinking and maybe it'd be a good idea if I did retire and move to Florida. Sooner or later he was going to buy me out anyhow, and he didn't want to wait till my price got too big. I said I had no intention of retiring, and Charney said the only way to keep the peace around here was if he bought me out before somebody like Williams came along and took my business away from me. Williams is a believer in rough stuff, and Charney is against it. The only thing Charney don't absolutely control is booze. 'You're greedy, Ed,' I told him. 'Yes, I'm greedy,' he said. 'But it's the only way to operate. If I let you operate independent, others will get the same idea and the next big thing is going to be the numbers racket.' If Charney lets me operate independent selling booze, the numbers guys will want to be independent, and that'll never be. The mobs all over the country are operating numbers. The profits are over ninety percent. It isn't like beer or booze, where you have to make the stuff and deliver it. In the numbers all you need is a few little pieces of paper and a few bucks to the winners. One man is your salesman for a thousand customers, and you have to take care of the cops and the politicians, but nowheres near the bastards you have to take care of selling beer and booze. So the next thing you're going to hear about around here is the numbers, with Ed Charney running it."

"But what about you and liquor?"

"Well, I said to him, 'Ed, I'll get out if you guarantee me the same income I got now for the next ten years. Otherwise, why should I retire?'

" 'What's your income now?' he said, and I told him. I gave it a little boost, but not much. But I could tell from the expression on his face that it was no deal," said Jimmy O'. "He said he'd have to think it over, and I told him to take ten years to think it over. That was when he got a little nasty. He accused me of being greedy, so I said to him he wouldn't get anywhere calling me names, and as far as that goes, I said I only had his word for it that Williams was operating on his own. How did I know that Williams wasn't doing exactly what Charney told him to do. 'You calling me a liar?' he said. And I said I wasn't exactly calling him anything—yet. Then he got tough. 'Jimmy,' he said, 'I was always against the muscle. You start using the muscle and it gets to be hard to stop. But if one man gets in my way, maybe the only way to push him out of the way is a little muscle.' So I said to him, 'Ed, would you knock me off?' And he said, 'Well, muscle is muscle. You use as much as you have to to make sure.' Then he walked out, and I been sitting here these last couple of months, you might say wrestling with my problem. Never another word from Charney, but every time I see a new face across the street I make sure and find out who it is. The young fellow studying to be a doctor was one, but he's legitimate. One thing I don't like about sitting here, I began thinking what if I used a little muscle on Charney? When a man threatens you, you're half dead if you're not ready to do the same thing to him. And I'm ready. I got this thing hanging over me now, Milo, and I keep thinking to myself, with him out of the way I could walk in there the same day and tell them others, 'All right, boys, go on back to Jersey City. From now on it's me.' That's if I had a good right-hand man. It'd have to be somebody my own kind. But there's millions in it, boy."

"Millions?" said Milo.

"Millions," said Jimmy O'. "You know what a million dollars a year is? It's under twenty thousand a week. He don't handle that much in a year, but I'm damn sure he handles it in two years."

"It's a hell of a lot of money. But how long would I be around to enjoy it?"

"How long do you want to be? You could of died for coffee and cakes the night you broke that bohunk's nose. The army used to pay me thirty-three a month, and my wife would of got ten gees insurance. I'm not asking you to go over there and put a slug in Ed Charney. But he made a threat to me, and I have to be ready. What's sauce for the goose is sauce for the gander, they say."

"My mother wanted me to be a priest, and here I am talking to another Catholic about—"

"You better not say it," said Jimmy O'.

"Why not say it, Mr. O'Dowd? If I go to work for you, it's what I'll always be thinking. You want me to be ready to kill a man. Why me?"

Jimmy O' again took out the roll of bills. "You see this? I could go in any number of poolrooms and find any number of young punks that would kill a man for $8,000. If that was all I wanted, I could get it done. I could probably go to Jersey City, New Jersey, and get a guy to do it for less. But I never said anything to you about a cold-blooded murder. I don't want to be going around with that kind of a fellow. On the other hand, I want a young fellow that if trouble starts, I can depend on him. Somebody my own kind that won't kiyoodle out on me if the trouble starts. Them fellows across the street, I know Ed Charney inside out, and when he gets an idea he worries over it, worries over it, like a dog with a bone, and I'm the bone he's been worr'ing over for these last three months. When he gets an idea, he won't give up on it, and sitting right there where you are now, he got the idea that somehow or other James Aloysius O'Dowd should have a solemn high Mass of requiem said over him."

"Why are you so sure?"

"I'm so sure that if I was to die of the pneumonia I'd know Ed Charney was behind it."

Milo smiled. "Pneumonia, maybe. The next time he has a cold don't let him blow his breath in your face. But the only rough stuff I ever heard of him in connection with was when they had that thing about swiping a truckload of beer in one of the patches. Some fire company helped themselves to beer for a picnic or something. It was in one of the patches near Taqua."

"You got the story all wrong, Milo, but it'd take too long to put you straight on it. Suffice it to say, the guy that hijacked the truck went off the road in a skidding accident, right? If it happens a whole year after the party stole a truckload of beer off of Ed Charney, who's going to connect up the two incidents?"

"Well, it was always hazy in my mind," said Milo.

"In everybody's mind. But that's what I mean about Ed Charney when he gets an idea won't give up on it," said Jimmy O'. "That's also about how much you can depend on Ed and his talk about him not liking rough stuff. Ed was in the army, too. Not the 28th Division. He was in the 49th. But he saw action, and us fellows that saw action, we never want to see it again, but you're not as afraid as you were the first time."

"Well I was never in the army, Mr. O'Dowd," said Milo. "I don't know where you got the idea that I could kill a man. Just because I went after a drunk in my saloon."

"A big drunk, a tough drunk. The toughest guy in your neighborhood, so I'm told. You had to come from behind the bar with your blackjack in your hand and go right up and slug him, half again your size. I got the story from witnesses, Milo. It wasn't like hitting a guy back that hit you first. You went right after him. And I understand you did the same thing with a couple others, not as big. When I heard about it I said to myself, 'Here's the young fellow I been looking for.' And you're not escared of me."

"Should I be?"

"Not exactly. But a lot of men twice your age come in here and they don't have your self-confidence. They act like they were afraid I was gonna take their business away from them. Not you. You speak right up, you say what you think. I like that. I know I can depend on you."

"Mr. O'Dowd, as far as I know I'm the youngest saloonkeeper in the county."

"Yeah, I wouldn't doubt that for a minute," said Jimmy O'. "You are, in years."

"I didn't start out wanting to be a saloonkeeper. My mother had me all cut out for a priest, and *I* wanted to be a doctor," said Milo.

"Go on," said Jimmy O'.

"But inside of the fifteen minutes I've been here you convinced me of my true vocation."

"And what is that, Milo?"

"You convinced me that I ought to be a gangster."

"A gangster? Oh, come now, Milo. You been reading too many newspapers."

"No, that doesn't have anything to do with it. You're a rich man, and you got that way partly by being a good judge of character. And I think you judged my character pretty well. You figured out that I like money, and I do. That's one thing you figured out. The other thing is that I'd do damn near anything to get it."

"Ah, then you'll come to work for me?" said Jimmy O'.

"Yes, I'll come to work for you."

"That's the way to talk, Milo."

"But wait a minute, Mr. O'Dowd. I didn't finish talking," said Milo. He reached in his pocket and took out the two $100 bills and handed them to Jimmy O'. "I'm giving these back to you."

"I gave them to you," said Jimmy O'.

"And I'm giving them back," said Milo. He held out his hand. "You have eight thousand on you. Give me four."

"Those kind of jokes I'm not partial to, son," said Jimmy O'.

"Me either," said Milo. He kept his hand extended.

"I'd kill you first," said Jimmy O'. "You mean cut you in for half of my business? Before I did that I'd kill you."

"Mr. O'Dowd, you as much as offered me a partnership a minute or two ago. You said there was millions in Ed Charney's business. What was I supposed to think? I understood you to mean that I'd be your partner. If you didn't mean that, you were stringing me along."

"I wasn't stringing you along, young fellow. But you're very hasty."

"Yes, I guess I am. But I'm not the same guy that came in here fifteen minutes ago. I know a lot more about you and a lot more about myself. As soon as you said 'millions' I suddenly began to realize that Ed Charney was nothing but a big fat Italian from Jersey City. Why should he have it all?"

"Go on home, young fellow. Go on back to your little saloon."

"No, I can't do that, Mr. O'Dowd. Not any more. If I go out of here, I go across the street."

"Is that what you are? You'd turn on your own kind like that? We'll see about that," said Jimmy O'. He reached for the telephone and lifted the receiver. "Six-four, six-four," he said. "Hello, Ed? This is Jimmy O'. Oh, I'm pretty good, Ed. Say, there's a young fellow by the name of Milo Brady. Brady. That's the one. Big Bart Brady's kid. I don't know what the hell's got into him, but all of a sudden he come storming in here and wanted to be my partner. My partner. In my business. He's sick in the head, Ed. I threw him out, but I wanted to tip you off. You're next on who he wants to be partners with. Oh, that's all right, Ed. These young guys. See you around." Jimmy O' slowly, carefully replaced the receiver.

"So you threw me out, eh?" said Milo.

"I could if I had to," said Jimmy O'. He picked up the two $100 bills that lay before him and put them in his pocket. "But if I's you, young fellow, I'd stay away from Ed Charney. Him and his buddies'll kick you to pieces. Even a year from now they'll kick you to pieces." He pointed to the folded newspaper at his side. "You know what? I think the Pirates are gonna win the pennant," he said. "It'll be the Pirates and the Senators." He stared hard at Milo Brady.

The Farmer

At the sight of a young woman sitting on a tree stump at the side of the road Kramer might ordinarily have slowed down, but he would not have stopped. This young woman, however, was wearing riding breeches and boots, was smoking a cigarette, was such a picture of dejection, that curiosity and the instinct to be helpful made him stop. "Can I do anything for you?" said Kramer.

She looked at him with hostility, impatience, and it was obviously against her will that she made the effort to be civil. "Yes, if you'll get me to a telephone," she said.

"We have one, the second farm down the road. Get in," said Kramer. He opened the door of the half-ton and she stood up. As she approached the truck she limped. She got in beside him and he put the car in low gear. "You get thrown off your horse?" he said.

"Wasn't *my* horse," she said. "I never would have been thrown off my horse."

"What'd he do? Shy up at something?"

"A snake. A nasty little snake went slithering across the road."

"Yes, we had a lot of copperheads around. The dry weather brings them out. I killed one this morning, right in my barnyard. Near the water trough."

"I wish you'd have killed that one."

"I noticed you limping. Where were you hurt?"

"At the base of my spine," she said.

"Oh," he said.

"He reared up and back I went."

"And ran away," said Kramer. "Well, he most likely headed for home. Where are you staying? Dr. Jones's?"

"Yes, how did you know?"

"They're the only ones still keep any saddle horses in the Valley. I can take you there, it isn't much farther."

And Other Stories (1968)

"All right, if it isn't too much trouble," she said.

"I guess you're a friend of Martita's. You're about her age."

"Yes, I'm staying there."

"Are you from town?"

"What town?"

"Gibbsville," he said.

"Yes," she said. "My name is Sheffield. Barbara Sheffield."

"Oh, Sheffield-that-has-the-lumber-company's daughter. Out there on Twelfth Street."

"Yes."

"I bought all the lumber for my tractor barn from Sheffield."

"That's nice," she said.

"My name is Kramer. Irwin Kramer. Your father wouldn't know me, but I know Gus Bohmer pretty well."

"Oh, yes. The foreman."

"Gus is related to my wife's people."

"Is that so?"

"Here's my farm, on your right. I'm on both sides of the road, but those are the farm buildings on the right."

"My, it's quite impressive. Quite an establishment," she said.

"It belonged to my father *and* my grandfather. I wasn't going to farm it, but I had my older brother was killed in the war in France, so I was the only one left. Two older sisters, but both married. One living in Reading and the other in Swedish Haven."

"What were *you* going to do instead of farming?"

"Well, I guess if I had my way I'd have finished my college education and maybe gone to law school."

"Oh, you did go to college?"

"For a year to Muhlenberg. But then Paul got killed with Company C, the 103rd Engineers. You know, mostly from Gibbsville."

"Yes. I had two cousins in that company."

"Sheffield?"

"No. One was a Hofman and the other was a Davis."

"Yes, I didn't remember any Sheffield in Company C. There was a Dayton Sheffield in Company D."

"He was another cousin," she said.

"I had my cousin Walter Kloster in Company D. I guess you saw my brother Paul's name on the roll of honor they put up at the armory."

"Yes, I must have," she said.

"Corporal Paul M. Kramer, under the killed in action," he said. "I guess you're a college girl?"

"No. I didn't go. I should have been a sophomore now, but I wouldn't have got anything out of it. I'm a non-producer."

"A what?"

"That's what a friend of mine calls me. He says I'm a non-producer. Anybody that doesn't work or do something he calls a non-producer. He's certainly right about me."

"Well, you have plenty of time, and I guess if your father owns the Sheffield Lumber Company you don't need the money. In other words, you don't have to go to work. I wouldn't work if I didn't have to."

"Not even as a lawyer?"

"No. I didn't take any special liking to being a lawyer. I just wanted to get away from the farm. But I never will now."

"Sell it," she said.

"Ho-ho. Sell it! Did you ever try to sell a farm? You never get what you put into it. Sure, I could sell it to my neighbor, for five thousand dollars. Take a mortgage and all that. Did you ever go to a farm auction? See those prices? Five dollars for a cultivator. Six dollars for a lime spreader. Fifty cents for a set of harness. Two dollars for a DeLaval. They come around like chicken hawks, looking for the bargains. Maybe you think your farm is worth twenty, twenty-five thousand, but wait till you go and put it up for sale. Georgie Laubenstein over in the next valley. Four hundred acres, thirty-two head of Holstein, a practically brand-new tractor, a house with running water, a new Delco. You know what Elsie Laubenstein got when she sold? Fifteen thousand dollars. Fif-teen thousand dollars. If you don't have a son that's ready to take over, and run your farm, your widow is lucky to get a quarter of the value for a quick sale. I bet you Dr. Jones put in thirty, forty thousand dollars since he bought the Snyder farm, but I'll bet you they don't get any thirty thousand for it when he dies. Not that he's a regular farmer. He's what they call a gentleman farmer, uses it for a hobby. Any time you see a saddle horse on a farm around here, that means a rich man that farms for a hobby. Do you have a horse at home, in town?"

"Yes. I hope I don't have to give him to Dr. Jones for losing his horse."

"Don't worry. The doctor's horse'll be in the barn when we get there."

"Would you mind stopping a minute?" she said.

"No. Is your back hurting you? This half-ton don't ride too easy."

"It isn't my back. I'd just like to smoke another cigarette before I have to face Dr. Jones and Martita. Will you have a cigarette?"

"I don't mind," he said. "I don't very often smoke a cigarette. In the house I smoke a pipe or an occasional cigar, but I never smoke anything around the barn. And I never took up chewing. Most farmers chew, but not me." He drew the truck over to the side of the road. "I don't even carry matches, so you have to light your own."

"What if that damn horse didn't go back to the barn?"

"He will. But even if he didn't they'd find him. Which one was it? The chestnut?"

"No, the white one. The white gelding. You seem to know the Jones horses," she said.

"Farming, you get so you know all the stock everybody has. There's not so many people to know, so the next thing is you know the stock. The cattle. The horses. Dogs. All the animals that last a few years. Not the poultry or the pigs. They don't last long enough. But there's not a farmer in the two valleys that wouldn't know Dr. Jones's white horse."

"I suppose not," she said.

"We're all used to him. The doctor comes down here all year round, not just the summers. And he'll go for rides on that white horse in all kinds of weather."

"Yes, I know," she said.

"Soaking wet I've seen him, the doctor. He must enjoy it."

"He loves his farm," she said.

"He can buy mine any time he wants to, providing he offers me a decent price. But his place is too far from mine. He wouldn't want to buy mine. Did your father ever think of buying a farm?"

"Not that I know of. His relaxation is playing golf. And he likes to go fishing, in the Poconos. As far as I know, he never showed the slightest interest in farming."

"I thought maybe if he knew my farm is for sale, he could come and have a look at it."

"I don't think there's much chance of that," she said. "You really want to get rid of it, don't you?"

"As quick as you say Jack Robinson, if I was offered a decent price. But that'll never be, and I know it. I'm tied down to it. Trapped."

"Maybe if you did sell it and went away, you'd miss it."

"Not me. I only had the one year away from it, one year in Allentown, at Muhlenberg. But my goodness, I made friends there with a Chinaman. A boy from China, a freshman with me. You'd never meet anybody from that far away living on a farm all your life. It's only by accident I met you."

"Aren't you married?" she said. "You are. Our foreman is related to your wife's people."

"I'm married," he said.

"Doesn't your wife like living on a farm?"

"She was never anywheres else. Not even to Philly, except when we passed through it on our way to Atlantic, on our honeymoon. She didn't like it. The farm she came from, over in the other valley, her parents didn't have any of the modern conveniences. They had to pump water by hand. Coal-oil lamps. No such thing as the telephone."

"So your farm is luxury to her."

"Luxury is right. Her mother brings her ironing over every Tuesday, because we have the electricity. The last baby, her mother stayed with us a week and she never went to bed till two o'clock in the morning, listening to the radio. I have such an Atwater-Kent set I bought last year. The old lady won't believe it that the music comes from Chicago, through the air. She thinks it comes over the electric power line, or like the telephone."

"Well, I don't understand it either."

"But you know it doesn't come over the telephone line," he said.

"I know it because that's what I was told. Understanding it is something else again," she said.

"Well, I guess if you're talking about the scientific part, I don't understand it either. You'd have to know more about electricity than I know."

"I don't want to hold you up," she said. "You were on your way home."

"No hurry. I don't so often have an interesting conversation," he said. "A person doesn't get to talk much to his neighbors. Like I'm out plowing or something like that, in the field, and I see my neighbor plowing in his field. 'Hyuh, Kramer,' he says to me, and I say hello to him. But we don't always stop and talk. When we do stop and talk, maybe he wants to borrow something off of me. I want to borrow something off of him. Or maybe they're going to vote on spending some money on the road. The road needs it, but nobody wants to spend the money. Every spring the road is so bad we have to spend the money, but it's township money, and township money is our money. The county won't help, the state won't help. It's all right if county people want to use the road, but they won't give us the money. That's why the road's in such bad condition. Look at the condition of this road."

"It's pretty awful," she said.

"They fill in with a wagonload of traprock, but that only lasts a little while. We ought to have a whole new road. You'd be surprised how long it takes to wear out a set of tires on this road, and tires cost money. They had this meeting of the township supervisors last Feb'uary and I went to it and I told them, I said let's do something about the road this year. Let's everybody vote to spend the price of a new set of tires, around forty dollars apiece, and get a halfway decent road. You would have thought I was a crazy man, the hollering and yelling that went up. So along comes April and they fill in the holes with some traprock, the same as ever. It's enough to make you sick. Next year it'll be the same, but I won't say anything. I said my say. It's hard to get a farmer to part with his cash, the little he has. But what they're afraid of most of all is raising the assessments. They figure if the road gets better, the assessments will go up. And they will, too. But we'll be getting something for our money."

"I never thought of farmers having these problems, but I suppose they do," she said.

"People are dumb, and there's nobody dumber than a dumb farmer. I'm the only farmer in the Valley that gets the paper in the mail. The only farmer in the Valley. It's two days old, but it's still news. Those that have a radio set can listen to what's going on in Pittsburgh, KDKA. But they don't know what's going on in Gibbsville, eleven miles away."

"There's not much going on there," she said.

"Oh, I don't know. My wife only reads the ads, but I like to read about what's happening. There's always something new."

"I wish I thought so," she said.

"I see your father and mother's name in the paper every so often."

"Always with the same people. Mr. and Mrs. Joseph Chapin entertained friends at dinner at their home on North Frederick Street. Among those present were."

"Well, yes, but they're not just sitting home every night."

"Nearly every night."

"Here it's *every* night," he said. "Three hundred and sixty-five nights a year. Up at six o'clock every morning, or earlier. Even when it's a heavy rain you have your chores to do."

"Well, my father gets up at seven."

"But he wouldn't have to."

"He's at the lumber yard every morning at half past eight."

"I'd trade places with him," he said.

"I hope you don't. He wouldn't make much of a farmer."

"Neither do I. I do what I have to do, and I earn a living, but by Jesus I hate it. Pardon the French."

"How many children have you got?" she said.

"Two, and one on the way."

"What are you going to do with them?"

"Well, the boy is three and a half. The girl is two. It's too soon to say, but I hope the boy finishes college and goes away. By that time I'll be about fifty, I guess. Maybe I could sell the farm and get work in town. Twenty years from now, who can tell?"

"Maybe the boy will want to be a farmer."

"If he listens to his mother he will, but not if he listens to me."

"She likes the farm."

"She likes it better than town. She doesn't know any better. I guess I oughtn't to said that, but it came out."

"Is she pretty? Your wife?"

"I guess you could call her pretty. She was only sixteen when we got married, and she put on some weight since. She's a farm girl. She's so Dutchy you'd have a hard time understanding her talk. She only went to the eighth grade. That's as far as most farm girls go. They don't need more than that. They're better off without it, I guess. She cooks, bakes, sews, all those things. And when she was living home she did the milking and all that. Butchered."

"Butchered?"

"Sure. Butchered. Made soap. She says she could shoe a horse, but I never saw her."

"You ought to be proud of her. She sounds like a very remarkable person."

"In some things."

"In a lot of things, it seems to me."

"You don't have to take her side against me," he said. "I appreciate her, and I'm good to her. Get that straight. I'm good to her. But I know what you're thinking. You're thinking I don't appreciate her."

"That's exactly what I was thinking," she said. "You have some idea that she's not good enough for you."

"She is now, because I turned into a dumb farmer and that's all I'll ever be any more. But what I should have done when my brother was killed in the war, I should have been smart enough to say I only had the one life to live. I should have stood up to my mother and said I wasn't going to run the farm."

"What could you have done? You were a freshman in college."

"What difference does that make? A man ought to be able to decide for himself. If he doesn't, then he has to blame himself for what comes after. I don't know where I'd be now, but I wouldn't be tied down to the farm, stuck away for the rest of my life, working from morning to night at work I don't like. Raising kids. Talking to myself. I used to hear about China, and I wanted to go there. I wanted to go everywhere, see everything while I was still young, not be like my father and my grandfather, stuck away on this God damn farm. Last summer one day I was so disgusted, I was out in the field getting in the hay, a thunderstorm was coming. I said to myself, what was the use of it all? And I stood there with a pitchfork in my hand and I held it up in the air for the lightning to strike. But it didn't. It hit a tree on my neighbor's farm, but not me. If I took my shotgun and blew my head off, they wouldn't get the insurance. But if I got hit by lightning they would. They'd have been all right, and so would I. Are you ready to face Dr. Jones?"

"I guess so," she said.

"O.K.," he said. He put the car in gear and they moved on. He was a man of about medium height, wearing overalls and faded blue shirt and a straw hat that was frayed at the brim. His face below the forehead and his hands below the wristbone were burned by the sun. A leather thong attached to a button on the bib of his overalls led to the watchpocket, and a blue bandanna handkerchief was tied about his neck. He looked like any ordinary farmer who would be driving a half-ton on a country road, who would come to the assistance of a pretty girl in riding breeches.

We'll Have Fun

It was often said of Tony Costello that there was nothing he did not know about horses. No matter whom he happened to be working for—as coachman, as hostler, as blacksmith—he would stop whatever he was doing and have a look at an ailing horse and give advice to the owner who had brought the horse to Tony. His various employers did not object; they had probably sometime in the past gotten Tony's advice when he was working for someone else, and they would do so again sometime in the future. A year was a long time for Tony to stay at a job; he would quit or he would get the sack, find something else to do, and stay at that job until it was time to move on. He had worked for some employers three or four times. They would rehire him in spite of their experience with his habits, and if they did not happen to have a job open for him, they would at least let him bed down in their haylofts. He did not always ask their permission for this privilege, but since he knew his way around just about every stable in town—private and livery—he never had any trouble finding a place to sleep. He smoked a pipe, but everybody knew he was careful about matches and emptying the pipe and the kerosene heaters that were in most stables. And even when he was not actually in the service of the owner of a stable, he more than earned his sleeping privilege. An owner would go out to the stable in the morning and find that the chores had been done. "Oh, hello, Tony," the owner would say. "Since when have you been back?"

"I come in last night."

"I don't have a job for you," the owner would say.

"That's all right. Just a roof over me head temporarily. You're giving that animal too much oats again. Don't give him no oats at night, I told you."

"Oh, all right. Go in the kitchen and the missus will give you some breakfast. That is, if you want any breakfast. You smell like a saloon."

And Other Stories (1968)

"Yes, this was a bad one, a real bad one. All I want's a cup of coffee, if that's all right?"

"One of these nights you'll walk in front of a yard engine."

"If I do I hope I'll have the common sense to get out of the way. And if I don't it'll be over pretty quick."

"Uh-huh. Well, do whatever needs to be done and I'll pay you two dollars when I get back this evening."

The owner could be sure that by the end of the day Tony would have done a good cleaning job throughout the stable, and would be waiting in patient agony for the money that would buy the whiskey that cured the rams. "I got the rams so bad I come near taking a swig of the kerosene," he would say. He would take the two dollars and half-walk, half-run to the nearest saloon, but he would be back in time to feed and bed down the owner's horse.

It would take a couple of days for him to get back to good enough shape to go looking for a steady job. If he had the right kind of luck, the best of luck, he would hear about a job as coachman. The work was not hard, and the pay was all his, not to be spent on room and board. The hardest work, though good pay, was in a blacksmith's shop. He was not young any more, and it took longer for his muscles to get reaccustomed to the work. Worst of all, as the newest blacksmith he was always given the job of shoeing mules, which were as treacherous as a rattlesnake and as frightening. He hated to shoe a mule or a Shetland pony. There were two shops in town where a mule could be tied up in the stocks, the apparatus that held the animal so securely that it could not kick; but a newly shod mule, released from the stocks, was likely to go crazy and kill a man. If he was going to die that way, Tony wanted his executioner to be a horse, not a God damn mule. And if he was going to lose a finger or a chunk of his backside, let it be a horse that bit him and not a nasty little bastard ten hands high. Blacksmithing paid the best and was the job he cared the least for, and on his fiftieth birthday Tony renounced it forever. "Not for fifty dollars a week will I take another job in a blacksmith's," he swore.

"You're getting pretty choosy, if you ask me," said his friend Murphy. "Soon there won't be no jobs for you of any kind, shape or form. The ottomobile is putting an end to the horse. Did you ever hear tell of the Squadron A in New York City?"

"For the love of Jesus, did I ever hear tell of it? Is that what you're asking me? Well, if I was in New York City I could lead you to it blindfolded, Ninety-something-or-other and Madison Avenue, it is, on the right-hand side going up. And before I come to this miserable town the man I worked for's son belonged to it. Did I ever hear tell of the Squadron A!"

"All right. What is it now?" said Murphy.

"It's the same as it always was—a massive brick building on the right-hand side—"

"The organ-i-zation, I'm speaking of," said Murphy.

"Well, the last I seen in the papers, yesterday or the day before, this country was ingaged in mortal combat with Kaiser Wilhelm the Second. I therefore hazard the guess that the organ-i-zation is fighting on our side against the man with the withered arm."

"Fighting how?"

"Bravely, I'm sure."

"With what for weapons?"

"For weapons? Well, being a cavalry regiment I hazard the guess that they're equipped with sabre and pistol."

"There, you see? You're not keeping up to date with current happenings. Your Squadron A that you know so much about don't have a horse to their name. They're a machine-gun outfit."

"Well, that of course is a God damn lie, Murphy."

"A lie, is it? Well how much would you care to bet me—in cash?"

"Let me take a look and see how much I have on me?" said Tony. He placed his money on the bar. "Eighteen dollars and ninety-four cents. Is this even money, or do I have to give you odds?"

Murphy placed nineteen dollars on the bar. "Even money'll be good enough for me, bein's it's like taking the money off a blind man."

"And how are we to settle who's right?" said Tony.

"We'll call up the newspaper on the telephone."

"What newspaper? There's no newspaper here open after six P.M."

"We'll call the New York *World*," said Murphy.

"By long distance, you mean? Who's to pay for the call?"

"The winner of the bet," said Murphy.

"The winner of the bet? Oh, all right. I'll be magnanimous. How do you go about it? You can't put that many nickels in the slot."

"We'll go over to the hotel and get the operator at the switchboard, Mary McFadden. She's used to these long-distance calls."

"Will she be on duty at this hour?"

"Are you trying to back out? It's only a little after eight," said Murphy.

"Me back out? I wished I could get the loan of a hundred dollars and I'd show you who's backing out," said Tony.

In silence they marched to the hotel, and explained their purpose to Mary McFadden. Within fifteen minutes they were connected with the office of *The World,* then to the newspaper library. "Good evening, sir," said Murphy. "This is a long-distance call from Gibbsville, Pennsylvania. I wish to request the information as to whether the Squadron A is in the cavalry or a machine-gun organ-i-zation." He repeated the question and waited. "He says to hold the line a minute."

"Costing us a fortune," said Tony.

"Hello? Yes, I'm still here. Yes? Uh-huh. Would you kindly repeat that information?" Murphy quickly handed the receiver to Tony Costello, who listened, nodded, said "Thank you," and hung up.

"How much do we owe you for the call, Mary?" said Murphy.

"Just a minute," said the operator. "That'll be nine dollars and fifty-five cents."

"Jesus," said Tony. "Well, one consolation. It's out of your profit, Murphy."

"But the profit is out of your pocket," said Murphy. "Come on, we'll go back and I'll treat you. Generous in victory, that's me. Like Ulysses S. Grant. He give all them Confederates their horses back, did you ever know that, Costello?"

"I did not, and what's more I don't believe it."

"Well, maybe you'd care to bet on that, too? Not this evening, however, bein's you're out of cash. But now will you believe that the ottomobile is putting an end to the horse?"

"Where does the ottomobile come into it? The machine gun is no ottomobile."

"No, and I didn't say it was, but if they have no use for the cavalry in a war, they'll soon have no use for them anywhere."

"If you weren't such a pinch of snuff I'd give you a puck in the mouth. But don't try my patience too far, Mr. Murphy. I'll take just so much of your impudence and no more. With me one hand tied behind me I could put you in hospital."

"You're kind of a hard loser, Tony. You oughtn't to be that way. There's more ottomobiles in town now than horses. The fire companies are all motorizing. The breweries. And the rich, you don't see them buying a new pair of cobs no more. It's the Pierce-Arrow now. Flannagan the undertaker is getting rid of his blacks, he told me so himself. Ordered a Cunningham 8."

"We'll see where Flannagan and his Cunningham 8 ends up next winter, the first time he has to bring a dead one down from the top of Fairview Street. Or go up it, for that matter. There's hills in this town no Cunningham 8 will negotiate, but Flannagan's team of blacks never had the least trouble. Flannagan'll be out of business the first winter, and it'll serve him right."

"And here I thought he was a friend of yours. Many's the time you used his stable for a boudoir, not to mention the funerals you drove for him. Two or three dollars for a half a day's work."

"There never was no friendship between him and I. You never saw me stand up to a bar and have a drink with him. You never saw me set foot inside his house, nor even his kitchen for a cup of coffee. The rare occasions that I slept in his barn, he was never the loser, let me tell you. Those blacks that he's getting rid of, I mind the time I saved the off one's life from the colic. Too tight-fisted to send for Doc McNary, the vet, and he'd have lost the animal for sure if I wasn't there. Do you know what he give me for saving the horse? Guess what he give me."

"Search me," said Murphy.

"A pair of gloves. A pair of gauntlets so old that the lining was all wore away. Supposed to be fleece-lined, but the fleece was long since gone. 'Here, you take these, Tony,' said Mr. Generous Flannagan. I wanted to say 'Take them and do what with them?' But I was so dead tired from being up all night with the black, all I wanted to do was go up in his hayloft and lie down exhausted. Which I did for a couple of hours, and when I come down again there was the black, standing on his four feet and give me a whinny. A horse don't have much brains, but they could teach Flannagan gratitude."

After the war the abandonment of horses became so general that even Tony Costello was compelled to give in to it. The small merchants of the town, who had kept a single horse and delivery wagon (and a carriage for Sunday), were won over to Ford and Dodge trucks. The three-horse hitches of the breweries disappeared and in their place were big Macks and Garfords. The fire companies bought American LaFrances and Whites. The physicians bought Franklins and Fords, Buicks and Dodges. (The Franklin was air-cooled; the Buick was supposed to be a great hill-climber.) And private citizens who had never felt they could afford a horse and buggy, now went into debt to purchase flivvers. Of the three leading harness shops in the town, two became luggage shops and one went out of business entirely. Only two of the seven blacksmith shops remained. Gone were the Fleischmann's Yeast and Grand Union Tea Company wagons, the sorrels and greys of the big express companies. The smooth-surface paving caused a high mortality rate among horses, who slipped and broke legs and had to be shot and carried away to the fertilizer plant. The horse was retained only by the rich and the poor; saddle horses for the rich, and swaybacked old nags for the junk men and fruit peddlers. For Tony Costello it was not so easy as it once had been to find a place to sleep. The last livery stable closed in

1922, was converted into a public garage, and neither the rats nor Tony Costello had a home to go to, he said. "No decent, self-respecting rat will live in a garridge," he said. "It's an inhuman smell, them gazzoline fumes. And the rats don't have any more to eat there than I do meself."

The odd jobs that he lived on made no demands on his skill with horses, but all his life he had known how to take proper care of the varnish and the brightwork of a Brewster brougham, the leather and the bits and buckles of all kinds of tack. He therefore made himself useful at washing cars and polishing shoes. Nobody wanted to give him a steady job, but it was more sensible to pay Tony a few dollars than to waste a good mechanic on a car wash. He had a flexible arrangement with the cooks at two Greek restaurants who, on their own and without consulting the owners, would give him a meal in exchange for his washing dishes. "There ain't a man in the town has hands any cleaner than mine. Me hands are in soapy water morning, noon, and night," he said.

"It's too bad the rest of you don't get in with your hands," said Murphy. "How long since you had a real bath, Tony?"

"Oh, I don't know."

"As the fellow says, you take a bath once a year whether you need it or not," said Murphy. "And yet I never seen you need a shave, barring the times you were on a three-day toot."

"Even then I don't often let her grow more'n a couple days. As long as I can hold me hand steady enough so's I don't cut me throat. That's a temptation, too, I'll tell you. There's days I just as soon take the razor in me hand and let nature take its course."

"What stops you?" said Murphy.

"That I wonder. Mind you, I don't wonder too much or the logical conclusion would be you-know-what. My mother wasn't sure who my father was. She didn't keep count. She put me out on the streets when I was eight or nine years of age. 'You can read and write,' she said, which was more than she could do. With my fine education I was able to tell one paper from another, so I sold them."

"You mean she put you out with no place to sleep?"

"Oh, no. She let me sleep there, providing she didn't have a customer. If I come home and she had a customer I had to wait outside."

"I remember you telling me one time your father worked for a man that had a son belonged to the Squadron A. That time we had the bet."

"That was a prevarication. A harmless prevarication that I thought up on the spur of the moment. I ought to know better by this time.

Every time I prevaricate I get punished for it. That time I lost the bet. I should have said I knew about the Squadron A and let it go at that, but I had to embellish it. I always knew about the Squadron A. From selling newspapers in the Tenderloin I got a job walking hots at the race track, and I was a jock till I got too big. I couldn't make the weight any more, my bones were too heavy regardless of how much I starved myself and dried out. That done something to me, those times I tried to make a hundred and fifteen pounds and my bones weighed more than that. As soon as I quit trying to be a jock my weight jumped up to a hundred and fifty, and that's about what I am now."

"What do you mean it done something to you?" said Murphy.

"Be hard for you to understand, Murphy. It's a medical fact."

"Oh, go ahead, Doctor Costello."

"Well, if you don't get enough to eat, the blood thins out and the brain don't get fed properly. That changes your whole outlook on life, and if the brain goes too long without nourishment, you get so's you don't care any more."

"Where did you get that piece of information?"

"I trained for a doctor that owned a couple trotters over near Lancaster. Him and I had many's the conversation on the subject."

"I never know whether to believe you or call you a liar. Did you get so's you didn't care any more?"

"That's what I'm trying to get through your thick skull, Murphy. That's why I never amounted to anything. That's why poor people stay poor. The brain don't get enough nourishment from the blood. Fortunately I know that, you see. I don't waste my strength trying to be something I ain't."

"Do you know what I think, Tony? I think you were just looking for an excuse to be a bum."

"Naturally! I wasn't looking for an excuse, but I was looking for some reason why a fellow as smart as I am never amounted to anything. If I cared more what happened to me, I'd have cut my throat years ago. Jesus! The most I ever had in my life was eight hundred dollars one time a long shot came in, but I don't care. You know, I'm fifty-five or -six years of age, one or the other. I had my first woman when I was fifteen, and I guess a couple hundred since then. But I never saw one yet that I'd lose any sleep over. Not a single one, out of maybe a couple hundred. One is just like the other, to me. Get what you want out of them, and so long. So long till you want another. And I used to be a pretty handsome fellow when I was young. Not all whores, either. Once when I was wintering down in Latonia —well, what the hell. It don't bother me as much as it used to do. I couldn't go a week without it, but these days I just as soon spend the money on the grog. I'll be just as content when I can do without them altogether."

. . . One day Tony was washing a brand-new Chrysler, which was itself a recent make of car. He was standing off, hose in hand, contemplating the design and colors of the car, when a young woman got out of a plain black Ford coupe. She was wearing black and white saddle shoes, bruised and spotted, and not liable to be seriously damaged by the puddles of dirty water on the garage floor, but Tony cautioned her. "Mind where you're walking, young lady," he said.

"Oh, it won't hurt these shoes," she said. "I'm looking for Tony Costello. I was told he worked here."

"Feast your eyes, Miss. You're looking right at him," he said.

"You're Tony Costello? I somehow pictured an older man," she said.

"Well, maybe I'm older than I look. What is there I can do for you?"

She was a sturdily built young woman, past the middle twenties, handsome if she had been a man, but it was no man inside the grey pullover. "I was told that you were the best man in town to take care of a sick horse," she said.

"You were told right," said Tony Costello. "And I take it you have a sick horse? What's the matter with him, if it's a him, or her if it's a her?"

"It's a mare named Daisy. By the way, my name is Esther Wayman."

"Wayman? You're new here in town," said Tony.

"Just this year. My father is the manager of the bus company."

"I see. And your mare Daisy, how old?"

"Five, I think, or maybe six," said Esther Wayman.

"And sick in what way? What are the symptoms?"

"She's all swollen up around the mouth. I thought I had the curb chain on too tight, but that wasn't it. I kept her in the stable for several days, with a halter on, and instead of going away the swelling got worse."

"Mm. The swelling, is it accompanied by, uh, a great deal of saliva?"

"Yes, it is."

"You say the animal is six years old. How long did you own her, Miss Wayman?"

"Only about a month. I bought her from a place in Philadelphia."

"Mm-hmm. Out Market Street, one of them horse bazaars?"

"Yes."

"Is this your first horse? In other words, you're not familiar with horses?"

"No, we've always lived in the city—Philadelphia, Cleveland, Ohio, Denver, Colorado. I learned to ride in college, but I never owned a horse before we came here."

"You wouldn't know a case of glanders if you saw it, would you?"

"No. Is that a disease?" she said.

"Unless I'm very much mistaken, it's the disease that ails your mare Daisy. I'll be done washing this car in two shakes, and then you can take me out to see your mare. Where do you stable her?"

"We have our own stable. My father bought the Henderson house."

"Oh, to be sure, and I know it well. Slept in that stable many's the night."

"I don't want to take you away from your work," she said.

"Young woman, you're taking me *to* work. You're not taking me away from anything."

He finished with the Chrysler, got out of his gum boots, and put on his shoes. He called to the garage foreman, "Back sometime in the morning," and did not wait for an answer. None came.

On the way out to the Wayman-Henderson house he let the young woman do all the talking. She had the flat accent of the Middle West and she spoke from deep inside her mouth. She told him how she had got interested in riding at cawlidge, and was so pleased to find that the house her father bought included a garage that was not really a garage but a real stable. Her father permitted her to have a horse on condition that she took complete care of it herself. She had seen the ad in a Philadelphia paper, gone to one of the weekly sales, and paid $300 for Daisy. She had not even looked at any other horse. The bidding for Daisy had started at $100; Esther raised it to $150; someone else went to $200; Esther jumped it to $300 and the mare was hers.

"Uh-huh," said Tony. "Well, maybe you got a bargain, and maybe not."

"You seem doubtful," she said.

"We learn by experience, and you got the animal you wanted. You'll be buying other horses as you get older. This is only your first one."

They left the car at the stable door. "I guess she's lying down," said Esther.

Tony opened the door of the box stall. "She is that, and I'm sorry to tell you, she's never getting up."

"She's dead? How could she be? I only saw her a few hours ago."

"Let me go in and have a look at her. You stay where you are," he said. He had taken command and she obeyed him. In a few minutes, three or four, he came out of the stall and closed the door behind him.

"Glanders, it was. Glanders and old age. Daisy was more like eleven than five or six."

"But how could it happen so quickly?"

"It didn't, exactly. I'm not saying the animal had glanders when you bought her. I do say they falsified her age, which they all do. Maybe they'll give you your money back, maybe they won't. In any case, Miss Wayman, you're not to go in there. Glanders is contagious to man and animal. If you want me to, I'll see to the removal of the animal. A telephone call to the fertilizer plant, and they know me there. Then I'll burn the bedding for you and fumigate the stable. You might as well leave the halter on. It wouldn't be fair to put it on a well horse."

The young woman took out a pack of cigarettes and offered him one. He took it, lit hers and his. "I'm glad to see you take it so calmly. I seen women go into hysterics under these circumstances," he said.

"I don't get hysterics," she said. "But that's not to say I'm not in a turmoil. If I'd had her a little while longer I *might* have gotten hysterical."

"Then be thankful that you didn't have her that much longer. To tell you the truth, you didn't get a bargain. There was other things wrong with her that we needn't go into. I wouldn't be surprised if she was blind, but that's not what I was thinking of. No, you didn't get a bargain this time, but keep trying. Only, next time take somebody with you that had some experience with horses and horse-dealers."

"I'll take you, if you'll come," she said. "Meanwhile, will you do those other things you said you would?"

"I will indeed."

"And how much do I owe you?" she said.

He smiled. "I don't have a regular fee for telling people that a dead horse is dead," he said. "A couple dollars for my time."

"How about ten dollars?"

"Whatever you feel is right, I'll take," he said. "The state of my finances is on the wrong side of affluence."

"Is the garage where I can always reach you?" she said.

"I don't work there steady."

"At home, then? Can you give me your telephone number?" she said.

"I move around from place to place."

"Oh. Well, would you like to have a steady job? I could introduce you to my father."

"I couldn't drive a bus, if that's what you had in mind. I don't have a license, for one thing, and even if I did they have to maintain a schedule. That I've never done, not that strict kind of a schedule. But thanks for the offer."

"He might have a job for you washing buses. I don't know how well it would pay, but I think they wash and clean those buses every night, so it would be steady work. Unless you're not interested in steady work. Is that it?"

"Steady pay without the steady work, that's about the size of it," he said.

She shook her head. "Then I don't think you and my father would get along. He lives by the clock."

"Well, I guess he'd have to, running a bus line," said Tony. He looked about him. "The Hendersons used to hang their cutters up there. They had two cutters and a bob. They were great ones for sleighing parties. Two-three times a winter they'd load up the bob and the two cutters and take their friends down to their farm for a chicken-and-waffle supper. They had four horses then. A pair of sorrels, Prince and Duke. Trixie, a bay mare, broke to saddle. And a black gelding named Satan, Mr. Henderson drove himself to work in. They were pretty near the last to give up horses, Mr. and Mrs. Henderson."

"Did you work for them?"

"Twice I worked for them. Sacked both times. But he knew I used to come here and sleep. They had four big buffalo robes, two for the bob and one each for the cutters. That was the lap of luxury for me. Sleep on two and cover up with one. Then he died and she moved away, and the son Jasper only had cars. There wasn't a horse stabled in here since Mrs. moved away, and Jasper wouldn't let me sleep here. He put in that gazzoline pump and he said it wasn't safe to let me stop here for the night. It wasn't me he was worried about. It was them ottomobiles. Well, this isn't getting to the telephone."

During the night he fumigated the stable. The truck from the fertilizer plant arrived at nine o'clock and he helped the two men load the dead mare, after which he lit the fumigating tablets in the stalls and closed the doors and windows. Esther Wayman came up from the house at ten o'clock or so, just as he was closing the doors of the carriage house. "They took her away?" she said.

"About an hour ago. Then I lit candles for her," he said.

"You what?"

"That's my little joke, not in the best of taste perhaps. I don't know that this fumigating does any good, but on the other hand it can't do much harm. It's a precaution you take, glanders being contagious and all that. You have to think of the next animal that'll be occupying that stall, so you take every precaution—as much for your own peace of mind as anything else, I guess."

"Where did you get the fumigating stuff?"

"I went down to the drug store, Schlicter's Pharmacy, Sixteenth and Market. I told them to charge it to your father. They know me there."

"They know you everywhere in this town, don't they?"

"Yes, I guess they do, now that I stop to think of it."

"Can I take you home in my car?"

"Oh, I guess I can walk it."

"Why should you when I have my car? Where do you live?"

"I got a room on Canal Street. That's not much of a neighborhood for you to be driving around in after dark."

"I'm sure I've been in worse, or just as bad," she said.

"That would surprise me," he said.

"I'm not a sheltered hothouse plant," she said. "I can take care of myself. Let's go. I'd like to see that part of town."

When they got to Canal Street she said, "It isn't eleven o'clock yet. Is there a place where we can go for a drink?"

"Oh, there's places aplenty. But I doubt if your Dad would approve of them for you."

"Nobody will know me," she said. "I hardly know anybody in this town. I don't get to know people very easily. Where shall we go?"

"Well, there's a pretty decent place that goes by the name of the Bucket of Blood. Don't let the name frighten you. It's just a common ordinary saloon. I'm not saying you'll encounter the Ladies Aid Society there, but if it didn't have that name attached to it—well, you'll see the kind of place it is."

It was a quiet night in the saloon. They sat at a table in the back room. A man and woman were at another table, drinking whiskey by the shot and washing it down with beer chasers. They were a solemn couple, both about fifty, with no need to converse and seemingly no concern beyond the immediate appreciation of the alcohol. Presently the man stood up and headed for the street door, followed by the woman. As she went out she slapped Tony Costello lightly on the shoulder. "Goodnight, Tony," she said.

"Goodnight, Marie," said Tony Costello.

When they were gone Esther Wayman said, "She knew you, but all she said was goodnight. She never said hello."

"Him and I don't speak to one another," said Tony. "We had some kind of a dispute there a long while back."

"Are they husband and wife?"

"No, but they been going together ever since I can remember."

"She's a prostitute, isn't she?"

"That's correct," said Tony.

"And what does he do? Live off her?"

"Oh, no. No, he's a trackwalker for the Pennsy. One of the few around that ain't an I-talian. But she's an I-talian."

"Are you an Italian? You're not, are you?"

"Good Lord, no. I'm as Irish as they come."

"You have an Italian name, though."

"It may sound I-talian to you, but my mother was straight from County Cork. My father could be anybody, but most likely he was an Irishman, the neighborhood I come from. I'm pretty certain he wasn't John Jacob Astor or J. Pierpont Morgan. My old lady was engaged in the same occupation as Marie that just went out."

"Doesn't your church—I mean, in France and Italy I suppose the prostitutes must be Catholic, but I never thought of Irish prostitutes."

"There's prostitutes wherever a woman needs a dollar and doesn't have to care too much how she gets it. It don't even have to be a dollar. If they're young enough they'll do it for a stick of candy, and the dollar comes later. This is an elevating conversation for a young woman like yourself."

"You don't know anything about myself, Mr. Costello," she said.

"I do, and I don't," he said. "But what I don't know I'm learning. I'll make a guess that you were disappointed in love."

She laughed. "Very."

"What happened? The young man give you the go-by?"

"There was no young man," she said. "I have never been interested in young men or they in me."

"I see," he said.

"Do you?"

"Well, to be honest with you, no. I don't. I'd of thought you'd have yourself a husband by this time. You're not at all bad-looking, you know, and you always knew where your next meal was coming from."

"This conversation *is* beginning to embarrass me a little," she said. "Sometime I may tell you all about myself. In fact, I have a feeling I will. But not now, not tonight."

"Anytime you say," said Tony. "And one of these days we'll go looking for a horse for you."

"We'll have fun," she said.

All I've Tried to Be

The building was not old as office buildings go. It had two elevators and a mail chute and a directory of tenants that was ornamental as well as practical. Throughout the building there were Savage burglary-alarm stations, the kind that set off a signal at police headquarters if the night watchman failed to make his stop at each station every hour. After twenty years the building was still no worse than the second tallest in the town, and had been the best investment the Masons had ever made. The lodge owned the building, but even without the members' efforts it would have averaged eighty percent occupancy through the years. In a larger town, or in a great city, the building would not have attracted any attention; it was only twelve stories high and there was nothing about the architecture that would have frightened Fouilhoux or Hood. Nevertheless Miss Lapham, visiting the building for the first time, was favorably impressed. The brightwork on the elevator doors and mail chute and directory had a nice patina and as she waited for one of the elevators she looked up at the marble ceiling, as one will while waiting for an elevator, and she was sure that there was not a speck of dust in the ceiling corners. The man she was going to interview, Mr. Lewis C. Craymer, ran the building, she knew, and she admired the way he ran it.

The elevator operator was a girl who bore a very, very slight resemblance to Dorothy Lamour. "Three, please," said Miss Lapham.

"Right," said the girl. She seemed to be counting the time she waited, or possibly was silently going through a song. In any case she suddenly closed the elevator door, as though she had reached the end of a count or a song, and took Miss Lapham to the third floor. "Three out," she said. "If you're looking for Craymer, it's to your right and another right."

"How'd you know I was looking for Craymer?" said Miss Lapham, with a smile.

Esquire (July 1972); *The Time Element*

The girl smiled back. "The other offices on this floor are the dynamite company, and I didn't think you'd be in the market for dynamite."

"You're right, but I might be looking for a job or something."

"They only employ the one woman and she'll be here forever," said the girl. "All the rest are men."

"That ought to be interesting, being the only woman," said Miss Lapham.

"It's plenty interesting where you're *going,*" said the girl, closing the elevator door.

Miss Lapham could not be sure whether the girl's manner indicated esprit de corps or disrespect toward Craymer. She went around to his door and knocked. "Come in," a man's voice sang out.

She entered a small reception room-outer office, which was unevenly divided by an old-fashioned oak fence, the kind once dear to country lawyers and justices of the peace. Beyond was a larger office, separated from the smaller by a wood-and-glass partition. The two rooms got the theme of their furniture and decoration from the oak fence. At a quick glance Miss Lapham was almost sure that there was nothing in either room, including the typewriter in the ante room, that was newer than the fence. As she had observed earlier, the building was not remarkably old but *was* remarkably well cared for. But Mr. Craymer's offices were of another day, and so was Mr. Craymer. It was like walking through the Presbyterian Hospital in New York and opening a door at random and discovering an abdominal operation being performed by a bearded man in a Prince Albert.

Mr. Craymer was clean-shaven, except for a small mustache, and he wore an ordinary three-button sack suit, but he wore a heavy gold watch chain, with a collegiate gold charm and an old-time large-size fraternity badge. His gray hair was parted in the middle. A nail-scissors job had been done on his cuffs, but not on his nails, and his stiff collar was cleaner than his shirt by at least one day's wear. He came around from behind his desk to greet her. "This must be Miss Lapham," he said.

"That's right," she said.

"I'm delighted to see you. Have a chair. I've just been getting things, uh . . ." He removed a pile of cardboard folders from a chair and dusted it off with a rumpled handkerchief. The chair was on one side of the desk, which was roll-topped and so crowded with papers that there was scarcely room for the outstandingly modern article, the telephone. "I was just signing some letters," he said. "My secretary only comes in in the morning." He cleared his throat.

"Go right ahead," she said.

He took an extraordinarily long time reading each letter, frowning and clearing his throat and apparently having trouble concentrating on the correspondence. Miss Lapham looked about her. Besides the desk and chairs there was a large plain table, on which were stacks of papers of assorted sizes; several piles of cardboard letter files on the composition floor (there was only one small green rug on the floor, under her feet); wire wastebaskets; a black tufted-leather sofa with a Navajo blanket folded in a corner; an oak filing cabinet with some of the tabs written on and some not; and a small safe with a letter press on top. She noticed also a pencil sharpener screwed into the wall, and quite naked without the covering that is intended to hold the vermicular pencil-peelings; a check protector under the pigeon-hole compartments of the desk; a russet leather shotgun case under the sofa; a man's pair of rubbers, also under the sofa; several rubber-tire ash trays; two unused memo pads for 1947 and 1948, which advertised the neighboring dynamite company; four blackened silver loving cups with crossed tennis rackets on two of them; a battery lamp, suitable for camping, boating, the farm, and countless other uses; and a large silver-plated carafe and tray and three Coca-Cola glasses on the plain-topped table. There were Venetian blinds on the three windows and the window glass was spotlessly clean.

"Mm-hmm," said Mr. Craymer, nodding to his letters. He had been standing; now he sat down in the swivel chair. "This office, we've been so . . . I don't see how we ever get anything . . . I'm sorry, Miss Lapham. Do you smoke?"

"I have some."

"Here. Try a—have you ever tried one of these? They're Fatimas. No gold tips, but finest quality. That's the slogan. . . . Now then, the *Standard* wants some help from me. Is that correct? Did you just start there?"

"I started Monday."

"And you're from?"

"Originally Cleveland, Ohio, but more recently New York."

"Is that so? Well, I imagine a writer can get a lot of experience working on a paper like the *Standard*. I happen to believe in the country doctor, too, you know." He scratched his head behind his ear. "Whenever one of the younger chaps comes to me for advice, I tell them they ought to practice in a small town first, before specializing. Now what was it you wanted to know exactly?"

"Well, part of my job, at least till I learn my way around, I'm supposed to go back in the files and write the thirty-years-ago and twenty-years-ago-today stuff. I guess you've read them."

"I certainly never miss them. I'm in them so often. One or the *other.*"

"Well, somebody sent us this photograph and asked why we didn't run it, but the only trouble was they didn't send the names of the people in the picture. Mr. Pierson said he recognized you, but you were the only one."

"Who's Mr. Pierson?"

"Why, he's the composing-room foreman."

"Oh, Jake Pierson. Jake, of course. The printer. Is that what he is? Composing foreman." Mr. Craymer nodded. "I've seen him going to work, to and fro all these years, and I never knew exactly what he did. Well, let me have a look at the picture."

She handed him the photograph and he immediately smiled. "Oh, my yes. Now I wonder who on earth sent you this. That's me, all right. I can give you the names right off the reel. There's m'self, with the cap in my hand."

"Can you give them to me left to right?"

"Very well. This short fellow, that's Henry Crowell."

"Henry H. Crowell, of the Keystone National?"

"Henry Crowell. Correct. Next to him is Sam Biggers. That's Samuel T. Biggers, the lawyer. Then myself. Lewis C. Craymer. Then Van Vandergrift. He's living in Philadelphia. Theodore P. Vandergrift, retired now, but formerly with Union Carbide. Very well-to-do. *Very* well-to-do. Arthur Schneider. He was killed at I *think* it was Belleau Wood. With the Marines, I know."

"Belleau Wood?" said Miss Lapham.

"Oh, this picture's over thirty years old. This was taken before the first war. You can't put this with your twenty-years-ago. A lot of people would know right away. Then here's dear old Charlie Watkins, my doubles partner for years. You'll see his name on two of those trophies over there. Charlie lives in New York City, and I'm sure if you were in the newspaper game there you've heard of Charlie. Charles W. Watkins. He has a house at 25 East Seventy-ninth Street, New York City, and a large country place at Amagansett, Long Island, where I've visited him many, many times."

"Charles W. Watkins. What does he do?"

"Oh, Wall Street. He's in all kinds of activities in the banking world, and still owns property here in town that I handle for him. Was there a letter with this picture? I wonder who sent it?"

"An anonymous letter, that's all."

"Man's or lady's handwriting, would you suppose?"

"I couldn't tell. It was printed. It just said 'I think many of your readers would be interested in this old photograph of prominent local citizens,' or something to that effect. It was a nice note."

"I don't remember the picture at all. I don't remember who took it or why, but of course I know where. It was taken at the old Tennis Club. This was our old team. Charlie played first man and he and I were the first doubles team. We beat all the good teams in this part of the state. In those days they didn't have as many country clubs, golf courses, that is, but every town big and little had a tennis team. Let's see, now, Charlie played at Yale. Henry at Princeton. Sam at Haverford. Van wasn't on the team at Lehigh, but he played a lot. Arthur Schneider at Princeton, not on the team, and I played on the team at Lafayette. I guess there weren't many better club teams in the whole East, when you think of it. How many other towns could boast of so many varsity players? And we had a ladder, you know. You weren't always sure of your place on the team, just because you made it once. We were always challenging each other, taking each other down a peg, so to speak."

"Did you have a name for your team?"

"Why, just the Gibbsville Lawn Tennis Club team. We always traveled by motor, too. The Watkins had a big Locomobile, and the Schneiders had a Lozier. There was room for all of us in one car, and a chauffeur, but not for our duds. After a match there'd always be *some* kind of party. A dance, sometimes, or a dinner party. We'd start out for a place like Scranton, or Fort Penn, in the morning. Have a very light lunch. Chicken sandwich or something on that order, and play our match in the afternoon. Take a cold shower—couldn't always get hot water when you turned on the hot water tap. Then dress and go to some party or other, and usually drive home the same night. Those distances don't seem very great now, but the roads in those days were a different proposition. Latham did you say your name was? No, it was Lathrop was the name of some people I knew then. They were Wilkes-Barre people. Before you were born. How old would you say I was?"

"I could never guess."

"Well, of course you know to some extent."

"Well, if you were twenty-two and out of college in 1916, before the first war. That's thirty-three years ago. You'd have to be fifty-five."

"You hit it right on the head. Fifty-five and play volleyball three times a week. Do you board in town or what?"

"I'm living at the YW."

"Well, if you'd like me to keep an eye out for an apartment, I sometimes hear of them, you know. It isn't my special line, but naturally I hear from time to time. It must get very boring for an attractive young girl, at the YW."

"Well, of course I've only been here less than a week. I only started Monday."

"That's true. You haven't met many people, I suppose."

"Not many."

"I'd like to see you get acquainted with some of the young people. I don't necessarily mean the country club crowd. I resigned there, a few years ago. I like a more active game than golf, and the people there—well, I used to go there and I'd know every single man, woman, and child, but there's a different crowd there now. It isn't what it used to be. Some of us'd rather go to one of the roadhouses, and of course I being a bachelor, I have a small but comfortable bachelor apartment where I do my own entertaining. More like New York than you usually find in a town this size. Nobody bothers me, you know. My little place is over a store that's closed at six o'clock and the people downstairs go home and I might as well be living a thousand miles away, unless I happen to want friends to drop in. What I mean to say is, a man does his work, and then he's entitled to his own private life."

"I agree with you."

"Good. You've been married, I suppose?"

"No."

"I suppose you're like me in that respect."

"What respect is that?"

"Well, I could never tie myself down to one girl. It wouldn't have been fair to the girl I married. For instance, if I were a married man now, I'd go home for dinner and all evening I'd be thinking of an attractive young lady that came and interviewed me."

"Well, I hope you're not going to forget me just because you're *not* married."

"Far from it. Anything but. In fact, I'd like to take you out to dinner this very evening, if you don't mind my terrible old car. I've made a trade on a new one and they're letting me keep this till the new one arrives. I'll sort of hate to part with it, but. . . ."

"Mr. Craymer, did you send this picture to the paper?"

"Did I send the picture? I never saw the damned thing before in all my life. What made you think that?"

"I had to ask you. I just had to ask you, that's all."

"God in heaven. Do you think a gentleman would do a thing like that? I never heard of such a thing in all my life. Why did you ask me that question?"

"I had to. It's been on my mind."

"But do you mean to say that after spending an hour in my company you still had to ask that question?"

"I had to ask you."

"Did someone put you up to it? Is that why? Someone at your office?"

"No, nobody put me up to it."

"I don't understand you, young woman."

The door opened and the elevator girl, dressed in her street clothes, appeared in the outer room. They looked at her and she at them. She said, "Oh," and went out again. Miss Latham stood up: "I didn't realize it was so late."

"I don't understand you," said Craymer. "Look at the picture. Look at it again. Study the kind of people that are my friends, that I grew up with. Then ask yourself, 'How could I ask that question?' "

"I'm sorry, Mr. Craymer. I realize it was a mistake."

"The greatest mistake of your life. My dear young woman—if you don't know people better than that, then you can't expect to get anywhere in writing. You have to know people to write about them. The great masters all knew human nature, and you've just been showing how *little* you know."

"I'll go now, Mr. Craymer," she said gently. "The elevator girl'll still be in your building."

"Oh, the hell with her," he said. "I want you before you go to give me your word of honor—you don't believe I sent that picture to the paper."

"I give you my word of honor. I don't believe you sent it."

"Thank you," he said. "If I thought anybody believed that of me— I wouldn't know *what* to do. All I've ever stood for, all I've ever tried to be. I'm fifty-five years old, and all my life I've believed there were some things you did do and some things you didn't."

"Mr. Craymer, why don't you take me to dinner?"

"You sure you want me to?"

"Quite sure," she said.

He took a deep breath. "Well, of course I will. But you've been very naughty. Very naughty. But I'll take you to dinner."

The Journey to Mount Clemens

We finished up at Number 4 in time for supper. The dining-room closed at seven o'clock and we just made it. There were five in our party and we all sat at the same table. The food was good; the hotel had a reputation for good food, and we all knew that the next place where we would be stopping had no such reputation. Nevertheless we were not sorry to be on our way. Nothing had gone right during the two weeks we had been at Number 4, on a job that should have taken much longer. Carmichael, the chief of our party, had been putting the pressure on us because he wanted to get back to the main office in New York. He would have two days in New York and then he would be off to another assignment in the Sudan, where the Company was building a dam. Carmichael was known as a slave-driver anyway, but during the two weeks at Number 4 he had outdone himself. Breakfast every morning at seven, lunches packed so that we could eat on the job, supper at the hotel, and then night work, and no time off on Saturday or Sunday. Carmichael wanted to have the Number 4 job all cleaned up before he went abroad, and he thus had an incentive that we had not had. It was characteristic of him that he had not a word of praise or thanks for the extra work we had been putting in, that made him look good but that did nothing for us.

Our work was not easy to explain. We were a valuation crew, which meant that we were putting a valuation on the entire physical property of an electric power corporation. Every item, from a box of paper clips to a steam turbine, had to be inspected and a price put on it. The purpose of the valuation was to enable the financial people in the main office to show what was being done with the corporation's capital. This information was doubly important: it was helpful when the corporation asked the power commissions for an increase in rates; and it showed the public that the corporation was a substantial enterprise when a new stock issue was offered. I was the only

Saturday Evening Post (August/September 1974); *Good Samaritan*

member of our party who did not hold an engineering degree, but even I had learned to identify such unusual items as a mercury arc rectifier and a Coxe traveling grate and a continuous rail joint. I was eighteen years old, knew nothing about electricity, had just been kicked out of prep school, and had got the job because Carmichael had been a patient of my father's. I was paid seventy-five dollars a month, but I was living on an expense account a good deal of the time, and I could count on at least five dollars a week from shooting pool with the other members of the party. They were not very good, and I was just enough better to win. But during the two weeks at Number 4 we had shot no pool, drunk no whiskey, chased after no girls. We had been working twelve-hour days, seven-day weeks; and we hated Carmichael, he knew it, and seemed to enjoy it.

Our bags were packed and waiting in the lobby as we ate our last supper at Dugan's Hotel. "Well, gentlemen, this time next Saturday I should be passing through the Strait of Gibraltar. No, not quite. I'll still be in the Atlantic a week from tonight. King, you've been to that part of the world. How long before I get to Gibraltar?"

"Depends on the boat. Eight or nine days. You stop at the Azores, more than likely, but I doubt if you go ashore. I didn't."

"I have no particular curiosity about the Azores, but I would like to see Gibraltar."

"See it is all you will do. You won't be going ashore there either, according to my recollection. You keep right on till you get to Naples. You can go ashore there."

"I've been to Naples," said Carmichael.

"Yes, I was a lot younger then," said King. "You can have a high old time in Napoli. Is your wife going with you?"

"Oh, no. Not on this trip. I'm afraid she's had her share of the tropics."

"Well, not me. One more winter in the North Temperate Zone and I'll be ready for the Sudan. Keep me in mind when you're out there, Carmichael."

"I'll do that," said Carmichael.

We all knew that King had once been Carmichael's boss, and that their positions had been altered by Carmichael's ambition and King's fondness for the booze.

"I'd go there in a minute," said King. "I don't suppose you know that I was the first man the company sent out there."

"I didn't know you were the first," said Carmichael.

"Well, I had another fellow with me. Ken Stewart. But he died while we were out there. Got one of those tropical bugs. But the original survey was done by me. I learned to speak Swahili. It's not hard."

"I didn't realize they spoke Swahili in the Sudan."

"I didn't say they did. I just said I learned to speak it. There's no damn use learning to speak those other languages. There's fifty of them, from one tribe to another. But if you learn Swahili you can get along. It's like French. You go anywhere in the world and if you speak French you'll find somebody to understand you."

"Swahili is like French? Come now, King."

"For Christ's sake, Carmichael. The French language isn't like the Swahili dialect. But if you speak Swahili in that part of Africa, it's like speaking French in the rest of the world. Now have I made myself clear?"

"Now you have, yes," said Carmichael.

King was the only member of our party who ever spoke that way to Carmichael. Indeed, I doubted that anyone else in the entire organization, regardless of rank, would be so disrespectful. The man was so austere, so inseparable from the tradition of efficiency and hard work, that no matter how much he was hated, his personal dignity was inviolate. We could share King's dislike of Carmichael, but I think we all felt that his behavior toward him was foolishness. But then there was a great deal of foolishness to be tolerated from King. To me, working at my first real job, one of the most fascinating things about the Company was that it could include and retain a Carmichael and a King in the same organization. Could it be that there was someone back there in an office on Lower Broadway who remembered that King had once learned to speak Swahili and remembered also that Carmichael had not always been King's boss? Reluctantly, inexplicably I was discovering that my pity for King could be changed into pity for Carmichael. The Company had got all it could out of King, and was now getting all it could out of Carmichael. I, eighteen years old, could see that Carmichael would some day be another King, bled dry, burnt out, and kept on the payroll in some minor job where former underlings would be disrespectful to him. In those days, on that job, I was fascinated by many things, but most of all by the subtleties and complexities of the relations among my superiors —and they were all my superiors. They were all anywhere from five to thirty-five years older than I; educated, experienced men who had, among them, been in just about every country on earth. Working with them, living with them, was rather like being a very junior officer in the regular army. As it happened, I was in home territory, never more than seventy-five miles from the place where I was born, but for the others in our crew Eastern Pennsylvania was only less strange than Shanghai or the Sudan or Ecuador. Indeed, they were more at home in the distant places, where they had spent more time, than in the mountains where I lived. One night before Carmichael arrived to deprive us of our free time, I had sat with them in the lobby of Dugan's Hotel and listened to King and Edmunds trying to carry on a conversation in Chinese, but they had made no sense to each other because King spoke one kind of Chinese and Edmunds another, and a word that meant duenna in King's dialect meant prostitute in Edmunds's. Then they had turned to me and asked me to spell shoo-fly as in shoo-fly pie, which we had had for supper. Then we all went down the street and I beat them at pool. It was a great job, just great.

Now it was time to get in the two Company cars and drive the twenty-eight miles to Mount Clemens, where there was a new sub-station. When we got outside the ground was covered with new snow. "Oh, dear," said Carmichael to the driver of his car. "How long has this been coming down?"

"A good two hours or more, ever since you was in the hotel," said the driver. "It's all right, though. I got the chains on."

"The chains? Will we need chains?"

"We'll need chains all right," said the driver. "We'd of needed them anyway, without this extra snow. Once you get off the main highway the road to Mount Clemens'll be slow going."

"Well, it's only about thirty miles," said Carmichael.

"*Only,*" said the driver.

"What?"

"You said it was only thirty miles, but I'm glad it ain't any more."

"How long do you think it'll take us?"

"Well, we better allow about an hour and a half."

"To go thirty miles?"

"I seen it take six hours, when there was big drifts. If I was you, Mr. Carmichael, I'd bundle up warmer than that. Don't you have a pair of arctics?"

"Not with me," said Carmichael. He was wearing a topcoat, fedora, and low shoes. "I've put away all my winter clothes. I'm on my way to Africa."

"Try Dugan. Maybe he has a pair somebody left behind. And maybe you could get him to give you the loan of his fur coat. He has a big fur coat he wears. You ought to have a muffler to go around your ears. And warm gloves. You want *me* to ask Dugan?"

Carmichael hesitated.

"Mr. Carmichael, I know you only think it's thirty miles, but it's liable to be five below zero by the time we get to Mount Clemens. And if anything happens to the car we could be out there all night."

"It's been nowhere near that cold here," said Carmichael. "I haven't needed anything heavier than this coat."

"Yeah, but your office was only two-three doors away from the hotel."

"Well, I don't want to hold up the parade," said Carmichael. He returned to the hotel, having paid no attention to the rest of us who had stood waiting for him to assign us to the cars.

"Pig-headed son of a bitch," said King. "While we stand here freezing." He turned to me. "You and Edmunds might just as well get in the Studebaker. He'll want me and probably Thompson with him in the Paige."

Carmichael came back wearing a bearskin coat, arctics, and sealskin cap. He was accompanied by Dugan bearing three Thermos lunch kits. Dugan gave one to Edmunds and me. "Don't know how long the coffee'll stay hot, but it's better than nothing," said Dugan.

"You don't happen to have a couple of pints of whiskey," said Edmunds.

"You know I don't handle it," said Dugan. "But you know where you can get it. There's two ham sandwiches in there for you."

"What about our driver? Doesn't he rate anything?" said Edmunds.

"Mr. Carmichael didn't say anything," said Dugan.

"I'll be all right," said our driver. He held up a pint of whiskey. "But thanks for askin'."

In a few minutes we were under way, and the moment we left the town we were in almost total darkness, broken only by the dashlight and the beam from the Studebaker's headlights. We lost sight of the Paige. "Carney must be in a hurry," said our driver.

"Carmichael," said Edmunds.

"No, I mean Carney. That's the other driver. But I ain't gonna try and keep up with him. I don't want to break a cross-link. The hell with that. You warm enough back there?"

"Fine, so far," said Edmunds.

"The secret is get one blanket under you and one over you. The best thing is if you have a dame with you. That keeps the old circulation going."

"The best thing is to stay home and have the dame in bed with you," said Edmunds.

"Well, you won't have a hard time finding them once we get to Mount Clemens. Lithuanian. Polish. Irish. But this being a Saturday night, some of them went to confession. Some of them won't go out with you Saturday night, or if they do it's a waste of time. They won't even have a beer with you after twelve o'clock midnight. Sunday night, that's an altogether different story. Talk about your hypocrites, them Catholics."

"You're talking to one right now," I said.

"Oh. Well, if you want to offer me out when we get to Mount Clemens."

"I will," I said. My stomach fell at the thought of having a fist fight at the end of our journey, but I had not learned to keep my mouth shut.

"I don't have anything against all Catholics. Carney's my best friend."

"Ah, shut up," I said.

"Both of you shut up," said Edmunds.

Conversation was suspended, but the absence of talk did not produce quiet. Now we listened to and thought about every sound, and most of the sounds were ominous, beginning with the rising and falling of the wind and the frequent changing down to second gear as we left the main highway. The side curtains were secure, we were not uncomfortable, but any minute we could expect the isinglass in the curtains to crack, and when that happened the wind and snow would rush in. Edmunds and I were dressed warmly in sheepskin-lined reefers, woolen helmets that rolled down over our ears and throats, and six-buckle arctics, the cold-weather clothes we had brought with us to Number 4. Our driver wore a plaid mackinaw and a helmet like ours. If the car broke down we would not freeze to death so long as we stayed inside—and the wind did not tear the curtains to shreds. We were moving slowly, very slowly. We came to a mining patch called Valley View—every county in Pennsylvania, I suppose, has a Valley View—which I knew to be less than ten miles from Number 4, and it had taken us half an hour to get that far. And the worst was yet to come. I had been over that road many times, in summer and winter, and one thing I remembered about it now was that between Valley View and Mount Clemens the road cut through practically virgin forest. There was no settlement large enough to be called a hamlet. My superiors, who had lived in jungles and spoke Swahili and Cantonese, probably had no idea how close they were to a wilderness. The bear and the rattlesnake were hibernating, but there were other hazards and the worst of them now was the cold. Every winter, in that part of the country, we would hear of men who had been found frozen to death and of others who had lost a foot by frostbite.

"You're not very talkative," said Edmunds.

"You told me to shut up," I said.

He laughed. "Well, I give you permission to talk now," he said. "I want to stay awake. I learned that in Wyoming and Montana. Don't fall asleep in this kind of weather, or you may not wake up."

"We'll be all right as long as we keep going."

"How much longer have we got to go?" he said.

"A little over half way," I said.

"We got about twenty miles to go," said the driver. "If we don't get to Mount Clemens by ha' past ten Carney said he'd come back and look for us."

"Well, at least we won't be stuck out here all night," said Edmunds.

"That's providing Carney gets through all right. If Carney gets stuck, we're stuck too."

"That's a pleasant thought," said Edmunds.

"Well, it's not so bad," said our driver. "If Carney don't get there by ten they'll send a Company truck out after us. We got nothing to worry about."

I was not so sure. "How big a truck?" I said.

"It's about a two-ton Dodge. One of them they got for the maintenance crews. They got them fixed up so they can stay out here all night if they have to. For when they have to repair a high tension line. I seen them go out when it was ten below. I wouldn't have that job if they paid me a hundred dollars a week. Sixty-six thousand volts. You don't even have to *touch* the God damn line. You get too close and the juice jumps out at you. I seen a guy got too close and it pops a hole right through the top of his skull. That's what sixty-six thousand volts'll do to you. Right through the top of your skull, a hole about the size of a silver dollar. I wouldn't work around that stuff if they paid me *two* hundred dollars a week."

"Well, it's better than freezing to death," said Edmunds.

"Maybe you're right at that," said the driver. "I never thought of it that way. Uh-oh."

Up ahead, in the middle of the road, stood Carney, waving both arms, flagging us down. The first thing I noticed was that the smoke was coming out of the exhaust pipe, which at least indicated that the Paige had not stalled.

"Get in," said our driver. "What's wrong, Carney?"

Carney got in the front seat, turned and addressed Edmunds. "You got another passenger. Mr. King is riding the rest of the way with you."

"How does that happen?" said Edmunds.

"Well, I guess that's not for me to say, but they had a little argument and Mr. King wants to ride with you."

"That's all right with us. Tell him to bring his blanket and come on back," said Edmunds. "Are you all right otherwise?"

"Yes, I guess so," said Carney.

"You don't seem too sure," said Edmunds.

"Well, I guess I ought to tell you. King took a poke at him."

"At Carmichael, I suppose?" said Edmunds.

"He gave him a bloody nose."

"A little argument. So Carmichael ordered him to ride with us."

"No. I did," said Carney.

"*You* did?"

"I told them, I said one of them had to change cars. They were swingin' away at one another back there, and I stopped the car. As far as I know they're still at it. They're acting like a couple of God damn kids."

"So you took charge. Well, good for you, Carney."

"I guess it'll mean my job, but those two bastards, rassling around back there, they could send me into a ditch."

"Sergeant Carney, of the 103d Engineers," said our driver. "You tell 'em, Carney."

"Supposed to be gentlemen, but acting like a couple of God damn hoodlums. I'll get another job."

"Don't worry about that now," said Edmunds. "Tell King to come on back here."

We watched King, being pulled out of the Paige by Carney and dragging a blanket along the snow, staggering toward us. He was talking to himself; you could see him.

Our driver switched his headlight off and on to signal to Carney that King was safely with us, and the Paige got under way again. King climbed in with Edmunds and me, and the Studebaker began to move.

"At your age you ought to have more sense," said Edmunds.

"Sense? If I'd had more sense, you're right. I'd have given him a *good* beating twenty years ago. I don't know why I didn't. He gave me plenty of cause to. In Quito, twenty years ago, I found out he was going over my head, sending back his confidential reports to the home office. That's when I should have given it to him, when I could have wiped up the floor with him. But I got in a couple of good punches tonight."

"Yes, and you've cooked your goose," said Edmunds.

"Have I? We'll see. And what if I have? They can retire me on half-pay and I'll open up a gas station in Florida. Maybe I'll let you come down and join me there, Edmunds. You're not getting any younger either."

"You're reverting to second childhood."

"Well, I hope it'll be better than my first," said King. "I grew up in a Methodist parsonage and that wasn't much fun." He took a deep sigh and turned over on his side. He was sitting in the left corner, Edmunds was in the middle, I was in the right corner. Now the going got really rough, and instead of being excited, as I had been, I was afraid. Up ahead the Paige, a heavier low-built car, was breaking the path for us, otherwise we could not have gone on. Several times we dropped down into low gear and our driver was zig-zagging to gain traction and keep moving. He was a good snow driver, I had to say that for him; he knew how to use the momentum of the car to keep from getting wedged in. Our undercarriage was higher off the ground than that of the Paige, but even so I could feel the transmission scraping the false crown in the center of the road. There was, of course, only one path. At best, in summer conditions, the road was narrow, not wide enough for two big trucks to pass. Now, if a third car had come from the direction of Mount Clemens we would have had to get out and shovel snow to make the path wide—and I knew who would be swinging the shovels: the two drivers and I. Maybe Thompson would have helped out; he was younger than the others of our party. But I was sure that Carmichael would have ordered me, as the low-ranking member of the party, to pitch in. I hoped that if another car came from Mount Clemens it would contain five hard-muscled Lithuanians.

As the Studebaker zig-zagged we in the back seat were jounced and jostled. "I'm lucky Gaston—in the middle again," said Edmunds.

"Do you want me to change places with you?" I said.

"No, stay where you are. You two keep me warm."

"Is King asleep?" I said.

"Yes, and I'm going to let him sleep. We must be more than half way," said Edmunds.

"We got about twelve miles," said the driver. The last four miles is the worst, all uphill. We'll make it."

"You're doing very well. What's your name?"

"Stone. Ed Stone. They call me Stoney."

"Well, I'm going to give you a good report," said Edmunds.

"That'll help, in case they fire Carney," said Stone. "I ought to be due for a promotion, but there's no job for me as long as Carney's there."

"Don't raise your hopes on that score. Knowing Mr. Carmichael, I doubt if Carney'll be fired."

"Well, maybe you could see I got some overtime," said Stone.

"That's not my business, but I'll give you a good report," said Edmunds. The car lurched, and I could not guess whether Stone was taking out his disappointment by mistreating the car or was making an honest zig-zag. In any case, King was thrown across Edmunds's chest and Edmunds impatiently pushed him back in his corner. I laughed.

"Lucky Gaston," I said.

"Don't get fresh," said Edmunds. "We've had enough for one evening, without a fresh kid to boot."

On the uphill climb I could almost literally follow each revolution of the wheels by the sound. The windshield wiper, operated by hand, gave Stone a view of the road ahead, but I could no longer tell where we were except to estimate by the steepness of the grade how far up the mountain we were. I had also lost track of time, and I was not sufficiently curious to take off my gauntlets and look at my watch. Over and over again I resigned myself to my fate, but the pessimistic composure did not last; the slightest change in the speed of the revolutions of the wheels put my imagination to work again. I had the disadvantage over Edmunds of knowing that the last mile or so was dangerous in daylight in any season; a car could drop three or four hundred feet before being stopped by timber, and here, of course, the wind was at its worst. I very nearly prayed, and my refusal to pray probably was prayer of a kind.

Then we were there. Out of the black darkness of the valley and the mountain road, and on the summit of Mount Clemens. Even through the isinglass and iced-over windshield we could discern the lights of the town, and we could feel the level progress of the car.

"Well, we made it," said Stone.

"Good work," said Edmunds. He reached over and shook King. "Wake up, fellow. We're almost there."

"You want to go right to the hotel?" said Stone.

"I sure do," said Edmunds. "Do you realize we never thought about the coffee? I'll bet it's still warm. But I'm going to have a drink."

"That's why I asked you," said Stone. "There's a couple places open where you can get booze. You can't at the hotel."

"No thanks, I have a quart in my suitcase," said Edmunds. "Come on, King. Wake up. I'm surprised he didn't wake up when I said I had a quart. King!"

But King was dead.

The Gentry

In that winter George Campbell hardly ever missed a Sunday afternoon call on his father and mother. The old man and George would sit in the bay window from some time after two o'clock until the town clock struck five. With the coal stove burning and the windows tightly closed, the bay window was blue with the lingering smoke of their cigars, and what with the air that way and their having eaten substantial Sunday dinners, the father and son would sometimes sit in drowsy silence and sometimes both would doze off. But as soon as one opened his eyes and resumed rocking, or scratched a match to relight his cigar, the other too would open his eyes and neither man would comment on his own or the other's nap.

There were plenty of things to talk about when they felt the need of conversation. There were business and money things, and local and state politics, and the federal government in Washington. Road-building in and out of town was a favorite topic of conversation, and so was building and rebuilding of structures for private or commercial use. And then there were the passersby. Men and women out for a Sunday stroll—or, more likely, walking from one house to another house—could see the two men in the bay window, and nearly all the people would bow to the Campbells and the Campbells would return the greetings with bows and waves. "The Frankenheimers," the old man would say.

"Yes," George Campbell would say. "Guess they were over at the Schultzes'."

"More than likely."

"Burying Adam Tuesday afternoon. Wonder why they're keeping him that long?"

"Your mother says it's to give Adam's sister time to get here from Iowa."

"Wasn't that sudden. She could have been on her way."

"No, the way we heard it, Adam was showing a big improvement

Good Samaritan (1974)

the early part of the week, then took a turn for the worse I believe it was Thursday night. Yes, Thursday night. They had the doctor in twice Thursday night. Got a tank of oxygen from the Outerbridge Colliery, but it was too late to do him much good."

"Well, Adam was one of those sickly fellows. He always looked on the verge of consumption."

"Yes, you remember his mother died of it, old Mrs. Schultz. It runs in the Schultz family. Marian's hardly more than skin and bones. And you look at Maude Frankenheimer. She'll be the next to go."

"Well, if she is I don't know what'll happen to that family. Felix Frankenheimer wouldn't be able to hold them together."

"Oh, Felix is a pretty good fellow."

"Oh, no, Pop, you don't know."

"You mean he gets liquored up? That's a well-known fact, George."

"I was thinking more of something else."

"Yes. Well, I guess not as many know about that, and voices carry. Your mother's in the bay window right above us."

"Thought she was in your room, taking a nap."

"She was, but not now."

"I guess they could keep Adam another week if they wanted to."

"Yes, what the embalmers can do nowadays."

"Not only nowadays. The Egyptians had the secret two thousand years ago."

"I guess they did, yes. Those mummies. But that was wrapping them up in linen bandages, wasn't it?"

"In something, I don't know just what it was. They were way ahead of their time in textiles."

"I just as soon be cremated, but your mother won't hear of it. I was going to put it in my will, but she wouldn't have it."

At five o'clock George would rise and say, without fail, "We're having early supper, so I guess I won't keep Lucy waiting." He would put on his overcoat and derby, call upstairs, "Goodbye, Mom," and wait for her reply, then he would speak to his father. "May see you next Sunday, if not before. Goodbye, Pop."

"Goodbye, son," the old man would say, and another Sunday would be gone without George's having said what was on his mind.

So it went all through that winter. George would drop in on Sunday afternoon and he would be pleasant company for his father, but Oscar Campbell would often hope during the week that on the next Sunday George would unburden himself. He was a good son and, as far as Oscar knew, a good man. He was certainly a good husband

and father. He seldom touched hard liquor, and considering that he was a good-looking fellow, he was extremely honorable about women. It was true that any deviation from the strictest observance of the marital vows would have put him in a conspicuously different category, and in Lyons there was little opportunity for adultery; but George was not even gallantly flirtatious. He had no special smiles for special women friends; he was equally polite to them all. And so Oscar Campbell ruled out liquor and women as his son's problem. George was in good health for a man near forty, putting on a little weight, but it was natural for a man that had a desk job to put on some weight. His children had gone through and were going through the illnesses of childhood, but nothing more serious that appendicitis had afflicted either child. Money worries? Well, everybody had money worries to some extent. Everybody wanted more money, to do the things he could not afford; to buy things for the house, to own a car or a bigger car, to save more for the children's education, to take out more insurance, to go away on a longer, distant vacation. There were not many men in Lyons who were better fixed financially than George Campbell; he pulled down a salary of $7500 a year, and he did not have the actual handling of money as a responsibility or a temptation. And George knew that in the event of some crisis, some emergency, he could always go to his father. At the same time Oscar knew that his son saved money, had a growing bank account, paid his bills promptly, had his wife and children looking neat and clean and nicely dressed for church and Sunday school. There was really nothing in God's world that should have been bothering George Campbell, but his father knew that something was eating George, and it was something either so piddling or so awful that he could not bring himself to talk about it.

The season for the Sunday afternoon calls came to an end with the arrival of warmer weather. They sat out on the porch now, and people would stop and visit with them, and in late May, George stayed away two successive Sundays and his father rightly guessed that his son would not resume the visits until they could sit inside again, just the two of them in the bay window. Maybe by fall whatever it was would have straightened itself out, and if not, maybe George would tell his father what his troubles were. It would not do to come right out and ask George if there was something bothering him; their relationship had been too long established as father and married son, heads of separate households, with separate family secrets and the son going his own way. Oscar Campbell was glad in a way that the summer came when it did: without the summer interruption he might have let his curiosity get the better of him and said something that would reveal to George that he had been noticing all winter that George had a problem on his mind, and that was the last thing he wanted to do. Surely, too, the last thing George would have wanted.

Immediately after the Fourth the elder Campbells closed their house and went on the trip to California that they had been planning most of their married life. They had postponed the trip four years earlier, when George went in the Army and was sent overseas. They had put it off again in 1919 and 1920 because Oscar had been worried about the state of the Union; it was no time to just pack up and leave the business and go sailing off to places three thousand miles away. If George had elected to work for his father instead of becoming superintendent of the stocking factory, the Campbell Hardware & Supply Company would have been in safe hands; but Oscar fully understood why George had made his decision. He wanted to be on his own, and there certainly was a bigger future with Acme Mills than with the Campbell store. Acme had small factories scattered all over the coal regions, where the women were willing to work for low wages, and promotion in the Acme organization was said to be rapid. In ten years, by 1931, George might expect to be working in the main office in New York City. Campbell Hardware & Supply offered no such inducements, and Oscar Campbell had his eye open for a buyer. It was a good business, he had made money at it, but he wanted to be able to sell it for a top price. Now he had two young fellows, local talent, interested in buying, and with two fellows interested, he decided to make believe he was not eager to sell. It was the right moment to go on a long trip . . .

When Oscar Campbell and his wife returned from California they had George and Lucy and the children over for Sunday night supper. The children were in excellent health: Andrew was brown from the sun, had grown nearly an inch taller since June, and had won the boys' ladder tournament at the tennis club. He was no longer the little boy who loved to tap his grandfather's cheek to make smoke rings. Fay, the granddaughter, had changed even more. She was excited and apprehensive about going away for the final two years of school; a boarding school would be so different from High. They were good-looking children. Lucy had brought them up well. After supper Oscar's wife and Lucy and Fay did the dishes, and the three males sat on the side porch behind the mosquito netting.

"Grandpa, why don't you put in wire screens instead of this netting stuff?" said the boy.

"Because your grandmother doesn't like the look of wire screens, not on this porch. She wishes this porch was in the front of the house and the front porch was back here."

"Why?"

"Well, I guess for show."

"Women have funny ideas," said the boy.

"Sometimes," said the old man.

"When I have a house I'm going to have a porch all the way around, full of swings and chairs and things. Upstairs, too. I'm going to have all sleeping porches."

"Do you expect to sleep outdoors all year round?" said the old man.

"Sure. That's healthy. Then you jump out of bed in the morning and go inside to a nice warm room. When I get rich I'm going to have my breakfast brought to my room every morning. In the winter I'll have waffles and maple syrup, or else some mornings I'll have fried scrapple and apple sauce with a lot of cinnamon. And every morning I'm going to have a glass of orange juice as big as a glass of milk. Every morning. Do you know the McMillans, Grandpa? The new people? They all have a glass of orange juice every morning. They just moved here from East Orange, New Jersey."

"Maybe that's why they drink so much orange juice."

"Oh, Grandpa, quit your kidding."

"I know some people live in Coaldale, but they don't eat coal for breakfast. Do you know how much a dozen oranges cost?"

"No, how much?"

"I think around forty-eight cents a dozen, somewhere around there. Do the people in Chestnut Hill eat chestnuts for breakfast?"

"Oh, Grandpa. Just because I said the McMillans came from East Orange . . . We live in Lyons, but we don't eat lions. Do you get it?"

The old man laughed. "All right, boy. Go help your mother and grandmother. I want to talk to your father private."

The boy left, and his grandfather said, "He's growing awful fast, George."

"Like a weed, but he's on the go from morning till night."

"Well, just as long as he gets his rest."

"He gets plenty of that. Is he hard to get out of bed in the morning? My Lord. When he said that about jumping out of bed into a warm room. That was a good one. Lucy and I have to call him three times to get him out of bed in time for school. I wish I could sleep like that."

"You did, when you were his age."

"Well, I'm not his age now."

"Why can't you sleep? What keeps you awake?" The old man was pleased that the conversation had taken this turn, but he knew he had to be carefully casual.

George hesitated only slightly. "Oh, I guess I oughtn't to drink coffee at night."

"I guess not. I'm only allowed the one cup a day, at breakfast. Some people it affects but others can drink it just before going to bed and they go right to sleep." The old man was voluble to cover up his inquisitorial moment, but he was not sure he was deceiving George.

"I used to love to sleep," said George. "I don't know just when I stopped getting enough. I guess when I was away at college. I guess that was it. Not that we had to get up any earlier at Spring Valley than I was accustomed to at home, but at home, in high school, you and Mom made me go to bed earlier. That was it. At Spring Valley, living at the Phi Gam house, we used to play pool till ten o'clock, then we were supposed to put the cover on the pool table and turn out the lights. That was a house rule, and the year I was king of Phi Gam I had to enforce those house rules. But then we'd sit up and talk till one, two, three o'clock in the morning, and that wouldn't leave us much time to sleep. You know, I never thought of that before."

"No, you never told me Spring Valley was like that."

"A lot of things you don't tell your father at that age. All ages, I guess. Andrew doesn't tell me much. He asks a lot of questions, but telling me things is a different story."

"Well, before you know it he'll be off to Spring Valley, and new friends and a whole new life, and you won't see much of him. That's the way it was with you. I'll never forget that year you didn't want to come home for Christmas. I thought your mother would cry her eyes out."

"For a girl in Detroit, Michigan. Adeline Halliday, Joe Halliday from Phi Gam's sister. Married a missionary and lives in China. I don't even know her married name. But you know, Pop, if you hadn't put your foot down and made me come home that Christmas, chances are Adeline and I would have gotten married. And who knows, I might have studied for the ministry. She had a lot of influence over me, Adeline."

"You weren't cut out to be a preacher."

"I certainly wasn't, but Adeline could have made me into one."

"You're much better off with Lucy. Lucy's the perfect wife for you, George."

"Yes. Yes, I know she is." George Campbell did not enlarge upon his compliment to his wife, and apparently wished to say no more about her. "I'm going to send Andrew to Mercersburg for his last two years of high."

"Well, I guess that's no more than fair. You're sending Fay."

"No, that isn't why. We don't expect Fay to go to college. But I'm not sure Andrew is going to Spring Valley. He wants to go to some place bigger, and if I get transferred to the main office we'll be living somewhere around New York and around there they never heard of Spring Valley. This McMillan, the new man in town, he went to Williams and I think he's been telling Andrew they have good tennis teams at Williams."

"Williams. Where would that be?"

"In Massachusetts. Oh, it's one of the best, but it's going to cost a lot more money than Spring Valley. But of course if I get transferred to the main office that'll mean more money for me."

"Well, you know there's nothing I'd rather spend money on than my grandchildren, so don't let that bother you. But on the other hand, you're not going to send Andrew to a college because it has a good tennis team."

"I might."

"You would?"

"Well, I might. I don't say I would, but if people know who you are, say you're a good tennis player, they like to do business with you."

"Well, you're his father, so I'll leave that up to you. But I couldn't tell you the name of any famous tennis player."

"That's because you don't read the sports pages."

"A waste of time."

"Not any more, Pop. In business nowadays you have to be up on things. The last time I was in New York the company took us all to a ball game and then we had a big dinner at the Commodore Hotel and they had entertainment."

"That's nothing new."

"A cowboy spinning a rope and making jokes about the government and Europe and all that? If you didn't read the papers you didn't get the point of half of his jokes."

"The sport page?"

"Well, I guess not the sport page so much, but things are changing in the business world, Pop. You ought to see the difference in book-keeping. We don't even make out our own timesheets any more. We send the time cards to the main office and they send back the pay-checks, all made out."

"I know. I've cashed some of them at the store."

"Efficiency."

"I don't call it efficiency to send a boy to college to learn to play tennis. I call it just the opposite. But your grandfather had the same doubts when I sent you to Spring Valley. 'How is that going to help him sell dynamite to the mines?' he said. And he was right. You're not selling dynamite to the mines. You're making stockings for some Jews in New York City."

"As long as they treat me right I don't care what they are. Jews or Christians."

"Oh, I have nothing against Jews. Some of them are fine people. But I wish you were going to stay around here, George. You have your roots here and your children belong here, not in some little town near New York City, where they won't know anybody and nobody will take any interest in them."

"Pop, there's nothing for them in Lyons, or for me. We're too dependent on the mines. The collieries close down for a couple of weeks, and if it wasn't for the stocking factory and the tap-and-reamer, where would a lot of our people be? I have eighty-five women and girls at my factory, and the tap-and-reamer has maybe sixty men working there. When the collieries shut down, or there's a strike, you know how it can be in Lyons. Seventy-five hundred a year isn't the most I hope to earn, but that's as high as I'll ever go if I stay here."

"Well, I'd like to see you get the promotion, but it'll be lonesome around here when you and the children and Lucy all move away," said Oscar Campbell.

"I've *got* to get away!" said his son. He spoke with such startling vehemence that the old man expected more to follow, but George Campbell had said all he was going to say. The old man avoided looking at him.

"Oh, I want to show you some picture postcards we collected on our trip. There's a whole stack of them in on the mantel, George. To the right of the clock, I believe I left them." He wanted to give his son a chance to recover from his outburst. Whatever was to be learned, he did not want to learn it until his son was ready to talk, for he was now convinced that George's trouble was not a piddling one. He was sure, too, that George's story would be a long one. "Bring along a couple of cigars, on your way back, George," said the old man.

"Just one for you, Pop. I'd rather have a cigarette if you don't mind."

"Well, then never mind the cigars. Just bring me the postcards. On the right of the clock, a whole stack of them in an elastic band."

"On the right of the clock."

"Yes, and while you're getting them I think I'll take a walk down to the end of the yard. My bladder's giving me a little trouble."

"Maybe you ought to let Sam Merritt have a look at you."

"Oh, it's just those six days and nights on the train. No exercise. If I don't get in a mile every day my whole system pays the penalty. I'll be back to regular after I'm home a few days."

The young and old spent the remainder of the evening over the postcards. "I didn't know California was so full of Catholics," said Lucy.

"I didn't notice that particularly. Did you, Mom?" said Oscar Campbell.

"We didn't see any," said Mrs. Oscar Campbell.

"But all these missions, and all those towns beginning with Santa," said Lucy.

"Oh, those are from the Spanish days. The Catholics don't cut much ice any more," said Oscar Campbell.

"Then why don't they change the names of the places?" said Lucy. "All those Catholic names would keep me from going there."

"Oh, you're always harping on Catholics," said George Campbell.

"Well, those missions are very pretty, *there*," said Mrs. Oscar Campbell. "They don't belong here, but out there they fit into the landscape and the climate. Here they'd look out of place, of course."

"I hope it doesn't get much hotter there than it does here sometimes," said George Campbell. "We're getting dog days again."

"Out there you don't seem to mind it as much. I guess it's dryer," said Oscar Campbell. "A lot of their land is real desert."

"That's where the twenty-mule team comes from," said Andrew. "They have to carry their own water. They have a cart as big as the borough sprinkler or else they'd die of thirst."

"I'd love to go there sometime," said Fay. "I'd never come home. I hate cold weather."

"You can play tennis all the year round out there. That's why they're such good players. McLoughlin. The cannonball serve. Whack! But Tilden is better, I have to admit that. But if I lived in California I'll bet you I could beat anybody around here, even Mr. McMillan," said Andrew.

"Stop boasting," said Lucy Campbell.

"It's not boasting, Mother. And anyway you wouldn't mind living in California. You said you'd rather live any place but here. I heard you."

"Well, I don't take that back," said Lucy.

The younger Campbells went home at nine o'clock. "I wonder what's going on there," said Mrs. Oscar Campbell.

"Why?" said her husband.

"There's something pestering Lucy. I don't suppose George let on what it was?"

"No."

"There's something pestering her, you must have noticed it. I had the feeling all last winter that there was something, but I didn't want to say anything. Not so much with Lucy as George, here every Sunday. But tonight Lucy was the one. And Fay, too."

"Fay? I didn't notice anything with Fay."

"You didn't happen to be looking in her direction when she said that about California and never coming home. She meant it. They're *all* acting different, except Andrew. I'm going to see what I can find out."

"Now don't you go asking a lot of questions or you'll start people wondering."

"Now don't you tell me what to do, Oscar. I know how to go about a thing like this."

"The best way is to not go about anything. You do no good stirring up a lot of curiosity."

"That's your way, not my way. Your way didn't find anything out all winter from George."

"My way didn't make a mess of things, either, and that's what you're liable to do. Don't start asking people a lot of questions." When he spoke in that tone, which was seldom, she did not oppose him.

They got through the dog days, and Fay went away to her boarding school, and it was Indian summer, and Andrew was picked for the high school varsity football team, and the older men changed to their long underwear. But George Campbell did not resume his Sunday visits to his parents' house. The father and son encountered each other on the street and George said, "You have a nice window for hunting season."

"Yes, we received a lot of compliments."

"Who did it?"

"Young Bob Frankenheimer."

"Well, he did a better window than I ever did."

"He used some of your ideas," said the old man. The Campbells had always been proud of their window displays at the hunting season and Christmas. Even after he went to work for the stocking factory George Campbell continued to do the hunting season window.

"No, mostly his own. I forgot all about it this year. Why didn't you remind me?"

"I thought you'd be too busy so I gave the job to young Bob."

"No, if you'd have reminded me I'd have done it, but I guess it's a good idea to break in a new man. And he deserves a lot of credit. How many guns did you sell so far?"

"Well, I know we sold five pump guns."

"Five? Boy, that's the most pump guns you ever sold."

"Three or four double-barrelleds. The single-barrelled are very slow this year. I think we only sold one. They all come in wanting to see the pump guns."

"You know why. The dummies young Frankenheimer had in the window, they all had pump guns. What else did you sell a lot of?"

"Three rifles. The high-powered Savages."

"Three in one year! We didn't use to sell that many .22's, or just about."

"No, there was some years we didn't sell a one of the high-powered rifles."

"You know why, Pop? That's young Frankenheimer again. He got hold of those deer heads. Where did he get them from?"

"I don't know."

"I used to have to get the loan of the moose head from the Moose Lodge, and they always made me have a card in the window, courtesy Loyal Order of Moose. I notice you didn't have the head in this year."

"No. Bob said he was going to do without those cards this year. No advertising cards, no courtesy-of. Just try to make it look like a hunting camp, as much as possible."

"Yes, I always used to have a lot of revolvers and axes and compasses and all that stuff lying there. His was more like a real camp. I recognized those dummies. They came from the clothing stores. But I always had to have a little card saying courtesy of the stores."

"Well, I know what he did there. He told Forrest Brown and Herb Hoffmann that any time they wanted to borrow guns from us they could, and we wouldn't insist on a card."

"I should have thought of that," said George Campbell. "Well, tell Bob for me, he did a darn good window."

"He'll appreciate that. You know it looks like I'm going to sell to him."

"I know."

"But he can't call it Frankenheimer's as long as I'm alive."

"Well, he'd be foolish if he did. You've been in business a long time."

"Yes, but his folks say he ought to be allowed to change the name. They don't want the town thinking you're a silent partner. They don't have anything against you personally, but they want Bob to start out with his name on the signboard."

"Is that what's holding up the deal?"

"No. What's holding up the deal is that I don't know what I'll do if I retire."

"Well, you've been talking about it a good many years, Pop."

"Yes, but when the time comes you don't want to. It'd be different if I could hand the business down to you and Andrew."

"Now, Pop, don't try to sell me that bill of goods. I'm leaving Lyons as soon as I get my promotion."

"Why do you and Lucy want to leave here in such a hurry?"

"What made you say Lucy?"

"Well, it's Lucy as much as you, isn't it?"

"It's both of us . . . I gotta go to the bank before it closes. So long, Pop."

It was a poor excuse; the bank was open until three, and it was only half past two. In the evening Oscar Campbell said to his wife, "I saw George today."

"Our George?"

"Sure."

"Did he have anything to say for himself?"

"No, why should he? You mean because he hasn't been here?"

"Well—he certainly stayed away all fall," she said.

"Well, is that against the law? If he doesn't want to come, he doesn't want to come. He will when he wants to. But I think he misses working at the store, down deep. He noticed young Frankenheimer's window."

"Is that what you talked about?"

"Mostly."

"Listen to me, Oscar. Don't you start trying to get him to stay here in town. As soon as he gets his promotion, I want you to do everything you can to help him get settled wherever he's going to live. If it looks like he needs money, you give it to him. And I pray it'll be soon."

"Woman, did you go and do the opposite of what I told you? You've been poking your nose into things that don't concern you."

"If you don't tell me about my own son, I'm going to have to find out for myself."

"I don't know anything *to* tell you."

"Then you better start finding out."

"What?"

"You won't get anything out of me. And don't accuse me of poking my nose into anything. What I found out was told to me without me asking anybody anything."

"About George? What?"

"No sir, not another word out of me. Find out for yourself."

It was now his turn to be respectful of her anger, as she had been of his. In the forty years of their marriage they had learned such things; how far one could go in taunting the other; when to keep silent; when to yield. In twenty years neither had struck a blow at the other, and in those years of controlled anger long silences had taken the place of the slaps and punches that were not uncommon among the couples of their acquaintance.

This long silence lasted for three or four days and nights. Except for nights spent in travel and just before and after her two accouchements he had always slept in the same bed with his wife, and he continued to do so now; but their sleep was not restful, and in the mornings they were tired and peevish. Oscar Campbell was the greater sufferer because he was a home man, never one to discuss family matters with outsiders; with no friend so intimate that he could make inquiries about his son, he could not now suddenly begin asking questions, to find out for himself.

Then on the fourth day of their silence he came home from the store and she was crying. She was sitting in the upstairs bay window and she called down to him. "Oscar?"

"What?"

She came downstairs and said, "What are we going to do?"

He was hanging up his coat and hat in the closet under the stairs. "About what?"

"You didn't hear about her? Stella Valuski?"

"Who is she? Paul's wife?"

"Daughter. She hung herself."

"Well, I'm sorry for Paul. He's a good honest man."

"Sorry for Paul? Be sorry for us. For George, and *his* wife and children."

"Are you saying there was something between George and this girl?"

"Oh, God. Do I have to tell you that too?" she said.

"George carrying on with a hunkie girl?"

"She's one of the girls at the stocking factory."

"Oh, God. I thought he was above that." He reached for his hat and coat.

"Where are you going?"

"To find George."

"Wait. Don't go there. Leave them alone. They don't want us

interfering now. Wait till he comes here and then talk to him, but for God's sake let him and Lucy be by themselves now."

Oscar Campbell put his coat and hat back on the hooks. "I don't know what to do," he said—having made one decision. "Let's go out in the kitchen and sit."

They did so, and he got a cigar but did not light it. "The last thing I hoped my son would ever do. Monkey around with one of those factory girls. Did she leave a note? Tell me about it. How did you know she was his strumpet? Where did you hear she hung herself?"

"If you'll let me tell you, I will. You can always hear gossip in this town if you're willing to listen."

"I want to know, without you going into a long story, who connected up George and this Valuski girl? Do you have any proof?"

"Nobody connected them up. They didn't have to."

"You mean it's only guessing on your part? Nobody told you she was his woman, but you know it anyhow?"

"Some things you don't have to have the proof for. Some things you know."

"Good God, woman. You must be losing your senses." He now put a match to his cigar. "It's all in your imagination."

"Stella Valuski hanging in the boiler-room at Acme, that's not my imagination."

"Where do you connect that up with our George?"

"You'll see, you'll see."

"Not a single person said anything about George and this girl. Is that right?"

"Yes, that's right. But they've been saying things about Stella Valuski. Where does she get the money for stylish clothes, on a factory girl's pay."

"There's a thousand other men in this town besides George."

"There's a thousand other men, but how many of them were worried sick about something for over a year, and now one of the girls in his factory hangs herself. You're trying to look in the other direction because you want to."

"To think that I was on the verge of going over to George's house, accusing him of the Lord knows what all. And all based on your crazy guessing. And you his mother, worst of all."

"You know there's something bad, only you don't want to admit it. Well, we'll see who's right."

They buried the Valuski girl in unconsecrated ground, without a requiem Mass. The town heard that the autopsy showed her not to have been pregnant, a discovery which added to the mystery of her death; but in the kindlier view she became a flighty girl, who smoked cigarettes during lunch hour, who wore silk stockings in the factory, although she could have bought cotton for wholesale; a flighty girl who laughed off the casual indecent invitations of the men in the factory; a flighty girl who may have been wild, and being wild, a bit crazy. In the town the final judgment was that she *was* crazy, and among the Polish element an effort was being made to obtain permission to have her buried in the Catholic cemetery. Among the other, non-Polish townspeople she had ceased to exist, ceased to have had an existence. In a month she was forgotten. No one wanted to remember a crazy young girl who had tied a rope around her neck and hanged herself from a steam pipe in the boiler-room of the stocking factory.

And yet in those first weeks Oscar Campbell could not bear to see his son, and he was relieved that George had not resumed the Sunday afternoon visits of the previous winter. No more was said between Oscar Campbell and his wife about the Valuski girl; indeed, they avoided mentioning George's name. She had been wrong, wrong, wrong about George, but Oscar Campbell was not a man to rub it in. She loved George as much as he did, and forty years of marriage taught you when it was best to keep still. You did not taunt a woman who had made such a shamefully wrong judgment of her only living son.

It was Lucy's family's turn to have her and George and the children for Thanksgiving dinner. At the store the clerks were working nights unpacking the Christmas goods. At church the women were busy in the basement selecting and wrapping clothing for distribution among the poor. The miners were pleased that they would be getting some overtime. The holiday season, everyone said, would be on you before you knew it.

And so it was, with its comings and goings and greetings and good wishes. And then it was over, the bells and the carolling and the three days of snow, and Fay gone back to her boarding school; and the January winds came down the valley and even on the brightest days no one was on the streets who could remain indoors. The paint salesmen were around, getting orders for spring, and the men who sold gardening tools and fishing tackle. There was skating in the Glen, and a tramp was found frozen to death under the railway freight platform. Farmers reported deer in their barnyards, and you could have venison and pheasant if you did not ask too many questions. There was a lot of pneumonia around, but not as much other sickness. People somehow took better care of themselves in the wintertime. They bundled up warm and they ate good substantial meals. And they slept better.

A Man to Be Trusted

When I was growing up there was one house I always liked to go to. It was in a town about fourteen miles away by the country roads, and though there were two ways to get there, neither way totally avoided the crossing of a mountain. Consequently I had never been to the town before my father bought his first automobile, in 1914. It is hard to believe now that a town only fourteen miles away was so remote or inaccessible and yet in the same county as the town where I lived, but that was how things were when I was a boy, before we had a car and roads were paved. We lived in Gibbsville, which was the county seat, but people in Batavia who had business in the court house mostly had to take a railroad train to a station in the next county, change trains, and in effect double back to get to Gibbsville. There was no direct rail communication between Gibbsville and Batavia, and as Batavia was a good five miles to the west of the river and the canal, the two towns might just as well have been in different counties. It just happened that Batavia was in Lantenengo County instead of Berks County, and Batavia people found it easier to go to Reading, the next big town, than to Gibbsville. I would be inclined to guess that Batavia people felt that they had much more in common with Reading than with Gibbsville, and not only because of the fact that it was easier for them to get to Reading. Traditionally Reading was a Pennsylvania Dutch town, while Gibbsville was a mixture of Yankee, English, Welsh, and Irish that together outnumbered the Pennsylvania Dutch. And on court days the Batavia people would also be encountering the Poles and Lithuanians and Italians who worked in the coal mines and the mills and car shops, whom Batavia people called foreigners. There were no foreigners in Batavia, although Pennsylvania Dutch was their second language and in the case of some of the older people, their only one.

To this town, late in the nineteenth century, had come a man

Good Samaritan (1974)

named Philip Haddon and his wife Martha. She was the daughter of old Mike Murphy, who had come up the hard way in the steel business in Ohio and had made enough money to send Martha to school in the East and then to Switzerland. The Murphys owned a big house in Cleveland, but Martha and her mother and sister preferred to live in New York, in a house that was less ostentatious but more elegant than the one in Cleveland. Martha Murphy was a handsome brunette, tall enough to wear her hair in a pompadour, and rich enough to attract titled Europeans who were her co-religionists and some American Protestants who could supply her with Knickerbocker names. But she fell in love with Philip Haddon and he with her, and he turned Catholic and married her. To the delighted surprise of Mike Murphy his new son-in-law went to work for Wexford Iron & Steel, which was named after Mike's home county in Ireland, and Philip was put in charge of a Wexford subsidiary in the town of Batavia, Pennsylvania. "It's nothing big now, mind you," said Mike Murphy. "But it's twice as big as when I bought it and there's over fifty second-generation puddlers on the payroll. It's got a future, Philip."

Martha would have lived anywhere with Philip, and Batavia looked nothing like a steel town. Indeed, it was not a steel town. It was a town on the edge of the Pennsylvania Dutch farming country that happened to have an iron foundry at one end of it. The foundry, as it continued to be called, filled special orders; deck plates and turrets for the Navy, parts for the independent manufacturers of automobiles and trucks; jobs that were too small to engage the facilities of the big mill at Wexford, Ohio. Philip Haddon ran the Batavia foundry efficiently and profitably, and was rewarded by his father-in-law's decision to promote him to an important post in the Wexford mill. Now Mike Murphy got his second surprise from Philip Haddon: Haddon told Murphy that he preferred to remain in Batavia, that he had no desire to move to Ohio, and furthermore had no ambition to be Murphy's successor as the chairman of the board of Wexford Iron & Steel. To a man like Murphy, who had fought his way up, Haddon's lack of enterprise was incomprehensible, and he did not hide his disappointment. He had a talk with his daughter Martha, hoping to persuade her to influence Philip to change his mind, only to discover that Martha was in agreement with Philip and was herself content to stay in Batavia. "Well, if that's the way you want it," said Murphy to his daughter.

"It's the way we want it, Daddy," said Martha.

"You're not saying why. In ten years Philip could be a rich man. In twenty years he could be as rich as me."

"Yes, he probably could," said Martha.

"He's not a lazy man. It's just that he don't have the ambition," said her father. "Maybe instead of a gentleman you'd have done better to marry one of my lads in the oil shanty, a fellow with more get-up-and-go."

"But I didn't. I married Philip, and you should be proud of him for making a success of Batavia."

"Batavia wasn't all his doing. He took over a going concern. He got no test of his abilities there. But if that's as far as he wants to go, he's not the man I thought he was. What I don't understand is why the two of you are content with Batavia. I gave you a million when you were twenty-one. He wouldn't have to work at all. How much of this is your doing, Martha?"

"Half of it, maybe a little less, maybe a little more," she said.

"I give up, I give up," said Mike Murphy.

"If you want Philip to resign from Batavia, he will. But if he does, you'll never see *me* again," said Martha.

"There's things you're not telling me, there's more to this than meets the eye."

"There always is, Daddy," she said. "There always has been."

"Now what do you mean by that remark? You're not resurrecting that old trouble between your mother and I."

"I'm not resurrecting anything, am I? You've always had someone else, and the whole world knew it."

"Your mother had a better understanding of that than you'll ever have."

"Acceptance of it, not understanding," said Martha.

"Ah, you're afraid that Philip'll get too big for you. Is that it, girl?"

"No, that's not it, Daddy."

"If he got as rich as me, you'd lose him. Is that it?"

"No. I'll never lose him. Or he me," she said.

"Well, that's something to be thankful for, isn't it now? To be so certain of everything the future holds for you. No temptations and deviations and allegations and fascinations and affiliations. Not to mention some other -ations I could think of."

"Yes, you left out fornications," she said.

"So I did, didn't I?" said her father. "Well, my girl, being's you have your future all worked out for yourselves, as your loving father I can only hope and pray that the good Lord concurs with your plans. It'd be a pity if ten or twenty years from now your husband belatedly suffered an attack of ambition. Belated ambition could be as bad in one thing as another for a man, whether it be business or pleasure. The time to pull a heat is neither too soon or too late."

"I'm sorry you're disappointed in Philip, Daddy. Maybe what I ought to be sorry about was that I had a sister instead of a brother. Then you'd have had a son and you wouldn't have counted on my husband."

"At that Margaret is more of a man than he is," said Murphy.

"Don't you believe it," said Martha. "Margaret's as feminine as I am."

The old man was too malleable to become misshapen by one defeat, and he sought and found a man of Philip Haddon's age whom he could train to succeed him at Wexford. The man he found was not a gentleman, and Mike Murphy lured him away from Pittsburgh and married him off to his other daughter, Margaret. It apparently made little difference to Margaret, who was unhappily married to a concert violinist of limited talent and strange ways. I was never sure what money changed hands in the process of Margaret's obtaining an annulment of her musical marriage and her union with her father's hand-picked successor. I was too young to know about such matters, and besides I never laid eyes on Margaret. In fact I was quite grown before I knew or cared that Martha Murphy Haddon had a sister. As far as I was concerned, Martha Haddon was the beautiful wife of Philip Haddon, and they lived in Batavia, fourteen miles from my home town, and I always liked to visit their house.

The Haddons had visited my house twice before we owned a car and paid our visit to Batavia. I must explain here—and especially now, in the seventh decade of the century—that the first meeting of the Haddons and my parents came about because my mother had gone to a Sacred Heart school. The Sacred Heart nuns are an order whose influence is world-wide, often compared to the Jesuits, but smaller in number and far subtler as a power elite. The children of the poor do not go to Sacred Heart schools, in Paris, in London, in Montreal, in New York, in Philadelphia, in Mexico City, in Madrid, in Vienna, and money alone was not an automatic qualification for admission to one of their schools, nor was membership in the Roman Catholic Church. What I might ironically call a freemasonry existed among Sacred Heart alumnae, and when Martha Haddon settled in Batavia, Pennsylvania, she got a letter from a Madame Duval, of the Sacred Heart order, who told her that my mother lived in Gibbsville. My mother likewise got a letter from Madame Duval, saying that one of her girls, Martha Murphy Haddon, had recently moved to Batavia. In due course my mother invited Martha to a ladies' luncheon at our house, and the ice was broken. My mother was older than Martha, and they had not been to the same Sacred Heart school, but they had friends in common among Sacred Heart alumnae in various parts of the world, and I suppose the two women looked each other over like two old Etonians who are thrown together on a rubber plantation in the Straits Settlements. Philip Haddon owned a green Locomobile phaeton, which was driven by a chauffeur without livery. We were accustomed to seeing Locomobiles and Pierce-Arrows and Packards, owned by mining superintendents and driven by men in business suits, and so I guessed that the Haddon car went with his job. I was about nine years old, impressed but not overawed.

A few months later my father bought his first Ford, and he and my mother and my sister and I returned the Haddons' visit. Batavia was a pretty town, much more countrified than I had expected, with great walnuts and chestnuts and elms on the principal streets. The foundry was at the southern end of the town, not noticeable from the Haddons' house except for a tall stack from which issued a thin trickle of smoke, the day being Sunday. "We usually go to Mass in Reading," I heard Mr. Haddon say to my father. "There's a priest that says Mass here every fourth Sunday, but the rest of the time we drive down to Reading."

"Oh, are you a Catholic too?" said my father.

"Yes, I became one when we announced our engagement."

"Well, I'd better be careful what I say. Converts are stricter than we are," said my father. The two men then talked about guns and shooting, and Haddon invited my father to spend the night when the season opened. Quail, and some pheasant, and always a good bag of rabbit.

"This young man isn't quite ready for that, is he?" said Philip Haddon, putting his hand on my shoulder.

"He's getting a .22 for Christmas, if he's a good boy," said my father.

"Well, would you like to go down in the cellar with me after dinner? I have a couple of .22's you might like to try," said Haddon.

"Me?" I said.

"I believe your father thinks you've been a good boy, don't you, Doctor Malloy?"

"Sometimes," said my father.

"Splendid. Dinner'll be ready in a few minutes," said Haddon.

"Oh, boy, thanks," I said.

"Not *thanks*. Thank *you*, Mr. Haddon," said my father.

"Thank you, Mr. Haddon," I said.

We had not finished dinner when the telephone rang. "It's for you, Doctor Malloy," said Haddon.

"Who could that be?" said my mother.

"I can guess," said my father. "Excuse me."
He came back from the sitting-room. "It's the hospital."
"Oh, dear," said Martha Haddon.
"Mr. MacNamara?" said my mother.
My father nodded.
"Won't you even have time to finish dessert?" said Martha Haddon.
"I hate to say it, but we have to go right away," said my father. "I apologize for this interruption—"
"Oh, not at all, Doctor Malloy," said Philip Haddon.
"Isn't that always the way, though?" said my mother. She was already standing, and my sister and I were rising.
"May I offer a suggestion?" said Haddon. "Why can't Mrs. Malloy and the children stay, and I'll drive them back to Gibbsville in my car?"
"In your Locomobile?" I said.
"Well, Katharine, it's up to you. I'm going to have to go straight to the hospital."
"Oh, no. That wouldn't be right. No, we'll go with you," said my mother.
"It's no distance at all, and the doctor's going to be busy all afternoon, I can see that," said Haddon.
"Well, you're right about that. I'm going to have to operate," said my father. "If it wouldn't be too much trouble, but I have to leave this minute. Katharine, you and the children finish your dinner and come home with Mr. Haddon."
"Good. Good work, Doctor Malloy. I can see that your mind is on more important things already. You just leave it all up to me," said Philip Haddon.
He was the first person I had ever known to make audible comment on my father's habit of distracting himself. We might not know which patient or which operation he was thinking of, but we knew the signs that his attention was elsewhere. Philip Haddon had recognized the signs, and what's more he had made so bold as to be frank about it. It was a rare thing when anyone made a personal remark to my father. Most people were afraid of him, in awe of him, but Philip Haddon was not. To a boy of nine it was an instructive experience to see someone unhesitatingly change my father's plans, and my father's submission. The moment my father left for the hospital a party-like atmosphere prevailed. We finished our dessert, the two women and my sister went upstairs, and Philip Haddon took me down-cellar to his rifle range. It was a gun room as well as a shooting gallery, with rugs on the concrete floor, glass-paned closets for his

rifles, shotguns, and handguns, and framed pictures on the panelled walls. That room was my first real introduction to Philip Haddon, and for the rest of the afternoon I kept learning things about him that added to my information and respect.

I remember that that day he was wearing a brown tweed suit and brown spats over wing-tip brogues. My father went in for tweeds but not for matching spats. Philip Haddon had an American face and gold-rimmed glasses, no moustache, smoothed-down light brown hair parted not quite in the middle. He was taller than my father, probably about six-feet-one, and built like an end. He had been to West Point. "Is that where you learned to shoot?" I said.

"Well, that's where I learned the army way, but I've always been fond of shooting," he said. "I must have been about your age when I started. What are you, ten?"

"My next birthday I'll be ten," I said.

"Good. Then you started earlier than I did," he said.

I was an inquisitive boy, especially if given the encouragement of sensible answers. "Why did you go to West Point? Did you want to be a soldier?"

"I didn't have much to say in the matter," he said. "My father and four of my uncles went there. But no, I didn't want to be a soldier. I wanted to be a painter."

"That paints pictures? An artist?"

"Yes. Do you want to be a doctor?"

"No," I said.

"What *do* you want to be?" said Philip Haddon. "Have you decided?"

"A state policeman," I said. "Or maybe own the circus."

"Yes, owning a circus would be fun," said Philip Haddon. "I'm not so sure about being a state policeman. Most of them were in the army, and I've *been* in the army."

"Why didn't you like it?" I said.

"Well, I suppose because I'm not very good at taking orders. As far as that goes, I didn't like giving them either. But that's something you can't avoid."

"You could run away," I said.

"Not really. You can't really run away."

"I'm going to. When I get bigger. When I'm twelve," I said.

"You're going to run away when you're twelve? Where to?"

"Out West. Wyoming, maybe. I can work on a ranch. Have you ever been there, to Wyoming?"

"Yes, I have, in the army. Twelve is a little young to be working on a ranch. Not that I want to discourage you, but I think you ought to wait a bit longer. Fifteen or sixteen. They have blizzards in Wyoming, and it gets awfully hot in summer. Much colder and much hotter than it gets here. Why a ranch? Do you like horses?"

"I'm a good rider," I said.

"Have you got a pony?"

"No, I have a horse. My sister has a pony but she doesn't know how to ride. She's too little, and she's scared."

"Well, she may get over that," said Philip Haddon. He opened one of the gun closets and handed me a Winchester .22 with a nickeled octagonal barrel. "Let me see you handle it."

"Can I fire it?" I said.

"You're on your own," he said. He was watching me carefully. I took it off safety, aimed at the target, and pressed the trigger. "Good. You proved the piece. You've handled guns before."

"You bet. Since I was little," I said. He handed me a box of ammunition. "I know how to load it, too."

"It's all yours," he said.

I fired fifteen shots, the full load, uninterrupted by him. "Very good," he said. "Your grouping was good, once you got the feel of it."

"I never got a bull's eye," I said.

"No, but you got some 5's and 4's, and only two worse than a 3," he said. "Naturally you have a lot to learn, such as breathing, but you have the makings of a good shot. If it weren't Sunday we could try a revolver, but they make too much noise. Now I think it's time we joined the ladies."

"Thank you very much," I said.

He ran a cleaning rod through the rifle barrel, and I picked the empty shells off the floor and put them in a wastebasket, in imitation of his neatness. We smiled at each other. "We're going to get along fine," he said.

"Do you have a little boy?" I said.

"We did have, but he died. Diphtheria. Your father's a doctor, so you've heard of diphtheria."

"Yes, my brother had it. They had to put a silver tube in his throat," I said.

"But he got well. That's good."

"I had anti-toxin. That *hurt,*" I said. "A needle in my back. But I didn't cry. My sister cried, but I didn't. All the kids in our neighborhood had anti-toxin, and I was the only one that didn't cry."

"You must be very brave," he said.

"My father said I had to set a good example. But it hurt that night and I cried then. It hurt as bad as the needle, only different. But I didn't have to set an example then, so I cried."

"It's very important to have to set an example," he said.

His wife called from the top of the cellar stairs. "Philip, Mrs. Malloy thinks it's time to go."

I wanted to stay, but the immediate prospect of riding in the Haddons' Locomobile was attractive. "Can I sit up front with you?" I said.

"Well, of course. Ladies in the back, gentlemen up front," he said. "Come with me while I get the car."

I accompanied him to the stable, where the green Locomobile, spotless and facing outward, occupied space on the ground floor. The car had Westinghouse shock absorbers, twin spotlights bracketed to the windshield, and a double cowl in the tonneau. Right there as it stood was one of the most beautiful cars in the world, and I was about to go for a ride in it. *"Some . . . car!"* I said.

"You approve?" said Philip Haddon.

Then I saw the box stalls at the other end of the barn. "Look! A white one and a sorrel," I said.

"Mrs. Haddon rides the white one, I ride the sorrel," said Philip Haddon.

Everything was so neat and orderly; each horse's halter hung outside his stall, half a dozen bridles and saddles—English and McClellan—were on pegs against the wall; brooms and buckets, curry combs and brushes, soap and harness oil and sponges were where they ought to be according to someone's plan. "The sorrel wants to go out but he ought to know better. We never ride on Sunday," said Philip Haddon.

"I do," I said.

"Yes, but you don't live in Batavia," said Philip Haddon. "Well, off we go." He started the motor, let it turn over for a minute or so, and we moved down the slag driveway to the porte-cochere. In the half hour that it took us to drive to our house I said not a word. Philip Haddon and his wife and my mother carried on a conversation that did not concern me, and besides I had things to occupy my mind: the location of electric switches and buttons and dials and meters, and an enameled-brass St. Christopher medal that said something in French, and a small brass plate that was marked "Built for Philip Haddon, Esquire."

My first day with Philip Haddon came to an end, and I had so many things to tell my friends that I did not know where to begin. The next day, at school and after school, I decided I would not tell anyone anything. Mr. Haddon and Mrs. Haddon—she was pretty and nice—were not to be shared with my friends.

Months passed before I saw them again, and the next time I saw him he was in the hospital, where my father had operated on him for appendicitis. "I'm taking you over to see Mr. Haddon," said my father. "He said he'd like to see you, I suppose he was only being polite. Anyway, you can only stay a few minutes. He had a close call."

Mrs. Haddon was sitting in a white iron chair. "I brought you a visitor," said my father.

"Oh, it's my friend," said Philip Haddon. He was weak and not wearing his gold-rimmed glasses, which made him look weaker and older. He put them on.

"I brought you some flowers," I said.

"Oh, are they from your garden?" said Philip Haddon.

"No, *they're* all *dead,*" I said.

"Well, I almost joined them," he said. "I can thank your father that I didn't."

"I'll be back in a jiffy," said my father, and left us.

"Does it hurt?" I said.

"No, not really," said Philip Haddon. "But it did."

"We were very lucky that your father was here," said Mrs. Haddon. "He was just getting ready to leave the hospital when I called. Dr. Schmeck and I drove Mr. Haddon to the hospital, and they had the operating room ready when we got here."

"Oh, yes. Peritonitis," I said.

"You know about peritonitis?" said Mrs. Haddon.

"I know that's what happens with appendicitis," I said.

"I notice you and your father pronounce it *eetis* instead of *eyetis,*" said Philip Haddon.

"That's the way they pronounced it when he was in medical school. Appendic*eetis,* periton*eetis.*"

"It must be the correct way, but I'll never get used to it," said Philip Haddon. "Well, how is school?"

"Oh—school. All right, I guess," I said.

"When I get out of here you must come down and see us again," said Philip Haddon. "I won't be able to ride for a while. I'm going to have to wear a big belt."

"I know," I said.

"But we can shoot," he said. "Your father and I were going gunning together when the season opens, but I don't think he'd approve of that now. So you come instead."

"All right," I said.

"As far as that goes, you could ride with me," said Mrs. Haddon. "You could ride the sorrel. That is, if you don't mind riding with a lady."

"Don't let that fool you," said Mr. Haddon. "She rides as well as any man."

Well, the upshot of that conversation was that the Haddons remembered their invitation, and many times in the next couple of years I went to their house and rode with them and shot with him. It did not matter that at first I was aware I was taking the place of their dead son. I would board the morning train and get off at the main line station where Philip Haddon or his wife would meet me and take me to their house for the day. In the mornings I would ride with one of them, and after lunch he and I would shoot. I would arrive dressed in breeches and puttees, and she or he would be in boots or breeches; but nearly always it was she who rode with me. After his operation he had never regained his interest in riding, and if it had not been for me they would have sold the sorrel, and Mrs. Haddon would have had no one to ride with. My visits were fortnightly, seldom oftener than that, and always arranged by the Haddons in advance. I came to look forward to seeing her as much as I did him, and I reached the age where I became more and more conscious of her figure. She got into my dreams.

One day she met me at the train and immediately announced that there would be no shooting that day. Mr. Haddon had been called to Philadelphia on business. He was very sorry—but I was not. She said that instead of shooting that afternoon she would, if I liked, take me to the foundry and I could see the sights, have a ride on the dinkey engine and the traveling crane. Mr. Haddon said I might enjoy that. And so she and I rode the white and the sorrel, and she said she was going to have to change her clothes because Mr. Haddon did not like her to appear before the foundry workmen in riding breeches. "I'll only be a few minutes," she said. "A quick tub and change." I waited downstairs until I heard the water running in the tub, and then I went upstairs and entered the bathroom without knocking. She was standing naked, feeling the water in the tub. "What are you *doing* here?" she said.

"I wanted to look at you," I said.

She reached for a towel to cover herself. "But you mustn't," she said.

"I only wanted to look," I said.

"Well, I should think so, at thirteen," she said. "Now you've seen me, you must go."

"I want to kiss you," I said.

"Yes, well I knew that," she said.

"I love you," I said.

"That's not love, Jimmy. That's something else," she said. "Can't you see that you're embarrassing me. All right, you can kiss me here." She lowered the towel and put back her shoulders so that her breasts stood out. I kissed each of them. "That's enough now," she said. "Go on downstairs and we'll pretend this never happened. Never." But I put my arms around her and was rough with her and she struggled. "Stop it," she said.

"You wanted me to. You did. I could tell."

"Wanted you to what? Thirteen years old, you must be insane."

"What he does, Mr. Haddon," I said.

"Huh. What you think he does," she said. "You could be wrong about that, too. All right, open your trousers." She got down on the floor and I got on top of her, but I could not control myself and she lay there, wanting what I could not give her. "Now let me have my bath, and you go make yourself presentable."

She came downstairs in about half an hour. "We can dispense with the visit to the foundry," she said. "I can take you to the station, there's an earlier train. We can't talk about it any more till after lunch."

"I don't want any lunch," I said.

"Well, you'll damn well sit here while I have mine," she said. "I have the maid to consider." She chattered while the maid came and went.

"He ain't eating," said the maid.

"He lost his appetite," said Mrs. Haddon.

"He always stuffs," said the maid.

"Well, not today," said Mrs. Haddon.

"Maybe because the Mister ain't here," said the maid.

"Very likely," said Mrs. Haddon.

Later, in the sitting-room, I said, "Are you going to tell Mr. Haddon?"

"No. It wasn't all your fault," she said. "I must have been leading you on, without knowing it. I've seen you look at me, so I should have been forewarned. Have I ever looked at you that way?"

"No."

"Have you ever thought I was flirting with you?"

"No."

"Well, if it's any consolation to you, my husband thought I was flirting with you."

"Me?"

"You, and not only you," she said.

"I never thought so," I said.

"I never did either," she said. "But my husband does. There are some women who give that impression."

"Not you, though," I said.

"Do other women flirt with you? Not girls, but women."

"I don't know."

"Oh, you'd know," she said.

"Some, maybe."

"And what do you do?" she said.

"I don't do anything. With girls I do, but not women. You're the only one."

"Failing the opportunity, I suppose," she said. "Well, I'll be more careful in the future. I'll lock my bathroom door."

"You're not cross at me?"

"More with myself than with you. This could have had serious consequences, you know. The maid. My husband. Your father. Nothing like this must ever happen again. If my husband gave you a good beating, your father'd give you one too. Not to mention the fact that I'd also get a good beating from my husband."

"I'd kill him if he did," I said.

"Mm. How chivalrous, and what a mess. Hereafter confine your attentions to girls your own age."

"I don't like girls my own age," I said.

"Well, a little older, when their busts develop. Thirteen is too young for you to *think* of older women. I'm old enough to be your mother, you know. I am, you know. I'm ashamed of myself. I gave in to you. No matter what happened, I gave in to you. You'll always remember that—and so will I. I have a husband that I love dearly, and he loves me. But a thirteen-year-old boy could make me forget that. Do you realize how much that's going to make me hate myself? Are you mature enough to understand that? You could lose all respect for women after today. It could have a bad effect on the rest of your life. Giving in, that was the worst thing that happened today. That was a terrible sin."

"Don't think that, Mrs. Haddon," I said.

"Do you deny that it was a sin? I can't. I've heard of women like that. When I was at school abroad there was a girl's mother that had a weakness for young boys. It was such a scandal that the girl was asked to leave school. A highly respected family. The girl's life was made miserable by the weakness of the mother, but am I any better?"

The flow of her self-castigation would not stop, and it began to frighten me. I wanted to comfort her, but I did not know how without touching her, and an instinct told me that she wanted to be touched and that that would lead to what she called giving in. She wanted to weep and would not weep. My instinct to comfort her was confused with the sight of the rise and fall of her bosom, and whatever was going on inside her was happening to the woman on the bathroom floor. I could not stand it any longer and I kissed her on the mouth. Her response was complete and eager, but then as suddenly she pushed me away. "God, what am I doing?" she said. "What am I *doing?*" She put her hands to her cheeks. "He's right about me," she said, and I knew she was talking about her husband.

"Get your cap, and we'll get some fresh air," she said. She stood up, only barely discernibly unsteady. "I'll drive you to the station." She had her own car now, a Scripps-Booth roadster, a three-seater with the driver's seat forward of the other two.

"You don't have to do that," I said.

"You're wrong, I do have to. I want the cold air on my face, to bring me back to my senses. And you need it too, young man."

Because of the odd seating arrangement I had to lean forward in the noisy, windswept, little car, and she had to repeat half of what she said. But our conversation did not touch upon our intimacies. The cool, cold air was having its effect on her—and on me. The newness, the uniqueness of our experience lay for me in the fact that I was learning for the first time in my life that a woman could actively desire a man. I had kissed girls and sometimes found them responsive, but I had never known, never even heard, that a woman was more than submissive to a man. Now I was learning that it was in the nature of a woman to have a hunger for a man or a boy of thirteen who had the functions of a man. This revelation, this discovery was so violent that I needed someone to discuss it with me, but my inexperienced contemporaries were out of the question; already in experience I was so far ahead of them that none of them would believe me. The superlative irony was in the circumstance that the only man, woman, or boy or girl in whom I had the confidence for confiding was Philip Haddon. On my visits to his house I had told him many things about myself and my family and enemies and friends, and he had always listened with more than perfunctory interest. I almost laughed at the thought of telling him what had happened with his wife that day. Well, at least I was sure that she was not going to tell him either.

Just before we reached the station she said, "I'm never going to say any more about today, to you or anyone else. And don't you."

"I won't," I said.

"The next time you go to confession—do you ever go to an Italian priest?"

"No," I said. "Why?"

"Because Italian priests aren't as easily shocked," she said. "I'd always much rather go to an Italian priest. Whenever I have something naughty to confess, I go to the Italian parish in Reading."

"That's not a true confession, if he doesn't understand what you're saying," I said.

"I don't hold anything back. I tell him everything," she said.

"You're not confessing to a man. You're confessing to God."

"I know all that," she said. "All the same, I'd rather say those things to an Italian. And another thing, don't turn pious on me."

I wasn't ready—but is one ever?—for the physical and spiritual revolution that began for me that day. I had yielded to strong impulse, I had seen her naked body and made an incomplete attempt to commit adultery with her, and I was entertaining doubts about the sanctity of the confessional. She became the most fascinating, evil, ignorant, cynical woman the world had ever known. I wanted to escape from her and sin, but I knew that I would have to go back to her and sin and her secret delights and godless thoughts and infinite pleasures.

"I'm not pious," I said.

"No, I know you're not," she said. "In fact, you're very wicked to know as much as you do." With that she won me over to the side of wickedness, completely. I could not say to her that I was ready to abandon the pleasures of wickedness; I could not say it to myself when the opposite attraction was so powerful. As she drove me to the station I was aware that I was being chastised for improper conduct, the misbehavior of a boy of thirteen with a woman of whatever age she was. It was as much as I could expect, and it was the right thing for her to do. But already I had been matured by the day's experiences to the extent that my childhood was in the past and I knew it. That was all I knew at the moment, but that much was certain.

We sat in the car, waiting for the northbound train, and she seemed fully to have regained her self-possession, her own place in the world, so that she was protected by her dignity and her tweed skirt and her accustomed manner toward me. She offered me a cigarette and I took it, although her husband had never offered me a cigarette because he respected my father's rule against them. In a strange, conspiratorial way she had somehow managed to join with me in an alliance that supported the smoking of cigarettes while, in the time remaining, totally ignoring our sins of thought, word, and

deed. The camelback engine came heaving up the track and I got out
of the roadster, took off my cap, and looked at her with what must
have been apprehension and longing.

"No, don't try to say anything," she said, and smiled reassuringly.

II

I went away to boarding school that year where I did not know a
soul. In the new life I made the new friends and enemies and the
associations with the new things that came out of old books. It was
impossible for me to risk the scornful disbelief of other boys with the
story of my experience with Mrs. Haddon, and I kept it to myself.
With girls my reticence was just as strong. They would let me kiss
them, but some of them, most of them, would fight or cry if I put my
hand on their growing breasts. They would threaten to tell their big
brothers, although they never did. During that phase of my adoles-
cence I had dreams about Mrs. Haddon's body, but they were so
secret that she as a living person did not exist. When I went home on
school vacations I did not see her, and the friendship between my
parents and the Haddons was never meant to flourish. Two or three
years went by, and Philip Haddon continued to be a patient of my
father's; once or twice a year the Haddons and my parents would
meet halfway for Sunday lunch at the Lantenengo Country Club; at
Christmas they exchanged suitable presents. But Martha Haddon, if
it was deliberate, managed to stay out of my sight, and of course I
was falling in and out of love with girls closer to my own age. I had
guessed her age to be about sixteen or seventeen years older than I,
so that by the time I got out of prep school and went to work on a
Gibbsville newspaper, she was in her late thirties. My father died,
and my mother had a letter from the Haddons, who were traveling
abroad and did not hear about his death until a month later. The
letter was written by Martha Haddon and Philip Haddon was only
formally included in it. "Mr. Haddon must not be well," said my
mother. "Otherwise I think he'd had written. He and your father
were closer than Mrs. Haddon and I."

"Well, some men hate to write letters," I said.

"Yes, but not Mr. Haddon," said my mother. As was often the
case, she was right, for the next time I visited the neighborhood of
Batavia I was on an assignment to cover a fatal stabbing, and because I was in the neighborhood I paid a call on the Haddons. From
my paper's point of view it was not much of a story. Some Negroes
living in a tent and working as day laborers on a highway construction had a drunken brawl in which one man was killed and the others

immediately fled. The state police were not even sure of the names, and I was sure that my paper had no interest in the story. But my curiosity about the Haddons was active, and I had the paper's Oakland coupé and time to spare.

It was a hot August day, toward noon. The smoke from the foundry stacks hung thick and low, as though waiting for any light breeze to take it away. At the Haddons' house on the other end of town the awnings and the wire screens seemed to darken the rooms, and there was no sign of life in the yard. But as I got out of the Oakland the porch screendoor opened and Martha Haddon descended. "Are you from the Light Company?" she called.

"No, ma'am," I said. "I'm from the dark company." It was a feeble enough joke, but I would explain it to her later.

"Don't tell me! It isn't who I think it is," she said, and called back to the man on the porch. "Philip, we have a visitor. James Malloy."

"Oh, good," I heard him say. "Dr. Malloy's boy?"

"What on earth are you doing here on this sticky, hot day?" said Martha Haddon. "Come in out of the sun and have a glass of iced tea."

Philip Haddon rose slowly and rested his palm fan and newspaper on a wicker table. He was wearing a pongee suit, striped blue shirt, white canvas oxfords. We shook hands and I explained my presence in the neighborhood and my little joke. "Well, you'll stay to lunch," said Philip Haddon. "You might even have a swim. I think the pool is new since you were here last."

"It is," she said. "This is only our third summer with the pool."

"Has it really been that long since we used to shoot? But then it must be. You're not a boy any more. You're quite a young man. Newspaper work, and watching people carve each other up."

"Yes, I remember when my father carved you up," I said.

"And you came to see me in the hospital," he said. "Well, damn it all, it *is* nice to see you again. Isn't it awful that we can live so near and never see each other? We've never even been to see your mother since your father died."

"Well, *you've* had some excuse," said Martha Haddon. "Mr. Haddon caught some kind of a stomach ailment in Italy."

"Say no more about it," said Philip Haddon. "I think it was nothing more than a recurrence of malaria. Everybody that was ever in the army got *some* malaria. Unfortunately, I've had to retire from the foundry, and we may have to move away."

"We *own* the *house*," said Martha Haddon.

"Yes, but the new superintendent may not like to have me looking over his shoulder," said Philip Haddon.

"As you've probably guessed, this is a frequent topic of conversation," said Martha Haddon. "But we don't really want to leave Batavia. Where to? Good heavens, we came here as bride and groom, and this has been our home, our only one."

"I'm sure Mr. Malloy'd much rather go for a swim than participate in our discussion," said Philip Haddon.

"No, I always liked this house," I said. "I hope you keep it."

"Then that settles it," said Philip Haddon. "You promise to visit us often when they finish the new highway."

For the first time ever I suspected that Philip Haddon was capable of subtlety. "I promise," I said.

"All right, fine, we'll hold you to that," he said. "Now if you'd like to have a dip before lunch, I'll get you a pair of trunks."

"Aren't you coming?" I said.

"No, if I get a chill I'm through for the day, maybe longer," he said. "But Martha will go with you."

"All right, we haven't much time," said Martha Haddon.

We put on our bathing suits and left him on the porch. The pool was in a corner of the yard, protected on four sides by a tall hedge, and on the way to the pool she and I wore bathrobes. "It's our one concession to Batavia," she said. "They wouldn't approve of a grown woman walking around in a bathing suit."

"Do you really like it in Batavia?" I said.

"I like it better than any place else," she said. "It keeps me on my good behavior—*most of the time.*"

"Oh, you remember," I said.

"Of course I do. It's not something you forget."

"Well, what about him, Mr. Haddon? Did he ever know about me?"

"I didn't tell him," she said.

"That isn't answering my question," I said. "Something a minute ago made me think he knew *something.*"

"You're a young man now," she said. "Yes, he guessed, but he never really wanted to know anything like that."

"Was there a lot to know?"

"You must think I'm very unattractive," she said.

"Far from it," I said.

"You must, if the best I could do was a thirteen-year-old boy," she said. "A twenty-year-old boy is better, but do you think there's been no one in between?"

"Well—*him.*"

"Oh, he's happy now. He likes being an invalid."

"He wasn't always an invalid," I said.

"Most of the time," she said. "Do you know why he liked being a Catholic? It was because he thought it'd make me behave. But it didn't turn out that way. It made him behave, but not me."

"I thought you were deeply in love with him," I said.

"I am. But you have a lot to learn about love."

"I guess I've learned more from you than from anyone else," I said.

"It doesn't really matter who you learn it from, as long as you learn it. I even learned some from you."

I laughed. "From me? A hot-pants kid?"

"An inexperienced kid. You're not that inexperienced any more," she said.

"No," I said.

"You didn't teach me anything, but I learned from you. It was about myself. That I could want someone whether he was thirteen or thirty, provided he wanted me enough, and showed it. You have always been someone who wanted me."

"Today?"

"Of course today," she said. "Look at you. Just look at you."

"Then why don't we?"

"Because you're not thirteen now, and we can wait," she said. "He knows every move we can make, and he's sitting on the porch imagining it. So don't be surprised if he comes down here at just the wrong time."

"What would he do if he caught us?"

"That's a chance we're not going to take," she said.

"What would he *do?*" I said.

"I said we're not going to take the chance, and we're not. Anyway, not today."

"Oh, all right," I said. "He likes to think about it, and you like to talk about it. Which one's worse?"

"Take your swim, and be more respectful to your elders," she said.

I stood on the diving-board and turned my back on her.

"Go ahead, it'll do you good," she said.

I plunged in and the water was a shock but I took a few strokes to get used to the temperature, and when I climbed out Philip Haddon was standing above her at the side of the pool. "You see what I mean about the chill," he said. "It's water that comes from a spring."

"I'll say it does," I said.

"Say, by the way, I brought something to show you," he said. From his jacket pocket he took out an automatic pistol. "Ever seen one like it?"

"No," I said.

"It's a Browning automatic," he said. He handed it to me, and I hefted it.

"It's loaded, isn't it?" I said.

"Oh, yes," he said. "But I know I can trust you with firearms."

"Philip always remembered that he could trust you with firearms," said Martha Haddon.

Tuesday's as Good as Any

Saturday afternoon, along about three o'clock, was George Davies's time for his regular visit to the establishment conducted by Nan Brown. The bank closed at noon and George could be finished up with his work by one o'clock. He would eat lunch at the Olympia—alone, and at the same table against the wall where he had lunch six days a week—and at the cashier's desk he would buy a cigar, light it, and smoke it on his leisurely stroll to Dewey Heiler's poolroom. Dewey's was the respectable poolroom, patronized by men who for one reason or another had not joined the Gibbsville Club and by a few who had. Dewey did a brisk trade among the ten-two-and-four customers, whose jobs permitted them to drop in for a dope, as they called it. A dope was only a Coca-Cola, but nearly all the men under the age of seventy called it a dope. Dewey did not bother with anything but dopes and chocolate milks. No ice cream. Nothing to eat but butter pretzels. And anyone who wanted to sit down had to go to the rear of the shop where there were benches for the pool players and spectators. But there were some customers who never set foot in the rear of the shop, and George Davies was one of them. You never saw a judge or a doctor in the rear part of the shop. They played their pool at the Gibbsville Club or at the Elks'. On the other hand, the younger element seldom lingered in the front of the shop. They would make their way to the pool tables and the benches. It took a bit of nerve for a young fellow to hang around in the front of the shop and try to join in the conversation with the business and professional men who were having their dopes.

Banking hours being what they were, George Davies was not one of the ten-two-and-four customers, but he was a Saturday afternoon regular, and he was welcome in the front of the shop. He had been a customer of Dewey's ever since the shop first opened, good for a box of cigars once a month and for boxes of the fine candies that Dewey put in for the Christmas trade. By and large, George was probably as

Good Samaritan (1974)

good a customer as any Dewey had, and in any case he was respectable, clean, never loud, and no one disliked him. At Gibbsville High he had been salutatorian and manager of the basketball team, and in the class prophecy it was predicted that he would one day be Secretary of the Treasury, a not entirely wild guess in view of the fact that it was known that he was going to go from high school to a job at the Gibbsville Trust Company. If his father had not died in junior year, George most likely would have gone to the Wharton School at Penn, but his mother was alone in the world and needed George at home. She was a fragile woman and terrified by the fear that she might fall down the cellar stairs and lie there while her cries for help went unheard, as had happened to old Mrs. Tuckerman on North Fourth Street. And so George went from high school to the bank, while his mother kept house for him on North Third Street.

"Seven o'clock, George," she would call to him in the morning, and he never had to be called twice. He would shave and dress, and breakfast would be on the table when he came down; ham and eggs or scrapple on the mornings between Hallowe'en and Decoration Day, corn flakes with a sliced banana or berries during the warmer months. It was a six-block walk from the house to the bank, and unless he had to leave a pair of shoes to be resoled or to do some other errand, George would follow the same route every day: a block and a half to Market Street, three blocks on Market, and a block and a half on Main. It was not a long walk, but at the pace George set for himself it was enough exercise to get the circulation going and the mind alerted for the bank's arithmetic, and, after his first three years, for the intercourse with the bank's customers.

As an assistant teller he enjoyed the contacts with the customers. He well understood that the customers he was likely to deal with were neither rich nor important, and that to them he represented the substance and prestige of the bank. Nobody knew that better than George. He could put himself in the place of a customer and imagine the customer's thoughts, see himself as the customers would be seeing him, a trusted custodian of their hard-earned cash and in certain ways the controller of their credit. Actually George was not called upon to make decisions on their credit; it was not part of his job to give his advice on loans. Nevertheless he encouraged customers to believe that behind his dignified friendliness was a shrewd judgee of character who had a good deal more to say in the bank's affairs than his modest title indicated. He would smile knowingly when friends casually asked him how things were at the bank. He was close-mouthed to such a degree that he conveyed the impression that discretion was demanded of him by the confidential nature of his duties. In due course his superiors and his fellow-workers at the bank began to accept his performance as generally desirable. Although his dealings were with small depositors on a small scale, it certainly did no harm if he could make people feel important.

It was not really so strange that George's Saturday visits to Nan Brown's establishment passed unnoticed. Without telling anyone where he was going, he would say so-long to the men in Dewey Heiler's poolroom and walk the half block to Main Street, making sure that he was not compelled to linger with anyone he encountered in the shopping district. Nan Brown's place was on Railroad Avenue, but in the immediate neighborhood there were warehouses and commercial enterprises such as tinsmiths and wholesale grocers, a nonresidential area usually frequented by men who would not know George by sight, and all, at that time of day, on business bent. The traffic in the area was nearly all trucks, large and small. George's only risk was if some friend happened to see him actually enter Nan's establishment; but the risk was not great, and it was one that George had carefully calculated. Three o'clock on a Saturday afternoon gave him a margin of several hours before the Saturday night customers would begin to arrive and all the time he needed before the late-afternoon drinkers. He would walk purposefully up Railroad Avenue at a steady pace that would be taken as that of a man who had a long way to go; then as he reached Nan's place he would abruptly turn left and enter the house, go to the room between the front parlor and the kitchen, and sit down and wait for Nan.

"Hello, George," she would say. "How's the world using you?"

"Oh, about the same. How are things with you?"

"Can't complain. Who do you want this afternoon?"

"I was thinking of Dottie," he would say.

"All right, she's awake. You want to go on up? Save me a trip. I got this God damn rheumatism and I can't seem to get rid of it. I decided it must be the climate. As soon as I get enough put away I'm moving out to the West Coast, California."

"You've been saying that as long as I've known you."

"Well, one of these days I'll do it. I got it all figured out. I could probably open up inside of a month or so, as soon as I got the name of a good lawyer. There'd be no trouble getting girls, all those kids that go out there looking for jobs in the movies. You never been out there, have you, George?"

"I've never been west of Pittsburgh, and then only once. I like it right here in town."

"Well, I wouldn't mind it if I didn't get this rheumatism. I hate to tell you how long I been here."

"I know how long you've been here."

"Then you can pretty nearly guess my age," said Nan. "I was twenty-two years old when I came here."

"You must be pretty well fixed, Nan."

"I didn't come here as the owner of the place. I was only one of the girls, working for Millie Harris then."

"I remember."

"You didn't used to come in as often then. I remember who you came in with, the first time. Fred Raymond, Lord rest his soul. He was one of my regulars. Millie didn't used to like it when a customer got attached to a girl, but I said to her, in this business the customer's always right. Give them what they want was my motto. Well, you want Dottie. Who'd you have last Saturday?"

"Arline."

"Next Monday I got a new girl arriving from Philly. I had good reports on her from different parties. I'll show you a picture of her."

"All right."

"Here, have a look. You can't tell if you're gonna like her by her picture, but you can't complain about that shape. She says the picture was taken last month. I'm putting her to work as soon as she sees the doctor. That always takes a couple days."

"Well, maybe next Saturday, Nan."

"Okay, George. Enjoy yourself in case I don't see you," said Nan.

He would be out of the house by five o'clock, at peace with the world and with himself, and ready for a shave and a facial at Lou Yoker's barber shop, where he would fall asleep in the chair. Sometimes he snored, and the other customers would laugh, but when he awoke from his nap, his face under the hot towels, they would stop laughing because they were to that degree respectful toward a man whose word meant something at the bank. Lou Yoker's barber shop was in the basement of the Y.M.C.A., and when he was finished with his shave and facial, George, carrying his coat and vest and hat and collar and tie, would go to the Y.M. locker room and take off the rest of his clothes and go for a swim in the deserted pool. Although he had been a member of the "Y" since its beginning, the only use he made of its facilities was his weekly dips in the pool. He liked to swim. There was a rule that forbade the wearing of bathing trunks in the pool, based on the theory that the dyes were not fast and contaminated the water. All swimmers therefore were naked. George would leave his glasses on a shelf in the lavatory, lower himself into the pool, and for half an hour (or fifteen minutes, if the hour was later than usual) he would luxuriate in his solitary possession of the pool.

"Did you have a nice swim?" his mother would say when he got home.

"Fine," he would say.

"Who did you see?"

"Oh, a few fellows," he would say. She was aware, he knew, of the Y.M.C.A. rule that required nude bathing, and for a few minutes in her imagination she could picture the friends of her son, splashing about in innocent nakedness. Once, a long time ago, she had expressed the thought that after a certain age the swimmers ought to be required to wear bathing suits. Senior members, eighteen and over, ought to wear *something*, she had said. But he had convinced her that a rule was a rule and must be obeyed by one and all. Besides, no ladies were ever permitted in the basement. "I should hope not," said his mother. "I should certainly hope *not*." She would give him his supper, and after the dishes were washed and dried she would join him in the sitting-room while he read the paper and smoked his cigar. It was their time for conversation that concerned the house and housekeeping, their relatives and neighbors and friends. Mrs. Davies did not like to bother George during the week, when he would have his mind on bank business. Saturday after supper was the best time, and really the only time, for conversation. At nine o'clock she would retire and he would hear the water running in the bathtub. Sometimes he would wonder why it took her so long to finish her bath, but she was entitled to take as long as she liked. After all, Saturday was his time for his visit to Nan Brown's and his shave-and-facial and his dip in the pool, which constituted his preparation for the best night's sleep of the week. Once she had retired to the bathroom he did not see her again until Sunday breakfast, but he knew that after her bath she took her tonic and went to bed and apparently slept as well as he did.

She kept one bottle of her tonic in the bathroom and another bottle in the kitchen closet so that she did not have to climb upstairs every time she felt the need of it. The label said "Dr. Fegley's Reliable Compound" and the tonic was manufactured in a little town in Ohio. George's mother had relied on it ever since he could remember, long before his father passed away. The label recommended it for the treatment of run-down and nervous conditions, thin blood, rheumatism, and organic disorders. The picture of Dr. Fegley on the label inspired confidence. He was a bearded man with half-spectacles and a shock of white hair, and his tonic had first been recommended to George's mother by old Mrs. Tuckerman, who but for her unfortunate fall down the cellar stairs might still be taking it. George had never inquired into Dr. Fegley's tonic. He had always assumed that certain women needed tonics for certain ailments at certain times, and his mother had been taking Dr. Fegley's as naturally as she wore a skirt. As long as he could remember, it had been delivered by the case, two dozen bottles at a time, with a discount on orders in case lots, and no danger that she would ever be without it. She spent so little money on herself that the last thing he would ever question her on was the cost of her tonic. She, of course, had no way of knowing that part of the money he said he spent on cigars was in fact a cover-up for the money he spent at Nan Brown's.

His mother, but no one else, was aware that George's forty-third birthday and the twenty-fifth anniversary of his going to work at the bank fell in the same week in June. His bank anniversary happened to be on a Tuesday, and he had hoped that the directors, who regularly met on Monday, would call him in and congratulate him. Monday passed, however, and it was not until closing time Tuesday that the president and the cashier, marching together and grinning, came to George's cage and Charles C. Williams, the president, said: "George, we have a little surprise for you."

"For me, Mr. Williams?"

"For you. Maybe it escaped your attention," said Williams, "but twenty-five years ago on this very day you joined our staff. Today is your twenty-fifth anniversary with the Gibbsville Trust Company. Don't tell me you didn't know it."

"Well, I won't say it never crossed my mind."

"Well, we didn't forget," said Williams. "And to commemorate the occasion I have here this token of our esteem. Open it, George." He handed George a parcel wrapped in tissue paper and secured with the seal of Lowery & Klinger's jewelry store. Other members of the bank staff had slowly gathered around to watch the ceremony.

"You want me to open it now, in front of everybody?" said George.

"Sure, go ahead. It won't explode in your face," said Williams. His laugh was jovial.

George undid the wrapping, tossed the tissue paper in a wastebasket, and looked at the black velvet box. "I wonder what's in it?" he said.

"You'll never find out if you don't open it," said Walter Strohmyer, the cashier.

George pushed up the velvet lid and saw the matching silver pen-and-pencil set. "Well, say, isn't that nice," he said. "A pen-and-pencil set."

"Sterling silver," muttered Strohmyer.

"Yes, it ought to last forever," said George. "Well, say, thanks. Thanks very much."

"Read the engraving," said Williams.

"'To George W. Davies, twenty-five years' service, Gibbsville Trust Company, June 1924.' Well, say." There was a light flutter of handclapping by the staff and handshakes by Williams and Strohmyer.

"There is also the usual cash bonus at the end of the year," said Strohmyer. "Being a twenty-five-year man yours'll be larger this year."

They were interrupted by a stenographer who told Williams he was wanted on the telephone.

"Did they say who it is?" said Williams.

"They said if you couldn't come to the phone to give you a message. It's Mr. Choate. He said they were starting without you and you could meet them on the third tee."

"All right," said Williams. "Tell him you gave me his message. I damn near forgot I had a golf date. Well, George, I hope we're all around when you make it fifty."

"Oh, I doubt that, Mr. Williams. I'll be sixty-eight then."

"What the hell, pardon my French, ladies, but wouldn't you say George looks good for another twenty-five years?" said Williams.

"Oh, at least," said one of the women.

"Well, give my regards to your mother, George," said Williams.

"Thank you. That will please her very much."

"I'm sorry I have to go now," said Williams. "But I always like to be around when we honor one of our faithful employees. George came here straight out of Gibbsville High and's been with us ever since. One of our old reliables, you might say. Very highly thought of. Well, George."

"The proudest day of my life," said George. "Thank you, everybody."

"And we'll see to it there's a little article in the paper," said Strohmyer.

On that note the ceremonies were concluded, and the bank employees, a little late, headed for home. The last to leave was George. It was a day to celebrate, and the usual way to celebrate was to drink some liquor. But George had no taste for strong drink and he had always stayed away from saloons and speakeasies. He thought of dropping in somewhere for a glass of beer, but it was not like George to drop in anywhere, and there was no one at the bank whom he might invite to join him. They were not beer drinkers at the bank. Walter Strohmyer was a Sunday School superintendent, and another of George's colleagues was prominent in Christian Endeavor Society activities. Even Murphy, the retired policeman who was the bank guard, practiced total abstinence and had not touched beer or whiskey since his thirtieth birthday, although he had a brother who ran a saloon near the steel mill. "Well, goodnight, Murph," said George.

"Goodnight, George," said Murphy. "See you in the morning."

"See you in the morning, bright and early," said George.

He had his pen-and-pencil set in his pocket, and he would have liked to show it to the men at Dewey Heiler's, but he was unequal to that kind of ostentation. He could not casually pull the box out of his pocket and say, "Look what the bank gave me." The men at Dewey's would all be polite and show an interest, but one of the regulars at Dewey's was a director of the bank, who just might not like the idea of that kind of showing off.

He walked along Main Street among the late shoppers and the homeward bound, the men and women waiting at every corner to take the trolley to the neighboring towns. It was one of the busiest times of day in Gibbsville, with the automobiles blowing their horns and the trolleys clanging their bells and the newsboys peddling the afternoon papers. "Get your late scores! Phillies win! Getcha paper!" He came to Market and Main, but he did not turn to the left. He knew where he was going, without knowing why. He turned right and irresistibly was drawn to Nan Brown's. She was standing in the downstairs hallway, talking to one of her girls.

"George, what are you doing here? It's *Tuesday*," said Nan Brown.

"It's all right if I come in, isn't it? Are you open?" said George.

"Oh, sure. Any time," said Nan. "Any old time, and Tuesday's as good as any. We were just starting supper."